the devil's city

PRISON FOR SUPERNATURAL OFFENDERS BOOK FIVE

MEGAN LINSKI & ALICIA RADES

We the authors acknowledge that the United States of America is a country formed on stolen land. We respect and honor the indigenous peoples who have lived here for centuries, and we recognize there is still much work to do to make reparations and heal the damage caused to the many indigenous nations who were first here, both in the past and today.

May we remember the atrocities once committed, create a better world in the present, and look forward together for our future.

ONE

Freedom had never been a privilege afforded to a guy like me. All my life, I'd been scraping by with the bare minimum, taking only what I needed to get by. I'd been really fucking good at it, too, but that life was over.

Now, the entire world was mine for the taking. Anything I desired, I could have.

And why not? I was a freaking demigod, and no one was going to stop me—not even the Warden. We'd escaped his prison, and we were finally free.

I held tight to my Familiar's scales as the wyvern flew high above the French nature reserve, where my friends and I had been hiding for the past two weeks since our escape from the Darke Institute. The wind whipped through my hair, and my Air magic buzzed throughout my body in exhilaration.

This was true freedom. There wasn't a soul around for miles, and I was completely surrounded by my elements. Earth and Air magic pulsed through my veins, and the setting sun touched my skin.

Hold on tight, Charlie, Oberi stated through our telekinetic bond.

He should know me better by now. I spread my arms out wide and let out a gleeful laugh as air rushed by me. Oberi dove downward, and my stomach leapt into my throat.

"Wahoo!" I cried as I plummeted toward the ground. I relished in the high. I'd never felt anything quite like it.

Oberi shifted his weight, and we leveled out over the treetops. He pumped his wings, pulling us higher into the air. I squeezed my legs against his form and held tight to the spines on his back. Oberi flipped through the air, and I laughed as my stomach flopped in my abdomen.

"Again!" I shouted over the roar of the wind.

As you wish, Oberi said. He was having just as much fun as I was.

Oberi reared his head upward and tilted his wings. We flipped over backward... and I loosened my grip. I slipped off his back, and although my heart hammered as I fell through the air, I'd never been more at peace.

I tumbled through the open air, my arms spread out wide as I took in the thrilling sensation. I couldn't see the incoming treetops, but I felt them with my magic. I intended to catch myself with my magic, but instead, a loud cry came from above me, and Oberi plucked me out of the sky with his talons. He tossed me upward, and I landed on his back again.

I'd never gotten to be a kid, or felt that careless sense of freedom other children had growing up. For the first time, no one was going to hurt me for letting my guard down, so I was going to enjoy it as long as possible.

I couldn't stop laughing as I clutched one of his spines and righted myself again. "That was incredible!"

You were about to become shish-kabobbed, Oberi said.

"Relax," I told him, patting his scales. "I'm a big boy. I can catch myself."

Playtime is over, Oberi said. *We're supposed to be scouting.*

"Well, what do you see?" I asked. Oberi was our eyes up here in the sky, but I could sense supernaturals with my Elf magic. I didn't feel a soul anywhere.

Nothing but trees and mountains, Oberi said. *No signs of life.*

"Perfect," I replied. If I could live in the wilderness with my friends the rest of my life and no one bothered us, I'd be golden.

We can't stay here forever, Oberi said, catching my thoughts. *Eventually, we have to get back to fighting the war.*

Out here in the nature preserve, it was easy to forget the supernatural communities were bombing each other. It had only been two weeks since we escaped the Warden, but already it felt like the man had only been a figment of my imagination— a specter I'd conjured up while being locked up in the Darke Institute for Supernatural Offenders. Of course I *knew* he was still out there, but some days it was easy to forget a whole world existed outside of this little slice of heaven my friends and I had created.

I spot a white wolf, Oberi reported.

"Let's see what she found," I said.

Oberi swooped out of the sky, and we landed in a small clearing. I beamed, still riding the high of the flight. I slid off his back, and he transformed into a husky beside me.

The white wolf approached. *"Did Oberi see anything?"* she asked.

"Nothing," I said. "What's your report, Kallie?"

My friend's heavy footsteps became light as she transformed back into her sorceress form. "I didn't pick up anything for miles— not so much as a scent."

"So we're still safe," I stated.

"For now," Kallie agreed as we started back toward our camp. "But we're going to have to get moving soon, Charlie."

"Why?" I asked. "If the Warden was able to find us, he would have by now."

"That's only because we have strong wards keeping him from tracking us," Kallie said. "But we can't survive out here without resources. Eventually, someone is going to notice us. We can't keep going into town."

Our first night here, we'd portaled to the nearest town to steal food. Ava was feeling reckless and wanted to shoplift, and Marcus was too chicken to stay in the woods by himself. Kallie and I were both strong illusionists, and our illusions were enough to give us shelter and clothing, but illusion food had no substance, and we'd starve without real food.

My illusions were getting better. The clothes I created were solid, and they'd stay that way forever, unlike Kallie's illusions that vanished when she got too far away from them. I'd even learned how to apply color to my illusions, which was significant progress. But any food I tried to create had no nutrition. It really fucking sucked, because I was all too familiar with the ache of hunger, and it seemed like the one thing I couldn't provide my family with at will.

My days of thieving and conning had come in handy, because at least if I couldn't conjure real food, I could steal it.

And maybe that was the problem. I'd grown up fighting for scraps, and my relationship with food was far from the best. I never once believed that food could be permanent, and so it was impossible to create it.

I knew how to get resources one way or another, but unlike before, I was no longer starving. I could take whatever I wanted, and not a damn soul on this earth was going to prevent me from doing that.

I'd never had so much fun stealing things than when I did it with my friends. I used to be scared that I'd get caught, but now, I was unstoppable. Ava didn't care one way or another if we stole shit or not, and I had to admit, her encouraging me to misbehave only made me want to commit more crimes. The Institute hadn't changed that part of me at all. If anything, it'd only made me a better thief, and my wife was more than willing to be my partner in crime.

Up ahead, I heard a door shut, then the sound of my wife's wheelchair on a ramp as she came out of the cabin. Our camp was nestled in a tiny clearing, just big enough for a cottage, a campfire, and a picnic table. Kallie had created a nice little cabin with her illusion magic that we'd been staying in, and it was spacious and comfortable. We had a roof over our heads, and really, that was all I could ask for.

"How's the temperature?" Ava asked in the distance. She must be approaching the campfire, where Marcus was brewing our potion.

"It could be hotter," Marcus replied. "I need the potion at a rolling boil."

"Here, let me help," Ava offered.

I heard the crackle of a fire, then the snap of bubbles.

"Perfect," Marcus said, though his voice sounded strained.

"Are you hungry?" Ava asked, sounding concerned. "We have a few extra rations."

"No," Marcus answered, almost too quickly. "Save it for the others. Charlie and Kallie will be hungry when they get back."

"You haven't eaten all day," Ava pressed. "There's enough for—"

"I *said* I'm not hungry!" Marcus snapped.

"All right," Ava huffed, and I knew she had to be rolling her eyes. I heard the rustle of a bag, then a gasp.

A twinge of agony rippled up my back, and I knew instantly it had come through our bond. The pain ebbed slightly, but Ava had failed to hide it from me. She was powering through and using her healing magic to help with the pain of dealing with her spinal injury, but it wasn't always enough.

Kallie grabbed my arm, and I stopped in my tracks. She pulled me behind a big tree and lowered her voice. "Charlie, they're getting worse. We need to make a decision."

"You're talking about leaving," I stated flatly.

"We have to do *something*," Kallie pressed.

It felt like an impossible ask. I'd never felt safer than I did in this forest, shielded from the world by these trees and encompassed by my element. Here, my wife had a warm bed to sleep in every night, and my Familiar could roam free. The last thing I wanted to do was leave. No one would bother us here. Everything would stay perfect.

"Charlie," Kallie prodded when I didn't say anything. "We can't keep hanging around. Marcus is on the edge of losing it because he doesn't have his antidepressants. If he's not brewing that potion, he's in bed, and it's only getting worse. Ava's off her bipolar meds, not to mention she's out of painkillers. That's dangerous for both of them, because Ava quitting her lithium and Marcus stopping his SSRI's abruptly could really hurt them. Ava's healing magic is only enough to prevent the worst side effects, but if she doesn't get back on something soon, she'll start having withdrawals or she'll go completely manic, not to mention Marcus is already showing signs of a depression relapse. None of us want him to get suicidal again. We need to go find some medication for both of them. And if you and Ava want to keep getting it on like you do, you're going to need a new dose of birth control."

I groaned. "Okay, fuck. I don't need a lecture on safe sex."

"You *do* need it if it's going to get you to move," Kallie insisted. "I know you were on birth control at the Institute, and that it was specially brewed using magic. I know where we can get our hands on more."

"If we run, we can't ward ourselves from the Warden," I argued. "Wards don't work that way. They're stationery, so our wards are the only thing keeping him from finding us right now. Besides, we don't know where the next key is, so why are we talking about leaving when we don't know where we're going next?"

"We've been here too long. We need to move to another isolated location," Kallie argued. "Wards or not, the Warden will eventually track us down."

"Okay, so let's do that forever, so we can't be found," I said, completely serious.

"You can't keep living your life only looking ahead for the next couple of days."

"Why not? It's worked before."

"Look, you can sit around and convince yourself that running is the only way to survive, but we all know what will happen if we don't find those keys," Kallie said. "What happens when you die and you're trapped in the in-between forever, just like all the other souls, because you never opened the Elven Gate? We can't do nothing while the Warden is taking over the world. I know you like it here, Charlie. But you have to decide once and for all if you're going to lie down and take it, or if you're going to go after the keys."

I rubbed my face. "We can't go anywhere, anyway. Moving is risky without the anti-tracking potion, and Marcus hasn't finished it."

"I know we should wait, but I don't think we can any longer," Kallie insisted. "Not when it comes to their meds, at least. These two need some happy pills."

I hated to even consider Kallie's argument, because all I wanted to do was keep my friends safe behind our wards, never to face the Warden again. But they weren't safe if they weren't getting the medical care they needed. I turned my attention back to my wife. In the distance, I could hear her rifling through papers. She'd barely taken her eyes off the files we'd stolen from the Institute since we got here. We'd been studying what the Warden knew, so we could accurately predict where he was going and how to face him. It was a long, arduous task that I could tell was weighing on Ava-Marie. Even from here, I could hear the quiet moans of discomfort as she shifted in her chair.

A ripple of pain slipped through our bond, and it felt like someone had lit my spine aflame. I grabbed the trunk of the tree to keep from falling over. Ava usually shielded her injury from me, but the fact that she couldn't anymore was telling. She was in far more discomfort than I could fathom, and the only reason she was getting by was because she was so used to being in pain.

"All right," I agreed. "We need to come up with a plan."

"Let's go talk to the others," Kallie suggested.

We approached the camp. Ava immediately slammed our bond shut when she heard us approaching. She hadn't realized we'd been in the trees, or that I'd felt her pain only moments before. It wasn't that she was trying to hide it from me. Rather, she didn't want me suffering alongside her, because no matter how much of her pain I felt through our bond, I couldn't take it away from her.

"How was the flight?" Ava asked, keeping her voice even.

"It was nice," I said, but the high I'd felt had vanished. Now I was more worried than anything. To steady my hands, I approached Rishi, who was lounging on the picnic table atop the files Ava was studying. I stroked the cat's fur, and he purred under my touch. Alette fluttered by and landed in my hand. Sprigs quickly joined her, tickling my fingers with his spindly legs. The sentient twig climbed atop the moth, and he gave a tiny cry before she took off, fluttering him around the campsite.

"The perimeter is clear," Kallie reported. "How's the research going?"

Ava shuffled papers around. "I found a file detailing the Warden's experiments. He's somewhat cryptic with his notes, almost like he was intentionally hiding details in case anyone came across them. But from what I can gather, stealing our powers and becoming a demigod himself is only the first step in his master plan. With enough power and inferichite, he should be able to make demigods out of anyone."

"So he's building a demigod army?" I asked roughly.

"In theory, he *could*," Ava said. "He's limited by inferichite, though, because it takes so long to grow."

"He's got plenty," I stated. "Now that the Institute is destroyed and we escaped, he has no reason to leave the inferichite perimeter around the property. He could've dug up all those crystals to reuse."

"Yes, but now they're *his* weakness, too, since he's a demigod like us," Ava pointed out. "Just being around inferichite is going to slow him down."

"Slowed down or not, he's still got to be going through with the ceremonies," Kallie said thoughtfully. "We already know he's had demigods working for him for a while, though I think we can reason that Esther and Mad Dog are both natural-born demigods. How many more do you think he's created by now?"

"And *who*?" I added.

Ava flipped through a few more papers. "I'm not sure. From what I can tell, the ceremony won't work on just *anyone*. The subject has to be strong enough to withstand a demigod's power. He killed a lot of people running his experiments, and he's surely killing again. But whoever he's recruiting, they surely have to be as loyal and crazy as Esther and Mad Dog—"

A sizzling sound cut her off, and we all whirled toward the fire.

"No!" Marcus exploded. "No, no, no, no, no!"

His voice grew with intensity with each passing word. It sounded like his potion had boiled over. No one had quite forgotten how he'd gone psychotic the night we broke out of the Institute. We'd all been a bit on edge, hoping it wouldn't happen again.

Kallie was right— he really needed his meds.

"Marcus, calm down," Ava insisted. "I've got this."

The temperature around us dropped, and the sizzling stopped. Ava had used her Fire magic to kill the campfire and stop the boiling.

Marcus began pacing back and forth. "This is all wrong. It's not working!"

"What's the problem?" Kallie asked. "Maybe I can help."

"You can't come along and fix this with your false realities and illusions!" Marcus raged. "We need better ingredients— *real* ingredients."

Marcus wasn't acting like himself. He didn't usually yell at her about things like this. He was losing his patience with Kallie, and that was telling of how low he felt. He definitely was getting depressed.

"Hey, I'm good for more than just my illusions," Kallie snapped. "Get me a list. I'll get whatever you need."

Marcus scoffed. "From where? I need *magical plants*, Kallie. In case you haven't noticed, they aren't exactly bountiful in this stupid forest."

Kallie walked over to Marcus, and his footsteps came to a halt as she shook him. "Marcus, I need you to pull yourself together and get me that list. I know a fae apothecary not far from here. Charlie and I will go. I'll portal us there, and we'll get everything you need."

"You're not going to find what I need at any random apothecary," Marcus insisted.

"I'll find it at this one," she promised.

The message was loud and clear. This wasn't just any fae apothecary, bound by the rules of Malovian law. She knew about black-market dealers, and she was willing to walk us into danger to get what we needed. It was either that, or eventually let the Warden find us. We really needed this potion if we wanted to move about without being tracked.

"What if someone recognizes you?" Marcus demanded.

"I can disguise us with glamour," Kallie said. "It's a simple illusion that will conceal our features. See?"

Magic tingled over my skin and across my nose. I had no idea what I looked like, but judging by the way Marcus gasped, I must've looked like a completely different person.

"What if the Warden's tracking you?" Ava asked nervously. "You'll be leaving our ward."

"We'll be quick about it, before his spells can find us," Kallie said. "We have to take the risk to get the ingredients."

"All right. Give me a minute." Marcus came over to the picnic table. He must've conjured a paper and a pen, because he began scribbling something down. The paper rustled as he handed it to Kallie. "I hope this place really has the stuff, because if it doesn't, we're fucked."

"We'll get it," Kallie promised again, though I heard uncertainty in her tone. "Charlie and Oberi are with me."

Magic bloomed in front of us, and Kallie took my hand and led me through the portal. The temperature dropped, and my feet hit solid pavement. Voices came from somewhere nearby, echoing off walls around us. It seemed we were in some sort of alleyway.

"Get down," Kallie hissed.

The three of us ducked, and I leaned against the cold metal of a dumpster. I knew that feeling all too well, after spending many nights on the streets. I missed the forest already.

"We're in the alleyway behind the pharmacy," Kallie said. "They're closed for the night, but there are cameras on both sides of the alley. I should be able to scramble the images with my magic."

"The pharmacy?" I asked. "I thought we were headed to a black-market dealer?"

"Two birds with one stone, Charlie," Kallie said. "The pharmacy is a front for the magical dealings that happen behind the counter. We're getting Marcus and Ava their meds *and* the ingredients for the potion. These places are usually warded against magic, so we'll have to get in the old-fashioned way."

We could try bartering first, Oberi suggested.

"With what?" I questioned. "They'll spot an illusion from a mile away."

"Come on," Kallie hissed. "We don't have much time. Oberi, keep watch."

On it, sister, Oberi said.

Kallie dragged me forward. She pulled something out of her hair and shook out the strands, nearly smacking me in the face. Kallie knelt beside the building, and the lock wiggled as she stuck her bobby pin inside it.

"Once I get this open, an alarm will go off," Kallie said. "We'll have to disable the alarm system immediately."

I smirked. Working with Kallie was better than any thief I'd teamed up with in the past. "I'm guessing you know how to do that."

"You learn security systems really quickly when you're a vigilante assassin," Kallie said proudly. The lock clicked, and the door swung open. "We're in."

We hurried inside, and Oberi slipped through the door behind us. A keypad beeped as Kallie hacked it to disable the alarm system before it could notify the owners.

"Done," she announced. "Come on. The pharmacy is this way."

Kallie led me down the hall, and the air expanded to a huge room, like the grocery stores back home. She picked another lock and disabled the alarm system again. I entered some sort of storage area. I reached out and felt shelves, all lined with bottles.

"You and Oberi find the meds," Kallie said. "I'll cover the apothecary and get the ingredients on Marcus' list, and get you your birth control. We'll meet back at the exit in three minutes."

"Got it," I agreed.

Kallie fled the room, and I heard her footsteps racing down the hall. Oberi was already sniffing around, searching the shelves for the medications we needed. In husky form, he was particularly sensitive to smell, and he didn't need to read the labels to know which meds Ava and Marcus usually took.

Here's the lithium, Oberi said, nudging his nose at a bottle on the shelf. I felt for it and gathered several in my arms. He hurried down the aisle and found the antidepressants, along with painkillers.

The bottles were big, at least a quart each. I wanted to take as many as possible, so we didn't run out. Whatever we didn't need, I could sell for real cash, so I could make sure my family had whatever they needed. I'd given up drug dealing a long time ago, but I'd do it again if I had to.

That should be it, Oberi said. *Let's go.*

I left the storage room, but two bottles slipped out of my arms. I knelt to pick them up, and another one slipped.

Screw this. I went to create a backpack so I could carry them that way.

An alarm squealed overhead, and my heart lurched. Everything happened so fast I couldn't quite process it. The magic concealing my features disappeared. Oberi barked once, then came the sound of her phoenix cry.

Something's wrong! Oberi screamed in my mind.

I felt her shift again, and Fire blazed across the bond as she became a Fire unicorn. Shelves knocked over as her form grew, and the smoothness of Water magic filled the bond. Her horn poked me, and I jumped out of the way before I could be impaled by her narwhal horn.

"Oberi, what's happening?!" I screamed.

I can't control it! she cried.

The bond shifted again, becoming masculine. I heard the unfurl of leather wings as he shifted. Oberi grew so large that his wyvern scales squashed me against the wall. The ceiling shook overhead, and dust rained down on me. Shelves crushed under his weight. Oberi barely fit inside the store.

The alarm came to a sudden stop. Although the room had gone silent, I could still hear the heavy pulse of my panicked heartbeat in my ears. Oberi shifted again, shrinking to the size of a husky.

"What the hell happened?" I demanded.

Some sort of magic, Oberi said.

"Yeah, I figured that," I growled. I slung the backpack over my shoulder, the medications rattling around inside of it. "Let's go, before it happens again."

I started for the hall to find Kallie, but the sound of a male voice stopped me.

"You're not going anywhere," he sneered. He spoke in a Malovian accent, so he had to be some kind of shifter. "Hands in the air, or your girlfriend dies!"

Kallie let out a pained cry, as if the shifter had her by the hair.

I went to cast a battle spell, but Oberi barked. *He's got a dagger to her neck!*

"Charlie!" Kallie cried, causing me to hesitate. She knew all too well what I'd do to this guy if given the chance. "If we kill him, we'll attract attention from the whole supernatural community!"

"The glamour's gone," I seethed. "Better to leave no witnesses."

"Kill me, and she dies with me," the shifter threatened.

Kallie could kill him in a heartbeat, but she was right. If we left a trail of bodies, other supernaturals would come after us. We had to get out of this clean, and without anyone on our tail.

"You think you can steal from *me?*" the shifter said with a laugh. "Some thieves you are, casting magic in my shop. My spells have revealed you for what you are."

I realized that I'd fucked up. Kallie had said we couldn't cast magic to get through the wards. I didn't realize a simple illusion spell would set things off, as it wasn't an outright attack. I mentally kicked myself for the stupid decision. The spell had stripped us of our glamour and forced Oberi to reveal all five forms, all for a dumb backpack.

I had to find a way to get through to this guy, because we weren't leaving here without our stuff. I didn't care if Kallie thought we couldn't leave bodies behind. I would if I had to.

"Please, sir," I said sadly, throwing in a voice crack for show. When you wanted to run a con, you had to play to what was important to the person you were trying to fool. Hopefully this guy had a shred of empathy. "We don't mean anyone any harm. My wife is in a wheelchair, and in a lot of pain. We have nothing left, and we just want to help her. Don't you have a family? Wouldn't you do anything for them?"

He didn't seem to care. Instead, he scoffed and said, "You think I'd believe a sob story like that? I should be turning you into the authorities right now!"

"So why aren't you?" Kallie asked.

"Because I've seen what you can offer," he practically sang. "I'm willing to forgive you for trespassing and sell you whatever you want, in exchange for one of those wyvern scales."

"What do you want me to do? Just pluck one off his back?" I sneered.

"If you don't want me turning you into the authorities, you will!" he demanded.

"That's a rip-off," Kallie spat. "One wyvern scale is worth a hundred times what we're here for!"

"You destroyed my entire pharmacy!" the shifter roared. "I think it's a fair trade."

"Or I could just kill you and walk out of here," I said with a shrug. Screw conning the man. I was ready to get this over with.

"Kill me, and other fae will be here in moments to hunt you down," the shifter said. "Now that I've stripped your glamour, I've got you on camera, and the recording has already been sent to an off-site server. Give me a wyvern scale, and I'll wipe any traces of you ever being here."

"Charlie, do it," Kallie insisted. The last thing we wanted was to be followed.

I gritted my teeth. I didn't like being pushed around by some sleazy black-market dealer, but no one could find out where we were. It was the one weakness we had, and this guy knew how to play it.

If it gets us out of here without a trace, I'll give him one of my scales, Oberi told me.

"Fine," I growled. I turned to Oberi, and he shifted. He didn't make the full shift, or he'd take up the whole room. It was just enough that I could feel his scales. I pinched a scale around his neck and ripped it out. Oberi winced.

I held up the scale to show the shifter, but I didn't hand it over right away. "Let my friend go."

"Give me the scale first," he demanded.

"I said—" I started, but Kallie cut me off.

"Charlie, just give it to him so we can get out of here."

I placed the scale in the shifter's outstretched hand, the same time I grabbed Kallie and yanked her away from him.

"Now get out of here!" he yelled. "I don't want to see either of you back here ever again."

We scrambled down the hallway.

"Did you get it all?" Kallie asked.

"Yes, you?"

"Everything. Including your anti-baby meds. Let's get out of here." Kallie created a portal in front of us, and we leapt through. We landed on soft ground, and the scent of the forest filled my nose.

Oberi shook out his fur. *I can't believe I gave a scale up to that stinky old dude! That guy was suspicious.*

"Of course he was," I said. "What else did you expect from a black-market dealer? Do you think he recognized you, Kallie?"

Kallie hadn't been seen around these parts in over two years, but the fae wouldn't soon forget the face of the young princess who'd been sentenced to prison for an assassination attempt on the king.

"I don't think so," she said. "If he had, he would've asked for a lot more. That wyvern scale should keep anyone from coming after us. It's worth a lot of money."

She seemed so certain, but I couldn't help but keep my attention on the forest, listening for footsteps or any other signs of life. I heard nothing.

We returned to camp, and Marcus and Ava were gathered around the fire. The sun had set by now, and the air grew colder.

Marcus scrambled to his feet when he heard us coming. "How'd it go?"

"We got it all," Kallie said, dropping to her knees beside the fire. Vials rattled, and bags rustled as she laid the contents of her haul out in the dirt. "How long will it take to brew the anti-tracking potion?"

Marcus mumbled under his breath as he looked everything over. "It'll have to simmer overnight. We should be able to leave in the morning. Once we take the potion, the Warden can't track us anywhere."

"Then let's pack up so we're ready to go as soon as possible," Kallie said. "We got something else, too."

I slipped the backpack off my shoulder and pulled the medicine out. Oberi sniffed the bottles, then took one in his mouth and walked over to Ava.

"Medication?" Ava asked.

"You both needed it," I said, handing a bottle to Marcus.

He hesitated, but took it anyway. "Thanks."

Ava didn't say much, but I felt her relief slip through our bond. She hadn't wanted to ask us to obtain her medication, but she was grateful it was there. At the very least, it would give her some relief from her pain, and we'd stolen enough meds to last quite a while.

"What happened to you out there?" Ava asked as we all sat around the fire. She must've noticed my agitation.

We told them about our run-in with the black-market dealer. Ava seemed nervous when we finished telling her what happened.

"Are you absolutely *sure* you weren't followed?" she asked.

"Certain," I said. "He got the better end of the deal, so he's not going to follow us."

"He sounds sketchy, no matter what you gave him," Ava replied.

"We portaled out of there, so I don't know how he'd find us, even if he wanted to," I said. "We didn't leave a trail behind."

Ava didn't say anything more, but I knew she was still concerned. She'd been paranoid since we'd left the Institute, worried the Warden was going to find us sooner or later.

Hell, let him. I'd kick his ass all over this forest.

Marcus mixed his ingredients together, and the potion bubbled lightly. Finally, he said, "The potion should be done in a few hours. We should all get some sleep."

We gathered our records spread over the picnic table, and Marcus subconjured them, along with the medication bottles. I helped Ava to bed, then gave Marcus her chair so he could keep it in his stash. That way we could leave as soon as possible.

Oberi curled up at Ava's feet, but I sensed he wasn't sleeping. The hair on the back of my neck stood, and I paid close attention to the sounds of the forest, but I heard nothing except the wind rustling the trees.

I tried to tell myself we were safe here. The Warden couldn't track us behind our wards, and the guy at the pharmacy didn't know where we'd gone. Still, I couldn't shake the odd sensation crawling up my back as I climbed into bed beside my wife. I didn't bother changing into pajamas, because I wanted to be ready to get the hell out of here as soon as the potion was ready.

I loved it here. I never wanted to leave. But now that we'd been spotted, I didn't think we could stay any longer. The fae apothecary hadn't been far from here, and even if our cabin was secluded, they knew where to start looking.

It was time to start moving and find the rest of the Divinity Keys before the Warden did.

I lay awake for a long time, unable to sleep, but eventually, I drifted off.

Bang!

I startled awake as the front door of the cabin burst open. I immediately reached over for my wife, and she grabbed on to me. Oberi barked loudly, and my heart hammered.

Ava's panic flooded through the bond. "Charlie, what's—?"

A deafening noise came from above us, and dust rained down on our heads. Wind came rushing into the room as debris flew everywhere. It was like someone had ripped the roof of the cabin off. I threw myself over Ava to shield her, wondering what the hell had happened now.

"Come out, come out, wherever you are!" a deep voice rang from outside.

Holy shit. That sounded like Mad Dog.

I didn't have a second to process it before the bed vanished from beneath me. Ava and I fell to the forest floor as the illusion broke, and the cabin around us vanished. Ava let out a pained cry, and Oberi shifted into a wyvern, spreading out his wings to shield us. I felt Sprigs jump into my pocket, and I heard a whizzing sound as Alette hid beside him.

We're under attack! Oberi cried.

I didn't care if Mad Dog was here or who he brought. We were demigods; we could take on anyone.

Oberi's venom sizzled as he shot it at our attackers, but it made a *splatting* sound, like it hit a pane of glass before disintegrating.

I can't get past their shields, Oberi panicked.

"Hold them off, Kallie!" Marcus screamed. The firepit hissed, like he'd spilled some of the anti-tracking potion into it.

Everything that we'd made with illusion magic was gone. The only things that remained were our real belongings, like Marcus' cauldron and the vials we stole from the apothecary. Marcus sounded like he was rescuing the potion, while Kallie fought off the attackers in the open clearing.

My whole body shook as I rushed to cradle Ava in my arms, but she was already blasting off magic. I felt Water and Fire converge through our bond as she used simultension on herself, creating that deadly blue Fire she'd made in the Darke Games. Ava shot it off, but I heard it fizzle out before it made its target.

"What the hell?" she growled.

She shot off another spell, but it ricocheted back in our direction, and the Fire seared the ends of my hair as I flinched away.

Someone cackled loudly. "You think your Fire is a match for us? We're demigods now, and we're stronger than you'll ever be. All the other Mission kids who wanted to become demigods died, but *we* were strong enough. Your spells can't touch us."

There was only one person who would brag that much during a fight. It had to be Deuce, the vampire who got sent to Cellblock 9 after I framed him for murder. Last I saw him, he was lying unconscious in Cellblock 9. The fact that he was strong enough to withstand demigod power was impressive, considering I'd knocked him out more than once.

Oberi threw himself in front of us again, letting out a loud, threatening cry.

Ava clung to me. "It's The Mission! Esther, Naya, Mad Dog, and Deuce. Charlie, they're stronger than I've ever seen them. I don't know how, but they're shooting my Fire back at me!"

I wasn't sure how they'd gotten here so quickly. The bastard at the pharmacy must've ratted us out!

"Stay low," I warned Ava. "I won't let them hurt you."

It killed me to leave my wife's side, but these fuckers would die before they touched her. I leapt onto Oberi's back and conjured a spear, which became solid in my hand. It was the easiest illusion that came to mind, and appeared almost without thought.

To the right! Oberi told me. Through the bond, I could sense the exact spot I needed to aim, and I thrust my spear forward.

Something shattered, and I realized my illusion spear had been broken. I blasted off battle spells, but each one fizzled out. Below me, Marcus and Kallie threw spells, but I heard their magic wither away before they could do any damage. I heard the shattering of glass, as if their shields had been broken.

"Stop playing this game, and submit to the lord!" a woman's voice came from above me. Feathery wings flapped, which meant it *had* to be Esther. Only she would try preaching about her god while actively trying to kill us.

"I think they're better off dead," a woman laughed. Her leathery wings flapped nearby. It was definitely Naya. We'd had far too many run-ins with this succubus for me to ever forget her voice.

Gathering all the magic I could, I thrust a heavy gust of air above me, and Esther went spinning downward. She knocked into Naya, and they both spiraled into the ground. A tree cracked and groaned, but Naya only laughed. The succubus was as hard as rock. I doubt I left so much as a scratch. Oberi lifted his head and spat venom at Esther.

Esther screamed. I expected the venom to encompass her and kill her like it did the guards the night we escaped, but she flapped her wings again, flying high above us.

"The lord has foreseen your deaths!" Esther shouted. "It is his will that you perish!"

She sounded perfectly fucking healthy to me. Damn angel healing magic.

Mad Dog laughed maniacally, like our magic was nothing short of amusing to him. "Your wyvern is weak, just like the rest of you," he sneered.

Something shifted in the bond, and I didn't know what it was at first, until I realized Oberi was *shrinking* beneath me. He shifted so fast that I fell out of the air and landed hard on the ground. Oberi roared loudly, but it morphed into a bark as he became a husky.

I can't shift! Oberi panicked. *It's some sort of compulsion!*

Mad Dog had used vampire compulsion to kill Thaddeus, but back then, he'd used blood magic to do it. It seemed that his demigod powers were growing, and he could compel anyone, blood magic or not. I barely had a second to take it in before Ava screamed my name.

"Charlie!" Her panicked cry cut through the forest.

I felt the rush of air swirling through the clearing as Mad Dog raced toward her at super speed. I moved so fast that I crossed the impossible distance in less than a second. I threw my hands upward and caught him around the throat before he could go in for the kill. Magic swelled through me as I siphoned his super strength and held him back. The magic felt familiar, and it occurred to me that I moved so fast because I'd siphoned his super speed at a distance, before I consciously decided to. They didn't know who the hell they were messing with.

Mad Dog hissed as his fangs protruded, pressing into the skin on my neck. He never got the chance to break the skin, because I used his super strength against him. I lifted him by the neck, then slammed him into the ground so hard that it left an impression. I forced the earth open beneath him, and it swallowed him whole as I buried him alive. It wouldn't kill a vampire, but it'd hold him off for a bit.

Esther's feathery wings continued to flap above us. She'd turned her sights on Kallie and Marcus as they shot spells in her direction. A clap of thunder rang out around us, and the air sizzled as we narrowly missed being struck by lightning. An explosion blasted off near Kallie and Marcus, and the whole earth rocked back and forth.

Fucking hell. Esther was one strong angel. She'd learned to manipulate energy to create electromagnetic blasts and bombs!

Kallie and Marcus were able to defend themselves— but barely. Deuce was killing their spells every chance he got and shattering their shields the moment they cast them. Esther aimed energy at them again, and they got out of the way just in time, their screams echoing through the trees. Dirt flew into the air and rained down on us.

Ava was casting whatever was in her arsenal— Fire, Water, Spirit magic— yet none of it had any effect. We were practically sitting ducks. A whine of agony sounded nearby, and I felt a slicing sensation across our bond as Oberi was cut open by one of Esther's spells.

"Kallie, get us out of here!" I screamed.

I heard the snap of her fingers... then the strangest sensation surrounded me. The sounds of the forest vanished. The rustling of the trees was gone, and the dirt falling from above halted mid-air. I could still feel pebbles of dirt on my skin, and I knew Kallie had stopped time.

So why did I still hear the sound of beating wings above us?

"Charlie, duck!" Ava screamed.

A wave of Fire blasted past me as she went to defend me, but Esther got to me first. The angel hit me so hard I nearly blacked out. Angels were fucking strong— I knew, because I'd fought them in the ring. But Esther was one hell of an angel. We'd severely underestimated her power.

I went flying across the clearing and landed against a tree. I felt something snap, and at first I thought it was my back, until I sensed the tree waver above me. The sounds of the forest returned, and time began moving forward again. The tree groaned as it began to fall, but I levitated it with my Earth magic and threw it at Esther. She let out a heavy *oof* as it hit her and she toppled out of the sky.

"Ooh, what's this?" Naya practically sang, sounding amused. "The fae princess can stop time?"

Fuck. Kallie had been learning how to stop time without influencing other demigods, but we were in too close proximity. She couldn't pick and choose to take us and leave them behind. Now they knew what she was capable of, and we'd revealed one of our greatest assets.

"It changes nothing!" Esther roared. She was obviously getting impatient. "Our lord wanted them dead, and so they shall be!"

All at once, my friends let out a collective scream. Oberi yelped like he was in pain, and Rishi hissed. I didn't know what had happened.

She's blinding us with her light magic! Oberi cried.

Did this bitch forget that I was blind? I was unaffected, and I went in for the kill. I had Mad Dog's super strength and speed, so I crossed the distance to Esther in a moment. I pummeled my fist into her face, and blood spurted over my shirt. Damn it all if that wasn't satisfying.

Esther got a hold of my wrist. She wrapped her legs around my middle, then curled her wings around my entire body as she dragged me to the ground. "Submit to his will," she demanded.

A familiar pain overcame my body, and my muscles seized up. I remembered it all too well. The Warden had used this power on me in Forevermore. It was a type of life-force manipulation angels had, a way to suck the life energy out of you by sheer will.

Back then, I couldn't defend myself from it. But I was stronger now.

My magic warred against her, siphoning my energy back into me. I tugged even harder, trying to take her power for my own, but I couldn't muster anything beyond her super strength. Her demigod powers were a match for mine, and I couldn't take anything more than her weakest asset. She was powerful— I'd give her that. All her healing abilities and energy manipulation powers were beyond my reach.

I threw a punch, but she dodged it, and my fist met nothing but air. I went to sink the other fist into her gut, but she drew her knee upward and blocked the attack. It was like she knew what I was going to do before I did it.

That was her demigod power, I remembered. She always had a way of reading our weaknesses, and now she knew how to read us better than ever. She knew every attack we were going to throw at her before we even thought of it ourselves.

This bitch may have been at the Institute voluntarily, but she was the worst inmate they'd ever let in that place. There were only so many ways to kill an angel. Let's see how well she functioned without a head.

I conjured a sword, and it pierced her wing. Esther screamed in pain as I yanked the sword downward, slicing through her wing. Esther leapt backward, and I jumped to my feet. I wasted no time aiming the sword at her head, but before it could make contact, it disappeared in my hands.

Shock must've crossed my features, because Deuce stood by the tree line, laughing maniacally.

Of fucking course; because he always needed someone else to fight his battles.

Before I could conjure another spell, the dirt beneath me shifted. I hadn't realized I was standing right where I'd buried Mad Dog, and he was making the climb out of his grave. A hand curled around my ankle and yanked me to the ground. I aimed a blast of battle magic at him, but panicked when the magic never came.

I felt Mad Dog's compulsion locking my powers down tightly, forcing me to hide my own magic from access. I wondered why he didn't just puppet us around and make us kill ourselves like he'd done to Thaddeus, but I realized we were too strong for that. He could compel our magic against us, but he couldn't overcome our consciousness.

Mad Dog let out an angry roar— almost animalistic.

"A little help!" I screamed.

"Let him go, you soulless bastard!" Marcus sneered.

I thought it was just an empty insult, because vampires still had a soul, until I realized what Marcus was doing. Mad Dog's scream came to an abrupt halt the same time an image formed at my feet. An ethereal picture of a furious vampire appeared, his spirit hand curled around my ankle.

If I could see him, that only meant one thing. Marcus had *ripped* Mad Dog's spirit out of his body.

"What have you *done?!*" Esther screamed.

I heard her footsteps racing forward, then felt her body land on top of Mad Dog. For the briefest of moments, his grip on me loosened. Then his spirit vanished and he clutched me even tighter, as if Esther had shoved his soul back into his body.

Obviously she did, because she could manipulate a person's life force. That had to have some effect on the soul. Even if Marcus could take someone's soul out of their body, Esther could just put it right back. I kicked Mad Dog hard in the face, and he dropped my ankle.

"Rishi, attack!" Marcus screamed.

Marcus cast a spell, and Rishi transformed into a deadly spirit. He dove toward Mad Dog and Esther, and his form swept through me for a moment. I saw the ethereal shape of a cat's face as he dove toward our attackers. As soon as he passed me, the image vanished.

Rishi hissed as he went in for the kill, but he never made it to Esther and Mad Dog. Instead, he shifted course, and turned straight toward Marcus and Kallie.

"Rishi, no!" Marcus screamed. Rishi lashed out, and I heard the tearing of fabric as he swiped his claws out at Marcus.

"Stop!" Marcus ordered. The spell broke, and Rishi landed on the ground.

Naya laughed, and I knew whatever happened had been her doing. She had some way of turning our powers against us.

This was *bad*. If Naya could turn our spells back on us, Deuce could break them, and Mad Dog could cut off all our magical access, we were fucking screwed. There was *no way* we could fight these people, no matter how much power we had, because their special demigod abilities prevented us from fighting back.

Our only option was to run.

I raced to Ava and scooped her up in my arms. Marcus and Kallie sprinted to our side.

"Kallie, a portal!" I screamed.

"I *can't!*" she yelled back.

Mad Dog must've been blocking her power. We had to get far enough away so his compulsion wouldn't affect us.

"You aren't going anywhere," Esther sneered. Her wings flapped again, which meant she'd healed already. A spell crackled, and Oberi barked loudly, warning us of the incoming blast.

Ava threw up her hands. Protection magic bloomed out of her so strong it seemed to rock the very earth we stood on. The explosion sounded all around us, but never touched our forms.

"Holy shit! Ava can make shields!" Kallie cried.

Magic smashed against Ava's shield, never touching us. Curiously, I reached out my hand, and my fingers connected with something solid. An image formed in my mind, because the shield was made with Ava's Spirit magic. I saw what appeared to be a big glass dome encompassing my friends and me, pulsing with spiritual power, thin beads of energy moving throughout. I'd heard Anichi could create shields, but I didn't know it was possible for Ava. I felt her strong emotions bleeding through the shield, created out of Ava's love for us and her fierce instinct to protect us.

"Get them!" Esther barked.

"Deuce can't break it," Marcus realized.

"Then let's go!" I demanded. "We need a portal now, Kallie."

"We have to get further away!" she insisted.

"I can't hold this for much longer," Ava whimpered. Her whole body quivered in my grasp as I felt the shield drain her magical energy.

We ran into the trees. The earth shook beneath us as Ava's shield grew stronger. A deafening *snap* sounded, and the earth split in two at the strength of Ava's Spirit magic. Trees groaned and toppled over once they hit Ava's expanding shield, and I heard Naya scream.

Good. I hope she'd been pinned under one of them.

A shattering sound filled the air, and Ava went slack in my arms as she passed out. Her shield broke and faded away, leaving us completely vulnerable. Esther's wings beat from overhead, and the others followed.

"We have to keep going! Mad Dog's cutting off my power," Kallie yelled.

"Submit to the lord's will, for he is always watching!" Esther screamed in the distance. She was coming for us quickly. We had mere moments before she caught up.

Then the air shifted around us. I felt familiar sparks as I heard a portal bloom in front of us.

"Thank the goddesses your ward finally fell," a voice came from the other side of the portal. "We've been trying to track you all for weeks!"

"Quickly, everyone drink the potion, so they can't follow us," Marcus insisted. He shoved vials into our hands. The vials were wet, as if he'd spilled a lot of the potion while he'd been trying to bottle it up. We downed the anti-tracking potion without question, and I tipped a bottle past Ava's lips. She coughed as she drank, but didn't wake up.

"Come with me," the strange voice said.

I didn't know who this guy was, but something told me we could trust him. Anywhere was better than here, at least.

Esther let out a primal scream as she dove for us. We jumped through the portal, and it slammed shut. Feathers drifted over me, but I realized they must've been cut off from Esther's wings as the portal shut, because she hadn't made it through.

I dropped to my knees and set Ava in the grass beside me. I pulled her into my lap and pushed her hair out of her face. "Pidge, are you okay? Wake up."

She took a rattling gasp, and breathed, "Charlie."

"Are you hurt? That was a pretty big spell," I worried.

"I'm fine," she said warily. "Just a little shaken up."

I held her for several long moments, then sagged onto my back, trying to catch my breath. Alette fluttered away, and Sprigs hopped onto my shoulder.

We made it! Oberi cried.

"Barely." I breathed a sigh of relief. We'd been training with our demigod powers for months, but we'd never had to go up against other demigods before. They'd caught us off guard, and we weren't prepared to fight them.

I would *never* let that happen again.

I got to my feet. I didn't know where we were, but I turned to the individual who'd portaled us to safety. I reached out a hand to shake his. "Thank you for coming to our rescue. We wouldn't have gotten out of there if it weren't for you."

He didn't shake my hand, though. Instead, he dragged me into a tight hug. He was taller than me, and I recognized his scent.

Holy shit. It couldn't be—

"Master! I'm *so glad* I finally found you!" my guard squeaked.

This couldn't be real. I felt the world tilt on its axis as I asked in complete disbelief, "Eddie?"

ava-marie

TWO

I was still spinning from my place on the ground. I didn't know where we were, though we were clearly in another part of some distant forest, different to the one we'd left. The trees danced overhead in circles as a familiar, loved voice broke into my dizzying thoughts.

I heard my husband say a name that I recognized. I managed to push myself upright. My lip trembled as I observed Eddie's form. He was just as I remembered him, standing tall, optimistic, that same goofy smile plastered across his face...

But there was an eyepatch over his right eye that concealed what lay under. My stomach dropped.

Eddie embraced Charlie so tightly he lifted him off the ground. Charlie gaped as he loosely held Eddie back.

"I can't believe you're here!" Charlie coughed as Eddie let him go. "You came at just the right moment."

"Not soon enough, I'm afraid," Eddie replied, pocketing a small hand mirror. "I was hoping to find you before anyone else did."

"Eddie, how did you survive? We were told you died in an explosion!" Marcus explained.

"Oh, yes, a very compelling story, that," Eddie said eagerly, excited to launch into the tale. Oberi bounced at his side, and Eddie reached down to pat his head. "But it'll have to wait until we get somewhere safe."

Apparently, hugs were more important than safety, because Eddie went around and embraced everybody. He got to me last, kneeling down before me and wrapping me in the tightest hug. "Dearest princess! Life's been dark without you."

"I missed you too, Eddie. What happened to your eye?" I asked.

"It was an unfortunate event of being in the Elvish concentration camps," Eddie informed me. "They tortured all of us for information, but I am proud to say, I never gave in! The Warden's tormentors grew tired of me eventually, and took my right eye as punishment, so to say."

"I'm really sorry that happened," I said sadly.

"On the contrary, when they took it, I considered it a privilege, because it helped me to better understand my master," Eddie said brightly.

Oberi gave a high-pitched whine, and Charlie's expression softened. "It's really nice to have you back. How'd you save us?"

"Elves can use mirrors to create portals," Eddie explained. "It is how we used the Mirror of Ingress to escape Forevermore when it was sieged."

Eddie fished in his pocket and took out the small pocket mirror again, displaying it to us all. "I used this to portal you here, to this waypoint along the path. Elves must have a mirror on the other side of their destination to make portals. Thankfully, the portal I created was able to generate off the reflective surface of Ava's Spirit shield. My instructions were to make sure we weren't followed before I brought you back to a safe place."

"It doesn't appear we've been followed. Otherwise, Esther would've blown our heads off by now," Kallie noted.

"I'd rather she do that, instead of listening to another one of her stupid sermons," Marcus complained.

Eddie nodded in utmost sincerity, then turned his attention back on me. "My princess, why are you still on the ground? Here, I'll help you stand."

Eddie offered a hand, but I cringed away and kept my gaze on the ground. "I can't, Eddie. Not anymore."

Eddie's look was so full of sorrow as his eyes locked on my legs. He glanced away regretfully. "Yes... it seems all of us have lost something, in these past months since we've been apart."

Charlie picked me up. I felt safe as he cradled me against him, and my head fell onto his chest. I was so exhausted after making that Spirit shield. I didn't think I could stay awake for longer than a few moments.

"Do you have somewhere for us to go?" Charlie asked.

"Of course. Follow me."

Eddie pointed the pocket mirror to the empty space in front of him, and as he did, a portal bloomed there. He gestured for us to go through it. Kallie and Marcus went first, while Charlie carried me forward. I didn't see where we were heading, because as we went through the portal, I fell into unconsciousness.

I lingered there, somewhere in the darkness and complete stillness, until I felt myself rousing lightly in a soft bed.

I knew Charlie was near before I saw him. I felt his weight on the bed, and I recognized the smell of bergamot. "Are we okay?"

It took a tremendous amount of effort to open my eyelids. The first thing I noticed was there was golden light everywhere, and the area I found myself in was pristine. I'd woken up in an elaborate bedroom, which was made of marble and decorated with gorgeous furniture. The bed I lay in was big enough to sleep four people, and it was layered with silk sheets and cashmere blankets.

A massive sliding glass door that led to a stone balcony stood open. Gossamer drapes drifted in the breeze, which smelled like sea water and was warm. I heard seagulls, and the muffled sounds of people below.

I expected to wake up in some sort of army tent, but I'd arisen in a palace.

"We're safe." Charlie stroked back a few strands of hair from my eyes. "We're with the Elves. Eddie took us to their new city."

"A new city?" I slowly sat up. Oberi licked my chin.

"After Forevermore was taken over by the Warden, my grandfather and the rest of the Elven refugees that got away built a city on an island in the middle of the Mediterranean Sea. It's surrounded by wards. No one's found it yet."

"The Elves built an entire city in a year?" I questioned.

"They used magic, but they had help," Charlie explained. "Apparently, a sorceress from Malovia took an abandoned Elven city from the fae realm of Edinmyre— a settlement named Ithriel— and moved it through a portal to this island. Then the Elves rebuilt the ruins of Ithriel and filled in the gaps with magic. Besides the old structures, the city is created out of illusions that are solid. The Elves can't do that, so the fae stepped in to lend a hand. Once the rebuild was complete, the Elves renamed the city Ilamanthe."

"So the fae are allies with the Elves now?" I asked. They'd been enemies during the last Great Supernatural War, with the fae being the greatest persecutors of the Elves, but I supposed Kallie's brother was running things in Malovia now.

"Seems like it. The fae want to make amends for the last Elven genocide, so they're here to help. The fae created this city for the Elves as a peace offering. It was a good thing they managed to build it so quickly."

I had to marvel for a moment. "What fae could be so powerful she could move an entire city from one realm to another?"

"I'm not sure, but hopefully we'll get some answers soon. Whoever she is, she must be one powerful sorceress."

As I got to a sitting position, I realized I was wearing some sort of pretty silk dress, soft enough to sleep in but definitely fit for a princess. "I'm assuming there's a dress code."

Charlie looked different, too. He wore a pair of black slacks, with a fine silk shirt that had a few buttons open at the top. He appeared positively dashing. "The servants gave us some new clothes. I dressed you when you were out of it. All of us were covered in dirt from the fight with Esther."

"How long has it been?" I was horrified important things might've been decided when I was sleeping. I didn't want to be behind on what was going on.

"You've only been sleeping for a few hours. Eddie had us rest here until we were ready to see everyone. This is our personal suite. Kallie and Marcus have rooms nearby. Basically, we have an entire section of the palace to ourselves that the servants are referring to as my quarters. All of our friends are rooming in this tower, which is reserved strictly for the prince and his guests, but you and I have the biggest suite."

"We have a whole tower to ourselves?"

"It sounds crazy, but it's actually nothing compared to the rest of the palace," Charlie informed me. "This place is enormous. It makes the Institute seem small."

"Well, I'm up now, so we better get to it."

My wheelchair stood beside the bed. Marcus must've dropped it off. Charlie helped me into it. I found a gold brush on a nearby vanity, and I combed out the tangles in my hair before we left the room.

The rest of Charlie's quarters were just as grand as his suite was. In the center of the tower was a living space, where all the bedrooms were connected. There was a massive fireplace in the main room, as well as floor-to-ceiling windows that displayed the city below. A widescreen TV hung on the wall, and large sectional couches were spread throughout the space, the walls lined with dozens of bookshelves. One of the walls housed a floor-to-ceiling mirror that made the space appear even larger than it already was.

It was even better than the rooms at the palace in Forevermore. Everywhere I looked, there was a new piece of art or another beautiful thing to look at.

I rolled myself to one of the giant windows and looked down, observing the scene. Hundreds of buildings were clustered around the city's palace. I recognized the beauty of ancient Elvish architecture in every stone structure. They really had taken the bones from Ithriel and turned those ruins into the incredible buildings they were today. Everywhere I looked, I saw tall spires, domed buildings, and formidably tall architecture, with massive gargoyles and stained-glass windows.

It appeared the palace itself had been built on the side of a mountain that overlooked the city, and the buildings that had been constructed around it were collected on the cliff sides below. Small dots moved within the city as thousands of Elves maneuvered throughout the cobblestone streets. The Mediterranean Sea spanned outward all around us, appearing endless, while a glistening sandy beach circled the island's edge.

I felt tears rise and nearly spill over. I couldn't believe the Elves had made it after Forevermore had been sieged. More so— they'd *thrived*. What an exceptional and resourceful people the Elves were. I thought for sure they'd be hiding in cities around the world, but here they were. Despite the worst, they'd gone on to survive.

The doors to the quarters opened. Eddie walked in, followed by Kallie and Marcus. When Eddie saw us, he hurriedly bowed so low it was nearly funny.

"My prince and princess," he gushed. "Welcome to the city of Ilamanthe. In Elvish, it means *city of new light*. Our Emperor thought it was a fitting name for the place that now resides us. He changed the name from Ithriel, because this place is no longer just an Elven city, but a city for all, and the freedom that inspires us to carry on."

New light indeed. I certainly felt revived.

Eddie took a seat on an armchair, while Kallie and Marcus went to lounge on the sectional— on opposite ends, I might add. I rolled to the end of the sectional where Kallie was sitting, while Charlie took a seat on an armchair opposite Eddie's.

"Okay, out with it," Kallie said. "How'd you escape the camps, Eddie? We were certain you were dead."

"I all but was, by the time I left the West Facility. That is the name of the place they kept us. It was a concentration camp on the other side of Darke Island, far from the Institute," Eddie said.

"The West Facility? Was that really what it was called?" Marcus asked.

"Yes." Eddie nodded grimly. "The Warden isn't a particularly imaginative person."

That was putting it lightly. He was about as creative as my left butt cheek, and I hadn't seen that create any masterpieces lately.

"The name just seems so... cold." Kallie scowled. "Like some sort of landfill."

"That is the point. As far as the Warden is concerned, once we're at the camps, we're garbage to be disposed of. We weren't afforded the right to a proper name, not even to terrify us." Eddie's shoulders drooped. "The angels are the ones running the camps. They starved us, beat us, and forced us to work making war supplies for the Warden day in and day out. Many of us got sick from disease and died, while most others starved to death. Others were merely tortured until their bodies could endure no longer."

"Elves are immortal and super strong. They aren't easy to kill. The angels must've been extra brutal to kill them this way," I said.

"Indeed. Their tactics went beyond the point of cruelty," Eddie admitted heavily. "They regulated us to one slice of bread and a watery soup with one radish per day. Elves are immune to magical restraints such as noxite, so starvation was their way of keeping our magic contained, as we were too weak to summon it. I spent most of my time carrying stones from quarries I could barely lift, and making bricks, as the angels needed them to rebuild Celestial City."

Eddie shrugged unhappily. "I thought, at times, of attempting to sneak out, or of creating a weapon with the bricks I was making, but I was so malnourished I knew I wouldn't win if there was a fight, and I didn't have enough energy to run fast enough to escape. When I wasn't being made to labor, I was being tortured for information. It is how I lost my eye."

"These monsters are sick," Marcus growled. "It's deplorable they can do this to people."

"That is not how the angels see it," Eddie stated. "In their eyes, these camps are a sort of purgatory, a method for cleansing sin. The angels who ran the camps allowed prisoners to leave, so long as they swore an oath to join a new religion and work as soldiers for the Warden and his cause."

"The Mission," Charlie said in disgust.

"Indeed," Eddie replied. "The prisoners who converted were stuffed into military vans and never seen again. Some of my company agreed to be converted, but most of us stuck to our faith. Eventually, the Warden got tired of waiting for answers. If we couldn't be converted, he wanted us to be exterminated. Myself and several other Elvish prisoners were taken out of the camp and into the woods. I realized that we were being moved out of the West Facility and to a new camp on the mainland. I knew that if we had any chance of escape, we needed to do it then, because once they took us to the larger camp there was no possibility of getting out alive."

Eddie smirked. "I was very weak and didn't have much magic left. But as we stopped for the night, I remembered my master, and all my friends, and I realized I didn't want to die this way. So when the backs of the soldiers were turned, the other Elves and I got together to join our magic with simultension, just like Charlie had taught us. We were able to create a magical blast that killed the soldiers. But we were unable to control the magic, so it backfired and killed a couple of us as well."

"Oh, Eddie." I was breathless with the admission. It was awful.

"We knew some of us could die if we resisted, but we didn't care. Death was acceptable, when compared to how we'd been living in those camps," Eddie replied. "Our magic left a crater in the ground. There weren't any remains of those who'd perished in the blast. We knew we had to leave there quickly. We scattered in all directions, so anyone following wouldn't be sure where we went. For a day or so, I survived off roots and tubers I found underneath the ground. I didn't mind— it was more than they were feeding us in the camps. I thought about returning to the Institute to find Charlie and help him escape, but before I could, the other Elves found us and brought us to Ilamanthe. I've spent the rest of that time recovering and searching for you."

"We're proud of you for staying so strong," Charlie said. "I can't even imagine what you've been through."

"It wasn't easy, and is still not. I have nightmares about the camps." Eddie shivered. "But I am comforted in knowing the West Facility no longer exists. Once I got to Ilamanthe and told the Emperor where the camp was located, we were able to send agents in to destroy the West Facility and rescue those we could."

Eddie smiled. "But I should pause the story, for now. You have others eager to join you."

I was about to ask who he meant, until the door to the room burst open. Elated voices rose throughout the room, and I gave a scream of joy as I watched Chancey, Ivy, Ez, Opal, and Alistair stampede into the room. Kallie, Marcus, and Charlie jumped up from their seats, and the room was quickly enveloped in a mess of shouting, joy, and love.

"You're alive!" I cried out. I instantly reached for my brother, who squeezed me tightly. His peryton Familiar, Tahoma, gave a gentle snort and nuzzled my cheek with his soft lips. I was so relieved that I let out a couple of sobs. The moment was overwhelming— *all of them* had gotten out, and unhurt. It was nothing short of a miracle.

"Fuck yeah, we are! It's gonna take more than a burning prison to get rid of us!" Ivy exclaimed as they embraced me. I let the tears fall, because it was a huge weight off my shoulders to know that, despite my choice to allow the Institute to burn, the people I cared about hadn't suffered the consequences of my actions.

"This is crazy! How'd you guys escape?" Charlie asked.

"Now *that's* a story," Chancey said, slinging his arm around Charlie's shoulders.

"See, as you know, shit was going *down* at the Institute that night," Alistair said. "Ez, Opal and I were still in the woods when you guys were taken to Cellblock 9. The guards never found us, but we spent days trapped out there, trying to figure out how to get over the fence. Eventually, the guards came looking for us. I was able to trick them with my Mentalist powers, and puppet them away from our location long enough to remain hidden. But then the fire happened, and everything started going up in smoke."

"You guys remember Ives and me got separated from the group when the guards started attacking students," Chancey said. "The mob carried us away, where we met up with Alistair and the others outside. It was complete chaos, I tell ya."

"The prison yard was in shambles," Alistair said excitedly— sounding like he was retelling the events of some rager party, and not a life-or-death situation. "We figured if we wanted to live, we had to get the hell off the island. So, we thought... why not take a bus?"

A huge grin spread across my face. I recalled the memory of the Institute's submarine bus smashing through the prison's fence line and ambling clumsily toward freedom the night we'd escaped. "No way! That was *you*?"

"Oh, yeah. We overpowered the guards protecting it, Chancey hotwired the rig, and we took off outta the Institute's cage," Alistair said proudly. "One of the grandest moments of my life, if I do say so myself."

"They came after us like hell, but everything was smooth sailing once we hit the water, cause they couldn't come after us. I gotta say, though, I mighta run over a couple of vamps on our drive out," Chancey added.

I nearly toppled out of my chair laughing. I pictured Chancey recklessly driving the massive submarine bus across Darke Island while being chased by guards, the rest of my friends clinging to the bus seats like cats in order to hold on.

"One of the angel guards smashed into the windshield and rolled off the top. It was *great*," Ivy cackled. "We popped open the back door and flung some battle orbs behind us before we hit the ocean. We watched a couple guards blow up. It was quite the *riveting* experience."

"Maybe for you." Ez scowled as he rubbed his head. "I still got the scar from when I hit my head on the ceiling. Chancey nearly rolled the damn thing."

"I got us out!" Chancey said defensively. "You should quit complaining and be glad you got a ride. It was hard enough squeezing your big ass Familiar on the bus."

Tahoma let out a sullen bray, and I asked, "Are the keys safe?"

"Yes. They're in a royal vault here in Ilamanthe, protected by Elven guards. I made sure I didn't lose them," Ez said.

My shoulders sagged. I was more than grateful the Warden hadn't gotten his hands on the Divinity Keys we had, because it'd taken a lot of sacrifice to obtain them. "What happened next?"

"We just kept driving until we hit land. By the time we pulled onto a beach, your dad was waiting for us," Opal informed me.

"My dad?" I tilted my head curiously.

"Our parents are here. *Everyone's* parents are here, actually," Ez stated. "We've got a bit of bad news... Kinpago and Octavia Falls were taken by the Warden."

"*What?*" Marcus asked, and my stomach twisted.

"They couldn't hold up. The Warden was going to destroy both cities if we didn't let him have them, so they decided abandoning the towns was the best way to preserve what was left," Alistair said. "The priestesses and the chieftains got everyone out they could. The elementals and witches that survived are currently living here, in Ilamanthe."

Then Alistair scoffed, and he mumbled under his breath, "Or at least, everyone who isn't a *traitor* is here."

"What do you mean?" I asked.

"Some elementals and witches surrendered to the Warden and joined The Mission when the cities fell. They didn't see a point in continuing to resist," Ez clarified. "As far as our side, we don't have many strongholds left. *Hok'evale* is safe, but we don't know for how long."

"Where did the Warden take all these prisoners of war?" I questioned. "If Kinpago and Octavia Falls have fallen, those supernaturals that didn't get a chance to flee had to be taken somewhere."

Eddie gave a heavy sigh. "Unfortunately, we believe they've been taken to the same camp the Warden had attempted to move me to. From the intel we've gathered, we know it is even larger, and more dangerous. The Main Facility is somewhere in the contiguous United States. It has many more Elves in captivity, and it is also where the Warden holds his prisoners of war. There are all kinds of supernaturals being kept in that camp, some even of the Warden's own race, angels who didn't support his cause."

"Then what are we waiting for?" Charlie demanded. "Let's go there right now to destroy it and liberate the prisoners."

"I wish we could, but it is very well hidden. We've been trying to find it for some time, but have so far been unsuccessful. It is a highly concealed secret of the Warden's, and until we locate where it might be, a rescue mission is impossible," Eddie said.

"I'm betting the Main Facility has to be near California. Darke Island is off the western coast of the United States," I said.

"Six hundred miles off the coast," Kallie objected.

"Yes, but it's still easier to transport people across the open ocean rather than thousands of miles across land where they might be spotted, and we know the Warden used Darke Island as his base for years," I said. "He's probably been building this camp for a while, waiting for the right time to use it against his enemies. The West Facility was just a holding center on the island he could use until the Main Facility was finished."

"What about the witches? Connecticut is a long ways away from the west coast. If the Main Facility is on the other side of the country, you must've found clues as to how the captured witches were being transported," Marcus asked.

"Unfortunately, we did not," Eddie replied. "The Warden must be using some type of magic we aren't aware of or don't have access to in order to transport all these prisoners from one side of the nation to the other."

"Why couldn't the Warden just conjure portals, and move people that way?" Charlie questioned. "They're harder to trace."

"Moving a lot of people through portals is hard. It's not easy magic, especially not across hundreds of miles," Kallie said. "Only the best supernaturals can pull it off, and the Warden doesn't have any Elves helping him."

"That we know of," Charlie mused. "He could be forcing prisoners to do his bidding."

"You would need many, *many* portals to transport that number of prisoners," Eddie explained. "Even if it was possible, which it could be, it's unclear as to how he could create so many portals without leaving supernatural traces that we could follow. But from what we can guess, the facility must be somewhere near the west coast, just as Ava predicted."

"That still doesn't narrow it down," Marcus grumbled. "The western United States is huge. There's massive sprawls of open desert that go on forever, without a soul in sight. The Warden could pick a million places to put this camp. It's like locating a needle in a haystack."

"We'll find it," Kallie said firmly. "And once we do, the soldiers who are torturing those poor people are going to beg for mercy."

"Which we aren't going to give them," Charlie added coldly, and Oberi gave a growl. I whole-heartedly agreed.

"I just don't know how the Elves managed to find somewhere so efficient to hide," Kallie said. "This area is perfect to hold the city of Ilamanthe. How'd they locate such a well-concealed area after Forevermore was sieged?"

"Your family, actually," Ivy stated. "Turns out that King Ethan and Queen Emmaline were the ones who found the island after Forevermore fell, and they helped the Elves build a city here with illusion magic. They've been busy doing that in secret while your brother and his mate have been running Malovia."

"If Kazim has ascended the throne, why are Ethan and Emma still referred to as king and queen?" Marcus asked.

"My parents aren't reigning monarchs anymore, but they still retain their titles," Kallie explained, before turning back to Eddie. "How are things in Malovia?"

"Apparently, after Octavia Falls was taken over, King Kazim aligned himself with the witches and officially declared war against the angels," Eddie said. "The fae have been providing endless resources to Ilamanthe to get the Elves back on their feet. Although many fae have sought refuge in Ilamanthe, their country is still standing— for now."

I was glad that the fae had chosen to side with us, because they were powerful allies. They were just as rich as the Elves used to be, and since the Malovian Revolution had been over for twenty years now, the country had plenty of time and resources to recuperate and help others.

Kallie nodded. "Kaz would do that. Is my brother here?"

"He is. There are many individuals waiting in the council room to speak with you all," Eddie noted.

"Then let's talk to them right away," Charlie said.

The room began to clear out as the group headed into the hallway. I went to follow, before I felt a light touch on my shoulder. "Princess, may I speak with you in private?"

Eddie appeared wholly somber. Charlie paused at the door, as he was the last to leave. But Oberi nudged his hand, and he continued after the others.

After the door shut quietly behind us and we were alone, Eddie hung his head. "Princess, I... I feel so much guilt."

"Why, Eddie? You didn't do anything wrong," I insisted.

"While you were sleeping, Charlie informed me of what happened. You and the others ventured into the Infernal Underground to find me. That attempt to rescue me led to you losing your ability to walk," Eddie choked. "I am no guard, but a coward. My duty in life is to protect my master and his princess, and you have sacrificed a part of yourself to protect *me*. There is no greater shame for an Emperor's guard. I am worth nothing if I cannot serve you. My failure to defend my life's purpose is what led you to this predicament."

"The Warden took you, Eddie. You did all you could, but you didn't have a choice," I pressed.

Eddie shook his head violently, and tears flung from his eyes as he fell to his knees before me. "You don't understand, princess! I deserve to be punished for my insolence."

"Oh, please, Eddie, get up." He was making *me* emotional, and I didn't blame him for what had happened in the slightest. "I'm not going to punish you — that's ridiculous. And please don't tie your self-worth to Charlie and me. You're worthy just by being alive. You don't need to prove yourself."

"I understand, but this is my culture, and how I was raised. I was born to serve, and be a good guard," he whimpered.

"You *are* a good guard, Eddie. You've never let us down, and I'm sure you won't in the future, so long as there's anything you can do about it."

"My princess is too kind." Eddie wiped at his face and sniffed as he staggered to his feet. "But if there is any way to repay this debt and make it right, I will."

"There's nothing you have to repay," I said kindly. "But if you want to escort us to the council room, it would probably be helpful. This palace is massive, and I don't feel like getting my ass lost."

Eddie laughed lightly. "Of course. May I?"

I gestured that he could touch my chair. He pushed me out of the room and into the hallway, where everyone else was waiting. Eddie pushed me at the front of the group, carrying on as he explained everything the palace had to offer.

"The servants are here to feed and clothe you, as well as clean your rooms and tend to anything you don't desire to do yourselves. We have a grand dining hall, magnificent private pools, theaters, magical creature stables, and a temple to our goddesses all within the palace walls, as well as a hospital, should anyone fall ill," Eddie stated. "Everything you need here is accommodated for, though if you wish, you may venture out into the city to explore."

The decoration of the palace was ornate and carefully styled. Every furnishing appeared elaborate. It felt so odd, leaving the despair and filth of the Institute to be welcomed into such a bright place that was clean, shining, and full of light wherever you went. I almost felt uncomfortable... like I didn't belong here.

But that wasn't true. I was an Elven princess now. I belonged here more than anybody. I just had to get used to living comfortably again. Here, the guards wouldn't bully and stalk me; they'd follow my orders, and protect me with their lives.

The Elves we passed in the hallway gave delighted noises, bowing and curtsying with glee. A couple of Elvish ladies had sparks in their eyes as they watched me roam by, whispering to each other in excitement.

Overwhelm settled in my bones. These people were looking to *me* to become the mother of their race. There hadn't been a female Elvish monarch in decades, and now that I was here, I gave them hope. I didn't think I was worthy of having that responsibility, but it was on my shoulders now, so I had to perform my duties to the best of my ability.

"You'll do well," Kallie murmured beside me, and she reached out to lay a hand on my shoulder. She knew what it felt like to be a respected princess, with a whole country waiting for her to make the right or wrong moves. I wish I could say I'd gotten better at making good choices over the past few years, but I wasn't so sure I hadn't gotten *worse*. Now my decisions affected more than just Charlie and me, or my friends. They affected a whole nation.

This was very different from being the daughter of a chieftain. I hoped I'd make the Elves proud. Or at the very least, that I wouldn't mess it up too badly... because I was good at destroying whatever I touched, including my own life. I didn't want to ruin the lives of the Elves as well, and I already had once, back in Forevermore.

I couldn't afford to screw up this time.

Eddie took us to a set of golden double doors, where a pair of guards were waiting. They bowed to Charlie, then to me, before they pulled the doors open.

The council room was absolutely massive. It was a circular marble room, with a glass ceiling that opened up wide to the sky. At the end of the room was a gigantic tree, with twisting limbs and large, multicolored fruit that hung off its branches, Elvish designs formed into the bark as if with magic. The tree reached upward to the high ceiling, framed by a lovely indoor waterfall that pooled around its roots. Someone was playing a soft flute nearby, but I couldn't see who. It looked more like a greenhouse to protect this beautiful tree, rather than a council room.

A massive round table stood in the middle of the room, surrounded by high-backed chairs. Gathered in front of the table were a large number of people, most of whom I knew.

"Daddy!" I cried happily. I threw my arms out, and he rushed forward to give me a hug.

"It's wonderful to see you, peanut. We had no idea where you were," Daddy said, giving me a kiss on the head.

"Though we were sure you were safe," Mama added, and she stroked my hair. "We had faith you and your friends made it out of the Institute."

"Yeah, seeing as how we weren't *completely* convinced you didn't cause the fire." Daddy laughed.

I cringed. He'd meant it as a joke, but it hit closer to home than I wanted to admit. I hadn't *started* the Institute fire, but I had let it burn... and that was still a decision I wavered on from time to time.

I noticed a certain red dragon was missing— my father's companion, Julian. He almost never left Daddy's side, and that worried me. "Did Julian make it?"

"Yes, peanut," Daddy said. "Julian is too large to navigate most of the castle, so he's spending most of his time with the Elvish military defending the city, but rest assured he is safe."

"Are the others here?" I asked them.

"Your siblings are staying with us right here in the palace. The Emperor has provided us, as well as Kallie's and Marcus' parents, and your grandparents, with the finest suites in all the castle," Mama said. "Your Aunt Imogen and Uncle Jonah, along with their families, are all in Ilamanthe. They have their own apartments in the city. We managed to get everyone out, even though some people couldn't be saved."

Mama gave Daddy a sad look, and I didn't ask about home. I didn't want to know what the angels were doing with Kinpago now that they had it under their control, because it would make me too sad.

Whatever the case, I was an Elvish princess. This was my home now.

My parents weren't the only ones I knew. Everyone else's parents were here, too. Nadine and Lucas were in the room, and both of them reached out to give Marcus a hug. King Ethan, along with Queen Emmaline, greeted Kallie warmly, pulling their daughter into an embrace.

Emperor Cassiel was surrounded by members of the Emperor's Guards, two of which I recognized. General Ibrahim and Colonel Amilda, whom we had met in Forevermore, stood guard at his side.

Cassiel approached Charlie. His grandfather gave him a gentle welcome as Cassiel reached out to shake Charlie's hand.

And Cameron. He was hanging back. I stared Charlie's father down. Although he glanced away from my glare, it was only for a moment.

"We're grateful to be together again," Emperor Cassiel said, clapping Charlie on the back. "I had hoped our reunion would come sooner, but you are here now. Your father is here as well, Charlie."

"Hello, son," Cameron said softly.

Charlie's tone became cold. "You haven't earned the right to call me that. You *left* us in Forevermore! You just fled, so that we could be captured by the Warden, and we remained locked in his prison for another *year*. How could you?"

"Charlie," I said gently. My husband wasn't on the best terms with his dad, but I didn't think it was fair of Charlie to blame Cameron for leaving us in Forevermore. "I *told* them to leave. They were standing by the Mirror of Ingress, and there was no way we were going to reach the portal with them by that point. They had to get out while they still had the chance, even if we didn't. They didn't need to be captured alongside us."

"I never would've left if I had a choice," Cameron replied, but Charlie only looked more disgusted by his response. "You had the chance to come with us, and you broke my arm to get away from me."

"To get to *Ava*," Charlie spat. "You may feel comfortable leaving your family behind, but I would never do such a thing."

By the ancestors, Cameron wasn't helping.

Emperor Cassiel quickly stepped in. "We wanted to take you with us, but we had to make a decision at that precise moment. As Emperor, it was a choice I had to make for my people. I realized as Forevermore fell that three Elvish royals were in danger, and if all of us died, the monarchy died with us. Our people would be completely unprotected, and left vulnerable in our absence. It was our job to lead the Elves to refuge here in Ilamanthe. One of us can die, but not all three, otherwise, our nation will die with us. Believe me Charlie; as my grandson, you are precious to me."

Charlie relaxed slightly.

"I knew the Warden would keep you alive, and there was nothing that would stop us from rescuing you in time," Cassiel added. "We've spent the last year building Ilamanthe and getting our people back on their feet, so that we could come back and get you. We had an extraction plan in place and returned to Darke Island the first chance we got, but by then, the Institute had already caught fire, and you and your friends were gone. We've been tracking you ever since, and were lucky enough to gain the narrow opportunity to portal you back here. I know you've felt alone, and had to go through a lot of things by yourself. But you were never *truly* alone, because I've always been trying to bring you back to the family, even if I wasn't successful. Can you ever forgive me for the decision I made that day?"

Charlie's hesitation was evident through the bond. It was clear he trusted his grandfather far more than Cameron— respected him, even. "I believe I can forgive you and learn to understand why you made that decision. We're all here and safe, so I guess it all worked out in the end."

I looked to the other people in the room, to those I didn't know. There was a small brunette girl that had to be Marcus' little sister. She appeared confident and held herself tall.

"I missed you, big brother." Erica gave Marcus a one-armed hug. "I want to hear all about how you busted out of prison. I'm sure it was epic."

"Hi, Erica," Marcus said. "Sorry about... home."

Erica shrugged. "Wasn't much left of home once we had to leave, anyway. I'm not too worried. I'm sure we'll get Octavia Falls back."

"What does it look like?" Marcus asked warily.

"It's a literal hellscape," Lucas said gravely. "When we left, the entire city was in shambles. There were cracks in the earth, and massive black tar pits had popped up all over the city to suck people to their death. The dark gods and The Mission destroyed the town. It was nearly uninhabitable."

"After everything you did to fulfill your prophecy and save it, now it's gone," Marcus nearly wept.

"He ain't the only one, kid," Liam grumbled. "Kinpago's destroyed for what has to be the millionth time. I'm starting to get used to it being on fire."

"We can get our cities back," Lucas said firmly. "This war isn't over, and everything isn't completely gone. We can rebuild once we win. The true heart of a community isn't the place; it's the people. We're still surviving, so they haven't beat us yet."

"Dad's right," Erica cut in. "We don't stop being a community just because we lost our home. Witches are still going through with their Evoking Ceremonies to awaken their powers, and they're still brewing potions, casting spells, and surviving no matter what. We don't stop being witches because there are people out there who want to take us down. No matter where we are on this planet, we're going to continue being who we are."

"You need to stay out of this, Erica," Marcus said. "You're too young. You can't fight yet."

"Actually, my birthday was last week, and my powers awakened," Erica stated matter-of-factly.

Marcus' features paled. "How long have we been on the run? What day is it?"

"It's July fifteenth," Lucas told him.

Marcus blew a breath of disbelief. "I didn't realize how much time had passed since we left the Institute. I'm sorry I missed your birthday, sis, and your Evoking Ceremony."

Erica nudged him. "It's fine. It's not like I expected my fugitive brother to break out of prison to show up for my birthday. But look— here you are. Just a couple days late."

Marcus choked back tears. He obviously really missed his family.

"Of course I'd break out of prison for you," he whimpered.

After all the complaining Marcus did about how perfect his sister was, I was surprised to see they had a good relationship. Clearly he'd just been talking out his ass.

"Can I see it?" he asked her.

I wasn't sure what he meant, but Erica obviously understood. She pulled down her shirt collar to show a tattoo of a skull across her collarbone.

"Mortana," Marcus said with a nod. "You got the powers of a Death Witch. What's your specialty? Necromancy? Can you control dead bodies like zombies?"

"Nah, it's not as cool as your powers, bro," she teased. "I'm a Reaper's Apprentice, just like Dad."

Marcus gasped and clutched his heart, until he nearly fell over. "Reaper's Apprentice? That's a super rare gift."

"The coven needs more reapers." Erica dropped her gaze. "I've already heard more voices in the last few days than Dad did in his first year. It's tough out there."

"Voices? What do you mean?" I asked. "What exactly is a Reaper's Apprentice?"

"I have the powers of a reaper," Erica explained. "In Miriamic culture, reapers are specialized spirits who greet witches at death and help them cross over to the afterlife. I hear the last thoughts of the coven's dead, and I carry them with me to the afterlife, to help make their transition easier. As a Reaper's Apprentice, I'm studying under Dad to learn my abilities, so that one day I can help the souls of the coven reach our spiritual realm."

"Did Kellen make it out of town?" Marcus blurted. "Is he here with you?"

Kellen had been Marcus' mentee before he came to the Institute. His older sister was Anya— Marcus' former girlfriend, who he'd accidentally killed years ago.

"I'm sorry, Marcus," Erica said gently. "I saw him get captured by The Mission before we left Octavia Falls. Neither me nor Dad have heard his last thought, which means he's still alive. We believe he's being held at the Main Facility."

"Then we need to get him out. The minute we find out where the Main Facility is, I'm going in there," Marcus pledged.

He turned his attention to two people standing near Kallie. "Let's get to work. Who are *these* people?"

He'd asked that question rather rudely. One of them had to be Kallie's twin, because they appeared to be very alike. Kazim didn't look much like a king, more like a scholar. He was scrawny and wore glasses that were slightly askew, his blond hair a mess on top of his head.

Nobody answered Marcus' question, because the twins were staring each other down.

"Kaz." Kallie observed her brother, unsure of what to say. This had to be the first time they were facing each other since she'd been sent to the Institute.

Kazim's face brightened into a wide smile. He embraced Kallie, lifting her off the ground with the force of his hug. "Never thought I'd miss you so much as the day you left for the Institute. It's a wonderful thing we're together again. Shouldn't have ever been separated."

Kallie gulped back tears as Kazim placed her back on the ground. "Shouldn't have. Wouldn't have, either, if not for Valen."

"Believe me, he's on my list," Kazim growled. "I've got guards crawling the country looking for his arse. If he's anywhere to be found, I'll have them bring him back to Malovia, so I can skin him alive myself."

Kallie leaned in to hold her brother again, like she couldn't get enough of him. "I can't tell you how much that means, Kaz."

"You know I couldn't believe it when you tried to kill me, even when the evidence was staring me in the face. I felt something was wrong. I should've put it together that Valen compelled you. Once the evidence came out against Valen, I ordered him to be found and brought to trial immediately. I felt terribly guilty you had to go through all that. I should've listened to my gut, and never allowed you to go to the Institute." Kaz frowned.

"We've all made mistakes," King Ethan said, coming between them both and laying a hand on each of their shoulders. "All we can do now is put the past behind us."

"Indeed." Kaz gestured to the woman beside him, speaking to the room at large. "For anyone who does not yet know, this is my queen, mate and soon-to-be wife, Sigrid."

Sigrid was tall, taller than Kazim, with black hair and dark, hooded eyes. She spoke with a slight Malovian accent as she nodded toward the rest of us. "We finally meet again, Kalina. As for the rest of you, I am pleased to make your acquaintance."

Kazim's eyes raked up and down Marcus' form, like he was expecting more than the man before him. "Is, uh... is this it?"

"*Kaz*," Kallie hissed.

"Oh, sorry, didn't mean to put it that way. Just... never seen one of our kind with a warlock before," Kazim said. He reached out to shake Marcus' hand. "You're my sister's mate, correct?"

Kazim's parents must've informed him about what was going on between Marcus and Kallie. Her parents knew she was mated, but beyond that, I wasn't sure what else she'd told them.

Marcus appeared to have no idea what was going on. "Ah... not really."

Kazim's eyebrows knitted together, like he didn't understand why Marcus didn't accept the title. He slowly let go of Marcus' hand and drew away. "Good to meet you, besides."

"I'm really happy to see you both," Kallie replied, quickly diverting attention away from Marcus. "From what I've heard, Malovia hasn't been seized. Shouldn't you be there, preparing for battle?"

"Mom and Dad are staying in Ilamanthe to support the fae who have fled Malovia, but I'll be returning to our country soon, as Sigrid and I need to maintain a stronghold in Dolinska," Kazim replied. "We're here to see you, and to speak with everyone about what's to be done about this war. We need to make some decisions on what to do next."

"Everyone take a seat," Emperor Cassiel instructed. Chair legs scraped across the floor, and a variety of noise surrounded me as everyone went to sit at the round table. Oberi changed into a phoenix and sat on the back of my chair, tilting her head inquisitively.

Cassiel took a breath, inclining his head. "Firstly, I wish to thank King Ethan once again for providing us this island where we can hide. I'd also like to thank him for lending his fae to help us to build this city. Your aid is greatly appreciated in a time of war."

King Ethan nodded. "I promised myself long ago that if there was another supernatural war between the races, I would do whatever it took to protect others, and do what is right. The fae made a mistake in the last Great Supernatural War, and my family is here to right the wrongs our race caused."

"Secondly, I would like to thank Queen Emmaline for providing an alliance with the dark fae city of Eiragrad, which is located in Edinmyre," Cassiel stated. "Assistance between the dark fae and ourselves has been vital to keeping the city alive, and the portal that's been sustained in Ilamanthe that leads to Eiragrad by your magic gives us an advantage. The magical pathway between the two cities enables us to exchange resources, and have an exit strategy if Ilamanthe is compromised. I would also like to thank you once again for moving the ruins of Ithriel from Edinmyre to Earth, which enabled us to build Ilamanthe from the bones of our ancestral city."

I nearly toppled out of my chair. Kallie's *mother* was the sorceress who'd portaled the city of Ithriel to Earth? That kind of magic would kill most fae instantly on attempt. Queen Emmaline was far more powerful than I could've ever conceived.

"The city was helping me, and the magic was working for me, not against me. Ithriel wanted to be inhabited again, and the spirit of the city enabled my powers," Queen Emmaline responded. "It wasn't a simple task, but it needed to be done, so I finished the job."

I could hardly take my eyes off such a powerful caster. If Queen Emmaline could do that— move whole cities across space and time to new realms— she was an ally we needed on our side. More than that, she was a woman I wanted to be like.

She caught me staring at her and looked my way. I felt a shiver roll up my spine as the queen set eyes on me.

She frightened me. Her power was so immense it was terrifying. And I wasn't an easy person to scare.

"All the same, moving a city from one realm to another is an incredible feat, one the very gods could be proud of," Cassiel responded.

"It is what my goddess expects of me, and I'm more than happy to be of help," Queen Emmaline replied. "It was the least the fae could do, to repay the Elves for what we did to them a hundred years ago."

"Isn't Edinmyre its own realm, one the fae and Elves come from?" Marcus asked. "If there's a portal open to Edinmyre, why don't the Elves hide in Eiragrad? Edinmyre would be safer than Earth."

"*Some* Elves have moved there," Cassiel said. "But migrating to Edinmyre is a permanent choice."

"Most supernatural races can't go there," Kallie explained. "Fae and Elves are able to handle the strange way time and magic works on that planet, but other supernatural races aren't able to spend more than a few hours there; otherwise, they become trapped and go mad."

"Isn't it better for the Elves to hide there, then, if the angels and other races can't stay in Edinmyre?" Marcus asked.

"It's difficult to move back to Earth once you've spent more than a few days in Edinmyre at a time, even for one of our kind," Queen Emmaline said. "The fae and Elves who choose to live in Eiragrad can never return to Earth once they've settled there, as the magic doesn't allow them to leave. If the residents of Ilamanthe were to migrate to Edinmyre, they'd be stuck there permanently, though it is a last resort if Ilamanthe is sieged like Forevermore."

"And we've settled here on Earth. We aren't going to let the other races push us out of our home, not when Charlie's prophecy is so close to being complete, and we have a chance to move on to the Blessed Haven," Cassiel said firmly. "If we move to Edinmyre, we have no way of coming back to Darke Island and communing with the gods again through the Elven Gate, or journeying to the Blessed Haven at all. Running isn't the way to solve this. We have to pursue some sort of peace."

"And opening the Elven Gate is the only way to do it," Charlie said. "We have five Divinity Keys now; the elemental, witch, fae, angel, and merfolk key. If we can find the vampire and Astromancer key, we can open that gate and put a stop to this. Not to mention if the Elves die out, all magic will as well, because the Elves are the original supernaturals and the magical world's connection to the Blessed Haven. So I'll lead the Elves to paradise, and perhaps then the war will be over."

"The war's never going to be over, not until we stop the Warden," I said. "Even if we open that gate, he's dead set on starting a war between the gods, so he can rule over the afterlife and life on Earth both."

Quite right, Oberi said. *Dominion over the spiritual realm is his top goal, and if he succeeds, there will be no hope for any of us, not even if we manage to open the Elven Gate.*

I repeated what Oberi said to the room at large. Kazim leaned on the table.

"What's his plan, here? How does he think he'll be strong enough to conquer all the gods in the Blessed Haven so he can seat himself as the only ruler of the afterlife?"

"He's set the dark gods from hell loose," Kallie said. "He plans on overwhelming the gods in the Blessed Haven, then once they're taken care of, he'll be making the rules."

"Then... what? He expects all these dark gods won't turn on him once they're done doing his dirty work?" Kazim asked. "They're not just going to fall in line and do as he says."

"There must be more to his plan that we don't know about," Lucas said. "He'd think farther ahead than what we're considering. There must be a way he can control them."

A shiver ran up my spine at the suggestion. I couldn't imagine what kind of power or weapon the Warden had that would make even the dark gods fear him.

"Do we have any clues on where the last two keys might be?" Nadine asked. She flipped open a notepad and clicked a pen, a detective gathering clues.

No one said anything. Ez groaned and said, "Come on, there has to be *somewhere* we can start."

"The Astromancer key will be the most difficult to find. The enchanters are a very reclusive society, and as such, information on where their key is will be almost impossible to locate. If anything, finding the vampire key should be the next step," Cassiel mused.

"Why don't we ask for their help?" I questioned. "The vampires have already taken the Warden's side, but maybe the Astromancers will want to lend us a hand."

"We've already sent a request to their leaders for an alliance, and have been ignored," Cameron noted. "The angels haven't outright attacked the Astromancer city yet, so we believe they're playing both sides."

"This isn't right," I said in frustration. "The Astromancers can't sit out and claim to be Switzerland when the supernatural world is in chaos. Whatever happens affects them as much as it does us."

"But that's the stance they've chosen to take," Daddy replied. "The Astromancers won't make an alliance until there's an obvious winner to the war. Then it'll be too late."

"If I know anything about vampires— and I do— they're all greedy bastards who want the most power for themselves," Ivy said. "So I bet the vampire key has been passing through the hands of dozens of vampires through the years, who kept on killing each other for a shot at having it. That'll leave a bloody trail we can follow, so we can start investigating."

"At least that's something," Charlie grumbled.

"What do we know about the gods— *all* the gods?" I asked. "Can we infer anything from there?"

"That's a very large subject. Where do you wish to begin?" Cassiel asked.

I sighed. "Well, the Hawkei god is the Great Spirit, who in our culture is above all beings. The Great Spirit split into hundreds of other Hawkei gods, such as Coyote Spirit and Whale Spirit."

I was worried about Coyote. He hadn't contacted me since I'd escaped Cellblock 9, and I wasn't sure what had happened to him, or if he was okay. And it wasn't like I had a way to get ahold of him, so I was left to wonder.

"Mother Miriam is the goddess of the Miriamic Coven, alongside her husband Santos, and the Seven Gods are the deities of the fae pantheon," Marcus said. "Hopefully they're still in the Blessed Haven, in their respected afterlifes, and defending their territories from these dark gods the Warden sent to take them down."

"How many of these dark gods are there, and why should the gods in the Blessed Haven be threatened by them?" Charlie asked.

"These dark gods are lesser deities that aren't as strong as the rulers in the Blessed Haven, but they outnumber them," Cassiel said. *"That's* where the threat lies. They were previously contained in the Eternal Torment, but now that the Warden has set them loose, they've become a threat."

"And these dark gods are angry," Cameron added. "They were banished to hell because they were weak, and unable to accumulate followers to worship them like the other gods did. They most likely seek to take the patrons of the more benevolent gods for themselves once their enemies have been destroyed."

"Not all of the dark gods are weak," Ivy countered. "The vampiric god resides in hell, and I can assure you, he's gonna want a piece of the action."

"What's he like?" Kallie asked.

"The vampiric god is a high-level entity named Uraeus," Ivy explained. "You can't get into his lore without learning about the angel deity, the Almighty One."

Chancey nodded. "The king of heaven, surrounded by all his archangels. His brother, Uraeus, used to be a god as well, but he got kicked out of the after-life after he tried to overthrow the Almighty One."

"So Uraeus is definitely on the Warden's side, because I'll bet he's pissed that the Almighty One kicked him out of the Blessed Haven, and wants payback," Ivy stated.

"How loyal are vampires to Uraeus?" Marcus asked.

"Uraeus created vampires to do his bidding, but honestly, he rarely calls upon us anymore. We don't have a holy book or morals to follow," Ivy said. "The vampires don't worship Uraeus; we just know he created us. I don't think Uraeus cares if we murder people. That's why vampires are more atheistic—not that we don't *believe* in our god, but that we live our lives on our own terms, because Uraeus won't interfere one way or another. He's a very uninvolved god, but if he shows up to ask you to do something, a vampire better damn well do it, or face his wrath."

"So we can't count on the vampire god to help us, because he'll want the benefits of working for the Warden," Kallie said. "Isn't the Almighty One worried about the Warden and what he's doing? I'm sure the so-called *king of heaven* doesn't want to be kicked off his high horse."

"Well it's clear he hasn't done anything about it yet, has he?" Chancey asked. "The Almighty One allowed the Deacons of the Celestial Church to rise to power and make the Warden what he is. Maybe there's another angle."

"There are other gods," I insisted. "Who else is on our side?"

"The merfolk worship an ancient pantheon called the Twelve Titans, but since the merfolk have joined the Warden, we don't know if they'll be of any help, because the merfolk have turned against their gods in favor of following The Mission," Cassiel said. "The Twelve Titans could be preparing to fight against their ex-followers. We aren't completely sure."

"Anyone else?" I was beginning to lose hope that we weren't on our own.

"There are the *shinrei* of the Astromancer culture. They are spirits, divinities and forces of nature that possess both positive and negative qualities, who love and destroy in equal measure. They are unpredictable, and extremely dangerous," Cassiel said. "The Astromancers believe that their powerful ancestors or rulers can become *shinrei* after death, although the main concept behind the spirits of the Astromancer world is animism— that objects, places, and creatures all possess an individual spirit, such as a mountain taking on a life of its own."

"It sounds similar to Hawkei culture. We too believe that everything has a soul, even if it doesn't appear alive," I said.

"Correct." Cassiel inclined his head to me. "The thought of what these spirits are is ever-changing, and the religion expands and grows, shifting to include new thoughts as they are conceived. A *shinrei* can be an ancestral hero, or something as simple as an idea that is worshiped as a god. From what I've heard, the numbers of *shinrei* rival the gods in the Hawkei religion, in the thousands. Since we're not Astromancers, these spirits will be difficult to connect with, as they will most likely ignore our requests."

"Do we have an Astromancer who's willing to help us commune with them, so they can help us find the Astromancer key?" I asked.

"We've been searching," Cassiel said. "We'll continue to look until we find someone who's willing to lend their aid."

"What about a half-Astromancer? There are plenty of those, kicked out of Astromancer society," Marcus said.

"Unfortunately, those with mixed blood are ignored by the *shinrei* as equally as those who have no Astromancer heritage at all. We will need a pure-blooded Astromancer if we would like the help of the spirits in locating the Astromancer key," Cassiel clarified.

"We could ask Professor Takahashi," I said. "He's a full-blooded Astromancer. He would help us."

The room became very quiet, and Daddy said, "We're very sorry to tell you this, peanut, but it seems Professor Takahashi has vanished. We can't find him anywhere."

"Professor Hemlock is also missing," Queen Emmaline added. "We haven't been able to locate either of them since the Institute was abandoned by Doctor Taurus."

"They must've been kidnapped before the Warden set fire to the Institute. We couldn't find them before we went down to Cellblock 9," Kallie said.

Cassiel nodded. "That is what we believe happened. It is our best guess that Takahashi and Hemlock are being imprisoned somewhere by The Mission. We've made efforts to find them, although we are unsure if they are dead or alive."

I felt very ill. If our teachers were still breathing, they were definitely being tortured by the Warden, and it was because they'd protected us. Hemlock and Takahashi had guided and mentored us for years. Besides aiding us with our demigod quest, they'd made life at the Institute bearable, sometimes even fun. I wouldn't forgive myself if something happened to either one of them.

"We won't give up until we find them," Daddy said, noticing the stricken look on my face. "I promise."

Cameron gave a huff. "Not like the Elvish goddesses have been any help. We haven't been able to commune with Idril and Caralyn for some time. They've been ignoring our offerings and prayers for help." He nearly sneered the words.

"They are not *ignoring* us," Cassiel said, sounding annoyed. "They simply cannot hear us. Something is wrong."

"The gods are having trouble reaching across the spiritual plane to communicate with us. Coyote Spirit told me so, before I left Cellblock 9," I said.

"You've spoken with a Hawkei god?!" Daddy yelped in alarm, and he leapt out of his chair.

"I've talked with Coyote, like, *a million times*, Daddy, get with the program," I said, rolling my eyes.

I guess I never *had* told anyone beyond my little group that I'd had full conversations multiple times with gods, because almost everyone else in the room appeared completely shocked. But it was old news to me, so we needed to move on with it.

"This is *not* information to glaze over," Daddy grumbled as he fell back in his seat, but Mama cut him off.

"What did Coyote Spirit say?" she asked curiously. Everyone centered their attention on me.

I crossed my arms. "Well, Coyote told me that the connection between Earth and the spiritual realm is closing, so the spirits of the dead can no longer cross over to the afterlife. They're stuck in-between, and because of that, the gods aren't able to influence things like they were before. Coyote insisted that it was really important for Charlie to fulfill his prophecy, because if he doesn't open the Elven Gate, the afterlife remains inaccessible for everyone, not just the Elves."

"I've been trying to move the souls of the coven to the afterlife without success," Lucas explained. "I knew something was wrong, but assumed someone must've been targeting my reaper abilities personally. Now we understand things are happening on a much larger scale. My magic isn't working correctly with the afterlife in such turmoil. I can't help anyone from the coven cross over. They're stuck, and I'm powerless to help them."

"It is even worse than we feared," Cassiel said darkly.

"Maybe that's why my birth mother, Neva, can't speak with me, even though I've tried," Kallie said. "The fae goddess of time should've come to me by now, in a vision or in person, for all the times I've requested her help. I'm her blood— she should be honor-bound to visit me. But I don't know if she can, with the boundary between the realms being broken."

"Princess Ava, if there's any hope of contacting the gods, especially our Elven goddesses, it is through you," Cassiel said to me. "You are now the mother of the Elvish race, and the only spiritual bridge we have left to our deities. Your experience in the afterlife could give us the connection we need to speak with them."

That was a huge responsibility. I nervously clasped my hands together under the table and managed to say, "I can try. I have a strong connection to the spiritual realm. I have ever since I came back from the Ancestral Lands.

Perhaps if I can commune with the gods, they'll be able to help us bring an end to the war on Earth, and we can help them stop the war in the Blessed Haven."

"If Ava's doing spiritual work to cross the broken boundary in order to speak with the gods, I can help, too," Marcus offered. "I can work on accessing visions in order to gain intel on the enemy with my magic. My mind reading abilities are growing. If I can access information that way, it'll be really helpful."

"Do you mean if we capture one of the Warden's higher-ups, you could look into their mind and see what he's got planned?" Kallie asked.

"Maybe. I've been getting better at mind reading, but when you're inside somebody's head, there are so many thoughts and visions that not all of it is useful, and important people like the Warden have wards against my powers," Marcus explained.

"You're a demigod. You should be able to get into anyone's head, even if they have wards on them," Kallie insisted.

"It's not that easy. Even if I *can*, that doesn't mean I'll find what I'm looking for," Marcus said. "When I'm in someone's mind, it's like I have access to a whole library, and what we need is a singular sentence in one book, so I don't know where to start looking. Unless someone is thinking of the exact thing we're trying to get information on, right at the moment I peek inside their head, I have to go searching, and rifling through someone's thoughts takes longer than you'd think. The brain has over six thousand thoughts a day, and I have to skim through all of that, and sometimes more, to even narrow it down."

"There are ways to make it quicker," Lucas said. "We'll find a witch who can teach you to be more efficient at mind reading."

"What I don't understand is why the Warden is keeping Elves in concentration camps instead of executing them on a mass scale," I said. "Why does he need to keep them around in prison camps? He's already unleashed the dark gods. What else does he need them for?"

"That may be the most worrying thing of all, princess," Cassiel mused.

"There's just so much to do," Charlie said in frustration. "How are we going to manage finding the rest of these keys while fighting a war?"

"I think it's best if we sort our efforts into three groups," Cassiel began. "My grandson, the princess, and their friends will spend their time investigating the Midnighters and searching for the vampire key. Myself and my son will do what we can to locate the Main Facility, and put an end to the Elvish concentration camps for good. We will also do what we can to learn more about the Astromancer key. The rest of us will occupy ourselves with helping the other races who've been displaced settle into Ilamanthe."

"That's a job for us parents," King Ethan stated.

"Agreed. We'll have the resources," Daddy added.

It was weird to see them working together, but I guess we all had to, now. There wasn't any other option.

Kazim rose from the table. "I'm going to focus my time on learning everything I can about the Warden and his defenses. I want to know what his weak points are, and if there are any gaps in The Mission we can use to gain the advantage. The Malovian army is large and strong, and the various races living here together in Ilamanthe are no small force. We have a shot at winning. The Mission won't be easy to conquer, but if we stick together, we just might pull through this."

"If you wanna kill the Warden, you better come up with a damn good plan, because nothing we've tried has worked," Alistair said dully.

"Did you get a chance to work your Mentalist powers on him, like you did Professor Mazur?" Charlie asked.

I shuddered at the memory. Before we'd left the Institute, Alistair had used his powers on Mazur to make her turn her own life-energy magic against her, draining her until she was nothing but a husk. Angels were all but impossible to kill, yet Alistair had done it, so we were hoping he could do the same thing to the Warden.

"I did. We ran into him before we stole the bus," Alistair said. "I tried casting the spell, and forcing him to drain his own life-energy, but it instantly rebounded. I don't think he had a ward on him, either. He was just so strong that the magic immediately backfired the second it hit him."

"We only got away because he was in too much of a hurry to summon the dark gods than to deal with us," Chancey said. "But he did send a nasty spell back, one that nearly cut me in half. If I wasn't an angel and didn't have self-healing abilities, I would've been sliced in two."

Chancey stood and lifted his shirt. A deep scar ran across his abs. Ivy winced, like recalling the moment pained them greatly.

Alistair was a talented warlock. If the Warden could brush off one of his spells like it was a nuisance and not an actual threat, we were in big trouble.

"The Warden has to die if we're ever going to finish this," I insisted. "There has to be a way to kill him."

"I'll research it," Ez offered. "I'm spending all my time learning about healing magic. I can learn about the systems of angels, too, and figure out any potential weak spots."

I slightly winced when Ez spoke. I hadn't had time to tell my brother what we'd discovered in the Warden's office. We'd found medical records from angel surgeons, who'd done a live autopsy on me during my spinal surgery after I'd gotten hurt in the Underground. Because they'd been experimenting on my body while my Anichi magic was attempting to heal my spine, the injury had set wrong, and there would never be a cure. Ez still thought there was a chance I could walk, and had been researching ideas on how I could make a full recovery for months. He was going to be devastated to learn the truth.

I'd tell him later. He didn't need to know right now. Not when he was doing the hard work of figuring out how we could kill the Warden.

"We can kill the Warden after we get the Divinity Keys," Charlie said. "And they're not here, so we need to pack our things and go looking for them again."

"I understand your impatience, but it's best for all of us to remain within the safety of Ilamanthe until we have iron-clad clues on where the keys might be. The supernatural world isn't safe," Cameron said.

"Don't tell me what to do," Charlie shot at him, and I watched Cameron recoil. "This is my responsibility. I'll fulfill my prophecy the way I see fit, and we can't be expected to find the keys while sitting around here, because they're obviously not in this city."

"Ehh..." Chancey started, and he shook his head. "Sorry to tell you this, pal, but it's not gonna be easy searching for these keys outside of Ilamanthe. The Warden's got wanted posters of you four painted all over every town."

"What?" Charlie's expression became dark.

"He put out a huge bounty on your heads," Chancey stated. "He's promised millions of dollars to the supe who can bring the four of you in, dead or alive, so you've got bounty hunters crawling all over the place just looking for a clue on where they can find ya."

I bet that sleazeball at the pharmacy recognized you, and called it in hoping to get the reward, Oberi remarked.

"That's great," Charlie growled. "Like we needed more complications. Guess we have no choice but to stay here."

"You'll manage. We all will," Mama said gently.

Daddy huffed. "Not like we all don't know what it's like to be hunted down."

"Very true." King Ethan nodded.

"This shit's getting kind of old," Nadine mumbled. Lucas reached out to grab her hand.

The door to the room opened, and two older women strode in. The first woman had caramel colored hair and wore a multi-colored dress. The second twirled as she entered the room, a variety of bangles jingling on her lithe form as she danced to my side with a broad smile.

"These are two members of the Demigod Guardians, Professor Wykoff and Professor Amber," Cassiel said, gesturing to them in turn. "Although the

Guardians prefer to keep their membership as secretive as possible, they have sent these strong women to stand in Takahashi and Hemlock's place."

"We will be taking over your demigod training from this point on," Wykoff said, stopping before the table. "It's important to advance your abilities so you can stay ahead of our enemies."

"And bless the world!" Professor Amber cheered. She had literal glitter in her pockets, and flung it upward so it tricked down onto the people closest by. I sneezed.

Daddy rose from the table. "It's good to see you again, Professor Amber," he said as he gave her a hug.

"And you too, dear," Amber said, placing a peck on his cheek. "It was a blessing to help you on your ascension toward enlightenment. Now I get to help your daughter. What a joyful time this is!"

I wouldn't call this war a *joyful time*, but I liked Professor Amber's style. She seemed like the kind of person who could turn anything into a spiritual lesson, no matter how crappy it felt.

"We're happy to see you again, Professor Wykoff," Lucas said, giving her a nod. "We need you on this team."

"Aren't you a member of the Union?" Marcus asked, looking up at Amber.

Amber gave a high-pitched giggle. "I *am* a member of the United Supernatural Union, representing the Hawkei, but as things have gone rather bottom-up there, I've decided to spend most of my time with the Guardians while keeping up appearances on the council. Not that anyone *knows*, of course, as the Guardians are a secret society. The Union members I cannot trust believe I am spending my spare time at a nudist colony in France."

"It's certainly something they'd believe you to be doing, Professor," Mama said with a smile.

"There are more Guardians than anyone realizes, scattered throughout the globe. We're wise supernatural elders concerned with the survival of the supernatural races, as well as this planet. Therefore, it is imperative that the demigods within our care are ready to take on the Warden," Wykoff added. "During your training, you'll be joined by another demigod in our care."

"Another demigod? Who?" I asked.

Somebody *literally* kicked the door in. Oberi gave a surprised screech from the back of my chair and fluttered her wings in alarm. I turned my chair slightly to see who had entered.

A tall, pale-skinned vampire entered the room with an enormous amount of swagger. He had a mess of red hair, and black sunglasses over his eyes. He was dressed in a way that flattered his form, and he was astoundingly attractive, even by vampire standards. He looked somewhere around nineteen, maybe twenty. The way he rolled his shoulders as he walked told me he thought he was the gods' gift to the world.

"That's my cue to join the party," the vampire sang loudly. The slightest of Irish accents tinged his tone. "Everybody, welcome to *my world*."

"Well hello, Danny," Ivy purred. "Wish I could say that I missed you, but I didn't."

Danny removed his sunglasses and pocketed them in his jacket. His eyes were an even redder sheen than his hair. "That's too bad, Ivy. I thought we had some fun back in our day."

Chancey put his arm around Ivy's shoulders, staring Danny down. Danny appeared gleeful at the negative attention. He wiggled his eyebrows at Chancey, who glared in turn.

Ivy rolled their eyes. "It wasn't anything like that. Stop implying things. You're not as hot as you think you are."

Danny grinned. His sharp incisors weren't as prominent as Ivy's, but I could still see them if I looked closely. "I'm here, aren't I?"

"A demigod. Hm." Ivy raised an eyebrow. "Didn't know you were that special."

"You better believe it," Danny said. "I'm strong enough your dad was hunting my ass down back in Chicago to work for him, and he wasn't gonna take no for an answer. It's a good thing the Demigod Guardians picked me up. Otherwise, I'd be taking jobs for Salvatore Bianchi, and we know he doesn't like me."

"*I* barely like you," Ivy shot back. "And you still gotta prove yourself to the rest of my friends."

When Danny saw me, he stuck his tongue between his teeth. "*Hello, princess.*"

He pushed Marcus out of the chair beside me and promptly sat down. "I'd like to get to know *you* better."

"That's my wife you're talking to," Charlie warned. Marcus grumbled as he got off the floor, and Rishi whined.

"Hey, you're welcome to join if you'd like," Danny joked.

I could tell when a guy was an actual threat and when they were just joking around, and for the five seconds I'd known him I'd determined that Danny was just another horny toad.

I shook my head with a wry smile. "You aren't making the best first impression."

"First impressions are widely misleading." Danny put his feet on the table and leaned back in his chair. "As far as I see it, I'm not joining you guys, you guys are joining *me*. So what do you have to offer?"

"Us?" Kallie asked ludicrously, and she gave a short laugh. "We're the best at what we do."

"You want proof of my abilities? I'll take any of you in a fight, right here and now," Danny offered. "I don't lose."

"I don't either," Charlie sneered.

Danny gave a loud, obnoxious sigh. He took his feet off the table and let his chair fall to the floor with a *clatter*. "Look, none of us want to live in a world— or go to an afterlife— where Doctor Taurus is making the rules. I've never met the guy, but from what I've heard about him, I'm willing to join the rest of you crazies in going against him."

"We aren't crazy," I said sharply.

"I took a look at your records, and I gotta say, the jury's still out on the four of you not being loony," Danny said. "But as far as I'm concerned, I don't care much about that, because I'm nutty, too. Besides... the Warden's gotta know there's only one king of the world, and he already exists. Me."

Danny was definitely a live wire. A *cocky* live wire. This was going to be fun. I couldn't believe he was acting like this in the Emperor's own palace, at his round table.

But Cassiel must've gotten used to Danny's behavior by now, because he said, "I'm sure the five of you will make a great team. Danny has shown us he's more than willing to help our cause."

Danny gave me a wink. I let out a skeptical noise and put my head in my hand.

"What about others?" Marcus asked as he finally got to his feet. "Are more demigods coming?"

"Er... no," Wykoff said, and she blushed slightly pink. "We've unfortunately lost them."

"Lost them?" Marcus said blankly. "How do you misplace a person?"

"She's trying to tell you they're dead," Danny said flatly. "The Warden's been using The Mission to hunt down any demigods the Guardians have been hiding, and he's exterminated them all— after draining them of their powers, of course. Besides the ones he's got on his side, which he made, the demigods left in this room are the only ones that remain in the world."

There was a very long pause, and Amber said, "Yes... sadly, that has been the case. But I'm optimistic the rest of you will pull through! After all, we're counting on you!"

She gave us a thumbs-up. It was far from reassuring.

"I think we need to bring this meeting to a close," Cassiel said. "We've covered much information, and I'm sure the prince and princess, as well as their friends, need rest."

Absolutely. I felt drained. There was so much for us to do, discover, and solve, that it felt overwhelming. Good thing we were demigods, because I felt like we had to be, in order to have a shot at fixing this.

There was assorted conversation as people got up from their seats. Marcus and Kallie went to join their families, while others went in different directions.

I really wanted to visit my parents, but I needed some downtime first. "Meet you guys for dinner?" I offered as Mama waved goodbye.

"Of course. And Ava," Daddy called before we left. I paused at the door.

Daddy's tone was heavy. "Your Aunt Maddie is in the city. She wants to see you, when you're ready."

My stomach became hollow, and I nodded vaguely in reply. My aunt had made my prophecy. Maybe she'd discovered something that could help. I'd have to visit her as soon as I could...

I didn't know if I had the strength. My prophecy had nearly killed me several times over, and had actually killed me once. I couldn't take more bad news if my aunt had any.

I felt my nerves waver as I turned to face Daddy. I needed to talk to him about this, if only briefly. "Daddy... if I'm an Elvish princess, what does that mean when it comes time for me to be chieftess of the Toaqua tribe?"

"Don't worry about that now, peanut," Daddy told me. "I'm not going anywhere, and I'm definitely not stepping down from the chiefhood while the supernatural world is going to shit. We can talk about it after the war is over."

I nodded, but I wondered if it ever would be.

Charlie pushed my chair into the hallway. Danny did a complete turn on his heel and gave us a roguish smile. "I'd love to get to know you better, but I've got more important things to do. See you at demigod training. That is, *if* you can keep up."

Danny took off down the hall at super-speed. The effect blew back my hair.

"I'm not sure if I like that guy," Charlie grumbled.

"He's not as bad as he seems. Danny's for show, all bark and no bite," Ivy said.

Then Ivy paused, and added, "Okay, maybe a *little* bit of bite. But not toward his friends, and he'll be loyal to us, if we're loyal to him."

"You got a history with that chump?" Chancey asked, totally jealous.

"He's blowing smoke. We pulled off a couple of scams together, but we never had any romantic involvement. He's not my type," Ivy said, and they kissed Chancey's cheek.

"But you *do* seem to know him well," I pressed.

"Danny's an immigrant. He left Ireland and hopped over to North America when he was a teenager," Ivy said. "I found him hanging around Chicago looking all sad and desperate, and sort of took him in. We helped each other get by. The last time I saw him was before I ended up at the Institute. I'd like to say I'm surprised he survived without me, but I'm not. The kid's got nine lives. Kind of like a cat."

Chancey scowled. "Or a cockroach."

Whoever Danny was, he seemed like the kind of guy that wanted to be the boss, and I knew that wasn't going to fly with my husband around. But they could work out their manly bullshit later, because as far as I was concerned, finding those keys and getting results was more important than any dick-measuring contest these two felt like having. Even if I'd always back Charlie up at the end of the day. It was good Danny didn't like to lose, because that meant he'd do whatever it would take to win. We needed people like that on our side, if we were going to beat the Warden.

I couldn't believe The Mission had eliminated all the other demigods. I knew there couldn't be that many, but their deaths proved our kind had to stick together. Alone, we were strong, but we couldn't resist the Warden unless we teamed up.

When we returned to our room, Charlie and I were alone with Oberi. As Charlie shut the door behind us, I said quietly, "You don't seem to harbor any resentment toward your grandpa."

Charlie gave a miserable shrug. "I'm still kind of pissed at my dad for everything that happened to me as a kid, though now that I've had some time to think about it, I can somewhat see that it wasn't *all* his fault... I don't know. I'm still on the fence if he did everything he could to find me, though I want to believe he did."

"Doesn't that mean you should be mad at Cassiel, too?"

"My grandfather is an Emperor," Charlie replied. "He's responsible for everyone, so I can understand his position. It would be difficult for him to look for me while ruling an empire and trying to keep thousands of people safe. But my dad was merely a prince. He was responsible for *just me*, and he still let me down. I can't get over the fact that I think he fucked up... but maybe he didn't mean to."

I didn't say anything. My hatred for Cameron was a sore subject. He wasn't my father, so I didn't have to love him, or consider forgiveness. As far as I was concerned, he was a sperm donor who'd created the love of my life, nothing more or less. We didn't need him to get by.

But maybe Charlie needed him, and I had to consider that.

A loud *bang* cut off our conversation. It sounded like a gunshot. When I heard it, I jumped in my chair. I felt my skin become cold and clammy as a tightening sensation clamped down on my throat, sealing off the air from my lungs. My chest grew heavy with a weight that was more than a million pounds, and as my heartbeat started thrumming wildly, I became dizzy.

I still remembered everything. How smooth the pistol felt in my hands, and the recoil as it went off. The spatter of blood across my face and the smell of brain matter as it spilled onto the floor from the bullet's blast. With that loud *bang*, I was no longer in the safety of Ilamanthe's walls, but trapped within Cellblock 9... choosing between my life or someone else's to survive.

The sense of panic lingered for only a few moments before it began to pass. But still— Charlie noticed. He must've caught my thoughts, because he ducked out the door for a second.

When he returned, he sat down beside me in a nearby chair and took my hand. "It wasn't a gun. A servant accidentally dropped something in the hallway. It was an innocent mistake."

"Oh." I let out a whoosh of breath, but the tension didn't leave. I was still frozen.

Charlie squeezed my hand. "Pidge, we gotta get you some help."

My fingers shook in his. We'd talked about what we'd been through down in Cellblock 9 once. *Once.* He'd told me what they'd done to him, and I'd told him what I had to do to survive. We hadn't been able to stomach going over it more than that.

But he was bringing it up again, because it was obvious I couldn't handle it. I hadn't been able to, not since we'd left Cellblock 9.

"The nightmares haven't stopped. You were tossing and turning in your sleep before I woke you up to go to that council meeting," Charlie insisted.

My head dropped. "I shouldn't be this upset. I've killed more people than the guards I shot in Cellblock 9."

"With your *magic*," Charlie clarified. "It's different, destroying people with your Fire or Water than it is killing them with a gun. The pistol made it... more personal."

It did. My magic was a barrier. It turned people to ashes, or my Water magic caused them to collapse on the floor without me seeing the internal damage my powers caused. Even with the explosion I'd caused in the Infernal Underground, all of that was at a distance.

Not in Cellblock 9. The Warden had stolen my magic then, so I had to steal a gun in order to escape, and shoot people at close proximity. I'd watched as the bullets made their heads explode. The blood spilled all over me with every shot. I was forced to *see* the damage I'd done, and acknowledge if I hadn't pulled the trigger, those guards, deplorable as they were, would still be living.

I wasn't remorseful that I'd killed them. More upset by the reality that I had to see those gory effects up close, because I didn't have a choice.

"You aren't sitting here upset that you've killed people," I mumbled. "I've seen you take lives with your bare hands, and you don't even seem like you care."

"I can turn that part of me off if I want to," Charlie said. "*You* can't."

I wish I could. I'd *tried*.

Though I wondered if Charlie wasn't lying to himself. Even though he didn't feel the effects of what had happened, I worried there would be long-term consequences to some of the things he'd done, both out of survival and out of anger. Maybe he was just stuffing it down and pushing it away.

I wasn't able to do that. What had happened in Cellblock 9 overpowered me like a giant wave, dragging me under. I wasn't sure if I needed to forgive myself, because these people had been trying to kill me and I had no other choice, or if I needed to get comfortable with the fact that we'd have to do a lot worse if we wanted to protect what little we had left.

One thing was for sure. I never wanted to touch another gun in my life.

Though who knew what else I would do, or what lengths I would go to, to keep this world from falling into the Warden's hands. I'd made peace long ago with the idea of becoming the villain.

But after what had happened in Cellblock 9, I was no longer sure if I had it in me to be that villain. And that was a problem. If I couldn't become someone my enemies feared, we'd lose.

And losing wasn't an option. Not even if I had to become the worst villain that ever was, and make a permanent decision to change things in this world for better or worse. Because as my prophecy stated, I was the only one strong enough to make those hard choices.

Even if they ruined me.

THREE

I couldn't believe we were here. Walking the halls of this palace felt like a dream. Eddie was alive, and everyone's families were okay. Sure, there were aspects of this palace that were made of illusion magic, but our friends were *real*, and it was a miracle beyond anything I could ever imagine.

I was still trying to wrap my head around it the next morning. When I woke up, I couldn't remember where I was. For a moment, I thought I had awoken in my cell back at the Institute. Then I felt the morning sun on my face, and the weight of Ava-Marie's head on my chest, and I remembered I was free of that place. Oberi was laying across my legs and snoring loudly. I ran my fingers across the silk sheets, then over Ava's soft skin. She stirred awake, and her form instantly stiffened in my arms as she startled awake with a gasp.

"It's okay, pidge," I whispered quickly. "It's just me."

Ava relaxed into me, giving a blissful sigh. "Oh, Charlie. I almost forgot we were safe."

I kissed the top of her head. "When you're in my arms, pidge, you'll always be safe."

Ava snuggled back into me, and her breathing slowed. I took in all the sensations around me, burning this beautiful morning into my memory. The birds were chirping, the sun was shining, and I had the most amazing woman in my arms. And the bed— dear ancestors, the bed. It was more comfortable than anything I'd ever experienced. War or not, life couldn't get any better than this.

Leaves rustled, and the sound came from our room, not outside. "What's that?" I asked curiously.

"Sprigs. The servants brought him a potted lemon tree to live in, and he's hopping from leaf to leaf," Ava explained. "He really likes it."

I was glad the little guy was enjoying himself, because I was, too. Ava and I stayed tangled up for a long time, until we heard servants enter our living quarters. The delicious scent of fried meat and fresh eggs filled my nose. Oberi perked up from the end of the bed and sniffed the air. His tail thumped against the mattress.

Bacon! Oberi exclaimed, before jumping off the bed. *Finally, the type of service I deserve.*

What a humble dog you are. I helped Ava out of bed and into her chair, then wheeled her out into the living area. The servants were already gone, but they'd left trays of warm food for us. I lifted the cover on one, and ancestors, the scent of bacon smelled like heaven. I wasn't entirely convinced I hadn't died and ended up in paradise.

I dug in, though not before Oberi snatched half the bacon in his mouth and ran off with it. I shoved bacon and eggs into my mouth, and washed it down with the most delicious orange juice I'd ever tasted. There were croissants, and mixed fruit, and all types of pastries I'd never even heard of. Every piece of food I put into my mouth was more divine than the last.

This was different from the Institute, where the cafeteria only allowed you to take so much, or you had to worry about other inmates stealing food off your plate. No one was bothering us here, and we could have as much as we wanted.

My stomach expanded the more I ate, and I realized for what felt like the first time in my life that I was *full*. Still, I couldn't stop eating. I didn't want any of it to go to waste. There were starving people all over the world, and it would be wrong to let any of this rot—

I paused mid-bite. I realized Ava was chewing slowly, as if this was a normal meal for her. Come to think of it, she'd only leaned over me once to grab a pastry. She'd hardly eaten anything.

"Pidge, how much food is left?" I asked.

"We haven't even eaten half of it. Why?" she replied.

My very full stomach sank, and I pushed myself away from the table. "This is too much. It's not fair that we're given more than our share. I'm a prince now. I won't sit here in gluttony while people in my kingdom go hungry."

"Charlie, there's enough food here for everyone in Ilamanthe," Ava said.

Her words barely registered at first, because I didn't think it was possible. After a few beats, it sank in.

"*Everyone?*" I wondered. "Even the people who don't live in the palace?"

"Yes," Ava said.

I furrowed my brow. "Food has always been a scarce resource in my world. How can there be enough for everyone?"

"There's always enough food," Ava said. "The people of Ilamanthe choose to distribute it fairly, rather than punish those without access. When people go hungry, it isn't because there aren't enough resources. It's because people in power choose to withhold them, because they make more profit when people have to struggle."

I felt resistance to the thought, even though I wasn't sure where it came from. "I thought there was only so much to go around, and not enough for everyone to share."

"That's just what you were taught. The world isn't a pie. Just because one person gets a slice doesn't mean they're taking something away from someone else. There's enough on this planet to support everyone, and for everybody to thrive. But some people don't see it that way, so they think that hoarding what they have is going to protect them somehow."

It was a completely new concept to me— everyone getting access to what they needed, regardless of how society chose to judge them. It was exactly what I wanted as prince.

"If we can give everyone food, then we can give them whatever they need," I realized. "Access to housing, healthcare... we could set up a universal base income so *everyone's* needs are met."

Nobody would have to be poor and homeless like I did. Nobody would have to starve, or fight to obtain what they needed to survive. It was an amazing way to think.

Ava reached out to touch my hand. "I know you aren't sure about this prince thing, but you're already thinking like one. And when the crown is passed on to you, you're going to make a great Emperor."

For the first time, I dared to dream what that would be like. Being Emperor wasn't about living here in this fancy castle, getting whatever I wanted. It was about helping the people out *there*. Ilamanthe may be a paradise on Earth, but there were still people outside of this city who needed our help. Once we rescued the supernaturals from the Warden's concentration camps, they could join us here, where everyone was taken care of. Sharing what we had was the only true way to end peoples' suffering. The Warden was going about it in all the wrong ways.

"I don't understand why the Warden is forcing people to follow him and join The Mission, if his true desire is to stop suffering. There are other ways to do it with the tools he already has," I said.

"Because the Warden doesn't really want to stop suffering. He just believes he does," Ava said coldly. "He likes the idea of keeping everyone under his control. He believes if he has ultimate power, he'll be able to craft the world to his liking. He wants everyone to think, act, and behave like he does, without any outliers. The world wouldn't be beautiful if everyone was the same. In fact, it's more dangerous if no one is allowed to be different."

Ava sighed. "People like us don't belong in the Warden's world. Which is why we have to stop him."

I thought about all the things I could do once I took the crown. It actually made me *excited* to think the kind of impact a guy like me could have on this planet. I'd seen so much shit in my life, and I didn't want my people to ever go through what I had.

I took another bite, but I barely thought about it. It was just... instinctual. Ava assured me there was enough to go around, and still, I didn't feel like I could let any of it go to waste.

It's okay to stop eating, Oberi assured me. *There will always be more.*

"It doesn't feel like it," I admitted. "I've never had this much food in my life. When you grow up with food as a limited resource, you learn to eat as much as you can when it's there, because you don't know when you'll be able to eat again. And the food is *so good.* Growing up, a meal to me was a plate of mashed potatoes, or a piece of bread for dinner— that was it. I never had so many options. I don't know what it's like to *choose* to just leave food off my plate."

Ava placed her hand on mine. "You're going to get used to it, because there's no way Oberi and I are letting you go back to that place again. You won't go hungry anymore, and you'll always have a choice from now on."

Her words were comforting, but I had to learn to believe them. It was so hard to trust that what I had wouldn't be taken away.

I stuffed myself until I couldn't take another bite. Just as Ava and I finished our breakfast, a knock came at the door, and the servants returned to take our plates. Several other people entered the room, and I heard the sound of something rolling in behind them.

"Sire, are you ready for your fitting?" Eddie asked.

"Fitting?" I wondered.

"Oh, yes, we have a very busy day," Eddie said. "The royal tailor has accompanied me this morning to get your measurements, so you can be properly fitted into your suit. Our royal stylists have brought some outfit options for the princess as well."

"Ooh, that dress is *pretty.*" Ava rolled toward the stylists, and hangers clicked together as she started looking through the outfits they'd brought.

You didn't tell me there'd be hats! Oberi ran past me, nearly knocking my chair over.

"Eddie, I really don't need a suit," I protested. "I'm fine in my regular clothes."

"The Emperor requests it," Eddie stated. "You're a prince now, and must look the part. Think of it as your uniform."

If the Emperor required it, then I guess I didn't have a choice. I wanted to show my grandfather I respected his position, so I would do as he said.

The tailor had me stand with my arms straight out while he measured what felt like every inch of me. I had no idea fitting into a suit could be so complicated. I thought it was as simple as grabbing a suit off the rack in my size and slipping it on. Turns out it was more like an intricate science, apparently.

Ava found a dress she liked, and the stylists worked on her hair and makeup while I stood there with the tailor. He got my measurements, then had me sit for the stylists. Several people surrounded me all at once. Someone ran their fingers through my hair and asked how I liked to wear it. I didn't care much for style, so I explained the way Ava liked it slicked back, and they began running gel through the strands. They even trimmed the beard I'd grown during our time on the run.

Oberi breathed a blissful sigh as one of the stylists brushed out his fur.

I shifted uncomfortably in my chair.

Is something wrong? Ava asked through the bond.

Nothing's wrong, I assured her. *It's just new. I'm not used to getting services like this.*

I really like watching you get pampered, Ava replied. *Maybe manicures can be our thing now. I'm loving it.*

Ava's enthusiasm bled through our bond, and I found myself getting a little excited, too. It was definitely strange, being waited on like I was someone *important*, but the way the stylists made conversation and were so nice to us, it felt natural. I didn't want to see myself as above them, or like their job was any less important than mine. They were merely my colleagues, helping to run this kingdom alongside me. The less I had to worry about how I looked, the more I could worry about my people. We all had a role to play, and just because my job was more public didn't make any one of these people any less valuable.

I vowed then to always treat these people as my equals. I wouldn't be the kind of prince that let this stuff go to my head.

When the stylists finished, the tailor helped me into a suit. I thought suits were supposed to be scratchy and uncomfortable, like the one I'd worn during the Villain's Ball, but this suit was soft and comfortable— like wearing pajamas.

Something in the room changed when I put that suit on. I felt like I stood taller, but there was also this energy coming off from everyone else that seemed... I don't know... more respectful?

"How do you feel?" Ava asked.

At the same time, her internal thoughts slipped through. *He looks so fucking hot. I can't wait to get that suit off him.*

I smirked. I stretched my arms out to the side, then took a few steps across the room. The suit moved with me like it was an extension of my body. Even the shoes felt form-fitted to my feet. I thought that in this suit, I would be respected.

"It feels great," I said honestly. *You're going to have a hard time getting it off of me,* I teased Ava.

Believe me, it won't take much, she joked back.

It was weird, because I wasn't the type of guy to wear suits. Put me in a pair of ripped-up jeans and a cotton t-shirt and I was good to go.

Or so I thought, up until this point. As I ran my fingers over the soft fabric, I realized how much I *liked* it. I used to think things like this were over the top and unnecessary, but maybe it wasn't that I didn't like nice things. Maybe it was that I'd never had the opportunity to enjoy them before.

That realization hit me *hard*, and I had to excuse myself from the room as the stylists cleaned up. I exited through the sliding door that led onto the balcony. Sunlight touched my face, and a warm breeze passed through my hair. Even though on some level I enjoyed the pampering and I *loved* the new suit, my stomach tangled into knots.

Ava wheeled onto the balcony. She must've felt that something was off, because she asked, "Don't you like it?"

I ran my fingers over the railing, because I didn't know what else to do with my hands. "Yeah, it's great... it's just—"

I cut off as my fingers trailed over various raised bumps engraved onto the railing. At first, I thought they were just pretty designs, until I realized I recognized the patterns. "This railing is engraved with braille," I remarked in awe.

Ava wheeled even closer. "The builders must've left some sort of message for you. What does it say?"

I started on the left side of the balcony and began reading. "It's a description of the view," I realized. "It describes the sea, reaching out to the horizon, and the skyscrapers... wow, I didn't realize the buildings here were so tall. I didn't know how big Ilamanthe was."

"It's pretty big. There are a lot of refugees from all supernatural races here," Ava said. "I've been looking around our room, and I noticed there's braille embedded in a lot of places, on plaques on the walls and such. This palace was made so you could get around easily, and see it the same way other people can."

I got choked up and turned away from her. Ava reached out for my hand.

"What's wrong?" she asked.

"This feels too good to be true," I admitted. "There's the food, then the stylists, and now this. Someone cared enough to make this view accessible to someone like me. I've never had that kind of equal treatment before. It's like I'm waiting for the other shoe to drop. There's still a war going on out there. It's weird being in this safe, happy place with more resources than I could've ever dreamed of, while other people are still out there suffering."

"You're not a bad person because other people are suffering and you're not," Ava told me.

She understood me far too well, because that was *exactly* what I was thinking.

"It doesn't seem fair," I stated.

"That's because it isn't," Ava said. "But just because someone else is suffering doesn't mean you have to suffer alongside them to even the scales. Why not indulge in the *good*, and then do what you can to make life better for others? Isn't it more fair if we all have it good, rather than using suffering as some sort of virtue?"

Her words felt heavy, but they lifted a weight off my chest at the same time. "I guess I never saw happiness as something that we could all have. It's just another limited resource in my world."

"You can't think like that," Ava said. "Happiness isn't a limited resource that only a few get access to. It's something that we create— and you know as well as I do that as demigods, we can create whatever the hell we want. Why not joy?"

I sighed heavily. "That's a relief to think that way. But I'm not sure I can. To me, happiness was always something I had to suffer to achieve, and if I was happy, it meant someone else was suffering."

"That's not true," Ava said. "Happiness isn't something that you steal from other people so you can make it your own. It can only come from inside of you. Anyone who thinks they have to steal joy from others to feel happy are miserable pieces of shit."

I smirked. "You're right. I guess that's why the Warden's still out there hurting people, because no matter what he does to make other people suffer, it will never be enough."

"Exactly," Ava said. "So don't feel bad about creating your own happiness in the meantime, because the more you and I can create for ourselves, the more we can share that joy with others."

"I may be a demigod, but I can't just *create* happiness and distribute it to the masses," I said.

"Why not?" Ava asked. "You can use the power you have, not just as a prince, but as an individual, to help others, and more importantly, help yourself. Because if we all took care of our own needs, the world would be a better place. When you're full, you can think clearly and make rational decisions that will keep your people from going hungry, too."

She was talking about more than just the food. This was like a spiritual hunger that had always been hard for me to satisfy.

"The difference between a good leader and someone like the Warden is that a good leader believes that joy is limitless and *everyone* should have access to resources," Ava said. "The Warden doesn't believe there's enough to go around. He thinks he has to take those resources away to end suffering, but in the process, he's created the suffering he says he despises."

"We aren't going to be like the Warden," I stated.

Ava took my hand and squeezed it. "Never."

The stylists had spent a lot of time on us, so it was almost eleven o'clock before we left our room. Eddie took us on a tour of the rest of the palace, though we didn't even visit half the rooms. It was a lot of work, walking around the whole building. I pushed Ava so she didn't get tired, but I figured by the end we must've roamed at least a few miles, judging by the amount of steps I took. There were elevators for us to use, and like Ava said, braille plaques lined the walls before every door and entrance, along with beside windows.

Ava typically had to describe everything to me, but she didn't have to this time, because the palace was accessible all on its own. It was nearly miraculous.

When we returned to our suite around one o' clock, Eddie said, "Sire, it's time for lunch."

I was still full from breakfast, though that'd been hours ago. "Thanks, Eddie, but I'm not hungry."

"You misunderstand," Eddie said. "This is a meeting. Your presence has been requested."

Eddie had said we had a full schedule for the day, though I wasn't sure what that entailed. Hell, I didn't even know who I was meeting with. But this was the life of a prince, and if I wanted to change the world, it was going to have to start by making alliances— both inside the palace and out.

"All right, let's go," I said as I reached for Ava's chair.

"The princess will not be attending lunch with us," Eddie said. "She will be having lunch with Kallie, to discuss her court selection. She is permitted to choose a selection of ladies to assist her in daily tasks."

Oberi shifted into a unicorn from the other room. *Count me in as a lady-in-waiting!*

Ava squeezed my hand. "You've got this, Charlie. You're the prince now."

And a fine prince at that, she added through the bond. I could practically feel her eyes roaming my form, and that made me relax.

"I'll see you later, pidge," I told her, before leaning down to place a kiss on her lips.

Eddie and I left the room, and he guided me down the hallway and through a twist of stairs. This palace seemed bigger than the Institute. It was going to take me a long time to learn the layout.

The delicious scent of steak and roasted potatoes filled my nose. I wasn't hungry, but that smell alone made my mouth water. I didn't know who I was meeting with, but when I heard the sound of voices making conversation, I stopped in my tracks.

It was a man and a woman. I didn't recognize her voice, but the man's was almost too much like my own.

My father.

Eddie paused in the hall. "Do you need a moment?"

Instinctually, I wanted to hightail it in the other direction. I wasn't interested in having lunch with the father who had abandoned me...

But I was a prince now. I had to learn how to be diplomatic, even with my adversaries. Maybe my dad and I could smooth things out. It didn't have to be bad between us.

I cleared my throat and straightened my suit jacket. "No, Eddie, I'm good."

Eddie opened a door, and I stepped inside what appeared to be a private dining room. My magic swirled around the room as I took in what I could. The room wasn't very big, but there was a large table set in the center. My father and the woman clinked their glasses together. I could hear Cameron's alicorn Familiar munching on hay nearby.

"Charlie," Cameron— I mean, *my father*— said. I still wasn't sure what to call him. "You're early. I was expecting your grandfather to arrive first. You look nice."

"The stylists did a great job," I replied, because I didn't know what else *to* say.

"Charlie," the woman gushed.

She got out of her chair and wrapped me in a hug. I stiffened. The woman smelled of flowers and seemed very friendly, but it was a bit off-putting considering I had no idea who she was.

Or... had we met before? I wasn't good with voices, except for my closest friends.

"It's so great to finally introduce myself," she said in excitement. "Cameron has told me so many good things about you."

"Hmph," was all I could manage. My father didn't know anything about me. What could he possibly have to say?

Eddie pulled out a chair for me, and I sat down. He quickly got to work on setting my napkin in my lap, but I took it from him. "I've got it. Thanks."

He stepped back, and my father cleared his throat. "Charlie, I'd like you to meet Drea."

"Drea's his guard, like I'm yours!" Eddie said chipperly.

"Yes," Cameron confirmed, though I sensed hesitation in his tone. "Drea is also my wife."

The room fell dead silent, and it took me a beat to process his words. I was certain I hadn't heard him correctly. A storm brewed in my abdomen, and it took everything I had to force it back. I hid my hands under the table so he wouldn't notice them shaking.

"I'm sorry," I finally said, as calmly as I could manage. "I must've heard you wrong. You said Drea's your guard *and* your wife?"

"That is correct," Cameron said brightly.

This was far from the great news he thought it was. It was wrong of him to marry his guard, on so many levels. My hands curled into fists.

"I understand this may be a lot to take in," Cameron said quickly. "I know this is all still so fresh to you. It took me a long time to even consider moving on from your mother—"

"So you forgot about Mom, like you forgot about me," I growled.

"Charlie, you know I went looking for you," Cameron insisted. "I never forgot about either one of you. Losing you both was the hardest thing I ever had to go through. It's been over twenty years—"

"I don't care how long it's been. You gave up!" I shouted. Forget acting like a prince. I couldn't contain my anger. "If I lost my son, I'd spend a hundred years looking for him. Is *she* the reason you stopped looking for me? Once you decided to settle down, I didn't matter anymore?"

"It wasn't like that," Cameron insisted.

"She's your *guard*, Cameron!" I shouted. I didn't miss how I'd let his name slip out. I didn't feel like calling him *Dad*, that was for sure. "How has anyone allowed this to happen? She can't consent!"

"Charlie, please," Drea said softly. "I assure you, I married your father of my own free will."

"Yeah?" I questioned. "Or has *he* told you to say that? Because I know damn well Eddie will do anything I say. He's magically bound to do it."

"I would never violate Drea's free will like that," Cameron said, his tone growing angry. "To even suggest such a thing is awful."

"Just because you didn't *want* to violate her free will doesn't mean you didn't unintentionally," I argued. "I could say, *Eddie, give me a blow job,* and regardless if he wants to do it or not, he's gonna do it, because as my guard he can't disobey a command."

"Very well, sire!" Eddie said cheerfully. He ducked under the table, and his fingers reached for my waistband.

I shoved his hands away. "Eddie, stop," I ordered. "It was just supposed to be an example."

Eddie poked his head out from under the table. "Oh. I see. Point made, my prince."

He squeezed himself out from underneath the table and went to sit back down, while I raged at my father. "See what I mean? I didn't intend the order, but he went to follow it anyway!"

"Charlie, this behavior is unacceptable!" my father snapped— like I was a child. "I won't have you insult my wife to her face like this."

"Then perhaps she should leave," I stated coolly. "Eddie, why don't you and Drea give us a moment?"

Eddie started for the door immediately, but Drea hesitated, until my father told her, "It's for the best. Charlie and I have much to discuss."

Eddie and Drea exited the room, leaving Cameron and me alone.

"I understand you've been through a lot, and all of this is overwhelming," Cameron said calmly. "It was too much when I was your age, too. That's why I ran away to Kinpago, where I met your mother. However, it's unfair to take that out on my wife. I love Drea very deeply. It's not fair to expect me to never love again."

"You may love her, but the power dynamic is off," I insisted. "You're always going to be above her, and even if she wanted to, she can't say no. There are lines that you should never cross, and this is one of them."

"Don't make me out to be the villain," Cameron warned. "You can't treat my wife like she's below me just because she's my guard. She and I are equals."

My jaw dropped. I couldn't *believe* he had the nerve to suggest what he had. "The last thing I'd ever do is look down upon someone for where they stand in society," I sneered. "Have you forgotten that I was homeless and living on the streets? I'm fucking blind, and have lived most my life with no accommodations, let alone any money or status. In case you've forgotten, I've lived at the bottom of the barrel. I've been a prince for *one fucking day*. I'm not going to forget everything that happened to me— I never will."

Cameron drew in a deep breath. "I understand how hard this must be for you, but please try to comprehend that my relationship with Drea is not what you think. Yes, we connected at a vulnerable time, but she was the one who helped me through your mother's loss. I never pressured Drea to do *anything*, let alone fall in love with me. When I was searching for you, it nearly killed me. After the Hawkei sent you away, I did my damndest to find you, but your records led me nowhere. I wasn't even sure if you were alive. I continued searching, but I only came up with more questions. Without knowing if you were dead or alive, all I had was false hope. I *wanted* to keep looking for you, but there was nothing else to look for."

"I don't believe you," I insisted. "Even if my records led to a dead-end, you had magic."

"I *tried* to use magic," Cameron said. "None of it worked. I thought that meant you were dead. It didn't make sense at the time, but now I believe that your latent demigod magic overpowered any tracking spells I had access to. I was obsessed with finding you, to the point where it nearly killed me. Drea was the one who convinced me to give up the search."

My stomach bottomed out. "So she was the reason nobody ever found me. How long did it take you to give up after you got together? A year? Five years? What, did you marry her, then decide you were going to forget about the first family you'd created because you got a new one?"

"It's not like that," Cameron insisted. "Drea saved my life."

"How, by fucking you?" I growled.

"Ancestors, Charlie, is that all you think about?" Cameron demanded. "My relationship with Drea goes far deeper than that."

"Yeah, I'm sure it goes *deep*," I muttered.

Cameron's voice turned stern. "I know you're used to speaking your mind and throwing punches, but you can't act like that in the palace. If you're going to be a prince, you have to leave your attitude in the past."

Great, now he was lecturing me.

"Regardless of what you think of your stepmother, you're going to have to learn to get along with her," Cameron said. "She's my guard, which means wherever I go, she goes. She may not become the queen, but she *is* my wife. I won't have you insulting her again."

"And why *can't* she become queen?" I demanded, already knowing the answer. I just wanted to hear him say it out loud.

"Drea was born into her role as my guard," Cameron explained. "As such, she is magically bound to her birth station. She can't climb ranks or become a princess as your wife can, regardless of our marriage license, because her magical duty supersedes any other contract."

"*There's* your problem!" I shouted. "You just admitted it. She's your guard first. Can't you see this marriage is wrong?"

Cameron shot out of his chair and slammed a fist down on the table. "That's enough! You don't know the first thing about what Drea and I have together. You've been married to Ava-Marie for barely a year. Don't act like you're an expert on marriage. I've been married to Drea for nearly twenty years, and I certainly know more about being in a committed relationship than you and your wife!"

That pissed me off more than anything else he'd said. Ava and I had managed to keep our marriage intact despite everything that had been thrown at us. It didn't matter how long my dad and Drea had been together. It didn't change that he was wrong and I was right.

"Don't you *dare* bring my wife into this!" I yelled as I jumped to my feet. My chair fell over, and my whole body shook. Magic rattled around inside of me, and I had the sudden urge to burst out of my skin and breathe fire out of my mouth. The familiar feeling of supernatural strength surged through me, and I knew I must be siphoning powers from someone nearby. "You don't want me insulting your marriage? Don't treat mine like it's invalid because you've been married longer! Ava and I have been through hell together, something I bet you and Drea can't say while lounging around in your fancy-ass dining room and sleeping on your silk sheets, being waited on hand and foot every hour of the day."

Cameron's breath wavered, like he was trying hard to hold back an insult. He spoke slowly and deliberately. "Don't make *any* assumptions about what I've been through."

"Oh, I think I've assumed enough," I growled.

Screw this prince duty shit. I was supposed to be in charge here, which meant I did whatever the hell I wanted. I turned from my father and stormed out of the room. It was better than throwing a punch at his head.

I was too furious to process my surroundings. All I knew was I had to get away from my father. I hurried down the hall and heard footsteps coming my way. I thought it was Eddie, until I heard the sound of my grandfather's voice.

"Charlie, slow down," Emperor Cassiel insisted. "There's no need to get angry."

I stopped in my tracks. "You heard all that?"

"Everyone in this wing heard it," my grandfather said, though his tone was hard to read. I noticed then that there were other footsteps and voices passing through the hall. We weren't alone.

Magic rippled up and down my form. I rubbed my arms to feel *scales* appearing along my skin. I didn't know what the fuck was happening to me. I began clawing at the scales like I could rip them off my arms.

Several people gasped. They'd all stopped to stare.

"You need to calm yourself," Cassiel instructed, sounding concerned. "You're siphoning magic from a dragon shifter in the kitchens."

My throat began to burn with the heat of fire rising up inside of it. I'd siphoned supernatural strength and speed from others before, but never anything as powerful as their shifter abilities. I wasn't even *touching* the dragon shifter. Hell, we weren't even in the same room. It really freaked me out.

Cassiel grabbed my shoulders firmly and shook me. "Charlie, you must get your anger under control, or it will control you. If you shift inside the palace, you could bring this whole hall down upon us."

"What the hell do you want me to do?" I demanded. "Take deep breaths and confess my *feelings?* Not gonna work, gramps."

"It'd be a pretty damn good start," he stated sternly. He wasn't being mean — it was more like... he cared.

"So I'm just supposed to walk out of there acting like everything is fine?" I asked. "My father married his *guard.* How could you allow this? Why didn't you stop him?"

I got even angrier, and I felt my grandfather's hands grow smaller on my shoulders as my legs lengthened.

Oh, shit. I was shifting.

People shouted, and footsteps retreated away from us.

"Eddie, get these people out of here!" Cassiel shouted.

I felt a powerful wave of magic yank my power away from me. I collapsed to the floor, suddenly feeling very weak. I hit the marble hard. The burning in my throat subsided, and I realized the scales on my arms were gone.

The room spun around me, and it took me a moment to find my bearings. I shakily pushed myself upright. "What just happened?"

"You were about to shift into a dragon that is far too big to fit inside this area of the palace," Cassiel said. "You would've killed half a dozen people. I siphoned the magic inside of you for my own, before you could hurt anyone."

"I didn't know you could do that," I admitted as he helped me to my feet.

"There's a reason I'm the Emperor," he reminded me.

My grandfather wasn't a demigod, but he was certainly a talented Elf.

I furrowed my brow. "You didn't shift, though. How can you control it and I can't?"

"Because I don't allow my emotions to control me," he said. "I was hoping to mentor you in Elf magic, beginning this afternoon. It appears we should start immediately. Come with me, Charlie."

My grandfather led me away from the dining room and through a twist of hallways. Footsteps followed us, and I realized it was his guards, though they kept a distance behind us to give us our privacy. We stepped outside, and his guards remained stationed near the doors.

The air was warm, and a light breeze touched my face. I heard the sound of a trickling fountain nearby, and my Earth magic tingled. The scent of lavender filled my nose, and something soft brushed against my skin as I walked by it. I reached my hand out to feel velvety flower petals all around us. He'd taken me to one of the palace gardens.

My grandfather stopped at the edge of the fountain. "Sit," he instructed.

I remained firmly planted in place. "I'm not doing anything until you answer my question. How could you let my father marry his guard?"

"I did not," Cassiel said. "Your father never consulted me, and frankly, he didn't need to. I did not approve of the relationship at first, but over time, I've come to accept it. Drea loves your father deeply, and he loves her. It is not my place to get in the middle of that."

"Even though it's wrong?" I demanded.

"Who are we to say it's wrong?" Cassiel asked. "The world isn't black and white. There are gray areas that we must learn to navigate, especially if you're going to be leading the Elves."

"Oh, believe me," I said. "I'm more than familiar with gray areas."

"And yet you have much to learn," Cassiel stated. "Now, sit."

This time, I did as I was told and sat on the edge of the fountain.

Cassiel sat beside me. "As you know, the Elves have long been involved in criminal activity to ensure our survival. We've been known to cheat and steal, though not without purpose. We engage in these activities as a means to better our society, and to right wrongs. People think that as criminals, we are driven by our rage, but that cannot be further from the truth. The reason we're so good at what we do is because we *understand* our anger, and we know how to utilize it to our advantage. As prince, you're going to be heading all kinds of questionable operations. You cannot lead effectively if you let your anger get the best of you."

"I don't get it," I said. "Are we the good guys, or the bad guys?"

"Who says there *are* good guys and bad guys?" Cassiel questioned. "Perhaps there are just *people* who are all doing their best. The difference is, who's better at what they do?"

I smirked. Here I was, thinking my grandfather was going to lecture me on shoving my emotions aside, but as it turned out, he really *got* me. I was liking him more and more.

"The reason our lineage has continued on after every war and genocide is not because our family is somehow virtuous and good," Cassiel said. "It's because we know how to utilize situations to our advantage. We may not have the numbers the other supernaturals have, but we know how to work with what we've got. And we've got a hell of a lot of trauma and anger. Anger is a tool, and just like every Elven Emperor who came before you, you must learn how to master it. And if you do, you can restore our people to a good standing in the supernatural world, and our community can thrive."

I liked the sound of that. "How do I utilize it?"

"You must first understand it," Cassiel said. "It's like your illusion magic. Allow me to demonstrate. Since you can create solid illusions, why don't we try... a gun?"

I wasn't surprised that a gun was the first thing to come to my grandfather's mind. He was, after all, the leader of the greatest crime lords in supernatural history.

I was getting better at illusions, and it didn't take much for me to form a gun in my mind. I imagined the feeling in my hand— the shape of the grip and the cool of the metal. A solid gun took shape.

"Now, aim it at me and shoot," my grandfather instructed.

"I'm not going to shoot you," I insisted.

"Go ahead," he encouraged. "Aim it right at me and pull the trigger."

"Are you insane? No."

"Aren't you mad?" Cassiel said. "Don't you want to take your anger out on someone? Don't you want to punish me for allowing your father to marry his guard? After all, why didn't I step in and stop it? How could I let your father move on from your mother, and stop looking for you—?"

Bang!

I aimed the gun at his leg and pulled the trigger. A loud noise sounded through the garden, but something wasn't quite right. I'd shot guns before, but this one had no recoil. It felt more like shooting a water gun than a real gun.

Cassiel laughed. "Very good, Charlie! I didn't expect the sound. It was very realistic."

I frowned. "Well, clearly I missed my target."

"Of course you did," Cassiel said. "That's because there was no bullet— you merely created a lump of metal and a nice sound effect."

I furrowed my brow and began running my fingers over the gun. I'd created an old-style revolver, and it *felt* real. I opened the chamber to find it was full of bullets, and I emptied them into my hand. I thought they'd be mere casings, but they were all heavy and hadn't been shot.

"In order to create an illusion and make it function properly, you must first *understand* the thing that you're making," my grandfather said. "Some illusions will be easy, while others require a deeper understanding. The bullets, for example, very likely could be shot, but you neglected other parts of the gun. You have the frame of the gun and the trigger, but where's the hammer? Without it, the bullets couldn't fire."

"Then why'd it sound like it?" I asked.

"Because you *believed* it would," he explained. "The sound was an illusion itself, spurred by your expectation. But when I told you to make a gun, did you think about what kind of gun you were going to make, and how it would be designed?"

"No," I admitted. "It didn't matter to me whether it was a revolver or a pistol. I didn't really think about it."

"That's why we *must* be intentional," Cassiel said. "If you understand the tool you're working with, you can utilize it most effectively. The same is true of our anger. Initially, anger makes us *react*, sometimes irrationally— just as your first instinct was to make the gun go off. You went for the quick result you'd come to expect, but underneath it, you forgot to utilize the real function of the gun. Anger can drive us to action, but if we react too quickly, all we get is a bang and no real solution."

"So how do I utilize it properly?" I asked.

"The first step is patience," Cassiel answered. "Our family does not simply *react*. We use our anger to devise strategy. I cannot cover strategy in a single lesson, but as you train with me, you will come to understand. Today, let's focus on shifting our mindset. You must get comfortable with the idea that anger does not require immediate action. Your rage is better utilized for long-term strategy. Furthermore, damage is not the only course of action. You know as well as I that you can channel your emotions into your magic to create things out of nothing, so why not transmute that anger into something that can help everyone, instead of hurting them?"

"I think I understand," I mused. "Instead of being bitter about everything I've been through, I can use that anger to enact policies that will ensure none of our people ever live the way I did."

"Precisely," Cassiel said. "I wanted our lesson today to cover mirrors and portals, as portals will be incredibly valuable to you. Perhaps we can use that to demonstrate some of these concepts. Follow me."

I stood and followed my grandfather across the garden. He led me into a wide hall that was open to the gardens. There was a roof above us, but I could still feel the breeze on my skin.

"This is the Royal Wall of Mirrors, one of our main portal hubs," Cassiel explained. "Although we try to limit our portal use as much as possible so we aren't discovered, this is where many of our agents portal in and out of Ilamanthe."

I reached out to feel the wall, and my hand traveled over a cold, flat surface. I felt an ornate frame that stretched taller and wider than I was. As I continued feeling the wall, I found more and more of these frames, all evenly spaced. There had to be a dozen of them.

"They're mirrors," I realized. "They're magical, like the Mirror of Ingress in Forevermore, but smaller."

"Yes, but you misunderstand," Cassiel said. "Elves do not have to use magic mirrors to create their portals. Any clear reflective surface will do."

I was excited to learn about portal magic. I'd never done it before. "How does it work?"

"Think of portals like a fold in the fabric of space," Cassiel explained. "The fae are able to connect any two points, but Elves are more limited in this power. We can connect any two mirrors to create a portal— or any reflective surface, such as a body of water that is still enough to be clearly reflected. But you must be careful, as this kind of portal magic can come with consequences."

"What kind of consequences?" I asked.

"There's a space between each entrance and exit to a portal— a separate realm, if you will," Cassiel said. "For a brief moment, you will pass through this realm before exiting the portal on the other side. This realm— the Mirror Realm, as we refer to it— exists outside of space and time. If your connection is not secure, you may find yourself entering a portal with no exit. When you are in the Mirror Realm, you are stuck between time and space, which means you can't even age to death. You simply go on existing for eternity, with nothing but your thoughts to exist alongside you."

"It sounds worse than death," I remarked.

"I would imagine so," Cassiel stated solemnly. "Because of this, we only use portals when absolutely necessary, as working with the Mirror Realm can be very risky. Once you get stuck, there's no escaping."

"So why do it at all?" I asked.

"Because when fighting a war, sometimes, the benefits outweigh the risk," Cassiel replied.

"What else is there to know about mirrors?" I ran my hand over another flat surface. "None of these mirror portals are activated, so I assume it's something that can be turned on and off?"

"Yes," Cassiel said. "An Elf must activate their portal, and then it stays open for just a few moments as the Elf passes through. You can take others with you, but an Elf must lead them through. You couldn't create a mirror portal, then walk away and expect it to remain active."

"How big does the mirror have to be?" I asked. "These mirrors are all large enough to walk through, but Eddie portaled us to Ilamanthe with a mirror he had in his pocket."

"We can use pocket mirrors, but they are a little trickier," Cassiel said. "One must use it to *project* the portal, reflecting the portal from the mirror itself onto the landscape. There must always be a reflective surface on the other end to portal through. You will soon learn that technique. Today, I want you to work on portaling through one of these mirrors to another on the other end of the hall. Do you think you can do that?"

I laughed nervously. "I can't make any promises. In theory, this all sounds great, but I don't know the first thing about how to actually achieve it. What if I get stuck like you mentioned?"

"I didn't warn you about the Mirror Realm to scare you," Cassiel said. "You are an exceptionally strong Elf. Traveling through mirrors should not be difficult for you. I simply wish to pass my knowledge on to you. Think of mirror portals like your battle magic. It's just another tool, and if you misuse it, it can do considerable damage. But if you use it responsibly, it can give you an advantage over your enemies."

I stepped up to the mirror on the end and pressed my hand to the glass surface. "So, how do I do it?"

"As with illusions, it simply takes imagination," Cassiel explained. "Picture this mirror connecting with another. Imagine the glass melting beneath your fingers, allowing you passage."

I shrugged. "Sounds easy enough."

I did as he instructed and pictured my hand melding with the mirror and coming out the other side through a mirror at the other end of the hall.

Nothing happened.

I tried again. Still, the glass beneath my palm remained solid.

I stepped back to think it through. I could feel my grandfather's curious gaze on me, but I ignored it. He wanted me to be strategic. I could try.

He also said I had to *understand* the tools I was working with. All right. I could do that, too.

He didn't say anything as I walked to the other end of the hall and felt the mirrors along the way. I stopped at the one on the end— my target. I was going to portal from the mirror on the other end of the hall to this one, but I had to understand where I was going first.

After feeling around for a while and getting an idea of what I was aiming for, I returned to the first mirror. I splayed my palm over it and imagined stepping through the mirror, and pictured myself coming out of the other across the hall.

Still, nothing happened.

"It's not working," I complained. Anger bubbled up inside of me again. I still wasn't totally over what had happened earlier, and my frustration only grew.

"Keep trying," Cassiel explained.

I drew a deep breath and tried again. This time, I pictured the entire hall bending to my will, imagining the mirrors connecting through space and becoming one. That was essentially how this magic worked, wasn't it?

The mirror remained solid, and I got even more frustrated. My grandpa didn't say anything as I tried to work it out, but I knew he was waiting for something to happen. I couldn't let him down. I had to prove to him I could do this. If I couldn't create a simple mirror portal, I certainly couldn't sit on the throne once he and my father stepped down.

"You've got this, Charlie," Cassiel encouraged. "All it takes is understanding and a bit of reality manipulation."

Something occurred to me, and it made my anger flare. "Then maybe that's the problem," I said, smacking my palm on the solid glass. "You say that like it's so simple, but maybe I can't manipulate reality the way that you can, because I don't *experience* it the same. You can look down the hall and see all these mirrors lined up, but I can only experience one at a time. I don't know how to combine these mirrors into one point in space at the same time, because I can't experience them all at once! I don't have any sight!"

I never used my disability as an excuse, but it was the only thing that made sense right now. Cassiel said this should be simple, and I was the greatest Elf to ever live, so why couldn't I do it like everyone else?

Cassiel spoke calmly. "You're reacting to your anger. Feel your rage in your body, but instead of releasing it right away, turn it into strategy."

"I don't know what that *means*," I insisted, whirling toward him. My foot hit a rock, and it went skidding a few feet away. "You're telling me what to do without giving me the steps to get there. I've got one mirror on this end of the room and another over there, but the steps between them aren't making any sense."

Magic swelled inside of me, and though it felt familiar, it was different from my own. I realized I was accidentally siphoning my grandfather's magic, like I had with the dragon shifter.

Cassiel placed a hand on my shoulder, as if that would calm me down. Come to think of it, it was helping. I could feel him tugging on his magic, drawing it away from me.

"You already have the tools, Charlie," Cassiel said. "Patience. Imagination. Creativity. You already know how to bend reality to your will— you've done it many times before. Bend this anger to your will as well. You've got to be strategic, and you can't do that by copying my strategies. You must make your own. You said yourself you experience the world differently than me, so what strategy is going to work for *you*?"

I rolled my shoulders, even though all I wanted to do was smash this mirror instead of portal through it. But my grandfather was right. Whatever I was doing wasn't working, so I had to change it.

Instead of reacting immediately, I turned inward. My grandfather was preaching patience and strategy, so how could I use those to my advantage? I'd been strategic all my life, conning people to get to where I needed to go. I just had to do the same here.

But I couldn't con a mirror. I had to con *myself.*

I stood in front of the row of mirrors and focused on the feeling of sunlight reflecting off their surfaces and onto my face. We were shaded by the overhang above us, but there was enough sunlight coming through the gardens that I could still feel it. Or, at the very least, I imagined it. It didn't matter if the sunlight was real or not, because whether I imagined it or not, it was real to me. I sensed all the mirrors at once, and I suddenly understood something I didn't before.

Of all the tools I had at my disposal, the ones inside of me were the strongest, and the easiest to manipulate. I thought creating this portal would prove something to my grandfather, but maybe that was the wrong way of thinking about things. If I had something to prove to him, then I was trying to prove something to myself, too, which meant I didn't actually think I could do this.

Anger led to solutions, or so my grandfather thought. Well, there was only one solution I could think of right now.

I leaned down to grab the rock I'd kicked earlier, and I tossed it in my hand.

The solution wasn't to prove what I was capable of. It was to know that I was *already* capable, no evidence needed. Kallie had been trying to drill that into my head since she first taught me about illusions. Portals were a manipulation of reality, just like illusions were. So I came to the conclusion that there was no reason to create the mirror portal in the first place, because the portal already existed.

I drew my hand back and threw the rock straight toward the glass. If it were any other mirror, it should have shattered, but the sound of breaking glass never came. Instead, I heard the rock clatter to the ground yards away from me, all the way on the other end of the Royal Wall of Mirrors.

I didn't have to celebrate it, because I wasn't surprised. I'd already made the decision that it would work, and I knew reality would warp to my command. That didn't mean I didn't feel damn good about it, though.

Just to enjoy my work, I stepped forward and walked straight into the mirror. It was solid only moments ago, but now, the glass melded around me like a viscous liquid. For a beat, I felt myself floating somewhere else entirely, then I stepped out onto solid ground.

Clapping came from far away on my left. My grandfather had been standing to my right a moment ago, and now, he was all the way on the other side of the Royal Wall of Mirrors.

"Excellent job, Charlie," Cassiel praised.

I turned back to the mirror and touched it, but the portal had already closed. The glass was solid again.

Cassiel approached me. "I wasn't sure you would master it so quickly, but you've done well."

"Thank you," I said.

I should've felt a surge of pride, but I just felt *normal*, like I knew all along how simple it was and I just had to remind myself of it.

"I wonder how far I can take this," I mused. "You said Elves could only portal through reflective surfaces, but what if there aren't any around? I've got to be able to get my people out of a bad situation in a pinch if it comes to that. I'm not your typical Elf, so what if I can make my own mirror?"

I concentrated, and the handle of a small mirror appeared in my hand, like what Eddie had used to portal us to Ilamanthe. I ran my fingers over the smooth surface of the mirror. Around the edge were intricate designs that reminded me of the Elvish carvings in my room. I could feel the mirror reflecting the heat of the sun. The mirror was completely solid, and I'd done a good job.

I turned the mirror down the hall to project a portal like Eddie had. I decided it was already done, but nothing happened. My magic seemed to be warring inside of me.

"It's a good theory, Charlie, but I'm afraid the mirror you created is not reflective— it's merely made of glass," Cassiel revealed calmly. "It will not work to make a portal."

I ran my fingers over the mirror again. The glass was smooth, and it *felt* like a mirror in my hands. "I don't get it. My illusion magic isn't like anyone else's. It's tied to my demigod powers. When I create something, it becomes reality and never goes away. This should be as real as the mirrors on the wall."

"As I said before, you must *understand* the tool you are using, in order to utilize it properly," Cassiel said.

I understood what he was saying immediately. "I see. I'm unable to replicate a mirror's reflection, because I experience it differently. It's like with the gun— I made the frame, the bullets, and the sound, but I didn't have all the other pieces in place. I understand how mirrors work, but I don't *experience* them the same way other people do. It's reflecting the sun's heat, but not an image, because my illusion magic is limited by my own understanding."

It was the same way I couldn't create nutritious food out of nothing, because I never trusted that the food would last.

"Don't be too hard on yourself," Cassiel encouraged. "If this doesn't work for you, we will simply explore other tools that will. You don't need to be able to use your illusion magic in a pinch if you are clever enough, because you will always find another way out— whether you have access to a reflective surface or not. In these lessons, I will teach you how to pivot in situations in which you might need to explore alternatives. You're a clever man, Charlie, and I trust that you will learn how to use that to your advantage in any given situation, just as well as you use your magic."

His encouragement meant everything. No one ever thought I had what it took, because they didn't want to take the time to teach me. They saw a blind guy and wrote me off as a lost cause. But my grandpa wasn't like everyone else who had thrown me out like garbage before. He was going to do whatever it took to turn me into the next criminal mastermind in the family. I would become the next great Emperor who would lead the Elves long after he was gone.

"All right, I'm ready for the next step," I told him.

"Excellent, because it's time to meet your team," Cassiel said. "If you're going to follow in my footsteps and become a criminal boss, you're going to need a specialized team. I'm going to teach you how to develop a strategy. You'll need people to execute it for you."

AN HOUR LATER, I was sitting in the palace throne room. The room was enormous, large enough to seat several hundred people. It was at the top of the palace, and open to the air through gigantic archways that displayed the rest of the city. I could feel with my Air magic that large banners hung from the cathedral ceiling, blowing lightly in the breeze. They probably depicted the symbol of my grandfather's house. At the head of the room was a raised dais, which overlooked the rest of the space. Dozens of stairs led up to the dais, where the thrones sat.

There were four thrones on top of the dais, which my grandfather told me were made of gold. The largest throne was in the middle, and was where Cassiel sat. At his right hand was a throne identical to his, but smaller in stature, which was the place for my father.

On the left were two other thrones in black wood, one that I currently sat in. They were for Ava and me, and signified our place in the monarchy. Underneath my fingers, I could tell that the thrones were carved with intricate designs. I was certain Ava would love them.

My grandfather ignored his own throne and stood beside me as we waited. His guards, as always, had followed us here, but they remained still as statues. I quickly learned that my grandfather never went anywhere without several members of the Emperor's Guard close behind. The doors to the throne room opened, and several pairs of footsteps shuffled inside.

"Sire," Eddie said. "Your entourage, as requested."

"These Elves are highly skilled in various specialties," my grandfather explained. "Each Emperor has access to his own team called the Elvish Associates, whose job is to carry out missions for the royal family. This team has been carefully curated for your purposes, Charlie, and you may direct them in any way you choose."

I was feeling pretty cozy in the throne, but I stood to greet each one of them in turn.

"This is Elyx," Eddie introduced as I shook the first man's hand. "He's a highly trained marksman, in both magical specialties and practical weapons. If you want a sniper, Elyx is your guy."

"Nice to meet you," I told him.

"The very same, your highness," Elyx said.

"The twins are Asa and Ares," Eddie continued.

I shook their hands in turn. Their hands felt similar, both rough and muscular. They were both much taller than me, and their hands were practically twice the size of mine.

"They're the muscle of the team, and both have trained in torture techniques," Eddie explained. "If you ever need to intimidate a witness, these guys have you covered."

"It's a pleasure to meet you both," I said.

"The pleasure is all ours," Asa replied in a deep voice.

"And this is Gavyn," Eddie introduced.

Gavyn... why did that name sound so familiar?

"It's nice to see you again, my prince," Gavyn said.

"Wait... you escaped the Institute after Forevermore was seized," I realized. Gavyn was one of the young Elves that had been captured in Forevermore and thrown into the prison with us. He'd siphoned angel wings from a guard and flew over the fence. It was a really big deal, because he was the first inmate to escape. "The Warden said you'd died."

Gavyn gave a smug laugh. "The Warden is a liar, but you already knew that."

I smirked. "It's nice to see you made it."

"Gavyn's more than an escape artist," Eddie said. "He's our communications expert. If you need a negotiator, a messenger, a PR guy... he's your man. He's also very skilled at blending in if you ever need to go undercover."

I nodded. "Sounds great."

"And finally, meet Max," Eddie said.

I reached out to shake his hand, but I was surprised to feel that he was smaller than the others, and his hands were smooth. He wore all types of rings, and bracelets jingled on his wrists.

"Max specializes in tech," Eddie said. "If you ever need to get past human technology or you need to hack into a high security system, just ask Max."

"I certainly will," I replied. "It's good to have a guy like you on the team."

Max gave a light laugh, but it came out higher than I expected. That's when I realized Max was a *woman*. She didn't correct me. Instead, she said, "I'm happy to be included."

"Sorry," I said quickly.

"Look, if you see me as one of the guys, I'm happy to be one of the guys," she teased.

I decided I already liked Max. She wasn't going to treat me like some stuck-up prince she had to bow down to, and I liked it that way. We were a team, and even though I was calling the shots, I wanted my team to work together as efficiently as possible. I figured I could really get along with these people.

"This is for you, Charlie." Max handed me a slim, rectangular item that fit nicely in my hand. "We have phones for you and all of your friends. They're completely warded and untraceable, magically or otherwise. Your phone is already set up with assistance technology to help you navigate the apps. I'll teach you how to use it."

"Thanks, Max." I slid the phone in my pocket before turning to the others. There were six of them total, including Eddie, and I needed to utilize their skills the best I could. "It's my job, and the job of the other demigods, to begin our search for the vampire key. We're still looking for a solid lead. What I need from all of you is intel on the vampires. Learn as much as you can about the Midnighters. I want to know how their society operates, and who their most notable leaders are. Report back to me on what you find."

Ivy had a lot of intel on the vampires already, but I need to give these guys something to do in the meantime. With Max's hacking skills, I was hoping we could learn some things Ivy didn't know.

"Eddie, you're heading the research team," I added.

Eddie gasped, but he tried to keep his excitement contained. *Barely.* "I'm the boss?!" he exclaimed.

"Yep," I said. "You're all free to go."

Eddie started barking orders at them right away, and I internally laughed at his enthusiasm. He seemed so happy to be useful, instead of waiting around for my instructions.

Before I left the room, my grandfather stopped me. "Charlie," he said lowly. "There's one thing you must understand as a leader."

He piqued my curiosity, and I listened closely as everyone else left the room.

"These people are devoted to you, but they are not your friends— not in the sense that you've become accustomed to," Cassiel warned. "Your Associates will lay down their lives for you, and if I know anything about my grandson, I know you would do the same for them. But you *must* remain focused on the long-term goal. Do not let yourself become a sacrifice for a single person. You are the Elven prince, and as a prince, you hold your people together. If you sacrifice yourself, you sacrifice us all."

His words chilled me to the bone. My grandfather's message was clear. My Associates were people I had to trust with my life, but I couldn't get too close. One day, I would be put in a position that I didn't want to be in... and I'd be forced to make a decision that could crush me.

What my grandfather didn't realize was that I'd been in that position time and time again, and if there was a mark of a true villain, it was that even though I'd already been there, I'd go dark again... and I knew exactly what decisions I had to make.

They weren't the right ones by any sane person's standards.

And somehow, I was completely okay with that.

I'd already grown too close to Eddie— he was my friend, but I had allowed that relationship to go too far. When the Warden had sent Eddie to the camps, I'd tried to save him. That action had gotten Ava hurt, as well as put me and the rest of my friends in danger. I couldn't make the same mistake again. I wouldn't allow myself to see my team as anything more than people who worked for me... *expendable* people, who I was willing to sacrifice for the cause.

"I understand," I told my grandfather coldly. Then I turned on my heel and left the throne room.

Eddie was waiting for me out in the hall. He fell into step beside me, though I wasn't quite sure where we were going.

"What's next on the agenda?" I asked.

"Well, you had a mentorship session scheduled with your grandfather this afternoon, but as I understand it, you've already completed your training for the day," Eddie said. "If I may ask, what did you cover?"

"Mirror portals," I told him.

"Oh, fun!" Eddie exclaimed. "It took me years to learn mirror portals. I was thrilled once I figured it out."

"It really took you that long?" I asked. "I already traveled through my first mirror."

I guess my grandfather made it sound easier than it was.

"You forget that when you and I met, I still couldn't siphon magic from other supernaturals," Eddie reminded me. "My powers have grown considerably in just a year."

"Yeah, I suppose," I said. It was easy to forget with his chipper attitude how much Eddie had been through. Trauma like that could really push a person to grow up quickly.

I stopped in the middle of the hall. "Hey, Eddie…"

He halted beside me, and I said, "When I told you to blow me earlier, it was just something I said to piss off my dad. You know I wouldn't make you do anything like that, right?"

Eddie instantly sounded confused. "Why not? It is a service like any other, such as arranging your schedule, or fetching your things would be."

"I don't think Alistair would see it that way," I pointed out.

"Whysoever not? I am merely serving my prince. There is no romance involved. It is simply my job to please you, in any way. Though he is not an Elf, certainly Alistair would understand I must serve you," Eddie said blankly.

He really didn't get it. Elvish culture had brainwashed him to be loyal to a fault.

I sighed. "Look, Eddie. You're not like the rest of my guards, okay? We're friends… probably closer friends than we should be. And because of that, I'm going to give you an order that overpowers all other orders for the rest of your time of service, understand?"

"Anything, sire. What is it you ask of me?" Eddie questioned.

"If I give you an order, and you don't want to do it, you don't have to follow it," I said firmly. "I want you to have free will, and this is the only way I can see getting around the magical contract that binds you to me. If I ask you to do something, and it goes against what you truly want, then you can refuse."

"I will follow any request my master demands. I can't imagine refusing you for anything," Eddie said in astonishment.

"Maybe you'll never have to. But at least this way, I know you're following my orders because you want to, not because you're required to by magic."

"If this is what you wish, then I will agree," Eddie said. "But it is a promise I will never have to keep, because I will never disobey you."

"We'll see. But keep in mind I *really* don't want to do anything sexual with anyone who's not my wife," I said as we continued walking down the hall.

Then I scowled. "I don't want to be like my dad."

"You are too hard on him," Eddie insisted. "I have known Drea for many years. She is a part of my family, as all guards who serve the Elvish monarchy are related, distantly or otherwise. I do believe her and your father are truly in love. I don't think he forced her into anything without her consent."

"Well, that's good to know." I still wasn't certain he hadn't given up on me, though. It would take some convincing to make me think my father actually cared about what had happened to me.

"Seeing as you've already figured out mirror portals, that brings me to an important feature in your room that we should discuss," Eddie said. "Allow me to show you."

Eddie led me back to my room. Ava and Oberi weren't there, and the room was quiet when we arrived.

"It's in here," Eddie said, leading me into the bedroom. He guided me to the wall across from the foot of the bed, and I reached out to feel a tall mirror attached to the wall. "This may appear as an ordinary mirror, but it is enchanted."

I furrowed my brow. "My grandfather said mirrors didn't have to be magical to pass through them. An Elf creates that magic themselves."

"This one is particularly special, because it's warded to keep anyone but you from accessing it," Eddie explained. "That way, enemies can't use it to pass into your quarters. There is one other mirror like it— a sister mirror, if you will. That mirror resides right behind this wall, past six feet of blast-proof and magic-repellent material."

"What, like some kind of bomb shelter?" I wondered. "Six feet seems almost... excessive."

"You are the prince," Eddie stated bluntly. "It's standard in all palaces to have some sort of safe room for the royal family. If we are under attack, you can pass through this mirror into the safe room, where enemies can't find you. Would you like to go inside?"

"Sure." I stepped up to the mirror and splayed my palm over the glass. I imagined the gap between the wall collapsing, connecting the two mirrors into one point in space. The solid surface seemed to melt, and my hand sank through the glass. I stepped forward, and Eddie followed behind me.

My magic swirled around the room as I walked inside. It wasn't very big, but it was spacious enough that it wouldn't freak me out to spend long hours in here if necessary. I couldn't make sense of anything other than the walls, though. There didn't seem to be anything in here.

"Eddie, it's empty," I remarked.

"Well, of course," Eddie said. "The builders didn't know when you would arrive. The room was sealed off when it was built, and we needed your magic to access it after that. Now that you're here, we can start stocking it with supplies. There's a closet for non-perishable food items, as well as a bathroom in case you're here for a long time. You have full access to electricity, and the room is equipped with a state-of-the art magical ventilation system that has been rigorously tested for security vulnerabilities— there aren't any. However, in the case of debris, there are oxygen tanks in the closet. There are no exits, apart from the enchanted mirror."

"What happens if the mirror breaks during an attack?" I asked.

"It's highly unlikely, due to other security protocols. However, if it truly came down to it, we'd be able to use machinery to get you out— it would just take some time."

"If you can get inside, that means so can our enemies," I pointed out.

"They'd have to know this place existed," Eddie replied. He smacked the wall and said, "This baby's completely enchanted so that even if someone's looking for signs of life, they won't find it. No amount of infrared cameras, tracking spells, or things like that can penetrate these walls, and they're completely soundproof. You've got complete privacy in here."

Soundproof. I liked the sound of that. An idea began to form in my mind.

"Just let me know how we can make this room the most comfortable for you, and I'll get anything you request right away," Eddie said.

I already knew exactly what I wanted. "Eddie, I'm going to give you a long list of things I need, but you've got to get them with no questions asked, all right?"

"My lips are sealed," Eddie promised.

Good, because I didn't want anyone to know what I had planned for this room. This safe room was built for me and my wife.

And I was going to make it our sanctuary.

ava-marie

FOUR

Charlie had a role to play here in Ilamanthe, and so did I. As Ilamanthe's princess, the Elves were looking for me to guide them. I planned to fulfill that role to the best of my ability.

An Elvish woman led me down the hallway. A servant offered to push my chair, but I refused, preferring to move myself. These people needed to see I could be a capable leader, not a precious little thing who expected everyone to wait on her.

"My name is Elrye. I am in charge of the monarchy's daily operations, as I have been for the past three-hundred years," the woman at the head of the group told me. She was tall and beautiful, with long silver hair and a staunch expression. "If you need to organize an event, summon members of the royal court for meetings, or are simply confused on what your duties may be, call for me, and I will be able to point you in the right direction. I have served many Elvish royals, and assure you, I am the best at my job."

I didn't doubt it. This lady was over three centuries old. I bet she saw me as nothing more than a child.

"As you've been told, the first item of duty is to decide your personal court. A princess needs allies and friends, and your court will be loyal to you alone," Elrye said.

She pushed open a door to a beautiful parlor room, one with an open balcony and flowers blooming along the walls. Elvish servants puttered around the room, taking care of the flowers and arranging the space.

Kallie was there, along with Opal. They were both dressed in lovely gowns, and were having tea by an open window. Opal gave me a nervous wave as she chewed on a pastry, while Kallie lounged against the chemise couch, indulging in the lap of luxury.

"I have summoned a few of your friends to help you with this task," Elrye noted. "Choosing a court is no small task, and your lady-in-waiting is the most important position."

"I thought Kallie would be my lady-in-waiting," I replied.

"The Grand Duchess is a princess in her own right, and will have other duties here in Ilamanthe working for the King of the Arcanea, serving as a fae diplomat on his behalf," Elrye said. "It wouldn't be proper of her station to be your lady."

"My brother needs me to do work here, as much as I'd like to always be at your side," Kallie said, and she slowly sat up. "But I can help you choose a valuable court. I have experience with this kind of thing."

"It's your decision on how large or how small you wish your court to be," Elrye noted.

"I think it's best to keep it small," I said. More ladies meant more people to watch, and I had more important things to do than keep an eye on potential traitors who'd stab me in the back.

"Very well. At the minimum, you will need a handmaiden to help you with daily tasks. This includes bathing, dressing, and getting ready for the day, as well as someone who can bring you food, who helps keep your quarters clean and fetches anything you may ask for. There are servants to help you with these kinds of tasks, but your handmaiden will be your own personal maid, in your service only," Elrye said.

It felt a little uncomfortable to have someone waiting on me so heavily, but I supposed that it was required— not to mention having a helping hand would really be beneficial now that I was a wheelchair-user. Charlie had to help me out a lot at the Institute, but he'd be busy with other obligations now, so I was glad someone else would be stepping in.

"I would like my handmaiden to be someone I personally know," I said. I wasn't comfortable with strangers touching my body, and if this person was going to help me bathe, I'd at least like to be able to hold a polite conversation when I was buck-ass nude. "I request Opal, if she's okay with it."

"I'd be happy to be your handmaiden," Opal said, in a voice so quiet I barely heard her. "I don't have a job here to do in Ilamanthe, and I think it would keep me busy."

A happy squeal erupted from the other room. A young girl with aquamarine hair in pigtails toddled in, running circles around Elrye before she tripped over her multiple skirts. She pushed herself up, and rushed to Opal with arms out wide.

"This must be your daughter," I said as I smiled at the child. She gave a wide grin back.

"Yes. Your parents brought her here," Opal said, and she lifted Marina onto her lap. "Unfortunately, the foster family who took her in died during an attack on Atlantis. The Elves worked together with the Toaqua to find her and bring her back to Ilamanthe. I'm very grateful."

I understood. Opal cared about me, and she wanted to help. But being close to me meant she and Marina could be in danger, because I was the princess, and therefore always a target.

But that also meant I had plenty of guards around to protect them at all times. I needed to keep them close.

"Excellent. Elves love children. We find, after living for so long, that they bring a sort of youthful energy to the room," Elrye replied. "You will also need a personal guard, princess. We have many to choose from."

She clapped her hands. From another door marched a variety of guards, who turned at-attention in unison. They were all brawny, tall, and armed to the teeth.

"Our guards are trained from the moment they are able to walk. All are skilled in both fighting and magic, and each one has taken a vow to lay their life down for any member of the monarchy should it be required. These Elves will fight to the death to defend you," Elrye stated.

I surveyed the faces of the guards carefully. Each of them looked the same, and there was nothing distinguishable about any of them. "Those who've seen battle, step forward," I said.

About half of the guards lined up before me. I tapped my fingers on the armrest of my wheelchair and asked, "Have any of you killed an angel?"

Only one guard emerged. I gestured for her to speak, and she said, "I have, princess. Only one, and he nearly killed me. But I harnessed my magic to drain his life-force energy, and used that power to end him."

The guard was over six feet tall, and had layers of muscle. I figured she could stop a train coming toward her head-on and throw it in the other direction. She looked like somebody who could keep her mouth shut if shit went south, and even better, she was a woman. I wanted an all-female team, and if she had killed an angel, she was strong enough to defend me against nearly anything. "Perfect. I want you."

"A fine choice. Eldin is at the top of her battalion," Elrye replied.

The rest of the guards left the room, and Eldin went to stand guard beside my chair.

"Finally, you must decide on a lady-in-waiting. Your lady is different than your handmaiden, as she is required to be Elvish, and is more of a companion than a servant. She will keep you entertained, and accompany you to public engagements," Elrye stated. "She is also responsible for arranging your schedule, and fulfilling any demand you may have of her."

Elrye clasped her hands together. "If you had been born an Elf, and married Charlie among us, your lady-in-waiting would've been bonded to you after the ceremony, much like the prince is bonded to Edwyrd. But since you are an Elementai, a change is in order, and you must choose your own. For all these reasons we simply *must* insist that the lady you choose is of Elven blood, someone who knows our customs and can teach you about our way of life. A princess usually has several ladies, but since you wish to keep your court small, we shall keep it to one."

I didn't want to be bonded to anyone but Charlie and Oberi. This position sounded like a big deal, and honestly, I didn't trust any random ass stranger with the job, although I would have to pick one.

"Choose carefully," Kallie warned me. "My cousins were my ladies-in-waiting, and they were very valuable to me. You lady-in-waiting isn't just a friend. She's a tool, one you have to use effectively to retain control of the court."

I looked to Elrye. "Who do you suggest?"

"In my opinion, I believe you should choose Abigail," Elrye said.

At the name, another person entered the room. The girl was around our age, and had beautiful brown curls with big hazel eyes. I was surprised to see she used a wheelchair, like me.

When she wheeled before me, she shakily stood, and gave me a short bow. "Princess, my name is Abigail. I am an Elvish lady here at the court, and am an ambulatory wheelchair user. I retain the ability to walk and stand, although I can't do so for long periods of time."

I noticed her ears weren't pointed. "You're only half-Elf," I stated. "What other supernatural heritage do you claim?"

"I am an angel. I am of the Taurus family— in fact, I am the sister of Esther Taurus, who I'm sure you've met," Abigail said dryly.

Revulsion churned my insides. I wanted to puke up my breakfast. "You're a *Taurus*? Why is she even here?" I demanded of Elrye. "She should be thrown out of the city! I want her out of here at once!"

I was *pissed*. The Elves had brought this girl in here because they'd thought we'd bond over being wheelchair users, but she was just another manipulator, and I didn't want that in my court.

"I understand your reaction. It's true that I am Esther's sister, but there's a long history between us," Abigail said. "In truth, I am half-angel, half-Elf. Esther and I share the same father, but not the same mother."

"Why do I care?" I spat. "Leave!"

"Please, allow me to explain," Abigail said, and she slowly sank into her seat. "I would like you to understand my position."

I was about to tell her to go to hell, but Kallie caught my gaze, and something in it said to let Abigail speak... even though all I wanted to do was to cut her throat. "Fine. But nothing you tell me is going to change my mind."

"Very well. May I come join you for tea?"

I didn't want her anywhere near me, but I felt Oberi prodding me through the bond. *This could be an opportunity*, she said gently. *Keep in mind you're in a royal court now, and this is how the game is played. Information is invaluable here, and if Abigail is a Taurus, she might have some.*

I couldn't let my personal feelings get in the way of gaining intel, so I said, "Sure. Whatever. State your case."

"Thank you." Abigail wheeled up beside me. She poured herself some tea, then took the cup and saucer in hand before she began to speak.

"Esther and I are around the same age. Our father had an affair with my mother before Esther was born. I am older, but only by a year," Abigail explained. "My mother was an Elf living among the angels in secret. After the Elven genocide during the Great Supernatural War, my mother went into hiding in Celestial City. Her entire family had been slaughtered, and she believed that she was the only Elf that was still left alive. To hide her identity, she cut off the tips of her ears, and made them round in order to fit in amongst the angels. She was beautiful, and immortal, so they believed she was one of them."

I wasn't buying this story just yet. "Go on."

"She met my father after he was already married to Esther's mother," Abigail said. "My mother didn't know that he was married, so she thought she was the only woman in his life. He was attempting to live a double life. As I've heard it, he liked the power it gave him, to have two different families."

The Taurus brothers loved toying with people's lives, apparently.

"The secret came out after I was born. My father couldn't hide the affair any longer, and he was found out," Abigail explained. "Once the affair was revealed, my uncle— Doctor Taurus, as you know him— discovered my mother was an Elf, and considered it proof that the Elves were still alive. He tortured her, looking for information on Forevermore. But my mother didn't know anything, because she believed herself to be the last Elf alive. She died under his questioning."

Although I didn't want to, I felt a small stab of pity for Abigail. No one was exempt from the Warden's cruelty. He'd harmed everyone I knew, whether they were a stranger or my closest friend.

"I was given to Esther's family," Abigail went on. "I was never told of my true heritage, and I was raised by Esther's mother. She treated me with kindness, but was distant and cold. I thought she didn't like me because Esther was her favorite. I did my best to earn her love, but she never showed any affection toward me. My father wasn't particularly warm, either. I don't think he truly loved my mother, just loved the attention she gave him. He didn't want a child to come out of the affair, but he was stuck with me."

Abigail sipped at her tea. "Despite feeling like an outcast in my own family, Esther and I were very close. I loved my sister, and I knew she felt the same way about me. We did everything together. There was a time in my life I would've died for her, had she asked."

Abigail's tone became flat as she said, "Then... Esther came of age and got her powers. My uncle discovered she was a demigod. Doctor Taurus told us the truth about everything, thinking I might've inherited some sort of spectacular magic as well from my Elven heritage. But I didn't show any signs of talent, so he lost interest pretty quickly. Esther, though..."

Abigail gave a sigh, one that was a combination of bitterness and hurt. "She couldn't handle the fact that our father had cheated. She wanted that reality to go away, and I was a reminder that he'd been unfaithful to her mother. Any love she had for me was lost. She used her demigod abilities to conquer me in a fight, when I was just trying to get away from her, and she ripped out all my feathers."

"That sounds awful," I said honestly. I couldn't believe Esther had done something so gruesome to someone she supposedly loved. She was worse than I'd ever dreamed.

"Angels are weak without their feathers, and they can't survive if both of their wings are taken. It's their connection to the divine and the source of their magic," Abigail explained.

"So you can't do magic anymore?" I asked.

Abigail shook her head slowly. "I have *some* Elven abilities. But they're not very strong, and I'm unable to harness angel magic at all."

Abigail stirred her tea with a slight frown. "Esther left me for dead. I probably *would've* died, had the Demigod Guardians not found me. They'd been looking to convince Esther to join them, but after spying on her and seeing it was a lost cause, they rescued me instead, and took me to Ilamanthe."

"When did you come here?" I asked.

"Around the same time Esther arrived at the Institute. So... nearly five months ago?" Abigail set down her teacup. "I've been studying to become an Elvish lady since my arrival. My mother had been a high-born Elf, and it would have been my station, had I been raised among the Elves in Forevermore. As I understand it, Elves are born into their roles, and study to become them their entire lives. I don't fit in anywhere else in Elvish society, and I depend on the monarchy to care for my needs, so I've vowed to serve them. As your primary lady-in-waiting, I'll be here to guide you in your new role as princess. I've been working very hard to learn the customs here. I can teach you everything you need to know about Elvish culture, and I can keep you company. I can even spy for you amongst the court, if you so wish."

"It's safe here in Ilamanthe. The Elves practically worship the monarchy," I rebutted.

"The Elves are a loyal people, but there are always one or two in any royal court who are only looking out for themselves," Abigail replied. "And it goes without saying that you have married into a mob family, princess. If you want to govern properly, and keep your head, you need allies who can slip in and out of places undetected."

"How can I trust that you'll be loyal to me only?" I crossed my arms. I wasn't so sure she wouldn't sell me out.

"My station here, as well as my reputation and my long-term stability, relies on me being a valuable member of the royal court. I have to be useful to my princess; otherwise, I can't stay, and I have nowhere else to go. I don't have much magic, and without magic in this supernatural world, I'll be at risk without the protection of the court," Abigail replied. "I can understand if you don't want to trust me, and I know I have to earn your respect. But you can believe me when I say that I am loyal to the Elven monarchy, and to you. Esther and my uncle think that I'm dead, but if they knew I was alive, they'd certainly kill me. If I want to stay alive, I must be of use."

I liked that she wasn't trying to bullshit me with noble proclamations of loyalty she didn't mean. She was intent on staying here in Ilamanthe, and I was a means to that end.

That was fine. Her goals aligned with my own, and people who were working for themselves were easier to control than people who served you because they loved you. I could predict what a selfish person could do; I couldn't predict what one of my friends might do if I or someone else they cared for was in danger. Abigail needed me to favor her for her own benefit, which meant I could use her as my pawn. But I wasn't convinced it was the right move.

"I need some time to think about this privately," I said.

"We shall give you a moment," Elrye replied. She and Abigail, along with all the other Elves but my guard Eldin, left the room.

I leaned in toward Kallie and Opal. "Did you buy any of that crap? That sob story she was spewing was such bullshit."

"I think she was telling the truth," Opal said, and Marina slid off her lap to go play with the flower petals scattered on the floor. "She seemed very serious."

"She's a very good actress." Whatever Abigail said, I didn't trust that she had completely lost her affection for Esther. There was a dark shadow in her eyes when she said her sister's name that told me she wasn't ready to let go of her yet.

Kallie tapped her chin. "I think we need to hire her."

"You *trust* her?" I asked in disbelief.

"It's not that," Kallie said. "But choosing Abigail is a clever move. She was close to our enemies. If we get to know her, we can pry her for information on Esther and the Warden. Then we can use that information against them."

A wise decision, Oberi agreed. *Keeping the enemy close, and learning about them in the meantime.*

"She knows Esther's weak spots, as well as the Warden's. If she turns out to be untrustworthy, we can get rid of her," Kallie said with a shrug. "But I think this is too valuable of an opportunity to throw away."

The way Kallie said *get rid of her* didn't imply firing Abigail. I supposed that was good enough for me.

I summoned everyone back into the room. Abigail appeared... almost nervous. She was excellent at keeping a flat mask, but I was good at reading people, and she definitely wanted this position. Whether it was to keep her place here in Ilamanthe, or because she wanted to spy on me for the Warden, I guessed we'd find out.

"I suppose you can stay," I said. "But it's going to be a while before I'll know for sure if this situation is going to work out."

"Understood," Abigail replied. "I will do everything I can to serve you well."

An immense rage boiled inside my chest and flooded outward. I found myself consumed by a red-hot anger that caused my skin to burn. I thought my Fire magic was going to come erupting out of my form and reduce everyone in this room to ash.

I didn't know where it had come from, but I thought my rage was directed at Abigail, and how absolutely insane it was she thought she could serve me when she had previously been connected to Esther and the Warden.

Then I realized the fury wasn't coming from me. Holy hell, Charlie was *mad,* and I could feel it.

"Is there something wrong?" Opal asked, and she wiped at her face with a napkin. "You've elevated the temperature around us by at least ten degrees."

Sweat formed on the faces of others in the room. I subdued my Fire magic and gestured for the servants to open a window. "It's my husband," I explained quickly. "He's absolutely fuming. Something bad must've happened."

I was really worried. Was Charlie safe? Who could even attempt to hurt him here in Ilamanthe, where he was a prince and had total control?

"I believe he was scheduled for lunch with his father," Abigail replied. "The servants were gossiping about it this morning."

That would explain why I wanted to pick this table up and hurtle it across the room. I didn't think the reunion with Charlie's dad would go well, but something hurtful must've been said. I felt Charlie's anger rise and fall, then explode. He briefly lost his bearings as magic was siphoned out of him.

Shit, he must be fuming. Someone— probably his grandfather, as I thought he would be the only Elf powerful enough to do so— had taken his magic for a moment to calm him down. I felt him come around, and magic flooded back into his body. I attempted to reach out, but he was so pissed I didn't think he heard me.

We should give him some time, Oberi noted. *This is not a problem we can fix. Charlie and his father must resolve it on their own.*

Or I could just settle it with Cameron myself, I shot back.

Unlikely. Let it be.

I felt Charlie's anger dim, and resolved we'd talk about it later. This was between Charlie and his dad, and I knew better than to get involved unless the situation absolutely required it... though if Cameron continued to hurt Charlie, I was going to lose my patience and take matters into my own hands.

"We should move along," Elrye stated. "There is still much to see."

Elrye took us out of the parlor room and down the hall, to another set of double doors. "This area is known as the Ladies' Court. This tower is strictly reserved for the women of the palace. Only females are permitted in this area, and it is an area that is under your control entirely. Not even the Emperor or the princes are allowed to enter."

A pair of servants opened the double doors, and we roamed inside. I was delighted to see a beautiful area that was full of Elvish women. There was a lovely round pool beneath a waterfall that fell from one of the palace roofs. Around the pool were lounge chairs, and there was a bubbling tub that had been built to resemble a hot spring. Palm trees provided shade, and a female band played relaxing music in the background. There were massage tables, and people were getting manicures near a drink station which served mocktails that changed color. A mini-workout station stood on a platform above the pool, where Elvish women lifted weights and practiced sparring.

"Awesome, no men around." Kallie gave a broad smile. "Might as well call it paradise."

Clearly she wanted somewhere to hide from Marcus.

I was ready to get in the pool immediately, but Elrye led me on. "There are other bedrooms here, if you wish to take some time to yourself."

"It's not like I'm going to need it." I couldn't imagine a situation where I'd need a bedroom separate from Charlie's. It wasn't like we'd ever sleep apart, but maybe I could use this place for a girl's night.

"Perhaps you will, one day," Elrye replied. "All your clothes and treasures will be stored here as well."

Treasures? I didn't know what she meant, until *I did*. Elrye led us to an absolutely enormous walk-in closet the size of a small house, and when I ventured inside, I nearly died of happiness. Clothes and dresses lined the walls on hangers at my level, and designer bags were lined on top of dressers according to color.

And ancestors, shoes, *glorious shoes* spanned the entire length of the closet in small cubbies that were easily accessible for me to reach. There were literally hundreds of them. I could wear a different outfit every day for a year and still not go through everything in the closet. I swear, a tear slipped out of my eye.

"We wanted to make sure the princess was well-dressed, as we heard from your friends that you enjoy fashion," Elrye said with a coy glimmer in her eye. "I hope that you'll come to cherish every piece."

"There's so much pink!" I squealed. I hugged the ballgown closest to me and buried my face in the puffy tulle skirt. I loved Charlie, but it would've been worth marrying him for the closet alone.

There was a dressing room area, where couches circled around mirrors. There, I could try things on. There was a ramp I could use to venture up onto the raised dais, so I could look at outfits in front of the mirrors. The entirety of the Ladies' Court had been built to be accessible to me in mind, and I could get anywhere and do anything without having to ask for much help. I was absolutely touched by how generous the Elves could be.

I wanted to start playing dress-up immediately, before Elrye hurried us along. "The back of the closet is my personal favorite."

Ancestors, there was more? How could there be *more?*

Elrye took us to a door and indicated that I should open it. I did so and almost passed out. Gorgeous necklaces, earrings and bracelets lay on velvet pillows underneath white spotlights. Priceless gems and jewels were everywhere, ready for me to wear. There was a literal *pool of fucking diamonds* in the middle of the room. I absolutely couldn't believe it. "Are those real, or illusions?"

"Real as can be," Elrye stated. "Everything in this room is certified and genuine."

I was completely blown away by the abundance the Elves had. "You can't give me all these diamonds," I insisted. "They belong in the royal treasury, to all the members of the monarchy."

"Oh, this is nothing," Elrye said with a casual wave of her hand. "Trust me when I say the Emperor has more than enough to spare."

"How'd you get it all out of Forevermore before the Warden took it over?" Kallie asked.

"We didn't store most of our treasures in Forevermore. The monarchy was careful to hide our true wealth in secret magical stores all over the world, just in case our city was discovered," Elrye replied. "Of course, we did lose quite a few treasures from the siege of Forevermore, but let me assure you that what we have here in Ilamanthe is more than enough for everyone."

She could say that again. Finally, I was living my best *Ava-Marie life* as I was meant to experience it. I was born for absolute luxury. I wasn't sure what to bathe in first, the pool or the diamonds.

Looking around at everything the Elves had, I was confused. "The Elves have so much wealth, and so many resources. Why didn't they use them to win the last Great Supernatural War?" I questioned.

"Money is a wonderful resource to have in a time of suffering, but diamonds don't win wars, princess. People do," Elrye responded. "We had three very powerful magical societies fighting us from all sides. The fae were as wealthy as we were back in that time, and the angels and vampires had their own stores of riches. Our allies, the Elementai and the witches, weren't as well-equipped, and we had to share what we had with them to bolster their forces as well as our own. We can throw all the wealth we desire at obtaining weaponry, but we were vastly outnumbered, and back then, most of the supernatural world had the goal of exterminating us, simply *because* we were so powerful."

"But you had everything at your disposal, magic and otherwise," I stated. I wasn't trying to argue, but understand. If I was to be the princess of these people, I needed to comprehend how the Elves had failed, so we wouldn't make the same mistake again.

"A beetle is far stronger and more powerful than an ant, but if a thousand ants swarm one beetle with the singular goal of destroying it, the beetle will die," Elrye responded. "Our enemies were wise, because they came together to capture our most powerful warriors, and either imprisoned or killed them all before the war truly began. It left most of us defenseless. Our money was all but useless by the time we had to go underground and hide within Forevermore. Hopefully we can utilize it better this time."

"Are you sure there's enough to go around?" Kallie asked. "The Elves are so generous. I can't help but wonder if it's going to run out."

"The Elves have a different way of thinking. We believe abundance is infinite, that there's always more than enough for everyone, and always more to be had," Elrye replied. "Yes, we did earn most of our wealth through crime, but we also elevated our society through trade and magical goods long before the first Great Supernatural War. Our people have been around since the dawn of time, and we've used that advantage to compile everything we've ever wanted. We offered to give away some of that wealth to the other races in times of need, but even as we did so, that caused many to resent us."

"No wonder people wanted to wipe the Elves out," I said quietly. The jealousy alone from the other magical races, witnessing the Elves living in such prosperity, would inspire hatred.

"Indeed. Many of the other races, most prominently the angels, didn't believe everyone could have what they needed. They thought that the Elves hoarded everything for ourselves, so they attempted to take what we had," Elrye said heavily. "But such conversations shouldn't be had on a day like today. You have some time before the next item on your schedule, princess. Feel free to use this area how you wish."

Abso-freaking-lutely. I spent the rest of the morning and a good portion of the afternoon basking in paradise. I put on one of the adorable bikinis I had in the closet and went to go swimming. It was much easier to get in the pool, due to the lift they had for wheelchair users. The Institute never had one, which meant someone always had to carry me in. The Elves had thought of everything to accommodate me.

I used my Toaqua powers to swim around by myself for a while, while Opal splashed with Marina in a shallow area of the pool. Her child had the cutest turquoise mermaid tail, and she could already swim well. Oberi busied herself with getting a massage, nickering as the therapist kneaded her back while two Koigni girls braided her Fire mane and tail.

Abigail and I had made small talk while we swam in the pool, mostly about the city. She'd brought me a couple of drinks and had offered to reapply my makeup once I got out of the water.

Having a lady-in-waiting felt like having a paid best friend, and I wasn't sure if I liked it much. It felt fake.

While Abigail was chatting with Opal, I took my chance to get away from her so I could approach Kallie, who hadn't said a thing since Elrye had left us to our own devices. Kallie lounged on a reclining chair by the pool and soaked up the sun.

I paddled up to her and rested my arms on the edge of the pool. "Hey. Why don't you come in? It's a beautiful day."

"I will in a minute," Kallie said. "I'm just... distracted."

"How come?" I rested my chin on my hands. "I know this is a lot to take in, but we should enjoy it while we can."

Kallie gave a sigh. "Honestly... I'm still thinking about the Dollmaker."

The hated name soured a beautiful day like today. The Dollmaker was a mass murderer who'd killed multiple young women in Malovia. Charlie and Kallie had done some investigating before we'd left the Institute, and they'd discovered the Dollmaker was actually Kallie's ex, Valen. He'd compelled her after she'd broken up with him to assassinate her brother, and although the attempt to take Kazim's life had failed, it had gotten her sent to the Institute. The police were looking for him, but at the moment, Valen hadn't been caught.

"You upset he's still on the run?" I asked.

"Yes, but there's more to it. I'm wondering how he was able to compel me to kill my brother, and not have me remember it. That's some strong magic," Kallie said.

"Wouldn't a fae be capable of pulling something like that off?" I asked.

"Fae magic *can* compel people, but it's very hard to do, and the magic requires a lot of effort. It's usually only something sorceresses can pull off, not shifters. Valen's good in battle, but his magic wasn't that powerful. I don't think he was strong enough to compel me on his own, especially not since I'm a demigod," Kallie said.

"You think he had help?"

"He must've. Either he had someone cast a compelling spell on me, or he had some sort of object that did it for him. I'm thinking it must've been the second option, because if he kept the item in his possession, he could've used it during other murders to keep his victims from fighting back or escaping," Kallie said.

"If it was an item, I bet a vampire created it. They're basically masters of compulsion magic. Valen either convinced one to give the item, or stole it," I said.

"Or he's working for a powerful vampire, one who's willing to give Valen materials as long as he kills people this bigwig wants out of the picture," Kallie noted darkly. "Gods, I hope the Union catches this bastard soon. I'd give anything to go through his tools of terror and see what he's got."

"They're too busy looking for us." I scowled.

"Yeah, and I can't exactly leave here to search for him while we're still looking for the keys. I know those have to come first, but I still wish that sick bastard was behind bars."

"He will be, Kallie. He can't run forever."

"I know." She sat up and braided her hair back. "If only I could be out there right now, hunting him down."

"I know you feel responsible for what he did, but you're not to blame for his crimes," I insisted.

"He started killing people because I rejected him," Kallie said. "If I had just said yes—"

"If you had agreed to be with him, you would've been miserable, and he would've made your life a living hell. Not to mention it probably wouldn't have stopped him from killing, anyway. He would've done it regardless, because he's wired that way to get a thrill out of hurting others," I pointed out. "You could've done *nothing*, Kallie. Let's get the keys first, then we'll kill him, and you can put it behind you."

"Right." Kallie gave a slow, thoughtful nod. "Put it behind me."

We munched on a charcuterie board for lunch, then sunbathed until Elrye told us it was time for my next appointment. I decided I was already bored of my outfit from that morning and decided to choose another one, although Elrye told me to be dressed for some exercise.

I chose the *cutest* two-piece tracksuit, and was feeling absolutely extravagant as Elrye led us to another area of the palace— a massive room that was open to the sky and the size of a football field. The walls were made of stone, and the floor underneath us was some sort of bouncy, cushiony material that would be supportive if someone fell.

"This is the palace's training arena," Elrye informed us. "It is where you'll be practicing your abilities. You don't have to worry about holding your powers back, as it has been magically reinforced for demigods."

Kallie looked around. "We could practically blow this place up with our magic and it would still be standing. We don't have to worry about experimenting with spells that are too powerful."

"Precisely," Elrye said, and she inclined her head. "I will leave you to it. Your companions and the Demigod Guardians will arrive shortly."

Charlie was already there, leaning against a wall and waiting for the rest of us. He'd slipped out of his suit and changed into a t-shirt and workout pants.

His expression was pretty flat— which I never knew whether to take as a good sign or a bad one. I felt his bitter emotions flood our bond, though, and they were pretty wounded. Something had happened.

"Hey, babe," I said lightly, trying to cheer him up. "How'd this morning go?"

Charlie frowned. "I met up with my dad. And his *wife*."

Oof. I didn't know Cameron had remarried. No wonder the conversation hadn't gone well. "Are you okay?"

"I'm fine, as long as he stays away from me."

Not well at all. "Do you want to talk about it?"

"What's to talk about? He's moved on. Why bother being upset about something that happened years ago, anyway?"

He shut off his half of our bond, so I couldn't feel his emotions anymore.

Charlie was obviously hurt, and I wouldn't make him talk if he didn't want to. I knew he'd come to me eventually, so I steered the conversation in another direction. "Did you see your grandfather?"

Charlie brightened considerably. "Yeah. It was great. He taught me how to portal through mirrors."

"That's awesome." At least the day hadn't been a complete disaster for him.

Marcus ambled in shortly after we did. He hung out with Rishi at a distance, and didn't make eye contact with any of us. He didn't say anything, not even a hello, which told me something was bothering him.

Professors Amber and Wykoff entered the room. This time, Amber was followed by her orangutan Familiar, who was carrying a harp.

"I hope you're up for a workout!" Wykoff announced. "Today we'll be doing some hardcore training."

Right. Couldn't just laze around all day. I was here to do a job, to protect the people of Ilamanthe, and it was time to work.

Abigail gave me a nod. "I'll leave you to it, princess. If you need me, I'll be nearby."

She exited the room, and Eldin went to stand guard outside the door. Hm. I suppose if Abigail was going to spy on me she'd stay to watch my magical performance. But not excusing herself looked suspicious, too.

I put Abigail out of my mind. I needed to focus on my training, not her.

"Danny's late," Charlie commented snidely. "Does he think we have all day to wait around?"

Wykoff checked her watch. She shook her head, gave a sigh, and stated, "We might as well begin without him. Who knows when he's going to show up."

"We're going to start with a meditation, to delight the senses and invigorate the mind," Professor Amber cooed. "This way, your body will be delightfully prepared for the intense experience you're about to endure all over your form!"

Is she talking about meditating or having an orgasm? Oberi asked.

We didn't know, but Amber gestured for us to sit. Everyone but me took a seat on the ground, and the orangutan began strumming the harp.

"Close your eyes," Amber hummed. "Let yourself float away on the waves of delectable delight. Feel the tremors electrifying through your skin as tingles run on energy currents, from your soul into your earthly form. Transcend the limits of time and space, and become an endless being, one that expands outward in order to encompass all the universe, indulging yourself in sensual pleasure."

I don't know what she's talking about, Charlie whispered telepathically.

I don't either, but just go with it. My dad had told me Professor Amber was a little weird, but he never explained how much. This was supposed to be an experience, right? Might as well play along.

Oberi was getting into it. *I am life. I am death. I am the ending, and the beginning. I am one with the earth and sky!*

I attempted to relax, but it was hard when I was connected to Charlie's mind. He kept thinking that this was pointless— that meditating was a waste of time and we needed to get to work on practicing, so we could be strong enough to beat the Warden.

I cut that connection off. I knew he was impatient, but I needed to ground myself before we began. I listened to the sound of Professor Amber's voice, and soothed myself to the music of the harp until I felt a faint buzzing throughout my torso. When I had a clear head, I could feel my Fire, Water, and Spirit magic resonating inside of me, and I had a stronger connection to it. Ideas of what I could do with my magic came to me, and how I could utilize them in battle. I was glad we'd started the session with meditation, because it enabled me to center in on the moment so I could think straight.

"Do you feel the vibrations?" Amber prodded. "Can you sense the titillating, intimate caresses of time and space—"

The meditation was brought to a screeching halt when one of the doors to the training arena *slammed* against the wall. My eyes shot open, and I jumped in my chair. Kallie gave a gasp, and Marcus fell over beside me.

Danny strutted into the room like a cocky rooster, did a spin on his heels, then flicked his hair out of his eyes. "I'm here, everyone. No need to get alarmed."

"Danny, you're late again," Professor Wykoff said patiently.

"I would've been on time, but the ladies needed me," Danny replied. "So are we working today, or what?"

Danny made a show of tossing off his jacket and doing a couple of arm stretches that were obviously meant to display his muscles. He was dressed in a tight shirt and pants, a hilt holding a short, small blade against his calf.

"I suppose the meditation is over," Wykoff noted. "Everyone rise, please."

The others got to their feet, and I said, "The ceiling's open to the sun. Why aren't you frying your ass off right now?"

"The palace has a ward around it so vampires don't burn," Danny said. "I can frolic in the sunshine as much as I please here."

Charlie scowled. "We need to move on. What's next?"

"We'll begin with sparring," Wykoff said. "The four of you will be going up against Danny. He'll be defending himself alone."

"The four of us against him? He's not going to be able to keep up," Kallie said skeptically.

Danny gave a small laugh. "We'll see, sweetheart. Unless you're too afraid to challenge me, even as a group."

"We're not afraid. We just know you're going to get torn to pieces once we're done," Charlie rebutted.

"Please," Danny scoffed. "You have no idea what I can do."

I expected this exercise to last all of five minutes. "Whatever you say."

Oberi knelt before me, and I slid out of my wheelchair and onto her back. The illusion saddle pad appeared as I got on, and Charlie fastened the straps for my legs before we faced off against Danny.

Amber and Wykoff moved out of the way. Once they were standing at the wall, Wykoff said, "I would like you all to treat this as an actual fight. Don't hold back. We have healers to help you recover, should you get injured, but we cannot afford for any of you to go easy on each other when we have so much at stake. Begin."

The four of us flung magic at Danny at once. I threw out a combination of Fire and Water, Charlie blasted Air magic, and Kallie and Marcus tossed battle orbs. Danny used his super speed to sprint out of the way, and all of our hits missed.

Kallie transformed into a wolf, so she could keep up with him. She ran after Danny and opened her jaws wide to catch him. He rolled out of the way of her snapping fangs and tripped her up. She went tumbling to the ground, and as he did so, he reached out.

Danny grabbed Kallie around the waist, spun her around and tossed her across the arena with his super strength. She smashed into the wall, and a bit of concrete crumbled off the side. She groaned as she hit the floor, struggling to get up.

"Kallie!" Marcus shouted. He created a battle orb and Rishi jumped into it, zooming around the room. Rishi went after Danny, but Danny grabbed the battle orb that Rishi was in and smashed it with his hands. Rishi yowled as pieces of magic shattered like glass, and he went skittering to the other side of the arena to hide.

Danny ran toward Kallie again. I wasn't sure why he was making her his target, as she was already down for the count, but Marcus didn't stop to think. He slid to a stop in front of her, putting himself between her and Danny. Marcus flung his arm out, and I watched as a silvery specter began hovering outside of Danny's body. Marcus was attempting to rip out Danny's soul as a gut reaction to protect Kallie.

Danny leveled Marcus with a heavy stare. Once Danny's eyes fixed on Marcus, he gave a cry of agony and dropped to the floor, landing heavily on his right arm. Danny had practically turned him into a limp rag doll.

"Don't try to rip my soul out of my body, pal," Danny warned. "You ain't gonna like it."

I wasn't sure what kind of power he'd used, but Danny's magic had completely incapacitated my friend. Marcus rolled on the floor, wincing in pain.

Danny had taken down two of our teammates in seconds. We were underestimating him. Oberi cantered around Danny in a circle, while I observed him as we went around. Charlie waited, looking for the right opportunity to strike.

This guy was too good. There was something off about him. We needed to figure out what that was before we tried to take him down. I blasted off different types of magic in succession— first a fireball, then a stream of Water, then orbs of Spirit magic, to see how he'd react to them and how he countered each one.

He didn't react how I expected. Instead of dodging the magic, he *ran toward me* and slid underneath the shots I was firing. He pulled a dagger from the hilt that was attached to his calf and slashed it upward. The cloth cinch holding the saddle pad in place was sliced clean through. With nothing to hold me on, I toppled off and to the ground. Oberi nickered in surprise as I crashed downward, and Danny sprinted to the opposite side of the arena.

I tried to push myself up, but I found that my hands were stuck to the floor, and I couldn't move any part of my body. I realized that when Danny had cut the cinch, he'd also nicked my knee, and a tiny cut was oozing blood there. I glanced up, and saw Danny focusing his gaze on me.

He was using my blood to compel me. I couldn't fight back. "Oberi!" I called.

I can't move, either, Oberi nickered, and she let out a huff. Danny had cut her, too, and although the injury was barely visible, the few droplets of blood that dripped out of the cut on her belly were enough to enable Danny control of our bodies.

When Charlie realized that Oberi and I were down for the count and that he was on his own, he went ballistic. Charlie siphoned Danny's vampire strength and speed. He hurtled at him, raising a fist to drive it into Danny's face.

It seemed like Charlie wasn't able to take all of Danny's magic, because Danny kept his abilities. Charlie did what he knew how to do best and began throwing punches that became blurs due to the high speed. I heard Danny laughing, like he thought this was a fun game as he flung back hits of his own.

Charlie realized this wasn't going anywhere. He used his Elven illusion magic to conjure a sword, and he swung it at Danny's head. I was pretty sure the Elven healers couldn't sew Danny's *head back on* should Charlie knock it off, but Wykoff and Amber didn't stop him. Danny ducked and allowed Charlie to swing at him carelessly time and again before eventually, Charlie lost his footing and stumbled.

Danny took the opportunity to twist Charlie's wrist, and Charlie loosened his grip on the sword. Danny ripped Charlie's weapon out of his hand and kicked his legs out from under him. Charlie fell backward, and Danny pointed the blade at his throat.

"Surrender," Danny said. "You're done."

Charlie sneered, and Danny took a few steps back. I felt the compulsion magic holding me and Oberi break. The unicorn knelt to the floor, and I pulled myself back onto her. My group hobbled our way to the center of the arena, where Danny tossed the blade to the floor.

"Are you *sure* these guys are demigods? They don't seem like they're at the top of their game," Danny said, gesturing to us.

"That wasn't fair," Charlie spat as he caught his breath. "What's his demigod power? It gave him an edge."

"I had an edge, sure, but you still should've been able to overpower me. You guys are untrained as a team," Danny said. "If you noticed, most of the maneuvers I did were to avoid you, not to fight back. I only went on the offense when I saw an opening and you guys left yourselves defenseless. I didn't have to kick your ass or be the strongest guy in the room. I just had to outsmart you. You guys fight well as individuals, but not together. We're not gonna last if we can't battle as a unit."

"I agree," Professor Wykoff added. "The four of you should be helping to protect each other, so there *are* no openings. Instead, each of you went on the most aggressive offense possible, instead of taking turns to attack while the others held the enemy off."

Talk about our greatest weakness. Danny was right. Esther and her demigod goons had been able to beat us the other day because they worked together, and we hadn't. He'd pointed out our biggest flaw.

"Can you see people's weaknesses, like Esther?" I asked Danny.

"Nah," Danny said. "I'm kinda the opposite. I see people's deepest desires — what they want the most. That's my demigod power."

"That doesn't mean anything," Kallie said. "You being able to see what we desire shouldn't have given you that much of an advantage."

"Sure it does. It was easy," Danny replied. "Once I knew what you all wanted, it was simple to manipulate. Marcus wanted to protect Kallie. I had to disarm her first, so he'd be too distracted trying to save her and would be unable to defend himself. Ava wanted to figure me out, and her trying to guess what my demigod power was threw her off, leaving her vulnerable. And Charlie was focused on beating me up, not *winning* the match, so I took advantage of his anger and used it against him. I knew he'd fuck up and get sloppy. I just had to wait for when."

"With that kind of demigod ability, you can do anything," Marcus said. His tone held a shiver of fear.

"It's not perfect," Danny argued. "I can see people's deepest desires, yes, but it's still hard for me to utilize. I can't tell when someone is lying, to me or themselves, and if someone has two opposing desires that are equal in want, I'm not always sure which one to manipulate. It's not a sure thing, and sometimes I get it wrong— and sometimes, I have to *ask* people what their deepest desire is before I can manipulate it, because I can't always see it. Wards and magical protections can trick me and get in the way."

"Marcus can protect our minds. It shouldn't have worked," I argued.

"I can't protect you from everybody, especially if I don't know what I'm protecting you against. I've protected us from Seers— witches who can mind read or predict our intentions— but some mind manipulators like Alistair can get through," Marcus panted. "Looks like this guy is one of them."

Danny chuckled. "What *do* you truly desire, Marcus? You don't need to tell me— I can guess."

Marcus flushed and turned his back on Danny, mumbling something under his breath.

"That's an unusual power to have," I stated carefully. Demigod powers were influenced by personality. Danny's demigod power indicated that for all his bravado, he was a huge people pleaser.

Danny let out a huff. "Yeah, well... as a kid, it was a lot safer for me to cater to what other people wanted. Having a super sensitive alarm system about my parents' feelings kept my ass out of some shitty situations."

It got rather quiet, and no one dared to ask him to clarify. I changed the topic, because I could sense this wasn't something Danny wanted to talk about. "What kind of magic did you use on Marcus?"

"Yeah, I wanna know. It dropped me to the floor," Marcus said, giving a grimace as he rubbed the arm that he fell on.

"Blood distortion. It's when a vampire takes control of a person's blood and uses it against them. Sometimes, a vampire can use blood distortion to make people their puppet. In some cases, a vampire can use it to disable a victim and make them feel pain, as I did with Marcus," Danny stated. "I don't need to make him bleed to do it. I can manipulate what's in his body from a distance."

"That's similar to what a Toaqua can do with water in the blood," I stated, impressed. I could use Water magic to move limbs, but was otherwise limited.

"Yeah, but I'm kind of shit at it, and I can only use it every now and then. Not to mention it doesn't last— I had to pull it back quick with Marcus, if you couldn't tell," Danny said. "But it's useful in a pinch. Maybe one day I'll be strong enough to use it properly, but for the moment, I still get too drained to harness it well. It's hard magic. Most vampires can't use it."

For Danny to admit that he couldn't do something told me how difficult blood distortion really was. Still, he was a tough demigod. I respected what he could do.

"Let's try working together as a team," Wykoff suggested.

We practiced for the rest of the afternoon. We sparred a little, though it was nothing as brutal as the first time around. Wykoff and Amber instructed the four of us to fight Danny again, but this time, she had us alternate who was on the defense and who was attacking, giving us instruction as we sparred.

It definitely made a difference, and I saw we were more effective. If we had worked together like this when Esther had found us in the woods, maybe we would've been able to chase her cronies off.

Danny kept trying to help, but he could be a little *too* honest, and his pointers pissed Charlie off more than they provided any kind of advice. By dinner, I was worn out and starving. Wykoff and Amber dismissed us, and Danny dipped out the moment we were let go.

"Ancestors, that guy's a prick," Charlie complained as we left the arena. "I didn't hit him hard enough, because if I did, he would've shut up. He was babbling the whole time."

"Danny pointed out all our weak spots. We learned a lot from him today. He can teach us what we need to know," I said.

"He's *so* full of himself. I've never met a guy more in love with a mirror," Charlie mumbled.

"I mean, he's kind of a jackass, but I really do think he wants to help. Being arrogant doesn't make him evil."

And I wasn't so sure Danny's attitude wasn't all an act, either. Charlie was a quiet guy, so it wasn't any surprise his and Danny's personalities clashed. But they'd have to figure out a way to work together, because we were on the same team.

Marcus and Kallie followed us as we were led to another beautiful balcony overlooking the palace gardens. A long table had been set up, and food had been placed out for us. Dinner was served— spinach-artichoke pasta, with glazed salmon on the side and lemon-lavender sponge cake for dessert. All of our friends were here, chatting as they ate.

I noticed Abigail was sitting beside Eddie. I acknowledged her with a nod, and she nodded back, although neither of us said anything more.

"Did you enjoy your first day in Ilamanthe?" Eddie asked as he took another slice of cake.

"I loved it. What's next on the agenda?" I asked.

"All that's left is a lesson after dinner. Since you are monarchs, you and Charlie will have to learn Elvish," Eddie stated.

Charlie gave a short sigh. "I feel behind. I don't even know Hawkei, and now I have to learn Elvish, too."

"I can teach you Hawkei, and we'll learn Elvish together," I told him.

"Easy for you to say. You already know four languages." Charlie frowned.

"It'll be five soon. I've been teaching her Italian," Ivy said— *very unhelpfully*, I might add.

Charlie's frown got deeper, and he poked at the food on his plate. He was getting so down on himself, and I didn't like it.

"You learned braille. You can learn this, too," I replied.

"I'm not fluent in it yet," Charlie argued. "I've been learning it for less than a year. I'm barely literate at braille."

"I believe in you. I know you can do this."

Ivy kept ducking their gaze. Every time a servant walked by, they hunched over and hid behind Chancey, avoiding attention.

I took an olive from my plate and threw it at them. It bounced against their head, and they yelped, "Hey, what was that for?"

"Why are you acting weird?" I laughed.

"I'm trying to keep a low profile around here," Ivy whispered, glancing from side to side.

"Why? There's nothing to worry about. The Warden can't find us here," I said.

"It ain't the Warden I'm worried about," Ivy replied. "It's people figuring out who I am. I'm in enemy territory."

"What are you talking about?" I asked.

"I'm a *Bianchi*. My family and Charlie's family have been going at it for centuries," Ivy said worryingly. "We're sworn enemies. My dad thought he'd gotten rid of the Elvish mob after the Great Supernatural War, but now he knows they're back, so some sort of gang war is bound to start up again."

"I didn't know the Bianchi family and the Wahkin family were rival gangs," Charlie said.

"Excuse me, but your family name isn't *Wahkin*, sire," Eddie piped up. "The Elvish royal family has a different title."

"Then why does it say that on my birth certificate? Why's my dad called that?" Charlie questioned.

Eddie cleared his throat. "Your father chose a different name once he fled Forevermore and hid himself in Kinpago, before he met your mother, in order to keep his identity hidden."

"Great, now my name isn't even real," Charlie growled.

"It *is* real. It's ours," I insisted, and I touched his hand lightly. "That's what makes it special."

"Aponi Wahkin was your grandmother's name on your father's side. She was the Air elemental married to Emperor Cassiel, so it does have some meaning to you," Eddie explained. "In Hawkei culture, it's traditional for the family to take on the mother's name. So it's actually accurate that your father took on the Wahkin name when he moved to Kinpago, as he was reclaiming his heritage."

Charlie relaxed, but his expression was still stony. "Okay, so what's the family's royal title?"

"Your grandfather's full name is His Imperial Highness Cassiel Majestica, Emperor of Ilamanthe, and your royal title, properly, would be Prince Charles Majestica, Grand Duke of Ilamanthe," Eddie said helpfully.

"Why don't I get to choose?" Charlie asked.

"Well, you do," Eddie said. "But your royal title is always going to be different from your legal name. Monarchs have many monikers that they go by, and always have been. It's your decision on how you want to be introduced, in what situation, though you'll come to find some names are more helpful than others in certain circumstances. It's not the same thing, sire. Names are power, and you want to utilize them as tools to get people to do what you want."

I'd say. If you wanted to walk into a room and make sure people knew you were powerful, being introduced with a long, formal title was better than some average name. Though I could sense through our bond Charlie didn't see it that way.

"Isn't it so wonderful to have so many titles?" Eddie gushed. "If you get tired of one name, you can just pick another! I only get to choose between Eddie and Edwyrd, and I am very jealous."

"Charlie Wahkin is just fine," my husband grumbled.

"Yeah, and the Majestica family ain't nothing to mess with," Ivy emphasized. "You wanna talk about bodies piling up on the streets, take a look back at some of the showdowns between the Bianchi mob and the Majestica family during the 1920s. The two sides *hated* each other, and if your grandpa decides that he doesn't want a Bianchi running around his palace, I'm dead meat."

"That rivalry was over a hundred years ago. I get that vampires and Elves are immortal, but not even they can hold on to bad blood for that long," I argued.

"Precious, you and your man have no idea what you've gotten yourselves into. These Elves like to play royal, but they ain't no saints," Ivy replied. "Both of you need a run down on how mob families work."

"So tell us." I leaned forward.

"First things first, you got the head of the family, which is the boss. In organized crime, there's a hierarchy. All major decisions are made by the boss, and power trickles down to other people within the family that are beneath him, such as underbosses," Ivy explained. "The wives of the family have their part to play, too, standing by their men no matter what goes down, prison, death or otherwise. You can't refuse an order given by the boss, or one of the underbosses, because otherwise, you're kaput. The dirty work is done by all the thugs at the bottom, but acceptance into the family isn't freely given. You gotta earn your place and swear to be loyal to the family above all, even over the gods and your loved ones, because the mob comes first. And you can't ever get out once you're in. If you try, you're sleeping with the fishes."

"Then why are you still here?" Kallie asked. "You left your dad's gang."

"I got tossed out on the street because my dad's the boss, and as much as he hates me, he didn't want to kill me," Ivy explained. "The only reason I'm still alive is because I'm my dad's only child. He thought throwing me out would make me reconsider my life choices and make me subscribe to living *his* way, since I'm bound to inherit the head position once my old man finally corks off— if he ever does."

Ivy sank down in their chair. "Which is *why* if your grandfather wanted to get a big hit on the Bianchi mob, all he'd have to do was make sure I was taken care of."

"My grandpa isn't going to hurt you," Charlie assured him. "You're safe here in Ilamanthe."

Ivy made a skeptical noise. "Sure, boss."

After dinner, we had a short lesson in Elvish before Eddie told us we were free for the rest of the evening and it was a good idea we get some rest.

One of the rooms in Charlie's suite had been converted into a mini-greenhouse for Sprigs. The little guy was enjoying jumping from leaf to leaf, sunbathing underneath the heat lamp. He gave us a *squee* as we went by, and I waved back.

Oberi wanted to fly around the city and stretch her wings. I watched the phoenix go as she leapt off the balcony, soaring over the palace towers as her white feathers contrasted against the sunset sky. Charlie leaned against the balcony, and I smiled as I observed the wind brush back his hair.

"How do you feel about being a prince?" I asked.

Charlie shrugged. "I'm torn. Some of this is great. I get to be part of a big family, one that has a noble cause and all this history."

His shoulders slumped. "Then, at the same time... it's also a lot to take in. Sometimes too much."

"It'll get easier. It's only the first day," I promised.

"I don't know if it will. My grandpa makes it sound like there's a lot of responsibility. If I had grown up with this, it might've been easier, but I've been thrown into it."

The setting sun cast rays across his darkened expression as he added, "I don't like my dad, but when I see things from his perspective, I can understand why he ran away. Even though I would never leave, because I *do* want this. It almost scares me... how easily I'm willing to do bad things for the family. My dad wasn't comfortable with it, because he grew up in Forevermore and never had to be that bad person in order to survive. I have. If my grandpa were to ask me to do something morally reprehensible for the family, I'd do it, because I've already done bad things, and I wouldn't flinch. I don't know if that makes me a bad person... and honestly, I don't really care if it does."

"It's okay to be conflicted." I took his hand. "Maybe you'll become sure of yourself once you spend more time here."

"Maybe." Charlie turned toward me and took both of my hands. "Let's forget about it. I have a present for you."

"A present? Where'd you find time to get me a gift during your busy day?"

"You'll see."

Charlie led me back to our bedroom and in front of a large floor-length mirror. He pressed his hand to it, and a portal began to open. "There's a panic room on the other side of this wall that only I can get into. It's meant to be a safehouse for us if there's an emergency, but I had a better idea for it."

I wheeled through the portal and into the room. An enormous smile spread across my face as I took in the area. In the middle of the room sat a king-sized bed with restraints attached to each of the posts, along with a bar overhead that had been drilled to the ceiling. On the wall hung all kinds of toys— whips, chains, rope and ribbons.

A dresser sat beside the bed. I went to it and began opening drawers. Vibrators, rabbits, cuffs, blindfolds and other toys were laid out on the velvet pillows within the drawers. Everything in the room was shades of black and green, and burning black candles hovered in the air as the only light.

"You turned it into a secret sex dungeon." I was absolutely *delighted.* It was better than Christmas morning.

"I knew you'd love it." Charlie's grin was just as eager as mine. "The best part is— it's soundproof."

"So I can scream as loud as I want?"

"Even louder, baby girl."

I found a set of black lingerie in one of the drawers. I'd never worn anything like this for Charlie before. This was going to be fun.

I unzipped my tracksuit hoodie. "Want to help me get dressed up?"

"As long as I get to touch you."

Charlie knelt before my chair. He slipped off my pants before his fingers caressed my legs gently. He pulled the lingerie bottoms over my legs and adjusted them around my ass, taking his time to touch my smooth skin. The panties were lace and had an opening at the bottom so I didn't have to take them off in order to fool around. There were straps that crisscrossed over my ass, and they matched the bra, which I fastened around my breasts. The top had slits for my nipples, too. I had never felt more alluring.

"I feel sexy." I shook my hair around my shoulders, which fell in waves. I knew I looked hot.

"You're always sexy." Charlie explored the lingerie. I shivered at his touch as his hands wandered everywhere, discovering where there was lace and where there was bare skin. I gave a small yelp as Charlie lifted me out of the chair.

He carried me to the bed and sat me down. "You're to do everything I tell you to, understand?"

"Absolutely." He'd get no protest from me tonight. I wasn't in the mood to be a brat. Right now, I just wanted to please him.

Charlie rummaged through the drawers, until he pulled out some sort of expandable stool. As he unfolded it, I observed that it was big enough for one person to lay under, and had two thick elastic straps with a slit in the middle. There was a handle on the top of the stool to grab, though I wasn't sure what it was for.

"What's that?" I asked curiously.

"It's a surprise. No more questions."

Charlie placed the stool beside the bed, then began undressing. As he slid out of his clothes, I observed him hungrily. We'd messed around after we'd left the Institute, but we could never be as crazy as we wanted to, because our friends had been around. Now that we were in this secret place, we could do whatever we wanted, and nobody would know but us.

Charlie sat on the bed. "Lie back."

I did so, lying beside him. He reached into a drawer at the bedside and pulled out a small device that was shaped like a budding rose. He turned it on, and it began to vibrate.

Charlie propped up my legs, then placed the vibrator directly on my clit. Holy hell, I swear, *the world* opened up when that happened. Sending me to a new dimension. The vibrator used air to suction onto my clit, and pulsed intensely. I usually had trouble distinguishing what was pleasure and what was just sensation during my spinal injury, but I had *no problem* knowing just how good this device felt. The effect was similar to Charlie's tongue. It was like he was giving me oral. I became dizzy, and fell into a lull as Charlie's other hand rubbed the inside of my thigh.

The moment I was about to go over the edge, he moved the vibrator from my clit to one of my nipples. The effect was just as delirious. Damn if this wasn't an amazing tool. He alternated from my nipples to my clit until I was writhing on the bed, before he drew the vibrator away.

"Don't edge me right now," I begged. I was way too close to getting off.

"I don't want you to come until you're on top of me," Charlie said lowly. "Be my good girl and behave."

I was confused. I hadn't been on top since my spinal injury. It'd just been too difficult, because my legs couldn't hold me up anymore.

Charlie set the vibrator aside. He leaned over to grab the stool, then set it so the legs of the stool were on both sides of his hips. He lifted me onto the chair, and as I sat down on the elastic straps, I finally got what he was getting at. Charlie adjusted my legs, and a thrill of exhilaration went through me as I imagined the possibilities.

Charlie adjusted himself, and I used the elastic straps to sink down. Delight exploded throughout my senses, and Charlie gave a sharp hiss. I realized that he was inside me, I was on top, and with this chair, I could ride him as much as I wanted.

This sex stool was my new favorite accessibility aid. I realized what the handle was for; it was posed in front of me, right before my breasts. I grabbed it, and used my arm strength to pull me up and down. The elastic straps I was sitting on helped me to bounce, and I found I could use them to adjust my position and go deeper without any effort. I didn't have to rely on my legs at all!

Charlie gave a moan, and I became completely invigorated. I used the sex chair to move on top of him, sinking down on him as far as I could and picking up speed.

Charlie let out a ragged gasp and managed to force out, "Slow down, pidge. You're going to get me off."

"That's the idea." I let out a wicked cackle, before giving a moan of my own.

"I want it to last. Go slow, now."

A command, not a request. I slowed up and used the chair to take long and teasing strides instead. Charlie fumbled for the vibrator and pressed it against my clit. My eyes rolled back, and I had to resist every urge in my body telling me to fuck him faster as I forced myself to follow Charlie's order. I felt an orgasm build and release, and as I clenched around him, Charlie made a gasping breath.

"A little faster," Charlie said, and I increased my pace. Charlie continued using the vibrator on me and reached up with his other hand to pinch and twist my nipple. I let out a soft sound and enjoyed the feel of his hand on my breast as we became entangled in the moment. I rode him for a long while, and changed up the angle, so I was taking him in deeper. As his dick rubbed against my g-spot, I swore, my body began to elevate.

"Faster," Charlie ordered, and I fucked him as hard as the chair would allow. I felt his release building quickly, and at his excitement my own began cascading, too. He fisted his hands in the sheets as he came, and I went right after, fireworks exploding behind my eyes as the world turned into a dazzling array of colors and light.

I had to take a few minutes to catch my breath. My arms were burning from lifting me up and down, but damn, it had been worth it.

Charlie appeared stunned. He took a few moments to recover before he helped me off the stool, then put it away. He reached into a mini-fridge sitting on the dresser, which was stocked with water bottles. He gave me one, then took a couple of long drinks himself. "Hell, it feels like we ran a marathon."

He winced, before he added, "Poor choice of words. Sorry."

"It doesn't bother me," I said. "You don't get offended when I tell people we *saw* something."

"I guess not." He got a bottle of lotion from the dresser drawer. "Lie on your front."

I turned over onto my stomach, and Charlie began rubbing my back. I almost didn't know what I liked more— the sex, or the aftercare. Even when sex wasn't particularly dominating, Charlie always spoiled me after. I think he liked taking care of me as much as I enjoyed being pampered by him.

As Charlie massaged my shoulder, I sniffed, and my lip quivered. I had tears in my eyes, though I tried to hide them away.

"Pidge, you crying?" He turned me over and wiped a bit of wetness away from my lashes.

"What you did was very thoughtful," I said shakily. "I never thought I'd get to have sex in that way again."

"It's not like I didn't get any enjoyment out of it," he said, amused.

"Yeah, but... you wanted to make sex accessible for me. How'd you even think of it?"

"I know it's a little weird, but I had Eddie's help setting this place up," he confessed. "I sent him with a list of stuff to get, and the chair was one of the things he suggested. It's a tool he and Alistair have used. He thought it'd be helpful for us to have one of our own."

I didn't think it was weird. On the contrary, I thought Eddie was being very kind, to be so open in order to help us. "Even if it wasn't completely your idea, I'm still touched. You remembered that I loved being on top, and you came up with a way to make it happen."

"Of course I did," Charlie said, and he tucked me into his chest as he kissed the top of my head. "I'd do anything to make my pidge happy."

I knew he would. This room was made for us, but he'd created it *for me.*

"It's wonderful," I replied with a sigh. "Our little sanctuary."

"I think this room needs a name," Charlie said. "That sounds about perfect. Our Sanctuary."

I snorted and put a hand over my mouth. "It sounds like we're screwing in a church."

"What we do in here is holier and more sacred than anything in any church could be." Charlie reached over to pull me on top of him. He gave me a light kiss, and I rested my head on his chest.

This place *was* our Sanctuary. We had tools we could use here that would make our time together truly ours. Nothing had to be missed, or left out.

Now that we were free, we could experience every aspect of our intimacy together, like any other couple would. There didn't have to be any barriers in our way. It made me dare to think we could just be... normal.

Though I cast that idea aside almost instantly. Now that we were part of the Elven mob family, *normal* would be something we'd never get a shot at ever again.

As THE DAYS passed in Ilamanthe, Charlie and I were kept busy with royal duties and growing our magic. We had demigod practice every single day, and it was made clear to us that harnessing our abilities to their fullest extent was our most important task. Charlie's team was looking into the vampire key, but so far, they hadn't found anything conclusive that could lead us to where the key might be.

One morning, while Abigail was curling my hair, she said that my family wanted me to visit for lunch. I kissed Charlie goodbye, then left him to go practice mirror portals with his grandfather. Opal, Marina, Abigail and I hurried off to the suite where my family was staying. Kallie didn't come, since she was in a meeting with a couple of Elven diplomats about fae relations, and I didn't want to bother her.

Oberi walked beside me with his head held high. Each day, Oberi wore an even bigger and more ridiculous hat. Today's hat was in the shape of a large mushroom, with a bunch of little mushrooms stacked on top of it. It was wholly obnoxious, and I knew that's why he loved it. He had his own personal room now in our quarters that was solely devoted to his hat collection, and I'd never seen him so happy.

A servant opened the door for me to my family's suite. The area was set up like a full-size condominium, with a kitchen, living room and all. Mama was at the stove, working on her famous Italian. The Elves were amazing chefs, but not even they could measure up to Mama's cooking.

Alana was sprawled out on the couch with her tigress Familiar, Zareen. She practiced Water magic by making a stream of water spin in mid-air. Maverick tinkered with tools and mechanical gears at a desk nearby, though the project was so jumbled I couldn't be sure of what he was working on. Daddy sat in front of the widescreen with a black cup of coffee. He watched the latest updates on the supernatural news with a scowl.

Daddy was always glued to the news stations these days. I was worried it was turning him into a different person.

"Oh, good, you're all here," Mama said as she set garlic bread out on the table. "Ez should be along soon."

Not a moment after she said that did my brother waltz in. Tahoma squeezed through the door behind him. The peryton had to tilt his antlers in order to fit through the door, even though it was wide. The moment she saw him, Marina gave a squeal and went tottering toward my brother.

"There's my big girl." Ez reached down and lifted Marina on his hip. She gave a happy squeal.

Ez kissed Opal, and added, "And there's my sweet girl."

Opal blushed, and I smiled. Opal and Ez were so cute together, and Ez did such a good job of taking care of Marina. Daddy side-eyed Mama, but she didn't say anything.

None of us had sat Ez down and had a private conversation about where his relationship was going with Opal. I was waiting for Mama and Daddy to bring it up, but so far, they hadn't. I thought it was pretty weird, seeing as how Ez was already acting like a dad to Marina. I figured they'd tell him to slow down or something, but nobody mentioned anything. I guessed we'd have to see where it led.

"This looks wonderful, Mrs. Mitoh," Abigail noted as she rolled up beside me, taking a napkin and putting it on her lap.

"I made more than enough. Take whatever you wish," Mama responded kindly.

Abigail got along well with my family, which was good for her, because I would've fired her if she didn't. Alana enjoyed her company, and I trusted my sister's judgment, so I let my walls down with Abigail just a little.

Throughout lunch, we talked about what everyone was doing in Ilamanthe. Mama and Daddy were doing their best to hold the tribe together with the other chieftains, while Alana and Maverick were getting accustomed to the schools in Ilamanthe.

"What about you, Ez?" I asked as I finished my plate. "I haven't seen you around much."

"I'm studying healing full-time. The Elves have a really intensive medical program, and I've immersed myself in it. I don't have time for much else," Ez stated.

"Ava, have you stopped by to see Maddie yet?" Daddy asked, abruptly changing the topic. "She's been waiting for you."

"I'm a princess. I've been busy."

The excuse was flimsy. I'd been avoiding going to see my aunt, because I wasn't sure what she'd tell me next about my prophecy. I knew that's what it had to be about. She wouldn't summon me for a friendly catch-up.

"Hm." Daddy made a face before he stood up from the table. "We have a surprise for you, peanut."

People hadn't stopped spoiling me since I'd become princess, and I found it delightful. "Ooh, what is it?" I asked eagerly.

"It's waiting outside."

A little while later, I found myself sitting by the side of the cobblestone street outside. The palace had a garage area to store vehicles in order to get around Ilamanthe. My gaze instantly jerked to the side when I saw a beautiful red sports car turn the corner. It was low to the ground, with big fat tires and an engine that roared so loud it made my heart stutter.

"No way?! You got me a car?!" I yelped.

"An *adaptable* car, one you can drive," Daddy clarified.

"Yeah! Me, Dad and Bren have been working on it!" Maverick added eagerly.

The car stopped in front of me, and Bren got out. He was a friend of the family, married to Chieftess Vanessa. He'd owned a shop for sports cars in Kinpago. I guessed he'd transferred his business to Ilamanthe after the Elementai had fled California. I couldn't believe he'd put this together for *me*.

"The look on your face is priceless," Bren noted with a chuckle. "Definitely worth it."

Maverick hopped up to the car and began explaining everything. "It has sensitive electronic controls for the fitting brake, and accelerator controls to the steering wheel, so you don't need to use your legs to drive. You can control everything with your hands. The accelerator is like a motorcycle's, and there's a knob on the steering wheel so you can steer with one hand, while controlling the speed with the other. It also has a rotating driver's seat, to help you get in and out, and a specialized space for your wheelchair."

"It can also convert to regular controls, just in case you need someone else to drive," Daddy added.

I figured I'd be driving some big-ass handicap van the rest of my life, and would never be able to tear up the roads again with a fast vehicle. I started blubbering. "I can't believe you did this for me!"

"We know you love going fast," Maverick replied. "It was so much fun to work on!"

"Can I take it for a drive?" I asked eagerly.

"Absolutely," Bren said. "Hop in."

I want to ride! Oberi cried out. His hat came tumbling off as he jumped into the back.

I was able to use the handlebars of the car to lift myself up and get into the driver's seat all on my own. My wheelchair folded up, and I found that it fit perfectly behind me. Daddy rode next to me on the passenger's side, and Maverick and Bren sat in the back. Mama and the rest of them waved me off as I revved the engine. Bren explained the controls to me, teaching me how to go forward, speed up and slow down.

I didn't want to take it easy, but Bren basically made me, because he didn't want me to be too reckless. I drove the car outside of the palace walls and into the city. We took a few winding roads that overlooked the ocean, and I experimented with the speed.

"I think you've got it," Bren said. "Just don't get too crazy, all right? I know this car can haul some ass, but I don't want you crashing it in the first week."

"I would never." This shiny new toy was my *baby*. I got such a hard-on for fast cars. Monica and I used to love them— probably why we'd stolen a few and taken them out for joy rides back in the day.

My husband was waiting in front of the garages when I returned, having a conversation with my mother. I rolled down the window and leaned my head out, revving the engine again and making the turbo pop.

"Charlie!" I screamed. "I have a new car!"

He laughed. "So I've heard! Let's go for a ride, pidge."

Daddy, Bren and Maverick got out, and Charlie got in the passenger's seat. We drove together through Ilamanthe, and now that Bren wasn't here to make sure I was a good girl, I was riskier. I took turns too sharp and pushed far past the speed limit. Oberi stuck his head out the window, panting as the wind blew back his fur, and Charlie let his hand fall up and down with the wind. Charlie didn't tell me to slow down, rather, only urged me to go faster.

This was seriously the best. The sun was shining and I was flying free, with my husband beside me and my dog in the back. Nothing could beat this feeling.

By the afternoon, I knew how to drive her like a champ. I was riding a high like never before. I'm telling you, living in Ilamanthe was the life.

I didn't want to beat on the car too badly, so we left her to cool off in the palace garage while Charlie and I headed back to our room to rest before our demigod lesson. I sat on the balcony, drinking pink lemonade. Oberi sunbathed beside me, soaking up the sun in his husky coat.

"Pidge?" Charlie came onto the balcony cautiously and took a seat beside me in a lounge chair. "Can I ask you something?"

I smirked. "If you want to eat me out later, I'd prefer it in the bathtub."

He smiled, but it wasn't as bright as it typically was. "I'll take you up on that offer, but... it's something else."

He sounded serious. I felt my insides drop as he reached out to take my hands in his. "I had an idea, but you're not going to like it."

Oberi lifted his head, appearing anxious. *What are you talking about?*

"Spit it out," I demanded. I didn't like being kept waiting, and this was really starting to worry me.

"To beat the Warden, we've got to be the best we've ever been, and use methods we never have before," he insisted.

"You know I'm willing to do whatever it takes."

"You sure about that?" he questioned. "Because I've had the idea that... we should start using pistols."

I felt sick. He'd just said a simple word, and I already wanted to throw up my drink. I thought about what happened when I'd used the pistol down in Cellblock 9, and already didn't agree with this. My hands began to shake. Charlie tightened his grip, so they steadied.

"Guns only have one purpose," I said. "It's not like magic, which can be used for good or bad. Pistols are only used to kill people."

"Which we've already done," he pointed out. "And we need to keep doing it, because unfortunately, this is a war and people die. As long as we aren't the ones six feet under, I don't know if it matters how we do it."

"I know I've killed people," I spat, and I wrenched my hands out of his. "But I don't want to see someone's head explode again."

"This will be different. I think we can use simultension to fuse them with our magic. It's the same as using a wand," he explained. "It's just a way to focus our powers."

"I understand where you're coming from, but pulling the trigger is different than casting a spell," I stated. "It's more personal."

"This fight has become personal, pidge. We can't avoid getting our hands dirty," he said. "And I'll do anything to anyone if it means protecting you."

"Every time I even *think* about using a gun, I'm back in Cellblock 9. I... I can't go back there."

"I don't want to make you repeat your trauma, but pistols could help us avoid something even worse in the future. If we had these pistols back in Cellblock 9, or even the Infernal Underground, maybe we could've avoided everything terrible that happened to us. We didn't have to be tortured, pidge. We can use these guns for good to protect ourselves and help people. They don't have to be used for an awful purpose."

I was unable to speak, so Oberi did for me. *Pistols are human weapons.*

"Not the way I've conceived them," he explained. "During my lesson with my grandfather, he had me practice creating a pistol. I've been studying them since, learning all the different parts and how they work. I understand them now, and how we can use them to concentrate our powers to the best of our ability."

Those late nights when he'd waited to come to bed until after I was asleep were starting to make sense.

I didn't like this. But if it helped us win, I was going to have to learn to be okay with this, because if the Warden was in my place he wouldn't think twice.

Charlie noticed my hesitation and rushed to say, "We don't have to use these if you don't want to. I don't want to force you to do this. I know you have a problem with guns, since—"

"How I feel about something doesn't matter if it can help us win," I said harshly, cutting him off. "Just... tell me how they work."

Charlie... Oberi warned. The unease throughout our bond told me my Familiar wasn't keen on this, either. I didn't like that Oberi was as clueless about this as I was. Charlie had kept both of us in the dark.

Charlie hesitated, before he began to explain. "It's not like it's a real gun. It's made of illusion— it shoots magic. It just enables us to cast faster, and the accuracy is more precise. It's much easier to harness our power through them.

We can fire a few rounds quicker than the time it would take to conjure and throw a single battle orb with our hands."

I felt the blood drain from my face as I said, "You've already created one."

He nodded. "Yes. I just wanted to see if it would work. And I tried it— it does. But it'll only work for demigods, so you don't have to worry about it being produced on a mass scale. I had Chancey and Alistair try to fire it, and it wouldn't work for them. Not just anyone can pull the trigger, because it focuses *your* magic. The magic doesn't come from the illusion. You have to combine your powers with the illusion of the gun, and only demigods are strong enough to fuse it with the technology. Normal, or even talented supernaturals can't access it, but we can. And this is a weapon we can use to beat the Warden."

It could be. These weapons could be the edge we needed. We had lost the fight with Esther and her demigod cronies, and we couldn't lose again. If these pistols could prevent that, I had to learn to get comfortable with them. "Are you sure these can help us?"

"We need to have something that can fire faster than our regular magic can, just in case we get outnumbered again," Charlie said gently. "I get that this is tough, but what happens if we aren't fast enough at the end of the day? We might lose a friend, or worse, we might lose each other. If you don't want to use it, that's completely fine, but I feel like *I* have to. To protect you, if nothing else, because you're the most important person in the world to me. Nothing's taking you away from me again."

"If you're carrying a pistol, I should be, too," I insisted. "I need to be able to protect you as best I can."

We need to be careful, Oberi objected. *I'm worried this could have more consequences than we realize between us.*

"Look. We weren't strong enough fighting Danny," Charlie said. "He wiped the floor with us, and he's not half as strong as the Warden is. But I think these will give us an advantage. Are you okay with going forward with this? Because we need an edge, and this could be it."

Charlie was right. I needed to get over it and get with the program. No matter how I felt about using pistols, we were part of a crime family. I had to be willing to do whatever it took to defend that family and make things right.

I was a chosen one. I didn't have the luxury of *making choices*, like normal people did. I had to do what was right for the world, no matter how uncomfortable I felt.

"I'll be fine," I stated. "Let's do it."

Ava, are you sure? Oberi asked. He knew I was lying, but I didn't think Charlie noticed.

"Yes. We have to at least try them out," I said. "Let's go early to our demigod lesson, to experiment."

Charlie seemed relieved. I caught a stray thought of his that I'd taken this idea better than he figured I would.

Yeah, well. If it came down to making myself comfortable or defending Charlie's life, it'd be Charlie, every time.

We left our suite and arrived in the training arena a short time later. The professors hadn't shown up yet, and neither had Danny. I waited by the door, while Charlie and Marcus got to setting up targets for today's practice.

Kallie strode in, carrying a wooden chest. She conjured a table, then set the chest on top of it.

"What's in there?" Marcus asked curiously as she opened the top.

"Pistols," Kallie replied. My stomach dropped as she began distributing them to Charlie and Marcus. "Charlie made them, but I perfected them with my illusion magic to work out any extra kinks."

Kallie hesitated as she looked at me. She knew my problems with guns and wanted to double check if this was okay. "Did Charlie talk to you about this before I made them, Ava? I didn't want to help create the pistols without you knowing about it first."

I frowned. "Yeah. Of course. Let's get started."

Charlie didn't say anything, and I bit my lip. I didn't like how he'd waited until the last minute to spring this on me, but I somewhat understood. He knew there was a risk I wouldn't take it well, and he didn't want to upset me before they were ready.

"Guns? *Really?*" Marcus asked skeptically. "This is stupid. Magic's much more powerful."

"These aren't your typical pistols. They shoot magic, not bullets," Kallie said.

She took her pistol and aimed it at a target. When it went off, I jumped in my chair. I watched as a bolt of purple illusion magic burst out of the gun and hit the target, completely obliterating it to pieces.

Well, I guess it was effective. And it was just like casting a spell, except you had to pull a trigger instead of wave your hands, so I guess it wasn't *that bad.* Just magic with fewer steps. Basically a wand, right? Witches used those all the time. It wasn't a big deal.

Charlie turned the pistol in his hand, observing it. The speculation on his face was curious.

"Do you think it'll help?" I asked him quietly.

Charlie nodded. "Marty was shot by someone carrying a gun. If I have one, too, I can stop that from happening to someone else."

I didn't know if that logic really worked out, but for Charlie, it was his way of justifying keeping the pistol.

We agreed that we'd have to make some tough choices in order to save the world, Oberi reminded me gently, and he put a paw on my knee. *This is one of those decisions.*

I nodded. "I know, Oberi. I just wish it didn't have to be this hard."

Kallie fired off a few more rounds, then turned to us. "They have silencers, so they shouldn't be as loud."

She paused, before she reached into the box and handed a pistol to me. I knew she'd added the silencers for me, but they didn't completely take away the sound of the gun as it went off.

I slowly took the pistol. The weight of it in my lap reminded me too much of what I'd done in Cellblock 9. It almost sent me careening back there again.

Marcus put two hands on the pistol and fired at a target. He screamed as it went off, and nearly fell over. The magical stream that had come out of the gun hit the top of the wall, and Rishi scattered out of the way as stone came crumbling down.

"Marcus, come *on*. You need to know how to do this," Kallie snapped. She stomped over to him and began teaching him, showing him the right stance and adjusting his arms so he knew how to shoot.

Charlie raised the gun. "Pidge, where should I aim?"

I indicated through our magical connection where he should fire, and the gun went off. Charlie's Air magic hit the target and made it explode instantly.

Charlie had practice knowing where to throw his magic, due to the three of us working on his general awareness through our magical bond. Oberi and I worked as an anchor for him, so he could understand his surroundings even though he couldn't see. Every time Charlie fired the gun off, the magical stream hit its target dead-on.

Charlie was *way* too much of a natural at this. But honestly, it was kind of sexy. He was a mob boss, so it made sense for him to carry a pistol. I was turned on by the sight of him firing the gun. It was so compelling to watch him shoot, because it made me view him in a light of power. The dominating aura he emitted while he shot at targets reminded me of how in control he was in the bedroom. It was hot.

Well, if I was attracted to the sight of my husband shooting a gun, I might as well give this a chance, right?

"Ava, do you want to try?" Kallie asked gently.

She seemed a little worried. It was wrong to make my best friend concerned. I needed to show her I could handle this. I lifted the gun and aimed, putting my finger on the trigger to fire.

Try as I might, I couldn't pull it. My hands shook, and I found my aim was unsteady. *Just do it. If Charlie can, you can, too.*

Though I attempted to force myself to pull the trigger, the movement wouldn't come. I sighed and lowered the pistol without success. This was much harder than I thought it was going to be. I still didn't understand how I really felt about this. How could I be perfectly fine with Charlie using a gun, but I still hesitated to aim? We were supposed to be one and the same, soul partners and equals. I needed to be comfortable with this if we were going to beat the Warden, so why couldn't I be? I was perfectly okay with Charlie using the pistol— even attracted to the idea. The temporary fantasy of him putting the gun to my head while we fucked in the Sanctuary immediately made me swoon, and I daydreamed about how pleasurable that would feel, no matter how messed up it was.

The thought of *me* pulling the trigger, though, and using a pistol to hurt someone again? Practically impossible. I didn't understand how I could find this romantic and traumatizing at the same time.

I didn't know how to feel.

"You don't have to right now," Kallie said. She took the gun from me and put it back in the chest. She sighed as Marcus fired his pistol again and missed.

Eventually, I grew somewhat desensitized to the sound of the pistols. They were going off, and nobody was getting hurt, so that was okay.

Maybe I was getting over it.

The doors to the training room opened a little while later, and we put the pistols back inside the chest as Professors Wykoff and Amber entered. Wykoff glanced at the guns, but she didn't say anything before Marcus subconjured the box. She didn't seem bothered by them— it was confirmation for me that pistols were basically the same as wands to witches.

Amber, though, noticeably scowled, which I'd never seen her do. She didn't approve, but didn't go to stop us, either.

"Danny won't be joining us today," Professor Wykoff said. This time, Amber's orangutan was carrying a small leather drum.

"Great, is he slacking off again?" Kallie asked sarcastically.

"I believe he is ill," Wykoff replied.

"Didn't know vampires could get sick," Charlie said.

"They can, with magical afflictions and other things. We've checked on him, and we think it's best to let him rest," Wykoff said.

Well, at least they'd double-checked that Danny was telling the truth, and not just blowing the lesson off so he could get laid somewhere. Though I had to wonder what was so bad it could make a vampire miss practice.

"It is nothing to worry over, for tonight, we descend into the past!" Amber stated triumphantly. "We shall guide you into the depths of the unknown, revealing what has previously been hidden from spiritual sight."

"What does that mean?" Kallie asked tiredly.

"Before he went missing, Professor Takahashi told us that you four believe you've been chasing after the Divinity Keys in your past lives, and have been hiding them throughout the centuries for your current selves to find now," Wykoff stated. "Professor Amber and I can put you into a trance, so you can insert yourself into a past life meditation and remember where one of you might've stored either the vampire or the Astromancer key."

"We should be careful with this," I said. The last time we'd put Kallie into a trance so she could remember her past life as Amalie, and recall where she'd hid the merfolk key, she'd almost gotten hurt. The practice had summoned a lot of dark spirits who were looking to hurt us.

"This is a safe place, and many precautions have been taken," Wykoff assured us. "I taught Meditation and Inner Magic at Miriam College of Witchcraft, so I am trained and experienced to guide you here. The meditation you're about to undergo is simple. Professor Amber will be leading the practice, using Elementai magic to induce the meditation. It is an ancestral technique, aided by the spirits of Hawkei who have passed on. I will be monitoring the situation. If any of you show any signs of distress, I'll pull you out of the meditation right away."

I trusted Hawkei magic more than any other kind, so I was ready to go in. Wykoff instructed us to lie down. Kallie conjured yoga mats for us, and Charlie helped me down to the floor as we sprawled out and got comfortable.

The orangutan began playing the leather drum, making a steady beat. Oberi lay between Charlie and me. He had already fallen asleep, giving loud snores— not exactly what we were supposed to be doing.

Amber began uttering a low chant, singing words in Hawkei as she cried out to the ancestors. I understood what she was saying, and allowed the words to wash over me as I closed my eyes.

> *"Ancestors, make what is unknown clear,*
> *Ancestors, show us the guided path,*
> *Ignite the things forgotten,*
> *And bring us to the past."*

The beat of the drum lulled me into a state where I felt my presence was no longer attached to my mortal form, but floating outside of my body. My soul hovered forward through a tunnel, racing forward to a stream of light.

"THIS IS *what must be done, Illari.*"

Red smoke filled the sky, blazing against the murky sunset. My husband and I stood at the edge of a pool, connected to a shimmering waterfall. Redwood trees grew around us. The forest was quiet, waiting for an impending doom to swallow us all whole.

Both of us were dressed in the respective Elder regalia of our tribes— he, Koigni, and I, Toaqua. A monstrous brown wyvern flew overhead, keeping watch as to warn us if someone was coming.

In my hand I felt the cool metal of a key. And the heavy burden of what would come if I threw that key away.

"Soleil, you don't understand," I insisted harshly in Hawkei. "This key— it can be used to cure the tribe of our problems. The Houses are already becoming divided. We can use the key to unite them again."

"Our ancestors have made it clear. The key must be hidden within the depths of this waterfall, so that a new Toaqua chief may find it, and bring it to the ones who will use it for good," he insisted.

"This is a risk. There is already talk of separating the Houses. If sides are taken and lines are drawn, our marriage is at stake, Soleil! Fire and Water will not be permitted to be together!"

"We are responsible for this. We're minai, ones who share a soul, and we are connected through one Familiar. This key has been given to us because of that gift, and it is our responsibility. We have to give up our lives, if we must, to keep it hidden from our enemies."

"The prophet has seen what will happen to the tribe if we don't use the key's power to bring them together. The Houses will go to war, and our future Elders will sacrifice our children in a trial, so they can prove themselves worthy. We can't allow that to happen!" I hissed.

"What will happen if that key isn't hidden is even worse," he insisted. "Trust me, Illari."

I trusted him with my life. Though I wasn't sure if he knew of the consequences this would bring.

I tossed the key into the water. I watched it float down to the bottom of the pool, and along with it, the tribe's future...

The vision changed. I found myself hurtling forward through the tunnel again, then coming to a harsh stop.

My hair was in a short bob, and the swish of fringe skimmed across my thighs as my flapper dress clung to my lithe form. The noise of a brass band struck up a jazzy tune as couples twirled on the speakeasy's dance floor, and a couple of vamps at the bar ordered some illegal booze.

I was thirsty for blood, but that wasn't anything unusual. I always thirsted for blood. What I was looking for tonight was a connection.

I skimmed the men in the room, but wasn't interested in any of them. They were the same old vampires I'd been with a million times before, nobody interesting or new. This town could be a real drag.

"What are you here for, honey? A dame like you shouldn't be drinking alone."

I swished my cocktail as I turned to take in the person who'd spoken. His voice was like velvet, warm and inviting. He was a tall, handsome vampire, one with dark hair and even darker eyes.

Instantly, I felt my cold skin begin to warm with desire. My body responded to his without him having to do so much as look at me.

"You're a sight for sore eyes," I stated, and took a sip of my drink. "Haven't seen you around this shindig before."

"Just got outta the pen, myself. One of my so-called pals ratted me out to the coppers." He gave a wink. "But between delivering shipments to the speakeasy, I've found time to call on sweethearts like you."

I had to smirk. "Well, aren't you the cat's pajamas."

"Lawrence, ma'am," he said, and he took off his hat to nod to me.

"Lucille," I purred. "And how do you know I'm interested?"

Lawrence grinned as he reached out and grasped me around the waist. He pushed me up against his bar, against his body, and I nearly writhed in delight.

"Come on, pidge. What's a fella gotta do to take you out on a date?" Lawrence smirked, and shivers rippled up my skin.

I didn't know who he was, because I hadn't met him before, but I didn't care. There was something between us that sparked and said this was the guy for me. It was just what I needed.

"Follow me out to the back." I took his hand, and we walked through a secret door hidden behind the speakeasy's stairwell.

We'd barely been alone for a few seconds in the alleyway before Lawrence gave me a rough kiss. I responded in kind, tearing at his suit jacket with my long nails and ripping it off.

Lawrence undid his pants, and hitched me up around his waist. He fumbled to push back my dress as he slid inside, and my head rolled back in ecstasy. He thrust into me, and I felt like the kind of connection we had could go on forever...

The vision abruptly shifted.

My hands were on a steering wheel, and a Model-T rocked back and forth as explosions rocked the car from side to side. I pinned the pedal to the floorboard, pushing the car as fast as it would go.

"Keep driving, pidge!" Lawrence held on for dear life as we sped away. Masci Taurus had sent angels after us, and they were hot on our tail, chasing us with several cars. We'd been fleeing them for days, and hadn't been able to shake them. I didn't think we'd survive this.

We'd been doing this for a while now, Lawrence and I. Our specialty was smuggling things nobody else wanted to transport, and we'd spent the past few years making good money doing it.

Until we stumbled upon something we shouldn't have. Something that was too strong for either of us to mess with.

I just wanted to pitch it. Get it away from us, before it killed us both. But Lawrence insisted we had to do the right thing, because this was bigger than us.

One last job, pidge, he'd told me. *We get the vampire key to Europe, we dump it in the vault at the* Banque Surnaturelle de Paris, *then it's easy street.*

Beside him in the backseat, another vampire clutched onto an ivory box. My soul jolted as I recognized him, and in a thick New York accent, the vampire said, "This ain't looking good!"

"Hold on, Mister Coffrey!" I yelled. "This isn't over!"

"Sure looks like it!" the vampire responded.

"We're gonna make it out of here, Frank!" Lawrence cried, but I heard the fear in his voice. He knew this was the end of the line.

Magic exploded ahead of us on the road. I swerved to avoid it, and drove right into an oncoming battle orb.

Frank jumped out of the moving vehicle with the box and managed to roll safely to the side of the road, but Lawrence and I didn't make it in time. The battle orb collided with the engine, and the car exploded. The screams of Lawrence and I mingled with the night as the flames instantly overtook the car, singing our marble bodies to ash.

My eyes shot open. I hurried to touch my skin, certain the flames were still licking up my sides.

They were gone. That had happened in the past, over a hundred years ago, and I was Ava-Marie now, not Lucille.

I managed to sit up. Charlie blinked a few times as he came to, and he instinctively reached for my hand. I took it. The feelings that flowed to him to me through our bond were powerful. We both remembered details of previous lifetimes, and though we couldn't remember everything, I knew we'd loved each other back then as much as we did now.

Amber gasped above me. Her orangutan Familiar was slumped on the ground, taking shallow breaths.

"Are you all right?" Wykoff asked in concern, and she laid a hand on Amber's back.

"I barely got through," Amber said weakly. "The ancestors nearly didn't respond to my request."

She put a hand on her Familiar, to steady her. Undergoing the ancestral chant and calling to the ancestors for aid had completely worn Professor Amber out. What she'd done had been difficult magic. She must be a talented supernatural for her to pull this spell off, especially since she'd had to reach past the broken boundary between Earth and the spiritual realm for the ancestors to hear her.

Oberi had changed into her phoenix form sometime during the meditation. She blinked her cool eyes and ruffled her feathers, seemingly puzzled.

"I had multiple visions," I said, and I looked at my husband. "What about you, Charlie?"

"I did, too," he confirmed. "In the first one, we were Hawkei Elders. Oberi was there. We spoke Hawkei, and though I don't know it, in the vision, I understood every word. We hid the key in a waterfall outside of Kinpago, because the ancestors had told us it would be safe there."

"I experienced it just like you said," I added. "Did you see the second vision, during the 1920s?"

"Yeah. But we didn't get to the end of that one," Charlie said darkly.

Hell no, we hadn't. We'd died in a flaming car wreck. "Masci Taurus— the Warden's father— he sent those men to kill us. He knew we had the vampire key. And that vampire who leapt out of the car with the key. Frank Coffrey— I remember his name," I said. "Do you think that was—?"

"It was definitely Chancey," Charlie confirmed. "I felt it, in my spirit. He was helping us. He must've died at some point after he took the key. That's why he's reincarnated now, as an angel."

"We were taking the key to some vault in Paris. Do you think Frank got the key to the vault before he died, or do you think Masci killed him first?" I asked.

"Either are possible," Charlie said. "We can't be sure."

"But we do know that in our previous life, we did our best to hide the vampire key," I insisted. "I think I can recall the name of the bank. It was the *Banque Surnaturelle de Paris*. We need to check to see if it's still there now, and if Frank made the deposit."

"I'll tell my team to look into it right away," Charlie said. "At least we're making progress."

"I'm glad you guys got some clues. I didn't see anything," Kallie said. "My mind was blank."

"Marcus?" I asked. "What did you see?"

He cleared his throat. "I... I saw..."

He jumped to his feet and swallowed visibly. "You know what? It's nothing."

Without another explanation, Marcus ran out of the training arena. Kallie's expression became deeply concerned.

Wykoff helped Amber to walk, and the orangutan Familiar hobbled after. "I think we've covered enough today. Well done, Charlie and Ava. Hopefully this tip about the bank vault will lead us somewhere."

"Are you going after Marcus?" I asked Kallie as she stood. Charlie helped me back into my chair. Kallie paused for a second before shaking her head.

"No," she stated. "I can't quite be sure, but I think whatever he saw has something to do with me. We still share a bond. And if I didn't see what he did, that means he's either blocking me out, or I wasn't around to witness whatever he did back then."

There were no clear answers, and until Marcus fessed up, we weren't getting any.

Kallie walked away, and I looked to Oberi. "Did you see anything, girl?"

Glimpses and pieces of the past, she replied. *But nothing that would help us, as far as I could tell.*

"Shit." I sighed. "I wish this was easier. I want to find the rest of the keys and get this over with."

You two think your quest is the hard part? This is merely the final step, Oberi said. *You've been chasing keys throughout the millennia, spending decades, sometimes even your whole lives, to locate and hide these keys, only for you to find them at the proper moment at this shred of time.*

"Were there any past lives for you to examine?" Charlie asked.

From what I can piece together, I don't really have *a past life, because I've never truly died— it's just one long continuation of this current life that I don't fully grasp. I kept bouncing between Earth and the spiritual lands in your various lifetimes,* Oberi replied. *When you were Elementai, I came here to be with you on Earth, then once you died, and transitioned into new supernatural forms, I remained in the spiritual realm until you summoned me again as your Familiar. The constant go-between from one place to another has completely altered my memory. I can hardly tell what is real and what may have been made up. It is why I cannot give you any clear answers.*

Oberi paused to contemplate. *If I recall correctly, I went into a deep sleep before the two of you were born into your current lives on this Earth, and I didn't awaken until it was time for Charlie to bond with me. Now we know why I was not there to defend you when you were children. I am very sorry, my beloved.*

"Did someone put you into this sleep, or did you do it to yourself?" I asked.

I don't remember anything about it, save for that I agreed to it. It must've been important. Oberi shook her head.

"What happened to us as kids isn't your fault," Charlie said kindly, and he stroked her feathers back. "There's a bigger meaning to all of this."

Though I may agree, it does not dull the sorrow. Oberi flew onto Charlie's shoulder and began preening his hair.

Charlie pushed me out of the training arena, and I gave a giggle. "We had some fun when we were a couple of horny vampires, screwing within five minutes of meeting each other," I cracked.

"In that lifetime, maybe, but we've been together forever," Charlie said. "It doesn't take long for the two parts of our soul to recognize each other."

My insides softened into goo. "We really *have* been together forever, haven't we?"

Centuries, even, Oberi said. *We cannot be aware of the time when our soul fragmented into two. We assumed it was at Charlie's birth, but clearly, it was not. You two have loved each other throughout time.*

If that didn't make me all warm and fuzzy to think about.

"I've gotten to love you through multiple lifetimes, and in a million different ways," Charlie commented. "It's incredible, really."

I reached over my shoulder to touch his hand. "Well, no matter how long it's been, I'm still your pidge."

"I guess part of me from back then bled over into this life." Charlie gave a laugh. "Thankfully, that was the only corny slang I still took with me."

"You've called me a dame before."

"Yeah, I have." Charlie brought me to a stop before we got to his suite. "Do you think we should check on Marcus? He ran off after the meditation."

"Probably. He was freaking out. Maybe if we talk to him, he can tell us what he saw," I said.

We returned to our quarters and headed toward Marcus' room. I heard a crashing noise long before we got to the door. The sound of things being smashed and torn apart echoed through the walls. My heart dropped.

"Marcus?" I asked. I put a hand on his suite door. My spirit tore as I took in the sight of the destroyed room. Paintings were laying all around the room with holes in them, the canvases shattered and torn in half. It was a complete mess. My voice became still. I was unable to speak as I watched Marcus stomp one of his paintings underneath his shoe, and punch a fist through the canvas of another.

He'd been doing nothing but painting since we'd gotten to Ilamanthe, because it seemed to be the only thing that soothed him. Now Marcus was turning his treasured works into fragments, destroying everything he'd created.

"Marcus, stop!" I cried. My shout mingled with Rishi's yowls. The cat seemed to be pleading with his warlock to take a moment to think. "You're destroying your paintings!"

"It doesn't matter! It's all garbage anyway!" Marcus raged. "My work sucks! It's trash, just like I am!"

"Marcus, calm down." Charlie hurried forward and grabbed Marcus, holding him in place. Marcus tried to fight back, but Charlie was stronger than he was, so Marcus was forced to stand there and take deep breaths in the remnants of his self-created disaster.

Charlie kept his voice even. "Marcus, why did you do this? You worked so hard."

"I don't know what's wrong with me!" Marcus replied tearfully, and he shoved Charlie away. "Why don't you just give up on me, huh? Why do you bother being my friend?"

"Marcus, *of course* I'm your friend. It's okay." Charlie wrapped Marcus in a hug, and Marcus sobbed on his shoulder.

Marcus didn't understand what was going on with him, but his meltdown was apparent to me. Whatever he'd seen in the vision had triggered him, and he'd been struggling with leaving the Institute worse than the rest of us had.

We all wanted out of there. Marcus didn't want to stay a prisoner. But the Institute had sunk its claws into him. He wanted to be out, but he'd become so accustomed to prison life he'd forgotten how to live outside of it. He was struggling to adjust now that we were in Ilamanthe, and that stress was making him lose his grip.

"What's going on?" I heard Kallie's voice echo from around the corner, and I froze. She walked in, and Marcus' expression went from enraged to devastated.

Kallie took one look at the mess around the room. Then she pinched the bridge of her nose and muttered, "For fuck's sake, Marcus."

Her lack of compassion shocked me. Couldn't she see how badly he was hurting?

"Kallie, don't start," Charlie warned. "He needs us."

She rolled her eyes. "He *always* needs us. You guys think it's disturbing because this is the first time you've seen it, but this isn't even the first time this *week* I've dealt with it."

"So don't," Marcus spat at her. "Leave me alone."

"Like you mean that. You'll be at my door in an hour or two with an apology, begging me to let you in," she sneered. Her words were so cruel.

"Kallie, why are you being this way?" I asked. I sensed Marcus wasn't the only one in pain here.

"Why shouldn't I? Marcus showed up to my room drunk off his ass last night looking for a booty call!" Kallie cried, flinging her hand out.

"It wasn't like that! I just wanted someone to *talk* to!" Marcus burst, and he staggered away from Charlie to face her. "Nobody understands how I feel!"

"And I'm here for you, but not if you're going to show up completely wasted!" Kallie said.

"I didn't know you've been drinking," I said. It *so* wasn't like him.

Marcus shrugged. "I haven't been. It was just the one time. I had a couple of drinks by myself last night, and got carried away, because..."

Marcus trailed off, and didn't need to finish. Because he got lonely, and he didn't know how to deal with it, or reach out for help.

"I've seen this movie before!" Kallie shouted. "You call me up, looking for a friend. We talk about things, we fuck around, then the next day you act like nothing happened, or *worse,* you get pissed off and purposefully act cruel, because you want to blame *me* that your life's fucked up. But in reality, you don't know what you want and you don't know how to make yourself happy! It's the same old story, Marcus, and I don't want to keep playing the reruns!"

"You can't keep *shaming me* for reaching out!" Marcus yelled back.

"I'm not shaming you for opening up! I'm just tired of being your punching bag, your emotional dumping ground, and your fuck buddy who you think doesn't deserve a commitment! I refuse to keep cleaning up your shit!"

"You're always trying to fix me and solve a problem, when I don't need a solution. I just need you to *understand,*" he begged. "Asking for help isn't easy for me, so I had to get drunk to do it. And every time I ask for help, you make me feel like shit about it. I try to get vulnerable with you, and you treat me like I'm a bad person for having feelings."

"Oh, really?" Kallie put a hand on her hip. "*I* make you feel like shit? I haven't sat there and listened to you for hours without a word when you needed a friend? I haven't held you when you needed someone to cry with? For fuck's sake, I haven't cried *with you*? I've done everything I can to make you feel better. Hell, I've done whatever I needed to just to get you through the night, and I'm still falling short. You act like I haven't sacrificed whatever I had to in order to support you, and even with all of that, you keep telling me that it's not enough. I keep trying to pull you out of this black hole of self-loathing that you've put yourself in, but you refuse to come out! What else do I need to do to prove to you that I want this, and that I'm not going to abandon you?"

"I know you've put in the work, but this shit is hard for me!" Marcus exclaimed. "I know it hurts you to see me this way, and I don't want to hurt you, so I try to help myself, but that doesn't always work. You obviously don't want me bringing all my baggage to you, so I feel alone, because you're supposed to be the *one person* I can talk to about this stuff. But I can't, so I haven't figured out how to deal with it yet."

"Oh my gods, Marcus, you're just making it *worse!*" Kallie screamed. "I can't be your everything and nothing all at once! What do you want?"

She spun on her heel to storm out. Marcus reached out to grab her shoulder. "Kallie—"

"No! I'm sick of this game!" She wrenched herself out of his grasp, and left the room. Charlie, Oberi and I hurried after her into the hall.

"Kallie, wait!" I cried out. My arms were burning trying to keep up with her. I could only spin these wheels so fast.

She paused to catch her breath. I brought my chair to a halt beside her. She hunched over her knees, quivering like she was about to cry.

"I can't... I can't keep *dealing* with him, Ava," Kallie said in a strained voice. "He's killing me."

I couldn't blame her. I felt sympathy for Marcus, and for his pain. I didn't know what side to take.

But I understood why Kallie wanted to give up, because watching someone you love fall apart without being able to do anything about it was basically hell.

I wasn't sure what to say, but I forced myself to find the words. "He's going through a hard time. The Institute left scars on all of us. He's just... not sure of how to heal them."

"I'm so tired of him putting me on a pedestal one moment and despising me the next!" Kallie yelled. "I'm either his savior or his devil, and I can't keep going in circles on this merry-go-round, because it's making me sick!"

"I understand that has to be terribly frustrating," I said. "But maybe if you just talk to him—"

"There's no talking! The guy's crazy! He's either sitting here proclaiming that he wants to have this big future with me, or he's screaming that I'm going to leave him and never talk to him again! There's no middle ground." She huffed.

"He's put you in the worst position ever, I agree. But I think there's something else going on here," I said. "He acts like he doesn't need you, but I promise you he does."

"I need myself. *I* need to be happy, more than I need to keep him in my life if he's going to act like this," Kallie said shortly. "I've dealt with this for over two years, and there's still no progress when it comes to us being together. If anything, we've backtracked, and my patience is running out. I don't want to be with someone who keeps accusing me that I don't love him."

"Kallie..." My voice got weak.

"I'm sorry." She staggered away, holding up her hands before she turned tail. "I can't handle him tonight."

She walked away. I didn't have anything else to offer that might comfort her, so I watched her go.

"I'll talk to her," Charlie said. "Maybe she needs someone to listen."

Charlie rushed after Kallie. I rolled my chair down the hall to return to Marcus. Oberi let out a coo as she settled on the back of my chair.

I found Marcus sitting on the ground, surrounded by his damaged paintings with his head in his hands. I rolled up behind him.

"She doesn't mean it," I whispered softly. Rishi gave a soft meow.

Marcus sighed. "I'm just... I'm having one of those really hard days where I'm trying not to hate myself."

I wrapped my arms around his shoulders and laid my chin on his head. "I know."

We sat like that for a while, before Marcus sniffed and wiped his face with his sleeve. "I think I need to talk to my Mom and Dad," he mumbled. "Catch you later, Ava?"

"Okay." I really hoped that's where he was actually going. His parents might be able to do more than I could.

I'll make sure he gets there, Oberi said, and she flew off after Marcus as he dragged himself out of the room.

All I could do was observe the mess Marcus had made, wondering if we'd ever find a way to fix it... fix him.

I couldn't lose another friend. But it seemed like Marcus was determined to push all of us away. He was sick. All my healing magic wouldn't do anything to cure him.

For as much as I loved Marcus, Kallie, and all my friends, I couldn't save them. I couldn't save *anybody*. No matter how much I wanted to take their pain away, I was helpless to stop their suffering.

That absolutely wrecked me. I couldn't live with it. The *world* couldn't go on when there were people who suffered so terribly in this way.

So I dared to think that one day, maybe it wouldn't have to. I was a demigod. I had the power to change things.

I swore to myself right then and there, whatever it took to make the world a better place, I'd do it. That way, people like Marcus didn't have to suffer...

And if there were consequences, I'd go through with them. No matter what they might be.

FIVE

I didn't know what kind of magic Professor Amber had performed, but it had far exceeded my expectations. I didn't expect the magic to be so powerful, or for the visions to be so vivid. Finally, we had information on the vampire key.

While my team worked on gathering intel, Ava and I paid a visit to Maddie that week. Ava *said* she wanted to visit her aunt, but I could feel her unease through our bond. It felt more like an obligation than anything, but at the same time, I could tell that Ava really missed her.

We drove into the city in Ava's new car. The ride was smooth, and the bucket leather seat gripped my body as I sank into it. I could definitely get used to it.

Ava slowed the car. "Oh, wow. This apartment complex must be twenty stories. Daddy says she's staying in the penthouse."

I hurried around to the driver's side door to help Ava out. She waited for me to open the door, and I got her wheelchair out for her, guiding her in.

"I can do it myself, you know," she purred.

"Yes, but you want me to pamper you," I replied. I felt her satisfaction, which stirred our bond.

She playfully nudged me. "I can get back in the car and turn us around."

"We can visit our Sanctuary later." I nipped playfully at her ear, and she giggled.

You two know I just had my breakfast. It's too early for all this foreplay. Oberi jumped out of the back seat and followed behind us in husky form.

"Take good care of her," Ava said to the valet as she tossed him the keys.

"I will, your highness," he replied, before the engine revved and the driver took off.

Hey! Leave a scratch and you're paying for it! Oberi barked, though the valet couldn't hear him.

I patted Oberi's head. "Let the poor guy have his fun. He'll get the car back to us in one piece."

Ava and I took the elevator to the top floor. The moment the doors opened, I heard a high-pitched squeal from across the penthouse.

"Ava, you're here!" Maddie cried. She rushed toward us, and we barely stepped off the elevator before she squeezed Ava into a tight hug. "I'm so happy to finally see you!"

"Auntie, you're suffocating me," Ava rasped.

Her aunt pulled away. "Sorry. I just haven't seen you in so long. And how are you, Charlie?"

I'd only met Maddie once, when she'd shown up at the Institute on the night of the Villain's Ball... and it hadn't gone very well. Though we'd spoken years ago, I was still rattled by what she'd told me in our first meeting.

I held out my hand, and she shook it. Maddie's hands were soft, but when I touched her, I sensed magic within her I'd never felt before. My Elven magic could feel her *naderei* powers— the abilities of a prophet. But there was something else about it... of all the powers I could ever take as an Elf, this was one I couldn't touch. No matter how strong I was, the ability to prophesy wasn't one I could siphon.

"I'm fine. Nice to see you again," I said, though I pulled away quickly. I hoped the meeting would be quick. Maddie seemed like a nice person, but she made me very uneasy, because I wasn't sure what she would say.

Another pair of footsteps came through a door to our right. "Is that Ava-Marie that I hear?" a male asked.

"Uncle Drew!" Ava cried.

A creature followed alongside him. The way its paws hit the floor and the sound of panting made me think it was a dog, but I couldn't be quite sure it wasn't a magical creature of some sort.

The creature approached Oberi while Ava and Drew exchanged pleas-antries. Oberi sniffed him, then huffed, like he wasn't pleased.

"Don't be rude," I scolded, before turning to Drew. "Can I pet him?"

"Yes, of course," he replied.

I bent to one knee and reached for the dog. He had soft fur, a long snout, and pointed ears. He thumped his tail on the ground happily, and his tongue rolled out of his mouth.

Ugh, he likes *you,* Oberi complained.

"Well, I've always been a dog person," I said. "Let me guess... a German shepherd?"

"Ace is a hellhound, actually," Drew said. "He has a Fire form when he's feeling protective."

My eyebrows shot up. "His fur is so warm."

That explains the smell of brimstone, Oberi remarked.

Ace stopped panting and turned to Oberi to bark. I knew Familiars could communicate, but I hadn't seen it first-hand until now. Whatever Ace said to Oberi made him back down.

I guess he's all right, Oberi admitted. *For a hellhound.*

"Oh, get over yourself," Ava said as she wheeled herself further into the room. "You're not the only magical dog that's ever existed— or reptile. Come meet Eirakari!"

I hadn't realized how big the penthouse was until we walked to the other side of the room. I could tell the ceiling was high because of the way my Air magic swirled through the room, but my magic kept going outward. A soft breeze traveled through the suite, and curtains rustled like the doors to the balcony had been left open. But there was another soft breeze that I couldn't quite place.

We came to something solid, and the breeze felt ice-cold. That's when I realized that it was a creature breathing.

"This is Eirakari, my aunt's Familiar," Ava said. "She's an ice dragon."

The dragon cooed as Ava began stroking her scales. It was like the dragon had missed her, too.

"It's okay. You can touch her," Maddie offered.

I reached out, and my hand connected with ice-cold scales that were smooth to the touch. Eirakari was a small dragon compared to Oberi's wyvern form, but she was still bigger than most creatures we encountered. I understood why Maddie required such a large penthouse, because otherwise, her Familiar couldn't fit inside. I figured the balcony doors had been left open so the ice dragon could come and go.

As I continued running my hands over her, I was surprised to find that her scales turned to feathers at her wings. She had spines growing out of her back and horns on her head.

"She's really gentle," I remarked. "I don't get to touch magical creatures often, so I almost never understand what they're like."

As if Eirakari could sense I needed to touch her to understand, she licked my arm, and I realized she had a forked tongue.

"She's very kind when she feels safe," Maddie says. "But the moment she feels threatened— or feels like my life is in danger— she can be downright vicious."

"A bit like your niece," Ava joked.

Maddie chuckled. "You have a bit of your mom in you, but you got your dad's side, too. Would you like some coffee? Drew just made a pot."

"Sure," Ava said.

Maddie led us to the dining room table, and Ava asked questions about her travels. Being a *naderei*, Maddie had journeyed all around the world looking for answers to prophecies she'd created... though none of them were as big or important as Ava's.

The atmosphere in the room was a little stilted. Nobody talked about the war, which meant Maddie's stories left out quite a few details.

Eventually, Ava set her cup down. "I'm really glad to hear you two are doing well, but I can't help but think we're all avoiding the dragon in the room — and no, I don't mean Eirakari."

"Your prophecy," Maddie noted. "It's why I summoned you here. I expect you wanted to talk about it."

"I don't *want* to talk about it," Ava said. "I'd rather there was no prophecy in the first place. But there is one, so let's figure out where to go from here."

Drew stood and cleared his throat. "I'll clean up."

He gathered our cups, then left the room. Ace followed behind him.

Maddie drew a deep breath. "I made the prophecy, but there's a reason *naderei* have to write everything down. My memories of the visions fade over time, and even if I did remember all the details, they're difficult to decipher. That job is left up to the one the prophecy is written about."

"You must remember *something*," Ava insisted. Pages rustled as she brought out her journal and flipped through the pages. "You don't remember writing any of this, or making these drawings? You don't recall how this page with blood from Erasmus Morelli got into my journal?"

"The page with blood...?" Maddie reached for the journal and began humming lowly as she observed it. "This journal was kept in your father's safe for ages. There's very little I remember, but this page... I think I recognize it. It's coming back to me now."

"You know where it came from?" Ava asked.

"It happened a long time ago," Maddie said, like she was still trying to recall the details. "I don't have a lot of memories from that time, because of what *that man* put me through."

"You mean Elder Oleander," Ava said sadly. "The major asshole Daddy fought during the Hawkei Civil War? He nearly destroyed the tribe."

"Yes," Maddie said. "Oleander captured me and tortured me for my prophecy powers. He tried to use me to predict his victory, but was unsuccessful, because prophets cannot be forced to see visions. They must come naturally. While I was his captive, I snooped around his office. I was looking for things your father could use against Oleander to end the Hawkei Civil War. While searching, I found files in Oleander's desk. One of these files had details about Darke Island. Oleander was working with Doctor Taurus to learn how to utilize other supernaturals' powers."

"Figures those two would be working together. They're two of a kind," Ava snarled.

"Yes. They were allies, although not on good terms. Both of them wanted to be in charge, and that didn't work well between them," Maddie said. "Although the Warden *did* supply Oleander with inferichite crystals, which he used to torture me in an attempt to harness my abilities. Obviously, it didn't work."

"The Warden was performing experiments even decades ago," I said. "This has been a long process for him."

"Indeed. The Warden's letters spoke of demigods and powerful keys—though I don't remember all the details. This bloodstained paper was in these files," Maddie said.

"But Erasmus was never arrested and sent to the prison on Darke Island," I remarked. "How'd the Warden get his hands on it to send it to Oleander?"

"Amalie and Dante were arrested," Ava said thoughtfully. "The Warden could've confiscated that page from Erasmus' allies and sent it to Oleander to gain information from it."

"When I touched the bloodstained paper, I received a vision of you, Ava," Maddie said. "I knew the page was important for your journey, so I kept it and snuck it out with me when I escaped Oleander. I sewed it into the journal later, for you to use to decipher your prophecy."

"Do you remember the rest of the journal?" Ava asked.

"I recall some of these drawings," Maddie admitted. "But I never quite knew what any of them meant. Lindsey and Miranda attempted to help me find the meaning, but nothing became concrete enough for me to point you in the right direction. Even if I tried deciphering these visions, they mean nothing without context of your experience, because they are meant for you alone."

Ava's disappointment sank through our bond. I was almost certain she'd been avoiding her aunt because she expected this very answer, but I also thought she hoped for more.

"What about the prophecy wording?" Ava wondered.

"I remember it well." Maddie paused, before she began to recite.

"The balance between the light and the dark

Will be brought together by the light of the new dawn

A discovery of the ancient ones on the island of shadow
Will change the course of our universe

A second war breaches the horizon
Mountains will fall and villains will stand

The heavens will crumble and hell will open wide
Unleashing the demons that fester within

The path she will walk determines our fate
She dances the line both dead and alive

A new world formed from gods of old,
One from ashes or one from light
The choice is hers alone."

Quiet harnessed control over the room, and Maddie stated softly, "I think you already know what it means. Most of this prophecy has already come to pass— all the signs leading up to the end. The discovery of the ancient ones, hell opening wide... these are all omens to tell you when it's time to make your decision. *The choice is hers alone.* Ava, all that's left of the prophecy is your decision on how to move forward."

"I was hoping a *naderei* could tell me how to make that decision," Ava said lowly. I felt her side of our bond flare.

"The prophecy is a warning about the end of days," Maddie explained. "You are in the center of it all, but how it plays out is up to you."

"That doesn't help!" Ava's tone was short. "You made my prophecy. I need you to tell me what to do!"

"You know I can't do that, and you also can't avoid it," Maddie replied calmly. "I don't want to worry you, but my visions were clear on the choice you were going to make. You don't have much time to divert the path of destiny and make a different decision."

"I'm not going to turn my back on the world," Ava said harshly. "I'm going to *save us*— all of us. The supernatural community is depending on me to stop the Warden's plans, and I swear I will."

"And what if you become just like him?" Maddie asked softly. "I don't say this to judge you. I merely intend to warn you of what you could become, while there's still time left—"

"How dare you say such a thing!" Ava yelled. "I'll *never* be the Warden. I'm sorry the past is difficult for you to revisit, but I am *not* who I once was. I'm not the villain you and everyone else are making me out to be!"

"Yes. And that's what frightens me," Maddie whispered.

Ava gave a dramatic noise. "Whatever. This is stupid. If all that's left is that I need to make a decision, then it's already made. We're getting those keys and defeating the Warden. We'll bring this planet into the light. I won't damn the world; I'll save it. You'll see I'm a good person... *all* of you will see. But until then, I'm out of here."

Ava wheeled away, and I heard the sound of the elevator's entrance to the penthouse *ping* as she pressed a button. I got up to follow her, but Ava was in such a hurry that the doors slid shut, leaving me behind.

Oberi shifted into a phoenix. She flew to my shoulder and perched there, ruffling her feathers in concern.

A silent beat passed before I turned to Maddie. "Ava's worried she'll make a mistake despite her decision. I can tell. But we'll be fine... right? I mean, the prophecy says the decision is hers alone, so as long as she decides we're saving the world, we have this thing in the bag. That's how these prophecies work... isn't it?"

"Prophecies are multi-faceted and nuanced," Maddie stated. "You're forgetting the final piece. The decision that *you* must make."

My blood turned to ice. I knew my part of the prophecy even better than Ava's. "We shouldn't be talking about this without Ava here."

"We must. Ava isn't listening, so I'm reaching out to you to be rational," Maddie begged. "If she's not going to take this prophecy seriously, *you* have to, because everything's riding on your decisions."

Maddie began to recite it, even as I wished she'd stop.

> *"A choice will be made by the twin of her soul*
> *To save her and damn the realm*
> *Or curse her, and save us all*
> *A fate worse than death*
> *Is the chosen one's destiny."*

"That part is already over," I replied in a hollow tone. "I made a choice when I brought her back from the Infernal Underground. She died, and I had to let her go, but it was *her* choice to come back to me. Ava didn't come back the same. I gave her up— I cursed her— just like the prophecy says. Now it's her choice to save us, which she *will*."

"This prophecy doesn't speak of death," Maddie said. "It speaks of *a fate worse than death*, which means your part of the prophecy has yet to be fulfilled."

A heavy weight dropped in my stomach. My tone grew defensive as I demanded, "What exactly does *a fate worse than death* mean? Ava's in constant, chronic pain. Isn't that worse than floating off to a utopian afterlife somewhere?"

"You don't believe that, Charlie. You know a life of disability is far from the worst thing that can happen to you, and sometimes, it can even be a gift. You're just repeating something able-bodied people say, because you want to avoid the problem," Maddie said harshly.

"But if I haven't fulfilled my part, that means Ava's destined to get hurt again, by *me*. I won't let that happen," I insisted.

"Your piece comes *after* Ava's decision has been made, after her choice to save the world or damn it has been proclaimed," Maddie said. "Which means you haven't gotten that far yet— but it's coming fast. You'll need to be ready to make the choice when the time comes, to side with or against her."

"This doesn't make any sense," I argued. "Ava's prophecy says that the choice is *hers alone*. So how can any choice I make possibly get in the way of hers? If it's true that I still have a choice to make, then the prophecies contradict one another. There's no way to win."

"I told you prophecies aren't always straightforward," Maddie reminded me. "There is much that is yet to pass that will influence the final outcome. Ava may wish to save the world today, but she can change her mind tomorrow. Whichever choice she makes will influence your final decision. I believe that Ava's portion is a warning, an omen like all the other lines before it. It will be *you* who will determine the final outcome. If you don't destroy her... she's going to destroy the world, Charlie."

Maddie's warning grew darker. "I know my niece. She wants to do good, but she's incapable of making the decisions she must in order to prevent damning us all. My visions aren't always clear, but I know one thing to be absolutely true. Ava *is* going to end everything. She was always going to. The only choice that's left to be made is if you're going to stop her, or help her do it."

"If you're so certain of her choice, then why are you pushing her to do the right thing?" I asked.

"Because it can still be changed, but *you* must be the one to change her mind. You have influence over her that nobody else has. We need to stop this, because if Ava goes down the road I think she's going to take, nothing will survive."

"I don't agree," I stated harshly. "You said it yourself that the interpretation is up to the prophesied one. Well, I say the destruction is already done. She *had* to go through dying in the Infernal Underground and come out different in order to choose to save the world. It's the only thing that makes sense. And because it's *my* prophecy, I get to assign whatever interpretation I want to it. And Ava can do the same for hers. She made the decision to save us. She's not going to turn her back on the world. She wouldn't."

"What if you're wrong?" Maddie asked gently.

"I'm not," I decided with firm conviction. I was a demigod, for heaven's sake. I was stronger than a prophet, and it was up to me to decide what my prophecy meant. Maddie couldn't help Ava decipher her prophecy's meaning, so I didn't know what she was doing lecturing me on mine.

"Are you sure?" Maddie pressed.

"Ava and I have promised each other we're going to do whatever it takes to stop this war, save the Elves and help people, even if it costs us each other," I said. "She and I are going to work together to make sure that happens, so there's nothing to worry about."

"Be careful," Maddie warned. "You believe that you can keep your promises to Ava, and perhaps you can. But when push comes to shove and your back is against the wall, you're going to find the options that are available to you are going to be very different from what you're considering now. When you're in the heat of the moment... are you going to be able to make the final call? Because I've foreseen what you will decide, Charlie— *both* options. And neither one is going to leave you anything but heartbroken. I only plead with you to make the *right choice*, because if you don't, you won't only lose Ava. Everyone will lose everything. And as much as I love my niece... preserving her life isn't a price I'm willing to pay for the world. What about you?"

I didn't answer, because that was a ridiculous question, and I couldn't believe she'd asked me to consider it. I turned on my heel and headed for the elevator, because I'd heard more than enough.

"Don't give me that look," I told Oberi once we were in the elevator.

You have no idea what look I'm giving you, she replied snidely.

"I can sense you're about to give me a lecture," I said.

Oberi sighed. *I'm not here to lecture you, Charlie. I just want to check in. I'm not going to try to change your mind. I know you won't listen to me, anyway—*

"I listen!" I defended.

You're interrupting, Oberi stated flatly. *I just want to understand. You aren't stronger than a prophet. Their magic is a power that goes beyond ours. Are you choosing to accept that your prophecy is fulfilled because you truly believe it, or because you don't want to face the chance that you still have a difficult decision to make?*

Her question struck a chord in me, and I immediately got defensive. "Do you *want* us to face a repeat of the Infernal Underground— or worse? Maddie said I get to choose, so I'm choosing this. The prophecy is done. We held a funeral for Ava. I've already destroyed her once. We're demigods, and we're strong enough not to let this happen again. If people can choose their own meaning of their prophecy, then I'll save Ava *and* the world."

I'm not suggesting you're bending the prophecy's wording too far, Oberi said. *I'm just not sure if you truly mean what you're saying. What if the Underground wasn't enough to change her mind? What if Ava chooses to destroy everything? Where does that leave us?*

"I guess that part would be up to her."

And you need to know how you'd respond, so you can prepare for it. That's why the prophecy exists, so you are ready. If Ava chose to destroy the world, would you stand by her and watch it burn, or destroy her to stop it?

"Ava and I have discussed this a million times. You know where I stand."

I know what you've said, Oberi replied. *But do you really believe that, despite your promises, you could choose to let her go for the sake of the world?*

"Why would I need to make a decision about something that's never going to happen?" I shot back. "It's silly hypotheticals, because I've already fulfilled my prophecy."

You didn't wish to discuss what would happen if one of you passed before you went down into the Infernal Underground, and Ava died that time, Oberi reminded me.

A heat of rage rolled through my body, though I forced it to stay suppressed. Bringing up what had happened still made me sick. "Yeah, and she's not dying again, certainly not by my hand," I spat. "What kind of a husband do you think I am? If it's a *fate worse than death*, it means something like torture, or inevitable, prolonged pain... do you really think I'd do that to her? It's unfathomable. Let's not worry about what's already come to pass."

Charlie, you don't understand. I will follow whatever you two decide, to save the world or damn it, because that is my responsibility and my oath as a Familiar. But you're brushing this off as unimportant when it means every-thing. Oberi gave an angry huff. *Maddie believes Ava is going to hurt people. Both of us find that hard to believe, because she wants to save everyone so badly. But what are you going to do if Maddie is right? If there's an emergency and we have to subdue Ava, we need to do it safely, so none of us get hurt. We should have some sort of plan we can execute together, just in case things don't go our way.*

"Fuck the plan," I said shortly. "It's not going to happen, and if it does, I'll deal with it myself."

Don't go making prophecies of your own, Oberi warned. *You aren't aware of how they might go.*

Oberi could say whatever she wanted. I wasn't giving in on this. We were demigods, and we decided our fate. Not silly prophecies, gods, or anything else.

Ava was waiting in the car when I came to the entrance of the building. I slid into the passenger's seat as Oberi flew in the back.

"You took a while," Ava stated, though it was hard to read her tone. "What'd you talk about?"

"The prophecy," I admitted. "But it doesn't matter. I told her it's not going to happen, and that we decide our fates. I honestly don't think there's anything to worry about."

Ava leaned over to kiss me. "Of course there isn't. We're calling the shots now."

My wife drove the car at high-speed back to the palace. I thought about my encounter with Maddie, but I resolved to let it go. Like I'd told Oberi, there was no point in worrying about what had already come to pass. There were more important matters at hand— namely, finding the vampire key. The sooner we had all seven Divinity Keys, the sooner we could end this war.

And her aunt was wrong. I was going to prevent this. Whatever her words meant.

Eddie greeted us inside the main doors of the palace. "Sir, your team has completed the first phase. When would you like to speak with them?"

"Now," I stated.

"I'm coming with," Ava added.

Eddie led us down a maze of hallways, and we came to a meeting room. Chatter filled the air. It sounded like Chancey, Ivy and Alistair were there, along with Kallie and Marcus, though the two of them sat at opposite ends of the table. The Elvish Associates spoke amongst themselves, but the chatter died when we entered the room. Eddie guided me to sit at the head of a large table, and Ava wheeled her chair up beside me. Oberi sat near my feet.

I crossed my hands in front of myself. "What have we learned?"

Chancey cleared his throat. "I met with Professor Amber. Since I was in your vision, we figured we might learn something from my past life. I was able to confirm through my past-life regression that I was the vampire you saw in your vision. I remember being chased, but I made it out of the crash that killed you guys. I went to Paris and got the key into a vault at the *Banque Surnaturelle de Paris,* but I was killed almost right after."

Max— our tech expert— spoke up. "We hacked into the bank's security system to confirm whether the key was still there, or if it had been moved. According to bank records, the vault Frank Coffrey placed the key into hasn't been accessed since the day he made his deposit over a hundred years ago. There have been no security breaches, either. The key is still there. It's the only thing inside this particular vault."

"Excellent," I said. "Let's blow the roof off this place and get us a key."

"It's not that simple, master," Eddie told me. "Gavyn has already surveyed the premises, and he found that the bank isn't secured only by human technology. It's protected by powerful wards. This bank is used exclusively by supernaturals, and the magic surrounding it is designed to protect the vault from supernatural attacks from all races."

I shrugged. "We're demigods. I bet their ward won't hold against Marcus' powers. He can break it."

"There's more," Gavyn stated. "Esther and her gang of demigods have been spotted in Paris."

"What?!" Ava demanded. "How can they possibly know where to look? The Warden has been searching for this key forever, and suddenly *now* he knows where to look?"

"We must have a mole in the castle," Marcus panicked.

"I had a feeling somebody was spying on us," Alistair said slyly.

"Relax," Ivy insisted. "You know who else has info about vampire doings? My father. And Erasmus was working for him— the same guy the Warden's men hunted down for slaughter. Erasmus knew enough about the keys to give up intel, whether he wanted to or not. Even if he didn't know exactly where the key was, he'd know enough to give the Warden a place to start. I'm sure the Warden has been hunting the key down for months, and their clues led them to the same place ours have."

"Regardless of how they got their intel, they're in Paris looking for the key," Gavyn said. "As far as we can tell, they don't know exactly where the key is hidden. They haven't approached the bank yet. If we go in guns blazing, we'll alert the other demigods to our presence, and they won't hesitate to kill us to get that key. We need to run a clean job, so that we don't alert our enemies."

I leaned back in my chair. "How do we do that?"

Max spoke up again, and papers rustled as she spread them across the table. "Along with bank records, we also hacked into bank surveillance. We've been mapping out bank processes, schedules, routines— everything we can possibly get our hands on. Security is intense on both the tech side and the magic side. We're going to have to be very strategic."

"We've been discussing an undercover operation," Eddie said. "Gavyn will be our undercover agent and get into the vault. Asa and Ares will pose as security guards in case anything goes wrong. Max will run tech surveillance from the van, while Elyx surveys from above. He'll set up his rifles from three buildings over. If Esther and her gang show up, they'll be dead before they can make it in the building."

"A bullet's not going to kill them. They're demigods," Marcus pointed out.

Elyx chuckled. "*My* bullets will slow them down, I assure you."

"Great," I said. "When do we leave?"

"We still have details to work out," Eddie replied. "We need to arrange fake IDs and disguises."

"Kallie can do that no problem," I stated. "Her illusion magic is powerful enough to disguise us as anyone. Plus, she can copy an ID like it's nothing."

"There are wards around the bank protecting it from magic like that," Eddie pointed out.

I shrugged. "Their wards have nothing against demigods if we use simultension. Our magic just has to be stronger than theirs."

"We can't be sure of that," Eddie replied. "No one's ever done it before."

I leaned back in my chair. "That's because no one's had *us* on their team. Get all four of us demigods in the bank, and we'll get that key no problem."

Eddie paused for a beat. "Um, my prince, you're not going with the team."

Protests rang throughout the room from my friends, and Oberi barked loudly.

My spine straightened, and my tone turned rough. "Like hell I'm not! What do you mean, Eddie?"

"The prince gives orders, but he does not carry out the mission, sir," Eddie said, like this was the way it had always been done. "Your Elvish Associates are here to do these dangerous jobs for you. The rest of you must remain safe here in Ilamanthe."

"Eddie, we've been to prison," Ava reminded him. "We're used to pulling off crimes."

"Yeah. Do you know how many houses I've broken into?" I asked. "I never got caught. You guys need demigods in there with you. We're not sitting back and doing nothing. The keys are *our* responsibility."

"I understand that, sir," Eddie said. "But I implore you not to underestimate your team. These Elves are the best in the business."

"And so are we," I growled.

"Yeah, we've seen hell," Marcus added. "Granted, it was a hole in the ground... but we've been through a lot!"

"Need I remind you I'm an assassin?" Kallie said. "I'm used to pulling off shit like this and not getting caught."

"Well, you *were* caught and sent to the Institute," Chancey said under his breath.

"All right, everyone settle down," I commanded. I couldn't have contention among my team. I turned to Eddie. "You *need* me on this job. I've used my Earth magic to crush iron doors like they're nothing more than a sheet of paper. I can knock the door off this vault no problem."

"That's not going to work," Eddie replied. "There's a fail-safe on the vault where if it's broken into by force, the whole bank will explode. We could shield ourselves from the blast, but the key could end up anywhere in the rubble, and that's time we don't have searching for it. The authorities will show up first. If you want this key, you need to do it properly. There are a series of codes and procedures we need to follow in order to unlock the vault without triggering alarms or explosions."

"If you're going to convince me to stay out of it, I need to know more. How long will it take before you're ready?" I asked.

Eddie sucked a breath. "At least a week."

That wasn't good enough. Esther was too close to the key, and she could be in and out of that bank before my team ever made it there. I didn't like this one bit.

Elyx must've noticed the look on my face, because he said, "My prince, this must be a clean job. We can't take any risks."

I wholeheartedly disagreed. You didn't walk into a high-security magical bank and expect to walk out with one of the most valuable items in supernatural history without taking risks. My team should know better, because we wouldn't win anything by playing it safe.

"I want files on everything you know about that security system so far," I ordered.

Max handed over a folder. Ava's brother Maverick had made me a new pair of reading glasses, and the glasses robotically read out the first few lines on the paper so I could understand what we were looking at.

When I'd gone through the entire file, I set it aside and stated, "I want the Elvish Associates to report back to me tomorrow with an update. Eddie, the five of you should get to work immediately."

"Yes, master," Eddie replied. He and the rest of the Associates hurried out of the room. I'd assigned him as the head of the operation, but it was clear I'd made a poor judgment call. These people weren't willing to do what needed to be done.

"What is it?" Ava asked when the Associates had left the room. We were alone with Kallie, Marcus, Alistair, Chancey, and Ivy. "You're thinking hard about something."

"I don't trust my team," I admitted. I was agitated, so I stood from my chair and began pacing. "Who are they to say we can't come along? *I'm* the boss here. If we *do* have a spy, it could be one of them. If we let them go through with this, we won't know until it's too late. I'm not letting these guys go without us and risk one of them taking the key. I don't know any of them well enough to allow that, except Eddie, and he's too trusting to think someone could betray us."

"So what are you going to do?" Chancey asked. "Demand to go with? You're the prince. You could get yourself killed."

"Isn't that what a demigod is supposed to do— be willing to die for the keys?" I demanded. "I'm not going along with them, Chancey. I've already got my team right here."

"You realize this ain't like breaking into a house, right? You ain't stealing a frickin' TV," Chancey said flatly.

"One break-in is just like the others. You just have to not get caught," I shot back. "And why trust strangers when we can do it ourselves?"

Kallie spoke up. "You're talking about going behind their backs?"

"Why not?" I said. "I don't owe these people loyalty. They're supposed to be working for me. I'm not going to hand this job off to them like I'm not the one in charge."

"It's called delegating," Chancey insisted.

"I'm the boss, and if they aren't going to do what I say, then I'll do it myself," I replied.

"I gotta agree with Charlie," Alistair said. "I mean, I love my man, but Eddie doesn't know what he's talking about. By the time the Elvish Associates stop dragging ass to get into that bank, Esther and her shitshow circus are gonna roll in there and take it for themselves. A week is too long to wait, especially when Esther's already in Paris. She could be planning to break in tomorrow."

"Exactly," I said. "Doing this ourselves, right now, is what makes sense."

Chancey sighed. "You think you can pull this off because you have experience breaking and entering, but you've never robbed a bank. It's not the same thing. I've seen this play out before. I lived a life of crime and got caught. I wasn't as smart as I thought I was— *none* of us were, pal. That's why we landed ourselves in the Institute. Now you wanna take a job a couple of weeks after your ass got outta prison. Are you nuts?"

"We've learned from that," I argued. "We're better than we've ever been, and we're demigods now. Look at us. Kallie's an assassin who can cast the best damn illusions I've ever seen. Marcus can get through any ward, and Ava's the baddest bitch I've ever known. She'll kill any fucker who gets in our way."

Ava laughed lightly. "That's the best compliment I've ever received from my husband."

"Our intel is right here," I added, waving the folder Max gave me. "Ava and I can plan a heist we can pull off tomorrow, not next week. We don't have that kind of time. Max has been poking around their computer system, and it's bound to trigger some sort of alert. The bank could move the key before we get there, or Esther could show up first. If the Warden gets his hands on the vampire key, we might as well kiss it goodbye, because we'll never get it back. We need to act fast, and we need to go *now*."

Ivy drummed their nails on the tabletop. "I think Charlie's right."

"Ives!" Chancey objected.

"Hear me out," Ivy insisted. "This bank is run by vampires, and vamps move fast— and I'm not talking about their superspeed. We've already been at this for a few days, and I guarantee you the second they get wind that *anything* is amiss, they're shutting that place down and hightailing the key out of there. I think Charlie's team is underestimating him. Vamps use a lot of human tech, and because of that, their wards and magic can't be too strong or it'll mess with the cameras, just like it did at the Institute. Demigods should be able to break in easy, but we have to do it before anyone suspects anything."

"If Ivy knows how this place operates, then we have the intel we need," I said. "Chancey, if you're in, you can run surveillance. What about the rest of you?"

"I'm all for it," Ava said, sounding excited.

Oberi panted. *Anything for those keys.*

"If you say we have a job to do, we have a job to do," Marcus added. Rishi meowed in agreement.

"You sure as hell aren't going without me," Kallie demanded.

Ivy's chair squeaked as they sat up straighter. "Whatever you need from me, just ask."

"I'm willing to create some chaos," Alistair added eagerly.

Silence fell, and we all turned to Chancey. Finally, he breathed a heavy sigh. "Yeah, all right. I'm in. But I don't like the look of this."

BY DAWN THE NEXT MORNING, we had a plan in place. Kallie, Marcus, Chancey, and Ivy had joined Ava and me in the privacy of our quarters before anyone else in the castle had awoken. We gathered around the couches in the main room. Oberi was coming with us, because we needed him, but Marcus had opted to leave Rishi behind just in case this went south.

The phones the Elvish Associates gave us were in a pile on the table. We were leaving those behind, because I didn't want the Elvish Associates trying to get in contact, demanding to know where we were while we were trying to pull off a robbery. We'd tell them everything once we were back in Ilamanthe with the vampire key.

Alistair was already in position and waiting for the proper time to set off his distraction. We'd be leaving once he did.

"Here's what we know from the file Max gave us," Ava started. "The wards cover a three-block perimeter around the bank, and portals won't work in that area. Marcus can't break the wards until we have the key, because otherwise, it'll alert the vampires in the bank that something is up. We'll have to portal into the city outside the wards, then drive the rest of the way to the bank. We'll take my car, along with one of the royal vans. Chancey and Ivy will be running surveillance from the van. Chancey will be our eye on the sky and the streets, keeping watch for any signs of Esther. Ivy will monitor the bank's live surveillance footage. Max has already hacked into the system. What she doesn't know is that she gave us enough information in this file to hack into *her* program ourselves."

Ivy rubbed their hands together. "I was starting to think my father's crime lessons would never pay off."

"They're paying off big time today," Chancey muttered.

"Marcus and I will get the vampire key," Ava continued. "I'll be the customer who comes in to open her vault, and Marcus will be the employee to take me back there. Kallie's already forged fake documents. As for getting into the vault, it requires a fingerprint and a retinal scan from a bank employee, along with the customer's passcode. We already have the code from Max's files."

"I've got an illusion potion that'll transform Marcus into one of the bank employees," I said, setting it on the table. "I snuck into the royal potions room and took a transformation potion from my grandfather's own stash, one that he brewed himself."

"I reinforced the potion using simultension, because demigod magic is the only thing strong enough to fool the wards and not set them off," Marcus added.

"But in order to transform Marcus into one of the bank employees, we'll need a DNA sample," Ava said.

"We already have our target," I added. "Every morning before he arrives at work, Louis Blanc visits the coffee shop across the street at seven-fifteen sharp. It's there that we'll immobilize him and get his DNA. He's one of their top dogs with high security clearance— a griffin shifter. Once Marcus takes the potion, the wards won't know the difference between Marcus and Louis Blanc."

"Paris is only an hour behind Ilamanthe," Ivy pointed out. "The bank will open soon. We don't have much time."

"No, we don't," Ava agreed. "Which means we have to move fast. The key is in a vault in the middle of the bank."

"You're sure we won't trigger the alarms?" Chancey asked.

"We shouldn't, but just case any alarms *are* triggered, Kallie has worked with tech before in her assassin days," Ava said. "She'll be on stand-by to disable the alarms if needed. As for magical alarms, Marcus can break those wards. However, that's going to alert the supernatural authorities, so we want to avoid resorting to that if at all possible."

"And if we trigger a fail-safe like Eddie talked about?" Chancey asked, before mimicking the sound of an explosion.

"We won't," I stated simply. "The Elvish Associates wanted to pull off a clean job, and that's what we're going to do."

What's my job? Oberi asked impatiently.

"Oberi will accompany Charlie inside the bank," Ava continued. "Charlie will be posing as a security guard, and Oberi will be his police dog. Charlie's job is to step in if any bank employees don't want to play nice. We'll all have earpieces so that Charlie can direct us. Once we have the vampire key, we'll quietly head back to our vehicles and portal home."

"Can Kallie portal two vehicles without being spotted?" Ivy wondered.

"We've already got an alleyway near the bank staked out, and it should be safe to portal there without being spotted," I said. "I'm bringing a pocket mirror, just in case we need to use one to leave quickly."

"And all of us will have our guns on us at all times," Kallie said. "Just in case things go south."

My pistol was holstered to the side of my body, underneath my suit jacket. The others were all hiding their weapons in similar places, just in case we needed them.

Ava unfurled a large piece of paper over the coffee table. "I've got blue-prints of the bank. Listen carefully, because we can't mess this up."

We went over our plan one more time. I was confident we could pull this off.

"Charlie and I are going to put illusions on everyone, to disguise our features," Kallie said. "Together, our magic should be enough to hold once we enter the ward perimeter. That way even if we get caught, people aren't going to recognize us."

Kallie and I used simultension to combine our illusion magic. The two different types of power melded together and settled over the entire group like a blanket of dust, save for Marcus, who needed to be himself in order for the transformation potion he was taking to work. I didn't notice much of a differ-ence, except my skin itched.

"Can't recognize any of you," Chancey said. "You all look different."

"That's the point." Ava checked the clock. "Time to go."

I snagged a pocket mirror from our room, and then waited by the door. "Come on, Alistair," I murmured. It was past the time we'd planned to pull off the distraction. Eddie would be coming this way any moment, and other guards constantly patrolled the palace at all hours. Alistair needed to hurry up.

A loud *boom* sounded, and the quake of a room exploding several floors down shook the entire palace. I heard the stomping boots of guards as they rushed down to investigate, and I smiled. Alistair had volunteered to create a distraction so we could slip out, as he was more than willing to experiment with the newest spell he'd created. It was a curse that caused multiple geysers to open up in the floor, spewing poison every time they erupted. Whoever touched the poison would get insatiable munchies, and all they'd become obsessed with was finding snacks... which would be a problem, because all the snacks were in the kitchen. The geysers would continue opening up, making everyone in the palace very hungry and not at all willing to work on solving the problem until they'd been fed.

That should keep them busy for a while, I thought, before gesturing to the team to follow me.

The halls were now devoid of guards, and we snuck down to the royal parking garage. I knew we had to move, because the second people noticed I was missing, the royal guard would start looking for me.

Ava, Oberi, and I got into her car, while the others piled into a van. The vehicles roared to life. I rested my elbow on the open window, and the air shifted as Kallie's portal bloomed in front of us.

Ava revved the engine. "Ready to rob a bank?"

A wide smile spread across my face, and I leaned over to kiss her neck. "Love, I was born ready."

Ava shifted into drive, and the tires squealed as we took off. My heart surged in excitement. The adrenaline rush felt so familiar, and I'd be lying if I said I didn't enjoy the thrill of breaking the law.

The temperature dropped a few degrees as we passed through the portal, and the sounds of Paris filled the air. Birds chirped, and voices from the street drifted in through the open window. I smelled fresh bread, and the sounds of conversation hovered over the space. In the distance, someone played an accordion. The morning sun touched my skin, and it was warm and refreshing.

Tires crunched through the alleyway behind us, and I knew the van had made it through. The portal closed, and Ava pulled out onto the street. She gave a gleeful laugh as she revved the engine.

"Hey now," I warned. "Let's not attract any more attention than we need to."

Ava snickered. "Why not make an entrance?"

It'd been a long time since I'd seen her this excited. To think, all we needed to do was rob a bank to make her happy. I was enjoying every second of this.

Look at the hats in that window! Oberi cried.

"If we get this key and end this war, you two will have plenty of time to go shopping," I said. "Hell, I'll conjure all the hats you desire. But first, we have work to do."

Ava slowed the car. "Speaking of which, here's our first stop."

A thrill traveled to my stomach. I honestly couldn't wait to get out there and do this. Though robbing a bank was technically a *bad thing*, I felt like I was made for it. "I'll see you inside the bank, my love."

I leaned over to take her face in my hands, and I placed a gentle kiss on her lips. Ava smirked under my touch. "I'll be the one robbing it," she teased as she drew away.

"Don't make me arrest you," I told her.

"I'm counting on it later." She snickered. "Now go."

Ava pushed me, and I got out of the car. Oberi hopped out of the back to help me navigate the unfamiliar streets. He wore a seeing eye-dog vest and a leash— though he wouldn't shut up about how much he hated it.

I don't see any other service dogs on leashes, he complained.

There aren't any other service dogs around, I replied flatly. *Now come on. We need to get inside.*

Ava had dropped me off at the coffee shop where Louis Blanc picked up his drink every morning. Oberi and I walked in, ordered an espresso, and sat down to wait.

Eventually, I heard the door to the coffee shop open again. *Target acquired,* Oberi said. *Louis is going for the table beside you.*

Louis sat down and unfurled a paper to read. I paid close attention to the sound of Louis setting his cup against his table, so I knew where it was.

I stood. Oberi guided me, much like he helped me identify targets during battle. I walked by, and pulled out a little trick I had up my sleeve— literally. As I passed, I slipped a few drops of potion into his coffee. It wasn't much; just a little sleeping potion that would kick in within a few minutes. I then headed around the corner to the back of the store, where the bathrooms were, to wait out of sight. Louis finished his drink, then exited the coffee shop.

Phase one complete, Oberi said, and we left the coffee shop. I slipped into the back alleyway, where the van was waiting for us. The doors opened, and I jumped inside.

"How's it going?" I asked Chancey and Ivy.

"We're right on schedule," Ivy said. Chancey hit the gas and we started around the block. Ivy tossed me some clothes, and I began changing into my security uniform. I switched my pistol from a holster on my side to one on my hip and secured it in place.

"Everyone else, what's your report?" I asked.

Kallie's voice came through my earpiece. *"I'm almost in place on the roof. I'm scanning for alarms now."*

"I'm parking the car," Ava added.

"And I'm tailing Louis," Marcus reported. *"The sleeping potion should kick right about... now."*

I heard Marcus grunt. He must've caught Louis as he passed out.

Ivy opened the back doors again. Marcus was right there, and he pulled Louis' unconscious body into the van. The doors slammed shut. It all happened so fast and casually I didn't think anyone on the street noticed.

"He'll be out for an hour," Marcus said. "I just need a cheek swab for the final touch... and there!"

The potion hissed from the vial in his hand. "See ya on the other side, boys."

I exchanged Oberi's service vest for a police vest before the van came to another halt.

"This is Charlie's stop," Chancey announced.

Oberi and I hopped out in our police attire, and he led me into the building.

Ava had said the bank was huge, but I didn't understand just how big it was until we entered. My Air magic swirled upward several stories, and I could still feel sunlight on my skin, as if the ceiling was made of glass. Voices came from so far away that I swore we could play football in this place.

There's a line of teller windows along the wall, Oberi told me. *A balcony surrounds the entire room on the second level. I see the hall that leads back to the vault.*

How's security? I asked him.

There are a few guards, but they haven't looked your way yet. You blend right in. Oh, shit.

I felt Oberi's gut sink, and mine did in response. *What's wrong?*

There are wanted posters... of you.

Are you fucking kidding me right now? I demanded.

Dozens of them, all over the place. They say that you, Ava, Kallie, and Marcus are dangerous criminals. Wanted dead or alive. Oh, there's a cash reward!

Well, what do you want me to do? Turn myself in for the money? I said sarcastically.

It's not that bad, Oberi insisted. *The photo they used is your old Institute mugshot, and you've grown a beard since then. You barely look like the same person.*

I sighed heavily. *That's not going to keep me out of prison. This illusion better hold.*

"Uh, boss? An update, please?" Ivy's voice came through my ear.

I kept my tone low as I whispered into the earpiece. "Oberi says that our faces are plastered all over the bank."

"*Just do the job and get out, before anyone suspects anything,*" Ivy said. "*A little wanted poster ain't gonna mean shit.*"

Before I could answer, Oberi cut in. *There's a guard coming your way. Eyes forward, keep walking.*

I pulled my hat further down over my eyes and focused ahead, like I belonged there. The guard passed by me without a word. I didn't think he noticed me, but I felt his magic rolling off him in waves. He was a dragon shifter for sure. Although we were in France, this property belonged to supernaturals. The guards here didn't answer to the French government— they answered to the United Supernatural Union.

In fact, every person in this building appeared to have supernatural powers of some sort. My Elf power picked up on other magic— mostly vampires and shifters, but I sensed a few Elementai and witches, too. The people here spoke all kinds of languages. I heard French, English, and a couple speaking in Hawkei.

"Ava, are you still good to go?" I asked.

"*I'm in disguise, and my chair makes people uncomfortable,*" she replied. "*People don't look me in the eye, anyway. I think we're good.*"

I positioned myself as close to the teller window on the end as I could, but I was on high alert.

"*Bonjour, Elise,*" I heard someone say as they passed the teller. She greeted them back, and they exchanged a few words in French.

"Is everyone in place?" I asked through my earpiece.

"*I'm good to go,*" Kallie replied.

"*Same,*" Ivy and Chancey responded.

"*I'm inside,*" Ava added. "*I see you, Charlie.*"

"*I'm right behind Ava,*" Marcus said, though his voice sounded deeper and unfamiliar. The potion had obviously worked.

I held my breath, half expecting some sort of magical alarm to start blaring and lock the place down. But nothing happened.

"*Ancestors, the wanted posters are everywhere,*" Ava mumbled. "*That's not even my good side.*"

I communicated to Ava through our bond. The less I said out loud, the better. *Focus, pidge. Approach the teller window next to me.*

Approaching now.

"*Bonjour,*" the woman at the window greeted Ava. She asked something else in French, but Ava replied in English.

"I'd like to access my vault," Ava said.

"Of course, *madame,*" the teller— Elise— replied in a thick accent. "We will need identification, a signature, and of course, your code to the vault."

Ava pulled out the documents Kallie had forged, just in case we needed them. "It's all right here."

"*Excuse moi?*" Marcus said as he passed by. He spoke in his best French accent. He sounded a bit nervous, but somehow managed to pull it off convincingly. I guess his days as a theater kid were starting to pay off. "May I be of service?"

"This woman wants to access a vault, *Monsieur* Blanc," Elise replied.

I quickly whispered into my earpiece. "Her name's Elise. Call her by name, and get rid of her."

"I will take it from here, Elise," Marcus said. "Please bring the *madame* a glass of water."

Elise sounded confused. "Yes, *Monsieur* Blanc."

Marcus went up to the computer and started typing on it. I didn't think he was doing anything more than mashing random keys. He made a show out of rustling through Ava's paperwork. Once Elise was gone, he said, "This way, *madame.*"

I must've been holding my breath the whole time, because when they disappeared into the hallway nearby, I finally felt like I could breathe. "Keep us updated," I whispered into my earpiece.

"*We're on our way to the vault,*" Marcus said, before quickly switching back to French. "*Bonjour, bonjour.*"

"How many people are back there?" I asked.

"*A few,*" Ava replied. "*So far, so good. Ancestors, how many wanted posters can they have?*"

I heard the sound of paper tearing through my earpiece. Ava was pulling the posters off the walls.

Ava, I warned through the bond. *We can shred this whole bank to pieces when we're done, but we need to get the vampire key first.*

I was just having a little fun.

Have your fun in the vault. How close are you?

The vault's just ahead.

I spoke into the earpiece again. "Marcus, report."

"Scanning now... fingerprint is good... retinal scan is... what the hell?"

My heart leapt, and a beat of silence passed. I started to panic. "Don't leave us hanging, Marcus. Report."

"The scan took, and we entered the code, but the vault isn't opening," he said.

"This should have worked," Ava insisted.

"Something went wrong," I growled. "Our magic must've triggered something. Kallie, what's happening?"

"There have been no alarms triggered on the tech end," she said.

"I can feel the bank's wards with my magic," Marcus added. *"Nothing's changed."*

"So what's going on?" I demanded. Oberi started to fidget beside me, and I could feel the panic rising in our bond between the three of us.

"Let me try again," Marcus offered.

Several moments passed where nothing happened, then I heard the sound of voices through the earpiece. They spoke in French, so I couldn't make out what they were saying.

Ava, report! I cried through the bond.

Two guards approached us— shifters, I think.

Marcus stammered a few incomprehensible things, then managed to squeak out, *"English, please. For the lady."*

"Monsieur Blanc, you should know better than to access the vault on your own," one of the shifters said harshly. His voice was loud enough to pick up in the earpiece. *"You know the procedure, and you know you need two bank employees to get inside."*

"Fuck," I growled under my breath. "I'm on my way."

Oberi and I quietly slipped down the hall, as to not cause a scene, then the two of us took off running in the direction of the vault.

"I've got you on the feed," Ivy said through the earpiece. *"To your left, Charlie."*

"Of course. I'm well aware of bank policy," Marcus continued, playing along.

I reached them just in time to hear one of the men ask a question in French. I didn't know what he said, and neither did Marcus.

"Is there a problem here?" I demanded.

The man simply repeated his question.

These shifters were highly suspicious, and I wasn't entirely sure how we were going to con our way out of this one.

He's asking Marcus what his wife's name is, Ava told me through the bond.

I quickly stepped in. "Well, go on, *Monsieur* Blanc. Tell him your wife's name."

"Y— you know my wife," Marcus stammered, still maintaining his French accent. "Delphine and I have lunch together every day."

We'd done our research, but this was cutting it too close. One of the guards instantly said, "Delphine doesn't take lunch in the city. She eats at her desk. You are not *Monsieur* Blanc."

Something in the air shifted. A high-pitched squeal filled the air, echoing throughout the entire bank.

A *clanging* noise came from the main entrance, and I felt noxite in the air. Ava gasped, *There are huge metal walls coming down around the bank, and they're full of noxite!*

Shit. We'd been fucking caught.

"Of course I'm him!" Marcus demanded, but his accent was no longer convincing. "Oh, fuck!"

"It's them!" one of the guards snarled. "The ones the Union is looking for!"

"You're under arrest, and the rest of you are coming in for questioning," the other guard sneered as he reached for Marcus.

Marcus let out a vile laugh. "Oh, yeah? Arrest this!"

A *thud* sounded, but it barely fazed the guard. I heard the shifter grunt and stagger backward a single step before he sneered, "That isn't gonna stop me from taking you in."

"Marcus, don't punch him!" Ava cried. "Cast a battle orb or something!"

"Uh... right!" Marcus squeaked. His magic swelled, then blasted down the hallway with the force of several bombs. Ava threw up a shield, and we were protected as Marcus' magic erupted.

The guards' bodies hit the floor, and the whole ground rumbled. Debris rained down from above us. I instinctually threw my arms above my head, even though we were in the safety of Ava's shield.

"We've lost visual!" Ivy barked in my ear. *"Can you hear us?"*

"Yeah, Ivy, we've still got audio," I said as my heart slowed.

The explosion settled. Ava dropped her shield, but dust continued to fill our lungs. Ava coughed. "Any chance the rest of the bank didn't hear that?"

I doubt it, Oberi stated flatly.

"What the hell?" Kallie demanded through the earpiece. *"I cut the alarms before you did anything. This was supposed to be a* clean *job!"*

"We didn't *know* about the two-man system," Marcus barked. "If you cut the alarms, I bet they had a backup."

"Well, you know now, so what are you going to do about it?" Kallie shouted.

The alarm stopped blaring. Marcus must've broken the bank's wards. Even so, voices shouted from down the hall. We had seconds to make a decision.

"Any chance the explosion rocked the vault?" I asked.

"Let's find out," Ava said breathlessly.

I felt Marcus put his hand to the vault door, examining it with his magic. "Fuck! This vault is locked down tight. It's on a separate system Kallie can't access, and it's got wards up the wazoo."

"So break them," I insisted.

Marcus sucked a breath. "I can't. I can feel they're attached to the fail-safe spell. If I break the wards, this whole place is going up in flames. It's nothing like I've ever seen before. You're basically asking me to defuse a bomb. Union authorities will be here before I can break it. It looks like there's a manual combination override on the vault mechanism in case an alarm is triggered. Without the override code, we're not getting in."

"Then we need to get Kallie down here, so she can break the combination and manually get us in," I said firmly.

"*Already on it.*" The shattering sound of a window breaking came through the com, and noise crackled as Kallie rushed to get to us from her place on the roof.

"We've gotta buy her some time to crack it open," Ava whimpered. "She's going to need a second."

I cracked my knuckles. "All right. Time for Plan B."

Guards flocked into the hallway, but before they could cast any spells, I'd already siphoned their magic dry. I drew the speed and strength of a vampire, along with the telekinesis of a warlock.

"What the hell?!" one of them shouted.

I barely gave them a chance to respond before I used telekinesis to toss them to the side. Their heads hit the wall hard, and the three guards slumped to the ground unconscious.

"If we're going to do this, we're doing it the right way," I said. I conjured two ski masks with my powers and handed one to Marcus, then put the other one on myself.

Oberi jumped at my feet. *Ooh, a hat! I want one!*

We really didn't have time for this, but I conjured one for him and put it on, anyway. Might as well go with it now, seeing as how our plan was royally blown out of the water.

"Does this mean I get to play damsel in distress?" Ava gushed.

I placed my hands on the back of her chair and leaned down to whisper, "Who said we're playing?"

I felt a thrill travel through Ava's belly, and I got a little excited myself. I reached down to pull out my pistol and showed it to Ava. "You okay with this, love?"

I think the sight of me holding the pistol turned her on. No matter how independent she claimed to be, I was her protector, and I wouldn't let anyone touch her.

"Green light," Ava breathed in admiration. "Whatever my dom wants."

Hell if that didn't get me going in a situation where I needed a clear head. These fuckers didn't know what hit them just yet. I grabbed the back of Ava's chair and started back down the hall briskly.

"Those noxite doors that shut all over the glass aren't going to be enough to keep the police out," I said. "They'll disable them to get in. We need more magic."

"*I'm going to put a shield on the place, so nobody can get in or out,*" Kallie said.

A shiver crossed over my skin as the shield took hold over the bank, and my Earth magic felt the marble walls ripple when Kallie cast her impenetrable shield. Once it was up, we didn't waste a second the moment we stepped into the lobby.

Pop, pop, pop!

People screamed and ducked for cover as Marcus and I aimed our guns at the ceiling and shot off spells. Gunshots rang throughout the room. People tried to run for the doors, then panicked as they realized that the noxite doors, as well as Kallie's shield, kept them locked inside.

"This is a robbery!" I screamed. "Everyone get on the ground!"

Oberi barked loudly. I couldn't help but crack a smile beneath my ski mask as every patron in the room followed my orders.

Well, almost everyone.

Something clicked, and I felt the *whoosh* of a dart fly through the air. A sharp pain entered my leg, and a magical substance emptied into me.

I yanked on the dart and tossed it aside. Laughter bubbled up in my throat. "Noxite? Please."

I aimed my gun forward.

The guard's at three o'clock, Oberi told me.

I pulled the trigger. A blast of Air shot with such clear precision that it went straight through the guard's leg. He let out a pained cry that echoed off the wall of the lobby. A *thud* sounded as he landed on the ground, writhing.

I could sense his magic. He was the dragon shifter from earlier, and I could feel it as he started to shift.

I hauled Ava out of her chair roughly with one arm, and held her body to mine as I pressed the end of the gun into the side of her temple. "Change, and I'll blow her brains out," I snarled to the shifter.

Ava began to sob loudly. "For the gods' sakes, do as he says!"

The guard hesitated, then came forward. Oberi growled, warning him to stay put.

"One step closer and she's dead!" I warned. I tangled a hand in her hair and yanked it to the side. Ava cried harder.

"*Please*! He's not fucking around!" Ava wailed.

"Let him do what he wants, so he lets the girl go!" a woman in the bank shouted. I heard the guards begin to back off.

You okay, pidge? I asked through the bond. I worried I was going too hard.

Perfect, she replied. *We've got to put on a show, right?*

She pressed her ass against me, and I got hard immediately. Her seduction called to me through our bond, telling me how much she was enjoying this— like this was one of the scenarios we played out in our bedroom and not life or death. We were playing it up, not just for the guards, but for each other.

This was hot. More than that, it was fucking thrilling, living on the edge like this with everything on the line, and both of us were getting pleasure from this sick performance. I would've thrown my wife on the floor and fucked her right there in front of all these people if we didn't have a job to do, but we did, so I just held Ava closer to me and pressed my dick against her so she knew it was there. She barely held back a moan of delight.

"Anyone else want to be a hero?" Marcus shouted, and he fired a few more shots.

People whimpered, but nobody moved.

I cocked my head to Marcus. "Clear out the offices."

Marcus disappeared into the hallway, while I continued pointing the gun at Ava's head.

"Ivy, an update," I ordered.

"*I'm getting the feed back now*," they said. "*Aaaand... I've got visual on you in the lobby.*"

"Kallie?" I asked.

"*I'm working on cracking the combination, but I need more time*," she insisted.

The sounds of frightened people increased in the room as Marcus returned. "I found a couple of employees hiding, including this big wig."

He pushed someone to the ground in front of me, and the man gave an *oof* as he fell at my feet. My Elven magic told me he was a vampire— probably the head of the bank.

I raised my voice as I said, "We need some *volunteers* to help us get what we came for. Anyone want to be kind enough to help us into a vault? We'd *so* appreciate the hospitality."

Not a damn soul stepped forward. The vampire on the floor let out a raspy chuckle. "You're dreaming if you think you're getting anywhere near that vault."

"I'll kill her," I warned, and I pushed the barrel of the gun against Ava's temple. She let out a pitiful whimper.

"Go ahead," he sneered. "She means nothing to me."

There was another explosion from outside. It boomed over the ceiling and shook the building. People screamed, and I became paralyzed as I felt magic wash off of me like sludge.

I realized that the illusions disguising our identities had fallen. The Union must've cast a spell around the bank to wash away all traces of magical influence. The magic was so strong it destroyed even the effects of my grandfather's potion.

If the spell was that powerful, only another demigod could cast it. That meant Esther was nearby, if her whole team wasn't here already. The hostages gasped as they recognized Ava's face from the wanted posters lining the wall. The ruse was up.

Ava knew how to fall safely. I pretended to shove her aside, and she made a show of collapsing dramatically while I kicked the vampire in the stomach. He let out a grunt, and I growled, "I don't think you realize I'm not fucking around. We're not leaving until we get what we came for, so we can do this the easy way, or the hard way."

"*I can't get into this fucking vault!*" Kallie screamed through the com. "*The combination isn't taking!*"

Screw this. The whole plan was taking way too long. We needed to get into that vault *now*.

"You think I haven't done worse than this little game you're playing? You're not as tough as you think you are," the vampire sneered, and he rose to his feet. Around me, the guards began to approach.

"Freeze! Nobody move!" Marcus bellowed. He fired off more shots, and a few people screamed. I heard a couple of spells being blasted toward me, and I had to duck as a fireball singed my shoulder.

The vampire I'd been speaking to took his chance to deliver a punch to my face that nearly knocked me out. It wasn't as strong as I was expecting— probably because the noxite doors around the bank were weakening people's magic. I fell over, landing heavily on my side. I pulled myself together and siphoned his strength so I could remain conscious. I got to my feet and faced him. He went to hit me again, but I shoved him downward as roughly as I could, knocking his feet out from under him.

The guards had gotten bold, and we couldn't have that, so I decided they needed to learn a lesson. Once I got the vampire off of me, I immediately siphoned the shifter powers of the dragon that I'd shot earlier, and I began to morph. Scales formed on my skin. My body began to grow, filling up the lobby. I was gigantic, and I couldn't see where I was going, so I was smashing countertops, furniture and registers trying to turn within the lobby.

Cries of terror could be heard all throughout the bank. Spells that guards fired bounced off my sides, and I heard the vampire that had been below me seconds earlier give a loud scream. I didn't even have to think about it before I lunged my fangs out.

His terrified yells were instantly cut off as I crunched him in my jaws. His body separated, and I let the two pieces of his deformed, mangled corpse fall to the floor. Wails shook the walls, and I heard the other guards fall over and crawl backward as they desperately tried to get away from me.

I shifted back. My chest heaved as I yelled, "Did you see what I did to him?! Do you want to join him?"

A few of the bank patrons began sobbing. Then I felt something strange and foreign...

Ava's slight disgust.

But I barely registered it, because there were so many other powerful emotions coursing through me. Soft steps moved forward, and a woman said, "We'll do it. My coworker and I. We'll get you into the vault. Just don't hurt anyone else."

I smirked. "Good decision. Let's go."

I reached forward to grab her, then pushed her in the direction of the vault, jamming the pistol into her back. Marcus walked forward to control the other employee, while Ava hoisted herself back into her chair.

"We're taking these hostages!" I yelled. "As some of you have already found out, we've put a shield around the bank, and not a damn one of you is strong enough to break our magic. Anybody who tries isn't walking away from this!"

Nobody dared to reply.

Once we were back in the hallway and out of sight of the lobby, I couldn't help it. I ripped off my facemask, leaned down and kissed Ava as roughly as I could. This was *such* a fucking thrill.

"Charlie." Ava laughed, pushing me away.

"You were a beautiful little actress," I hushed, and I kissed her hair.

"As long as you liked my performance," she murmured, and kissed me back.

The employees we'd taken hostage didn't say anything. They knew we'd played them, but they were under our control now, so there wasn't anything they could do that could help them except comply with our orders.

"About damn time you showed up," Kallie complained as we approached the vault. "Can we hurry up and get out of here?"

I nudged the pistol into the spine of the woman in front of me. "Go ahead. Just open up the vault, so we can get what we came for. Then my friends, myself and my sweetheart will be on our way."

The woman walked forward slowly. She and her co-worker approached the vault. I heard some technical noises before the spinning mechanism on the vault's door audibly opened.

"There. We did what you asked," the woman said in a quivering tone.

"You can go. We don't need you anymore," I said, before stepping inside. The woman and her coworker ran off as my friends and I entered the vault.

Everybody went dead quiet, and my friends paused once we were inside. None of my partners stepped forward, or even *breathed*.

"So? Get the key," I ordered.

"Charlie..." Ava said, but her sentence faded away. Marcus and Kallie didn't add anything.

It was like nobody wanted to tell me what they saw.

"Oberi, describe the room," I ordered.

The vault is a fairly large area, he said. *It's empty, save for a rotary phone attached to the wall, and a pedestal in the middle of the room that has a glass case display on top of it. Inside is an ivory box— open, with a silk pillow where I assume the key was kept... but it's empty. The vampire key was definitely here a few hours ago— I can feel its resonance. We just missed it. Someone must've gotten here first.*

"*Fuck!*" I screamed. I kicked a wall, absolutely enraged we'd done all this to get shit in return.

Ava told the others what Oberi said, and Kallie noted, "Who has the key?"

"Probably Esther. She must've gotten here first," I snarled. "We need to get it back from her."

"We can figure that out later—" Ava started, but her voice was cut off as a blaring noise resonated through the com in my ear.

"*It's the fucking feds!*" Chancey roared. The sounds of noxite guns went off, and shots fired from a regular pistol Ivy was carrying. I heard both of my friends scream before the com faded into static.

"Ivy? *Ivy?!*" Ava yelped. "Fuck! We've lost communication."

"Which means we have no idea what's going on out there," Marcus panted.

"They might've gotten caught," Ava said weakly.

"Feds can only mean one thing. The United Supernatural Union is here," Kallie said. "They must've ordered all the Union police who work for them to—"

"*Put your weapons down, and come out with your hands up! We have the place surrounded!*" A voice on a megaphone boomed so loudly, I could hear it through the walls.

Yeah, the cops had definitely shown up. My mind raced to come up with a way out of this, until Kallie said, "Hold on. If the key was just here, I can reverse time up until the point that it left. Then we can take it and leave."

"Do it, then," I snapped. We were cutting this too close.

Kallie snapped her fingers. Then a second time.

I didn't feel anything happen. No dip in my stomach, no shift in reality. It was as if an invisible hand wrapped around my throat and cut off my access to air.

"No," Kallie groaned, and she snapped her fingers a third time. "No, *no!*"

"What's wrong?" Marcus asked.

"I can't reverse time," Kallie gasped. "It's not working."

"Is there inferichite somewhere in the bank?" I asked in a panic. We should've felt it.

"No," Kallie said in horror. "This... this is me. I don't have any access to my time powers."

I struggled to understand what she meant, but Ava got it first. My wife's understanding of the situation rushed across our connection, and it hit me so hard I almost fell over.

Shifters were weak if their bonded partners left them in limbo for too long. Marcus' failure to either accept or deny Kallie as his mate was draining her magic, and now she couldn't access it without the help of their bond.

I realized Kallie putting the shield on the bank had drained up what magical reserves she'd had, and it needed time to replenish. Power was supposed to flow equally between two bonded partners, like it did between Ava and me, but with Marcus blocking his half of the bond off, Kallie couldn't access what she needed.

We'd warned him about this. I'd *tried to tell him*. And now it was happening, at the worst possible moment it could.

Marcus knew it, too. His voice was strained as he rasped, "Kallie."

"It doesn't matter. There's nothing we can do about it now," she snapped.

The phone on the wall rang. We all jumped at the noise. It kept ringing and ringing. I wondered if anyone was going to answer it, or if we even should.

Then, Marcus' footsteps echoed across the floor as he picked up the phone. "Hello?"

There was a pause, and Marcus said, "They're asking for you, Charlie."

He shakily handed the phone to me. I picked it up and barked, "Yes?"

"Hey, Charlie. It's nice to speak to you again."

It took a moment, but I recognized that voice. It was Killian Ryan— the supernatural bounty hunter I'd met before I'd left the Institute. He and his partner, Colter, had come to thank me for my criminal profile about the Dollmaker, which had led to the warrant for Valen's arrest. They'd thought I had potential as a future bounty hunter, and wanted me to join their team once I'd graduated. They must've shown up with the rest of the Union reps to help bring us in.

"What do you want?" I kept my voice flat. I didn't want to give these guys an in.

"We want to help," Killian said. "We're outside. You guys have gotten into a bad spot."

I huffed. That was undermining the situation as much as fucking possible. "You can't help us. We come out, you'll take us away."

"We can work something out," Killian promised. "We know you kids aren't bad people— you're just confused. It's normal, after everything you guys went through, trying to escape the Institute the night it burned. You're upset and acting out. We've found other students like you, and we've helped them."

Yeah, right. I knew *exactly* what had happened to those inmates who'd managed to escape the burning prison and gotten themselves arrested again afterward. They'd been sent to Mission indoctrination camps, and that was the last place I wanted to go.

"We're in too deep. If you want me, fine, but I'm not letting my friends take the heat for this. Arrest me, and let the others go," I said.

"You know we can't do that. Come on, Charlie, this isn't the way you want to do things. You're a good guy," Killian insisted. "You don't want to scare all these people."

I knew what they were doing. They wanted to get on my good side, appeal to any sort of empathy I had, so they could save hostages and hopefully make an arrest in the process. I wasn't going to bend.

"I'm doing the only thing I know how to do," I said blatantly. "This is what the world made me to be, so now it has to pay the price."

Killian must've handed the phone over to Colter, because the next voice was deeper. "We know you've got your wife and friends in there with you. You don't want to put them in danger, do you? You're the leader of this group, aren't you, Charlie? You want everybody to get home safe."

I gave a soft laugh. "I've learned not everybody gets to go home at the end of the day."

"Don't do this, kid. You've got a bright future," Colter added. "If you turn yourselves in now, there might still be a chance you could join us someday. We know you want to be a bounty hunter like us. You can have that, Charlie. Think about it— you could provide for Ava, have some kids, a good life. You don't want to throw it all away."

His words made me second-guess everything. Maybe I *shouldn't* be doing this. Maybe this was the wrong thing to do. I was hurting people, and I didn't want to do that.

But if we didn't get this key, *everyone*— on the Earth and in the afterlife— would get hurt. These guys didn't understand that I had to make some impossible choices.

Yet even the good guys working for the Union had been compromised by the Warden. The Union was under his control now, and I knew if we surrendered we'd never see the light of day again— if we even made it to the next morning.

I had dreams. Dreams that I desperately wanted. But I should've known they would never pan out. I wanted to be a supernatural bounty hunter, but I wasn't, and I never would be. I needed to make a choice. I could keep chasing after a foolish hope, or decide to become the villain my family *expected* me to be.

It wasn't like I had much of an option. I had to let that dream go now. What I wanted in the face of what my family needed absolutely didn't matter.

The phone shook in my hand. I could physically feel my future crumble into pieces as I replied, "I'm the grandson of Emperor Cassiel Majestica, and an underboss of the Elven crime family. This is what I was born to be. *This* is the life I choose."

I hung up the phone. Seconds later, it rang again. I thought of the pleading words of Killian and Colter, and I felt guilty. Perhaps I could explain things to them. They didn't know about the keys and how important they were. If I told them about our destiny, they might understand, and want to help.

I hesitated before I picked it up again. "Hello?"

"Hello, Charlie! We've missed you!"

It wasn't Colter or Killian this time. It was fucking *Esther*. Revulsion churned my innards as I snapped, "Fuck off, Esther. How'd you convince them to let you talk to us?"

"I told them we were *such* good friends at the Institute, and you just needed to hear a familiar voice!" she said chipperly. "Please come out, so this can all end happily!"

"The minute we step out of this building, you and your demigod buddies are going to obliterate us," I hissed.

"You should be more concerned about your immortal soul," Esther crooned. "The only way to salvation is to seek refuge under the wings of The Mission's god. You don't want to be *judged* in the afterlife, do you? The god of The Mission doesn't forgive without repentance. But if you hand over the key, and plead for his forgiveness, I'm sure my uncle will—"

Nope. I slammed the phone back onto the receiver. Any doubts about the choice I'd just made flew out the window once I'd spoken to Esther.

Everybody on this planet wanted to use and manipulate us, and I knew better. I berated myself for being so stupid to nearly fall for the Union's pleas... told myself I was an idiot for being so *weak*.

I'd made my decision, and I was never looking back.

"That was Esther. She's here," I said. "She doesn't have the key. She asked us to hand it over, so she thinks we stole it first."

"That means the Warden doesn't have it in his hands yet, but somebody else does, somebody that doesn't work for him," Marcus whimpered. "We've been played."

"I bet it's that fucking spy we've got hanging around at the palace. The bank knew we were coming. Whoever the mole is, they raised an alarm, and somebody moved it just before we got here," I seethed.

"If Esther's here, the Warden isn't far behind. He could arrive any minute," Kallie worried.

"We can't fight them all off. We need to *go*," Marcus insisted.

A loud voice drifted through the walls of the bank. Esther had transferred to using a megaphone, and was screaming religious propaganda. "THE GOD OF THE MISSION WILL DESTROY THOSE WHO DO NOT WORSHIP HIM! SUBMIT NOW, AND BE CLEANSED OF YOUR SIN—"

I blocked her out as I shouted over the sound of the megaphone. "Kallie, make us a portal. It's time to leave."

She let out another pained noise. "I can't do that, either. It's not just my demigod abilities. Everything's affected."

"What can you still cast?" I asked desperately.

She gave a gasp of pain as she attempted to create a spell. A spell flickered out and died. "All I've got is battle orbs. I can still use my gun, but I don't have access to anything stronger."

"It's okay. I've got a pocket mirror, I can portal us out—" I began.

But as I reached into my pocket, I gasped as my skin cut on bits of shattered glass. I drew the mirror out of my pocket and ran my fingers over it.

It was just a frame. There was no reflection. I'd landed on my side during the fight with the vampire. It must've broken then.

I couldn't use it to make a portal and get us home... which meant there was nowhere else to go.

This was it. We were trapped inside the bank, surrounded by enemies with no way out.

ava-marie

SIX

"Charlie, what do we do?"

My question failed to rouse a response. He wore a blank expression, even as Oberi nudged his side.

"Where the hell are we supposed to go?" Kallie cried. "Esther is going to break through our shield eventually!"

"They've got us pinned," Marcus half-sobbed.

Charlie remained silent. He was completely helpless, which meant it was time for me to take action. We'd been cornered back in the Infernal Underground, and I'd go to hell before I allowed something like that to happen again.

"If you can get me to my car, I *promise* I can get us out of here," I swore.

"Where is it?" Charlie asked. His voice was hoarse.

"Still parked in an alleyway at the front of the bank." Even as I said it, my heart fell.

"That means we'll have to fight our way through the barricade and hope the cops didn't take the car," Marcus moaned.

"It's our only shot," Charlie said. "Let's move."

The sirens were closing in all around me, intermingling with the voices in my head, which were starting to blare out warnings. Oberi ran out of the vault and back down the hallway, and my friends raced after him in a dead run.

"Kallie, take down the shield," Charlie ordered. "We'll release the hostages and blend in with the crowd as it leaves. I'll disguise us with illusion magic so they don't notice us slip out."

Kallie nodded. Tingles crawled over my skin as I felt the shield lift. We hurried into the lobby, where the hostages had figured out the shield had dropped and were racing for the door.

I hardly had time to take a breath before Union reps stormed into the bank from all sides. Noxite darts and spells flew everywhere. I flung myself out of my chair and onto the floor as magic flew over my head. A second later, a battle orb slammed into my chair and blasted it to pieces.

Well, so much for that.

"Oberi, I need to be on your back," I instructed. She instantly changed into a unicorn and knelt to the floor. I pulled myself onto her. The saddle pad formed beneath me, and I strapped my legs tightly to her sides.

Oberi raced me behind a corner while Charlie, Kallie and Marcus ducked behind a counter to take cover.

Hostages were hit with multiple noxite darts or pelted with spells. They immediately went down. Holes formed in bodies as supernaturals took magical blows that were meant for us. Chaos ignited the area. Union cops collided with the fleeing bank patrons, until the crowd formed a literal mob. This was an absolute shit show.

Our plan to get out had failed, because we hadn't thought the Union members would kill civilians in order to get to us. Who were the real villains here?

"Why are they putting the hostages at risk?" Kallie asked.

"Esther must've lost her patience and ordered them to go in!" I yelled. "She doesn't care who lives or dies, so long as they arrest us!"

"You'll never take us alive!" Marcus screamed. He fired off six rounds, and I watched Union cops go down once his magical bullets hit.

There was so much noise, and everything was in mayhem. A lump lodged in my throat, and I clung to Oberi's mane. "Charlie, I'm scared."

"Don't quit on me now, pidge." Charlie poked around the corner and fired three shots before pressing his back to the counter. He went to shoot again, but a battle orb collided with his shoulder, and he gave a gasp. I felt the pain ricochet across our bond as blood spewed out of the wound. I saw that the orb had wrecked his shooting arm, to the point I could see muscle and bone poking through the tear in his clothes. He slid onto the floor as he struggled not to pass out.

I'd failed to use my pistol before this moment. I didn't think I had the strength. But Charlie was hurt. Seeing him like that, in desperate pain and trapped in this goddamn bank, erased the part of me that was afraid.

Fuck my earlier reservations, my morals, whatever it was that held me back before. I'd use this pistol to take as many lives as I had to in order to keep Charlie safe, and I'd feel no guilt about it whatsoever afterward.

Taking a life for him, in whatever way I had to? Simple. Easy.

I reached into the lining of my jacket, where my pistol had been concealed, and drew it out. I urged Oberi forward, right into the line of fire, and raised my weapon to pull the trigger.

I couldn't even see straight— I must've blacked out. All I could feel was the recoil of the pistol in my hand as it went off, and felt my Water magic rushing through the gun to create ice bullets. Union cops screamed in terror and went to take cover behind objects as my shots hit their target. Oberi helped me by launching fireballs from her horn, and as our hits connected, I realized something terrifying and invigorating.

I didn't need to be trained. I was an excellent shot.

Even so— more Union cops kept flooding in, and they made a small army. We might be demigods, but being outnumbered had stopped us before.

"We need to clear a path, or we're never getting out of here!" Kallie cried over the noise.

Charlie managed to stagger to his feet. Through a heavy breath, he gasped, "Light it up, pidge."

I was more than happy to oblige my dom. Each wall of the bank immediately ignited into gigantic flames the second I thought of it. My Fire magic licked up the marble, so hot that it even melted the stone, causing the building to buckle. Any furniture within the bank was instantly set ablaze and turned to ash. Several Union cops standing near the flames spontaneously combusted. Oberi shook her head in fury. An enormous jet of fire resembling a flamethrower shot out of her horn, helping me turn the bank into a pyre.

The incredible heat in the building caused all but the grittiest Union police to flee the bank. We picked off the rest of them with our pistols as we fled toward the doors.

The cool air outside kissed my skin. It was just as chaotic outside the bank as it was inside. Squad cars surrounded the bank, but the Union cops were divided on whether to go after us or stop the fire. Around the area, humans had surrounded the bank with expressions of shock, videoing the scene with their phones as both we and the police shot off spells.

Supernatural secrecy was apparently gone. I searched for my car and saw with relief that it was still in the alleyway I'd parked it in earlier, and it had gone completely unnoticed by police. We could still make it.

I looked up when I heard wingbeats. Esther was here, hovering in the sky before the bank, her angelic wings spread out wide like she owned the very world.

But we'd gotten fucking lucky, because none of her friends were with her. They had to be doing other dirty jobs for the Warden.

Wasn't going to prevent her from trying to kill us. Shrieks rose throughout the street as Esther used her light magic to blind us. I cringed away from the harsh light, and Oberi whipped her head away.

I heard the sound of a pistol going off, and Esther screamed. Abruptly, the blinding light immediately ceased, and a crashing *thud* boomed ahead of me.

Charlie had taken a shot with his good arm, and he'd managed to hit Esther in the wing. She'd fallen from the sky and landed on a squad car, breaking the windshield.

She cringed and went to get up, but I was already firing. Blood spurted from her front as several of my shots connected, and she collapsed flatly on the broken windshield with a pained groan.

My Fire bullets weren't going to kill her, but they'd keep her down for a while. I flattened myself to Oberi's neck, and she galloped through the zigzag of patrol cars as Union cops flung spells after us. Oberi jumped, sailing us over a squad car as Kallie and Charlie darted around it and Marcus slid across the hood.

My heart was pounding when we finally reached my car. Charlie swung me off of Oberi's back with one arm and threw me in the driver's seat before he slipped into the other side. Oberi changed into a husky, jumping onto Charlie's lap. Kallie and Marcus barely had time to jump in the backseat before I revved the accelerator.

I was a damn good driver, and I knew I could outrun these assholes. We were pinned back in our seats by the force of the car shooting forward. I immediately turned out of the alleyway and onto a side street, racing down that before I got to the main road.

The Union cops were immediately on our tail. Red and blue lights flashed behind us, and police sirens wailed as squad cars followed us on a high-speed chase throughout the streets of Paris. Pedestrians screamed and dove out of the way as iron tables and chairs bounced off the hood. I winced as the furniture scratched the paint and left dents in the hood of my new baby.

My car was faster than theirs, so I was able to make it to the highway, where I had more room to maneuver. I swerved around other vehicles as I pushed the odometer past a hundred.

Marcus and Kallie leaned out the windows in the back and fired shots at the chasing patrol cars. They clung to the sides of the car to hang on as I swerved to avoid battle orbs whizzing toward us from behind. Squad cars tried to avoid their shots. Several ended up spinning off the road or crashing into each other, tumbling over into the ditch.

Traffic slowed up ahead due to construction. I went around it and started driving on the median, though it slowed us down. As we sped past the traffic and into the construction site, I searched the surrounding area, looking for something we could use to escape.

Oberi barked like crazy. One patrol car sped past us and went to box us in, but I spun the car around in a one-hundred eighty degree turn and got back on the gas, driving head-on toward a line of approaching squad cars.

"Ava, are you fucking nuts?!" Kallie screamed.

Absolutely. I had the balls to pull this off. Monica and I had stolen a car before, and the race we'd had with the cops back then hadn't ended well. I was determined not to let this be a repeat.

There was a ramp to my right, used by construction workers for repairing a nearby overpass. I jerked the car to the side and drove up it, launching the car off of the ramp. My stomach dipped as the car went airborne, and we flew over the squad cars that had been racing toward us seconds before.

Kallie, Charlie, and Marcus screamed as we sailed through the air, but I tightened my grip on the steering wheel until my fingers were white and my arms were shaking. *Come on, baby, you can do this.*

The car slammed against the concrete, bouncing off the tires. I swear I heard a couple of parts in the undercarriage come snapping off. The windshield cracked with the force of the fall.

Holy shit, that was going to be a lot of repairs. I nearly wanted to cry.

"We can fix your car later, let's go!" Charlie shouted, reading my thoughts. I pushed the car even faster, laying on the turbo.

The cars we passed became a blur, and dismay built inside my chest as we drove down the wrong side of the highway. I jerked the car to the side several times in order to avoid slamming head-on into vehicles that were barreling straight toward us.

"They've got people in the sky!" Marcus cried. I noticed out the front of my cracked windshield that several helicopters were trailing us from overhead, and getting closer.

I couldn't outdrive a fucking copter, that was for certain. We needed an escape, somewhere to take the car and hide. If we didn't disappear, and fast, they'd catch us, because I couldn't keep this up. Eventually, the car was going to break, and if that happened, we were fucked. I had to get this car to a place we could take a portal out of here without them following.

I had to get us out. Losing the cops and portaling away was our only shot.

Then I saw a line of patrol cars up ahead. The highway was blocked behind us, and the Union police had set up a barricade in front of us. It looked like the highway was blocked off at all angles. I needed to go back into the city.

I immediately slammed to a stop. I heard Marcus yelp as his face hit the headrest behind me, and blood spurted from his nose onto my arm. The vehicle made a screeching noise as I threw the car into reverse, and I painfully turned in my seat so I could look out the window behind me. My spine screamed in protest— I still didn't have great control of twisting my upper body, and fuck if it didn't hurt like hell to do so, but I had to right now. I drove backward at over sixty miles an hour, before I whipped the car back around and took an exit that curved into Paris.

The Union was waiting for us off the exit, of fucking course, and they'd laid down spikes on the road ahead. I did my best to swerve, but I couldn't avoid them all. I groaned as I heard the spikes pop the right tire.

"Great! Now we're screwed!" Kallie snapped as the car leaned to the side. I didn't slow down, but kept on the gas as we sped back into the streets of Paris— this time, a business district with a variety of expensive skyscrapers.

"We can still drive on the rim for a minute, but we have to get away from them," I insisted. "Kallie can't portal us away right now, which means Charlie is the only one who can."

A singular Union squad car had managed to keep up with us the whole time, and they were still sticking with us. It wouldn't be long before my car gave out, or they caught up to us.

"I need a mirror!" Charlie yelled.

"Where the hell are we gonna find *that*?" Marcus cried.

I was debating on pulling this bitch over and convincing the others to scatter out of the car and make a run for it while I held the cops off with my magic, until Oberi stood on Charlie's lap.

There! That skyscraper has a reflective surface, Oberi said, pointing with his nose.

It did. There was a building straight ahead that had a mirror-like surface coating the entire building. We could use it.

Drive through it, pidge. Charlie's thoughts were full of determination. *I'll get us home.*

I didn't think twice as I pushed the car in a straight line toward the skyscraper, the odometer climbing past one hundred and twenty. If Charlie said he could do it, he would do it. There was no fear, only complete and absolute trust. I'd put my life in this man's hands more times than I knew, and he'd never let me down before. He asked, I answered. He ordered, I complied. That was my role, and that was who we were. I'd crash this car and kill us all before I denied his command.

Yeah, I was fucking crazy. I loved it. *He* loved it. And riding this high and feeling alive, playing with the lines between life and death, was the most exhilarating thing we'd ever known.

Kallie and Marcus hadn't heard our conversation, and had no idea what we were planning. Kallie's voice got nervous. "Ava, what are you doing... AVA!"

I closed my eyes and braced myself, fully expecting to feel the car collapse around me as we crashed into the building.

But... I didn't. I pried open my eyelids, and my mouth dropped open in amazement as I observed the space around us. Mirrors surrounded us everywhere, reflecting our appearance millions of times. My face flew by in a blur as the car continued moving steadily past. It appeared we'd stepped *into* the mirror... like we'd entered another world.

Charlie had done it. He'd opened up a portal through the reflective surface in the skyscraper.

But we weren't the only ones who'd driven through it. The squad car who'd followed us was sailing behind us through the Mirror Realm, almost like we were moving in slow motion.

A portal blossomed ahead of us, and I saw the sea that surrounded Ilamanthe. We drove through the portal and came out at ground level on a highway outside of the Elven city.

I stopped the car on the side of the road. I turned to see what we had come through, and saw that the mirror behind us was some sort of reflective billboard, welcoming refugees fleeing The Mission to the city of Ilamanthe. On the right side of the highway was a cliffside, lined by a guardrail. Beside the cliff was the open ocean, a wide expanse of the Mediterranean Sea.

Charlie leaned out the car window, aimed his pistol, and fired a shot at the mirror we'd come through. Disbelief pierced my chest as I watched the bullet shatter the billboard into pieces.

The last thing I saw as the portal closed was the shocked faces of the two Union representatives as the portal slammed shut.

The fragile bits of the mirror fell to the pavement. My heart stuttered. A broken mirror couldn't reflect clearly enough to make a portal. Those people had no way out.

Marcus turned green. He swallowed thickly as he asked, "Are... are those Union cops stuck in the mirror?"

"I had to seal off the portal. Otherwise, they'd follow us and expose Ilamanthe," Charlie said roughly. "I didn't have a choice."

Something gnarled inside of me like jagged thorns. *A lie.* He did have a choice, and he'd made it.

But Charlie was right. We couldn't afford to put the Elves in danger again, not for anything... *we couldn't.* The city was more important than whoever had been in that patrol car, even if they were now stuck in the mirror world. The lives of thousands meant more than the existence of a few, and they'd chosen to chase after us when they knew we were demigods and what we were capable of. We'd done all we could.

I opened the car door and bent down to pick up a large fragment of the broken mirror lying on the road.

In its reflection, I could see the pale, terrified expressions of the Union representatives stuck inside the mirror. They were screaming.

Charlie stumbled out of the car and took the broken shard from my hand. Then he walked to the edge of the cliffside, beside the guardrail, and pulled his arm back to toss the broken mirror as far into the ocean as he could.

Nobody said a damn word.

When Charlie got back in the car, I managed to rasp, "We can't leave Chancey and Ivy."

"We have to. We can't go back for them," Charlie said heavily. "Whatever happened, we'll put ourselves in danger if we try to find them now."

Ancestors, I prayed they got out somehow. I couldn't handle it if the Warden captured them because of us.

I drove slowly back to Ilamanthe, where we got a lot of attention from the curious Elves on the streets. They were all too keen to gawk at the damage to my expensive car.

We managed to pull into the royal garage within the palace boundaries unseen, by some fucking miracle, but I bet the guards were already running to Emperor Cassiel to tell him we were back. Shit. I'd hoped when we'd returned, we'd have the vampire key in hand to calm some of his anger. Instead, we'd completely blown the whole operation and nearly gotten killed in the process.

I parked the car within the enclosed garage. Under the hood, the engine was smoking. Dammit all, Bren was going to kill me.

Kallie huffed. "Time to face the music, I guess."

"Not yet. This was my idea. I want a chance to explain things to my grandpa, before the rest of you get in trouble," Charlie said heavily.

"Fine by me." Marcus was out of that car in a flash. Kallie waited for a minute or two before she left.

After she was out of the garage, Charlie opened the door, and Oberi hopped out. *As much as you need to learn the consequences of your actions, beloved Charlie, I don't wish to see them put upon you,* Oberi noted. *I will cover for you. If people see me, they will follow. Perhaps it will give you time to seek out your grandfather and come up with an explanation.*

"Thanks, Oberi," Charlie said, and he ruffled his ears. Oberi trotted off, leaving Charlie and me alone in the car.

There was silence for a moment, before I asked with a smirk, "Baddest bitch you've ever met, huh?"

"You definitely live up to that reputation." He leaned forward, and I lightly touched his shoulder. The arm that had been fried by the battle orb mended, healing over until the injury was completely gone.

"Better?" I asked.

"Yeah. It no longer hurts."

We sat in the car for a few moments. Then Charlie reached out and snagged me across the waist, hoisting me out of my seat and into his lap.

Both of us were breathing raggedly, and he was already hard. I had no desire for foreplay, and he fucking knew it. He pushed the skirt of my dress up, and I hastened to unfasten his pants. Charlie ripped my panties off of me, grabbed my hips and thrust up. I sank down, letting out a loud moan as he went all the way in.

Charlie matched my noises with a moan of his own, and he started fucking me hard, lifting me up and down on his dick. I grabbed the car seat, and my nails dug into the leather as his movements went deeper. I felt my eyes roll back as the pieces of our soul connected, his body slamming against mine. I looked deeper inside our bond and felt his side of our spirit resonating against mine with a pure, clear warmth, his dominance wrapping around my half in a way that felt like I was being bound to his will. He kissed me hard, just as roughly as he had in the bank. I drank darkness from that kiss, licking up every drop.

It didn't take me long to come— he'd been edging me for what felt like forever, so my body was ready for it. The whole robbery, and the car chase afterward, had been like a BDSM scene created straight from our deepest fantasies. We'd totally fucked each other's heads, and the rush was even better than the one we got from sex. I'd been dying for a release ever since he'd put that gun to my head, and the thought of the cool metal pressed against my temple as he toyed with the trigger made me delirious... exhilarated. As my thoughts crossed across our bond, Charlie's excitement increased, telling me he'd liked it, too.

This was wrong. We were twisted as all hell. And we fucking *loved it.*

Charlie grabbed my hair and pulled as he came, and I screamed his name as we rode through it. Sweat beaded our faces, and I could feel his heartbeat pounding through his shirt against my own.

We put our foreheads together and just *breathed.* I was spinning in place and grounded all at once. This was better than any high I could get from any drug on this planet. I didn't want to get off his lap.

Charlie brushed my face. "Apparently we've found a new hobby."

I smirked. "Robbing banks isn't a hobby."

"Might as well be, if it can get us going like that."

I let out a soft laugh. He'd certainly started my engine.

I jumped as there was a sharp knock on the glass window beside us. I turned my head, and was *absolutely mortified* to see my mother standing there, her arms crossed with a disapproving frown.

"If you two are finished, Charlie's grandfather would like to speak with him," Mama said shortly. "I hope you have a good explanation for the damage you caused."

charlie

SEVEN

I felt the blood rush to my cheeks in utter embarrassment. I sure as hell didn't mind getting it on with my wife in our own fucking car, but did it have to be her *mother* who walked in on us?

"I'll give you two a minute, then you need to come with me," Sophia said.

Ava and I scrambled to get decent as Sophia turned away. Ava opened her door to let her mom know we were finished.

"I heard your wheelchair got destroyed," Sophia said as she wheeled a chair to Ava's door. News really traveled fast around here.

"Oh, wow. This is uncomfortable," Ava said when she transferred into the chair.

"It's temporary," Sophia promised. "We found this one in storage and figured it would work in a pinch."

"I guess it's fine, for now," Ava grumbled.

Sophia led us inside and through the palace. The only sounds were the click of footsteps and the roll of Ava's wheels. Obviously no one wanted to talk about what Sophia had just witnessed.

Sophia dared to break the silence first. "I didn't see anything, just so you know."

Dear ancestors, I did *not* want to have this conversation.

"Mama," Ava groaned. "Can we pretend it didn't happen?"

"There's nothing shameful about a married couple enjoying a bit of fun," Sophia said. "Your father and I have enjoyed time together in some interesting places—"

"Mama, *stop!*" Ava cried.

"I just don't want you to be embarrassed," Sophia said.

"I wasn't, until you brought it up," Ava replied.

"All right. It never happened," Sophia agreed.

She approached a door and opened it. I could feel the air shifting around the room as people breathed, but no one said a damn thing.

It was quite eerie, and my stomach twisted into knots. I wasn't looking forward to meeting with my grandfather after everything that had happened. I could imagine how disappointed he'd be already.

In the silence, I took a moment to assess the room. My Elf powers sensed demigod magic, and I noted that Marcus and Kallie sat on opposite ends of a long meeting table. The guards must've picked them up somewhere in the castle, along with Oberi, because he was ducked under the table in husky form. I could feel his guilt through our bond and knew his ears must be lying flat on his head. He felt bad for getting caught.

Others stood around the room. I picked up on the energy of two witches, along with a fae sorcerer and a wolf shifter. Marcus' and Kallie's parents were there, though my father was notably missing.

Fucking fantastic. Everyone *else's* parents had shown up, and my dad didn't care. Couldn't say I was surprised, but it still stung.

They weren't the only ones there. I also felt the energy signatures of a vampire and an angel.

"Ivy, Chancey!" Ava cried. "How'd you guys get out? We were worried sick!"

"The Elvish Associates pulled off a rescue," Chancey said.

"Yeah, *barely*," Ivy noted sourly. "They got rid of the Union cops and got us out before we could be arrested. What a shit job that turned out to be."

Ivy didn't get to say anything else before the door burst open behind us.

An Elementai strode in, and it was far too easy to recognize him by the way his energy commanded the room. "Sit," Liam ordered.

I pulled out a chair and did as I was told. Ava wheeled up beside me. Sophia remained standing with the other parents.

Liam began to pace around the table. It felt like he was boxing us in. I counted his steps. Ten... eleven... twelve...

He stopped at the head of the table and turned to face us. "What the *hell* were you thinking?"

"We're sorry." I ducked my head, and my voice came out smaller than I intended.

I hated feeling this way. I wasn't a kid anymore. I was a grown-ass man, and a prince at that. I was supposed to be a leader, not cowering to people who called my choices into question.

But still, this guy was a chief of our tribe *and* Ava's father. I didn't want to fuck up and make him disappointed in me, though I had. His piercing silence made me feel like a child.

"Sorry isn't going to cut it," Liam said roughly. "Do you have any idea how worried we've been? You tried to *rob a bank.* Do you realize how serious this is? What is *wrong* with all of you? And then you left us with a mess to deal with here at the palace. Don't try to tell me that curse wasn't your doing."

"I spent all morning breaking it," Nadine said. "I had to track down everyone it affected and remove the magic from them personally."

Marcus blew a breath. "Don't look at me. *I* didn't cast the curse. That was Alistair."

"I'm not *mad* at you," Nadine said gently. "I'm worried. You could've gotten yourself killed."

Marcus groaned. "Mom, I'm a demigod. You don't need to coddle me anymore."

"We're concerned," Lucas cut in. "We know things have been hard for you, especially in the last couple of years. We had hoped when you went to the Institute that it would help you, but now you're robbing banks? Marcus, what happened to you at that horrible place?"

Marcus nearly snorted. "Believe me, Dad, you don't want to know."

"We *do* want to know, because we care," Nadine insisted. "If we understood, maybe we could help. What you did was dangerous, and we don't want to see you get hurt. We'll get you a therapist—"

"I don't need a fucking shrink, Mom," Marcus snapped.

"He's right." Queen Emmaline broke in. "Why are we talking about therapy when we should be discussing the matter at hand? Our children have caused magical chaos! Maybe if you didn't sit back and put up with your son's shit, Nadine, none of them would be in this mess!"

"You think this was *our son's* idea?" Lucas demanded.

"I know our daughter is smarter than this," Emma replied.

"Indeed," King Ethan agreed. "We raised Kalina well. She understands this type of work takes secrecy. My child, you should've known your plan needed better execution."

"Dad, *seriously?*" Kallie complained. "I know how to pull off a job! Things got out of hand."

"This isn't helping—" Sophia started to say, but the others weren't listening.

"Kalina, if you and your friends wanted to rob a bank, you should've done it under the cover of night," King Ethan reprimanded. "To pull off something like this in the middle of the day is ludicrous. Did Marcus convince you otherwise?"

Nadine scoffed. "You think Marcus dragged your daughter into this? May I remind you that you're promoting criminal activity, *Phantom.*"

"My vigilante days are behind me—" King Ethan started.

"Apparently not, if you're giving her tips on how they could've committed a felony better!" Lucas barked.

"Well, if she's going to be a criminal, she might as well do it the right way," Queen Emmaline shot back. "Kallie, you're a member of the royal family. If you're going to break the law, at least don't get caught. I expected more from you."

"You're being too hard on her," Nadine insisted.

"And you and your husband are a soft cinnamon roll," Emma sneered. "Parents need to push their children to do better."

No wonder Kallie was so tough. Her parents loved her, and they were fair, but they could be a bit too strict.

I'd had enough of listening to this. I shot to my feet. "Kallie's a vital member of this team, and her skills are invaluable to us. The last thing she needs is a lecture about how much of a screw-up she is. And this wasn't Marcus' idea, or his plan— it was mine."

I'd felt like such a coward when I walked into the room, but I wouldn't let these people belittle my friends. Our parents might be disappointed in us, but they could only make us feel guilty about it if we let them. We were the ones in charge here, and we hadn't done anything wrong.

"You know what? I'm not sorry about any of it," I decided. "I'm in charge of this operation. I shouldn't be apologizing for making the right call. Kallie got us into the vault. We almost had the vampire key, but—"

"I don't want to hear excuses," Liam cut me off roughly. "I don't think you realize the gravity of the situation. Allow me to show you."

Something clicked, and a TV on the wall started to play the supernatural news. "*The suspects have been identified as the infamous Villain's Club, the gang name which they were known by during their time spent behind bars at the Darke Institute for Supernatural Offenders. Reports say the robbery was led by Charlie and Ava-Marie Wahkin. Witnesses are calling this husband-and-wife duo the supernatural world's own Bonnie and Clyde.*"

Oberi gave a low whine at my feet. *They're rolling security footage of you two inside the bank,* Oberi told me. *They've got a video of you two kissing while you were attempting to break open the vault.*

Internally, I groaned. The parents did *not* have to see that.

"Ava, wipe that smirk off your face!" Liam burst.

"What?" she asked innocently. "I thought it was sexy!"

"This isn't *sexy*! This is *disturbing*!" Liam bellowed. "Robbing a bank should *not* be making you think about—"

The broadcast continued. *"These partners-in-crime were not working alone. A female accomplice has been identified as none other than Kalina Nowak, former fae princess turned assassin for hire."*

Marcus shifted in his seat. "Great. They said terrible things about you guys. I can't wait to hear them blast my screw-ups all over the news."

The news anchor paused, as if checking their notes. *"The fourth member of their team is Martin Tyler, a rogue warlock born on the streets. He spent his childhood as a famous circus performer, not knowing where he came from, until a Ponzi scheme involving performing elephants landed him at the Darke Institute."*

"What?" Marcus asked in disbelief. "WHAT?!"

"That's unfortunate," Nadine whispered quietly.

"They got my name wrong! I'm not Martin Tyler!" Marcus yelled. "And I've never been in a damn circus! Why did they get my friends' information right and not me?!"

"I mean, it might be a good thing they don't know who you are," Ava offered feebly.

"No way! I always get the short end of the stick!" Marcus slammed his fist on the table. "It's all bullshit! Who's writing these news reports?"

"At least they mentioned you," Chancey said. "Ives and I didn't even get credit."

"This isn't something you want to take credit for!" Liam growled. "You *exposed* the supernatural world. The humans are preparing their nukes to mount them against us! I don't care how powerful you think you are— you aren't surviving a nuclear explosion."

"The United Supernatural Union was quick to execute their Exposure Protocol," the newscaster continued. *"Human witnesses have had their memories wiped, and all video content has been scrubbed from the Internet. The Union is working diligently to explain away the events as an elaborate hoax. For now, the supernatural world remains a secret, but until these criminals are caught, there's no telling what damage they'll do to our communities next."*

The television clicked off. Nobody dared to say anything— that is, until Ava opened her big mouth.

"I guess that means no nukes," Ava said happily, as if that was the end of it. "Problem solved!"

"No, not *problem solved*," Liam replied snidely. "The humans may have their memories wiped, but they're still on edge. They know something's up, even if they can't remember what it is. You guys really blew it, and you didn't even get what you were looking for."

Ava sighed. "We don't need the lecture, Daddy. We're adults, not children."

"Apparently you do, because you're behaving like kids," Liam accused. "You're like reckless teenagers acting on impulse!"

"Well, I'm twenty-one, so I'm not a teenager anymore," Ava said flatly.

Liam sighed, and his voice softened. "My point is, you can't keep making rash decisions. Because if you do, they're *going* to end badly."

"You made difficult decisions during the Hawkei Civil War," Ava reminded him. "We have a prophecy to fulfill, too. You need to let us make our own choices."

"I made tough choices because they were my only options," Liam emphasized. "You're making purposely bad decisions because you *want* to, not because you *have* to. There's a big difference, peanut. And I'm really concerned about how this is going to end if you and your friends keep going down the wrong path."

"That's not true," I defended. "You think this was a choice? We knew there was a chance someone else could get to the vampire key first, and we were *right*. We had to act fast, and it turns out, it wasn't fast enough. We could sense its resonance— we only missed it by a few hours. We should've gone last night, while the key was still in the vault. You're not mad that we tried to rob the bank. You're mad that someone else got there first. We *need* that key, and it's going to take criminals to get it. Would you rather us choose to sit back and do *nothing*?"

"You could've asked for help, but you didn't!" Liam insisted. "Charlie, if you don't learn how to trust people, you're going to end up in a bad situation. One we won't be able to get you guys out of."

I scoffed. "Forgive me if I don't trust anyone but the few people who have ever shown up for me my whole life. I *did* put my trust in people— *my friends*— and we managed to make it out alive. I call that a win."

Liam sighed. "You can trust us, too. We're here to support you."

"If you wanted to support us, you wouldn't be berating us," I sneered. "You say you're there for us, but where were you when we were in Cellblock 9? Because *no one* was there to get us out. We got ourselves out."

I didn't like mentioning Cellblock 9. I barely held it together as I forced the words out, and even then, my voice still cracked. I could feel tears brimming at the corners of my eyes, too.

But I hadn't cried since the day that the guards had broken the organ and all our musical instruments at the Institute, and I'd be damned if I let any tears fall now, in front of these parents who weren't mine.

"Charlie, we don't always agree on how to help you kids," Sophia offered. "But we parents are here for you. We've all had to deal with prophecies, and destinies that were too big for us to handle, at an age when that responsibility shouldn't have been on our shoulders. The adults in our lives who tried to help us often ended up dying, or went missing. Sometimes we couldn't rely on them because they ended up betraying us. We're trying to give you the resources we didn't have."

"Yes. As tough as we can be, we want to give you support," Queen Emmaline insisted. "We're upset because this could've gone worse than what happened today. One of you, or all of you, might've ended up hurt."

I knew I'd gambled with everyone's lives today. I'd put the people I'd cared about the most at risk, and if anything had happened to any one of them, I wouldn't have been able to live with myself.

But that didn't change the fact that I didn't believe the adults in this room actually *wanted* to protect me. No parental figure had ever shown up for me. I'd constantly been let down, and I wasn't going to take the bait this time.

My voice got rougher. I was more bitter than I ever had been. "The only heroes in this room are the ones who were with me in Paris this morning— and the people who were down there with me in Cellblock 9 when we were all dying. Don't sit there and act like you give a shit about anyone in this room but your own kid. My father didn't care enough to show up here, so I don't know why the rest of you pretend like I'm important."

Truth was, I wished Cameron *had* been waiting to yell at me. Everyone else's parents were here. At least if my dad was in this room, he'd fucking realize I was alive. I wouldn't be invisible to him. He talked a great game about missing me and wanting to be my father, but I *needed* him to be here, and he was off screwing around doing who knew what when I'd just made one of the biggest mistakes of my life.

He wasn't here to guide me like he'd promised. He'd brought me into this world just to leave me here. If he wasn't going to be my dad, why had he bothered to give me life? What had I done to make him hate me so much?

Charlie, Oberi said calmly. *We all know you've had to fight your whole life, but this robbery isn't about only you. Your actions have an impact on all of the supernatural world, and the human world as well.*

I don't know why I should care about the world, because the world doesn't care about me, I replied through the bond.

Then why are you doing any of this? Oberi asked.

His question struck me, and I wasn't sure how to answer. I didn't get a chance to respond before Liam was speaking again.

"You can't make emotional decisions because you think no one cares about you," Liam said softly.

I shook my head. He didn't get it. "You're just lecturing me because I'm married to your daughter, and you're afraid of how hard I'll fight for her."

"Yeah, you *are* married to my daughter," Liam said bluntly. "Which is *why* I care about you. You're family, Charlie. Everyone here cares. And because we care, we're telling you that you can't save the world by yourself. What you did at the bank this morning was impulsive and rash. You can't think that way if you're going to fulfill your prophecy, because it's going to get you hurt."

"Liam, stop," Sophia said gently. "This is unhelpful. Can we just be happy our children are alive?"

Liam drew a deep breath. "Yes, of course. We're happy you made it back safely. But if you need help in the future with all of this, please— ask. Because you don't need to do it alone."

The door opened, and everyone turned to see who walked in. My Elf magic sensed who it was immediately, because Emperor Cassiel had such a prominent and powerful presence.

My stomach dropped, and my heart sank to the bottom of my chest. *Oh, great, here it goes.* I bet he was going to read me the riot act about what a fuck-up I was, and tell me no prince had ever disgraced the family so shamefully. Not like I didn't deserve it.

My grandfather cleared his throat. "Charlie. I'd like a word."

His voice remained surprisingly even, and somehow, that made it even worse. I was *really* going to get it now.

"Let's go for a walk," Cassiel suggested.

I couldn't read his tone. Reluctantly, I stood and followed him. I kept my head down and my shoulders slumped. Didn't think I could feel any lower, at this moment.

"The events that transpired this morning in Paris were... unexpected," Cassiel began as he led me through the halls of the palace.

"Well, that's what you get when you rob a bank," I said flatly.

"Is it?" Cassiel asked. "I know what the news reports are saying, but why don't you tell me your side of the story?"

I was caught off guard. No one had asked me that... ever, really.

"We received intel on the vampire key," I started, before explaining everything that had transpired between last night and this morning. It kind of just came out of me, and I couldn't hold it back. I left out a few parts regarding my wife and myself, for obvious reasons. But otherwise, I told him everything.

Even what I felt, and what I'd thought prior to making the decision to leave for Paris.

By the time I finished, we had reached the gardens. A light breeze swept across my skin, and a lavender scent filled the air. It was a peaceful place. I wondered if the servants would hear my grandfather screaming at me from out here.

I expected Cassiel to respond, but he didn't. Not right away, at least. We paced around the gardens, until he said, "I'm disappointed in you, Charlie."

His words were like an arrow to the gut. There it was— the beratement.

I was fully prepared for him to chew me out, so I was surprised when he added, "I apologize for my role in this. I don't believe I've explained myself very well."

I furrowed my brow. "Aren't you going to yell at me?"

"For what, exactly?" Cassiel asked. "Failures happen. If you're going to take my place as the head of this family, you need to learn how to deal with failure in stride. The mark of a good mob boss is not a perfect track record. It's learning how to adjust when needed. That, and not getting caught. You barely made it out alive, but you're here with me now."

All I could do was gape. "I don't get it. Shouldn't you be ready to rip my head off? We exposed the supernatural world."

"What good would that do?" Cassiel asked. "I'm not here to guilt trip you. I'm here to train you, and I haven't done my job as of yet."

If he was yelling at me, I'd know how to respond. His behavior was weird, and I didn't know what to do with it. Cassiel sat on a stone bench, and I took my place beside him.

"I think it's evidenced by the way things turned out this morning that this cannot happen again," he said.

"So what do you suggest I do differently?" I asked, rather harshly. "I did what needed to be done."

"This isn't how this family operates. You're supposed to send *other* people to do your dirty work. You're the boss."

"Which is exactly why I took matters into my own hands," I stated.

"You got your hands dirty," Cassiel countered. "A good leader keeps his hands clean."

"So everyone else can take the fall for me?" I demanded. "I took a chance, and we got closer than we've ever been. I can't trust anyone else to get that close. It took a lot of demigod magic to get as far as we did. I've always done things by myself. I don't know why I can't do that now."

Cassiel sighed. "You're not the criminal you think you are— you're so much more. You've lifted from cash registers and stolen a few electronics. I've robbed royal vaults and taken jewels from high-security museums. I've stolen ships and navigated their route through treacherous waters. All of this was done from the comfort of my own castle. I'm going to teach you how to be a bigger class of criminal."

"What fun is sitting around giving people orders?" I questioned. "I should be out there breaking into bank vaults and cracking through museum security. Hell, I should be on the ships captaining them myself— not sitting here on the phone while someone's shining my shoes. Forgive me if that's worked out for you, but you don't get it. While you were building this palace and restoring Ilamanthe, I was rotting in a prison cell. If you could get past security in a museum, why couldn't you get into the Institute and get us out of there?"

"You think I didn't try?" Cassiel asked. "Patience is a vital tool in our family. These things take time."

"That's the *problem*," I insisted. "I acted fast on that key, and it wasn't fast enough. You tried to get me out of the Institute, but I couldn't sit around waiting for someone to save me. My friends and I saved ourselves."

I felt like I was talking circles with these people. No one was hearing me.

"I understand that you're upset," Cassiel started.

"No, I don't think you *do* understand. You're safe here in your palace. It makes you feel like you have time. But when you're out there on the streets, your clock is always ticking."

My grandfather thought about this for a moment, then said, "I see. Be that as it may, you can't put yourself in danger just because there's limited opportunity. If you are to take my place when I'm gone, you must produce an heir when this war is over."

I didn't understand why he was bringing this up now. Once I inherited all of this, I'd love to have kids and give them everything I never had. I wanted to build a perfect world for them.

But at the same time, Ava wasn't sure about having kids, and I wasn't going to make her be a mother if she didn't want to be. And I certainly didn't want to have kids as some sort of *obligation* to the throne. I knew how it felt to have a big responsibility you'd been born into, not chosen yourself, and it was heavy.

"Heirs are irrelevant," I stated.

"They're relevant if we hope to continue our family legacy," Cassiel insisted. "You're the prince, which makes you the brains of the entire operation. You can't have a bullet wound to the brain, or it compromises our entire existence as a society. Furthermore, you dragged Ava-Marie into the line of fire. She isn't just your wife. She's your *princess*. Soon, she will become the spiritual mother of our people, and she's your greatest treasure. You can't bargain with her safety like that ever again, because the monarchy won't survive losing another queen."

"I would never let Ava get hurt," I snarled.

"You almost did," Cassiel reminded me. "Our people look to Ava-Marie above anyone else. Once she completes her spirit ceremony and accepts her role as the mother of our people, she will be able to communicate with the goddesses. Our nation will look to her for answers. She is more vital to the Elves than either of us."

"The Elves have survived without a queen before," I pointed out.

"Barely," Cassiel replied. "You're correct that there hasn't been an Elven queen in years, and look at what has happened to us during that time. We barely survived extinction. We haven't thrived as a society since my wife died. That is why Ava is so important to our people. If she dies, so does our symbol of hope and rebellion."

Guilt twinged in my guts again, but I refused to feel guilty for this. I wasn't going to push my wife into this if she didn't want it.

"We all have different roles in our society," Cassiel continued. "As the Elven heir, you will take the role as our male leader. The Emperor is responsible for governing our society, fighting wars, and making decisions. But you cannot rule alone. The queen is our spiritual guide, and the mother of our race. She consults with the goddesses and sees what the Elves need to do as a people to prosper. As Emperor, you *cannot* make decisions without your queen. She is here to guide you. And so, you can see where I've had trouble without a queen at my side."

"Ava's already got enough responsibility on her shoulders. It's not fair to put this on her. I don't even understand how she's supposed to communicate with the Elven goddesses, when she isn't an Elf herself."

"If you are at all familiar with fae tradition, then you know that intention becomes reality. We came from Edinmyre, from the same place as the fae, so we hold many of the same beliefs. As with the Arcanea, the Elves believe that if you adopt a child or marry into a family, you become part of that family, regardless of your magical talent or genetics," Cassiel explained. "You are my heir, and I chose you to follow my legacy. You chose Ava as your queen. Because we made those choices, the Elves choose you, too. Ava is an Elf because she is your wife, and as we say, the blood of your blood. You have Elven heritage, and she is married to you, which makes her one of our own. She became a part of our race the moment she said her vows. Ava can communicate with our goddesses because they will accept her as their own daughter. It is her fate. The goddesses destined her to do this job before she was born, because she wouldn't be your wife if they *hadn't* picked her."

"Why Ava?" I asked. "Why not Drea? She's married to my father."

"Elves are born into their roles," Cassiel said. "Drea wasn't predestined to become queen, so she never will be. Elves believe that before we are born, our spirit enters into a contract, one that outlines our destiny. Although your father and Drea are partners in *this* lifetime, they are not destined mates. He was destined to be with your mother, but once she passed, her role among our people cannot be handed to someone else who did not agree to it before this lifetime. Cameron and Drea didn't *have* to end up together. It's just something that happened."

"So the gods and the ancestors meet in the Blessed Haven to decide our fates before we're born?" I asked harshly.

"Pieces of your life are predestined, yes," Cassiel confirmed. "But you were there, too. Your soul agreed to all of this."

I scoffed. "That's bullshit. Believing that way allows people to blame the victim so they don't have to work to change things. You can't sit here and tell me I *chose* to be homeless, or that I *chose* to be sent to prison."

"The Elves do not believe in victim blaming." He sounded a bit disgusted that I even suggested it. "This belief system should be utilized to empower you. It allows you to reclaim your power, and to find meaning in things that otherwise disempower you. There is, of course, room for one to experience the world, but certain fates cannot be avoided."

Kallie had said something like that a while ago, because as a fae, she believed in things like destiny. But I wasn't sure.

I shook my head. "I don't know if I can get on board with all of that."

"It's not your fault people treated you the way they did," Cassiel said gently. "But if you see yourself as the one in control, you may find meaning in what you experienced."

"There isn't any *meaning* to trauma," I argued. "It didn't make me *stronger*. It turned me into a criminal. I always had to hide or run from people who wanted to hurt me."

"You must find your strength in that," Cassiel said. "The monarchy mirrors its people, and our lives will reflect their struggles. The Elves have been in a state of poverty, hiding from the authorities of the magical world for years. Perhaps you had to undergo what you did in order to gain a better understanding of life, so you could be a better leader. It's you, Charlie, who will lead the Elves to a greater place."

He was talking about my prophecy. I liked to think I understood the Elves and how they thought, but I couldn't accept that I'd somehow chosen to go through all this shit to get there.

Ava and I were fated to be together— of that, I was certain. But he was wrong about me choosing the rest of it.

I didn't want to hear more about it, so I turned the conversation back on him. "Is that why you never remarried? Because you'd found your fated mate, and even if you met someone else, they'd never be *her*?"

"Yes," Cassiel said, and I sensed a hint of sadness to his tone. "Aponi was it for me. I was only capable of loving one woman, and I'm still only capable of that, even though she's been gone all this time."

I instantly understood how he felt. I didn't know how my father had remarried, because I could never do it. Ava was the only person in this world for me, and my grandmother had been the only person for Cassiel. I felt a connection with him, because we shared that kind of understanding.

"Ultimately, I want you to comprehend how important it is that you keep yourself and your family safe," Cassiel said. "At the moment, we can't communicate with our goddesses. Ava's the only way we'll be able to. She will be undergoing her spiritual process as soon as possible, and you'll have to help her. If you'd have grown up here, I would've taught you this early in life, but we must work with the time we have and start now. There's a hierarchy here within our system you've never dealt with before, and I must teach you how to utilize it, before you make another mistake."

"Maybe that's our problem," I said. "I *didn't* grow up here, so I have to make decisions from the harsh lessons I've learned, Grandpa."

"Please, call me *seanari*," he requested. "It's the Elvish word for grandfather."

The request struck me momentarily. I'd never called him Grandpa to his face, and I hadn't meant for it to slip out.

I didn't know if we were close enough for that yet, or if we'd ever be. But we wanted me to call him *seanari*, because... that meant we were family.

"Okay. *Seanari*," I repeated, testing the word on my tongue. I liked it, and I suddenly felt much closer to him. Almost like I could tell him anything. "But... I'm not like you."

"Do you not want to lead our people?"

I leaned back in my seat. "I do, but I need to do it *my* way. Either deal with that, or take my title from me, but I'm not going to stop doing what I believe is right."

"And that's why you'll make a good Emperor. I've chosen you for a reason, to take over the throne once myself and your father are both gone, should I meet an early end. You weren't merely born into this role; I knew you had the capability to become what our people needed you to be once I learned where you came from and everything you went through in order to survive," Cassiel said. "You went through so much to get to Forevermore, before you even knew what it meant to you, and that proved to me you were willing to fight for our people."

"I was fighting for our people when I broke into that bank."

"Yes. I saw the security footage on the news," Cassiel said in amusement. "It was easy to see that you and Ava were having the time of your life out there. I understand how you feel— your grandmother and I had some great times together when we were young."

"Really?"

"Oh, yes. We loved committing break-ins and all kinds of petty crimes. Your grandmother was a fantastic pickpocket, just like you. You've certainly inherited her skill."

"No one's ever told me I've inherited anything," I said. "I guess we're more alike than I thought."

"You remind me of my younger self, in a lot of ways. But I knew when I had to be a criminal and when I had to be an Emperor," Cassiel said firmly. "We had our fun, but when it came time to take on the bigger jobs, I knew I had to be a leader rather than the one pulling off the heist. You have people here willing to do these things for you, and you need to utilize them."

"How can you utilize people you don't trust? I'm always expecting someone to stab me in the back."

"You don't have to trust everyone who's working for you— in fact, many of them *will* try to stab you in the back. But I'm your grandfather, and you can trust me, because I vow that I won't fail you. I'm going to teach you how to find the right people to get the job done. I'm always going to be here for you, so if you need guidance, all you have to do is ask. You're my grandson. And because you are, I'm going to show you the way."

I'd had many mentors before, but I never felt I had anything to learn from them. I was always more powerful, or they didn't understand my disability, how to make accommodations for me, or how I felt. I had Marty for a few years, but he was a friend, and his guidance only kept me alive. It got me into trouble more than once— it almost got me killed.

My grandfather understood the thrill I got whenever I committed a crime, but he also had power and knowledge that I didn't. He knew how to keep his emotions in check and how to see the crime from a different angle, in order to pull it off in the most effective way. I knew I could learn a lot from him— if I could open myself up enough to allow him to help me.

And if I was really honest with myself, I really needed a role model. I never had a father figure in my life, and Cameron wasn't really there for me, even now.

But my grandfather was willing to step up and help me figure out how to be a man in a world where I'd struggled to learn how to become one by myself. Everyone around the palace really respected my grandfather. I wanted to command that kind of respect, too.

"I'm going to take your advice," I promised. "I'll ask for help next time."

I smirked, thinking about what we'd done. "Even if I *did* have a good time."

"I don't blame you for enjoying yourself. It's in your blood." Cassiel laughed. "But there's a time and a place, and it's important to discern where you're needed and where you need to give orders. When you're attempting these kinds of jobs, you can't be so attached to the outcome, because it won't always go in your favor. And sometimes, you need to have others take the fall for you."

"I guess I'm going to have to get used to that, because with what's at stake, not everyone's going to make it. I just have to make sure Ava and I do."

"Exactly. Now you're thinking like an Emperor," he praised.

We went quiet for a moment, and I listened to the wind whispering through the flowers before I felt pressed to say more. I didn't want to ask him this, but I needed to. "Why didn't my dad show up to the meeting? Everyone else's family was there. It was embarrassing I was the only one without a parent."

"Your father should've been there, but in my honest opinion, I don't think he knows how. Your father never got to be a dad, so he doesn't quite understand what that entails. He thought after you made such a big mistake, it would be best to give you space."

"I don't want space. I want support."

"You don't have to beg your father for his support, because the people who will support you will naturally show up, no questions asked. I'm here for you, and we're family. I can promise that I'm *always* going to be here."

I didn't care about my dad. He could go to hell. But my grandpa was genuine, and he wanted to help me. There was no point in focusing on the father who'd abandoned me when there was one right here offering to take my hand.

"Thanks, *seanari*. It's nice to have somebody who... finally gets me."

Tears welled in my eyes. I didn't want my grandfather to see me cry. I stood and cleared my throat. "Ava's, uh, waiting for me. I should let her know that you and I are all right."

"Of course. Go tend to your wife."

I left the gardens as quickly as I could before my grandfather could witness me break down. I turned the corner and leaned my back against the wall as tears slipped down my cheeks. No one had ever been a parent to me before, and for the first time in over twenty years, I had a relative who actually gave a damn.

Ava nudged me through our bond. *Everything okay, Charlie?*

I wiped my face and took a deep breath. *I'll be fine. Where are you?*

Oberi and I are back in our room.

I'm on my way.

I returned to our room and found Ava in the living area. I sank down onto the sofa and pressed my face into my hands. It had been a long day, and I didn't realize until now how exhausted I was. Oberi jumped onto my lap and licked my face a few times before he lay across my legs.

"What did your grandpa say?" Ava asked gently as she wheeled up beside me. She didn't ask the obvious, but she knew I'd been crying.

I sighed. "He wants to mentor me, and I think I'm ready for it. He's understanding, but he's disappointed I didn't send someone else to do my dirty work. He says you and I have to hang back because we're the leaders. We have roles, I guess. I'm supposed to be giving orders, and you're supposed to be communing with the goddesses and leading us spiritually."

"Pft, screw that," Ava said, trying to lighten the mood. "I'm not going to sit around and *pray* all day. I have a destiny to fulfill."

"I agree, but maybe my grandfather is right. I don't want you to get hurt. Every time we go out there, I'm putting you in harm's way. At least here in the palace, you're surrounded by guards."

Even now, Eldin was stationed just outside the room. The royal family could hardly go anywhere without a guard or two close behind.

"I can't blow off saving the world," Ava argued.

"Neither can I. But you need to hear everything he said."

I went over the entire conversation, and when I finished, I took her hands in mine. "We need to make a decision and stick with it. This is our last chance to walk away from this. I want to follow my grandfather, but you come first. If you don't want to do this, we don't have to be monarchs. I know it's my bloodright, but we're allowed to refuse the throne. You've already got a prophecy to fulfill. You don't have to be their spiritual leader, too. After we find the keys, we can run away from all of this and travel the world, like you wanted. We've got the power to do whatever the hell we want. No one is going to have the ability to stop us."

Silence settled over the room as Ava thought about my suggestion. Finally, she said, "This *is* what I want, Charlie. I want to follow where our destiny takes us. I don't mind being a leader, and I think you were born to be one, too."

I nodded. "That's exactly what my grandfather told me. We need to take his advice. We were sloppy with the bank robbery, and it cost us the key. We can't keep going in guns blazing. We need to be more strategic and fly under the radar. We're going to increase our demigod training sessions, and the next time we pull off a job, we bring the Elvish Associates on board. If we're going to live a life of crime, we can't afford to screw up next time."

I wanted to make my grandfather proud. Letting him down today had been worse than not getting the key.

He believed in me, so I was going to give him something to believe in.

WE MET ALONE in the demigod training room the following week. Marcus was notably missing, but Kallie and Danny were there before Ava and I showed up.

"Marcus got it easy. His mom and dad believe in the *gentle parenting* thing. My mom chewed my ass out, like any strong Malovian woman would do," Kallie groaned. "That was in-between my dad trying to give me pointers about how to break into places better."

"Daddy freaked out and Mama was concerned, but it's not like that's anything out of the ordinary for me," Ava said brightly. "This whole robbery was typical Ava being Ava. They should've expected it, really."

"Awesome for you that your mom didn't explode," Kallie grumbled. "To make it worse, my brother heard about it and called to complain. He doesn't like that I put my diplomat spot at risk for this job."

"Yeah, Ez didn't take it very well, either," Ava said reluctantly. "I was really hoping he wouldn't hear about it. Thanks, supernatural news!"

Kallie sighed. "Good thing you didn't come with us, Danny. You're lucky you don't have to deal with the 'rents."

Danny gave a dark, cold laugh. "Funny you think my Ma and Pops would give a shit."

Oh, Oberi noted softly. *So it's that kind of situation.*

Danny took a step toward me. "What about you, Charlie? I heard your old man didn't show."

"Danny, *shut up,*" Ava hissed.

I pretended I hadn't heard either of them. "I want a report on everyone's powers. I want to know where we're at, so we can discuss our potential. We need to get more strategic with our magic if we're going to figure out who took the vampire key from the vault and steal it from them."

"You don't have any leads?" Danny asked.

"Max combed through the surveillance footage, and the feed was cut the night before we arrived," Ava told him. "Whoever took the key from the vault covered their tracks. It could've been anyone from a number of supernatural groups that know about the Divinity Keys."

"So it's up to us to track them down," I said. "Kallie, how are things on your end?"

"I've been working on my time powers," she replied. "Back at the Institute, the wards and inferichite messed with my abilities, but here, I'm away from all of that, so my time powers are unbound."

Then she growled under her breath, "Or, they *would be*, if Marcus and I were getting along..."

That was a whole can of worms no one wanted to open.

"What can you do without him?" I asked curiously.

"I can stop time for as long as I want, without affecting other demigods," Kallie said. "I've been able to go back years in time, though I haven't ever stuck around long. I don't want to change anything. I can combine my time powers with my portal magic so I can take us anywhere I want in space and time. The only thing I can't seem to do is go into the future. I can only go back, but I'm hesitant to push too far, because my powers aren't super reliable at the moment. They come and go, and because my bond with Marcus remains unsealed, I don't have access to them all the time. If we get into another emergency, there's no promise I'll be able to access everything."

Danny groaned. "This is getting old. No wonder you guys fucked up the bank robbery."

"That wasn't Kallie's fault," I growled.

"Look, I'm just saying, you're presented with a problem, and it's clear what the solution is," Danny said. "If you guys want to unlock your full potential with time travel, you've got to figure out this fated mate situation. Kallie, you either need to break your bond with this guy, or be with him and have it over with, because if you don't fuck *him*, the Warden is gonna fuck *us*. And it won't be no tender loving, but a dick up the asshole straight to Shitsville."

"It's more complicated than that," Kallie sneered.

"Is it?" Danny asked simply. "Do you love him or not? A simple yes or no is all it takes."

"Kallie doesn't need this," I snapped.

"Someone needs to say it!" Danny insisted. "The world is *relying* on her. Kallie can't save the supernatural community if Marcus is dragging her along. From what I've heard, this has been going on for years, and it can't go on any longer. Kallie needs to make a decision on what she wants to do, because we're all tired of waiting here."

"Which she'll do on her *own time*," I stated firmly, before turning back to

Kallie. "We might still be able to use your powers. You've been going back in time, and none of us are getting sick, so it must not affect us like it used to."

"Charlie's right," Ava mused. "My symptoms haven't flared at all since we've been in Ilamanthe, so your powers must not be affecting me the same."

My main hesitation on using Kallie's time powers was that it could put Ava back in the hospital. The last time we tried to change things, Ava's symptoms had flared really badly. I'd never get that night out of my head— how she'd been in so much pain she'd begged me to smother her, and I'd actually reached for the pillow. I wouldn't put Ava through that ever again, not even for the vampire key. But if Kallie had been practicing her powers and it didn't affect us, then perhaps that was a problem that only existed back at the Institute, some side effect of time-traveling around inferichite.

"It's safe now, as far as physical symptoms go," Kallie promised. "My powers are getting stronger, and I can prevent us from getting sick because it's easier for me to do this. Before, you were getting sick because it's difficult magic that I was struggling to pull off, and that was triggering your body because people aren't supposed to be able to move through time and space. The way my powers work, I'm not screwing with the timeline; I'm manipulating your *place* on it. Your bodies were resisting because you aren't supposed to be there, but now I'm powerful enough to put you wherever I want on the timeline without it having an effect on you."

"If your time travel is unrestricted, we can pull off the bank heist again— the *right way* this time," I said. "We'll go in before anyone else gets the keys, so we can steal it before they do."

"We have to be careful," Kallie insisted. "If we take the key before your team can confirm it's still in the vault, we'll have changed the timeline. Then we'll never go to the bank in the first place, and we won't have the idea to go back in time to take it. It could create a paradox, which could be catastrophic. We could get stuck in a time loop, or cease to exist at all."

"When you and I went back in time at the Institute, we merged into the same timeline. We remembered both," I pointed out.

"I told you my time powers don't work the same way as they did at the Institute, and I don't know the full extent of what that entails yet," Kallie reminded me. "I promised before that I'm only going to observe. Changing things is dangerous, as you well know."

Kallie is right, Oberi advised. *Misuse of her power could be worse than catastrophic. She could end up unraveling the fabric of the entire universe.*

"There has to be a way we can use her powers to our advantage," Ava mused. "Can we steal the key without changing anything?"

"We could replace it with a fake," Danny suggested.

"And how exactly would that work?" Kallie asked skeptically.

"If you want to interfere as little as possible, you'd have to intercept the key before it was placed into the vault," Danny said. "Go back to the 1920s and get your former vampire friend to put a fake in the vault, so when your enemies come to steal it, they've got the fake one, and you've taken the real one through time travel."

"That might actually work," Ava said.

"And what if we accidentally change something?" Kallie pressed. "It could prevent us from being born. We don't know what kind of effect something like that could have."

"If no one knows anything has changed, then the events would play out exactly the same, wouldn't they?" Danny asked.

"This might be the only chance we have," I said thoughtfully. "If we can intercept Chancey— I mean Frank Coffrey, the guy he was in his past life— on his way to the bank, he'll put the fake key in the vault and be none the wiser. It's an easy pickpocketing job. Then we just portal the key back here. Nothing has to change except the future."

Kallie remained quiet as she pondered the suggestion. "It *could* work, but are we certain we're willing to risk it?"

"I don't know if we have a choice," Ava said. "It's either risk changing things, or let someone get away with stealing the vampire key. We have no leads, but we do have your magic. You have this power for us to use it, or the gods wouldn't have given it to you."

"Oberi, is this something we can pull off?" I asked.

Oberi huffed. *It's possible, but you'd have to be extremely careful not to change a single thing. Frank can't know you swapped the keys.*

"Oberi's on board," I announced.

Kallie sighed heavily. "I wouldn't be doing this if we had any other choice."

"We don't. Let's get ourselves a key, then," I said.

"I'm coming with," Danny insisted. "You guys fucked up the last robbery. I'm not sitting this one out."

The last thing I wanted was a fight. Danny wasn't going to take no for an answer, so I guess that meant he was coming along.

"Fine," I agreed. "But you answer to me. When I give orders, you follow them, no questions asked. Got it?"

"Understood, *your highness*," Danny said, in the most irritating way he could. He was obviously trying to annoy me.

I didn't like the guy, but I was going to have to work with him. "All right. We're going to need help from the Elvish Associates."

"You know they can't come with us," Kallie pointed out. "Only demigods can travel through time with me, along with Oberi because she's an eternal being. Rishi no longer freezes when I stop time, ever since he stepped into his demigod abilities in the Infernal Underground, so I'm certain he could come, too, since his powers are linked to Marcus. But that's it."

"I'm not suggesting we bring the Associates with us," I said. "But I resolved to let people help us. At the very least, we need to know when Frank made that deposit. Max has the bank records, so she can get us the exact day and time."

"You really think they'll go along with this?" Danny asked. "Everyone was up in arms the first time you tried to rob the bank. It's best if we keep this on the down-low."

"They don't need to know where we're going," I said. "We're just getting information. I'll be right back."

I marched down the hall and took a couple of turns until I reached the door where I'd met with the Elvish Associates many times before. I entered the room and heard the clacking of a keyboard.

"Your highness." Max was startled at my arrival. "What can I do for you?"

"I need you to search the bank records," I told her. "Find me the time and date when Frank Coffrey made his deposit into the vault. We know we're looking at the 1920's, but I want the *exact* date and time."

"I'm on it." Max turned back to the computer.

I expected her to ask questions, but she didn't. She must've felt unease in the silence. "Is everything okay, your highness?"

"Don't you want to know why I'm asking for this information?" I wondered.

"If it was important enough for me to know, you would've told me already," Max said. "The Elvish Associates don't ask questions; we follow orders. We aren't here to be your friends. We're meant to work for you. If you don't want to tell us anything, you aren't obligated to."

"You aren't mad at me for going into the bank without you?"

"I don't have a right to be angry, your highness," Max explained. "If that is what you thought was right, we have to back you up even if we believe it is wrong. From birth, we're taught to follow you without question."

I frowned. "Eddie's made it perfectly clear he's upset with me, and he's my guard."

"Eddie's closer to you than he should be," Max stated plainly. "He's breaking the rules by making his opinion known. He has been taught to comply without question, and that is what he should be doing."

I knew it was a bad idea to get close to Eddie. I needed to start putting some distance between me and my guard. Otherwise, we weren't going to be able to do our jobs properly.

"Here we go..." Max mused. I heard the whir of a printer, and Max handed me a thick sheet of paper with braille letters and numbers across the top— the exact time and date of the deposit.

"Thanks, Max," I told her. "You're a lifesaver."

I returned to the demigod training room, waving the paper at the others. "I've got it!"

We went over everything we knew— when Frank showed up at the bank, how we were going to pull off the switch, and what to do if anything went wrong. When we were ready, I created a solid illusion of a false key, so I could swap it for the real one and Frank would put the fake in the vault. Kallie crafted us period-specific clothes that would help us blend into the 1920s, as well as an oak antique wheelchair for Ava that fit the time period we were headed to.

"This thing is ridiculously uncomfortable," Ava complained as she sat in it.

"You won't have to use it for long," I promised.

Something clinked as Danny withdrew it from his pocket. "Bottoms up."

I scowled, but he'd already downed the liquid. "Drinking on the job, really?"

"Relax, it's not a shot." Danny chuckled. "Though, now that you mention it, I should think about keeping a flask on me at all times for jobs like this. It's a potion to protect me from the sun. I'm a vampire, remember?"

"Whatever you need to get the job done, I guess," I replied. "Let's get ourselves a key."

A portal bloomed in front of us. We traveled through it, and my stomach flip-flopped the way it always did in response to Kallie's time powers. The sounds around us changed as we were transported somewhere outside the palace. Chatter filled the air around us, and I heard the honk of a horn, but it was higher pitched than I was used to.

"We're definitely in the past," Ava noted. "All the men are wearing suits, and the women are dressed in day coats and flapper dresses. The cars here are accurate for the era, and so are the advertisements lining the buildings."

I was born for the 1920s! Oberi cried. Look at all the hats!

"Can we stop it with the hats?" I demanded. "We're here for the key."

"We're three blocks from the bank, outside the boundary of wards. We've arrived just a few minutes before Frank makes the deposit," Kallie said. "He should be around here somewhere. Come on."

We roamed through the streets until we were a block from the bank. We were careful to avoid other people, as to not interfere with anything in the past. It wasn't easy maneuvering the old wheelchair through the streets, either— things had definitely improved in that area since our time.

"I shouldn't have come. I'm attracting more attention than I should," Ava said timidly.

"You're fine, pidge." I cringed as a man passed by us and gave us a warm greeting.

"There's Frank, across the street," Ava said. "I recognize him from the vision."

Danny clapped me on the back. "Charlie, you're up."

I started across the street, keeping my head low.

He's approaching the crossroads, Ava told me through the bond. *On your left. You're ten feet away. Keep going.*

Her instructions helped me hone in on my target. *On target... Three... two... one...*

I expected to bump into him and make the transfer, but a soft breeze passed by me, then... nothing.

I lost him! I panicked.

What do you mean? Ava demanded. *He was right there! Did you make the transfer?*

I never touched him. Where'd he go?

He's past you now.

I hurried back to my friends on the other side of the street. I grabbed them and pulled them into a quiet alleyway. "I don't know what happened. I had him, and then..."

"It's like you went straight through him," Kallie finished for me.

"But I can touch all of you," I said. "What's going on? Are your powers slipping?"

"It's not that," Kallie replied. "My powers are working fine, but I've never gone back this far before. This is long before we were born, and we shouldn't exist in this timeline. I'm not sure we can influence anything around us outside our own lifetimes. We can touch *each other*, because we're from the same time, but as for everything else... it's like we're ghosts."

"That guy tipped his hat at us on the street," Ava pointed out. "We must be able to be seen and heard, but we can't touch anything. Hold on. Let me try something."

Flames crackled in Ava's palm, but she gave a thoughtful sigh. "My Fire doesn't burn anything."

"Oberi, why didn't you tell us?" I asked.

I don't know all the rules, he defended. *Mutabeecha exist throughout all time and space. I've never had this issue before. Let me try to change something.*

He skittered away. I heard a *crash*, like the sound of a garden pot falling from a windowsill. He came tottering back and said, *I still appear to be solid, and I can influence things, but none of you can. It makes sense, as I am eternal. I was alive at this point on the timeline. Though where I was, I cannot say.*

"If you exist everywhere, then you shouldn't have this same problem," Ava pointed out. "Let me try again."

Ava wheeled away for a moment. Her tone was disappointed as she said, "I can't touch any of the flowerpots— or anything else here, for that matter. The ground is solid, but it doesn't look like anything else is. I think people from this period can see my wheelchair, but not touch it, because we brought it here from our time."

I explained what Oberi had said, and Kallie groaned. "So we're intangible if we time travel outside of our own time period. Great."

Ava huffed. "We're going to have to think of something else— dammit, where the *fuck* is Danny?"

I whirled around, but I couldn't feel the pulse of his magic anywhere.

"He's fucking ditched us!" Ava sneered.

"We need to find him!" Kallie cried. "If he changes anything, he compromises reality!"

"I'm right here." Danny's voice came from around the corner, followed by the sound of footsteps. "And I brought a friend."

Though I couldn't touch anything outside of my timeline, my Elven magic could sense the vampire in front of us.

Kallie smacked Danny's arm. "You *idiot*! You know you can't change anything!"

"We *need* that key," Danny insisted. "I came along to make sure you got it this time. If we can't touch him, we can at least talk to him."

Ava's wheels inched closer to the vampire. "Chancey?"

"I don't know anyone by that name," the vampire said. I didn't recognize his voice, but I sensed something in him that reminded me of our friend. He still spoke with a New York accent, which was nearly odd. "Though, I believe I understand why you would call me that."

"I explained everything to him," Danny said. "He's going to give us the key."

"Fucking hell, Danny," I growled. "You used your powers on him, didn't you?"

Danny could see people's weaknesses by tapping into their desires. He was abusing his power.

"Look, everyone's got a weakness, all right?" Danny said nonchalantly. "And I've got my strengths, so I'm gonna use 'em. This guy needed to be convinced, so I told him what he needed to know."

The rules of time travel weren't clear, and it made my head spin. Outside our own timeline, we could be seen and heard, and my magic still worked to sense the world around me, but it was like we weren't *completely* here in the flesh. Danny's powers worked through perception, so I guess his powers were still good, too.

"I'm not gonna hand over the key without proof I can trust you," Frank said.

"You can trust us," Ava promised. "I'm Ava-Marie, and this is my husband, Charlie. You don't recognize us, but we used to be your friends in a past life. I was Lucille, and Charlie was Lawrence. We died in a car accident trying to get a special key away from Masci Taurus. Our friend is Kallie— she has the ability to time travel— and she brought us here so we could get the key before anyone else could steal it from us."

"I don't know if I believe you," he said skeptically. "You're gonna have to give me more than that."

Something sparked inside my mind. It was a memory, buried deep in my subconscious. I knew it had to be something from my past life that my soul had carried with me into this one. I'd never recalled it before, but the memory ran smoothly off my tongue. "The night before I died, you told me you didn't want to go on that job to steal the vampire key. You thought it was a bad idea, and you had somebody back home you were sweet on. You wanted to go into hiding. But I promised the pay was good, and we had to, so I made you promise not to back out. You swore on your lover's life that you'd see it through. Irene, wasn't it?"

Frank's voice was thick with a combination of shock and emotion. "Yeah, I remember. I never told anybody else about that night and what was said, and I didn't tell anybody I loved Irene but Lawrence. He would be the only one who knew. I guess I believe ya. Not like I got anything more to live for, anyway."

"What do you mean?" Ava asked.

"Irene is gone," Frank rasped out. "The wrong people knew what we were doing with the key and went back to Brooklyn to take her out. Slaughtered her in a club right in the middle of her song. If I find out who did it... but it doesn't matter now, does it?"

His coat rustled as he pulled something from his pocket.

He's got a box, Oberi told me. *The same one we found in the vault.*

"This key was meant for you, and I made a promise to ensure it got back to you. It's yours," Frank offered.

I pocketed my fake illusion key, because it was no use to us anymore, seeing as we were outside our own timeline. It was nothing more than an image here, the same way we were.

"Keep the box," I told him. "You need to put it in the vault as if it held the key, because we need to keep things as similar as we can to the way they originally played out. If you don't make the deposit, we won't go looking for it, and we won't come back here to get the key from you. We have to do everything the same as it happened the first time, except we're taking the key."

"I can't say I get it, but I figure you know what you're doing. Lawrence always had some kind of crazy plan. Just wish they didn't go so wrong as often as they did," Frank said.

Apparently I'd taken that trait into my next life, too. I wasn't going to keep making the same mistakes.

He opened the box. Oberi took the key in his mouth, since he was the only one of us who could interact with this timeline.

"Thank you," I said, and Kallie cast a time portal. It bloomed in front of us. Its power was so strong I stumbled back a few steps.

Oberi went to step through it first, but a loud *thwack* sounded through the alley. Oberi was blasted backward, and he gave a pained whimper as he smashed into the side of a building. Everyone gasped in unison, and I felt my insides twist in fear.

"Oberi!" I rushed to him and knelt down beside my Familiar.

Oberi shook his head as I cradled him in my arms. *Well, that was quite the experience.*

"What happened?" I demanded.

I tried to pass through the portal, but it won't let me through with the key, Oberi said sourly. *I don't think the Divinity Keys are capable of traveling through time. Their magical ability overpowers the timeline, so they can't be moved through it.*

"What's he saying?" Kallie asked. "My portal feels fine!"

"Oberi says the Divinity Keys can't be taken through time," I translated. "They must be too powerful."

"So what are we going to do?" Kallie asked in frustration.

"What if we hide it somewhere else, so we can find it in the future?" Ava asked.

"That changes too much," Kallie insisted. "We've already altered enough as it is. If we hide it somewhere else, who's to say the Warden won't find it before we make it back to our time? That could change *everything.*"

"There is no safer place than that bank vault," Frank said. "If I had put the key into the vault in your timeline, then I'm gonna do it again. I can't delay it any longer. I'll place the key in the vault, as it should have been all along. It'll be safe for you there until you figure out another plan."

"There has to be another way," I insisted.

"There isn't," Ava said. "This plan failed. There are too many variables we can't account for. We have to follow through with how things should've been and come up with something else."

It's our only option, Oberi agreed, before giving Frank the key once again.

"Go," Kalie pressed. "We've already wasted too much time."

"Guess I'll see ya in another life." Frank took off at vampire speed and was gone.

"Are you *crazy*?!" Danny yelled. "You can't send him off! We were *so close*."

"Hardly," Kallie said flatly. "You're a fucking moron, you know that? You don't know what you could've changed by telling him about us!"

"It doesn't matter if I broke the rules, because I actually did something about— whoa!" Danny cut off as Kallie pushed him through the portal. He gave a scream as he tumbled into it and through time.

"Let's get out of here," Kallie said.

Before Ava went through, she said to me, "Should we have warned Frank? We know that he's killed after he puts the key in the vault."

I hesitated. "If we did that, Frank would've survived, and the Chancey from our timeline wouldn't have been born, because Frank's soul wouldn't have incarnated into our angel friend. And my gut is telling me Irene was one of Ivy's past lives."

"I agree. They deserve to be together in our timeline," Ava said. "It's good we didn't say anything, even if it means Chancey's past life has to end."

We followed Kallie through the portal, and my stomach churned until we were back in the training room.

Danny must've tripped coming through the portal, because he was on the floor. I marched straight up to him and grabbed him by the collar. I immediately siphoned his vampire strength without thought and yanked him upright, pinning him to the wall.

"Are you insane?" I roared. "You were supposed to follow my orders! Do you have any idea what you might've done?!"

"Things didn't go according to plan," Danny said in a casual tone. "You said anything to get the job done. I had to improvise."

"Improvise?!" I growled. "You didn't just compromise the mission, you could've screwed up all of time! I'm not just the leader of this team; I'm a fucking prince! You need to learn to do as I tell you!"

Danny shrugged. "Well, you're not *my* prince. I didn't vote for you."

"Princes aren't voted for, dumbass," Kallie grumbled.

"Either way, I'm a vampire, not an Elf. I don't have to do what he says," Danny argued. "As far as I'm concerned, we're equals."

"Like hell. You are *never* coming with us on a mission again," I growled.

"Is that so?" Danny asked coolly.

"*I'm* in charge here." To reinforce my statement, I slammed my fist into the wall near his head. Danny barely flinched, but a piece of cinder block clattered to the floor.

"Charlie," Ava said softly. The sound of her voice was the only thing that slowed my heart rate. "Danny made a mistake, but we still need him."

"You might want to listen to your girlfriend," Danny teased.

I didn't know what kind of threats he was *trying* to make, because I was certain I could take him.

"That's my *wife*, you jackass," I sneered.

Danny chuckled. Then it hit me what he was doing. Ava was my weakness. Every fucking time. Nobody talked down to my wife, and he fucking knew it'd get on my nerves.

I dropped Danny and stomped toward the other side of the room. "He can be useful somewhere else."

"He could help," Ava insisted.

The door opened, and Kallie announced, "The rest of the palace looks to be in order. I don't think we changed anything significant."

I hadn't even realized she'd left the room; I'd been so angry.

"See? It's fine," Danny said.

He was so fucking cocky. I hated him.

"That doesn't change that you went against my orders," I said.

"Look, we're back, we're all in one piece, and we get a second shot at it," Danny stated nonchalantly. "It's all good."

I pressed my fingers to my eyes. This kid didn't get it. He was a poor substitute for Marcus, who I really wished had showed his ass up today. Where the hell was he?

I breathed a heavy sigh. "All right, time for Plan B. We need to time travel back to when the key was in the vault the night before the robbery and steal it without incident. Our first robbery attempt didn't work, so we'll have to come up with a different plan."

"Easy," Danny said. "You guys made it too complicated last time with all your disguises and potions. You had too many moving parts. *Of course* something was bound to go wrong."

"And how exactly is robbing a bank easy?" I demanded. "Have you ever done it before?"

Danny noticeably ignored my second question. "Look, we don't need disguises if we go back far enough that no one will recognize us. Kallie can get us as far back in our *own* timelines as possible, when we're technically still babies. We won't be on anyone's radar at that point."

"We're not going to become babies if we travel that far back, will we?" Ava asked.

"No. I've gone back pretty far, and my age never changed," Kallie said. "Our child selves will still exist out there somewhere. We just can't run into them, or we'd create a paradox."

When Kallie and I time traveled at the Institute, there were two versions of us— the original us from the timeline we first experienced, and the version of us that was time traveling. It was only when we returned to the present that our timelines melded together. We'd show up back wherever our present selves were after the timeline changed.

It was a good sign that we'd returned to the demigod training room just now, because it meant any minor changes we might've made had still led us to the same place we'd left, here in the present. But I was wary about continuing to fuck with this, because I didn't think we could keep doing it without consequences.

"All we have to do is get into the bank. Then I work some of my compulsion magic, and we get into the vault," Danny said. "I can compel the employees to forget, so they never suspect a thing. Simple as that."

"Don't you think they have wards against compulsion?" I asked.

"I'm a demigod," Danny said. "Their wards aren't going to contain my abilities."

"Marcus is a demigod, too, and he couldn't break the wards into the vault," I pointed out.

"I don't need to break any wards," Danny stated. "I just need to get in without setting off any alarms."

"The wards prevent Kallie from portaling closer than three blocks, or it'll alert security," I added.

"Because she's working against the bank," Danny said. "I'd be working my magic on *individuals*, so it's not going to set anything off."

"I think Danny's right," Ava said. "His magic is different from what we used before. I think we could slip under the radar."

I was skeptical of Danny's plan, but it was clear we needed him. We didn't have compulsion the first time around, but it was insane of us to have access to it and not use it. I didn't have to be his friend, but I could sure as hell use him to my advantage.

"You follow orders this time," I warned. "I don't care if you're a demigod— I *will* kill you. I won't stand to have you compromise our mission."

"Fuck, man, okay," Danny said, and I *swear* he had to be rolling his eyes. "You're the boss. God."

I hardly believed him.

"All right. Danny's the youngest, and since he's nineteen, then I'm taking us back eighteen years," Kallie said. "We'll all be kids, and we'll be within our own timeline. We'll be able to interact with our surroundings this time, but no one will recognize us. Don't touch anything or talk to anyone unless *absolutely* necessary."

We must've gone over the new plan a dozen times before we tried it. We weren't screwing anything up. When Danny started to complain he was getting bored and we just needed to do it already, Kallie created another portal, and the five of us stepped through.

Chatter filled the air, and the vehicles in the distance sounded more modern than the ones I'd heard in the 1920s.

Like when I'd time traveled at the Institute, I had a strange sense of *déjà vu* as we started through the streets toward the bank. Oberi stayed close to my side, and I pushed Ava's chair across the sidewalk.

We reached the bank, and I paid close attention to my surroundings as we entered.

"The wanted posters are gone," Ava remarked. "That's a good sign."

Nobody said much else as we marched straight past the teller windows and into the hall toward the vault, as if we belonged there. Nobody stopped us or questioned us, until we turned a corner.

"*Excuse moi,*" a female voice said. She said something in French, then switched over to English. "You cannot be back here. I will need to see some form of ID— ah!"

She gave a gasp, then her tone turned soft. "Right this way."

"What did you do?" I hissed at Danny.

"I only pricked her with a needle I keep on my person," Danny said. He sounded really chill about it, too. "I only need a drop of blood to work my compulsion magic. It's not going to hurt her. She'll just be confused when she comes out of it later."

I heard footsteps coming our way, and I leaned over to Danny to whisper, "We need two employees to get into the vault."

"Yeah, yeah. I got it. You can unclench your mangina."

A man let out a sharp hiss, and I heard something drip onto the floor— probably blood. A second later, he was following beside us. The two employees stopped at the vault, and Danny compelled them to run their scans and enter the code.

The vault opened, and Danny took a casual step back. "So simple. You should've brought me along the first time."

Fucking hell. I couldn't believe it actually worked. There were no alarms, no sirens— no one shouting at us through a megaphone.

"The box is here!" Kallie cried. She rushed over to the pedestal.

Oberi stepped into the vault beside me and sniffed the air. *Something is wrong.*

I stilled. I felt it, too. "Hold on," I told Kallie before she could open the box. "The magic is off."

When we entered the vault before, I could feel the residual magic from the vampire key, Oberi said. *This time, I can't feel anything.*

My stomach hollowed, and I slowly approached the pedestal. Hands trembling, I opened the glass case, then lifted the top of the box.

My fingers met nothing but the soft silk of the pillow inside. The key was gone.

"Frank conned us!" Danny cried.

"No, he wouldn't," Ava insisted, though she sounded unsure. "Something else must've happened."

I grabbed the box and twisted it around in my hands. We were too late... again.

Fuck!

I threw the box at the wall, and it clattered to the ground.

Kallie hastily picked it up and put it back on the pedestal. "Calm down. We'll figure this out."

"Not from this time period," I snarled. "Let's go back home. Danny, release the employees and get this vault sealed back up again. Kallie, get us out of here."

"It's cute you're addressing me by name, toots," Danny cooed.

If I ever wanted to hit somebody, it was him right now.

We returned to the demigod training room. That was good news, because it meant when we went back eighteen years, we didn't change enough to affect our location in the present.

It was the only bit of good news I'd had all day.

"Fucking hell!" I roared as I paced around the room. "What is it going to take to get this key?!"

"I don't understand what went wrong," Ava mused. "Frank had to put the key in the vault, because the box was there when we arrived. The key should've stayed there until the night before we broke in, when someone else stole it out from under us. Except this time, someone got to it decades before."

"We can't know that for sure," Danny pointed out. "Frank could've changed his mind."

"Great," I snarled. "You scared him off. I knew telling him about us was a mistake."

"There's a way to figure that out," Kallie stated. "But we're going to need Chancey's help."

Kallie left the room. I paced the area impatiently, waiting for her to come back. I was so pissed off nobody said anything— not even dumbass Danny.

She came back a half an hour later with Chancey in tow. "Chancey's agreed to do another past-life regression, so we can learn what happened after we spoke to him in Paris."

"I'll help in any way I can," Chancey offered. "But this better not hurt."

"It'll be just like taking a nap," Kallie promised.

Kallie conjured a bed and instructed him to lie down. I heard the rustling of pages as she rifled through a book.

"What spell are you going to use?" Ava asked.

"The same one from my grimoire that Marcus used on me months ago to make me remember my life as Princess Amalie," she responded.

"We shouldn't use that spell," I immediately objected. "It went wrong the last time we tried."

"The spell has to be performed by an Unseelie sorceress, and I've got Unseelie blood. We fucked it up last time because Marcus cast it. This time, it'll go right," Kallie promised.

I hoped it did, because we needed some confirmation. Kallie took a breath and began to recite. "*Phantom Doe of Shadow, Neva, Goddess of Time, take us back through distant past, make clear through path divine. Answers found in ancestors, hidden soon be known, through graves of ancient ones we dig, blood to blood, bone to bone.*"

Unlike the last time we performed this spell, everything was still and quiet. No monsters or spirits appeared to interrupt the meditation, and Chancey didn't start to shake. I didn't hear anything except Chancey's soft breaths. Everyone else was too on edge to even dare to make a sound.

"Go back to the time when you were Frank," Kallie instructed. "What do you see?"

"I see you," Chancey said calmly in his trance-like state. "All four of you and Oberi. We're standing in an alleyway, talking about the key."

"Good," Kallie encouraged. "What happened after our meeting ended?"

"I see myself approaching the *Banque Surnaturelle de Paris*," Chancey recounted. "The employees are leading me to the vault."

"Is the key with you?" Kallie asked.

"Yes," Chancey confirmed. "I'm looking at it now, and I'm closing the box. I placed it on a pedestal and left it there. I'm walking out of the vault, and it's sealing behind me."

"How is that possible?" Ava asked. "If this vision's correct, the key should've been there."

"Shh..." Kallie quieted her, before addressing Chancey. "What happened after you left the vault?"

A beat passed before Chancey answered. "It's hard to tell. I'm getting two sets of memories."

"He shouldn't remember two timelines," I pointed out. "He isn't a demigod."

"But we're using *my* demigod magic to bring his memories to the surface," Kallie reminded me. "So it's entirely possible he'll recall two sets of memories, because he lived two different timelines after we spoke with him, and he's channeling those memories through my demigod abilities. Chancey, what happened to you in the first timeline?"

"Someone was following me," he admitted. "They caught up to me after I left the bank, and slaughtered me on the street. They'd must've thought I still had the key on me. I remember thinking before I died that I'd gotten to the vault just in time, because they wouldn't find the key now."

"What happened the second time you died?" Kallie asked.

"I was delayed getting to the bank by a few minutes," Chancey said. "I remember feeling like I was being watched when I went into the vault. I think whoever was following me caught up with me at the bank. They must've seen what I'd done with the key. I went to a vampire bar afterward. That's where they found me."

"Chancey, do you know who killed you?" Kallie wondered.

"I don't," he said. "Both times I died, they approached me from behind and cut off my head."

"Thank you, Chancey. You can wake up now." Kallie led him out of the meditation, and we gathered around to discuss what we learned.

I felt Chancey shiver beside me. "You okay?"

"Peachy, man," Chancey grumbled. "It was a blast, remembering someone knocked my head off twice."

"Sorry," I apologized. "We had to know."

"Yeah, yeah." He crossed his arms. "But I ain't doing it again."

"It had to be Masci Taurus and his men," Ava said immediately. "They were already on Frank's tail, ever since Charlie and I— or Lawrence and Lucille, rather— died in that car wreck. Only a strong supernatural could behead a vampire so effortlessly, which means the person who killed him was either another vampire, a shifter, or an angel."

"My money's on the angels," Chancey agreed. "That was too clean a hit to be anyone else."

"Let me get this straight," I said. "In the *original* timeline, Frank made it to the bank and put the key in the vault. Masci's men found him after he left the bank, without any clue where he'd gone with the key. The key remained in the vault for the next hundred-and-twenty years until someone was tipped off the night before we went in for the robbery. We don't know who stole it— it could've been anyone."

"Yes, but things changed after we talked to Frank," Kallie said.

"The second time around, we delayed Frank a few minutes by talking to him. Masci's men caught up, and saw him put the key in the vault," I mused. "Then they stole it, before hunting him down to kill him at the vampire bar."

"That lines up with what I saw," Chancey confirmed.

"So we're in a *new* timeline now," I said. "One where the key has been in the hands of the angels all this time."

"If things changed, did we even rob the bank?" Ava wondered.

Yes, Oberi said. *It will take some time for you to recall the events, but I remember them. In our new timeline, Max was able to confirm through inventory records that the box was in the vault. You went to get it, but when you got there, you found nothing in the box, just like before. Everything else played out the same.*

Could the Warden have the key then? Ava asked. *He could've inherited it from his father.*

I don't believe so, Oberi said. *Esther still showed up looking for it, so the Warden is on the hunt for it as well. He too believed the key to be in the vault.*

Ava quickly told the others what Oberi said.

"Even so, the Warden is closer to the key than ever, because of what we changed," I growled. "We didn't know which of our enemies took the key in the original timeline, but in this one, it's got to be the angels."

"It makes sense that Masci wouldn't have given the key to the Warden," Kallie pointed out. "The Warden killed his father. They weren't on good terms."

"That doesn't mean the Warden won't find it among the other angels," I said. "Masci must've given it to someone before he died. The Warden is closer to the key than ever before because of what *we* changed. We can't keep doing this. Going back in time isn't safe, nor effective. If we keep trying, we're going to seriously screw something up— even worse than we already have. Regardless, we can safely assume the angels have the key, so we've just got to focus on the future and follow the clues to its next location."

"I want to go back and see who killed Frank, just to be sure," Kallie argued.

"*No,*" I stated firmly. "The last time we went back, we changed things. The key ended up with the angels this time, who are too close to the Warden. If you travel back again, you could change something else, and the key could end up in the hands of the Warden himself this time. We can't afford for that to happen, because if he has it, we'll never get it back."

"I understand what you're saying," Kallie said. "That was a close call— too close. But what other options do we have?"

"I'll put the Elvish Associates on gathering intel about Masci Taurus and his people," I offered. "They can find out who was working for him at the time, and who might've been involved."

"I'll hold off on time traveling for now while your team investigates. But if this takes too long, I'm going back myself," Kallie insisted. "I'm not taking any of you back anymore, unless..."

Kallie trailed off after realizing she'd said too much, but I'd heard the heartbreak in her tone. *Unless it's to save my mate's life.*

I didn't blame her. I'd do the same for Ava. Hell, I'd *tried* to do the same for her last semester.

Time travel was dangerous. Kallie couldn't keep casting it, but she *had* to do something about her and Marcus. This relationship was killing them both, and it was really affecting the team.

"I'm making the call. No more time traveling," I stated sternly.

This time, the team *better* fucking follow my orders. I was tired of not being taken seriously.

"I guess if this is a bust, I'm going back to my room to play with myself," Danny joked, and he collided into my shoulder to swagger away. "I suggest you all do the same."

My fists became tighter as I heard him slam the door to the training room shut. I couldn't believe the nerve of this guy. I hoped we found the rest of the keys soon, because I couldn't take working with him for long.

"It's always a bust, isn't it?" Kallie said hopelessly. "My time powers might as well not exist at all, for all the good they do."

It wasn't like her to get so down on herself. Danny's words from earlier had to be taking a heavy toll. He didn't understand this situation with Marcus wasn't as easy as he'd made it seem, but Kallie was definitely taking his words to heart.

"Do you want to talk?" Ava asked her softly.

"Let's just go somewhere," Kallie noted sullenly. "Somewhere *without* men. The Ladies' Court has never looked better."

Ava checked in with me, and I told her through our bond, *Go on, pidge. She needs someone to listen right now.*

I'll be back for dinner, like we promised, Ava responded telepathically, before she said aloud, "The female area of the palace is all yours. We can bitch about it in the hot tub. Come on, Oberi."

Oberi changed, and her hooves clattered against the floor behind Ava and Kallie as they left the training arena.

I sighed and rubbed my face before I headed back to my quarters, where my designated court lived. Kallie wasn't the only one who needed to talk, and I had to check up on Marcus. It really worried me that he hadn't shown up for practice.

At this point, Marcus was more like my little brother than he was my friend. We'd been through a lot together, and I was super protective of him. I really cared about him, and I wanted him to be okay. I wasn't ashamed of letting anyone know that. So if I had to bang his door down to get through to him, I would.

I knocked on the door to his suite. No answer came, except for the faint sound of a cat's meow.

"Marcus, open up," I called. "I know you're in there."

"No, I'm not— fuck. Go away!" he shot back.

I grabbed the door handle, fully expecting to have to work some magic to get it to open, but the door swung open effortlessly.

Marcus scratched away at a sketch pad, and the couch squeaked as he shifted. "I'm not really up for visitors," he stated flatly.

Rishi hurried over to me and began purring as he rubbed against my leg.

"Rishi seems to want company," I said as I sat beside Marcus. Rishi jumped onto my lap and kept nudging my hand.

I waited for Marcus to say something, but he didn't. I knew I would have to make the first move. "You weren't at our demigod lesson."

"So?" Marcus asked. "I'm sure you figured that out on your own."

"It wasn't a question," I said. "We needed you there, man."

"No, you didn't."

"Of course we did."

Marcus slammed his pencil down and tossed his sketchbook aside. "You don't have to lie to make me feel better. I know what the *Villain's Club* actually thinks of me. None of you really want me around."

"That's not true," I insisted. "Marcus, you're as much a part of our team as anyone. Hell, there wouldn't *be* a Villain's Club without you."

"Of course there would. I don't contribute anything, and I don't have a purpose. I'm supposed to have all these powers, but I'm not as talented as you guys."

"Marcus, that's bull, and you know it," I said. "You can break wards, summon spirits, read minds—"

"Hardly!" he cried. "I can't hone in on anything anymore. It's all useless chatter. I can't puppeteer people like Alistair can, or survive a knife to the heart like Chancey, and I'm not fast or strong like Ivy. Even Ez has healing powers, and Opal can talk to marine life. You're better off with average supernaturals than you are with me."

"It's our differences that make us stronger," I encouraged. "You've got all sorts of strengths. You were incredible when we broke out of the Institute. Your magic was unstoppable."

"I can't even remember doing that, so thanks for bringing it up that I lost my mind," he growled. "Apparently I can't access my full abilities unless I'm fucking crazy."

I took a breath. "Even if you can't pull off everything a warlock could possibly do, it doesn't make you weak."

"You don't understand the potential I have!" Marcus insisted. "Witch powers are diverse, and most witches and warlocks only have one specialty. When Mother Miriam came to me to unlock my powers, she said I was different. Most witches can't harness more than one power because it's too much for them. Their bodies will give out. My goddess said that I'd be able to harness them all. She said I needed the power of all five Casts to accomplish what I was put on this earth to do. I didn't get it at the time, but I understand now that she gave me access to all Miriamic powers because I'm a demigod. And my body can handle it... but I don't think my mind can."

"Is that what this is about?" I wondered. "You're afraid you'll never reach your full potential because of your depression? Marcus, you've barely scratched the surface, and you're already the most powerful warlock I've ever known."

"Maybe... I don't know. I met with my parents."

Several moments passed, but he didn't elaborate.

"What happened?" I asked carefully.

"They told me they knew I was a demigod." Marcus shot to his feet and began pacing around the room. "They've known all this time, ever since I was a baby."

"Why didn't they say something earlier?" I demanded. I hated Lucas and Nadine for keeping this from him.

"They wanted to— or so they said," Marcus admitted. "I guess there was some sort of magic, a curse, that prevented them from telling me— a spell so powerful even my mom couldn't break it. I had to figure it out on my own before they could talk about it freely. I just feel... betrayed. Even if it isn't their fault, they could've tried harder to get around the curse, you know?"

"Maybe they did try," I offered. "We don't know the parameters of this spell you mentioned. Marcus, I know your parents really care about you."

He scoffed. "Yeah, I'm sure they care about the *screw-up* of the family. My parents were *so proud* of me when I came home with a mark from all five Casts. They said I had to be destined for great things. But then my magic got out of control, and I killed all those people in the town square. If they could've at least *hinted* at something, maybe I would've understood the extent of my powers. Maybe I could've controlled them better."

"Marcus, I think they *did* try to tell you," I pointed out. "And you know what else? They fought for you. You told me your mom spoke to the rest of the witch's council to get you sent to the Darke Institute. I'm sure she didn't know how bad it was there and just wanted to see her son get help at a reform school. She did what she thought was best for you, because your coven was going to hang you if you didn't go. Your parents didn't abandon you, and neither have we. I don't understand why you're afraid people are going to leave when they never have in the past."

Marcus sank back into the couch. "I don't know, to be honest. I ask myself that question every damn day. The best guess I've got is that I was abandoned in a previous lifetime, and now my soul is permanently damaged."

I wanted to tell him he wasn't damaged, and to knock some sense into him, but I didn't think that would help. Marcus didn't need tough love right now. He needed to be heard.

"I've spent most of my life feeling broken, too," I admitted. "But if there's one thing I've learned about damage, it's that it can be healed. Yeah, maybe things won't ever look the same, and there will always be scars to remind you what happened, but you don't have to keep bleeding out."

Marcus didn't say anything, but he rubbed his hands together, like he was really thinking about what I said.

"Maybe you should take a break," I suggested.

"Take a break from saving the world?" he asked skeptically. "I'm not sure that's helpful to anyone."

"If it helps you, then it's worth it," I said. "You can't be out here saving the world when doing so keeps busting your wounds back open. You need time to heal, Marcus."

"I can't just step away," he insisted. "What will I do with myself? I'll get bored, and that'll just make things worse. Everyone else here has a super important job. You're a prince, Ava's a princess, Opal's her lady, Kallie's a court diplomat, Ez is studying medicine... and what am I doing? Sitting on my ass making art. Like that helps anyone."

"Art is important," I insisted. "And it's not like Ivy, Chancey or Alistair have jobs."

"Ivy's keeping a low profile, Alistair's busy experimenting with his magic, and Chancey doesn't *want* any responsibilities. He's happy to sit on the couch with a beer watching baseball for the rest of his immortal life," Marcus shot back at me. "But me? I can't just... bum around. I need something to *create*. But that's not saving lives. No one's even bothered to ask if I'm needed. So obviously, I'm not."

Marcus needed a job here in Ilamanthe. Something that wasn't as stressful as demigod work, and something where he could put his talents to good use. I was prince, so I was going to have to come up with something.

"I need a court bard," I said quickly. "Someone needs to sing and entertain the palace. We've got to keep spirits up around here."

"I can't keep a tune to save my life," Marcus said glumly. "You know that."

"So put on plays," I offered. "I'll be in the front row on opening night."

"Maybe..." Marcus mused, but I could already tell he was liking the idea.

Music, art, and theater were Marcus' healing modalities. Maybe if he spent enough time on his art, it would help him through some of his internal struggles.

"Come *on*, Marcus. We need to keep morale up around the palace," I insisted. "The war really brings people down. Giving them some entertainment could help."

"I guess you're right," Marcus finally said. "You guys have been telling me for a long time I need to work on myself, and now's the time to actually do that. Plus, I really *could* use a break from my powers. It's too much."

"That's good news," I encouraged.

"But," he added, and my stomach dropped, "I need to stay away from the team while I get my stuff in order."

"We still want you around," I promised.

"It's not that," Marcus said. He got to his feet and gave a sigh. "I can't work out my shit and save the world at the same time. I'll feel better once I figure myself out, and I need to do that alone. I can't talk to any of you guys for a while. I need... space."

The suggestion made me feel uneasy, but I knew protesting would only drive him further into his shell. We needed a healed Marcus if we were going to get anywhere— not a broken one.

"All right," I finally said as I stood. "If you need anything, my door is always open."

"I know," Marcus replied.

I reached out an arm for him, and although he hugged me back, his form remained rigid.

I left the room feeling disheartened. I wasn't entirely sure Marcus was taking my suggestion seriously. It more or less felt like he was agreeing to work on himself in an attempt to avoid us. I *really* hoped his time away helped him feel better, because I cared about him, and we all needed him. The team felt broken without him.

And no matter what he thought, we couldn't win this war without Marcus.

ava-marie

EIGHT

Ilamanthe smelled like fresh linens and sunlight. I awoke slowly, enjoying the sound of the birds outside as the curtains blew in the wind. Charlie was asleep on my chest, an arm wrapped protectively around my waist.

Last night was great. We'd messed around in the Sanctuary before we'd moved to the bed. I didn't want to stop, but I'd been so worn out I'd fallen asleep after he'd blown my mind. Charlie really knew how to push me to my limits.

I let a hand fall back above my head as I thought about how amazing life had become. Sure, there was a supernatural war going on, but I'd nearly forgotten about it here in Ilamanthe. We were doing all we could to stop the Warden, looking for the vampire key and practicing our demigod powers, but in the meantime, there was always something new to explore in the city or the palace. We got to spend a lot of time together with our friends, without having to watch our backs, and the Elves took care of us here.

This place was awesome. I'd never been happier in my life. I didn't ever want to leave.

Charlie stirred. He squeezed me sleepily. "Hey, you."

"Hey *you*." I smiled as I trailed my fingers through his hair. "You slept well."

It was really nice, watching Charlie rest. He never had the best sleep— he was always tossing and turning, talking in his sleep to some kind of nightmare. I'd observed him during long nights at the Institute when my bipolar kept me awake, and it was really hard for him to rest. But since we'd gotten to Ilamanthe, his dreams were always undisturbed. It was the best thing watching him be at peace, sometimes even *smile* in his sleep. He'd really changed for the better since we'd gotten here.

"I'm hungry, and I want breakfast." Charlie lifted the blanket over his head and ducked under it. His fingers caressed my skin as he pushed up my nightgown, and I felt his lips press against my clit before his tongue dove inside of me.

"Charlie…"

"I was dreaming about you last night. They were good dreams."

I let out a giggle that turned into a moan as his tongue licked me up and down. "You said you wanted breakfast."

"Why should I get out of bed when I can just eat you?"

I wasn't going to object. Charlie pushed my legs open wider, and I sank into the pillows as his mouth kissed my thighs. *Good morning to me!*

Oberi landed on the open balcony, back from her morning flight. The phoenix turned a beady eye on us as my fists bunched in the blankets.

Wrap it up, you two. Oberi ruffled her feathers. *I appreciate you're enjoying the moment, but there's a big day ahead... just like every day here, I suppose.*

"Tell them we're busy." Charlie licked me again, and my back arched off the bed.

I would, but your grandfather is expecting you both. You wouldn't want to be late, now would you? Oberi asked.

This made Charlie pause. He kissed the inside of my thigh. "We'll have to pick this up later."

I wasn't disappointed. Charlie liked to edge me, and making me wait all day would give me a bigger thrill later.

Charlie helped me into that awkward wheelchair I'd been given after I'd broken my other one, and he rolled me into the living area. The servants had already dropped off a fresh pot of coffee with a rack of newly baked blueberry muffins. I heard Sprigs sing a song from his potted lemon tree in the corner of the room and decided he needed more plants to hide in. We'd have to ask the servants to pick some up.

I wheeled up to the serving cart, poured a cup of coffee, then dropped in two sugars and a spoonful of cream before handing it to Charlie with a bowed head.

"Thank you, my love." He took a sip. "I have a surprise for you."

"A surprise?" I asked cheerfully as I made my own coffee, then took a bite out of a muffin. "What is it?"

"Once we're dressed, I'll show you."

I practically choked down my muffin. I loved presents, and I wanted to see what Charlie had gotten me. I was so spoiled.

After we'd gotten ready for the day, Charlie took me back to the living room. I squealed when I saw Kallie was standing by a brand new wheelchair, though it wasn't like any I'd ever seen. It was really fancy, with a bucket seat and padded leg rests.

"It's *pink!*" I screeched.

"Of course. I wanted it to be your favorite color. I knew you were uncomfortable in that chair." Charlie put a gentle hand on my shoulder. "It has all the latest advancements. It's a hybrid manual and motorized wheelchair, so if you get tired of pushing yourself around, you can use the remote to go forward, backward, or turn."

"It also tilts and reclines," Kallie said, pressing a button. I watched as the seat of the chair moved forward, then tilted backward. "And guess what? The wheels light up."

A hot-pink light emitted from the spokes of the wheels, and I went giddy. "I can't believe it glows!"

Charlie stroked my hair. "Only the best for my pidge."

I yanked on his arms and he stumbled forward. I wrapped my arms around his neck. "Oh, Charlie! It's perfect!" I kissed him on the cheek.

"Plus it's got padded seating, so you'll be able to sit on your ass after Charlie spanks you too hard," Kallie cackled.

"I want to try it out right away!" I gushed. They helped me into the chair, and it was super comfortable. I already loved it. I began pressing buttons, doing circles around the room. Oberi's head went back and forth as she watched me whizz by.

"Let's see how fast it can go," I blurted. Kallie opened the door for me to the outside hall, and I pressed the accelerating button down on the wheelchair as hard as I could. I was thrown back as the wheelchair jolted forward, and servants jumped out of the way as I went racing down the hall. I headed directly toward a curved ramp, which led to a lower level of the palace.

"Wee!" I cried. "This is so much fun... oh no!"

The chair had picked up too much speed on the ramp, and I lost control. I tried to correct it, but the chair jerked to the side and I tumbled out of it.

"Ava!" Charlie and Kallie's hurried footsteps clattered on the stone floor as they raced to catch up with me. I groaned, pushing myself onto my back.

"Are you okay?" Charlie worried, stooping to the ground.

"I'm all right." I blew a lock of hair out of my eyes. "I need to try that *again.* I think if I slowed down on the turn, I could make it—"

"No," Charlie scolded as he helped me back into the chair. "You went too fast."

"Why'd you put a motor on it if you didn't want me to race?"

"If you don't use it nicely, I'll take it away and get you something else," Charlie warned.

"No! My shiny toy!"

"Then behave."

Kallie put the chair back up, and Charlie deposited me into it. Kallie brushed off my dress as she said, "You need to get moving or you're both going to be late. You're supposed to have your spiritual initiation today."

My stomach sank. Right. That. Couldn't wait.

"I don't know if I'm ready for this," I said warily as we proceeded in the direction of the Elvish temple.

"You have to be," Kallie insisted. "You're the princess."

"But I don't know what they expect me to *do*." I'd been filled in on my responsibilities, but I didn't think I could pull them off.

"I'll be behind you," Charlie promised. "This is only the first day. If it goes bad, you always have the next time."

Sure, if the Elves don't kick me out. Their goddesses were sacred to them. It'd been stressed to me how important this was, and I was worried about messing it up.

Abigail met us outside the temple doors. My lady-in-waiting gave a kind smile. "Are you ready, princess?"

"Hardly." I had trouble meeting her eyes. I wasn't so certain my lady-in-waiting wasn't the spy we'd been looking for. She was such an obvious choice, and that's why I hesitated calling her out.

But at the same time, she was the only one I knew of who had a connection with the Warden. She was a Taurus, after all. I was almost certain she was feeding information back to her uncle about us. But if that were true, why didn't the Warden have the key already?

I wasn't sure, but I was keeping an eye on her.

"Can we go over what I'm supposed to do again?" I asked warily.

"The ceremony will begin, then once the opening rites are finished, your initiation will start," Abigail said. "You'll take your vows and allow the mystics to help you make the transition into a vision from the Elven goddesses."

"Great," I said. "Hopefully they're talkative today."

"Once your initiation is over, you'll be expected to participate in temple services at least once a week, helping the mystics hold ceremonies and getting messages from the goddesses," Abigail informed me. "But don't worry about all that right now. What's most important is this ceremony."

Awesome. If I didn't burn the temple down by accident during any of these ceremonies, I was golden.

A few guards opened the temple doors to us. We wandered inside, and I looked around in awe.

The temple was beautifully elaborate. Pews carved from the interior of massive tree trunks were splayed out in a circle around a large elder tree, which was growing in the middle of the room. The trunk of the elder tree had been shaped with magic, to form the image of two Elvish women entwining their bodies within the bark— the Elvish goddesses, Idril and Caralyn. Beside the Elder tree was a wooden altar large enough for a person to lay, with ivy that wound up the base, and a stone basin that held shimmering silver water. A long aisle started at the double doors and led up to the center of the room, through the middle of the pews. The windows were stained glass, depicting the story of how Idril had found Caralyn and bestowed upon her the powers of a deity. Emerald banners hung from the stone walls beside the windows, displaying the sigil of the Elvish house of Majestica— a tree surrounded by seven keys. The ceiling had a huge skylight, and yellow sun poured in from above to ignite the entire space. Everything was bathed in lovely tones of red chestnut, gold, and green. The entire room smelled of incense and mint.

"Wow. It's pretty in here," Kallie said as she looked around. Oberi soared over the pews, describing what she saw to Charlie.

"It would be a beautiful place to hold a wedding," I said, looking around. "So much sun."

Opal was here as my lady, as well as my guard, Eldin. They curtsied to me, and Abigail introduced me to a *very tall* Elvish mystic standing before the elder tree, who wore robes that seemed to be spun from the wings of moths, if such a thing were possible. The robes were that beautiful, and were in metallic colors. From my studies, I'd learned that initiates wore copper, regular mystics wore silver, and the highest roles in the temple wore gold. Other Elvish mystics were gathered around her, but they had their hoods up to conceal their faces. The tall Elf was wearing a gold diadem with a white pearl dangling from the center, so I figured she had to be in charge.

Abigail gestured to the tall Elf before us. "Princess, this is Valindra Essiel. She is the Great Mystic of our temple, and has been for over five-hundred years."

She didn't look a day over twenty-five. Valindra inclined her head to me and said, "Welcome, princess. Let us proceed with the initiation."

"You'll do fine," Charlie whispered to me, and I swallowed. I wasn't so sure about that. I was eager to step into this role, but now that my time was here, I was afraid. What if I wasn't able to do this, and I let the Elves down? So much was riding on me to be a good princess, and if I failed, the entire nation would come crumbling down. It was almost more pressure than I could handle. What if the goddesses didn't accept me, because I wasn't an Elf? I couldn't serve Charlie's people properly if the Elvish goddesses didn't want anything to do with me.

I had a hard time making normal people accept me, and now I had to impress *two* deities, neither of which I shared a bloodline with. I didn't think this was going to go well.

The mystics took me to the back of the temple. Opal helped me into a white dress so I could bathe in a circular pool beneath a thin waterfall. The Elvish mystics threw diamond dust into the pool as I bathed, and Opal washed my hair in rosemary perfume. They put a golden robe upon my shoulders that shimmered whenever I moved, and dotted my face with makeup they'd made from powdered flowers. Oberi sat on a perch over the pool and hummed a low tune as the mystics intricately braided my hair beside the water.

When the mystics wandered away to prepare the needed elements for the ceremony, Opal leaned in to whisper, "Don't worry. The goddesses will accept you."

"What if the goddesses think I'm a bitch?" I whispered back.

"You *are* a bitch. That's probably what they like," Opal joked.

After I was finally ready, it was time for me to be presented to the public. When we came back to the worship hall of the temple, the patrons of the palace had gathered in the pews for the ceremony. I peeked out from behind the door to the back and almost choked. Shit, the room was already full of hundreds of people. Everyone was going to see it if I made a mistake.

My grandparents were sitting close to the door I was peeking behind. "Ooh, I've always wondered how Elvish religious ceremonies would be performed," Grandpa Elliot whispered in excitement to my grandmother. "Now we get to observe one in person!"

"Such a joy," Grandmother Eleanor said dryly. She saw me and gave a firm nod.

I knew what that meant. *You can show them— don't screw it up.* My grandmother didn't care if I was queen of the elephants as long as it put me in a position of power.

Opal asked if I was ready, then wheeled me out. Whispers went up around the room as people saw me. Everyone looked excited and happy, though I wasn't sure if they should be. There hadn't been a female Elvish monarch in such a long time, but I couldn't say for certain I was the one they'd been waiting for.

I spotted a couple of friends gathered in the middle of the hall. Opal's daughter sat in Ez's lap, and he held her up so she could wave at us as I rolled by.

"I can't believe you guys dragged me out of bed so I could go to church. Last place I wanna be," Chancey complained. He actually looked *nervous* as he glanced around— like he thought an Elvish mystic was going to jump out from behind a pew and start beating him over the head with a holy book.

"This isn't church, dumbass," Alistair told him.

Ivy wiggled their manicured fingers at me, and I managed to grimace back.

My parents sat in one of the front rows. Mama gave me an encouraging smile, though I still must've looked worried, because my father reached out as I passed.

"You can do this, peanut," Daddy hushed, giving me a little pat on the back.

I was the daughter of a chieftain, and I had helped my dad with all kinds of ceremonies back in Kinpago. After all, as the firstborn of a chief, I could summon my ancestors, so I was used to being put on the spot.

But this was so different from Elementai lore. After all, who was I to initiate myself into this? I was trying to learn an entirely new religion on top of the one I'd been raised in. This was my specialty, and I was good at understanding other cultures as an anthropologist, but learning something and actually putting it into practice were two very different things.

My eyes scanned the room for anyone else. Marcus wasn't here, and my heart dropped. I knew he was taking time to himself right now, but this was important. I really wished he'd shown up to give some support. I guess he really had been serious about needing space.

Charlie was in the pew closest to the elder tree, sitting beside his grandfather. Elvish men didn't typically participate in spiritual ceremonies, as the Elves considered temple rites a consecrated act, where only women were sanctified enough to communicate with the goddesses.

I wanted his ass to be up here. If I had to do it, he should, too.

Cameron was here with his wife, though I'd noticed they'd chosen a pew opposite Charlie's. Hopefully they could keep the family drama to a minimum. This was a sacred place, and it didn't need to be ruined by arguments.

Opal pushed me to the center of the circle, in front of the elder tree, before she went to sit down. Oberi nestled in the branches of the elder tree above my head. Before the ceremony began, I took one last look around the sanctuary.

Coyote Spirit wasn't here. I really wished he was. I could've used his guidance right now.

I expected the Great Mystic to say something to start the ceremony, but instead, someone began singing in Elvish.

It was *Eddie*. Wow, he had a lovely tenor voice. I turned my gaze upward to see him on a balcony above the pews, standing beside a group of musicians who held drums, flutes, harps, and violins. He sang out the first hymn, and his voice vibrated around the sanctuary.

The Elves began to beat the drums with their hands, and other voices joined in. A choir of Elves standing on the balcony stepped forward to sing the song alongside Eddie. It didn't sound like the heavenly chorus of angels, but rather, a robust folk song that was bright and vibrant. As the song continued, the rest of the musicians joined in, their instruments weaving together in an intricate harmony.

Ancestors, the Elves were so talented with music. I'd rarely heard such a gorgeous song. The influences of the song were Celtic, or perhaps, Welsh... until it occurred to me that the Elves were so old that their culture had probably influenced *those* societies, not the other way around.

Elvish was very new to me, so I didn't comprehend most of what was sung. At least I was *kind of* getting the message. Poor Charlie looked completely lost. He hadn't been as quick to pick up Elvish terminology in our lessons, so I tried to interpret what I could for him.

The song is telling the story of your people, I explained to him across our connection. *It explains how the Elves left Edinmyre and came to Earth to worship your goddess here.*

He didn't respond, but still, I could tell he was appreciating the song just as much as I was, because it was so beautiful.

I was just starting to relax when the music faded away. The Great Mystic held up her hands, and everyone looked at her.

"It has been many years since a new princess has risen to be our messenger, one who may speak to the goddesses on our behalf," she announced. "Our mystics have tried and failed to contact Idril and Caralyn, most sacred of all goddesses within the Blessed Haven. Today, we pray that we may be enlightened through the eyes of she who has been sent to us."

The Great Mystic gestured to me. "Dear child, what is your name?"

"Ava-Marie Wahkin, Princess of Ilamanthe, wife, fated mate and soul partner of Prince Charles Majestica, Grand Duke of Ilamanthe," I stated. Abigail had gone over what I'd needed to say a million times, but I nearly stumbled on the lines.

"Why are you here?"

"To become the messenger of the goddesses, and guide my people into their light."

"What tree do you choose to mark your path?" the Great Mystic asked.

Trees were generally important to most supernatural societies, but Elves especially revered them. "I choose the poplar tree, the tree that has no secrets—

a tree that whispers, that can be cut down, yet will always grow back. A tree of Water."

Sounded like me when I'd looked it up in the royal library. Can't shut it up, can't kill it either.

"And who do you choose to be your guide?" the Great Mystic asked coolly.

"The phoenix, the spirit of transformation," I replied.

Like the trees, the Elves had animals that were sacred to them that they chose to follow in their life paths. I'd decided on the phoenix, because the concept of rebirth was important to me. I had left yet another life behind at the Institute and was stepping into another role, and so, I had to become something new once again. I had chosen a tree that symbolized the energy of Water, so I felt my guiding animal had to be something of Fire, to suit two of my elements.

"Then let it be so," the Great Mystic responded. "Let us prepare you to meet our goddesses and receive the message they shall send."

The Great Mystic dipped her fingers in the basin of water, then ran it across my forehead. The other mystics began stirring small pots of paint with brushes. They drew Elvish runes on my skin in golden paint, humming a chant. I swallowed a lump in my throat as they fixed a crown that was similar to the rays of the sun to the top of my head. The eager eyes of every Elf in the room fixated on me.

I was the symbol of their goddesses on this Earth. In the palace, I was the princess, but from this moment forward whenever I stepped into the temple, I would be the living incarnation of Idril and Caralyn, and would be treated as such. The goddesses would speak through me, and I would voice what they wanted to the Elves, whether I agreed with it or not. It was such a heavy responsibility that I nearly collapsed under the weight of it, but the Elves were depending on me, so I kept it together.

I didn't *feel* like a goddess, and didn't believe I could step into the role of one, but I'd been chosen for this one way or another. I had to transform into what my people needed me to be.

Once the preparations were done, the mystics lifted me out of my chair and carried me to the wooden altar. I gritted my teeth as I endured the sensation of their hands all over my limbs, and didn't breathe a sigh of relief until they'd deposited me on the altar, though it didn't last long.

This part was what I was most worried about. The trance. If I didn't receive a vision, it would be proof the goddesses had rejected me, and what would happen then? No one had actually told me— when I'd asked, Abigail made a face and said, *Let's hope it doesn't come to that.*

I didn't think I could make something up, or fake it. From what I'd read about Elvish religious ceremonies, this part was actually a huge show for the audience.

The mystics began chanting an ancient song. I felt my body tremble as a feeling like shivers raced up and down my skin. My eyes closed, and my head tilted back as a comfortable weight fell down onto my chest from above...

*M*Y FOOTSTEPS WERE *soft upon the sand. I was walking on a beach... the sky was red around me, casting forlorn shadows onto the bloody waves.*

Oberi was flying above me. She came down to land upon my shoulder. We looked at each other, then forward, casting our gazes forward to seek Idril and Caralyn.

As I kept venturing forward, I heard noises. Magic clashing, thunder raging — the sounds of battle. We climbed a dune, and the sight below paralyzed my chest with fear.

Gods— thousands of them— were scattered along the shores below, and it was their blood staining the sea red. They warred with dark gods who were riding monsters, and the monsters were climbing out of the sea. They came from a black portal swirling within the water. There were so many of them I couldn't count them all.

The many animal gods of the Hawkei pantheon were here, their bodies tumbling with the anthropomorphic forms of evil beings. Whale Spirit was in the water, using her large frame to crush a long worm with thousands of spinning teeth.

Alongside the Hawkei gods were other deities— giants who wore robes and capes, who were throwing massive spears and shooting arrows that were longer than my body at the monsters. I suspected these were the Titan gods of the merfolk. Alongside them were massive deer— the Seven Gods of the Fae— spearing monsters through with their antlers.

A woman in a black cloak tossed battle orbs over her shoulder that exploded on impact and shook the very fabric of time. By the magic she cast, I knew she was a witch, and had to be Mother Miriam. A tall monster with the body of a man and the head of a ram hurtled toward her, and I cried out a warning, but the dark entity stooped down and helped Mother Miriam to her feet before pushing her behind him, giving her time to flee. I knew it had to be Santos, Miriam's husband and protector.

There were other gods amongst them, but I couldn't recognize the others, because the battle was so chaotic. There was so much carnage all around me, and I was caught in the middle of it.

Ava, love, run! Coyote Spirit's voice echoed over the sounds of the fight. I saw him in his animal form as he crouched beneath a monster, his back pressed against a boulder. Leave this place!

I turned to flee. Just as I did, the entire firmament quaked beneath my feet, and the spiritual plane I was on went dark. I tripped, falling onto the sand, though I didn't feel it beneath me— it was as if it wasn't even there. Oberi was hurtled off my shoulder and sent flying several feet away.

Screams from gods and monsters both filled the air, until light suddenly reignited the beach. I looked up and saw that cracks— like those that would fill broken glass— were scattered across the sky. The colors around me bled together, turning into a mess of shapes. I attempted to reach out and touch a seashell, but my hand went right through it, and the shell dissolved into a streaming mess that resembled paint.

Everything started melting, then. The spiritual realm, the gods, and the fight, until the only things that appeared stable were Oberi and myself...

Oberi said my name, though I couldn't hear her. She put her beak to my third eye, and I felt myself tumbling out of the vision, returning back to where I came...

♂⚲

THE STONE ALTAR beneath me seemed incredibly stable. I couldn't believe I could feel something *solid* beneath me, because in the vision, it'd felt like I was falling since I'd tripped on the beach.

Oberi lay on my chest. She must've passed out and fallen onto me once I'd received the vision. She hopped onto the altar, and the mystics helped me to sit up. The expectant faces of the Elves shone back from me all around the temple.

I trembled. The vision had felt so real, more real than this Earth was. Being there in the spiritual realm was true living. Existing here was like watching someone else's life through a television screen.

It couldn't compare— I'd forgotten since I'd come back, but now, I remembered.

"Did you see our goddesses?" the Great Mystic pressed. The other mystics leaned in to hear my answer.

How could I tell them? What I'd seen was horrible. I nearly wanted to make up a lie, because the truth was so heavy. But the goddesses had entrusted me with this information, and I was obligated to share it, my opinion be damned. In any other circumstance I'd do as I pleased, but this was different. This was my duty, so I would follow what the goddesses had asked of me.

I was able to interpret the vision instantly, without having to consider what any of it meant. "I didn't see the Elven goddesses, but the spiritual plane was on fire with the blood of the gods. Every god I knew, and many I didn't, were battling with dark gods and monsters. A portal has been made that connects hell to the Blessed Haven, and the dark gods are trying to take over. The fight is making the spiritual realm weak and breaking it apart. It can't handle the disharmony between the gods. The entire plane is unstable. The gods are officially at war, and if it keeps happening, there won't be a Blessed Haven anymore to sustain them."

The terrified voices of the Elves filled the temple at my words. Emperor Cassiel rose to his feet to calm them. "Silence," he ordered. "We must hear the rest of this vision."

"Did you witness Idril and Caralyn in the fight?" the Great Mystic asked.

"I searched the battle, but the Elven goddesses weren't there," I replied. "Wherever they are, they're not near the Blessed Haven, but somewhere else. Perhaps they're hiding from the dark gods— and if they are, it makes sense you haven't been able to contact them. Ophio Taurus has helped the dark gods create this portal to the Blessed Haven, and as the gods continue fighting, we're going to see the effects here on Earth. This could damage more than our magic. It could end the whole world. I'm not sure if we could exist without the Blessed Haven, but I am sure that it's in danger. We have to do all that we can to help the gods here on our plane, and that means doing whatever we can to stop Taurus and his followers from gaining more power... because the stronger they get, the less chance we have of the spiritual plane surviving this."

An undertone of panic suffocated the room, but Emperor Cassiel turned to his people and said, "This vision foretells dark things, but it is still a blessing, for it gives us a warning. We have time to prepare and mount our attack. The gods need our help. Every Elf in Ilamanthe must be willing to lend themselves to the cause, so we can defeat Ophio Taurus."

There was a murmur of agreement. Cassiel swept his cloak behind him as he faced the Great Mystic. "Valindra, what is your decision on consecrating the Princess of Ilamanthe into your temple?"

The Great Mystic hesitated as she pondered her answer, and for an awful moment, I thought for sure she was going to kick my ass out and say that I'd failed. "It is unknown to us why Idril and Caralyn did not make an appearance to our princess. Yet, she *did* receive a message from them, so I proclaim her to have passed their test. She is now inducted into our temple, and will be known as our messenger, the Holy Mother to our kind."

"*Hail to our Holy Mother, and blessed be her name,*" the other mystics chanted.

The Elves in the congregation repeated their words, and Cassiel tilted his head to me. "Consider this ceremony complete. Well done, princess. You've made us all proud."

Didn't seem like it. I felt like a harbinger of doom.

The temple emptied out. Many Elves came up to congratulate and bow to me, though the mood was definitely dampened.

"Good job, pidge." Charlie gave me a hug. "I knew you'd pass."

"Thanks," I said glumly. "I just wish I'd delivered better news."

"The ceremony was beautiful. Elvish is interesting. It's very close to Malovian," Kallie said. "I couldn't interpret everything, but I could understand most of what was said."

"Makes sense, since the fae and Elves were neighboring nations in Edinmyre." I waved to Opal, who rushed up to me.

"Ava, that was amazing!" she gushed. "I can't wait to see it again!"

"What happened when I was in my vision?" I asked.

"Once you fell into the trance, your body writhed on the altar," Kallie explained. "Oberi passed out and fell from the tree onto your chest, then you began to *glow*."

"Yes. Your skin sparkled and turned golden. You shone like the sun! Then your body and Oberi's levitated off the altar," Opal said in excitement. "You appeared so beautiful, like a celestial being. It really was something to see."

"I was going to get up and wake you, but my grandfather grabbed my arm and told me to wait," Charlie noted. "It didn't seem like you were in pain, so I did."

His grandpa had to have some major pull on Charlie. He never hesitated when I was potentially in danger. But I wasn't the one in trouble— the gods were.

"Are you okay, Ava? You're really pale," Opal said with worry.

"Well, declaring that the spiritual realm is in chaos made me really hungry," I said. Though the vision had only lasted minutes, I felt so tired, and the preparation had taken all morning.

"Some food will help," Opal said. She escorted me to the back of the temple and washed the golden paint from my skin before removing the golden robe and helping me back into my dress.

Charlie pushed me across the palace to the outside dining area. The servants had already set out plates of lobster linguine with lemon orzo salad. I sipped at tea and tried to keep my churning stomach steady in-between bites of seafood.

Beside me, Kallie scowled. She'd been scanning the dining area for Marcus all hour, and now that the meal was basically over, it was obvious he wasn't going to show. "Okay, so he skips your ceremony, and now he's not showing up for lunch?"

"Marcus hasn't been around a lot, anyway," I reminded her.

"That's the point! Something's up," Kallie spat. "I bet *he's* the spy."

The idea was so silly I laughed out loud. "That's stupid, Kallie."

"No it's not! Who knew about our plan?" Kallie asked.

"Sure, but Marcus?" I raised a skeptical eyebrow. "He's been through a lot to get us here, just like we all have."

"He's *changing*, Ava. He isn't the same, not since we broke out of the Institute. I'm not officially mated to him yet, and maybe there's a reason why, because if I was, I'd be able to get into his head. What if there's a reason he doesn't *want* me in there? What if he's been hiding something from us all along?"

"Kallie, you're being paranoid. I understand if you can't trust *all* our friends, because someone has to be betraying us. But us four? We need to trust each other completely; otherwise, this isn't going to work," I insisted. "We can't turn our backs on each other like this. We're family."

"We're not family. If we were, he'd let me in, and he isn't," Kallie stated bluntly. "He's hiding something, and I'm going to find out what."

She was hurt because of how Marcus was acting, so I wasn't going to convince her otherwise. She skulked off with her food half-eaten, and Charlie said, "She's just being dramatic because Marcus didn't show up."

"We don't need any more drama around here," I grumbled. At this point, these two were being obnoxious.

Abigail approached me. "Your day is free, on account of your ascension to the status of Holy Mother this morning. I suggest that you spend it resting. The spiritual process to access the goddesses is exhausting."

She didn't need to explain that, because I was dead tired. I barely stayed awake through lunch, and Charlie noticed I was nodding off. He ducked his head to whisper lowly to me. "You okay, pidge?"

"I don't feel good." It was a crappy day as far as my body was concerned. The spiritual ceremony had drained me. I'd pushed myself too hard, but I didn't regret it. We needed that message if we were going to take action.

That was all I had the energy to say, and he knew it. Charlie lifted me out of the chair and onto his lap. I curled up against him and laid my head on his shoulder. We were in the middle of the dining area and surrounded by people, but Charlie's countenance dared anyone to come up and say something.

Eddie fetched a blanket, and Charlie laid it over me before he wrapped me up in his arms. It felt nice to be held like this, and I felt myself slipping off.

Here. This will help. Oberi landed on the back of Charlie's chair, and her beak began to preen my hair. Her healing magic washed over me, and I found, try as I might, I couldn't stay awake any longer.

I woke up a few hours later, still sore. Oberi was perched on the bedpost, cocking her head as I sat up.

I assumed my husband had carried me off to bed. "Where's Charlie?"

He went to train with his grandfather, Oberi noted. *Would you like me to fetch him?*

"Please." I missed him and wanted him around. When I checked in, I noted Charlie was so immersed in the conversation with his grandfather he didn't notice me brush up against his mind.

I'll go get him, Oberi offered. *Be back in a jiffy.*

She flew out of the room through the open balcony. I let out a small breath. As a princess, I never got time alone these days, so it was nice to have a moment to myself for once. I got myself into my wheelchair, then rolled to the vanity. I began brushing my hair, contemplating how I wanted to spend the rest of my evening.

"You look very lovely, my dear. Being a princess suits you. I suppose *both* of us crave power," a familiar voice said.

My fingers tightened on the hairbrush. I was never truly alone. *He* was always here.

I set my mouth in a thin line and turned my chair to face him. "What do you want?"

An image of the Warden peered back at me, his face set in that disgusting gloat I knew so well. The hallucination appeared so real, as if he was standing only a few feet away from me.

But I knew he wasn't, and so, I'd chosen to give him another name; The Beast. Because that's what the Warden truly was, deep inside. A vicious animal that needed to be put down.

"I'm merely here to keep you company," The Beast replied, sounding smug.

I gritted my teeth. At some point during my stay in Ilamanthe, the voices in my head had somehow morphed into The Beast. He was always lurking around, standing in the corner of every room I inhabited.

He didn't always speak. Most of the time, he remained silent. But when I had a spare second to contemplate my thoughts, there he was, ever creeping at the back of my mind.

I knew he wasn't real. This was just a part of my psychosis. If anyone walked in, they'd witness me talking to nothing.

But he was in my head, and he was real to me. Some demons stayed with you. The Beast was an infestation inside of me that had been planted there sometime during my time at the Institute, and for as much as I wanted to get rid of him, I'd be terrified if he didn't stay. Because I wouldn't know who I was anymore if that hatred for him was gone.

I scoffed. "You're a very unwelcome guest."

"It does you no good to lie to yourself," The Beast soothed, and my skin crawled. "If you didn't want me here, I'd leave."

"I don't. Go away."

"Come now. I think we could have an interesting conversation."

"I'm going to beat you," I said. "I get stronger every day."

The Beast narrowed his eyes. "You don't have to defeat me, because no matter what you do, I've already won. You only have to live long enough to become what you fear the most."

I tossed the hairbrush at him. It sailed through his wispy form before he vanished.

I sighed and dropped my gaze. Ilamanthe had isolated me from the reality of the war, but some scars didn't heal. The Beast was still in my head, and he wasn't going anywhere. As much as I hated to admit it, the Warden was a part of me now, just as I was a part of him, and he damn well made sure to haunt me every day. I was afraid if we got rid of him, it still wouldn't do any good, because he still lived in me.

And I didn't trust what that part of me wanted to do. Because anything was on the table, and if I lost any self-control... if the Warden was able to take over and do what he wanted...

There wouldn't be anything left of our world. Let alone me.

NINE

Ava's ceremony had been beautiful— powerful, even— but it'd put the entire palace on edge. I passed by people speaking in hushed whispers on my way to the gardens. We knew the war was out there, but today, it had hit a little too close to home. This war was getting worse, and if I didn't do something to stop it, it wasn't going to end. I needed to become a better demigod and prince, because the fate of the entire world hung on me. I couldn't depend on anyone else to stop this. This was my responsibility, and I was learning every day that there needed to be no limits to what I would do if I was to save these people.

My grandfather was already waiting for me when I arrived at the gardens. His guards remained at a distance to give us privacy. "Please sit beside me, Charlie," he said coolly.

I took a chair beside a patio table. Warm sunlight touched my skin. In the distance, I could hear laughter coming from the palace. It made it easy to forget there was a war going on outside of Ilamanthe, but I knew the darkness that lurked beyond this island.

"What are we going to do?" I asked. "The Mission is gaining power, and it appears the gods are falling. I can't just sit here on my throne in all this sunshine and laughter while people are out there dying."

"You need not worry," he assured me. "Our people are safe here in Ilamanthe. However, you must be told that in the past few days, The Mission has launched an attack against the fae. Our allies gave us this home, and now, we must protect theirs. I'm sending all the Elven soldiers we can spare to Malovia, to protect the fae borders and the residents still living there."

"How can you be sure we're safe here?" I believed my grandfather wanted to keep the Elves safe, but I was more than worried. I was almost petrified with fear that this perfect city couldn't last, and that it would somehow be taken away.

"I would never leave my people in danger," he promised. "We are well-guarded and have soldiers stationed at all times. Doctor Taurus doesn't know we're here, and we intend to keep it that way."

"But he *will* find us eventually," I said. "He's not going to give up. Once he does, how do we prevent him from destroying the city, like he destroyed Forevermore?"

"I have personally put up preventative wards around the city, to alert us immediately if any demigods besides the ones that are living here enter. The Warden is now a demigod, so we must be notified early if he arrives. We are also much more prepared than we once were. Our army is fortified and strong, and is able to hold the city under heavy attack. We weren't prepared when Forevermore was sieged, and were caught by surprise, but we won't make that same mistake again. I know the Warden has demigods on his side now, but we have demigods too, and I trust that you and your friends will be able to defeat them if the worst happens and we have to go on the offense. That is why I'm teaching you."

"You don't understand. The Warden is incredibly strong. I've seen him in action. Once he finds this place, he'll burn it to the ground," I insisted.

"We don't just have Elves living here, Charlie. We have the fae, who are a formidable supernatural force on their own, able to stand up to angels and vampires, and we also have the witches and the elementals within our ranks. Even if the Warden was to show up here with his army tomorrow, we wouldn't be easily defeated. The Warden won't attack until he is certain he can win, and certainty is a difficult thing for him to attain when Ilamanthe is as strong as it is currently."

"What about the dark gods?" I demanded. "He unleashed them on Earth. We saw him do it at the Institute, and we know they're working for him."

"Ava's vision showed us that the majority of the dark gods are battling the other gods in the spiritual realm," Cassiel pointed out. "*Some* dark gods roam among us, but you must remember that there is a potential for gods that are on our side to be living on Earth as well, either incarnated or in their true god forms. You think we're outnumbered and overpowered, but if we weren't strong enough to give the Warden a hard time, he would've already eliminated us by now. He can't simply walk in here and destroy everything as he did in Forever-more. We can be just as strong as he is, and with enough time, we can be better. We just need to buy ourselves some."

"I want to help," I said.

"The greatest thing you can do is grow your powers, so that you may assist when the time is right. The demigods here are our greatest asset, but we cannot send you into battle until you are ready."

"I've fought the Warden before," I pointed out.

"And how did that turn out?" he questioned rhetorically.

He was right. I'd faced the Warden multiple times, but we'd never actually defeated him. Now that he had stolen our magic for himself, and had Esther and the other demigods on his side, he had a miniature army that was crafted to kill us.

"This war isn't going to wait around until I'm ready," I insisted. "It could be years until I'm properly trained. How many people are going to die before then?"

"In any war, there are going to be casualties," he replied. "These soldiers know what they signed up for, and it's their job to hold off The Mission until you are ready."

"What about the civilians?" I questioned. "They didn't sign up for this."

"What are you suggesting you do? Go into battle and get yourself killed? What good are you to your people if you're dead? You can't help them. By *trying* to help, sometimes you hurt people more than you help them. Attempting to stop this now will hurt them in the long run, because if you get hurt, it will set the entire war effort back. A good leader amasses power to strike when the time is right. Don't forget that the Warden has demigods fighting for his side, too. And may I remind you that one of those demigods you haven't beaten in a proper fight yet."

Fucking Deuce. He was always slipping right out from under my fingers. He beat me in fight club, survived the Darke Games, and nearly killed us while we were on the run. One of these days, I was going to send him straight to hell, and I would enjoy every minute of it.

But my grandpa was right. Next time I ran into this guy, I better be sure I could completely obliterate him.

"I guess it's not enough to be the best out there," I said. "I have to be the best anyone's ever been."

"Precisely. You're strong, but you can become even stronger. That's why I've summoned you here today. I'm going to teach you to utilize one of your greatest Elven powers— bond breaking."

I leaned back in my chair. "I'm listening."

"Bond breaking is very powerful magic that can be used for good, but it can also be used to destroy your enemies."

"Breaking a magical bond sounds terrible. How can it be used for good?" I tried to imagine what it'd feel like for my bond with Ava or Oberi to sever, and I couldn't do it. Our souls were one and the same, and breaking our bond would destroy me completely. There'd be nothing left, no point to me existing.

But I supposed, if I thought about it in a strategic sort of way, that was the point— to leave my enemies so broken there was nothing left of them to fight.

"Bonds are incredibly powerful, and most of the time, they help the parties who participate in the bond do better. But sometimes, bonds can be suffocating. In such cases, you must break the bond to allow each party to grow on their own. Take this plant, for example." My grandpa placed a large pot on the table with a heavy *thud*. "Go ahead."

My fingers roamed over broad leaves, which crumbled at the ends. I reached a flower at the center with hard petals. My Earth magic tingled, but just barely. This plant was dying.

"What is it?" I asked.

"It's a suklune plant. It's a magical plant the Elves have tended for centuries. It contains powerful pain-killing properties that we use in our medicine. However, one must take special care tending them, because they're actually two plants in one."

I ran my fingers over the tough flower again and realized it wasn't really a flower. It was an entire plant that was separate from the first— some sort of succulent.

"These plants share a magical bond that allows them to grow together through a symbiotic relationship. It is only together that they produce their pain-killing properties, which in turn promotes a harvest that allows the plants to reproduce effectively."

"Each plant is so different," I remarked as I felt along the leaves. "Yet my magic can't tell the difference between them."

"Yes, because bonded, they're technically one being," my grandfather confirmed. "The broad leaf portion of the suklune plant comes from marshes, while the succulent grows in deserts. The leaves are good at pulling water from the soil, which nourishes the succulent. The succulent can store the water. Together, they may withstand a variety of environments. Traditionally, both of these plants would benefit from one another, but in this case, the succulent is overtaking the leaves."

I noted that the succulent felt firm and healthy, while the leaves were crusty and breaking off.

"They can no longer survive in the same soil. For both to live, the magical bond must be broken, so that they can grow separately."

My chest felt heavy. I knew it was just a plant, but it made me really sad to think about breaking them apart. "So all we have to do is break the bond and replant them?"

"You must take special care. Once separated, they must return to their respective environments to survive. They can either live together or live apart. There is no in-between."

"So I can use this against my enemies to divide them from the people they love? Not just the people they love, but the people who make them... *them*. I can destroy their spirits." I shuddered, because it was a big responsibility— a choice I hesitated to make, even on someone as evil as the Warden.

"Yes," my grandfather confirmed. "If your enemy happens to be magically bound, and you can get close enough to them to break the bond, a decision such as this can win you a war. But you must understand how powerful this magic can be. Once you break a bond, there is nothing but the power of the gods that can restore it. This type of magic can save your people, or ruin you. I've seen Elves lose their temper and break bonds they can never restore, even accidentally break their own. You have a bond yourself, and you must tend to it with care."

"I would never break my bond with Ava or Oberi," I snapped. "I don't care how angry I get. That's never happening."

"Hold on to that promise," he urged. "I've broken very few bonds in my time, yet there are several I deeply regret. The only reason I'm teaching you this is because it might be necessary to use it against your enemies. One day, you might run across a magical being that is so powerful, the only way for you to stop it is to break a bond they hold."

"You mean... I could potentially take away someone's casting abilities if I severed their bond?" I asked.

"Yes. Bonds hold magic, and sometimes, if one piece of a bond is cut off from their partner, they will lose access to their powers entirely," he instructed. "Though this isn't always the case. For example, if a fae's bond is broken with their mate, both parties will still retain their own magic, because their power comes from Edinmyre, and that's a channel they can still access without use of the bond."

"They might still be able to fight, but the loss would be crippling. They'd lose the will to keep going," I said.

"Precisely. But as you know, if a Familiar dies, so does an Elementai. And if you were to break an Elementai's bond with a Familiar, the elemental would lose their magic."

"Wouldn't the Elementai die, then, without the bond to hold them here?"

"It would be a possibility, but in this circumstance, we're considering splitting a soul," my grandfather said. "It would be more likely the Elementai themselves would remain alive, but be unable to cast or communicate with their Familiar. The body would remain, but the spirit would be separated."

I felt sick just thinking about it. I nearly wanted to run back to my room, clutch Oberi to my chest and never let her go. "It wouldn't be much of an existence."

"No. It would be a cursed life. Which is why you must understand how absolutely cataclysmic this ability to break bonds is. It's not a power to use lightly. In some circumstances, you're playing the role of the gods. Which is why I beg you to use it only when absolutely necessary."

The Warden may not be magically bound to anyone, but I was sure as hell some of his followers were. We needed every advantage we could get.

"I want to be powerful," I stated. "Teach me."

My grandfather sounded more than proud. "First, you must find the bond and draw it out. Observe the plant, and use your powers to explore the magic inside of it. It will feel like a rope, tethering one bonded partner to the other. Gently draw back your magic, pulling that bond to the surface."

I did as I was told, tangling my magic within its leaves. I could feel every leaf and every pulse of water through its vascular system. The plant seemed to *breathe*, and I could sense it as if it were my own body... but I didn't feel any magical tether. Beneath my fingers, the withering leaves began to grow stronger. But it lasted for only a moment before the succulent took the energy for its own. The leaves withered once more. I realized I was inadvertently using my Earth magic on them.

I drew back my elemental powers and focused on my Elf magic. Illusion magic tingled through my fingers. I pulled back on that and tried to find an energy signature within my body I'd never used before.

My grandfather waited silently. Minutes must've passed as I meditated, quieting my body and mind so that I could tune into my magic. My mind brushed up against something centered in my heart. It was a smooth magic I hadn't ever noticed before, but it was powerful, too— waiting dormant until I was ready to give it purpose.

I drew the magic to the surface and funneled it into the plant. To my amazement, I quickly found the tether that my grandfather described. My magic curled around it as surely as if I had touched it with my fingers. I dragged my magic back, pulling the bond with it.

I gasped as an ethereal strand took shape in my vision. I could *see* the bond tying these plants together, because it was a spiritual connection, and I didn't need my eyes to observe it, just my soul.

"I've got it," I announced.

"Good," my grandpa encouraged. "Now, wrap your magic around either end of the bond, and pull."

Mentally, I curled my magic around the string, and I yanked in either direction. The bond fought against me, as if I were stretching a rubber band. I pulled harder...

Snap!

The magical tether broke, and the thread withered from my view. My breath hitched as all my magic came rushing back into me.

"I did it!" I cried. "It wasn't that hard, either."

"You are a strong Elf, Charlie. Now that you understand the process, I'm certain you'll learn to break any bond you please. Observe your work." My grandfather pulled the plants apart and slid the pot toward me. He'd removed the succulent portion, and only the leafy part remained.

"It's okay now," I told the plant.

I infused my Earth magic through the pot, and the leaves became strong and healthy once more. I ran my fingers over the ends of the leaves, and the dry, crusted parts had vanished. I noticed the soil was dry, so I carried the plant over to the fountain to give it a drink.

Water droplets rolled off the dirt. The soil couldn't hold the water the plant needed. Carefully, I uprooted the plant and dumped the dirt out. I combined my Earth magic with illusion powers to conjure the damp soil the plant craved. I replanted it and watered it, until it seemed perfectly at ease in its new environment.

I returned to the table and realized my grandfather was still holding the succulent. I formed a pot of sand with my illusion magic. "Put him in here."

I pulled a bit of sand aside, and my grandfather placed the plant in the hole. Now both plants were potted and thriving.

"What should we do with them?" I asked.

"You can keep them, if you'd like," my grandfather offered. "I'm sure your little Sprigs would appreciate the variety."

He really would like it. The rest of the afternoon, my grandfather brought me more suklune plants that were overgrown, and I practiced breaking their bonds and regrowing the separated plants in different pots. By the time evening rolled around, I figured I was getting the hang of it. It was a simple process to break a bond... which bothered me, because something so powerful and sacred shouldn't be so fragile.

But I supposed that was one of the things that made a magical connection so special. One mistake, even something you didn't intend, could upset the balance and ruin things. I knew how strong a bond between two life forces could be, but I had a newfound respect for them after learning how easily they could break.

When the air had developed a slight chill from the setting sun, I felt Oberi approach. She perched on my shoulder and said, *Ava's awake. I think she needs you.*

It felt good to be needed. I stroked her feathers and fed her a blackberry I picked off a branch. "You're a good girl, Oberi."

Why are you being so nice? she asked suspiciously, though she gobbled up the blackberry and nudged me for more.

"Just... trying to appreciate what I have."

I said goodnight to my grandfather, and we returned to our quarters. I placed the succulent in the window where it would get plenty of sunlight, then gave the leafy plant a home in the corner of the room. Sprigs was excited about the new plants, and I heard him singing to them softly in a squeaky tone.

When I entered the bedroom, I found Ava at the vanity.

"Ow," Ava complained as the brush caught in her hair, making a ripping sound. "Dammit. My hair's all messed up. I slept on it wrong."

"Here, let me help," I offered. I took the brush from her hands, while Oberi flew over to sit on her armrest.

"How did things go with your grandpa?" Ava questioned before I had a chance to ask how she'd slept.

I worked a tangle out of her hair. "Good. He taught me about bond breaking."

"Oh?" she asked curiously.

"Yeah. It's an Elvish thing only the strongest can do."

"I'm sure you pulled it off no problem— *ow!*" Ava cried as the brush snagged.

"Sorry, pidge." I ran the brush through her hair again, slower this time.

"Don't be sorry. Do it again."

I furrowed my brow. "Like... this?"

The brush caught the knot in her hair again, so hard that her wheelchair pulled in my direction. I worried that I'd hurt her.

"Yeah. Just like that," she practically sang.

"*Oh*," I teased. I suddenly wasn't worried anymore. I yanked on the brush again, and she let out a moan of pleasure.

"I like it when you pull on my hair," she breathed.

"I like it when you moan."

Dear ancestors, Oberi groaned. *I do not want to see where this is going. I'm going to heal some people at the hospital. I'll be of more use there, I'm sure.*

Oberi sounded sarcastic, but I knew she was being serious. She spread her wings and flew out the window, leaving my wife and me in privacy.

I barely heard Oberi's retreating wing beats, because my attention was laser-focused on Ava. My pulse quickened as I leaned down to whisper in her ear. "You like *that*?"

I pulled the brush again, and she gasped as I yanked her head close to my chest.

"Harder," she begged.

Her wanting drove me insane, and my cock hardened. Memories of this morning flickered through my mind— all the things I wanted to do to her and never got the chance to follow through on. I'd been thinking about it all day, to be honest.

I ran the brush through her hair with one hand, then took the other and tangled it in the strands on the side of her head. I tugged lightly, before drawing my lips over the sensitive area behind her ear. "You want it like this?"

She moaned again, and that was a good enough answer for me. I set the brush aside. I leaned over her from behind. My fingers trailed her legs, which had warmed several degrees. I dipped my fingers between her thighs and was pleased to find she wasn't wearing any panties. She hardly did these days. She said it was more comfortable in the chair, but sometimes it was damn hard not to slip my hands up her dress at the dinner table. I'd had the thought that she liked doing it just to drive me wild.

I pulled her dress up over her head, then tossed it aside so she was bare. Without a word, she reached up and grabbed the tie around my neck. She wrapped it around her wrist a few times, before clutching it tight with her fingers and dragging me closer.

"I bet you can't break *this* bond," she teased.

I couldn't help it when a sigh of pleasure escaped my lips. My craving for her intensified. I wanted to taste her sweetness all over again, and to bury myself deep inside of her and make her come until she was screaming my name. "The anticipation from this morning must've been killing you all day."

She dragged me closer, then leaned her head back and pressed a soft kiss to my lips. "I need you to quiet my mind."

"I can do that, my love."

I came around the side of her chair, though she never loosened her grip on my tie. I scooped her into my arms and led her through the mirror into our Sanctuary. Ava shivered with longing as I placed her on the bed. I loosened my tie, and she eagerly offered me her wrists. Slowly, to make every moment count, I curled the tie around her wrists and secured them with a knot. I'd left just enough fabric to tie the end to the headboard.

Ava lay with her hands above her head, breathing heavily like she yearned for my touch. "Ancestors, Charlie, you look so fucking hot in that suit."

I slipped my suit jacket off and hung it on a hook near the bed, then slowly started unbuttoning my shirt. "It makes me feel powerful out there— makes me feel like I'm in charge. But I like it better in here with you, where the real me can come out in the bedroom."

I pulled the shirt off, and Ava gave a light gasp at the sight of me. Desperate longing passed through the bond, sending a thrill straight down to my cock.

I undressed, then knelt on the bed over top of her. Ava wiggled, like she was trying to touch me, but she couldn't when she was bound.

I wanted her so fucking badly. I parted her legs, then gently ran my fingers over her warm silkiness. She didn't react, and I worried she couldn't feel it. I pressed against her clit the same time I sent a light breeze to tickle her skin. Ava arched off the bed and gave a tiny moan. The sound drove me insane.

I ducked my head to brush my lips across her nipples. They were hard in anticipation. I sucked one into my mouth, and Ava breathed a wavered breath.

I want more, she begged, writhing on the bed.

I slid my fingers deep inside of her while I worked her nipple with my tongue. I bit down ever so slightly, and a wave of pleasure crossed through the bond.

I want you to fuck me, she requested.

I chuckled. "I want this to last."

"So make me come six times. I don't care," she moaned. "I thought you were hungry for me."

I smirked. "Love, I'm starving."

I resituated until I knelt between her legs. Slowly, I trailed kisses down her body, letting my breath tease her inch by inch. The bed squeaked as she yanked against the tie, anxious for her release.

I couldn't hold back my need for her any longer. I sank lower, until my head was between her legs and my tongue was circling her clit. My fingers moved in and out of her, stroking her pleasure centers with intent and precision. It had taken us a long time after her injury to find our rhythm, but now that we had, it was magical.

I worked her clit long and hard, until passion swelled across our bond. My fingers were starting to tire, and the muscles in my neck ached, but I didn't care how long it took to get her off, because every moment was worth it. Ava reached her peak, and her moans filled the room. Tingles spread up and down my arms, and the mattress beneath us seemed to turn to water for a moment as we both melted into it.

The wave of pleasure passed, and the bed became solid again.

"Do that again," Ava begged with a blissful sigh.

"Shh..." I warned, placing a wet finger to her lips. Ava sucked the finger into her mouth, and ancestors, I nearly lost it right there. I had to force myself off of her. "Give me a moment."

Ava snickered in delight. She could tell there was a surprise coming. We both liked to try new things, but there was something I'd been dying to try for a long time. I really liked surprising her like this, giving us new things to experiment with. It kept things interesting, and Ava was always open to whatever I came up with. She was my good girl.

I went over to the dresser, where we kept our toys laid neatly in a row. Ava wasn't allowed to open it, because I didn't want her to see all the fun things I had planned. I felt around until I found a toy made of two silicone rings with a small mechanical device attached to one end. I grabbed a bottle of lube and returned to the bed.

Ava gasped when she saw the toy. "Is that a cock ring? Ooh, I've been wanting to try one forever."

"Me, too," I admitted. "It's supposed to make me last longer."

"Is it? I don't know how it works."

"Well, sometimes it's hard for you to come, so I want to try and last until you do," I admitted.

"Charlie..." Her tone softened, and nearly broke. "You were thinking of me."

"Of course. Always."

"Accessibility is sexy," Ava gushed. "I bet we can fuck forever with that thing on."

"That's the idea."

I was already hard, and the inner ring wasn't very big, so I knew it wasn't going to slip on easily. I covered my cock with lube, then slipped one ring over my length, then stretched the outer ring around my balls.

"How does it feel?" she asked.

I winced. "A bit tight. I think I was supposed to put it on before I got hard, but you're just so damn hot. It should still work."

The cock ring had a small device that sat at the base of my dick to stimulate Ava's clit. I knelt between her legs again, then pressed the button on the side of the device. Ava let out a gleeful laugh as the soft vibration sounds filled the room. Her laughter was the best sound in the world.

Wanting flared through my veins, and I couldn't tease her any longer. I slid inside of her, taking in every sensation as her warmness enveloped me. Euphoria passed between our bond, and the room spun around us. I thrust into her harder, and she moaned loudly.

I was a fool to think I could keep this slow. I could no longer hold back my desire, and I slammed into her. With each thrust, she let out a moan. I had to brace myself against the headboard as I filled her up again and again.

The cock ring made me last longer than I thought was possible. It was passionate and rough— everything both of us desired.

Right there, Ava begged as I came close to my peak.

I thrust one more time, then buried my cock deep inside of her as I pressed the ring's vibrator to her clit.

"Charlie," Ava gasped, before tumbling into another orgasm. The exhilaration of orgasm kicked back through the bond, until I felt what she felt throughout my entire body.

Surprisingly, though, I didn't come. I smirked. This cock ring was quickly becoming my favorite toy.

This time, the high of orgasm didn't settle. Instead, something broke free inside of us, and I went mad for her touch. My lips crushed to hers, and her tongue slid inside of my mouth as I moved inside of her. I tangled my hands in her hair and tugged, and she responded by biting down hard on my lip. An intoxicating fervor overcame us as we made out. My lips moved down her neck, then back up to her mouth, where I could tell she desperately wanted me.

Ava drew away, gasping. "Talk dirty to me in Elvish."

"Oh. Um..." I'd been taking Elvish lessons, but I hadn't picked up on that much yet.

"Do it," she begged.

She could ask me for anything right now, and I'd be a slave to do it. I tried my best. "Uh.... *tiya kopala seksona sofine?*"

Ava snickered.

What are you doing? Oberi's thoughts cut through the bond.

I'm talking to my wife. Go away.

I tried to shove Oberi out, but she responded dryly, *You just called your wife a sexy sofa.*

Ava burst into laughter. "You can be *my* sexy sofa, Charlie. I'll sit on your face."

"Maybe later."

I slammed Oberi's side to our bond shut, leaving Ava's wide open and surging with passion. Sweat began to drip down my chest the longer I moved inside of her. I could have slowed down, but she was so damn sexy I'd thoroughly lost control. I sought a much anticipated release.

It could have been fifteen minutes or a whole hour— I wasn't really keeping track of time. All I knew was there was no better place in the world than deep inside my pidge.

Ava's passion built up again, and her nails clawed into my back. "Fuck," she rasped.

Her cry was my undoing. The room seemed to flip on its head as an intoxicating sensation burst through our bond and down my entire body. My cock contracted, filling her up as I curled my body close to her. Ava became tight as she spiraled into the orgasm alongside me.

I fell to the bed, panting. In my delirious state, I forgot that the cock ring was still vibrating. The world seemed to settle around me, and I realized how uncomfortable it had become. It was really tight and almost hurt. I pressed the button to turn it off, then slipped it down my length.

"You went for a really long time," Ava remarked breathlessly.

I smiled. "You want to go again?"

She sighed happily. "I thought you promised me I'd come six times."

I beamed. "Six times it is, my love."

Ava and I went at it until our bodies couldn't do it any longer. It must've been really late by the time we finished, though I wasn't exactly keeping track of time. I cleaned up while Ava rested on the bed, then I carried her back through the mirror and into our bedroom. I threw on a t-shirt and a pair of sweats, then left the room to get her glass of water. It was pretty late by this point.

"Aw. We missed dinner," Ava said, checking the clock.

I snickered. "I didn't."

She slapped my arm. I stepped out for a moment and asked a servant to bring us something from the kitchens to eat.

I was hungry, because I'd just put in a lot of work. I ate an entire slab of ribs, while Ava nibbled at a fruit salad. When I was done eating, I fed her strawberries while she sat on my lap. I felt her contentment across our bond, and I knew neither of us would ever want to be anywhere else.

She was nearly half asleep once we'd finished dinner. I helped her into the bathtub, and we washed up together while I gave her an entire body massage.

"I don't know why I'm still so tired. I slept most of the day, and you did everything during sex." She sighed as I lifted her out of the tub, and I set her in a chair so I could wrap her in a towel. She had learned to do a lot of this stuff by herself since she'd gotten injured, but I didn't let her do it most of the time, because I liked doing it for her and she liked being taken care of.

"The ceremony this morning took a lot out of you. I could feel it draining you across our bond when you were experiencing the vision," I said. "It's okay to rest. We'll get back to normal life tomorrow."

She nodded, because she was too tired to give much more of a response.

I pulled a nightgown over her head, then rubbed lotion over her wrists to treat the fabric burns from the tie. The cream was infused with special healing herbs. Eddie suggested it after he'd seen the marks one day. I hadn't realized I'd been leaving any behind, and I wasn't thrilled at the idea. Ava seemed to like them and wore them as a badge of honor, but I'd insisted all marks remain in non-visible places and that we didn't get too rough. It was non-negotiable.

Once I put her down, Ava sank deep into the bed, and her breathing rate slowed as she drifted off into a peaceful slumber.

I was crawling into bed when a light knock came at the door. Ava gave a soft sigh as I pulled the blanket up around her shoulders and kissed the top of her head. She completely relaxed as I tucked her in. I crossed our suite to answer the door, hoping this didn't take too long. I wanted to get back to bed.

"Hey, Charlie," Kallie greeted in a small voice. "I came to talk."

She barely sounded like herself. It was obvious something was really bothering her. I could hear the whizz of Alette's small wings hovering slightly above Kallie's shoulder. The faekin let out a few tiny noises that sounded deeply upset, and I knew she was concerned for her sorceress.

"Sorry. Ava's already in bed," I started. I didn't want to disturb her.

"I don't want to talk to Ava," Kallie stopped me. "I came to talk to you."

My brow furrowed. "Me?"

"I need advice... about Marcus," she admitted.

I leaned against the doorway. "You're upset he wasn't at the ceremony."

Kallie sighed. "That's part of it... but it's more than that."

"How can I help?"

Kallie hesitated, like she had a hard time talking about it. "You almost lost Ava, but when the time came, you were ready to let her go. I need advice from someone who's *been* where I'm standing. Ava's my best friend, but if I talk to her, she's going to convince me to keep holding on... and I don't know if I can do that anymore. I know you'll be straightforward with me and tell me how it is. Not how I want it to be."

Holy shit, this was really serious. I wasn't sure how much I could help Kallie, but she obviously needed a friend right now.

"Let's take a walk," I suggested. I put on some shoes and shut the door quietly. Kallie followed me out of my quarters and down the empty hall. "You're talking about breaking up with Marcus?"

Kallie scoffed. "Breaking up? We're not *really* dating. And that's just it. I can't keep going back and forth with him. He says he wants to be with me, but he won't make the commitment."

I shoved my hands into my pockets. I wished I had some insight to help Kallie, but I couldn't say I understood Marcus. I knew if I were in his position, I wouldn't think twice about committing to the woman I loved. And I knew he loved Kallie— without a doubt. So I wasn't sure why he kept holding back.

Still, I tried to comfort my friend. "I'm sure he'll come around."

I flinched as soon as I said it, because I knew it wasn't the right thing to say.

"People keep saying that, but the longer this goes on, the less hope I have," Kallie admitted. "Danny was right when he said I need to make a decision. And I don't think I can until someone hears me out."

We stepped onto a large balcony. The air was cool outside, and the city was quiet.

Kallie leaned against the banister. "I figure I can either stay and let Marcus string me along, or I can leave and have my heart broken. Either way, it's *really* fucking hard. I just want to understand why you didn't walk away from Ava. She's put you through so much."

I shrugged as I came up beside her. "Even when things are hard, I know we'll get through it. Things keep getting better between us, because we're both committed to growing together. Even when we were having problems, Ava was willing to put in the work. Do you think that's something Marcus will do?"

Kallie didn't answer right away, like she was mulling over the idea. "I want him to, and that's what's kept me holding on this long. But I haven't *seen* any progress."

"The way I see it, you've got two choices— leave, or stay. Both options are going to be painful, but one of them is going to hurt less. I don't know which one that is for you. You need to make that decision for yourself."

"It doesn't feel like I have a choice." Kallie's voice broke. "Even if I walk away, Marcus and I are still magically bound together. I just feel..."

Kallie sniffled. It was so quiet up here on the balcony that when her breath caught, it seemed to shatter the air around us.

Kallie was *crying*, which was a big fucking deal, because she only ever cried when things got *really* bad. Out of all the terrible shit we'd been through together as friends, I'd only witnessed her break down twice— once when we found out Marcus had joined a prison gang, the other when Ava was fighting for her life in the hospital. Kallie always held it together— always kept her guard up and presented a rock-hard exterior. For her to cry meant she was already beyond her breaking point.

Kallie turned away from me. "I just look up at the stars and realize how fucking massive this universe is, and I feel so *alone*. Marcus is supposed to be my person, but I'm so *lonely*."

She broke into full sobs that racked her whole body. "I've tried to... break our bond, but I'm... not strong enough to go through with it. I don't want to let him go... but I *know* I have to. Because if I don't, this connection is going to kill me."

My heart broke for her. I was really rooting for Marcus and Kallie, but this wasn't my decision. If Kallie didn't want to be in this relationship anymore, she shouldn't be bound by the magic of their bond to stay. It wasn't fair.

"Elves can break bonds, too," I told her. "My grandpa taught me how. If this is really what you want, I can help you."

Kallie grabbed my arm so hard that I thought it might bruise. "Will you? Because I can't do this alone. I need you to support me."

"What about Marcus?" I asked. This could destroy him.

Kallie dropped my arm. "What about *me*? Everyone's always concerned about Marcus and how fragile he is, but nobody asks what I want. This relationship isn't all about him. I'm a part of it, too, and if I don't want to be anymore, then I shouldn't be forced to!"

I frowned. "You're right. It's not fair."

"Not even close," Kallie bit. "Believe me, I've thought about the consequences a million times. The last thing I want to do is hurt Marcus, but I don't think it's fair for me to stay in a situation that's hurting both of us. I can't be in a relationship with someone who isn't there for himself, let alone there for me. I'm terrified Marcus is going to hurt himself one day, and I can't be there to wonder if it's my fault."

"Do you really think he would?" I knew Marcus had attempted to take his own life before, but I assumed he was past that.

"I'm not talking about suicide, Charlie." Kallie's voice grew heavier than before. "There's a *reason* he has so many tattoos on his arms. I've gotten close enough to see what he's covering up."

My heart plummeted to the bottom of my abdomen. I hadn't realized. "Has he stopped?"

"He swore to me he hasn't done it since he got to the Institute, but who knows. I'm worried if we get into another blowout argument, it could start up again. And I'm really tired of having these fights. We never resolve anything, we just go in circles. It's the same issues over and over."

"If it does happen, it's not your fault, Kallie. He's always been in a really dark place."

"It is if I don't make a decision to change things between us, instead of dragging it out. I want to help him more than anything, but I only feel like I'm making it worse. I think it'd be better for both of us if I'm not around. I just want us both to stop hurting."

Kallie was *begging* me, and her vulnerability made me want to shred her bond right there on the spot. I knew her relationship with Marcus wasn't great, but I hadn't realized how bad it truly was.

"What does the future look like if I break your bond?" I asked. "Because if we do this, it's permanent. It's not something you can take back, or something I can fix once it's gone."

Kallie took a moment to catch her breath. "I still have a duty to fulfill. I'll save the world with you guys, but once that's over, I can't talk to Marcus anymore. It's too painful to be reminded of how much I love him. I'll have to move on and go live a different life, and I can never see him again. So tell me, Charlie. Is this the right decision?"

A lump formed in my throat so large, I could barely speak past it. "If you're looking for me to talk you out of it, I can't do that. Because one way or another, you've already made up your mind. You just have to admit to yourself what you really want."

I wasn't sure which side she'd chosen, to be honest, but I had my suspicions. If Kallie had her way, she'd have broken her bond by now. I knew fae had the ability to sever their own mating bonds, and Kallie had tried, but she was too attached to Marcus to go through with it. That's why she needed me to do it for her.

It was overwhelming to consider. The Villain's Club wouldn't be much of a club without Kallie and Marcus. We'd never hang out as a group again. I knew once this happened, the four of us would never get to connect as friends like we had before. If I did this, it would create a broken family. I couldn't imagine the weight Kallie took on in making this decision.

But it was *her* decision, and as much as I didn't like it, I had to respect it. I just wished they could work this out, because following through on this would be life-altering— hell, it was a soul-altering decision.

"You should talk to Marcus," I encouraged. "Give him one last chance to convince you to work this out, and if you still mean it after you talk, I'll break your bond."

"That's it?" Kallie asked. "One conversation, then you'll break it?"

I nodded. "One conversation. Then you make the call."

"I just want this to be over," Kallie insisted. "I'm texting Marcus so we can do this right now."

I heard her furiously typing on her phone. Kallie paced around the balcony as we waited for Marcus to get her message and meet us here.

It was only a few minutes before his footsteps approached.

"What's so urgent?" Marcus asked. He'd come so quickly it appeared he'd left Rishi behind in his room. I had no idea what the text had said, but it'd made him move.

"You might want to sit down," I told him. Kallie and Marcus took a seat at a patio table overlooking the city, while I remained standing.

Marcus' voice raised a pitch. "You guys are freaking me out. Where's Ava?"

"Sleeping." I crossed my arms. "This is between you and Kallie. She has some things she'd like to say to you."

Marcus' chair squeaked as he shifted uncomfortably. "I'm listening."

Kallie drew a deep breath, but her voice wavered. "I'm thinking that maybe... maybe we should..."

She trailed off, then turned to me. "Charlie?"

The desperation in her voice was heartbreaking. She couldn't do this on her own, and that said a damn lot for a girl like Kallie.

"My grandfather taught me how to break bonds," I blurted.

"Uh, okay..." Marcus sounded confused— until it hit him. "Wait. You mean... you want to break *our* bond? You can't do that, Charlie!"

"It's not my decision," I stated coolly.

Marcus huffed. "What is this, some sort of threat? An *intervention?*"

"No," Kallie insisted. "I just can't keep doing this anymore."

"So you're just going to give up on me?" he demanded.

"You say that like I *want* to!" Kallie shouted. "Marcus, all I want is for us to get along. I want to secure our bond. I want us to be *together*, and it's killing me that we aren't. If you can't do that, fine, I'll respect your decision. But you need to respect *my* decision to walk away, because I can't stay here and love you if I can't love you fully."

Marcus surprisingly kept his cool. "You're giving me an ultimatum. You're threatening me so I'll *behave.*"

"If I have to do that, clearly you're misbehaving!" Kallie snapped. "This isn't some empty threat. I need to know where this is going, and if you can't make a decision, I'm done trying to beat an answer out of you."

Marcus sat there in silence for a few beats. "I don't believe you. You're not going anywhere."

His words hit *me* heavy, so I couldn't imagine how they must've affected Kallie.

"Oh my gods," Kallie said in realization. "Is *that* why you're doing this? You're stringing me along because you know I'll never leave? That's abusive as fuck, Marcus!"

He blew a breath. "Wow. That's a strong word. I would *never—*"

Kallie slammed her hands on the table and shot to her feet. "I don't care what you *think* you're doing. I'm telling you that I'm hurt, and you don't seem to care!"

"Of course I care!" Marcus insisted.

"Then why don't you want to *be with me*?!" Kallie screamed.

"You think that's why I won't secure our bond— because I don't want it?" Marcus raged.

"It sure as fuck feels like it, because why else would you avoid it this long?" Kallie demanded. "There's no reason why we can't be together! Nothing is stopping us but you!"

The air shifted around us, and magic tingled up and down my arms. A glowing rope appeared in my vision, and I realized the heat of their argument had brought their bond energy to the surface, where I could see the spiritual tethers tying them to one another.

The rope was so thick I didn't think I'd be able to wrap my hands around it if it were solid. An ethereal glow pulsed back and forth between them as passion surged across their bond.

"I want you to have the world," Marcus said.

"All I *want* is you!" Kallie shot back.

"You're not going to have any options if you're stuck with me!" Marcus shouted. "Once we secure our bond, that's it. *This* is all you're ever going to get. I'm a sorry excuse for a mate, and I don't deserve you."

"What's going on?" Ava's voice cut across the balcony. We all turned as she wheeled outside beside us. Her voice sounded groggy, like she was still trying to wake up. "I could hear you guys screaming from our room."

Kallie plopped back down into her chair. "We're just having a *friendly chat*."

"Kallie wants to break our bond!" Marcus cried.

I felt my wife's panic flicker across our connection. Ava's tone turned sympathetic. "You can't do that. Kallie, I know you're hurting, but you two can work this out."

"I know you think that because Charlie would never give up on you, but Marcus has already given up on me," Kallie said sadly. "He did a long time ago."

"You're the one giving up," Marcus sneered.

"Marcus, you aren't even *trying*," Kallie stated firmly. "We haven't made any progress in our relationship— and don't act like fooling around is progress. If anything, it hurts even more. Do you understand how fucking shitty it feels to be intimate with you, then just gather my shit and leave instead of staying the night? You didn't even *say* anything the last time. After it was done, you just let me walk out!"

"For fuck's sake, Kallie, it's not like we've slept together!"

"I don't care if we haven't had sex. By this point, we've done everything else, and it still means something."

Marcus let out a scathing sound of disgust. "Well, you fucked Scarlet, so I guess you would know."

"How dare you throw that in my face. We weren't together, so I don't know why you're upset."

"Because we're mates! I'm still pissed you did that."

"We're *supposed* to be mates, but we aren't, so why does it matter who I sleep with?"

Kallie wasn't even yelling at him anymore. She was too upset to do much of anything but protest and cry.

Ava grabbed my hand, her unease growing through our bond. This was hard to watch for both of us, but we had to let them have it out.

Marcus sighed. "I just don't get why you want to be with *me.*"

"Because *I love you,*" Kallie urged. "I love the way you express yourself through art. I admire that about you, because I can't express myself the way you can. I have to be so tough all the time, because that's what the world expects from me, but you're such a gentle person. You soften me up."

I could understand that. It was one of the reasons Ava and I worked so well together. I was a guy who had a pretty cold exterior, but Ava could melt me with just one touch. When I was with her, I could just be *me.* I knew Marcus was that for Kallie.

"You teach me how to see things from a compassionate perspective when I'm being too hard-headed," Kallie continued. "Nobody gets me like you do. Being at the Institute was hard, and there were times when you were the only thing holding me together. But ever since we broke out, it's like *you're* the one tearing me apart. Sometimes I wish we'd *stayed* there, because at least things wouldn't be different now."

"They're not all that different," Marcus muttered.

"And that's a problem!" Kallie insisted. "They *should* be different. We should be a couple. When things are good, Marcus, they're really fucking good. You surprise me with gifts, and even though we're not technically dating, you take me on the *best* dates. And when you go down on me... holy hell. It's moments like that when I know you really care. Sometimes, things will be really good between us, and I'll think everything is perfect."

She blew out a breath. "But gods, when it's bad, it's fucking awful. We'll have these big heated moments where you think I'm going to leave, and I promise you I won't, but I can't seem to convince you otherwise. You won't let me in, no matter how hard I try to help you. I'm just *so sick* of having this fight. It's really easy to see who you care about, because you're always there for them. I love how much you care about people, yet when it comes to me... you either care too much, or not at all."

"I care more than you know," Marcus said harshly. He wasn't being kind; he was being defensive.

"If you care so much, then show me," Kallie begged. "I love you so damn much, but I'm terrified you can't say the same, because it seems you only want me around to torture yourself."

Ava's grip tightened on my hand, and the tension in the air grew. We were both terrified of where this argument might end, and yet nothing we could do could stop what needed to be said.

"Maybe I *am* tortured," Marcus spat. "The view you have of me is false. I'm not this kind, noble guy you talk about. I'm just Marcus Taylor— some nobody theater geek who was smoking weed in his bedroom while you were being a princess by day and assassin by night. Before you got to the Institute, you were making the world a better place. I've done *nothing* with my life. One day you're going to wake up and realize that. Eventually you're going to get sick of me, and someone better will come along. It's easier to prepare myself for the disappointment."

I understood feeling inadequate, but Kallie was right. Whether Marcus realized it or not, he was doing this to punish himself, and he'd let that consume him to the point where he was only thinking about how to protect his feelings. Kallie desperately wanted to be with him, and he couldn't see *that's* what would make her happy. He was afraid to be happy with her, so he deliberately made them both miserable by pushing her away.

I'd made the choice to let Ava go because I loved her. Marcus wanted to keep Kallie in this limbo state where he could claim her as his own without ever having to take responsibility. That wasn't a relationship. It was a prison.

Kallie blew a breath in disbelief. "I'm so tired of being your fucking idol. I'm not some god to be worshiped; I'm just a woman who wants to be loved! You're not preparing yourself for disappointment, Marcus. You're already disappointed— constantly! You're making it worse by expecting the worst. It shouldn't matter if you lose me. What matters is if we're together *now*. You're so afraid of losing me in the future that you don't even want to try. You need me, but you're not willing to give me what *I* need."

The passion surging between their bond grew in intensity. Magic pulsed back and forth across their spiritual tether so fast that it was making me dizzy.

You aren't really going to break their bond, are you? Ava worried telepathically.

My stomach hollowed. *I don't want to, but it isn't my decision. It's Kallie's. And this isn't fair to her. She doesn't consent to being in this relationship against her will, and I'm not going to violate that.*

Ava understood deeply. So deeply, she didn't object further.

"Because I'm just so inadequate, aren't I?" Marcus sneered. "No matter what I do, I'm always going to be living in your shadow."

"You're being a coward," Kallie spat.

That really pissed Marcus off. "Forgive me if I know what it's like to lose someone! No matter how much I love you, I'm not a safe choice. So let's just keep what we have going, without putting any labels or obligations on it, and enjoy ourselves for whatever time we have left."

Marcus wanted to remain in the comfort of his despair more than he wished for Kallie to have peace. He didn't care if she was suffering, as long as she didn't leave him.

If that's how he was going to treat her, I didn't think they should be in a relationship at all. My job was to provide whatever Ava needed, even if there was a price I had to pay for it. And Marcus' complete refusal to make himself even the slightest bit uncomfortable so Kallie felt secure angered me. Greatly.

Kallie sighed in defeat. "You don't get it. Our time is up. I know you went through something hard, but you've deliberately made this harder for us. And you know what I think? I think you know exactly what it's like to lose someone, and you're okay with that. What you're *really* afraid of is that someone might actually want to stay, because you can't handle things going right. So maybe I should give you what you really want, and we'll both get our way. I'm sick of having this argument. This is the last time I'm having it. If this is how things are going to be, I can't be happy *with* you. We could have been happy together, but not anymore."

Ava's heartbreak filled our bond. We both knew where this was going, but Kallie had made her decision. We couldn't stop her now even if we tried.

"You're really going to walk away?" Marcus demanded. "Go ahead, but it's not going to mean anything. I'm your mate. You can try, but you can't be happy without me. You're not going anywhere."

I didn't need to have a connection with Kallie to feel how winded she was at Marcus' words. What he'd said had completely crippled her, and she was my friend. I wasn't going to allow him to keep hurting her like this.

Something broke within me— within us all. The spirit rope tethering the two of them together shattered like glass. A gust of wind blasted across the balcony, blowing my hair back. Fatigue washed over me, hitting me so suddenly that I fell to my knees.

"Charlie!" Ava gasped. She reached out to try and yank me to my feet.

"What— what just happened?" Marcus panicked. His voice was full of terror. "What did you *do?*"

He didn't need to ask me. He'd felt what had happened. But he had to hear me say it.

"I... broke your bond," I rasped.

I hadn't meant to do it... or maybe I *had*. Kallie had made her decision, and I was going to help her one way or another. I just hadn't meant for it to happen that soon. My grandpa had warned me this could happen if I lost my temper, and I didn't realize what I'd been doing until it was already done.

"You *broke our bond*?!" Marcus screamed.

He crossed the balcony in less than three paces and grabbed me by the collar. He yanked me to my feet and shoved me against the side of the palace. I should've been able to fight him off, but the spell had left me exhausted.

"Put it back!" Marcus shouted in a pained voice that echoed across the city. "*Put it back*, Charlie!"

"Marcus, stop!" Ava yelled, but he didn't listen.

Feathery wings flapped from overhead, and talons scratched against the banister. Oberi panted, like she'd flown as fast as she could get here.

Oh, no, Oberi whispered. *I'm too late to stop it.*

"You shouldn't have done that!" Marcus raged. "You had no right!"

Air swirled around his fist as he drew his arm back to punch me, but Kallie caught him and yanked him back.

"It's not his fault!" Kallie yelled. "I *asked* him to do it."

"No... no!" Marcus insisted, as if he could deny the truth.

I righted my shirt and stood up straighter. "I'm sorry. I really am. But I wouldn't have done this if Kallie hadn't asked. Whatever the situation is between you two, Kallie doesn't consent to being a part of it. She was born into this, and she didn't have a choice. All I did was give her that choice back."

Ava reached out for me. *Do you think this might've been a mistake?*

No, I told her. *This is what Kallie wanted.*

Marcus shuddered so violently beside me that I felt his tremors against my arm. All the rage melted from his tone. "I— I can't believe you did this."

Kallie breathed a sigh of relief. It sounded like it was the first unlabored breath she'd taken in ages. "This was the right thing to do."

"But you broke our bond," Marcus whimpered, as if it needed repeating... like he wasn't quite convinced of it.

"I told you I was going to! You didn't take me seriously," Kallie replied.

Marcus began to weep. "I didn't think you'd actually do it. I'm— I've been *blindsided!*"

Kallie huffed. "Charlie's blind. You're just a fucking moron."

Marcus dropped to his knees. "You can't leave me, Kallie! We're mates. We're—"

"Don't," she warned. "We're not mates anymore. I don't have any obligation to you. I'm never going to let you touch me again."

Sobs broke from Marcus' chest, and he turned into a blubbering fool at her feet. "I'm sorry. I'll do anything. I can change! Just give me one last chance."

"You had your chance. You didn't want commitment, so I gave you exactly what you wanted."

Marcus wailed. "I didn't want this!"

"Marcus..." I started, but he turned on me.

"Leave me alone," he snapped. "How could you do this?"

"You couldn't make up your mind. Kallie wanted this, and it'd be wrong of me to say no. I didn't do this to hurt you. I did this to help her," I replied.

Marcus got to his feet. He stood so close to me I thought he might try to throw another punch.

Instead, he sneered, "You know what, Charlie? I thought you were like my brother, but you're no brother of mine. Now that you've done this, you mean nothing to me. Just... go to hell."

I gaped at him. How could he say that after everything we'd been through? How could he throw our friendship away, when he was the one who'd caused all this in the first place?

Marcus shoved past me. His footsteps echoed down the hall as he ran away. I turned to go after him, but Ava grabbed my wrist.

"Let me," she offered. "You're the one who broke the bond. I need to be the one to talk to him, because he won't listen to you right now."

My shoulders sagged. I wanted to be there for my friends— both of them— but it seemed impossible, and that was more than devastating. To help one friend, I had to hurt another. There'd been no good way to solve this, and the damage had been done. This was a permanent decision, and now, it was over with. The only thing left to do was pick up the pieces.

Ava followed Marcus, and Oberi flew behind her. Silence settled over the balcony until Kallie turned to me.

"Thank you, Charlie," she said in a stronger voice than I'd heard her use all night.

"Are you sure this is what you wanted?" I asked.

"Yes. This was the right decision."

"How is this going to affect your powers?" I asked. "I know fae magic is closely linked to their mating bond."

"Now that the bond is broken, my powers won't be as strong as before, but it's worth it," she admitted. "I'm certain I wouldn't be able to time travel right now, but I'll be able to once I recover. My demigod magic will regenerate my powers eventually. It just... *sucks* that I never got to see how strong I could really be, because Marcus and I never secured our bond in the first place."

"You're strong without him," I told her. "You don't need him to be everything you were born to be."

"I know. I'm glad for it."

Then Kallie did something unexpected... she pulled me into a hug. Tears rolled down her face and soaked into my shirt. "Thank you so much."

I hugged her back. "I'm really sorry, Kallie. I wished this could've ended in a different way."

"Don't be. I know I made the right choice," she whispered. "Now, I'm finally free."

ava-marie

TEN

This was a fucking disaster. And I'd been involved in enough shit shows to know when things were going south, and when things had ended up in the pits of hell, and this was absolutely the second one.

"Marcus, wait!" I cried out. My wheelchair couldn't go as fast as he could run, and I was losing him in the palace halls.

I'll go after him, Oberi said, sailing forward.

I was too tired to push myself, so I used the remote on the chair to hurry after them. I followed my bond to locate Oberi. She was perched in a tree in the palace gardens a few branches below Marcus. He'd climbed into the limbs of the tree and was crying. Rishi had found him, and the cat was lonesomely mewling in his lap.

I stopped my wheelchair below the tree and looked up. "You've gotta come down."

"Go away, Ava. Go back to your bastard husband."

I felt Charlie's hurt twinge across our bond. He'd heard that.

I blocked Charlie out, because Marcus needed me right now. If he had to vent some frustration, he needed to be allowed to do that without my husband getting hurt.

"I'm not going anywhere," I replied. "You need to talk about this."

"Talking isn't going to do any good. She *left* me. There's no way to fix it now."

He sobbed harder. I was pretty lost on how to help him, because there was no way to express how absolutely devastating this was for him.

Then I realized... he *had* to express it. He was in so much pain all that anguish needed to go somewhere. He needed to do art.

"Hey, Marcus?"

"Yeah?" He sniffed.

"I've been wanting to get another tattoo," I tried. "Can you give me one?"

"Right now?"

"Yes. Please?"

He gave another loud sniff, then wiped his face and muttered, "Okay. I'm coming down."

Marcus let out an *ouch* as he cracked branches on the way down the tree. He almost tumbled out of it. I had to hold my breath, because I worried he was going to fall. When he got down to the ground, his face was so blotchy he didn't look like himself.

"Let's do it here." He sat down on a chair beside a fancy outdoor table, then conjured the tattoo quill I'd seen him use so many times.

"You have it in your stash?" I asked as I rolled up to the table.

"I always carry it with me, in case I get any urges." He gave a miserable shrug. "It's a replacement for... other things."

My mind didn't have to wander far to imagine what he meant. I'd seen tiny slit marks hiding underneath the colors of his tattoos once or twice, when we sat close together or when he pointed something out.

I'd noticed for years, but never said anything about them, because they didn't make Marcus any different to me. I destroyed others; Marcus destroyed himself. It's just what we did.

But that's exactly what I needed to talk to him about, because this conversation didn't really have anything to do with Kallie.

"It's good you're investing in your art," I said, not knowing what else to say.

"I'm running out of places to put them. I wanted to draw one on my elbow, but I can't reach around that way without making the drawing look like shit."

"You should open up a part-time tattoo shop," I suggested. "You're so talented that you should share those gifts with others."

"Maybe. I'm gonna have to start moving on to my legs next. There's a lot of empty skin there."

Marcus conjured a drawing pad. "What did you want to get?"

"A unicorn, on my right wrist."

He began to map out the idea for the design. I let him work in silence, observing as he put curled lines and intricate loops onto the paper. When he was done, he turned the pad around to show me.

I nodded. "It's perfect."

I liked it. It was really girly, but I also thought it signified Oberi. The design said something about being really strong when you didn't have any other choice. He'd definitely put his feelings into it, and that's what made the tattoo so heartfelt. The design was complicated and would take time to finish tattooing.

Good. It would give me some time to talk to him, and this conversation was going to be a deep one. I didn't want him running off until I got my point across. Marcus wouldn't leave a piece of art unfinished, even if he hated it. It wasn't in him. So he'd stick around to finish the tattoo even if he didn't like what was being said, and there were some things he needed to hear.

I laid my arm on the table. Marcus bent over and began to draw. The cool edge of the quill's tip laid ink into my skin, and the familiar feeling of getting a massage drifted across my wrist.

I didn't know how to start the conversation, until Marcus said quietly, "I don't know what I'm going to do now. She was the center of my universe."

If that didn't cut me through. An image of Charlie suddenly vanishing broke into my head, and I felt completely gutted. "I'm sorry, Marcus. I wish it could've turned out differently."

"Doesn't matter. I guess it's over now."

"It *does* matter, Marcus." I wanted to cry for him, because this was terrible, but I managed to keep myself together. "Kallie and Charlie aren't like us. They think with their heads, and we think with our hearts."

"Is that why she did what she did?"

He stopped drawing to look up at me. His eyes were so full of heartbreak. It was like looking into the eyes of a little kid. He seemed like a little boy who'd been abandoned, and he didn't feel the need to mask it around me like he did the others. It showed.

I was honored he felt he could be that vulnerable with me. But we understood each other like that. "Marcus, she asked Charlie to break your bond because she physically couldn't hold on any longer. I know her— she tried, with everything in her. If she had remained bonded to you, it would've eventually killed her. I know you don't want that for her."

He nodded thoughtfully. "I understand. I always knew I was bad for her."

Impatience flared within my chest, but I placed it aside. "It's not about that, Marcus. You're bad for her because you *believe* you are. You could've made a different decision. But now that it's over, you've gotta think about what you want to do next. Not what you and her are going to do, but *you*, and the life you want to live. That's the only thing that counts from this point out."

"Why does it matter if I'm not with her?" he asked. "Everything's pointless now."

I knew his mental health was on the edge. I completely got it, because I understood what it was like to feel like you were free-falling through life with no way to see the bottom, or know if the impact was going to hurt once you finally got there.

"It's not pointless. You don't need her to be yourself."

"But it feels like I need her to keep breathing," he argued. "Logically, consciously, I know Kallie loves me. I *know* we belong together. But there's something inside of me that can't accept it, and I always felt like she was going to leave me, so why make it permanent if I'm just holding out to be abandoned? I feel like I have to test her loyalty, even though I know that's unfair. I don't *want* to be this way, and I don't know why I am. But I can't make this go away, no matter how hard I try to logic my way out of it."

He gave a shaking sigh. "My dad's got depression, and he promised me if I went on meds this weight on my shoulders would be lifted. But I feel like it's never been heavier. He doesn't *get* me. And I thought that Kallie did, but I ended up being too much for her."

This was the part where I prayed he wouldn't run away. I'd suspected this for a while, but hadn't been sure until tonight. "Marcus, maybe you were misdiagnosed. Maybe it's not depression. Maybe it's BPD."

"What's that?" He shook his hair out of his eyes and looked up.

"Borderline Personality Disorder is—"

"Oh, that's great, so it's a personality disorder, like narcissism," he grumbled. "I'm an even shittier person than I thought."

"Let me talk," I said gently, and he shut up. "As I was saying, being borderline is a pattern of having unstable and explosive emotions. It messes with self-image, makes people impulsive, and leads to having chaotic relationships with others. People who are borderline can't tolerate being alone. They feel empty often, get angry at inappropriate times, self-harm, and have an intense fear of being abandoned. Suicide attempts are common with untreated BPD, too. Sometimes, it can masquerade as depression, though that's not really what it is. Maybe that's why nobody's caught it."

"I mean, it sure sounds like me," he said. "But I'm still not convinced it's that bad."

"It *is* that bad. Marcus, look at how it presents. You're always talking shit about yourself, you have a hard time controlling your anger, and you're always afraid you're going to get left, to the point you blow up your own relationships with the people you care about the most."

"But how do you know this is something I potentially have?" he pressed.

I wasn't surprised he was in denial. There were times I tried to talk myself into believing I didn't have bipolar, either, but it never worked. "It's just a guess. But I spent a lot of time in and out of the mental hospital growing up, and I know what it looks like. I've seen other patients with it."

He scowled. "I don't want these labels. I'm so sick of being told something is wrong with me."

"I've been labeled my whole life. I didn't like my diagnosis at first, either, but I learned that the label isn't about marginalizing ourselves, but about making sense of it, so we can find the tools that work for us," I explained. "Without my bipolar label, I wouldn't understand what was going on with me, or how to manage it. I think you need to see a psychiatrist and seek a formal diagnosis so you can get the help you need. You need mood stabilizers. Your antidepressants aren't enough. They might not even be the right prescription for you."

Marcus focused more intently on the tattoo as he asked, "How does somebody develop BPD?"

"Usually, it happens due to childhood trauma. Being in an unstable household and that sort of thing."

"That doesn't make sense," he argued. "I had really good parents, so I can't have it. My childhood was overwhelmingly positive, as far as my family goes."

"Usually, people with BPD have abusive or narcissistic parents, but that isn't always the case. Your parents might've loved you so much and been so overprotective that it started to become intrusive, and that made it hard for you to understand what you needed emotionally."

"Having helicopter parents isn't enough to cause this kind of mental pain," Marcus argued. "There's gotta be some traumatic event in my past that caused all of this."

"Maybe it's trauma you don't remember, because you were too little. But it could've had a big effect on your development," I said. "Do you know if there was anything bad that happened to you when you were a toddler, or even younger?"

He seemed contemplative. "Well, my brother died when I was young, but that wasn't the only thing. When I spoke to my parents, and they told me they knew I was a demigod all this time, they explained something *bad* happened to me when I was an infant. That's when I was cursed so they couldn't tell me what they knew about my powers. Apparently, it was terrible enough that I summoned my god Santos to protect myself. I was in danger, and people were hurting me."

Marcus acted like nothing bad had ever happened to him in his childhood, but he'd just listed off so many things that could be the cause of his struggles.

"You don't have to give any details on what happened," I said quickly. "But if what your parents say is true, then it explains why you're hurting so badly.

Most of our personality, and our insecurities, are formed before the age of five. My concern here is that BPD is usually formed from consistent trauma over a long period of time, and not just one instance. There are also genetic factors which can make you more likely to develop BPD even if you came from a good family. High emotional sensitivity can be an inherited trait, and that doesn't mean it's a bad thing, but it can lead to problems if it's not managed well. But maybe we're not looking at the big picture. There's not necessarily clear causes for a lot of mental illnesses, and that could apply here."

Marcus scoffed. "I've been fucked up since I came out. I've always struggled with depression and stuff like that, even when I was a little kid. Other kids picked on and bullied me mercilessly because I just didn't come out right. How I was as a child isn't normal."

"Well, I was diagnosed with bipolar really young, far younger than usual. Typically, bipolar isn't recognized until late teens or early twenties, and I was having severe symptoms by the time I could talk," I pointed out. "Marcus, we know having demigod abilities fucks with our brain chemistry. It wouldn't be unusual for your magic to mess with your brain, like my abilities worsen my bipolar. And you killed eleven people by accident when you were eighteen, which probably made it worse. You were barely an adult, and it was really traumatic. Do you realize you probably have PTSD on top of all of this? It might not be just one thing, but a lot of different things contributing to how you feel. The trauma from your infancy, your demigod powers messing with your brain chemistry, the bullying when you were younger, and potentially, trauma from your past lives could all be contributing to why you feel this way."

His response was thoughtful. "I guess that's true. But if I really do have BPD, it's not fair, and it's not okay for you to have bipolar, either. Why did we get the shitty end of the stick? Charlie doesn't have to deal with this. He's fine."

I nearly scoffed, because whatever Charlie was, he was never *fine*. "He does have to deal with it. He doesn't have BPD, but he gets angry and destructive. It's just in a different way. And Kallie struggles, too. But this is how you personally struggle."

His lip quivered. "I want to be with Kallie, but it's like I *can't*."

"Marcus, I really need you to hear me right now." I reached out to lay a hand on his arm, and he stopped drawing long enough to look up. "This isn't about Kallie. This is about your mental health. You're really sick. You need help. I'm worried you're not going to be around if this goes on for much longer. And no matter how bad things have ended up between you and Kallie, I want you to get treated for what's bothering you. Because despite what happened, I can't handle losing another friend. And none of us want to lose you, because your life is worth more than what you're willing to admit. You've *always* mattered. So as much as you think everyone else has given up on you, don't give up on yourself."

His eyes watered. "Can you promise me that it gets better?"

"I think it does. And it gets worse. Then it gets better again. Bipolar is shitty, and having BPD can be just as awful. But I still think life is worth living with it. There are ups and downs, but this world is so big and beautiful. It's not worth missing out on just because our brains are being assholes."

I paused before I added, "People who have borderline personality also fixate and obsess about one certain relationship. They choose somebody called a *favorite person* who they idolize and rely on for constant validation and comfort, but they typically blame the favorite person whenever they feel insecure. The BPD individual craves the favorite person's attention, but when they're triggered, the one with BPD will test the favorite person and push them away to see if they're going to leave or not. And I think we know who your favorite person is... and how you've been treating her."

"If that's true, then I can't have BPD, because I only push Kallie away," Marcus said. "I don't think she can love a guy like me."

"That's the BPD talking," I replied gently. "Marcus, you *did* latch on to Kallie. She's the person you seek all your love and adoration from, but at the same time, you don't believe it when she shows it. You also don't believe you can ask for validation, because you think that if you do, it doesn't count. You pushed her away because you wanted to see her fight harder for you, but that only became a self-fulfilling prophecy. She loved you so much, and it became too exhausting for her to give her love to someone who didn't receive it."

Marcus dropped his gaze. "It's all my fault, then."

"I'm not saying that, and I don't think it's helpful to think that way," I told him. "Relationships take work from both sides, and there were times when Kallie didn't treat you right, either. Having a greater understanding of this isn't about assigning blame, but about acknowledging the role you played and taking responsibility for making improvements. It's important to recognize what was helpful and what was harmful. With that understanding, you can find the right tools that will help you in the future. Neither of you have to excuse how you treated each other, but you do have to forgive yourselves, because you can't move forward if you're resentful towards Kallie or yourself. It's about getting the help you need, Marcus."

His hands shook, but he took a moment to calm them before he returned to working on the tattoo. "Do you think me having BPD is the reason I lost it at the Institute when we broke out?"

I didn't know. Marcus had turned into someone else that night, and from what he said, he couldn't remember going manic and developing a personality that was so contradictory to himself. But I had struggles remembering things when I developed psychosis, too.

"I'm not saying that psychosis episode was related to you having BPD," I started. "But the thing is... if a mental illness gets bad enough, almost *all* of them can result in people hearing or seeing things, even with something as common as depression. That's why it's really important to get some sort of treatment, because the longer you let it go, the worse it can get. You just get more and more paranoid, and more scared, and upset. Eventually your mind starts making up shit that's not there because you're sick and not getting help. It's like the progression of any disease. And I think you're at a point where you can't handle this by yourself."

Marcus nodded. "I can agree with that. There's something dark within me that I don't understand, and I don't think it's related to whatever's going on in my head. Back there, when we were breaking out, it was like something *else*... took over me."

"Maybe it wasn't BPD. Maybe it wasn't even a psychotic episode," I suggested. "Maybe it was the villain inside of you, coming out to protect yourself and all of us."

"I agree with that," he added. "Everything you've said so far about BPD makes sense, except for this. I don't think that episode and what's going on in my head are related."

"Do you think it was magical?"

"Possibly. That's what it felt like. It didn't seem like something that was going on inside my head, or something I was being possessed by, but something my demigod magic was *channeling*. I'm not really sure what happened."

"Whatever it was, I don't think you want it to happen again."

"No. It was scary, blanking out like that. And if it *does* happen again, I want to be in control of it this time."

I dropped my gaze. "I know how you feel. It's no fun, losing yourself."

"No. I hated it." Marcus scowled.

"If you don't want it to happen again, you've gotta work on understanding yourself, and what your triggers are. It's important for you to manage your condition, so it doesn't interfere with your life anymore. Or at least, as little as possible."

"It's not like I'm disabled like you and Charlie are."

"BPD *is* a type of disability, because it's disabling to live like this," I insisted. "You shouldn't discredit how painful this type of disorder can be."

"How can you say that?" Marcus asked. "You definitely have it worse than me. You're in a wheelchair."

"Big deal. That doesn't mean I get more disability points than you," I said.

"Yeah, not being able to walk isn't exactly ideal, but there are times where my bipolar gets so crippling that it becomes more of an obstacle to my life than being a paraplegic does. It's not a competition to see who's suffering more. You're in pain, so you should get what you need to get better. That's not taking anything away from me."

"Okay. I suppose you're right." Marcus leaned back as he finished the tattoo. "I'll go see a psychiatrist as soon as I can— tomorrow, even."

"Thank you. It means more to me than you know that you're taking this seriously." I raised my arm to observe the finished tattoo. I almost went breathless at how elaborate it was. "It's beautiful, Marcus."

"If you say so." He shrugged. "The nose is too long, and I put too many lines in the mane."

I didn't see it. "Well, whatever you think, the world shouldn't live without a gift like this, or without *you*. And despite your bond being broken, maybe things between you and Kallie can get better once you find what works for managing your health."

"She's never going to take me back. It's done," he replied despondently.

"I'm not saying you guys are ever going to be romantically involved again," I added. "But she means a lot to you, and you mean a lot to her. And though she needs her space, maybe there's still room for you somewhere down the line, once you get better. Being friends is a lot better than being nothing."

Marcus subconjured the drawing pad and quill. "I don't know if I can get better. But I want to at least *try*. Thank you, Ava. For being there."

I always would. Marcus and I shared something with each other the other two couldn't comprehend, a wordless understanding that agreed we were very similar and struggled with similar things. Charlie struggled at points with connecting with my turbulent emotions, but Marcus didn't, because he had to battle them himself. We couldn't shove down our feelings and hide them like my husband and Kallie could; we had to fight with them every day. So I would be someone who Marcus could battle his feelings with, because I knew better than anybody no one could do this alone.

Marcus agreed with me that he shouldn't be alone right now, and that he should stay with his parents for a while instead of in Charlie's suite with the rest of our friends. I figured it would be best if he didn't cross paths with Kallie or Charlie right now, and that his family would look out for him until he got to a more stable place. I personally escorted him there. I explained the situation quickly to Nadine and Lucas before I left with Oberi to travel back to our quarters.

By this time, it was pretty late at night, and I was longing for bed. But I really wanted to talk to Kallie before I turned in.

She opened up her door immediately when I knocked. I had the thought she appeared to be completely renewed. She stood straighter, and there was a reignited light in her eyes that I thought had gone out a long time ago.

My heart sank as I realized she looked like a girl who was relieved to finally be out of a bad relationship. My own feelings about the whole matter were complicated. I'd be cheering for her and opening a bottle of wine to celebrate if this had been some douchebag she'd dumped.

But it wasn't. The person she'd left was one of my best friends. I was happy that she was finally free of a situation that had been suffocating her. But I was also sad for Marcus that he'd lost her.

"Hey. You talk to Marcus?" she asked.

"Yeah." I entered her room, and she shut the door behind me. "He's with his parents."

She nodded slowly. "Good. I won't have to worry about him. I can focus on... me."

"How do you feel?" I asked. We roamed to the balcony, and she took a seat in one of the chairs while Oberi perched on the ledge.

"Honestly? Like I can finally breathe," she admitted. "It's no longer about what makes him happy, or what makes us happy, but what makes me happy. I can think about what I need, and I haven't in so long. I lost myself in what we were, and to find myself again... I can't even tell you how much that means."

"I'm glad you're getting your identity back."

"I had to. It's hard for me to remember who I was before him." She crossed her arms, holding herself. "At least now I can make decisions for myself without some jerk trying to run the show."

"There might be more to it," I said slowly.

I explained the conversation I had with Marcus, and told her my thoughts about him potentially having BPD. She seemed thoughtful when I finished explaining.

"This makes sense. If you're his favorite person, it explains why he has such intense feelings about you that go back and forth between positive and negative," I said. "He projects these big fantasies onto the relationship and needs your approval to feel good about himself, but he also lashes out because he's trying to test if you'll leave. It can be hard being with someone who has BPD, but if he gets treated, this relationship isn't doomed to fail. You guys could still make this work and set up healthy boundaries."

"Maybe that could've happened before, but the bond is broken now. The magic is gone, so I'm not interested in trying again," Kallie said shortly.

"Not even a little?" I whispered.

"No. He hurt me more than you realize. I can't sit around and allow him to treat me poorly because I feel bad for him."

"I get it. I have bipolar, but it doesn't give me an excuse to treat Charlie like shit." I shook my head. "But at least now you know why he acts the way he does. He doesn't want to, Kallie. He's not just an asshole."

Her mouth remained flat. "It's not an excuse for the way he treated me. I never thought he *wanted* to hurt me, Ava. But I don't want us to get back together. Ever. I don't want to even be his friend. And until he's better, I think it's worse for him if I'm around."

My heart broke into a million pieces for them. "I agree. Still sucks, though."

"It does. But I'd rather live with a broken heart than with regret that I never took the chance to see what life could be like without him hurting me," Kallie stated. "He might be able to recover and live a happy life, and that would be really awesome. Me and him, though? Never again. I wish him all the best, but he needs to leave me be."

Oberi cooed, then hopped onto her lap. Kallie stroked her feathers, and whatever hope I still had left for her and Marcus died within me. I really thought my intuition was right about them, but guess not.

It was contrary to everything I believed in, but I really had to wonder if love was able to fix the worst situations. At the very least, if they couldn't be happy together, maybe somehow they could be happy apart.

Time, I supposed, would tell.

⛓

THINGS WERE REALLY quiet after what went down with Kallie and Marcus. Charlie and I didn't see either of them around, just kept to ourselves.

Charlie felt guilty about what he'd done, but he didn't regret his decision. I thought that Kallie and Marcus had to grow separately before any progress could be made on reconciliation, friendship or otherwise, and Charlie had done all he could to help our friends. It was up to them now to see what the future held.

A few weeks later, Abigail delivered a letter from my Auntie Imogen, asking me to come visit her. I hadn't seen her in ages, so I was delighted. She was spending the day at *Uni Essentials*, a place in the city, and asked me to swing by. I wasn't sure what the location was, but it sounded magical, so I was looking forward to going. I took a carriage, and Eldin escorted me downtown.

From the moment I entered through the glass double doors, I was instantly transported to a fairy land. The doorway was a portal, and it took me to a room that had been placed under a wonderful illusion spell. The area around me was a massive flat plane surrounded by mountains, bathed in golden sunlight. The very air sparkled, and I inhaled the scent of wildflowers. On the cliff sides of mountains were gigantic mushrooms in pink, green, and light blue, so large they rivaled the size of trees. The sky seemed to span overhead, though if I looked closely, I could see wooden beams where the ceiling was high above.

There were unicorns everywhere, grazing on the mountain and napping in the sun. A river ran through the middle of the room that the unicorns drank from, and the water came in rainbow colors. Balloons filled the air, and the entire area smelled like birthday cake. All around the room were different vendors— chocolatiers, candy carts, and ice cream. Nearby, there was a white barn. On the wall were mounted all kinds of bridles and saddles, which the Elves tacked onto the unicorns to ride. Elves were bathing the unicorns, brushing their coats and feeding them treats. A big smile bloomed on my face as I watched unicorns bounce off of gigantic marshmallows into candy cane clouds.

"It's a unicorn stable," I said in wonder. "With all the things a unicorn could ever need."

Oh, goodness, I appear so silly, Oberi said in embarrassment, hiding behind her phoenix wing. *I need to fit in.*

Oberi changed into a unicorn and pleasantly stomped her hoof. *There. I am no longer a faux pas.*

I saw Auntie Imogen standing near a long stage at the bottom of the mountain that looked like a runway. She called me over, and I rolled across a pink bridge to where she was standing.

"Hey, Ava. Glad you could make it. You're the go-to girl on fashion, and we really need your opinion," Aunt Imogen said in a fluster.

"I'll say!" A high-pitched voice rang out from behind a rack of clothes. A blonde woman with large glasses poked her head out of a mess of gowns. "And to make things worse, I don't think this is my color."

The blonde woman waddled out from behind the racks, and I had to slap a hand over my mouth to keep from belting out with laughter. The *color* wasn't what was wrong with it. In fact, the lavender shade was the only thing saving the dress— if you could call it that. It was more like one big ball of tulle, shaped in a way that made the wearer look like a massive puff ball. The sleeves were so huge that the woman's arms stuck straight out, and she couldn't bend them.

"I designed that dress myself, Odette!" Aunt Imogen shouted. "I think it's great on you."

"It makes my ass look huge!" Odette countered. "I look like one big butt cheek!"

I knew her. Odette was one of Kallie's aunts— an alicorn sorceress, who was married to an alicorn shifter. There was an array of mischievous giggles. Three clones of Odette stepped out from behind the curtains. I assumed they had to be around my age. One of the girls was stuffed into an outfit that made her look like a walking avocado, while her two sisters wore equally outlandish garments— one an outfit that looked like a variety of long stuffed gloves sewn in a mismatched array, another a gown that appeared to be a bunch of pillows taped together.

"Theodora, take that off," one of the girls snapped, poking the avocado outfit. "You look ridiculous."

"Absolutely not, Odessa! It's in *style*," Theodora purred.

"Well, I suppose it *does* suit you, because you're always green with envy," Odessa said, fluffing her hair around the pillows.

"Says the girl who's cosplaying a mattress!" Theodora squawked. "Back me up, Kiara!"

"I'd rather look like a mattress than a hand job," Kiara said sourly in her glove dress. She'd definitely gotten the worst pick.

The triplets began to squabble. It was hard to tell who was saying what, because all of the triplets sounded identical.

"Girls, please, we don't have time for this," Odette told her daughters. "Let's see the opening dance again."

Theodora, Kiara, and Odessa lined up on stage before they broke out into a coordinated ballet sequence, which would've been lovely to watch... if Odessa hadn't stepped on Kiara's glove skirt and caused the three of them to come tumbling down in a heap.

I couldn't hold it in anymore. "What are you guys doing?" I asked with a laugh.

"We're putting on a fashion show," Aunt Imogen explained. "It was your friend Marcus' idea. Help morale around the city and all that."

"Yeah, except *my* morale is in the toilet, because this is a disaster!" Odette cracked. "The show is tomorrow, and it couldn't be more of a mess."

"Things would've been fine if my nephew hadn't insisted on turning the whole show into a musical." A petite brunette woman emerged from behind the scenes, holding a collection of sheet music and looking flustered. A white cat purred at her side. She hastily rearranged her sheet music. "I was good to go before Marcus came and made all these changes, and now, I'm more confused than ever."

"It wasn't such a bad idea, Talia," Aunt Imogen started. "Marcus is a good director, and he had some splendid ideas."

"Except I demanded that I play the lead, because my singing voice is *beautiful*, and he said no!" Odette squeaked.

Odette broke out into a croaking ballad that made several of the unicorns around us bray.

I winced. "What did Marcus think of all this?"

"Unfortunately, after seeing the first run-through, our director got frustrated. Marcus gave up and went home," Talia explained. "So Imogen decided you'd be the first one we should call for help. After all, a fashion show endorsed by the princess herself is sure to get attention."

"I don't know what to do. Jonah and I spent all week making these dresses, and it's too late to change them now," Aunt Imogen moaned.

That explains why they look so ridiculous. "I'm sure if we put our heads together we can think of something," I insisted. "Run the whole thing over again from the beginning, and I'll tell you what I think."

"Very well." Odette pulled at her dress. "I swear, this gown is giving me a wedgie."

"As long as a unicorn horn isn't where it shouldn't be," Talia joked.

Odette's mouth fell open in outrage. "Don't speak about my husband's endowments that way!"

A light laugh caught my attention, and I turned my chair. Queen Emmaline was sitting on a stair by the stage. I didn't know Kallie's mother would be here. She'd been so quiet I hadn't noticed... though it was easy to get overlooked when Imogen and Odette were in the same room together.

Queen Emmaline didn't exactly make me uncomfortable, but she was an intimidating figure. I suppose she had the right to be here just as much as I did, so I did my best to focus on the performance and not on impressing her.

I spent the rest of the afternoon watching the rehearsal. I made some suggestions and helped Aunt Imogen with the alterations for some of the garments. After all, I wasn't going to put my name on this fashion show unless it was as good as I could possibly make it.

The other models in the show were actually unicorns the girls had dressed up in different outfits. One had a doughnut-shaped hat around her horn with a cape draping down her back that looked like sugar sprinkles, and another was dressed to look like a scarecrow. The unusual garments looked very pretty on the unicorns. I thought Aunt Imogen should start designing clothes for animals instead of people, because they made more sense.

Of course, Oberi insisted she wanted to be a part of the show now, too. My Familiar proudly strutted her stuff up and down the stage in a giant green hat that was adorned with fake flowers. It was so heavy that it almost toppled off her head and killed me on one of the walk-throughs.

Seriously, though. That thing hurt coming down. I was going to have a bruise. By the end of rehearsal, everyone was feeling much better.

"You've saved the show, Ava," Aunt Imogen insisted. "We wouldn't have known what to do if you hadn't gotten here. We really needed an outside opinion."

"Glad I could be of service." I wasn't fully on board with the entire production, but I'd done what I could to save it. Odette had insisted on coming down from the ceiling in her puff ball outfit riding a giant plastic banana to start the show, and we hadn't been able to talk her out of it. She'd declared it would *make an impression.*

It would certainly do that. However this show performed, it would certainly be one the Elves never forgot.

As I turned away from the stage, Queen Emmaline rose. "Princess. If we could, I think we should have a conversation."

She wanted to talk to me? Why?

Queen Emmaline wasn't the kind of person you said no to, and even though this was my kingdom, she was a guest in my court. I wasn't going to refuse her. "Sure. Where should we go?" I asked.

"I pay for a personal parlor room in the store," she said. "We can talk there."

Oberi followed me as I trailed the queen. She came to a white door with golden swirls that was set into the side of the mountain, and she opened it wide for me.

We roamed inside, and I softened at how beautiful it was. We'd ventured into another illusion room. This one had been transformed into a beach, perched at what seemed the edge of the world. It appeared there was a setting sunset on the horizon, bathing the entire beach in shades of pink. On the beach near the water was a table set up with a grouping of chairs. There was a paved area beneath my wheels, so I could roll up to the table easily. There were unicorns here, too, and they frolicked in the water when they saw us approaching.

The queen sat down at the table and ordered tea from a waiter, while I bit into a cupcake that had already been set out.

"What a pretty room," I remarked. "I love it."

"I write poetry here. It's a hobby of mine," she explained. "The unicorns are inspiring, and sometimes I need a bit of space to myself."

I understood that. From the pocket of her dress, a little faekin came whizzing out. He was a miniature tiger no bigger than a dragonfly, with monarch butterfly wings and feelers on top of his head. He rubbed his face against the queen's cheek, then greedily got to licking up a spoonful of honey she set out for him.

"How wonderful! Is he your faekin?" I asked.

"Yes. Tygrys has been my constant companion and protector since I was nineteen," she replied. "He goes everywhere I do."

The queen gave Tygrys a cookie to nibble on, which he jealously guarded from Oberi with tiny, growly teeth. She waited until the staff brought the tea, and didn't begin speaking until we were alone again.

"You have to be wondering why I brought you here." The queen dropped two sugar cubes into her tea, before silently gesturing if she could give some to Oberi. I nodded, and my unicorn lapped up the sugar cubes in her hand greedily. "If we can, I'd like to get straight to the point."

"I appreciate that," I confessed. "I'm not someone who enjoys small talk."

"I'm not, either." She tapped her stirring spoon against the teacup. "And I believe this needs to be said, because no one else will say it, and you'll understand if it comes from me."

"Please, Queen Emmaline—"

"Call me Emma. At least, when we're alone," she insisted. "I know we have to follow royal protocol, but at heart, I'm still just a fae girl, and always will be."

I nodded. "Okay. Emma."

I dared to take another cupcake, because they were really fucking good. "Sorry if I'm awkward. You just seem so... strong."

"Strong?" She raised an eyebrow.

"Yes. No-nonsense."

She gave a wistful smile. "That actually encourages me to hear. Reminds me of someone I used to idolize. Perhaps I've become a little like her."

Emma sighed and added, "Well, the point is, I know you have a heavy burden. You're a royal now, so you have to act like one and manipulate the court in your favor. I want to help make that process easier, if you're open to the idea. I could tell during your spiritual ceremony that you felt out of place."

I blew out a breath. "I guess I couldn't say this to anyone else, but it *is* hard. I like being a princess, but there are so many things to learn. I wasn't born into this. I'm the daughter of a chieftain, but Hawkei culture is so different from Elvish. And the Elves have become important to me. They're now my people, but I feel like I'm going to fail them."

"It's typical to feel that way after marrying into a monarchy," Emma said. "It can be overwhelming at first, but you'll get used to it."

"You weren't born royal, were you? You came from America."

"I did," Emma said. "I became queen when my mate ascended to the throne, though I do say he couldn't have made it without me."

Her eyes narrowed as she mumbled, "At all."

"I guess you had a lot to do with it?" I asked.

"We both did a lot of work to save Malovia and become the rulers our country needed us to be, but if I'm speaking bluntly, I put him there. When I became Ethan's mate, I wasn't just choosing him, but choosing the crown and all its responsibilities."

I shrugged. "I guess it wouldn't have made a difference. I married Charlie knowing who he is. Even if I'd realized the role we'd have to step into down the line, I still would've married him."

"Being a royal becomes you, the longer time passes," Emma stated. "I can't imagine not living this life now, but there was a time when I was younger where I really had to weigh if this was what I wanted."

"How did you deal with the pressure?"

"I had a great many mentors who believed in me," Emma said. "And I wanted to change things in Malovia for the better, no matter what the cost. I knew I wasn't going to be able to do that unless my mate and I were the ones in charge. The fae are a stubborn people— but I'm worse. I was determined to set things right and get my way. And in the twenty years that my husband and I ruled, we certainly pushed things in the right direction."

"People say you're the greatest fae queen there ever was," I whispered in near awe.

Emma scoffed. "They certainly didn't talk like that when I was first crowned."

"You moved an Elven city from Edinmyre to Earth. That's an incredible feat."

"Perhaps. It's not that impressive. It's just what had to be done."

I wasn't buying it. No other fae on this planet would be able to do that but Emma. She'd accomplished something amazing, and no matter how high the queen's standards were, she was more powerful than I had anticipated her being.

"It's still a big deal," I stated. "I can't imagine anyone going up against you."

"Anything worth doing is going to meet with opposition, and quite frankly, the fae are assholes," Emma replied. "They worship me *now*, but it took years of ruling with grit and iron to get them to see things like I did. I was never cruel, but I wasn't going to allow hatred and bigotry to exist in Malovia if I had something to say about it."

"I want to be like that." I leaned closer. "I want to be a good Empress, someone people talk about for ages after I'm gone."

"Consider yourself lucky— you already have an advantage. The Elves nearly consider you a deity, so they'll be easily persuaded. But that's a heavy responsibility in itself. You're young, so you're going to make mistakes. All rulers do. The best advice I can give you is to think of the world before yourself. And don't make a move until you're certain your orders are going to help more people than they hurt... because someone *always* gets hurt at the end of the day, Ava. You can't prevent that as a princess. Only try to mitigate the damage."

"I don't believe that," I argued. "Charlie and I agreed we're going to make a better world for everyone."

Emma gave a thin smile. "You'll learn."

Oberi was begging for another sugar cube, rubbing her soft lips on Emma's shoulder. She fed the unicorn another, then gave Tygrys a second spoon of honey. "My daughter told me about your... death, so to say, after your encounter in the Infernal Underground. Firstly, I would like to apologize. No one should have to go through such a thing. I should be the first one to know."

I had heard the stories. "You went to the afterlife and returned too, didn't you?"

Emma went slightly pale, but I didn't see any other signs of her inward crumble. "I did. I had to imprison an evil entity on my quest, a very powerful dark creature. He wasn't easy to defeat. Putting him back in his grave took my life, as my prophecy had foretold."

"Yet your gods allowed you to return."

"They did. Someone I loved very much took my place." She gave a sad smile. "I had to leave them behind, as well as my goddess, Milonna. I haven't seen her since I departed the fae afterlife, the Great Hunting Grounds, and I miss her dearly."

"Why'd you come back if the Great Hunting Grounds were so wonderful?"

"I returned for my husband. I wanted to live a full life with him, and I felt cheated that I hadn't been given that."

"But you came back," I said. "Just like me."

"Yes." She nodded. "But I didn't come back the same."

I got it. Probably a little too well. "I wish others could understand. I've tried to make them get it, but they can't."

"Because no one will ever be able to comprehend what we've been through except each other," Emma told me. "You and I are the only ones I know of that have been to the land of the dead, existed amongst them *as* the dead, then returned to life on Earth. It's not enough to merely visit the spiritual realm and understand what it's like. You give up yourself as you die. Your soul becomes different. So walking amongst the living afterward, who have no idea what that experience is like, feels... empty."

I fiddled with my teacup. "Marcus said his parents visited one of the afterlives during their quest."

"Yes, but visiting it as a living person and being a part of it as a deceased individual isn't the same," Emma noted. "You and I both thought we were there to stay once we arrived, and then we had to leave. It's confusing to our souls, not to mention our mortal bodies remember dying, and what it's like to be dead. So it feels off to be living and breathing. Though we're happy to be alive, we're also sad we're not... there."

Ancestors, she understood exactly how I felt. "Being in the Ancestral Lands... it was the most unconditional kind of love," I said. "I've never experienced anything like it. I love others, and others love me, but nothing comes close to that feeling of peace and complete acceptance on the other side. And I was fine— it was the people back on Earth grieving me who weren't."

My throat constricted. "I came back because of Charlie. I definitely would've stayed in the Ancestral Lands if he hadn't called for me."

Emma nodded. "The things we do for our mates. You have a soul bond with Charlie as well. Though from what I understand, it goes deeper than other bonds I've heard of."

"It can be all-encompassing sometimes," I admitted. "We're not just soul-mates, we *share* a soul. Things have stopped being about me or him, and have become about us. And I like it that way, because I think we work best when we're acting as one being, instead of two separate people. It's the way our magic works. But I love him so much that sometimes, that love is scary. I don't know what I would do without him."

I sighed and leaned back in my chair. "Though there's one thing he can't really understand. My brain's never been right, but things have gotten worse since I came back. It's hard for me to remember things from the Ancestral Lands. I get mixed up on what happened and what I'm making up. Part of me still thinks I died young— because I did— and the other part thinks that since I'm alive here, that never happened. Because logically, it *couldn't* have happened if I'm still around. I have a hard time keeping things straight."

"I believe that's normal. Our soul isn't able to comprehend how powerful the spiritual realm is when it's stuck in a mortal body," Emma explained. "I have trouble with that, too. You're not crazy. Just trying to figure out what's real and what's in your head. Though that doesn't help, because I suppose it's *all* in your head."

"I'm just trying to put the pieces back together, one step at a time," I hushed. "But there are gaps. And I'm never going to be able to see the whole picture until my soul goes somewhere else."

"It's not a simple process. I've had to deal with this alone for almost twenty years," Emma said quietly. "And though I'm sad that you had to go through it, too, it makes me happy I have someone to share this experience with, because we can lean on each other."

My eyes watered. "Thank you, Emma. I'm... I'm really glad you understand."

We sat in silence for a moment. I played with my napkin and said, "It's too bad Kallie's not here. She used to tell me she missed tea parties back in Malovia. It'd be nice, the three of us."

Emma chewed slowly on a cupcake. "I asked her to come today, and she didn't show. She has to go through the grieving process, because her mating bond didn't turn out to be the happy ending fae society promises."

"What do you think she should do?" I dared to raise my eyes.

"I'll support whatever Kallie needs. I told her before her bond was broken to keep fighting for Marcus. But now that bond is gone, and I understand why she's tired of trying." Emma frowned. "Losing a mate is a devastating experience. It's soul-damaging. I nearly went through it myself. I think she and Marcus would be good together. But that's only if they can get out of their own way, and it seems too late to turn back now."

"Maybe," I said sadly. "Losing a bond is the hardest thing I could imagine."

It was unfathomable to think about losing that connection to Charlie. I wouldn't want to live anymore. Yet Kallie seemed like she'd needed the bond to break, so she could heal herself. I was both proud of her that she could be that strong, and sad things hadn't worked out.

"Let's hope they can keep working together," Emma added. "Because even though their bond is broken, I'm not convinced they can cut each other off completely."

I really hoped so, too. I went to say something else, but the door to the room creaked open. Aunt Imogen stuck her head in. "Ava, I hate to bother you, but Ezekiel is asking you to swing by as soon as you can."

She closed the door, and Oberi nickered. "I'm sorry," I said. "I can stay—"

"It's fine." Emma put her teacup down wistfully. "I said what I needed to. Go spend some time with your brother."

Her eyes glimmered as she whispered, "It's more important than you know."

I said goodbye, and Tygrys waved his feelers in farewell. The servants took me back to the palace, Eldin following behind. All of our friends had rooms in Charlie's quarters, and Ez and Opal shared one there. I noticed my handmaiden wasn't around as I entered the space. I told Eldin to stand guard outside.

My brother was pacing on the balcony. He looked... nervous. Tahoma was spread out across the bed and snoring loudly. Apparently *he* wasn't worried about Ez's freakout.

"You're the only one who can summon a princess and get away with it," I said as I approached my brother. "Look how much I love you."

"Thanks for coming by on such short notice," he said. "I didn't want to lose my nerve. It's about Opal."

I gave a dramatic sigh. "*This* again? Look, Ez, I'm sorry that you're tired of other guys hitting on her. I don't know how many times I gotta tell you, but Opal's technically an available lady. *My* lady. The Elf dudes at the palace couldn't give a flying fuck if you're her boyfriend. All of them want to elevate their positions, and marrying the princess's handmaiden makes them look good to the Emperor. If you want to keep her, you're gonna have to lock that shit down."

Ez took a breath. "Actually... that's what I wanted to talk to you about."

Ez dug in his pocket. He took out a tiny box and opened it. Inside was a rose-gold engagement band with a fire opal set into the center.

"Well?" he burst anxiously.

"No way." I looked up. "You're really gonna ask?"

"Well, since she's your lady, you technically have to approve any marriage proposals she's given," Ez said sheepishly. "And I figured I'd better ask you now, before you get pissed off at me for some stupid thing and tell me no."

"I wouldn't do that, shut up." I leaned closer to inspect the ring. "That's a pretty nice gemstone."

"Yeah, it is. I don't know *when* I'm gonna ask her, but when I found this ring, I decided I should go for it." He shrugged. "What do you think?"

"Wow, Ez." I looked up at him. "Have you talked to Mama and Daddy about this?"

"Yeah, and they're on board. They know I'm gonna do it anyway, whether they approve or not, and she's the one." Ez swallowed as he put the ring back in his pocket. "I think we'll wait to get married until the war's over, though. I want this wedding to be about her, and I know Opal. She won't focus on planning stuff because she'll be too busy worrying about what's going on out there. Not to mention med school is kicking my ass right now. I need to focus on passing some classes before I can actually tie the knot."

"I'm happy for you guys. Really." I leaned back in my chair. "You ready to be a dad?"

"I've been ready. I love Marina, and she loves me. Opal's daughter is the best, and I want to be her dad. I know you think this is fast, which is why I'm gonna give it some more time before I ask her, but I've made up my mind."

"Then I'll support you." I reached out and gave him a hug. "I'm so proud of you, Ez. You're going to be a great husband, and you'll make Opal happy."

"I hope so," he said, and he gave an anxious laugh. "I guess we'll have to see, right?"

There wasn't any doubt in my mind. I knew they'd be happy together. And it would be nice to attend a big, fancy wedding, since I hadn't gotten one of my own. I couldn't wait to help Opal with whatever she needed.

Though I hoped the day would actually come. Ez didn't want to marry Opal until after the war, and who knew how long things would drag out.

I hoped love would find a way through all things, but I wasn't sure if it would. Not when the world was this dark.

I felt the world tilt as my mind twisted, and my stomach lurched as I saw The Beast appear in a darkened corner. There he was, looming in the back of the room and observing me with a cruel smile. His gaze nearly promised that Ez and Opal would never get to be husband and wife, because he would kill them both before they had a chance to wed.

Over my dead body.

"You okay, Ava?" Ez asked warily. He knew when I was slipping; he'd grown up alongside me and could see the signs.

I glared at The Beast, refusing to take my eyes off of his as I replied, "Of course, Ez. Everything's just fine."

charlie
ELEVEN

Things had changed in the palace since I broke Kallie and Marcus' bond. Kallie's voice was brighter, and she walked with a spring in her step.

Marcus, on the other hand, didn't speak to me. I'd tried to talk to him more than once, but every time he knew I was around, he scurried in the other direction— as if he could hide from me just because I couldn't see him there. His energy was stronger than any other warlock's, though, and I could sense it easily with my Elf magic.

I understood he was mad. Ancestors knew I'd be pissed at anyone who tried to come between Ava and me. But I'd resolved to give him space. I didn't know if he'd ever understand why I did what I did, but I hoped he'd forgive me. It was hard not having my best friend around, and we were all worried about him.

At least there was some good news, lately. Ava told me Ez was planning to propose to Opal, though she didn't think he'd pop the question for a while yet. I wish he'd just do it already. He loved Opal so much, and they deserved their happily-ever-after. If it were me, I wouldn't wait another second to ask Ava to marry me. We never had a proper wedding, and I knew we both felt like we'd missed out. I didn't want Ez to wait for this war to end, because if he did, he might miss his chance. Ilamanthe was the perfect place for him and Opal to tie the knot, and he needed to get on with it already.

As if to prove my point, the sun shone down on me, and a warm breeze touched my skin as I made my way through the castle. It was a beautiful day, but so was every day here in the Elf city. Oberi walked at my side, leading me to the front doors. Eddie had informed me this morning that my grandfather changed our meeting location from the gardens to somewhere outside the palace.

When I asked Eddie why he'd do that, he simply said, "You're going to need more room."

I wasn't sure what my grandfather had in store, but I was excited. I never quite knew what to expect from him, so every lesson was always interesting.

Several servants greeted me at the doors, then guided me into a limo. I rolled the window down, enjoying the sounds of Ilamanthe as we drove through the streets. Oberi stuck his head out the window and panted happily. I tried to guess where the driver was taking us, but I didn't know the city well enough.

Soon, the sounds of the city faded, and the smell of salt water touched my nose. When I stepped out of the car, Oberi took off running. I went to follow him, and my feet sank into the sand. The guards that always followed my grandfather hung back.

"Charlie," Cassiel greeted. "How was the drive?"

"Great," I told him. "Oberi loved it."

You didn't tell me we were going to the beach! Oberi cried as he ran around. *I would've brought my beach hat. Here, throw me this stick.*

Oberi shoved a stick into my hand. I tossed it, letting my Air magic carry it far away. Oberi sprinted down the beach, barking happily.

I turned to my grandfather. "Why are we here?"

"I have a theory," he said. "But in order to test it, we had to get out of the castle."

Magic tingled across the bond, and I heard a big splash as Oberi shifted into a narwhal.

"Unfortunately, we will need Oberi for this exercise," Cassiel said, and he laughed.

I whistled to her. "Oberi! We've got work to do."

She smacked her fins against the surface of the water a few times in protest.

"Oberi, get your ass out of the ocean right this second!" I yelled. "If you're in there too long, the war will be over before you get out of the water."

Oh, yeah? What are you going to do about it if I stay? Oberi challenged.

"I might've gotten you a special treat earlier, but I'm not sure I feel like giving it to you now," I teased.

Hm. All right, but I want some belly rubs later, she grumbled.

She shifted into a husky and came out of the ocean. He shook his fur at me, getting me all wet.

I patted his head. "Good boy."

Yes, master? he said snidely.

"We're learning a new trick today." I turned back to my grandfather. "So what's this theory?"

"As an Elf, you know you can siphon energy from other supernaturals and take on their power," he started. "You shifted into a dragon at the bank. I wonder if you could take Oberi's powers."

"Won't that drain him?" I asked. "It's one thing to take magic from an enemy, but another to take from our own side. I can't leave Oberi helpless."

"That's what we're here to find out," Cassiel said. "The war is getting worse. There was recently a battle in Malovia between the fae and The Mission. We lost a lot of people and had to go on the retreat. More still, we lost ground in Malovia, and now that ground is outside of King Kazim's control... which means it's outside of ours. The capital city of Dolinska is still under our command, but we lost the outer villages."

"Why haven't I heard about this until now?" I pressed. I was a prince, and I needed to be informed.

"Because we have enough soldiers fighting this war. Your attention can't be divided from getting those keys, especially when there's not much you can do from here," he stated. "We have many generals, but only one prince. Remember what we talked about when it came to prioritizing your attention?"

I nodded. I understood what he was getting at. My attention and effort was a limited resource, and we had to utilize it properly... even if that meant taking a few losses. "If Kazim's no longer in control of certain parts of Malovia, that's a hard hit for us to take. We already lost Kinpago and Octavia Falls. We can't lose more ground than we already have. Otherwise, we're going to be overwhelmed."

"We may have lost the battle, but we *will* win this war," Cassiel vowed. "To do that, we must think of things Doctor Taurus has not. Soon, you will be ready to lead our people. In order to defeat him, you must become the most powerful Emperor this world has ever seen. So let's make you as powerful as possible."

"Siphoning shifter magic from Oberi shouldn't be hard," I said with a shrug.

You think your Elf power is stronger than mutabeecha magic? Oberi challenged playfully. *You're on.*

Oberi growled, but I quickly siphoned a bit of his magic, and he quieted instantly. I could feel the magic surging through our connection. It was easy. I couldn't believe we hadn't thought to try it before.

I guess you are *strong,* Oberi admitted reluctantly.

I tried utilizing his shifter magic for my own, but nothing happened. The magic tingled throughout my body, then just *stopped.*

"It's not working," I noted.

"Let's try it in a different form," my grandfather suggested.

Oberi shifted into a Fire unicorn, and we tried again. This time, the connection was even weaker. I could hardly siphon her magic at all. She shifted into a phoenix, and then a narwhal, but the result was the same each time. I could *feel* her magic, but I couldn't use it as my own.

"I can feel your Earth form strongest," I said. "Maybe because it's the weakest of them all."

Who are you calling weak? Oberi demanded. *You don't want to be caught under these claws.*

"Or perhaps you're more connected to Oberi's Earth form because it's your own element, and not part of Ava's," my grandfather countered. "Why don't we try Oberi's Air form?"

My eyebrows shot up. Oberi's Air form *was* his strongest... but it was also my strongest element, and Ava had told me before she guessed this particular form was connected to my half of our soul bond. "It's worth a shot."

You might want to take a step back, Oberi warned.

Magic built up throughout the bond as Oberi shifted into wyvern form. He grew to massive proportions, blocking the sun's rays from touching my face. Oberi let out a loud roar that seemed to shake the whole beach.

"He's an impressive beast," Cassiel stated proudly, before clapping me on the shoulder. "Take his power, Charlie. *Become* as powerful as he is."

My grandfather walked off, leaving us space so he wouldn't be squashed by one of Oberi's massive talons.

I focused on Oberi's power. His Air magic pulsed through me, more powerful than any of his other forms. I reached out for him, and he ducked his head so I could run my hands over his scales. Our connection ran deep, and magic sizzled over his form. I tangled my Elf magic with his power, and it came flooding into me. I took his magic into my body, willing myself to shift.

My legs elongated, and huge leathery wings grew out of my arms. The temperature of my body dropped, and my skin turned to scales. A warm sensation grew in my throat— the taste of poison I could now use to harm my enemies. I felt massive— over twenty feet long, at least.

My grandfather's applause came from far below me. "You did it! By the goddesses, you appear identical to your Familiar!"

Wow. I guess I did! I tried to say, but the words didn't come out. Oberi heard me, though.

I don't feel a thing, Oberi told me. *You aren't draining my power at all. It's like I'm sharing it with you, but I'm still as strong as ever.*

This is awesome! I raved. *I wonder what I can—*

I went to take a step, but I stumbled to the side and fell onto my shoulder.

My feet were *huge*. I wasn't used to being this big, or moving this much weight around.

Oberi let out a roar that sounded like a laugh. *Still a clumsy ass.*

From below me, my grandfather said, "You'll need to be more coordinated than that if we want to use this power in battle."

I stood straight up and shook off the fall. *I've got this. Come on, Oberi. Show me how to fly.*

You can't even walk yet, and you want me to teach you how to fly? Oberi joked.

I'm a fast learner, I replied. *I don't want to walk. I want to soar.*

It's not hard at all, Oberi said. *All you have to do is open your wings and let the wind carry you off.*

Oberi launched into the sky. I spread my leathery wings and kicked off the sand to follow him. My stomach dropped for a mere moment before settling, and as I pumped my wings, I felt the wind underneath me rise to support them. I used Air magic to bolster my place, raising me up quicker than I would without help. If I thought siphoning Oberi's magic was effortless, it was nothing compared to flying. Flying was as easy as walking down the street— easier, even. I felt like I'd been born to do this. I could fly as an Air Elementai by shifting the wind currents around me, but this was different, as I didn't have to do anything but allow my wings to carry me to where I wanted to go.

I was acutely aware that I had shifted into a twenty-foot-tall beast, but as I launched myself over the ocean, I felt weightless. My wings kept me up with no effort at all, and I could easily shift my weight from one side or the other to guide my path through the air.

Follow me, Oberi instructed, and he guided me through our bond.

Air rushed across my face as I pumped my wings, and we climbed higher into the sky. Moisture tickled my skin, and then came the warm kiss of the sun on my scales when we broke through the other side of the clouds.

The sky felt so expansive in front of me. I could go anywhere, and nothing could get in my way.

Woohoo! I shouted to Oberi through the bond.

There's no need to speak through the bond, Oberi said. *Use your voice.*

I opened my mouth, and a gleeful cry escaped my throat. It was deep and powerful. I tested a terrifying roar and was surprised to feel my whole body shake. It would certainly make my enemies think twice about facing me.

That's more like it! Oberi cheered, before letting out a deafening roar of his own.

A grin spread across my face, and I noticed my teeth were razor-sharp. I could snap the Warden's head off with a single bite. Just the thought gave me so much joy that I let out another cry, which sounded a bit more like a deranged laugh.

I'd like to see the Warden try to stop me now.

I spun through the sky, spiraling upward and downward, and doing flips from side to side. I'd spent so long locked up, but out here, I was free. It felt as natural to exist in this form as it did to be an Elementai.

Check this out! Oberi called through the bond.

I felt a shift in the air, and he went diving back down toward the clouds. I dove to follow him and heard the ocean crashing below me. When I felt the spray of the sea touch my claws, I caught myself at the last second and spread my wings outward, skimming my talons over the water.

Cold ocean water sprayed into my face, and I nearly fell out of the air in shock. Oberi tried to hold in a laugh.

Hey! I splashed him back with my tail, but he dodged out of the way. I flapped my wings and went after him, but Oberi was faster than me and ducked. I flew over top of him.

You can't catch me! he alleged.

Oh? Want to bet?

I chased Oberi through the sky, twisting and turning, but every time I thought I'd caught up to him he pulled away from me.

Watch out! Oberi called.

He warned me too late, and I flew straight into a flock of birds. One of them landed in my mouth and crunched against my teeth. My first reaction was to be disgusted, but I found I *enjoyed* the taste of blood on my tongue. I ate a few more, just because I was hungry.

The beach is up ahead, Oberi warned me.

I heard him land. I came down right on top of him, tackling him playfully to the ground. I couldn't really land well, so might as well fall on top of him. Oberi nipped his sharp teeth at me and tried to buck me off, but I had him pinned down.

Told you I could catch you, I teased.

Oberi's teeth connected with my wing a moment later, and he yanked me into the sand. He was gentle with me, and it didn't hurt, but it sure as hell made my heart rate spike. I got my legs under him and shoved him off of me, then twisted to get on top of him again.

Yield, I told him.

Oberi laughed. *Never!*

We roughhoused for a few moments more, shoving at each other. He was heavy, and just as strong as I was, so it was fun tossing each other around. We caused earthquakes on the beach as we wrestled, spraying sand everywhere with our tails. If this was a real fight and not just playing around, we'd be well-matched.

When I'd pinned Oberi underneath my talons, he shifted into a husky and slipped out from under me. I spun around to try to find him, until I felt a sharp sensation travel up my leg.

"Ow!" I screamed. This time, it came out audibly as I shifted back into an Elementai. I ran my hand over my ankle, but I found no injury. "Did you just *bite* me?"

As if my canine teeth could penetrate wyvern scales, Oberi responded.

I noticed he hadn't exactly denied it. He was stronger than he was letting on.

Footsteps came from down the beach. "Excellent!" my grandfather exclaimed. "You will need more practice, but now we know what you're capable of."

I got to my feet and dusted off my pants. "It was definitely something. It was different than when I use Elf magic on other people, though. It didn't feel like I was *stealing* Oberi's magic, so much as borrowing it, like I can borrow Ava's Fire."

"As I suspected," my grandfather said. "You two are bonded, so your power is one and the same. You are unique in that you are an Elf who can utilize Oberi's power, but it is part of you nonetheless."

"I could only shift into a wyvern, though," I stated. "Why can't I shift into his other forms?"

"You can take on Oberi's form because you share a soul— other Elves can't overpower a *mutabeecha*, but your magic is deeply connected to Oberi's. You're borrowing his power the same way you do with Ava's Fire, but you're limited by your own identity. Elves can take magic from other shifters for a short period of time, but it doesn't last, because shifter magic is an identification of the soul. It's more about who you are than it is about the ability itself. You are more Yapluma than anything else, so your magic identifies with Oberi's Air form. His other forms are mostly identifiers of Ava's piece of your soul. With practice, you may be able to take on Oberi's Earth form as well, but Air has always been your dominant trait. Was it difficult?"

I shook my head. "Not at all."

"It certainly looked easy," he said thoughtfully. "I wonder... Elves can't siphon from other Elves, but you're a demigod. You may be able to overpower another Elf."

"What good does that do me if I already have Elf magic?" I asked.

"Not *all* Elf magic," he reminded me. "Talented Elves each have a unique gift. You may be able to use it. Try it on me."

I hesitated. "I don't want to hurt you."

"You won't. If we want you to become the strongest Emperor ever, then you need to *be the strongest Emperor.*"

His meaning was clear as day. He wanted me to be stronger than him, and to prove it, I had to overpower him.

"What's your specialty?" I asked.

He paused a beat before saying, "Why don't you tell me?"

He wanted me to figure it out on my own. I nodded. "All right."

I faced him and concentrated. His magic was difficult to sense, and that's because it was so strong it was like running head-first into a brick wall. My hands curled into fists, and my teeth gritted as I tried chipping away at that wall.

"Keep going, Charlie," he encouraged.

I shifted on my feet and tried again. "You're holding back."

"Yes," he said calmly. "Show me that you're stronger than me. Show me that you have what it takes to be Emperor."

I poked and prodded at his magic, slamming against it with my own like a battering ram, over and over again, but I couldn't access his magic.

I didn't understand. I was a demigod. This should be easy.

"It appears I'm not the only one holding back," Cassiel stated.

He was right. I didn't want to hurt him, so I wasn't using my full power.

But we didn't have time for games. People's lives were at stake, and though I didn't want to hurt my grandfather, I also had the feeling he could take whatever I threw at him.

I threw the full force of my power at him, and I felt the mental wall crack, but I still couldn't get through. Magic sizzled over my skin, and I pulled from Oberi without thinking. Within an instant, I was a wyvern again, baring my razor-sharp teeth at him.

My grandfather stumbled backward. I'd completely caught him off guard. A second later, I had him pinned to the ground under my talons. The mental wall completely crumbled, and his magic poured into me.

Visions flashed through my mind— images and concepts that didn't quite make sense at first. I began to see colors spread out in front of me, as if I'd never been blind at all.

I saw a woman with dark hair emerge within the murky depths of the vision. She was beautiful, and as I gazed at her, something in my gut told me I was deeply in love with her.

No, not me... *Cassiel.* I realized that the vision was actually a memory, and I could see it through his eyes.

He stood beneath an archway made of flowers. All around me was the beach, and the wide expanse of the ocean. His other surroundings had been forgotten, but what he remembered most was the woman. She had flowers in her hair and was walking down an aisle surrounded by people. He couldn't take his eyes off her. I could feel the smile on his face.

The memories flashed again. I saw him place a ring on her finger— a square rose-quartz gemstone surrounded by miniature diamonds on a golden band. Then I saw her spinning around in the sand while distant music played through the memory.

The memories faded from my mind. I found myself on the beach in Ilamanthe once again, back in Elementai form. I was on my knees in the sand, and my grandfather lay on the ground beneath me.

"Did you see it?" he asked as he slowly sat up beside me.

The magic receded, and I shook off the strange sensation. I stood, then reached for his hand and helped him to his feet. "That was different than anything I've felt before. You can read people's memories."

"Yes," Cassiel said. He placed a hand on my shoulder and led me toward a nearby rock to sit down. "I can read all memories, except those of a demigod's."

"So, you've never read mine?" I asked.

"No. You're stronger than me, so I've never been able to see your memories," he explained. "The memories I read aren't always clear, though, nor reliable, as memories can alter with time, or be tampered with by magic. It is a useful tool to gauge allegiances within the castle, but there are limitations to what I can do."

"The woman I saw was my grandmother, wasn't she?" I asked. "I remember you told me about her— how her family fled Kinpago during the Great Supernatural War and sought refuge on Darke Island. Years later, after the refugees fled into the caves and built Forevermore, she saved you from a *serpens spelunca* attack."

Cassiel's voice turned reminiscent. "Yes. That was Aponi. We were married on a beach in Forevermore. An illusion, but beautiful all the same. I come here often, as this place reminds me so much of her."

"It seemed like the perfect wedding," I remarked. I hadn't been able to see much in the memory, but I'd felt what he did, and he'd had a wonderful day.

"It was a grand celebration within Forevermore," Cassiel recalled. "All the Elves came, and we sang and partied all night. The Elves made flowers bloom and butterflies dance, and the sunset turned the sky pink. Your grandmother was the most beautiful bride. The party went on for several days."

"It sounds lovely."

"All Elvish weddings are," Cassiel said. "They are the most important ceremony our people have."

"I wish Ava and I could've had something like that," I admitted sadly. "She proposed last-minute, and we got married later that day in an abandoned chapel on prison grounds—"

"Excuse me," Cassiel cut in, sounding appalled. "Did you just say *Ava-Marie* proposed?"

"Yeah. I mean, we didn't have much of a choice. We had to get married so the Warden couldn't send me down to the Infernal Underground, because there was a rule that he couldn't attack a family member of a chieftain without inciting a war against the Hawkei. Ava was Liam's daughter, so she asked me to marry her, to protect us."

"This is not how things are done in the Elvish monarchy," Cassiel insisted. He sounded truly offended. "Where's the romance, the beauty? When I proposed to Aponi, it was a three-day event! Charlie, you are a prince. It was your responsibility to ask the princess for *her* hand."

"Well, I didn't really get that option," I grumbled. "Our friends put together what they could, but it was no Elvish wedding."

Cassiel shot to his feet. "This isn't right! No prince and his princess should be wed in such a manner. You should have only the finest wedding! I won't allow a grandson of mine to be married in this way."

I shrugged. "There's not much we can do about it now. Ava and I are already married."

"Nonsense," Cassiel insisted. "You are the heir to the throne. You can throw any party you want whenever you please. You may be married under the law, but you never had a proper Elvish wedding— let alone a Hawkei wedding on your mother's side— and therefore, you are not married in the eyes of the goddesses and ancestors. So we will begin preparations immediately."

A royal wedding! Oberi cried. *Get my veil. We're getting married! Again!*

My grandfather had clearly made the decision for me, so there was no arguing against it. But you know what? I didn't want to argue. I'd always regretted that I couldn't give Ava the wedding she wanted, because I knew in my heart that she desired it. She thought she'd never get to have the pretty dress or her big day, but this was a way I could change all that and make her dreams come true. We could do it all over again and get married the right way this time. It'd make her so happy, and gods only knew that was the one thing I aspired to in this world.

Besides... I was obviously not going to convince my grandfather otherwise. Couldn't really tell the Emperor no, especially about a free party he wanted to throw for me and my wife. This was important to all of us, and I'd never gotten to have a huge celebration with all my friends and family. Might as well go along with it.

"I'll tell Ava right away—" I began, but my grandfather cut me off with a guffaw.

"You'll do no such thing," he said. "You'll get down on one knee and beg for her hand, like any decent prince should do. And make it a surprise. A grand gesture, if you will!"

"I'm sure Ava will love the surprise." *And the fanfare.* I wasn't sure who was going to be more excited about planning this— my wife or my grandpa.

"We shall perform the ceremony in the temple within the palace," my grandfather informed me. "Your wife will walk down a stone aisle surrounded by sunlight, with flowers in her hair and ivy hanging from the trees. We will sing and dance, and you will have the wedding you both deserve."

I started getting excited, because this actually sounded like fun. "You know what, you're right. If we're going to do this, I want to do it right. I never got a chance to ask her family for their blessing, and neither of us got a proper proposal."

"Yes, indeed. And you need a proper ring."

"Ava has a ring," I stated.

Cassiel laughed. "I've seen that ring, and it is not fit for a queen. It is merely a band, and the princess deserves a marvelous gemstone."

"I really would like her to keep the original ring," I said. Kallie had made it for her when we'd first gotten married, and it was special to her because of that.

"If you wish to keep the original band, we can solder it to a new one. I have just the ring in mind."

I furrowed my brow. "What were you thinking?"

"Follow me."

My grandfather led me off the beach and to the limo. The driver took us back to the palace.

Wedding bells are ringing once more! Oberi sang the whole way back, though it was hard to hear him over my grandfather carrying on. Cassiel really had a thing for weddings, it seemed, because he kept throwing plans at me while I just nodded stupidly. I had to propose to Ava fast, so she could handle all this and decide what she wanted. I didn't care what the details were, as long as she was happy and we both had a good time. Let her and my grandfather decide on what color the decorations had to be or whatever. I was fine with anything.

Guards followed us to a secluded area of the castle, one where we had to wander through a lot of doors. Something on the wall beeped, and I heard a loud *thunk*, like a lock disengaging on a massive safe.

"This is the royal treasury," my grandfather said.

He led me inside. Oberi spun around, taking in all the jewels. *It's so shiny! Ava would love it here.*

"Your wife deserves a ring fit for a queen, and so, she will have this." Cassiel stopped in front of one of the displays, then placed a ring in my hand.

I ran my fingers over it. The stone was large and square, and it had a smaller collection of stones around the edge. It reminded me of the ring in Cassiel's vision, before I realized it *was.* This was my grandmother's ring. It had to be.

"I can't just... take this out of the treasury," I stated. "This has sentimental value to you."

"And that's exactly why I want you to have it," Cassiel said, closing my hand around the stone. "This ring belonged to the love of my life, and now, I want it to belong to yours. This ring is meant to be worn by an Empress."

My breath caught in my throat. I couldn't imagine getting rid of something of Ava's if I lost her, but that's what my grandpa was doing for me. He was willing to let go of this part of his wife to make me happy. I could never thank him enough.

"Then I guess there's just one more thing to do," I stated. "I need to talk to Ava's father."

ỡð

AFTER MY GRANDFATHER and I had discussed plans about the proposal, Oberi and I left the treasury and headed toward Ez's suite. Ava was busy in mystic training with Abigail, learning Elvish customs and about the goddesses, so I knew she'd be preoccupied all day. Now was the perfect time to talk to her brother.

Why do you feel the need to ask her family's permission? Oberi wondered on the way. *You're already married. It's not like you can take it back.*

I frowned. "I'm not asking permission. I know I don't need it. I'm respecting our culture and following tradition. In Hawkei weddings, the whole family is involved. The tradition isn't about asking for their permission to marry her. It's about asking if they'll accept me as part of their family. I know Ava will choose me either way, but I never got a chance to ask if her family will. My culture was robbed from me as a child, and Ava and I never got to get married in the traditions of our tribe. I want to do it right and gain their acceptance."

Oh, I understand, Oberi said brightly. *You're looking for a family.*

"No!" I shot back. Something inside me recoiled, though I wasn't sure what it meant. "I don't need anyone but Ava."

That's not correct, Oberi insisted. *You were taken from your family before you can remember, and you grew up without a home. You were on the streets, and then you went to prison. You never had a family. Now your estranged father isn't there for you—*

"I get it," I snapped. "You don't have to make a list."

It's fine, Oberi said nonchalantly. *Liam will be a better dad for you, anyway.*

My breath caught in my chest, but I wasn't going to tell Oberi he'd guessed what I'd secretly been hoping for. "I don't need a dad," I mumbled.

Of course not, because Liam's already there for you!

I wasn't talking about this. We reached Ez's suite, and I knocked.

He answered right away. "Hey, what's up?"

"Can we talk?" I asked. "Alone?"

"Sure. Opal's at the temple with Ava, and Marina is at a playdate. I was just studying for my med class." Ez opened the door and invited me inside.

I sat on the couch, and Oberi hopped up beside me. "Ava told me your plans to propose to Opal. I came by to congratulate you."

No, you didn't, Oberi said snidely. *Stop lying.*

A half-truth is still a truth. Shut up. I need to concentrate, I replied.

Ez instantly began gushing. "Yeah, I'm really excited. I've got the ring picked out and everything. But I'm going to wait until her birthday. I want to take her out on a special date, but if I do anything before her birthday, she'll suspect something. I want her to be surprised."

"Cool," I said. "When's her birthday?"

"January. There's an ocean sanctuary on the other side of Ilamanthe. In January, they're doing an open swim so people can swim with the animals," Ez said eagerly. "I think that'd be cool to take Opal to and propose there."

"That's a few months away," I pointed out. "I don't want to steal your thunder, but there might be another wedding before then."

"Cool. Who's getting married?" Ez asked. "Wait— did Alistair propose?"

"Uh, no. I'm sure if he did, Eddie wouldn't shut up about it," I joked. "I'm actually talking about me and your sister. We never got to have a traditional wedding, and I wanted to do it over again."

Ez let out a huge gasp. "Ancestors!" He threw his arms around my neck and squeezed me tight. "That's a great idea! Man, this is so cool. I can't wait for you to be my brother again."

See? Family! Oberi barked.

"I can't breathe," I rasped.

"Sorry." Ez let me go, but his voice cracked when he spoke. "This is going to mean so much to Ava. When we were kids, she would go on and on about what her wedding was going to be like. It was kind of sad to see you get married so fast, because I know that ceremony wasn't what either of you wanted. I'm so glad that you're going to give her her dream wedding."

"Are you sure you're okay with this?" I asked as he sat back down. "Because we're already married, and you're next on the list. I don't want to take any attention away from you."

"No, this is perfect. If there's a royal wedding, it'll take the heat off me asking Opal before I'm ready. Mom can worry about you two instead of harping on me to get on with it." Ez chuckled. "Going to your wedding is going to give me ideas. I can't wait to attend!"

I took a pause. "Well, actually... I'd like you to be a groomsman."

Ez's voice raised a few pitches. "*Me?* A groomsman? Wow. I'd... I'd be honored."

I laughed. "I guess I don't have to ask to be your brother, because that sounds like a *yes*. I still need to talk to your parents, though. Can you get the rest of your family around tonight for dinner?"

"Don't worry about a thing," Ez said. "I'll make sure everyone's there tonight."

I was hoping Ez kept his mouth shut long enough for me to actually talk to the rest of the people in Ava's family, and even though I only had to wait a few hours to ask them, it felt like time dragged by until it was time for me to leave.

At seven o'clock, Oberi and I arrived at the Mitoh residence. The door swung open before I could knock, and Sophia threw her arms around me. She still had her oven mitts on, and the scent of fry bread and smoked fish filled my nose.

She must've been standing there watching through the peephole, just waiting for me to show up.

"Charlie, it's *so* good to see you!" Sophia said brightly. "I've been cooking all day. Come, have a seat!"

She led me over to the table and practically shoved me into a chair. I was able to gather that there were already several people in the room, by the sound of the chatter around me. I barely took a breath before she started scooping food onto my plate. "Here, try the mashed potatoes."

"Mom," Alana said from several seats away. "That's too much."

"Nonsense!" Sophia replied. "He's a growing boy."

"*I'm* a growing boy," Maverik pointed out. "*He's* twenty-four!"

Ez sighed. "Ancestors, Mav. You make him sound so old."

"You boys don't know what old is," Liam complained beside me. He was obviously in a *great* mood.

"Liam, please," Sophia said. "You're in your forties."

Ava's father leaned back in his chair. "And every one of these years I've lived has been long."

A knock came at the door. Liam sighed and got up from the table to get the door.

"We brought cake!" a woman exclaimed.

"Imogen, Jonah." Liam said their names like he was sick of them dropping by unannounced. "You weren't invited."

"We just *had* to come," Jonah insisted.

Ava's aunt and uncle barged past Liam and pulled up a chair on either side of me. Jonah draped an arm around the back of my chair. "Ah, the man of the hour!"

I turned to Ez. "You told them, didn't you?"

"They hounded me!" he defended. "And how could I keep such great news to myself?"

I sighed and decided there wasn't really a point in making small talk. "Well, now that everyone knows, I guess we can just get to it. I know Ava and I are legally married, but I never got to give her the traditional wedding she deserved. My grandfather wants to throw us a royal wedding, combining both Hawkei and Elvish traditions. Because of this, I came to ask for acceptance into your family."

This was kind of hard. I'd been rejected one too many times before, and now I was basically asking for it. It took a lot for me to open up like this. I practically had to force myself to do it.

But I knew this was important to Ava, and she'd be so happy once she found out I did this for her. Plus, if I knew for certain her family really did accept me, it'd make things easier for everyone down the line. I wanted to make sure there were no objections when it came to our marriage, and that everyone got along. This was the first step.

I pressed on. "I know you don't know me very well, and I didn't come from the best background, but I was born Hawkei. My tribe was stolen from me, and I want to find my way back to it. Ava has taught me so much about who I am and what it means to be part of this family, but we never got a chance to unite our families properly. My past isn't the best, but I'm going to do better by her in the future. I know if I had a daughter, I'd never want her to marry someone like me. But I'm asking you to look beyond my flaws, accept me as your son and help Ava and I create a brighter future together. I love Ava very deeply, and would do anything for her. So starting now, do you accept me as I am, and will you support us going forward?"

"*Of course* we accept you, Charlie," Sophia replied, and she reached out to give me another hug. "What happened to you wasn't your fault, and we don't judge you for your past. What matters is that you make Ava happy, and that you're here to protect her. We know you do both of those things, and we couldn't be more thrilled to accept you into our family."

The others echoed their agreement. There were so many people talking I couldn't understand most of it.

Jonah clapped me on the back. "You have no idea what you've just done, kid. You're one of us now. Now you can *never leave—*"

Jonah was cut off by the sound of the door bursting open, as if someone had literally kicked it down. I jumped from my seat, but the others remained calm as I heard a pair of high heels click across the floor.

"How *dare* you plan my granddaughter's wedding without me!" a woman cried.

"My dear, I'm sure our invitation got lost in the mail," a man replied in a bumbling voice.

I recognized him. It was Professor Baine— Grandpa Elliot, to Ava— and he'd brought along his wife. Grandmother Eleanor— Madame Doya, to me, certainly— was not happy.

Ez leaned over and whispered, "Are you *sure* you're ready to join this family?"

I had better rectify this. But I knew how to kiss ass when it was time, and Ava and her grandmother weren't so different. Flattery went far with both of them.

I stood and shook Baine's hand. "I would *never* do something like this without such important people present."

Before either of them could reply, I took Madame Doya's hand and kissed it, before I added, "Especially not the *matriarch* of this family."

Madame Doya relaxed, and I swear, I heard her let out a slight giggle. "You're lucky you're so charming, young man."

We had to pull up two more chairs for them. Everyone started eating, and throughout the meal, we were laughing and having a good time. They asked me about Ava, and I told them stories about our time together. There weren't a lot of good stories from the Institute— all the fun ones were inappropriate, and obviously stuff I could never tell her parents— but I told them about how Ava and I did physical therapy together, and how I'd helped her recover after she got out of the hospital. I knew I could take care of her, and I wanted her family to know I was in this for the long-haul.

Over an hour passed, until we finished eating and people started to go home. Oberi and I stayed to help Sophia with the dishes, but before I could lend a hand, Liam stopped me. He put a firm grip on my arm.

"Charlie, come with me," he ordered bluntly. "We need to talk privately."

Nerves tangled in my gut. I'd noticed that Liam hadn't said much at all throughout dinner. I expected he'd try to talk to me afterward, but I didn't know what he'd say. The guy was a chieftain, and he wouldn't be convinced easily, especially not when it came to his daughter.

Secretly, I cared about Liam's opinion more than anyone else, and I wasn't sure if I had his approval yet. He was a hard man to read.

Liam led me to a sliding glass door and onto a rooftop terrace. Oberi followed behind, and I felt his unease through the bond.

Once the door was closed and we were alone, Liam turned to me. "Look, kid. Your smooth talk and charm isn't going to work on me."

My heart turned to stone in my chest. I guess we were going to do this the hard way. Fine. I was used to it. If Liam wanted to fight me on this, I could play. I was already married to his daughter. He couldn't exactly tell me to stop.

"I know you think I'm not good enough for your daughter, and I agree with you, because who could ever be? She's perfect," I said. "But I'm going to be Emperor soon, and as a chief, that should be good enough for you."

Liam laughed lowly. "You haven't been married to Ava long enough if you think she's perfect. You can drop the tough-guy act. I just want to talk."

I shoved my hands into my pockets, and my spine stiffened. "All right. What do you want?"

"I know Ava loves you more than words can say," Liam started. "But she's my peanut, my firstborn, and as much as I know I have to let her go, it needs to be to the right person. I can accept that you love her, because I've seen how well you've cared for her, especially after she got hurt. You've cared for her mind and body, but I need to know you can care for her heart."

I was baffled. How could he even say that? "Of course I care about her heart. She's the most precious thing to me. I promise to keep her safe, no matter what."

Liam's tone, if possible, got even blunter. "I'm not asking you to make promises, or if you *want* to be there for her. I'm asking if you *can* do it, because one day, Ava's going to push you past your limit. I need to know that you can handle it, because I'm her father and *I* can barely do it. I need to know you love her as much as I do— no, *more* than I do— because otherwise, this isn't going to work."

I could appreciate that he was being upfront with me. I guess if I had a daughter, I'd probably be the same way. I'd rather he give it to me straight than pretend to accept me, then privately disown me down the line. I just wanted to prove to him that this was the right choice.

"Ava and I care about each other," I said. "I understand you're worried, but whatever she throws at me, I can take it."

"I know you say you understand, and I really want to believe you. But kid, I don't," Liam said flatly. "You've been through a lot, but you're not old enough yet, nor have you spent enough time with Ava to realize what's really coming. You just don't have the experience. I'm here for you guys if you're going to see this through. But neither of you had the chance the first time around to decide if this marriage is what you really wanted, because you were forced into it. All I'm asking is if this is something you'd choose for yourself if you weren't already tied to her. Because it's not a small decision."

It was hard for me to comprehend wanting anything other than my marriage. Ava was my only choice, the only person I'd ever want to be with. I didn't get what he was trying to say.

"Even if I hadn't married Ava before, I'd still want to marry her now," I swore. "I just want you to back me up. If I'm not good enough—"

"That's not what this is about," Liam insisted. "Kid, I'm going to be frank with you. There are times when this marriage is *going* to get hard, and you'll have a chance to walk away. In fact, I'm going to guarantee you'll want to."

He didn't know me if he thought that was the case, but I figured I'd hear him out, just to acknowledge his fears so he'd approve of me. "Okay. I'm listening."

"I need to know if you can stay in this marriage for the long-haul, because I know my peanut. Ava's the strongest person I know. She's been through hell and back, and she always comes out stronger, but the one thing I know she won't be able to come back from is losing you," Liam emphasized.

"I'd never ask for a divorce." I couldn't fathom being separated from Ava in any way, or worse, *wanting* to be apart from her. It was incomprehensible to me.

"You say that now, but you two haven't pushed each other far enough for that to have crossed your mind," Liam said. "I promise you that it will. But a passing thought doesn't have to be what you decide."

I was certain he was blowing things out of proportion. I couldn't imagine anything worse than what Ava and I had already endured, so I wasn't concerned about the future, because I wasn't leaving her side. "Why is this such a concern for you?" I asked.

"Because when you got married the first time, you didn't have an option. This... what you're doing right now... is a *choice*. And once you make this choice, you'll have to stand by your decision no matter what happens," Liam said. "That means I'm asking you no matter how hard it gets, that you'll stick around to figure it out, and you won't walk away from this marriage. Because if you do... you need to know she won't survive that. And if I'm telling the truth, I don't think you will, either. So make sure this is what you really want, before you make vows to each other you can't take back."

I lifted my chin. "Respectfully, sir, you don't know what Ava and I have already been through. If we can get through that, we can get through anything. I'm here for good."

Liam took my hand and shook it firmly. "If that's the promise you're making me, then I consider you my son. Welcome to the family, Charlie."

I felt relieved. If I had Liam's acceptance, the rest of the family would follow him, and I could truly be a part of it. I wasn't bothered by his warnings. I knew Ava and I were good together, and always would be.

Now all that was left to do was ask my wife if she wanted to marry me all over again.

I RODE a high of euphoria after talking to Ava's family. I wanted my wife to have the very best of everything, and here in Ilamanthe, she would. Ava's family seemed over the moon about the wedding, and I couldn't wait to reveal the surprise to her.

The next morning, I excused Abigail from her duties, and I helped Ava get ready for the day.

"This is... different," Ava remarked. "Usually you're hurrying off to some meeting or in the gardens with your grandpa."

"He gave me the day off," I told her as I brushed out her hair. I *loved* brushing her hair. It was so soft and silky, and she gave little moans when the brush tangled. I knew she was doing it to try turning me on, and it was working — but that would have to wait.

"That's strange," she said. "I never thought your grandpa would give you the day off. He's kind of a hardass."

I shrugged. "He has a soft side. I must've impressed him enough yesterday to earn it."

Charlie shifted into a wyvern! Oberi exclaimed. He jumped up and down, panting. *He was almost as impressive as me.*

"Almost," I scoffed.

Ava reached behind her chair and inched a hand up my thigh. "I'm sure there are some *very* impressive things about being a wyvern."

My dick hardened, and I had to take a step away from her. If I stayed close, I'd have her undressed in moments. "Look, I know we're into some kinky things, but I didn't think that was one of them."

"I want to know," Ava teased. "How big can you get, Charlie?"

I leaned down and pressed my lips to the side of her jaw, then whispered in her ear. "Bigger than you can handle."

Ava leaned her head into me. "Keep talking."

"So big that you—"

Can you not? Oberi huffed. *I'm right here. There's no need for a wyvern anatomy lesson.*

"I'm just curious!" Ava defended.

You'll have to satisfy your curiosity later, Oberi said as she shifted into a Fire unicorn. *We don't want to waste any time. We're going shopping!*

Oberi strutted out of the room, but paused at the door to quickly add, *And you're buying me a hat.*

"Ooh, shopping!" Ava raved. "Charlie, I can't wait."

She was being literal, because she was already shoving me out the door. It wasn't even breakfast time before we met up with Eddie.

"I hear we're going shopping today, sir," he said brightly. "I know all the best shops and restaurants in Ilamanthe. You won't be disappointed. I believe the princess would enjoy the mall."

Ava grabbed my sleeve. "Charlie, are you seriously taking me to the mall?!"

I placed my hand on the side of her face. "Anything for my princess, love."

We had a limo take us to the mall. Word must've gotten around that we were coming, because most of the shops were open early when we arrived, and there was quite a crowd lingering around waiting for our arrival. People cheered as we drove by, and Ava rolled down the window to wave back.

"They love us," she gushed. "It's like we're celebrities."

"You *are* celebrities," Eddie said. "You're the prince and princess! No one is more interesting than you, not even the Emperor."

I guess not. I'd never had so many people appreciate that I was around. It was weird, when I'd grown up in a world where nobody gave a damn if I lived or died. Now I was surrounded by a whole country who wanted to know everything about me, and I didn't do anything to gain their admiration except exist. It was wild to me.

The limo pulled into a private underground parking lot of the mall that was reserved for the royal family. My security team was already waiting for us when we arrived. We couldn't really go anywhere in the city without protection, but my guards had promised to give us space.

We took a private elevator up to the main floor. Eddie kept babbling.

"There are other shoppers here, but they've been advised to keep their distance, as the prince and princess are visiting," he informed us. "But don't worry. The area has been locked down for your arrival, and is perfectly safe, though the Emperor has arranged for an informal meet-and-greet before you begin."

"What are you talking about...?" Ava asked, but her voice dropped off as the elevator doors opened.

Another massive cheer erupted around us.

There's a red carpet with velvet ropes leading into the mall, and a ton of guards, Oberi explained. *There are hundreds of Elves in the mall's courtyard, and they're all jostling the guards for a chance to greet you.*

My stomach dipped. This was a little much.

"Your grandpa wants to show us off," Ava muttered lowly.

He definitely did. Ava and I hadn't gone out in public much. This was our first time.

But it was a requirement for the job, so I grasped Ava's shoulder. "We can do this. Why not put on a show?"

"It might be fun," Ava said, and we headed forward.

Cameras clicked as journalists took our photographs. The press was here, too. Bet they'd have a story running before we even left the mall. Ava signed autographs, while people asked to shake my hand. I didn't catch much conversation, as a lot of people were talking at once, but the Elves were so thankful that I was back, and they were excited that I was living here in Ilamanthe.

It was really humbling to have so many people interested in my life. More so, they all depended on me, because they believed I could be the one who could lead them out of this war and into the Blessed Haven, as my prophecy foretold.

People placed flowers into my arms and threw petals at Ava's feet. She was more popular than I was. A couple of women started to cry when Ava said hello to them.

"Princess!" I heard a man's voice over the crowd, struggling to get through. He pushed people aside to get to the front of the line. "Princess, please, help me!"

He sounded pretty desperate. "Let him through," I ordered, and a group of Elves parted to let him to the front of the line. The guards stepped in closer to protect us if something went wrong, but this guy didn't seem dangerous— just hopeful that he'd get a chance to speak to us.

Ava rolled up beside me and asked, "You wanted to speak with me?"

A rustling sound came as the Elf knelt before us, and I heard him lift something above his head. "Princess, please. My child is sick. No one can help her, and without your intervention on behalf of the gods, she may die. Please, lay your hands upon her, and plead to our goddesses that they may show her mercy."

Ava reached out and took the baby into her lap. Oberi snuffled his nose into the bundle the baby was wrapped in, and I felt Ava heavily concentrate as she focused her magic on the infant.

"Hm," Ava whispered. "I think I can fix this."

Some of Ava's magic flowed out from her form and into the baby. The crowd around us gasped, and from beside me, the child gave off some kind of warm glow. I figured she had to be lighting up.

As the gossip around us died down, Ava handed the baby back to the man. "There. She should be all better now."

He wept with joy. "The princess has cured my daughter! She has been blessed by the goddesses!"

"No, not really. I'm just a healer," Ava explained. "My Anichi blood gives me healing abilities."

"You can heal what most Anichi cannot. You are a miracle worker!" the man gushed.

The crowd around us began singing Ava's praises. I felt her uncomfortably stiffen beside me. I knew Ava was supposed to be the Elvish goddesses incarnate on this Earth, and their representative here in Ilamanthe, but I hadn't imagined the Elves took her title so literally.

Ava was a chieftain's daughter, and she knew what it was like being in the public eye, so she handled it all so gracefully. I honestly felt like I was balking whenever people wanted to talk to me. I held several bouquets that I didn't know what to do with.

"I'll have them delivered back to your room at the palace," a guard said. She took the flowers out of my arms and handed them off to a servant.

For as awkward as I felt, I think I could get used to all this.

The guards began shooing off the crowd, and Eddie announced, "That is all the time the prince and princess have for today! Thank you all for coming! The monarchy appreciates each and every one of you!"

The crowd slowly drained out of the area, and the guards led us to a more secluded part of the mall. Ava's chair squeaked as she sagged in relief.

"Finally," she breathed. "Alone at last."

"You okay?" I asked.

"The appreciation is fun and all, but I'd really like to get to shopping, seeing as how I haven't seen the inside of a mall in over two fucking years," she grumbled.

"We're getting right on it," I promised. "What did you do to that baby?"

"She had some kind of hole in her heart. It was so small it wouldn't show up on x-rays. I'm not surprised the other Anichi healers couldn't do anything, because when I first inspected her, I felt something was wrong with her *blood*, not her organs, so that concealed the true problem," Ava explained. "But I followed the clues, and realized there had to be an underlying issue. Ez has been teaching me a lot about healing since he's started med school. It's gotten easier for me to heal, now that I know certain things to look for."

"Well, now the Elves think you're a miracle worker."

Ava sighed. "Yeah. Just what I wanted to be."

I knew Ava didn't want to be put under any more pressure than she already was. I resolved to take her mind off things, because I wanted her to remember this day forever.

As we went further into the mall, Ava gasped. "Wow! I didn't realize it'd be so big. I'm officially in love!"

"You haven't even started shopping," I teased.

"Well, what are we waiting for?" Ava wheeled forward as quickly as she could. Eddie and I had to practically run to keep up.

The mall was outdoors and open to the air, with several levels of shops lining a smooth walkway. I could feel the plants and trees potted every few feet, and a fountain trickled nearby. In my opinion, the shopping center was more like a garden than an actual mall, because there were plants everywhere. It was a similar feeling to being within a beautiful jungle.

Ava dragged me into a shoe store first, and automatic doors opened to an air-conditioned shop.

"Oh my ancestors. Finally, a pair of shoes that aren't absolutely ghastly," Ava said brightly.

Look at the hats! Oberi exclaimed. She trotted toward the back of the store.

"You might want to shop in husky form," I warned her. "You're going to knock over shelves."

I'm fine, Oberi insisted. *These aisles are wide enough for me to navigate no problem.*

Her hooves smacked against the floor as she spun around. Amazingly, she didn't knock over any racks of clothes.

"Oberi's right," Ava said. "The aisles here are simple to navigate. I can get my chair around easily!"

That was so rare. Usually, there were a lot of places Ava's chair didn't fit, but the aisleways here were wide enough that she could not only roll down them, but turn around.

I reached out to feel the racks of shoes, and my fingers landed on a box. I felt around and noticed dots that I easily recognized. They spelled out the word *Medium.*

I was completely floored. My hands traveled along the boxes, and I found that *every single product* was marked with braille, so I could easily read what it was.

It was so unusual. I always had to have someone help me when I was shopping, because nothing was ever marked in a way I could understand. Now, I could read whatever was in front of me, because all the information was there in a way I could comprehend.

It was marvelous.

"Hey!" I called to Ava, who was already halfway down the aisle. "The sizes are marked with braille!"

"What?" she sounded astounded. She rolled beside me and studied the box I held in my hands. "Holy shit, you're right! You can *read* all the labels!"

The box nearly shook in my hands. This was such a gift. Were all the stores here like this?

At this point, I was having just as much fun as Ava was. Shopping had never been a good time before— kind of a pain in the ass, really— because nothing was accessible. Now, I had a better understanding of what was going on around me, and it was great.

"Charlie, come here." Ava handed me a denim jacket when I approached her. "You'd look hot in this."

"You think?" I took the jacket off the hanger and slipped it on.

"You look particularly dashing," Eddie said.

I shifted uncomfortably. "I don't like the way the fabric feels on my skin. Let me try a different one."

I ran my fingers over the racks to find my size in the men's section— which had tags that were all marked with braille, I really couldn't believe it. I felt the fabric until I found one that was soft. I tried the jacket on, and Ava gasped.

"Yes, absolutely, that's the one. We *have* to get it!" she insisted.

What's the point? Oberi cracked. *You're just going to take it off of him.*

"That's the fun of it," Ava teased.

She took the jacket from me, and I continued flipping through clothes on the rack. Ava tried on a bunch of dresses and modeled them for us. I had to feel each one, and Oberi kept cracking jokes.

Eddie liked all of them. I couldn't decide if he was being a kiss ass, or if he really did enjoy this. The employees were really nice and helped us find anything we asked for. Although I knew they'd be nice to us because we were royals, I genuinely thought they were the kind of people who'd help anyone no matter who they were.

We must've stayed in the shop for over an hour, until Eddie reminded us there were tons of other places to visit. I didn't really want to leave, because the shop was so accommodating. It was a rare experience, for sure. I was certain the other shops wouldn't be like that.

Ava must've bought at least six dresses. With my jacket and several hats for

Oberi, we left with tons of bags that Eddie *insisted* on carrying. As we took an elevator upward, Ava tugged on my arm.

"Look at that!" she said as she rolled out of the elevator and onto the second floor. "There's an information center where you can get audio headphones to assist you when shopping."

That was exciting news. "I've never been to a place that had something like that before," I remarked. "Let's check it out."

Eddie cleared his throat behind us. "There's no need for that," he insisted sourly. "*I'm* here to assist you."

"I just want to see," I told him. He shut up, but let out a haughty grumble. Hell, he was jealous over a pair of headphones taking away my attention. I get he wanted to be our only guide, but still. This was cool.

We approached the information booth. An audio recording started before we made it to the counter. "*You are now approaching the Ilamanthe Mall Information Center. Please wait behind the raised line until an attendant is ready to assist you.*"

I felt a groove under my feet, like the ones at a traffic intersection. Raised dots on the pavement were there to guide blind people, to let them know where to wait before they walked into the road by accident, but I'd never seen them be used for something like this.

A couple of quick footsteps approached us. "How can I help you?" the attendant questioned.

I asked for the audio commentary headphones. I put them on, and I was amazed at how detailed the descriptions were. A slightly robotic voice spoke. "*You are standing on the south side of Ilamanthe Mall near the information booth. To your right, you will find The Crystal Corner. To your left is the food court.*"

I took a few steps to my right, and the commentary continued. "*You are approaching The Crystal Corner. Doors are automatic, and the retail desk sits at the back left corner of the store.*"

I turned to Ava. "You were right. I'm officially in love with this mall."

"What do they do?" she asked.

"The headphones direct me wherever I need to go, based on where I am in the mall," I said. "It kind of works like a GPS system. I can find my way around by myself without having to rely on someone to direct me."

"Charlie, that's really great." Ava's voice had become soft. "I wish things had always been like that for you."

"I'm really happy to have it now," I said. "Come on, let's keep exploring."

With the use of the headphones, *I* was able to lead the way, for once, and it actually felt like I had a layout of where I was going with the headphones directing me. We entered The Crystal Corner, which I could tell without having to be told was a store full of magical crystals. The power from them resonated off of every shelf. It smelled of incense, and I could feel the crystals interacting with my magic— like they were inviting me to take them home.

"Kallie would love it here," Ava said. "We need to bring her next— *ooh,* quartz dicks!"

"Are you kidding me?" I asked.

"No way! There are crystals here that are literally shaped like penises! I *need* one!" she shouted.

Ava went off to look at the unfortunately-shaped crystals, but I wandered to the other side of the store. I was less intrigued by the crystals and more interested in how accessible the mall was. I ran my hand over the braille plaques that labeled each aisle, and stopped next to a display of bracelets and felt each one.

An employee approached. "Is there anything I can help you find, my prince?"

Ava's laughter rang across the store. I smiled. I was glad this was making her so happy.

"I'd like to buy something for my wife," I said. "What are the different crystals used for?"

"You have a lot of options depending on what you're looking for," she said. "All our crystals are cleansed and charged under the full moon. Amethyst is used for healing and spiritual connection. Rose quartz is a crystal for love. Citrine is excellent for manifesting wealth. Lepidolite stabilizes emotions."

The last crystal had my attention. "Tell me more about that one."

The employee picked up one of the bracelets and handed it to me so I could feel the stones. "Lepidolite comes in shades of purple and pink. It's known to naturally contain lithium, which can be used to treat mood disorders, release stress, and promote better sleep. It's long been believed that lepidolite can help people overcome mental trauma, and protect them from negative influences."

Everything about the stone sounded perfect. This would really help Ava.

"This is the one I want," I stated confidently.

The employee took me to the counter, and I quickly checked out before Ava placed a few items for herself at the checkout. I noticed the counter was low enough for her to check out comfortably in her wheelchair. She could see over the top of it easily.

I was so surprised that everything in this mall was so accessible. I kept thinking this was a dream, and at some point we'd run into a really rude person or an inconvenience we couldn't get around. But so far, we hadn't hit any yet.

"Look at what I got." Ava pressed a cold crystal into my palm.

I ran my hand over it and scowled. "Ava! This is a dick."

"I know!" she replied happily. "Isn't it great?"

"You know this is for *display only*," I scolded.

"Well, that's limited thinking."

I sighed, before I handed it to the cashier. "This too, please."

The cashier gave a slight giggle, before she handed me another bag. "That rose quartz phallic crystal is a customer favorite. It inspires romance and passion."

"Then it'll look great in our bedroom," Ava said eagerly.

I sighed. "Anything for you, princess."

When we left the store, Ava snatched the crystal cock out of my hand. "Here, Eddie. Carry this. We have more shopping to do!"

"Hold on," I told her. I reached into the bag and pulled out the bracelet. "A gift. For you."

I slipped it on her wrist, and her elation came through our bond. "It's so pretty! What is it?"

I smiled. "It's lepidolite. It's supposed to stabilize moods. I thought it would help you not to struggle so much."

Her voice became so soft. "Oh, Charlie! I love it so much."

I knelt down to give her a hug. She squeezed me tight, and it was obvious she was very appreciative of the gift. I really did hope it helped.

The air around us expanded as we entered a big department store next. I was certain they wouldn't have the adaptations we needed here. Such a big store with so many customers wouldn't bother to accommodate people like us.

I was wrong, though, when I heard Ava exclaim beside me, "This is really cool. They have a cart that's adapted to work with my wheelchair, so I can attach it to my chair and push it along, like an able-bodied person could do with a regular shopping cart."

"Like you need the ability to grab more stuff," I joked.

She ignored me. "I'm going to use it!"

Ava rushed from aisle to aisle so fast that I could hardly keep up with her. She grabbed things off the shelves and tossed them into her cart until it was almost full. At this point, I wasn't even sure what she was buying.

"The jewelry is downstairs. We have to check it out!" Ava insisted.

"Where's the elevator?" I wondered.

The headphones I still wore responded automatically. *"The elevator is two aisles to your right, next to the perfume counter."*

It was easy to find my way to the elevator, and even easier to feel which buttons to push by the braille engraved on them.

We took the elevator to the main level, and Ava tossed more things into her cart. It was overflowing by the time we checked out. Eddie was carrying so many bags out the door that he nearly toppled over.

I don't think either of us were prepared for Ava at the mall. She'd scared me quite a few times in the duration of our relationship, but this was her most terrifying form yet.

We must've been shopping for hours before we stopped at the bathrooms. I was amazed to find they had several private handicapped restrooms. Ava took one, and I took the other. Audio played when I entered.

"Wave your hand to the left of the door for audio assistance."

Curiously, I tried it.

"The toilet is three meters behind you. The sink is located to the right of the toilet. The soap dispenser can be found directly above the sink, and the paper towel is on the wall to the right of the sink. The garbage bin sits beneath the paper towel dispenser."

I'd never been so excited to piss in my life. Seriously. The audio descriptions and accommodations in this place were a game-changer. Now I didn't have to fumble around to find what I needed.

I left the restroom and heard Ava approaching. "They have audio description in the bathroom!" I said.

"I know!" she cried. "And the bathroom is big enough for my chair. It's so rare to go anywhere where my chair actually fits in the stall. So many places label their bathroom handicap accessible, but if I can't close the stall door behind me once my chair is inside, it's not actually accessible. There should be bathrooms like this *everywhere*."

"Not just the bathrooms," I said. "The whole mall. *Everything* is accessible. I could actually go shopping by myself, without any help. I've never been able to do that, because big places like this are usually too hard to navigate."

"It is strange to me that other communities wouldn't make such accommodations for their people," Eddie remarked. "These kinds of things are no hassle for the Elves. It's natural for us to provide simple features, to help make the lives of others easier."

I scoffed. "Never leave Ilamanthe, Eddie. You'd be shocked at how the rest of the world treats people like us."

"I certainly don't understand," Eddie said in confusion. "None of these things are particularly hard to implement. Why wouldn't all societies have functions in this way, so all kinds of people are able to act as individuals? After all, a disability is only one if it prevents someone from doing something others can."

"Everyone else acts like we're such a burden," Ava said bitterly. "But here, our disabilities are hardly an encumberment, because the Elves are naturally accommodating. Charlie hasn't even seen half of it. I saw a carriage earlier transporting people around who couldn't make the long walk from one side of the mall to the other. There are benches everywhere for people to rest if they can't walk far, and there was a mother's lounge next to the bathrooms for pregnant people and those with small children. We've passed a few designated quiet spaces and meditation areas for people who get overstimulated to calm down, and there's water bottle refill stations everywhere. And I can see over the counters at *all* the shops, which I haven't been able to do since I lost the ability to walk! I barely notice the difference between shopping in a wheelchair and how I used to shop before, because everything I need is provided for. I fucking love it here!"

"Alistair said something similar about the counters when we visited last, but I wasn't sure what he was saying. Is this not something that's common everywhere?" Eddie questioned.

"Not at all," I said. "In fact, if you tried to introduce a lot of these ideas in other societies, people would probably get pissed."

"They'd be... angry?" Eddie seemed mystified.

"Oh, yeah. Some jackass would say that the world doesn't need to cater to sick people and that we should be grateful for whatever minor help the ableds are willing to dole out," Ava spat.

"Very rude," Eddie commented. "At any rate, it's not like that in Ilamanthe. And I would like to say that although you may be in a wheelchair, princess, and master, although you may be blind, these aren't things the Elves talk about much. Disabilities are just seen as something that *is*, not something that makes you different."

It was revolutionary to think like that. "Thanks, Eddie. I wish all people thought that way."

The mall was bustling by now, and although our security team kept people at bay, we still heard a lot of cheers as people took pictures of us roaming by. It was around lunch time, so we made our way to the food court. Eddie must've been carrying twenty bags, and they kept bumping against me while we walked.

"Do you want me to take some of those, Eddie?" I asked.

"Oh, no, sir," Eddie said brightly. "I'm more than happy to carry them."

"You should see the smile on his face. He's having a blast," Ava snickered.

Eddie knew a couple of people here at the mall, which wasn't odd—honestly, he knew everybody, and could strike up a conversation with a complete stranger without batting an eye. He'd managed to befriend some random guy in the food court within five minutes, and was chewing his ear off about everything and anything.

"Quite a lot of bags you've got there," the Elf said. I knew he had to be gesturing at the mountains of bags Eddie was hauling around.

"Oh, yes. I wronged the princess badly in the past, and deserved to very much so be punished," Eddie raved. "But she is so merciful and kind, and therefore, sentenced me to a lifetime of carrying her bags whenever she went shopping as justice! I am happy to serve this sentence with pride!"

"I only told you that because you wouldn't shut up about it," Ava grumbled.

I had to laugh. In previous months, Eddie kept carrying on about how guilty he felt that Ava had gotten hurt in the Infernal Underground when we'd been trying to save him. To shut him up, she'd *sentenced* him to be her personal shopping assistant whenever she wanted to go for the rest of his days. I didn't know who enjoyed this more, her or him.

We ordered noodles at a place Eddie swore was the best in Ilamanthe, then took our trays to find a table.

"Hey!" Eddie exclaimed. "There's Alistair and the others."

We went to sit with them. Ivy, Chancey, Alistair, and Ez sat around a big table.

"We heard you'd be around today and decided to stop by," Ivy purred. "Your security team played nice and let us through."

"Only because you have the princess's *brother* with you," Ez boasted. "What does that make me, anyhow? A duke or something?"

"Mind if we join you?" I asked.

"Pull up a seat," Chancey said brightly.

I sat down, and Ava pulled up her chair beside me at the end of the table. I noticed the edge extended longer, so that she could fit her chair easily.

I'm going to splash in the fountain, Oberi said bluntly. *Peace out!*

Water sprayed against my face as she changed into a narwhal and jumped in. I took a bite of noodles. They were so good and slathered in a creamy sauce that burst with flavor. Why was everything so delicious here? I hadn't had a bad meal yet.

"What brings you to the mall today?" Eddie asked the others.

"Ivy and I are shopping for... things I probably shouldn't say out loud," Chancey said. "Alistair had to tag along as soon as he heard."

"Ooh, what'd you get?" Eddie asked him.

Alistair leaned over and whispered something I couldn't hear, and judging by Eddie's laughter, I was pretty sure I didn't *want* to hear it.

As we kept on eating, Chancey scooted closer to me. "So, how'd you like the ring?"

"Shut up," I said harshly, but thankfully, I didn't think Ava heard. "It's not time yet."

Chancey guffawed. "I wasn't talking about *that*, pal. The other ring."

Oh. I got what he was implying. I dropped my voice. "You were right, it did make me last longer. And it's pretty good, but if I'm being honest, it's a bit uncomfortable. Is it always like that?"

"Nah, it gets better the more you use it," Chancey insisted. "The first few times it's kinda tight, but you get used to it."

"Are you guys talking about testicles?" Alistair asked loudly, and I groaned. All attention immediately turned to us.

Chancey and Ivy knew about the cock ring, because they'd given me recommendations on which one to try, but I wasn't about to go telling everyone else about it.

"If we are, it's none of your business," I said.

"Bullshit!" Alistair exclaimed. "Whatever conversation you're having about sexy sacks, I want in!"

"Are you kidding me?" I asked.

"I'd say. Look, there's no *sexy* way to describe balls," Ivy argued.

"Sure there is! There must be!" Chancey burst in. "You got treasure chest, knapsack, coin purse, come fountain, precious jewels, tea bags, scro-tagonal—"

"What was that?" I asked.

"Scro-toe-na-gal." Chancey enunciated the word.

"That's a big word for you to use," Ivy teased.

"Lay off it," Chancey growled. "Anyhow, you got sperm shelter, jumbo junk..."

"Yeah!" Alistair eagerly agreed. "There's crown jewels, family jewels—"

"Hey, we ain't talking about the Elvish family jewels. Show some respect for the Emperor," Chancey blurted, and he smacked Alistair on the back of the head.

I gaped. "Why the *hell* are you guys talking about my family's—"

"Bean bag, dangly bits..." Chancey continued.

"Mayo sack," Alistair grumbled.

"Ugh! What is *wrong* with all of you?" I shouted.

I just wanted to enjoy my afternoon, and here all my friends were— my *buddies*, for shit's sake, not even the girls— carrying on about Nutsack Gate.

"Ooh, ooh, I've got one!" Eddie gushed. "What about..."

He gave a tee-hee, like a little kid, then whispered, "*Sexy droopers*."

"Wow, Eddie. Come up with that one on your own?" I asked.

"Oh, yes. Aren't you proud?"

His tone held no sarcasm, but I wasn't going to give him a treat for this one. "Not particularly."

Chancey was still rambling on. "You've got your wrinkle berries, your brass and tacks..."

"Chancey, I've never met anyone so knowledgeable on all the different ways a person can describe testicles, so well done," I stated.

"Don't tell him that, he'll get a big head," Ivy said.

"Which one?" Alistair asked.

The table broke out into laughter, until someone behind us said, "You could always call them sugar lumps. Bit unknown."

My heart skipped. That was Marcus' voice. I hadn't spoken to him in at least a month.

Nobody said anything for a couple of long moments, until Ivy questioned, "Hey. Found your art supplies?"

"Yeah, finally." Marcus strolled up close to me and took a seat. "Looks like I came in at just the right time."

He seemed friendly today, and in a good mood. I didn't want *this* to be the topic that revived our friendship, but if it got me and Marcus talking again, I'd take anything.

"Hey." Marcus reached out to nudge me.

I swallowed a lump in my throat. "Hey. You doing all right?"

His voice was playful. "Well, everyone isn't talking about *my* balls, so I'm doing pretty great."

"Yeah, thanks for that." Despite the conversation not being my favorite, I was really glad Marcus was here.

"I always liked referring to Charlie's balls as my personal fun bags," Ava said dreamily. "Isn't it so sweet?"

Now Ava was joining in, and since she knew more about what was going on down there than anyone else here, I had to put a stop to this. I stood and said, "Look, people, I don't really mind if you guys know about *some* of the stuff Ava and I do. I'm fine with sharing details about one of the most private parts of my life. I'm *not* okay with the community discussing my balls en masse."

"You said they could share *private parts*!" Ava cackled.

"I—"

"I love them, so should everyone else!" Ava nearly hit me as she raised a fist in the air. "Who's with me?"

Everyone gave a collective cheer, and I slapped a palm to my face. There was no stopping it now. I'd created a monster.

Marcus climbed onto the table, standing to recite lines as if he were upon a real stage. "They were two eggs wrapped in a silk scarf, a velvet satchel adorned with the soft hairs of a ripe peach. When the light hit his bulging sack just right, the eyes shone like jewels."

"Nay, good sir!" Alistair bellowed, clambering onto the table to stand beside him. "For thy scrotum remindeth thee of a disco ball, or perhaps, the beauty of blue marbles, which is sustained by the refusal of your love."

Chairs scraped the ground as everyone at the table leapt to applause. Somehow along the way, this had literally turned into a three-act play.

About my balls. Fan-fucking-tastic.

Other people climbed onto the table to offer their own renditions. Marcus hopped down and came over to me. "Can we talk?"

I was really scared about where this was going, but I wasn't going to back down. "Okay."

Marcus and I walked to a quieter area of the food court, away from our friends. Neither of us said anything right away, so I felt like I was forced to, in order to break the silence.

I cleared my throat. "Marcus... are you good?"

He gave a sigh. "No. Not really. But I'm better than I was."

"What does that mean?"

"I'm going to therapy, and I got a diagnosis," Marcus explained. "Ava was right. I do have BPD. She was spot on."

I didn't know what to say. "Wow. I'm sorry."

"Don't be. The diagnosis has been helpful, because at least I know what's wrong with me now, and I can find tools that work and help me feel better. They switched up my medication, and I actually think it might be working this time."

He scuffed his shoe on the floor. "Plus, I've been working on my art, and that's really helping. Working on a new play and stuff."

"I'm happy you're feeling better. Though I have to take some of the blame, because it's partly my fault," I said. "I'm sorry for what happened and for what I did."

"No, you're not," he replied gently. "And that's okay. I understand you're sorry for hurting me by breaking my bond, but you did the right thing. I know my actions were hurting Kallie, and I needed a wake-up call, because I wasn't thinking about her and what she needed. I see now that you didn't do this to hurt me, but to help her, and I'm glad you did."

His voice dropped as he added, "Kallie's much happier now, and I'm getting the help I need, so it's better for both of us. I know it'll take time, but I think I'm finally on the right track. Being borderline isn't easy, but at least I can have terms and an understanding now on what's going on with me. I have you to thank for that, because if you hadn't forced me to face reality, I'd still have my head in the sand."

I still felt pretty guilty. "I care about you. But I understand if you don't want to talk to me anymore."

"No. I still need you," Marcus said abruptly. "I know I've been a jackass lately, and you haven't been great either, but you're still my best friend."

My heart stalled in shock. I didn't think I'd ever hear Marcus say that again. I thought for sure he'd want nothing to do with me after I broke his bond, even though I missed him.

"I need you too, Marcus," I admitted, choking up. "You're one of the most important people in my life. I consider you a brother."

"We *are* brothers," Marcus said. "If you need anything from me, all you have to do is ask. I really do mean that."

I paused briefly. "Actually, there is one thing... I'm going to propose to Ava properly, today. You've been through everything with us, and I couldn't get married to her again without you. I don't know what I'd do if you weren't here. I was really hoping you could be my best man."

Marcus sounded confused. "Why would you want to pick *me* after the way I've treated you these past couple of weeks?"

"Because I don't care about all that. You've been there for me when I didn't know who else to turn to. I can't just forget about how much that meant to me."

"You want me to be your best man, but I'm not the *best*," Marcus argued.

He might be taking this too literal, but I needed to make him see he was the friend I needed the most.

"Yes, you are," I said. "You're the best at making me laugh when I'm down, and the best at accepting people for all their flaws. You're the best at seeing the world in a way no one else can. You're the best at listening, and you play the harp like no one's business."

"Yeah. That night in the chapel was pretty special, wasn't it?" he admitted sheepishly.

"You're the best at aiming spitballs at the back of Professor Jobe's head— no one could hit him square every time except you. You're the best at making cat costumes for Rishi. That taco costume was to die for. You're the best male cheerleader the Institute ever had."

"I was the only one," he stated flatly.

I ignored his comment. "You make the best sonnets about my balls."

"That actually wasn't a sonnet," he corrected.

"And..." I said finally. "You're the best at being my best friend."

I could hear the smile in his voice. "Fair enough. I am a pretty good friend, aren't I? But you know what, Charlie? It's not hard to be a good friend to a guy like you."

I didn't think I could have a friend get as close to me as Marty had been, but Marcus blew all my expectations away. I'd never had a friend be there for me like he was. And it was pretty awesome that he was in my life.

Marcus reached out to hug me, and I let him. I even hugged him back. I wasn't the best at this kind of thing, but I was getting better, and not having Marcus around had affected me more than I wanted to admit. I wanted him to know he was important to me, and I was glad to have him at my side. Because him not being there had been pretty empty.

"Of course I'm going to be your best man," Marcus said, and he clapped me on the back. "Now go ask Ava to marry you."

He pulled out of the hug and pushed me playfully back in the direction of the table. I started over there, relieved this whole argument with Marcus was over. I hoped we could all get to a good place again, as a group... but I guess that was up to Kallie.

When I got back to the table, I took Ava's hand. "We have one more place to go today. Are you ready?"

"Yes. But where are we going?" she asked.

I did my best to keep the grin off my face. "It's a surprise. Eddie, can you call the car around?"

"Absolutely, master!" Eddie nearly screeched. "After all, next is the main event of the day!"

"The main event?" Ava asked curiously.

"Eddie, shush," I snapped. He thankfully shut his mouth.

Oberi was still soaking wet when we got in the limo. Ava used her Water magic to dry his husky fur, and we traveled to the botanical gardens located on the other side of the city.

It was completely quiet here, and Ava noticed. "Where is everyone?"

"My grandfather reserved the gardens. It's only us here," I explained. I didn't want anyone else around for this, because I wanted it to be a private moment. I knew if there were people around they'd swarm us with cameras the minute I went to ask. The guards backed off to surround the perimeter of the gardens, finally leaving us alone.

We reached the gardens, and I pushed Ava through the gate. Oberi shifted into phoenix form and flew above us. Floral scents hit my nose, and a fountain trickled nearby. The sun was warm on my skin, and the air was pleasant, with a slight breeze. The gardens were peaceful and full of birdsong.

"It's really pretty here!" Ava said brightly. "There are flowers of every color, and hedges surround the perimeter. You won't believe the size of these sculptures. There are two massive sculptures of the Elvish goddesses, both covered in ivy and flowers. One of them has a fountain coming out of her hand that flows into a pond. That's Idril— I recognize her from paintings in the palace."

There were statues and sculptures all throughout the gardens. Ava explained that they looked like trees of twisting metal rising into the sky hundreds of feet. Hanging plants, ivy, and vines dangled from the tree limbs. The pathways were made of cobblestone, and we had to cross a couple of intricately crafted bridges over a winding river to journey around the gardens. My Earth magic felt how much plant life there was here, and it was incredibly abundant. The Elves had spared no expense in crafting this garden to be as beautiful as possible.

"There are ancient ruins here, unchanged from Ithriel. I can tell by the architecture and the quality of the stone that it's genuine," Ava said. "But the Elves have fashioned the plants to grow up the stone columns. The landscape is accommodated within the gardens, not the other way around. The Elves worked with the land, instead of destroying it to suit how they wanted the layout to be, but the pathways are still smooth and level enough that I can get through."

It seemed to be a theme of the Elves. Instead of changing things or forcing them to adapt, they worked with what was available to suit everyone.

And you know what? They always made something better than the other supernatural societies did, because of the way they thought about things.

I heard the rushing of water nearby, and my breath caught, because I knew we were close to our destination.

"There's a waterfall up ahead," Ava said. "But the path looks like it goes right through it."

"We have to go through the waterfall to get to the other side of the gardens," I said, and I grabbed the handles of her chair. "You ready?"

"Absolutely."

I picked up the pace and started jogging forward. Ava let out a little noise of excitement as we approached the waterfall, but instead of getting wet, the waterfall parted like curtains, allowing us through. As we stepped on through to the other side, I felt the Air around me vibrate with the sensation of hundreds of little wings.

"Oh," Ava said in glee. "It's a butterfly garden."

"What's it like?"

Oberi nestled in the trees above us. Ava moved forward and said, "There are so many I can't even count them all. There's monarchs, swallowtails, painted ladies, and others I can't name. The butterflies look like a rainbow flying through the sky, crawling on all the different flowers. There are so many."

She wheeled forward and laughed. "They're landing on me. It tickles."

Her back was turned to me. This was it. The big moment. I wanted this to be perfect, and I had to remember everything that I wanted to say.

I reached out to pick a flower. I felt the petals and realized it was a peony, still not in bloom. The petals hadn't opened up yet.

I slipped the ring inside, took a deep breath, and stepped forward. "Ava. We've been married for almost a year, and you know how much I love you."

"Of course. I love you, too. More than you'll ever realize."

I slowly got down on one knee. "Enough to marry me again?"

She turned around. I used my magic to make the flower I was holding bloom. Inside was the ring.

Ava let out a loud, surprised scream, like I'd jumped out from behind a corner. "What are you doing?!"

That wasn't the reaction I'd been expecting. "I'm... asking if you'd like to get married again."

I could feel her pounding heartbeat quivering across our bond. She was in shock. "But... why? We're already married."

"Because I love you. Because I want to live the rest of my life with you. Because every moment with you is like living another lifetime, and I want to live a thousand more. Because you deserve to have a gorgeous wedding and be a beautiful bride. Because I want to tell the world that you're my wife, and I'm your husband."

"I don't need any of that, because I have you," she insisted.

"But you never got the pretty dress, or the celebration, or the traditional ceremony, and I want to give all of that to you. I know people say that doesn't matter, but it matters to *us*, and I want to provide that. I have the opportunity to give you your dream, and I want to make you happy. So what do you say, pidge? We didn't get to choose last time, but we can make a choice now. Do you want to be mine, forever?"

Ava started crying. She wailed as she said, "I'd marry you a thousand times over. Yes, absolutely! Now give me that ring!"

It wasn't like I'd been expecting a different answer, but I was relieved all the same. I took the ring out from the petals and slipped it on her finger. It fit perfectly next to the original wedding band she had on. She threw her arms around me and flung herself forward so eagerly that she fell out of her wheelchair. I caught her, and we fell against the ground.

"Oh, Charlie! This was so perfect!" Ava kissed me over and over. "I can't wait to start planning everything!"

"Wow, you're really eager," I said with a laugh.

"Well, yeah. Weddings make me horny!"

Everything makes you horny. Oberi flew down from the treetops and landed beside us.

"I can be as horny as I want! I've never had a *fiancé* before," she gushed.

You guys were engaged last time for an hour. Still counts, Oberi argued.

"I don't know who's more excited for this wedding, you or my grandpa. That ring you're wearing was my grandmother's," I said, stroking her hair back.

"I love it so much. You couldn't have picked out a better ring. And it fits so perfectly with my first," Ava babbled.

She started yanking at my shirt. "Put me back in my chair. Let's get back to the palace right away, so we can have sex, then start planning this thing!"

Does it have to be in that order? Oberi asked.

Then she nuzzled our hair and said, *I am truly happy for both of you. This is what was always meant to be.*

It was. Ava was my destiny, and I wanted to show everyone just how much she meant to me. This wedding would be the start of it all.

I figured we'd return to the palace and spend some private time together, but the moment we stepped foot back through the double doors the room erupted into cheers.

"SURPRISE!"

My magic sensed that dozens of people were gathered in the main hall. Confetti fell from the ceiling, and a balloon bounced against my head.

"Congratulations to the happy couple!" My grandfather boomed. His footsteps approached beside me before he leaned in to whisper, "You *did* propose, correct?"

I laughed. "Yes. I did."

"Wonderful! The prince and his princess will be married again, in a royal wedding unlike any our empire has ever seen!" Cassiel cried out to the crowd. "Tonight, we celebrate!"

The rest of the room cheered, and music broke out. Ava leaned against my side and asked, "Did you know your grandpa was planning this engagement party?"

I smirked. "Nope. Told you he was excited."

The party went on all night. There was music, food, and dancing, and about a million people came up to us to say congratulations.

It was... different, being welcomed by a big crowd of people who were excited for me. I hadn't gotten that kind of support in my life before.

After we finished dinner, Alistair returned from the buffet and exclaimed, "They've got ass tons of chocolate cake! The damn thing's taller than I am."

The scent filled my nose, and my mouth was already watering. I got out of my chair.

"Where are you going?" Ava asked, though she already knew.

"I know you want some," I teased. "I'll bring you back a slice."

I made my way over to the dessert table. I didn't have a chance to grab a plate before someone shoved a dish in my hand.

"I already got you a piece," a sultry female voice said. It must've been a servant.

"Thanks, but you really didn't need to," I said. "I know you guys are meant to do things for us, but I enjoy serving my wife personally."

"Oh," she said flatly. "I didn't know it was for *her*."

"That's a rude way to address the princess," I sneered. I guess I understood why the women around here were jealous of Ava, because they all wanted to get in the prince's bed. Wasn't going to happen.

"A prince should be able to have whatever he wants," she replied. "After all, I'm here for you, Charlie."

I hesitated, because it was such a strange offer. This was definitely out of line and made me uncomfortable. I thought about reporting her to a guard, but I didn't want to get her executed for flirting with the prince. The Elves didn't fuck with that kind of shit when it came to the monarchy.

The best thing to do was put an end to this and walk away. "If I need you, I'll summon you."

I turned on my heel and hurried back to my table so fast I forgot to grab a slice of cake for myself. No way was I going back to the buffet alone, though. That serving girl had really creeped me out.

The party was still going on late in the evening, far past midnight, and the Elves were no closer to quieting down. My grandfather drank a whole tankard by himself and danced to nearly every song. He was having more fun than anybody.

I was considering telling everyone goodnight and taking Ava back to our room, because she was starting to fall asleep in her chair. It'd been a big day for both of us with a lot of activity, and as much as I was certain she wanted to celebrate our engagement in a much more private way, she needed to rest. We could wait until morning.

"Hey," I heard Kallie say, and I nearly startled. I hadn't heard her come up behind me— she was super good at sneaking up on people. "Congratulations."

"Thanks," I told her. "I hope the proposal was everything Ava wanted."

"It was, trust me," Kallie said. "You did great."

Her voice dropped to a serious tone. "I don't want to ruin your party, but we need to meet tomorrow morning as soon as we can. Demigods only."

"You found something?" I wondered.

"Yes," Kallie confirmed. "I learned more about the vampire key. And if we don't act fast, it might slip out of our hands again. So be ready. Tomorrow, we're moving in."

ava-marie

TWELVE

Kallie's words were urgent. We hadn't found a lead on the vampire key in what felt like ages, and now she was insisting that we could have it in our possession— today.

I hoped whatever information she had would give us some results. The entire summer had come and gone, and we had nothing. The Warden was growing stronger every day. We couldn't afford to keep giving him more time to get stronger while we kept following false leads. Charlie's team had been searching for the vampire key since the bank robbery had failed, but every trail they picked up went cold. We needed a win, and fast.

We got ready in a hurry that morning. But when I opened the door to our bedroom, I hitched a breath. Over a hundred roses were scattered in front of the door, their heads cut off. Petals and thorny stems were everywhere.

Okay, weird. Oberi scampered to our side and put his nose down to sniff the mess. *Hm. So this isn't creepy.*

"Are you getting a scent?" I asked.

No. All I can smell is roses. Oberi sneezed. *But truly, a strange mystery.*

"Charlie," I called. He came over, and I said, "Somebody left a mess in our suite."

He ducked down, and his fingers skimmed the ruined flowers. He frowned. "Who got into our suite? Our friends are the only ones who have access to my quarters, and the guards won't let just anybody in."

"Somebody must've put them here a few moments ago," I said. "Otherwise, the servants would've noticed and cleaned it up by now."

"Probably just one of our friends, playing a prank," Charlie said. "I bet it's Alistair. He was pretty wasted last night from the party."

I bet it was. He'd do something odd like this as a joke. "He's got a bizarre sense of humor."

Oberi wagged his tail. *I did see him sneak magical fireworks into Chancey's room last week. When he walked in, they all erupted on cue. The whole room nearly caught on fire before the servants had to put it out. It was quite dangerous, but Alistair thought it was funny.*

"So that's settled," I said. "Alistair thought it'd be a huge gag to leave cut-up roses outside our door the day after our engagement. Kind of messed up, but he's known for taking it too far."

"We've got no time for games." Charlie rose to his full height. "Let's go."

I rolled over the flowers, and we left them behind as we made our way to the practice arena to meet up with Kallie.

"I don't like not wearing my wedding ring," I complained. "It feels weird."

We'd dropped off my ring at the treasury last night, so the Elvish jewelers could solder my original wedding band with the absolutely gorgeous ring Charlie had proposed with yesterday. Hadn't even had that beautiful rock for a full day, and already, I was parted from my beloved.

"You'll get it back at the ceremony," Charlie soothed, and he brushed back my hair.

"Too long to wait." I'd be planning this wedding right now if we didn't have to work on demigod business, so whatever dumbass had the vampire key needed to cough it up, so I could get home and start looking for my dress. "You know, if I can't wear my wedding ring, you shouldn't be wearing yours, either. It's only fair."

Charlie scowled. "No."

You'd have to cut his finger off before he removed it, I was sure.

When we walked into the training arena, my jaw dropped. Kallie and Marcus sat at a table that she'd conjured in the middle of the room, and they were actually *talking*. What was more, both of them were *smiling*. She drank a coffee that I assumed Marcus must've brought her, while they eagerly engaged in conversation. It didn't look awkward, or weird.

Were they actually *getting along*? It was a little nuts. I'd assumed after they broke their bond they'd never speak again, but here they were, acting like everything was fine. When Marcus saw me, he cheerfully waved. I decided to play along and act like this wasn't fucking bizarre.

The Elvish Associates were here as well, along with Danny, Ivy, and Chancey. I wondered who exactly we'd have to take down if we were bringing along this many people.

"Hey," Kallie said as I rolled up beside her. "Glad you're here. We can get started."

"What's this all about, Kallie?" Charlie demanded as he took a chair beside me. "Do you really have a lead on the vampire key?"

"Of course I do," Kallie shot back. "I didn't call everyone in for teatime."

"Then why didn't I know about it earlier?" Charlie asked. "This shouldn't have been kept from me."

He was being kind of bossy. I laid my hand on his, to tell him to cool off. His shoulders slumped, and he didn't say anything more.

Kallie huffed. "I only learned of this yesterday. I called everyone together as soon as I could. I got tired of waiting for your team to find us some answers, so I took the risk and time traveled."

I knew Kallie's powers had been weakened by her bond breaking. She must've time-traveled the first chance she got, when her powers were strong enough again.

"Kallie, that's dangerous. You should've consulted us before you did it," Charlie hissed.

"You would've stopped me if I had," Kallie insisted. "Anyway, I went back to the day that Frank put the key into the vault, to see who took it. It worked, because I was able to watch who took the key from the vault before he was killed, and I also saw who murdered Frank."

"So do you know who he is?" Charlie asked.

"Yes. I learned his name, and he's still alive. Your team was able to track him down," Kallie informed us. "It turns out Masci Taurus wasn't the only person hunting for the key, and the angels weren't the ones who took it from the vault. The thief was someone named Lorenzo Gallio. Take one guess who he works for."

Charlie groaned and rubbed his face. "Not another vampire mobster."

"He's one of my dad's cronies," Ivy snarled. "And unfortunately, this guy is one I don't know."

"Or fortunately," Chancey subbed in. "Because if he doesn't know you, he'll be easier to fool."

"If that's true, we can assume that Salvatore Bianchi has the vampire key," Marcus said. "Great."

Charlie scoffed. "The head of the bank was a vampire. I bet he had ties to Salvatore. If he did, that means Salvatore knew all along that the vampire key was in the bank, but kept it there because that's where it was safest. Our first time around, we must've tripped the bank's security system when Max hacked their files. That's how they knew we were coming. Salvatore moved the key the night before we got there, but it was an inside job. That's how he got away clean."

"What about the second time, when we went back in time and changed things?" I wondered.

Charlie mused for a moment. "It's possible Salvatore didn't have people inside the bank back in the 1920s. We learned from Chancey's past-life regression that Frank was killed on the street the first time, like his killer thought he still had the key on him. That would mean Salvatore didn't learn about the bank vault until some time later. Originally, he must've spent years sending that bigwig up the corporate ladder until he gained control of the key in the vault."

Ivy drummed their fingers on the tabletop. "That certainly sounds like my father. He's no stranger to playing the long con."

"But the second time, after we changed things, Lorenzo followed Frank to the vault and stole the key that same day, before killing him," Charlie said. "Which means in the timeline we're currently in, Salvatore has had the key all along, even though bank records showed Frank made the deposit. Ivy, any idea where your father would've hidden it all this time?"

"It's hard to say," Ivy admitted. "Dear old Dad is headquartered in Chicago, but it could really be anywhere. He hides his riches all over the world, so that if his main casino is targeted, he doesn't lose everything. Wherever it is, it's in a highly secure location."

"We can be thankful it's in his hands, at least," Kallie assured us.

"Why?" I asked. "He's the most powerful vampire mob boss in the world, and he's not a good guy."

"Because my dad won't play ball with the Warden," Ivy informed us. "Two peas in a pod, they are. My dad and the Warden both have to be the biggest dick in the room, and my dad ain't gonna make a deal with the Warden, because he doesn't want to feel like he's beneath people. The vampire key gives him some sort of power he can hold over the Warden's head, and he'll get off on that."

"But the vampires have sided with The Mission," I pointed out.

"Yeah, the vampiric government, not my dad's mob. They're two separate groups, and my dad and the governing body of vampires are always going at it. They're sworn enemies," Ivy stated.

"That's putting it lightly. Salvatore Bianchi works for himself, and only himself," Danny added. "He hates the vampiric government more than he despises anyone else on this planet. They've gotten in the way of his plans one too many times."

"Salvatore Bianchi won't join The Mission?" Marcus asked.

"Aw, no fucking way," Ivy insisted. "My dad wants to be in charge. He's fine letting the Warden do what he wants with the rest of the world for now. But the moment the Warden sets foot in Chicago, which is his turf, he's gonna light him up."

"Hopefully they'll kill each other," Kallie grumbled.

Ivy sipped at their tea and continued. "So we know my dad won't hand over the key to the Warden... bad news is, he shouldn't have it in his possession, either."

"But we might be able to get it back today," Kallie added. "Max, if you would."

Max stepped forward. She laid a file on the table. "We know everything about Lorenzo Gallio. Where he hunts for blood, his schedule, what time he brushes his fangs in the morning. We also know... that he's a major pervert who likes to frequent strip clubs and brothels in every city he's in."

"How does this help us?" Charlie asked.

"We found out that Lorenzo is going to be in Las Vegas tonight, making a deal on a shipment for Chicago," Kallie said.

"What's he buying?" I asked.

"Blood slaves," Ivy replied regrettably. "One of the reasons I left the mob. I refused to deal in transporting people for slaughter. Unfortunately, trafficking of people, both human and supernatural, is my father's favorite method of business."

"We can't let Salvatore sell those people," I insisted. "We have to do something about it."

"We're already on it," Max said. "We have Elvish task members working on getting those blood slaves out of confinement and into refugee housing in Ilamanthe."

"Which Lorenzo doesn't know about yet, but he'll find out," Kallie said. "The deal is supposed to take place tomorrow morning. Lorenzo is arriving in Vegas tonight, so he can get his rocks off at the local vampiric strip club the night before."

"Charming," I said dryly. "So how do we get him?"

"That's where Ivy comes in." Kallie gestured to Ivy, who stood.

Ivy took a breath. "The vampire that owns the strip club has chains of supernatural brothels all over the world. I did a lot of work for him, and used to be his most popular dancer. He flew me all over the world as a performer and escort, because I brought in a lot of cash. He's a rat, but he's our way in. I've already reached out requesting to return and bring a couple of my dancer friends with me. He was chomping at the bit to have me back on stage."

"Who are these friends?" Charlie asked apprehensively.

"That would be us," Kallie said. "We pose as staff within the strip club, get Lorenzo alone, then figure out what he knows about the key."

"And if he doesn't want to talk?" I asked.

"Then we bribe him. Heavily," Max said. "Or resort to other methods. With luck, the slimy worm will betray Salvatore, tell us where the key is, and we'll bring it back here."

I glanced at Ivy. "Will Lorenzo risk betraying your dad? You don't turn your back on the vampiric mob without paying for it."

Ivy shrugged. "It depends on where his loyalties lie."

"Or how much he values his life," Charlie said darkly. "Salvatore will kill Lorenzo if he turns on him. He knows *we'll* kill him if he doesn't talk."

"It might not come to that," Max added. "The Elvish treasury is endless. We can give Lorenzo a more comfortable life than Salvatore can, and even better, we can hide him."

This sounded like a fairly solid plan. I was pretty confident it would work.

"There are wards set up all around the strip club, not to mention there are magical alarms placed in every major city around the world by The Mission to locate demigods. You'll have to portal outside city limits, then drive in to make sure they don't know you're coming," Max informed us. "You can't portal in or out of the club— there are wards there preventing access or departure once you're inside."

"Road trip!" Chancey shouted.

Charlie ruffled Oberi's ears. "I'm sorry, boy, but you can't come with us this time. You're too recognizable for a Familiar, and a strip club is no place for a dog."

I disagree, but point taken, Oberi said. She changed into a phoenix. *I will make use of my magic in the healing quarters where I am most needed, until you return. Be safe and well.*

She flew out the open door, and Kallie stood. "Everybody pack up. We're leaving immediately."

"We should visit my uncle first," Marcus said as he stood up. "He's staying in a penthouse in the city. He's an Alchemist, and he has a potion we can use to disguise ourselves."

"We could just use illusions," Kallie suggested.

"This potion is stronger, because I've infused my demigod magic into it," Marcus assured us. "I've been working on it with my Uncle Grant for a few weeks now, experimenting. It'll last even if there are wards or spells set up meant to break deception magic."

"Wow, Marcus. Nobody's ever pulled off a potion like that before," I said in surprise.

"Yeah, well, I decided it was time to start putting my demigod powers to good use," he said with a shrug.

Treatment really had to be helping him. He was finally going after his full potential.

"That sounds great. You did some awesome work, Marcus," Kallie said, and I nearly fell out of my chair at her compliment. "Let's go."

"I'll stay here and work on the final details of the plan with the rest of the team," Charlie said. "You guys go on ahead."

Danny flung an arm around Charlie's shoulders. "So who wants to play stripper, pal, me or you? I'll give you a lap dance to test it out."

Charlie scowled. I was interested on what exactly was in this potion, so I decided to go with Marcus and Kallie. We had a driver take us to Marcus' aunt and uncle's penthouse in the city.

"I don't think anyone's home," Marcus said as he opened the door. "They've been very busy lately—"

He stopped mid-sentence as we walked in. The place was a mess. There were empty bottles of alcohol everywhere, along with take-out boxes and party favors. A bag of chips looked like it'd exploded all over the baby grand piano in the corner. A framed photograph of Marcus' Uncle Grant carrying his Aunt Talia on his back was lying cracked on the floor. On a shelf, a collection of potion bottles had been knocked over, though thankfully none had been shattered.

My father, along with King Ethan, were sprawled out on the floor. Sleeping, I might add. King Ethan was in his wolf form. Daddy was literally cuddling him, holding on to the shifter for dear life and burying his head in the wolf's fur as he slept.

A guy I supposed must be Marcus' uncle stood at the stove, flipping pancakes. He didn't look anything like Marcus, with darker skin and black hair that stood straight up. He wore an apron and appeared positively chipper when we entered. "*Hola, sobrino!* Nice to see you, Marcus! I wasn't expecting you, but I'll put on some extra bacon."

He seemed like the only one who didn't have a hangover, though there was a cauldron on the table full of something that looked suspiciously like alcohol. It looked like something he'd been brewing himself.

"Uh, no need. We're not hungry," Marcus replied as he took in the aftermath of what looked like a freaking frat party.

Lucas stumbled in from the next room, looking hungover as all hell. "Hey, kids," he slurred. "What's happening?"

"Dad, what the hell?" Marcus gestured to the mess.

"It's a very long story," Lucas moaned, holding his head.

"We'd love to hear it," Kallie said, nudging her dad with her shoe. He let out a growl in his sleep and turned over, effectively smushing my dad. Daddy startled awake and shoved Ethan off of him, who rolled over the other way and kept on sleeping.

Daddy blinked sleep from his eyes, realized he was on the floor, and groaned as he pulled himself onto the couch. "Oh, dear ancestors."

"You lectured *me* about acting like a teenager, but obviously you four got carried away," I indicated, crossing my arms.

"It was all of us," Daddy grumbled.

"Yes," Lucas noted. "You all know we were there at the engagement party last night, and we decided to go out for a drink afterward."

"With our wives," Daddy added.

"I know we haven't gotten along well in the past, and have had our differences, but since the war is going on we decided to settle them over a few drinks," Lucas said.

"A *few*?" Marcus asked.

"That wasn't how it started," Daddy defended.

Marcus crossed his arms. "Dad, you told me to never cave to peer pressure. Now *you're* the one caving! To other adults!"

"Yeah..." Lucas trailed off. "The night got a little wild. All us parents decided to share our own stories, our history with our former prophecies and what not."

"And it was really creepy," Daddy deadpanned. "The similarities really threw us off."

"Then we all got depressed because of what we went through as kids, and all the stories kept on getting *worse*..." Lucas shivered. "Well, what we came to is that we're all more alike than we realized, that all of us have been through some shit trying to save the world, and now our kids are going through it, so we might as well forget about it and try to live while we're still young."

"So... you partied the night away," Kallie stated.

"We did our best," Daddy confirmed. "It was a fun night out at the bar, but us men had enough and wanted to continue the party back home. It was too far to walk back to the palace, so we crashed here. The ladies weren't up for coming back."

"Where are our moms?" I exclaimed.

"They didn't want the night to end, so they went out to the club." Lucas hiccupped, before he fumbled in the cabinet for pain reliever. "Haven't seen them since."

"For shit's sake, Dad." Marcus sighed, before turning to Grant. "I swung by to get the potion we've been working on. Is the latest batch done brewing?"

Grant nearly dropped his spatula, and his eyes widened. "You're using it?"

"Yes. We're going on a mission tonight," I said.

"Hold it right there, young lady," Daddy said. "What's this mission about?"

We painstakingly had to explain the whole thing to our fathers. Daddy sneered when we'd finished. "A strip club? You shouldn't be going into those kinds of places."

"I don't need the lecture, Daddy," I replied. "I'm sure you and Mama have never been to a strip club, but we need to do this."

Daddy's chest puffed up. "I'll have you know, your mother and I can be adventurous, and we *do* visit these types of establishments every once in a while. After all, your mother appreciates looking at other women—"

"Oh my ancestors, I don't want to hear about this!" I shouted. Apparently, all of our parents were more wild than we thought, even in their forties with grown-ass kids.

Daddy coughed to clear his throat. "Fair enough. Though I don't like that you're going into the line of danger tonight, I can't get in the way of it, and I'm not going to stop you. But please be careful, peanut."

"I will. We'll get the key and come home straight away," I promised.

Not like the thought of messing around in Vegas wasn't tempting, though...

Marcus ducked into a back room, then came out with a vial full of glowing purple liquid. "This should be enough," he said. "I'll leave the rest of you to your hangovers."

"Please do," Lucas noted sickly. King Ethan gave a particularly loud snore as we closed the door behind us.

"Didn't you realize your parents were missing all night?" Kallie asked Marcus as we left the penthouse. "Haven't you been staying with your mom and dad?"

"I have, but I feel better now, and you guys need me at the palace," Marcus stated. "I moved all my stuff back last night."

Kallie almost seemed to glow. "It's good to have you around."

We took the car back to the palace. While we were waiting at a stoplight, I looked to my left and had to do a double take. There our moms were, still in their clubbing gear and having mimosas at one of the nicest brunch bars in Ilamanthe, acting like they hadn't been out drinking all night. Emma and Nadine clinked their glasses together with huge smiles, while Mama ate avocado toast.

My mother saw me poking my head through the window of the limo. She gave a huge smile and waved. I slowly waved back as I rolled the window up.

Kallie gaped just like me. "Damn. I hope *we're* that cool when we get older."

"They could be on a supernatural reality show. *Party Moms!*" Marcus exclaimed.

I groaned. "Don't even *think* of mentioning anything like that to Cassiel," I warned. "He'll take any publicity for the monarchy, good or bad. Next thing you know, our moms will be the next big Elvish reality TV stars."

"Yeah. Probably a good thing to keep this little event under wraps," Kallie said with a nod.

"Your parents have corrupted mine," Marcus accused. "My mom never drinks."

"That might be a virgin mimosa in her hand, but it sure looks like she had fun last night," I teased. "She's missing a shoe."

Marcus groaned.

We spent the rest of the day going over the plan, then once we were ready, gathered together in our meeting spot in the parking garage.

"Where's Danny?" I asked when we arrived, noticing he wasn't around.

"He's sick again, unfortunately," Max said. "We'll have to do this without him."

Again? What was going on with Danny? He seemed fine this morning… though he'd never come back after we'd split up to go get the potion.

It wasn't my place to pry. After all, I didn't like when people tried to get the worst details about my spinal injury, especially when I didn't know them well. I wasn't good enough friends with Danny to ask those kinds of questions yet. If he couldn't come, we'd have to do this without him.

We drove my car through a portal that bloomed on the outskirts of Nevada. Charlie, Marcus, Kallie and I were in my car, which had finally gotten fixed from the bank robbery, while Chancey, Ivy, and the Elvish Associates were in a van behind us.

"Finally. Out on the open road," I said. I'd been looking forward to driving the long, winding roads of Nevada my entire life. I never knew I'd get to do it so soon.

"We're here to get the key," Charlie reminded me from the seat beside mine. "Don't attract attention."

"Of course not. Wouldn't dream of it."

I couldn't resist temptation, though. We were flying down the road at ninety miles an hour before the rest of them could tell me no, taking sharp curves at way too high a speed.

"By the goddess, Ava, slow down!" Marcus snapped from the back seat as Kallie fell into him around a turn. We'd lost the van a while ago, because it couldn't keep up.

"We need to get there on time," I argued. We merged onto the highway, and some jerk in a pickup truck tried to speed up so I couldn't get on.

No, thank you. I kicked my car into high-gear and cut him off, forcing him to slam on his breaks. The jerk responded by speeding up again, swerving around me and pulling ahead.

I had a smoothie from earlier we'd grabbed from the palace for a quick lunch, and this dickhead was about to wear it.

"ASSHOLE!" I rolled down the window and chucked the drink, which splattered all over the opposing driver's windshield. The truck immediately skirted to the side of the road and slammed on the brakes, which forced me to come to a dead stop so I didn't rear-end him.

I could've taken off, but I didn't. A big, burly looking dude with a buzzcut got out of the truck with his fists clenched, yelling some not-nice words. I grinned.

"Great, now he's coming this way," Marcus complained.

"Charlie, go beat him up," I said.

He guffawed. "Excuse me?"

"I mean, I'd do it myself, but then I'd have to get my chair out, and then get *into* my chair. It would just take too long, and we're in a hurry," I explained. "This guy looks like he's a human, so in the name of supernatural secrecy, we're gonna have to resort to some good old-fashioned ass-kicking. That's on you, babe."

"I'm not going to kick some guy's ass just because you cut him off!" Charlie yelled.

"You didn't see what happened! Don't you believe *me*, your *wife*?"

"Gee, I wonder why that'd be hard for me to imagine you didn't cause this."

"He's getting closer..." Marcus whimpered.

"Whatever happened to forsaking all others?" I asked.

"I don't remember traffic violations being a part of our wedding vows, but you can add them into the upcoming ceremony if you like," Charlie offered.

I huffed. "Wow. Just wow. Okay, Marcus, you're up!"

"Me?!" Marcus yelped.

The dude had gotten to my window and was banging on the door. He broke off my mirror, which made me gasp. How dare he touch my baby!

I poked Charlie's arm. "Ancestors, what a dick! You know, if he threatens me, you *have* to punch him, then."

Charlie let out an irritated noise, clearly contemplating it.

"Oh my gods," Kallie grumbled, and she got out.

Five minutes later, Kallie had dusted off her clothes.

"That loser got his blood on my shoes. You were right, Ava, he *was* a dick,"

Kallie complained as she wiped them off outside the car. The other guy, who Kallie had pelted to bits, stumbled back into his truck and drove off.

"You're all terrible people." Charlie shook his head.

I gave a happy sigh. "Well, now that's over with, we might as well get on down the road!"

"No, you lost your privileges. You're sitting in the back with me," Charlie said, and he snatched the keys out of the ignition. "Marcus is driving."

Marcus *did*, which was absolutely terrible, I tell you, because he went ten miles under the speed limit the entire time.

"Are we going to get there today, grandma?" I mumbled.

"Cars are dangerous. They are potential weapons, and therefore, should always be driven safely," Marcus replied.

Maybe it wouldn't be so bad if Marcus didn't have to sing along to *every single show tune* that played over the speakers. He'd hooked up his phone to the car stereo, and his playlist was extremely one-sided. I liked musicals, too, but it was hard to enjoy the music when Marcus was belting out *Waving Through a Window* at the top of his lungs for the third time in a row… with accompanied hand movements and expressions.

After I'd nearly aged ten years, we finally arrived in Vegas. This was one of the few places in the United States where I'd never been, and it looked amazing. The strip was full of fancy casinos that towered into the skyline, and neon lights beamed everywhere into the desert night. Hundreds of people filled the streets, and the whole city seemed to buzz with an undertone of excitement and danger.

"We could get into some trouble out here, honey," I said to Charlie as I looked around.

"There's a reason it's called Sin City." Kallie pointed to a tall building at the edge of the strip. "Here. The strip club's inside that hotel."

Marcus pulled into a parking garage. The van was already waiting inside.

We got out of the car, thank the ancestors for it. I was tired of driving with Miss Daisy over here.

"Marcus, you drive so slow that you lost the lead I had on the van, and they still arrived here earlier than us," I complained.

"But we made it here safely, and that's what counts," he shot back.

We all gathered in a circle outside the van, and Marcus conjured the potion. He passed it around. Each of us took a drink, save for Ivy. I waited for it to change my features, but nothing happened.

"Are you sure this spell works?" I asked, looking at the remnants of the potion vial.

"I'm positive," Marcus insisted. "I've tested it out a bunch of times. We don't look any different to each other, because we all took the potion, but anyone else who looks at us is going to see a completely different person. They won't be able to tell who we really are."

"Come on, we gotta go." Ivy checked their hair in the van's side mirror. "He ain't gonna wait forever."

"We'll be there at the designated time," Charlie said, and he swooped down to kiss me before he wandered off into the hotel with Chancey.

Everyone had their role; the Elvish Associates were going to hack into the club's security cameras and do surveillance. Ivy, Marcus, Kallie and I would go to the meeting with the club's owner, and hopefully, be able to pose as the staff within the club whenever Lorenzo showed his ass up. Charlie and Chancey were posing as guests, and would do their best to spy on Lorenzo as he moved throughout the club.

Ivy escorted us into a hallway that was connected to the parking lot, and led us to a glass elevator. We got in and rode the elevator up fifty floors, to the top of the building.

"It smells like blood in here," Kallie complained as we took the elevator up.

"Well, yeah," Ivy responded. "Vampire's lair and all."

The elevator doors opened. As we walked through, I felt something heavy press in around me— a ward meant for breaking enchantments. I felt the potion's effects waver, but they still held.

Marcus was right. Even if Kallie cast an illusion, the wards were so strong here that they would break, and a weaker potion would've definitely failed to hold up. The potion he'd made was incredibly unique.

The hallway we stepped into was dark and lit with blacklights. A tall, muscular vampire in a suit was blocking the door ahead.

"Hey, Biff. How's it going?" Ivy purred to the guard.

"Ivy." The vampire nodded and stepped aside to let us through. "It's great to have you back."

"I've been away too long." The way Ivy swayed their hips as they strutted into the club was even more seductive than usual. Although Ivy had promised to leave this life behind them, clearly it was still a world they fit into and knew well.

The club itself was massive. The tables and chairs were made of glass, and it was so dark inside I could hardly see. The area was dimly lit in purple and blue show lights, and there were multiple stages with spinning dancing poles. It was pretty empty here, as the club wasn't open yet. The room was nearly vacant, except for one person.

I officially knew the exact scumbag we were working with when I saw him.

He was a short, ugly ass looking vampire counting hundreds at one of the tables. When he saw us, he stood up and held out a hand.

"Ivy. You're as lovely as ever," he said, and he gave a slimy kiss to Ivy's fingertips. I don't know how Ivy managed to stand it, because this dude might as well be Creepzilla.

Ivy, though, didn't flinch, merely put on a smirk. "Darius Freyden. Can't tell you how *excited* I was to reach out."

"Heard you did some time in the pen." Darius stepped back. "You ain't still mad about those last clients I sent ya, right?"

Something dangerous flashed behind Ivy's eyes, but they quickly camouflaged it. "Of course not. I know the risks of this job. I'm here to work."

"That's what I like to hear." Darius' attention immediately turned to the rest of us. "This who you brought in? I'm not impressed."

"There's more to them than meets the eye," Ivy promised. "The girls are Lux and Blaze. And the guy's Marco. He ran security at the last club I danced for."

Darius huffed. "This guy ain't security," he said, thumbing at Marcus. "He's a pretty boy if I ever saw one."

"I beg your pardon?" Marcus squeaked.

"Look, toots, we take all kinds here," Darius spat. "Don't be shy. You ain't gotta pose as security. You're going up on the main stage tonight."

Marcus blanched, but I elbowed him and he peeped, "Whatever you'd like."

Darius turned toward Kallie. "Sorry, sweetheart, but we got enough blondes."

Kallie scowled. "Fine. I'll wait tables."

"Lucky you. Our last hostess just quit." Darius gave a smile that had fangs missing, but it fell as he glanced at me. "Get lost, wheels. This ain't a place for you."

"And why not?" I asked. "I've performed before."

One time in The Devil's Playground, but still.

Darius sneered. "Why would I want to hire a bitch in a wheelchair? Strippers gotta walk."

I gave a careless shrug. "I'm a fetish. You'd be surprised how many guys wanna fuck a girl with no legs. I'm a special order."

Darius scratched his dirty beard. "Guess you're right... the clients like variety on the menu, and we've never had a broad like you before. And you've got a nice rack. Fine. You're in."

Thank the ancestors Charlie wasn't here to listen to Darius talk to me like that. Guy would be dead in an instant and the whole operation would've been blown.

"Can we get ready now, or what?" Ivy asked bluntly. "I need to make some money tonight. I'm low on cash."

"Sure, sure. Take your whores backstage," Darius said carelessly, going back to counting his money.

Then Darius froze. "Your dad doesn't know you're here, does he?"

"My father never knows where I am. You can relax, big guy," Ivy said bluntly.

Darius definitely relaxed. "Good. We don't want no trouble from Salvatore."

"None here." Ivy turned on their five-inch heels and strode off the main floor, leading us to the back where the dancers got ready.

The moment we were in the locker room and out of his sight, Ivy's slick smile immediately slid off their face. "Ugh, what a roach." They wiped their hand on the edge of their short dress. "I'd gladly do another month behind bars if it meant never seeing his ass again. Darius made a lot of money selling me to people I had no business being with. After what happened, I... well. It was the reason I overdosed."

"Hopefully this will be the last time," I said gently.

"It will be," Ivy promised, a deadly note to their tone. "I ain't walking outta here without getting my revenge on that piece of filth."

"Why did he pick *me*?" Marcus whined. "I don't want to be a stripper!"

"This is a good thing," I pointed out. "Your mind reading is clearest when you touch people. If we get Lorenzo to feel you up, you can look inside his head and find out what we need to know."

"Awesome, because that's just what I wanted. Some sicko grabbing my junk," Marcus complained.

"We won't let him hurt you," Kallie promised, and she put a hand on his arm. "We'll get what we need and go."

"But I don't know if I can do this!" Marcus protested. "I'm not a dancer."

"Yes, you are. Marcus, this is just like theater club. You're playing a role—the stripper Marco," I encouraged. "Just go out there and act how *Marco* would act, not you."

Marcus immediately lit up. "Can I give him a backstory?"

"Sure." He could knock himself out if it got us that key.

"We've all got a role to play tonight," Ivy said as they sat at a makeup station. "And no using real names, here. Stick to your stage names, unless you want somebody to figure out the gig and rat us out."

Ivy dug in a box and handed Marcus a pair of tight gold briefs and knee-high boots. "Knock 'em dead, scamp."

Marcus frowned, but took them anyway. "Marco would love these. So I should, too."

We didn't have a lot of time to get ready. Most of the other dancers were already here, but they ignored us when we came in. I saw a couple of dancers whispering to each other and glancing at Ivy as if they were a legend. Hopefully the rest of us could play the part. I threw on a matching black bra and panty set before I curled my hair and did my makeup.

Ivy, as always, looked incredible. And, I noted, miserable. They'd moved on from this life and didn't want to go back to it.

They wouldn't have to. This would be their final time, I promised myself.

Poor Marcus was sour in his get-up. The briefs were definitely too tight on him.

"I'm cold." Marcus shivered, before he paused and said, "Just like how Marco was cold the night his mother abandoned him, in the freezing rain..."

"Whatever helps," Kallie said, and she nudged him forward. "Get out there and show them what you've got."

The club hadn't been open long, but there were already a ton of vampires here, filling up all the booths and tables. They sat at the edge of the stage and watched the dancers twirl around the poles with looks that more or less disgusted me.

Kallie went to the bar to start taking orders. She jerked her head meaningfully at Marcus, who gave a little groan and climbed onto a stage opposite Ivy. He twerked his butt very pathetically, drawing the attention of a couple of onlookers.

It would've been funny to watch if this wasn't so dangerous. People were doing drugs right out in the open. I watched as vampires fed from the dancers until they were almost bled dry. The girls had passed out by the time their clients were done drinking from them, and had to be carried back-stage by security to recover. The vampires who'd fed off of them didn't care, just acted like they'd finished a steak instead of sucked a person dry.

This wasn't your typical strip club. It had no rules, and was full of some really bad people. We had to be very careful.

"You okay?" I whispered to Ivy as we passed a whole crowd of clients doing nightshade. This had to be triggering as hell for them.

"I'll be fine," Ivy whispered back. "Let's just do what we have to and get out of here."

Couldn't agree more. Ivy sighed. They frowned for a moment, before something shifted in them and became plastic. Ivy pasted on a velvet smile and strode onto the stage, taking place at a pole. They were mesmerizing, and immediately drew the attention of everyone in the room as they began to twirl, becoming a precious diamond that every greedy bastard in this club wanted to have.

I lifted myself out of my chair and onto the stage. I had some exceptional upper-body strength now from pushing myself around all day, and I could hold myself up for long periods of time. I manually adjusted my legs so they were wrapped around the pole, and lifted myself onto it. I held on to the pole with one arm as it spun me around.

Marcus' slow driving had given me one advantage. I'd done some quick research on my phone before we arrived, watching videos of wheelchair users who'd modified pole dancing to make it accessible for paraplegics. I couldn't do anything half as complicated as what they could, but some of the moves were simple as well as sexy. I only had to adjust my body and hold on as the pole spun.

Besides... I just had to look hot until Vampire McWeirdo showed up. Which I hoped was soon, because I'd caught the attention of a couple of guys nearby, and I didn't know how satisfied they'd be with looking at my ass before they wanted to touch.

I felt on edge until I saw Charlie stride through the door with Chancey. Once I recognized my husband's frame in the low lighting, I immediately relaxed. Nobody was going to bother me with him around.

The security guard we'd talked to earlier blocked his way in. "Hold on. Do you have a pass?"

"Do I need one?" Charlie snapped back, playing all the part of the arrogant prick.

"This club's heavily vetted," Biff growled. "You don't have a pass, you're not getting in."

"I'm sure we can find some sort of understanding." Charlie was loaded with money we'd taken from the Elvish treasury before coming here. He plopped a massive stack of bills on the counter next to the guard. "I'm Cal Bently. Billionaire. Maybe you've heard of me."

Darius heard the word *billionaire* and came running. "Right this way, sir," he said, putting an arm around Charlie's shoulders and leading him to a table. "We have a private VIP booth just for you."

"It's nice *someone* knows how to treat people around here," Charlie replied snidely, and he plopped another stack of cash in Darius' hand as he sat down at the booth. The greaseball almost melted.

"I assure you, sir, we have the finest girls Vegas has to offer, and they're willing to perform extra services," Darius added. "Would you like us to set you up in a private room with Cashmere, or Misty? They are our most experienced ladies, and I assure you that you'll be pleased."

Chancey shook his head. "Nuh-uh. The boss has specific tastes. He likes girls like *her*."

He pointed to me, and Darius had to do a double take. "You want wheels?"

Charlie didn't visibly react, but his reaction across our bond was absolutely livid. I prayed he didn't reach out and strangle Darius for being such a moron. "Are you questioning my preferences?"

"N-no, sir, of course not," Darius stammered. "This club has a wide variety of whatever you're accustomed to, and if you like Blaze—"

"Good," Charlie barked back. "Girl, get over here."

I knew we were just playing a part, but I couldn't help but get a thrill when he talked to me like that. I slid off the pole, got myself back into my chair offstage, and came over. Charlie yanked me out of my chair and onto his lap to straddle him. He pulled me in closer, yanking my hair. I gave a moan for show, though it wasn't really fake.

"This one's mine for the night," Charlie said. He tossed another stack of money at Darius, which he fumbled to catch. "Now go get me a fucking beer."

Charlie gave my breast a squeeze, and I let out an exaggerated giggle. Darius hurriedly nodded his head. "Right away, sir."

When Darius hurried off, I leaned in to whisper, "You're very good at being a playboy."

I nipped at his ear, and he grinned. "And you're lucky we're in public."

His finger toyed at the edge of my panties and dipped down. I nearly let out a low gasp.

Chancey was on the other side of the table and couldn't see what Charlie was doing, but he still rolled his eyes. "Hey, I know you two get off on shit like this, but this ain't the time. We got a job to do. Keep your head on your shoulders and not in your pants, pal."

"Are you worried?" I asked, casting a glance back at him. I pressed my chest against Charlie's. I felt the weight of his pistol tucked into the holster there, hidden underneath his suit jacket. I felt safe, but maybe I shouldn't.

Chancey hadn't taken his eyes off Ivy, who was currently collecting dollars scattered all over the stage. "Yes. Ives shouldn't be here."

"Then let's find Lorenzo, so Ivy doesn't have to be. You guys see him yet?" Charlie asked.

My eyes scanned the club, until I noticed a vampire who was identical to the photographs that Max had shown us earlier. "Yes. He just walked in."

"With a whole entourage, no less. There are at least five other vampires with him," Chancey complained. "Good luck getting him alone."

Kallie watched Lorenzo as she poured drinks at the bar, tracking his movements. She wasn't going to let him out of her sight until we got what we needed.

Marcus noticed Lorenzo had showed up. He slid his way off stage and made his way over to the group of vampires, giving a flirty wave. At least he was getting into his role. He made a beeline for Lorenzo, but another vampire grabbed Marcus' arm and pulled him to his side. Marcus scowled, and Lorenzo's attention went to a different dancer nearby.

Ivy noticed the scene go down. I watched as Ivy gave the stage to another girl and strutted across the club to help Marcus, batting their eyelashes as they gave a friendly hello.

"We can't be staring at him," Chancey said under his breath, and I ripped my eyes away from Lorenzo. "It looks suspicious."

"What are we supposed to do?" Charlie hushed back.

"Just let Ives and Marco do their thing," Chancey whispered. "For now, act normal."

Well, *normal* in this strip club was a pretty good way of getting both me and my husband turned on. We both had to play our respective parts, and since I was a stripper and he was my client, there was no better way than a lap dance. Chancey left us alone at the booth, milling throughout the club to talk to the other dancers— and see if he could pick up any information on Lorenzo while he was at it.

"This might be the most fun I've ever had on a mission," I said as I sank down against Charlie's dick, moving in circles over his pants. He was trying not to be hard right now, and totally failing.

"I hate that we can't do anything right now," he nearly moaned, and he ran his hands through my hair.

"Back home," I promised. Once we got the key, we were picking this up where we left off.

An hour passed of Charlie and I absolutely edging each other, but it wasn't as fun as we wanted it to be, because it didn't look like we were making any progress on getting the key. Chancey slid back into the booth, and I whispered, "Did you find out anything?"

"It's like trying to yank off a limp dick," Chancey complained. "Nobody's talking."

"They're probably too afraid. Lorenzo has a reputation," Charlie added. He helped me off of his lap and onto the seat next to his. "We gotta try something else."

Two seconds later, a high-pitched voice stung my ears. "Hey there, big boy!" Marcus said outlandishly as he slid onto Charlie's lap. "You want to ride the carousel?"

Marcus began gyrating against Charlie's legs in a very terrible impression of what had to be the worst lap dance ever performed, tossing his head back. Shit, he was really bad at this. If anything blew our cover, this would be it.

"Marcus, what the fuck are you doing?" Charlie hissed under his breath.

"I'm *trying* to pass on information," Marcus snapped back. "For shit's sake, at least act like you enjoy it."

"Just sit down," Chancey growled, and he yanked Marcus into the booth. "Did you find out anything?"

"Lorenzo's not interested," Marcus insisted. "I tried to get him to touch me, but he's clearly not into dudes, and if I can't touch him, I can't read his mind— not clearly enough to find what matters, at least. He's not even falling for Ivy's charm."

"What about his friends?" Charlie demanded.

"That's not working, either. Everyone's mind is blocked here," Marcus said. "Even with my demigod powers, I can't get through long enough to see what's important."

"These guys work for Salvatore Bianchi. They know how to protect themselves. It's not weird they're warded at all times," Chancey pointed out.

"Exactly. What I'm trying isn't working," Marcus insisted. "You've gotta do something, Blaze."

Guess it really was up to me. "Okay. Let's switch gears."

We didn't have long to come up with a new plan, so we threw something together in five minutes. Charlie got up, then stomped over to Darius and shoved him.

"I need a private room to make a couple of phone calls," Charlie barked. "Are you going to find me one, or do I have to go somewhere else?"

Darius was temporarily flustered. He glanced at me, and I lifted my hands in surprise.

Darius visibly swallowed before he said, "Certainly. Right this way, sir."

Chancey hopped up to guide Charlie behind Darius. We were doing a good job of keeping his blindness under wraps, for now, but eventually Darius would notice Charlie's blank stare. Lorenzo needed to spill what he knew so we could leave.

I got into my wheelchair. Darius slithered back to me a few minutes later. "That billionaire hotshot who came in here hasn't stopped blowing dollars on you since he walked in," Darius said eagerly. "You might be my next hot item, sweetheart."

"Glad to help, so long as I get my cut." I forced a smile, which was more like a sneer.

"Oh, you got it, honey. Whatever you want. You just keep the fat cat's wallet flowing."

I scoffed. "I wish. I was doing pretty good, until he glanced at some stupid stock ticker on his phone. Then he started freaking out."

Darius curled his lip. "Typical. He saw his investments falling and needed a room so he could yell at some poor bastard on Wall Street. All these rich types care about is how big their wallet gets."

That was a bit hypocritical, wouldn't you think?

"So what am I supposed to do until he comes back?" I pretended to whine.

"Go find some other sucker to bleed dry," Darius sneered. "You're on the clock. Every minute you're not pulling in money is my time you're wasting, and I *always* make my money when it comes to the bitches I hire."

His meaning made my blood run cold. I thought about the women who'd been fed on earlier. He sold the girls who didn't perform well to be blood slaves.

Screw this motherfucker. I flung my hair over my shoulder. "Fine, whatever."

I acted like I was pissed off as I rolled away, but Darius didn't know he'd given me an opening. I fixated my eyes on Lorenzo and popped out my chest. Showtime.

He immediately noticed me. I rolled up to his table and said, "You seem like you've been here before."

Lorenzo's eyes wandered my body, then my face. "I'm a frequent flier here at the club. But I've never seen you around."

"I'm new." I leaned forward, trailing my fingers up and down his arm. "My name's Blaze."

Lorenzo blinked as he took me in, like he was starstruck. "You... you look like my wife."

Ew. I flashed my teeth and asked, "Is that a bad thing?"

"Not at all," Lorenzo promised. "She was a very beautiful woman."

I wasn't about to feel sorry for this bastard when I knew what kind of shit he'd done. I grasped his arm and said lowly, "Well... maybe I can help you remember her."

"Yes. I think you can," Lorenzo said softly. "She was a sickly, poor thing, like you."

Don't hit him. Don't hit him.

"I'm sorry to hear she passed away," I forced out, while thinking it might be a good thing she was in the afterlife and away from this asshole.

"I have a very dangerous career, with a lot of enemies," Lorenzo explained. "Sometimes, in my line of work, the people you love get hurt."

I was a mob wife. He wasn't saying anything I didn't already know, and I could guess what had happened. Lorenzo had taken a bad job, and his wife had paid the price for it.

"That's too bad," I said gently. "Do you come to these kinds of places often?"

"I never used to, until my wife died. Now I'm just trying to pass time and ward off the loneliness," Lorenzo replied.

"Well, you can spend some time with me," I invited. "I'm easy to talk to."

My skin crawled as Lorenzo's hands began to stroke my skin. "I might like that."

He hadn't made a move to fondle me, like I'd watched him do to the other dancers who'd come by. His hands on my skin were respectful and gentle. He really did want to pretend I was his dead spouse.

I didn't understand how someone who sold blood slaves for a living could hold so much affection for another person. Did he think his wife mattered, and all the other lives he ruined didn't?

"Do you mind if I call you Mabel?" Lorenzo asked. "Just for tonight."

This was going way too far, but he'd opened up to me, so this could be my way in. "You can call me whatever you'd like. Do you want a private room, so we can talk more... personally?"

"I'd love that, Mabel," Lorenzo said. "You don't know how much it means to have you back."

I was doing grief therapy in a strip club for a known supernatural trafficker. Not how I expected to spend my evening.

Lorenzo followed me to the back of the club, where the private rooms were. The sounds of sex were everywhere behind these doors. One of the bouncers opened up a private space for us, and Lorenzo paid him before the door slammed shut, locking me in with the vampire.

Lorenzo sighed. "Here we are. Alone at last."

He took a seat on a plush couch within the room. "It was a very hard day, Mabel. Would you mind rubbing my shoulders? You know I love your backrubs."

This guy was certifiably off his rocker. But he wasn't asking me to screw him, at least not yet, so I pulled myself onto the couch and sat beside him to rub his shoulders.

Massaging a vampire was like trying to knead a stone. It made my fingers ache.

"Any interesting jobs lately?" I asked. Maybe I could get this guy to spill without resorting to darker methods.

"A few, here and there, but I dislike talking about work when you're around," Lorenzo replied. "There are more interesting things to discuss."

I wasn't giving in. "Did the boss have you steal a special item, or—"

"Enough talking, Mabel." Lorenzo turned to face me, then grabbed the back of my neck. "Let us feed like we used to, *mi amore*. Just a drop."

I saw his fangs elongate as he leaned in. My side of our bond flared in alarm, and the door burst open. Lorenzo reeled back as Charlie forced himself into the room, holding up his pistol.

Lorenzo staggered to his feet as he looked at me, but I already had a ball of Fire in my hand. "Hands up, fuckface."

He did as he was told. His expression didn't reveal any betrayal, merely acceptance, as if he knew this was going to happen.

"You stole a valuable key in Paris over a hundred years ago, and killed Frank Coffrey afterward. We know you were the one who took the key, and we know you gave it to Salvatore Bianchi," I said coldly. "Tell us where it is, and we'll let you live."

Lorenzo let out a cold laugh. "And betray my boss?"

"We can hide you. We have the resources," Charlie added.

"There is nowhere I can hide from my past. That is something I will never escape," Lorenzo said lowly.

His eyes locked on mine. "Thank you, whoever you are. You gave me five more minutes with her. That's all I wanted in the world."

He dropped his hands, and one fumbled in his pocket.

"No!" I cried out, but it was too late. Lorenzo had opened his mouth and popped something in before we could stop him.

Charlie rushed forward and yanked his mouth open, but Lorenzo had already swallowed. The vampire began to gag as a dark foam sputtered out of his mouth, and he instantly collapsed on the floor.

A sour smell filled the room, like burning sulfur, and the vampire gasped in pain. Then Lorenzo twitched twice before he went still.

"Fuck!" Charlie yelled. I immediately got to the floor and put a hand to Lorenzo's chest, to see if I could save him.

My healing magic recoiled inside of me as it surveyed Lorenzo's body. He was already dead. There was a massive cavity in his chest where his heart used to be.

I let out a frustrated sigh. "It was a death potion capsule. The components were made of Fire magic. Once he swallowed the pill, it combusted in his chest and turned his heart to ash. The pill was probably something Salvatore had him carry, in case there was a risk he got captured and interrogated."

"And he just *took it* instead of fighting back?" Charlie asked. "He's a vampire. He could've run away."

"I don't think he wanted to live anymore, not without his wife. He knew how valuable the key is. He didn't want to risk giving it up."

"Guess we were wrong and his loyalty to Salvatore and the mob was worth more to him than his life," Charlie growled. "Goddammit."

I stared at Lorenzo's corpse. "I don't get it," I said. "He sold people. He *ruined lives*. He was an evil man, but he acted like he still loved her. How can a bastard like him love someone so much, when he's done what he has? Didn't he only care about himself?"

"I don't know, pidge. I don't think we can understand someone like him."

Charlie ducked to the floor and rummaged through Lorenzo's suit jacket. "We need to search his body. He's got to have something on him that'll give us a clue on where we can go next."

I helped him. We didn't find much in Lorenzo's pockets besides his wallet, which was more or less useless to us. But then Charlie flipped back the edge of Lorenzo's jacket, and I found a thin discrepancy in the lining.

"Here," I said, skimming my fingers over the lopsided stitching. "Someone's sewn something in."

Charlie ripped open the lining, and I reached inside the hole. I pulled out a folded piece of parchment. On it were six names written in fine ink.

"A list of contacts," I mumbled as I looked it over. "People Lorenzo associates with, potentially people who helped him steal the key."

"One of them has to know more," Charlie insisted, and he slipped the list into his pocket. "At least we aren't leaving here empty-handed. Let's go, pidge."

Fine by me. We left Lorenzo's corpse behind us and ventured back into the main part of the club.

"We've gotta get out of here," I said. "Let's find Marcus... *Marcus!*"

He'd apparently found his stride here at the club, because Marcus was fully in his element. He was up on the main stage, surrounded by a massive crowd of people as music thudded in the background. He spun around the pole, shook his ass and did some moves before spinning into a freestyle breakdance.

Wow. I didn't know Marcus could do that. The club patrons absolutely loved him. There were dollar bills sticking out of his briefs, the top of his boots and all over the stage.

Kallie came up behind us and crossed her arms. "I think he's taking this a bit too seriously."

"I'm impressed," I said as Marcus tossed back his hair and ran a hand over his abs, to the enthusiasm of the crowd. "He really is getting into it, and he knows how to put on a show."

"Well, was it worth it? Do you know where the key is?" Kallie questioned.

"Lorenzo's dead. We didn't get much out of him," Charlie informed her. "We need to leave."

Kallie's face fell. "Aw, dammit! You can't tell me this is another dead end!"

"We'll find that out once we get home," I said. "For now, we need to book it, before his body is found and it leads back to us—"

Pop! The sound of a regular pistol firing off shots echoed through the room. A couple people in the club screamed, but most of the vampires merely looked around curiously to see where the noise was coming from.

Ivy stormed out of the door that led backstage, slamming it open. The guests cleared a pathway as Ivy vengefully left a trail of blood dripping from their fingertips. Chancey walked beside them, his face unreadable.

As the door swung back open the other way, I saw Darius lying on the floor. His disembodied head lay beside his corpse, a bullet hole right in the middle of his forehead. His expression was frozen in shock.

"*Now* let's go," Ivy seethed. The pistol in their hand was still smoking.

The club's security team immediately reacted once they saw Darius was toast. They rushed toward Ivy with super speed, but Ivy and Chancey were ready for them. They took the guards head-on. Ivy was untouchable as he shot and decapitated vampires on the spot with brute force. I saw Chancey take a couple of bullets, but his angelic blood protected him as he started ripping the limbs off vampires.

The dancers in the club began screaming, and vampire mobsters drew pistols out from their suit jackets. Supernaturals didn't really use human guns, but apparently, vampires didn't give much of a shit. They wouldn't kill most supernaturals, but they'd certainly slow them down. Bullets and spells began flying. Kallie put up a shield around us, and I watched as silver bullets and blood magic bounced off the walls.

Marcus scampered off the stage and came running our way. Kallie let him through the shield, and he leaned on Charlie to catch his breath. "Whew! It's getting a little hot in here, hasn't it?"

"I'd say," I replied. "How do we get out?"

The entire club was a mess, but through the chaos, I saw a couple of bulky Elves force their way through the doors to the club. They were the twins, Asa and Ares. They were a part of Charlie's team. Kallie let them into the shield, where they started speaking at once.

"We've been compromised, your highness," Asa said to Charlie. "The United Supernatural Union is on their way here as we speak. You need to leave immediately, by use of a portal."

"I thought we couldn't use them here," Kallie yelled over the noise.

"We've broken down the barriers preventing portals from forming inside the club, and avoiding the alarm wards now is useless, seeing as how they've already been triggered," Ares replied. "The vehicles have already been transported back to Ilamanthe."

"We can't leave Ivy and Chancey," I protested, who were still in the middle of their brawl— and winning.

"Don't worry about them," Asa said. "We'll get them out. Just go!"

I glanced backward reluctantly, but I knew he was right. Ivy and Chancey had definitely come here with their own agenda. It wasn't our job to end their crusade for revenge and drag them back to Ilamanthe. That was the responsibility of the Associates.

Charlie took a mirror out of his pocket and projected it forward. A portal blossomed within the confines of the shield. I sagged in relief as I saw the beautiful, sunny pathways of the palace gardens shine through the portal's window. We hurried through, and the moment we were back in Ilamanthe, the portal closed behind us. We came through on the other side of a mirror that was within the palace's gardens, surrounded by wildflowers and roses.

The noise and violence abruptly halted, leaving only birdsong. I shuddered. That was *not* how we'd planned to end that operation, but clearly, Ivy and Chancey had other ideas.

"Look at how much cash I made!" Marcus cried, pulling dollars out of his shorts.

Kallie smirked. "They must've loved your dancing."

"I learned from my dad," Marcus gushed. "He really knows how to throw down."

Didn't know Lucas could break dance, but I guess that was cool.

Kallie snickered. "I guess you always have a career in erotic entertainment to fall back on."

"It was pretty fun," Marcus admitted. "Once I got over the embarrassment, and was *out there*, under the lights with the crowd cheering for me, I felt *alive.*"

"We're happy for you, Marcus. At least something came out of this," Charlie grumbled.

Marcus' smile fell. "You didn't learn anything about the key?"

"No," I said. "All we got from Lorenzo was a potential list of names on who he might've given it to."

"Shucks." Marcus' shoulders dropped. "Guess this really was a bust, huh?"

"Eh, not really," Kallie said. "I got to see you in booty shorts, so that was a plus."

She and Marcus both laughed. He slung an arm around her shoulder. "Well, maybe Marco will make a comeback someday. Smaller venues, though, more intimate settings."

"I'll be there, so long as you bring the boots," she joked. Both of them laughed.

It was nice they were getting along, but it was really depressing we hadn't made any progress on the key. These names might not connect us to anything important.

I could tell Charlie was thinking the same thing. As we headed into the palace, I said, "These names better lead somewhere, because we paid a high price to get them. Once this gets back to the Warden what we did at the club, he'll put two and two together and assume that Salvatore Bianchi has the vampire key."

"Salvatore will never give the Warden anything, so the key's safe for now," Charlie stated.

"Yes, but that also means Salvatore will go to farther extremes to keep it hidden," I pointed out.

It was a race against The Mission. Salvatore wouldn't hand over the vampire key willingly, but the Warden would do everything in his power, and use everything in his arsenal, to take that key from Salvatore's cold, dead hands.

Somehow, we had to outwit both of them. And with three powerful supernatural forces... demigods, vampiric mobsters, and the Warden himself... fighting to take ownership of the vampire key, who knew where it could end up next.

charlie

THIRTEEN

We'd retrieved the list of names from Lorenzo's body, but it seemed we were further away from the vampire key than ever. A week passed without any word from the Elvish Associates, and I was getting impatient. They were supposed to be investigating the names on that list, but so far, it didn't seem like they'd made any progress.

I kept busy by training with my grandfather in the gardens, while Ava spent most of her time with Oberi in mystic training or planning the wedding. We were preoccupied, but I was still on edge. Every moment we didn't have the vampire key in our hands was another second closer to the Warden finding it before we did, and we couldn't allow that to happen.

I'd been practicing my Elvish powers all morning when my grandfather finally excused me hours later. I'd skipped lunch, as I was too immersed in practicing to take a break. Eddie had been waiting for me at the garden entrance and quickly fell into step beside me as I left the area.

"Your highness, I have news," Eddie said.

"It better be good," I told him. I was too tired for another crisis— though now that I thought about it, it might be Ava's fatigue coming through our bond. She'd been more tired than usual, and her daily naps were stretching longer. Mystic training was difficult, and it often wore her out. Attempting to contact the Elvish goddesses was highly difficult. She hadn't done it yet, which meant whatever Eddie had to tell me needed to be a win. We couldn't take any more setbacks.

"Very good news," Eddie replied chipperly. "The Elvish Associates have a development for you."

"That's the best thing I've heard all week," I said. "Lead the way."

Eddie led me to the Elvish Associates' headquarters. They were all there, waiting for me.

I sat in a chair reserved especially for me and turned to the team. "I hear you've made progress on the list."

"Yes," Max said. "We've been able to verify that the men on this list are among the oldest and most highly trained vampires working under Salvatore Bianchi. Our intel confirms these are the men Salvatore has hired to guard the vampire key."

"Great. Let's find one of them, and get them to tell us where the vampire key is," I said.

"It's not that simple," Max said. "Salvatore was smart. He didn't tell these guys everything— only certain things that each of them need to know to defend the key. For example, one person might know the city the key is in, but not in what building. Another person might know the combination to the safe where the key is kept, but has no idea of its location. This prevents one of them from betraying Salvatore, as nobody has all the information needed on where the key is or how to get to it— except for Salvatore, and we know we're not getting anything out of him. Since we believe he's given information out in pieces, if we want to get the location of the key, we'll need to obtain all the pieces of information at once from all of the people on this list so we can put them together."

It seemed impossible. We'd barely scraped by with information from Lorenzo, and it was by sheer luck we got anything from his list. Now we had to try to get information from six separate people?

"How are we going to do that?" I asked.

"We need to get them together and read their minds," Max said.

I shook my head. "There's no way it's going to work. They've got wards over their minds, and Marcus couldn't even sort the information for *one* person, let alone six at the same time."

"That's because Marcus hasn't received proper training," Max argued. "We found a witch who can mentor him— a friend of his parents. Marcus is being summoned to the demigod training room as we speak to begin his training. It's going to take time for him to learn how to break past mind wards and read minds properly, but he *has* to learn the technique if we're going to get the information we need. It's the best chance we've got."

"How do we get these people on the list together?" I wondered. "They have to be in the same place at the same time for Marcus to be able to read their minds. If we go one by one, and isolate them in separate locations, one of these guys might figure out what we're doing and alert the others— even if we're doing it in disguise. We'll only get one shot to read all of their minds collectively, and I'm not sure what we can do to get these guys in the same room."

"We're working on that," Max said.

"If I may," Eddie offered. "I might have some suggestions."

I stood. "Excellent. Eddie, you stay here and work with the Elvish Associates. I'm going to find Marcus. I want to see what this training is all about."

"Very well," Eddie agreed. "We'll meet back at your quarters before dinner."

I left the Elvish Associates' headquarters. By now, I knew my way around the palace pretty well, and I could find the demigod training room on my own. On my way, I felt a familiar presence approaching me from the opposite direction. Her demigod magic rolled off her in waves.

"Hey, Kallie," I said.

She slowed her step. "You haven't seen Marcus anywhere, have you? I've checked his suite and the art room, but I can't find him anywhere."

I paused in the middle of the hallway. "Is something wrong?"

"No. Actually, it's the opposite," she admitted. "Oh, shit."

She dropped something, and I bent down to pick it up for her. It was a thin, smooth piece of wood with some sort of intricate carvings along the outside. If I had to guess, I think they were cats, intertwined with swirls. On the end was a carving in the shape of a wolf's head, with two gemstones embedded for the eyes, though I couldn't tell what kind they were.

"A wand?" I asked. Why was she carrying this around? Fae didn't use them.

"It's for Marcus," Kallie admitted as I handed it back. "I made him something— a sort of peace offering. I wanted to give it to him."

I tilted my head curiously. "I thought you two weren't planning on staying friends after everything that happened."

"I thought so, too," Kallie admitted. "But things are different than I expected them to be. I thought it would hurt to be around him, but now that the bond's broken, it's easier than ever. There's no romantic pressure anymore. We don't have this magical tether chaotically pulling us together and then pushing us apart. The energy between us is steadier. I think we can both think more clearly now— I know I can. Marcus and I will never be a couple, but I think we can still be friends."

"Are you sure? You seemed pretty done with him when the bond broke," I said.

"I was, but I've had the space I need, so it's not a big deal anymore," she said. "We can hang out now without it being awkward. It's actually really fun.

Plus, he's getting treatment for his BPD, so I don't feel pressured to save him like I did before. We can just... be cool. It's nice."

That was a relief to hear. I worried that the Villain's Club would be no more, and that was really sad to think about. It was nice to see them getting along for a change. I knew they'd never hook up again, but I honestly thought that was better for them, anyway. Now they could be friends without all that stuff getting in the way.

Kallie must've created a gift bag and tissue paper, because I heard it rustle as she placed the wand inside. "I want to give this to him right away. Do you know where he is?"

"Marcus is in the demigod training room," I told her. "I'm on my way there now. You're welcome to tag along."

"Thanks." Kallie tried not to let her emotions show, but I could tell her steps became a little lighter. She seemed more than a little excited to see Marcus again on good terms.

We entered the demigod training room and found Marcus seated at a table, while Rishi purred softly in front of him. They appeared to be alone.

"I didn't expect to see you two here," Marcus said. "I've got this room reserved for a mentorship session. She should be here any minute."

I sat in a chair opposite him. "We're not here to take the room from you. We're here to observe. If we're going to pull off another intel operation, I want to know everything. We can't afford any mistakes, so we've got to be confident we can pull this off."

"I can handle it, Charlie," Marcus said. "You don't have to babysit me to make sure I do it right."

"I know you're capable. I just want to learn how this works," I replied.

Marcus sighed, but he didn't insist I leave, so I stayed.

Kallie sat beside me and reached across the table to place her gift in front of Marcus. "I came to give you this."

"Oh, uh... thanks," Marcus said. "But it's not my birthday."

"It's not a birthday present, dummy." Kallie giggled. "I just wanted to do something nice for you."

"Wow, thanks," Marcus said, like he was baffled she would. "I don't know what to say."

"Don't say anything. Just open it," Kallie said in excitement.

Marcus was already tearing at the wrapping. He opened the bag and gasped.

"You got me a wand?" he squeaked. Sounded like he had tears in his eyes and everything.

"I didn't buy it. I *made* it," Kallie explained. "It's carved from a branch from the oldest tree in Ilamanthe. The gemstones in the wolf eyes are polished lepidolite and rhodonite."

I recognized the first one, because it was the same stone I'd gotten Ava for emotional healing. I didn't know the second stone, though.

Marcus must've, because he mused, "A stone of forgiveness."

"Yeah. Rhodonite heals wounds caused by... past relationships," she said, a little lamely. "I figured we're on the same page now, so maybe we can move forward as friends. I know we needed some time apart, but I have to admit I missed having you around. I want my best friend back, you know?"

"But Ava's your best friend," Marcus said, confused. "I didn't know I was in the top spot."

I nearly facepalmed. Marcus really had to stop taking the *best friend* label so literally. He did the same thing when I asked him to be a part of my wedding. It wasn't a competition, for fuck's sake.

"She is, but you are, too," Kallie confessed. "I miss goofing around and talking all day. I figured we could have that again, since, you know, there's no more pressure."

I held my breath, thinking Marcus would turn her down or have another explosion, but his clothes rustled as he reached over to hug her. "Thanks, Kallie. This is the best present I've ever gotten. I love it so much."

Rishi meowed, and Kallie mumbled, "It really was nothing. It was easy to make."

I didn't believe her. Wands were strong magical objects, and this wand had to be fortified with powerful demigod abilities to be able to withstand casting Marcus' magic without blowing itself apart. She'd poured a piece of her own power into this. It showed how much she still cared.

"I can't wait to try this out," Marcus squealed as he sat back in his seat. "This is awesome."

"Well, you deserve it," Kallie said quietly, though I didn't think Marcus heard her.

I drummed my fingers on the tabletop. "Who is this witch you're meeting with, exactly? Max said she was a friend of your parents."

"Yeah. She works with my mom, but they've been friends since I was born," Marcus explained. "She used to babysit me when I was little, and she comes over for family parties all the time. She's not my aunt, but she might as well be. When I was in the hospital after my first attempt, she came to talk to me and gave me some tough love. My parents are always soft and gentle, but she knew what to say to me to get me out of it. She says what she means, and she doesn't sugarcoat anything. Sometimes it can be rough, but more often than not, it's helpful. She's a very powerful witch, and we can trust her to teach me what I need to know to get the job done."

The door opened, and a woman walked in. Her heels clicked against the floor, and I could feel the air swirling around a cloak that billowed at her ankles.

"Marcus," she said brightly. "It's good to see you again."

Marcus immediately stood, and I knew this woman commanded respect. "It's been a while. Guys, this is Priestess Chloe."

I was shocked. Nobody mentioned anything about this mentor being a Miriamic priestess. That meant she was one of the people who'd sentenced Marcus to the Darke Institute. He didn't seem to hold any animosity toward her, though. Rather, he seemed to respect her. She must've advocated for him alongside his mother, to avoid a harsher sentence.

"Marcus, I babysat you for years. Just call me Chloe," she offered. "Have a seat. The technique you're about to learn is very intensive, so you'll want to get comfortable for it."

Marcus sat, and Chloe took the chair at the head of the table. "Chloe, these are my friends Kallie and Charlie," Marcus introduced. "They're demigods, like me, and we're working together to find the Divinity Keys, open the Elven Gate, and fulfill Charlie's prophecy as the Elven heir. We believe that by growing my power and learning how to read minds, I'll be able to obtain the valuable insight we need."

Not just anyone was privy to this information, but Chloe was a Miriamic priestess. She was practically a queen among the witches, and she was privileged to possess any and all information any other rulers had. Marcus trusted her, so I did, too.

"I can help with that," Chloe began. "As you know, various members of the Miriamic Coven possess the ability to read minds. But these powers have limitations. While each witch's specialty differs, I have yet to meet a witch or warlock who can fully intercept another person's thoughts with precision. A member of the Mentalist Cast may have the unique ability to read thoughts that you freely share with them, but they aren't able to see what remains hidden. A Seer might be able to interpret messages through feelings, but aren't able to get the exact thoughts in words."

"What's the difference between the Mentalist Cast and the Seer Cast?" Kallie wondered. "They sound so similar."

"They are, in a lot of ways," Chloe admitted. "And there's some overlap between the two Casts' powers. What separates a Mentalist from a Seer is *how* they use their power. Mentalists toy with the mind or have the power of telekinesis, while Seers are more adept at perceiving emotions, reading information from a distance, or obtaining visions about the past or future."

She turned back to Marcus. "Since you have the powers of both Casts, I believe you may be able to combine these powers to read minds more effectively. It's a technique I developed long ago alongside your Aunt Talia, who is a Seer. It's called teleinsight."

"Forgive me," Marcus said curiously. "I know you're the Mentalist Priestess, but how were you able to develop a mind-reading technique? I thought you had the powers of telekinesis."

"I do," Chloe confirmed. "Unfortunately, teleinsight is not something I'm able to do without the proper tools. Talia and I were in possession of powerful objects that granted us access to immense power. We no longer have those objects, so we can't perform the technique anymore. In fact, I don't believe any other witches could pull this off. However, I remember it well and can teach you. Since you have demigod power *and* the power of all five Casts, you should be able to do this. First, you'll need a wand so you can focus your powers. As the technique is very direct, I don't believe even you will be able to perform it without assistance. A wand is required for this technique to work."

"I've got one," Marcus said, and he waved his wand in the air. He almost poked me in the eye.

"Ouch! Be careful," I snapped at him, rubbing my cheek where he'd stabbed me.

"Sorry," Marcus apologized.

Maybe this was the weapon we needed. Get the Warden in here and we could just have Marcus gouge his eyes out by accident.

"This will work well," Chloe said. "What you're going to do is take your Mentalist powers and your Seer powers and combine them together, then direct that magic down into the wand. If you are focused enough, you should be able to pierce through any mental wards the subject has protecting them."

"So it's like using *simultension* on yourself, like Ava does when she combines Fire and Water magic to make blue fireballs?" Marcus asked.

"That's what I've heard when it comes to your friend, yes," Chloe responded.

"Ava's magic is stronger than ever when she combines her powers. Maybe if I do this, I can use teleinsight to read the Warden's mind," Marcus said.

"I wouldn't jump to conclusions just yet," Chloe warned him. "While the technique is powerful, other demigods are an even match for you. I don't think you'd be able to overpower another demigod's mind without their consent. Plus, this spell works best in close proximity, so even if you *could* read the Warden's mind, you'd have to get close enough to him to do it."

"All right," Marcus said. "Let's stick to these vampire baddies for now. What can I do once I'm inside their head?"

"You'll be able to quickly search for the information you desire, rather than being overwhelmed by too many thoughts and memories," Chloe explained. "You can force them to tell the truth if you so desire, or you can learn it yourself without them ever suspecting a thing."

"This sounds really useful," Marcus remarked. "There's got to be a special trick to it."

"The trick is to use their own mind against them," Chloe explained. "Before we proceed any further, I'd like to assess where you're at. I want you to demonstrate your mind-reading abilities on me. Somewhere in my mind, there is the name of a girl I once called a dear friend. Find her name."

Marcus cleared his throat. "All right. I'll give it a shot."

"Use the wand, and direct your magic," Chloe encouraged. "When you're ready, speak this incantation; *By the goddess' light and candle fire, illuminate the information I desire.* In time, you will learn how to perform the spell without speaking the incantation out loud."

"All right, I've got this," Marcus said; more to himself than to any of us.

Usually, he seemed so apprehensive when trying a new spell, especially one so powerful. Today, he seemed really confident in his abilities. Marcus began muttering the incantation under his breath.

I felt his magic swelling over the room. Though he directed his power at Chloe, I could feel it tingling over my skin. This spell was a lot, even for Marcus.

Several moments of silence passed. Kallie and I waited, but neither Chloe nor Marcus said anything. I must've been holding my breath, because I had to remind myself to inhale.

After a full minute, Marcus breathed a sigh. "I can't see it. There's too much information."

"I could feel you poking around in my mind," Chloe said. "You were flipping through my memories, trying to figure out on your own which one was important. You're trying to label these experiences for yourself, but you cannot rely on your own discernment. You're trying to observe, when you must *command.* You must rely on the subject's mind, because it's already cataloged and labeled these experiences. It already knows what information is important. Once you're inside, you must order the mind to bring the information to the surface. Forget about your own experiences and what you believe to be true, because you're not in your own mind anymore. You need to become a part of the subject's mind, until the subject is no longer the master of their own mind, but *you* are their master."

"Oh, I think I get it!" Marcus said brightly. "Can I try it again?"

"Certainly," Chloe responded.

Magic swelled over the room again, and Kallie leaned over to whisper to me. "Marcus isn't moving. He's gone into some sort of trance."

"Oh, wow," Marcus didn't *sound* like he was entranced, but I trusted Kallie that it must've looked that way. "I can see things more clearly. It's a lot more organized. Now I just have to find what I'm looking for... Was her name Lily— no. That's not it. Hang on."

We sat in silence for a while. Marcus kept pushing, never once giving up or criticizing himself for not getting it right away. He was more determined than ever.

Then Marcus snapped his fingers. "Got it! Her name was Gwen— no, Camille!"

"Well, which is it? Gwen or Camille?" Chloe replied harshly.

Marcus hesitated. "It was both. You loved them both dearly, and they turned their backs on you."

Chloe clapped her hands together. "Marcus, you did it! And it was so direct, I couldn't even feel you poking around."

"It worked!" he cried in relief. "But man, that's a powerful spell."

"I want you to try it on one of your friends," Chloe pressed. "As demigods, they'll be harder to read, and therefore, more similar to our warded vampire friends."

"I thought Marcus couldn't read demigods," Kallie pointed out.

"He should be able to if you open yourself to him," Chloe said. "As long as consent is provided and you let him in, he'll be able to see what's inside."

"No," Marcus objected. "I know I need to practice, but I'd rather not read Kallie's mind. I hope you understand, but it's kind of a respect issue."

That was putting it lightly. Digging around in someone's head, when you were their ex and things were already fragile was definitely uncomfortable. There were times I'd been in Ava's mind when we'd been broken up, because I couldn't help it, and it had been damaging to us repairing our relationship. Marcus didn't want to put this new friendship with Kallie on the line, even if he needed to practice this spell.

"Thanks, Marcus," Kallie said, almost in relief. "I appreciate that."

"You need to practice," Chloe insisted. "Someone has to be willing."

"Try it on me," I quickly offered. "I'm up for it."

"You sure you want me inside your head?" Marcus teased.

I shrugged and gave an uneasy laugh. "I tell you everything, anyway."

"All right," Marcus replied skeptically. "You asked for it. What am I looking for?"

"Find one of Charlie's secrets," Chloe encouraged. "Something he hasn't told you— something he may not even realize he hasn't revealed."

There wasn't much Marcus didn't know, but even so, I stiffened. I didn't want him finding out about *everything*. Some stuff I wasn't ready to reveal.

"Here we go," Marcus said. He began muttering under his breath again.

I opened up my mind to him and waited, then waited some more. I felt his magic swell and settle over the table, but I never felt it enter me. "So... are we going to get started, or what?"

"Shh..." Marcus hissed. "I'm concentrating."

That's when I realized he *was* working his magic on me. It certainly was a tricky spell, because I couldn't tell he was inside my mind. I didn't feel it at all.

I was anxious about what he might find, until Marcus burst out laughing, startling me. "*That's* your secret? Sounds like some kinky shit."

"Hey," I snapped. "I don't want you looking at any memories of me and Ava."

"Relax," Marcus said casually. "I only saw where that mirror in your bedroom leads. I didn't know you two had a secret sex dungeon."

"Marcus," I warned.

Marcus snickered. "I always wondered why we never heard you guys going at it from the other room, because you're literally right next to us. I know Ava's a screamer."

"Leave my wife out of this," I growled.

"Please," Kallie chuckled. "It's not like it's a secret. Some nights I could swear I heard Ava screaming at the Institute, and I wasn't even in the same cellblock as you. And let me tell you, those were *not* screams of torture."

I shrugged. "Yeah, I guess you're right. Ava would wear this information as a badge of honor."

Chloe gave a sigh. "Goddess. Do I remember what it was like to be your age. Not much has changed, has it?"

"*Please* don't tell me any stories about you and Uncle Miles. I've heard enough about my Mom and Dad's super happy fun times, and don't need to listen to yours, thanks," Marcus grumbled.

"You deserve it, for poking around in my head and immediately finding mine and Ava's hidden room," I replied. He didn't discover the worst things he could've, but he still found one of my secrets, so I guess that was great progress. This spell was actually going to work to get us the information we needed.

Marcus slumped in his chair. "It took a lot of energy for me to get just that little bit of information. I need time to perfect this strategy, because if I'm tired now, it's not going to look pretty if I go poking around in six people's heads at once. I need to learn how to do this with more people without getting so tuckered out. Otherwise, I'll pass out when I'm trying to read the minds of those vampire gangsters, and they're not gonna stop to ask if I need a minute. I've got to be able to do this flawlessly when the time comes to do the job."

Chloe stood. "Take the afternoon to recover. We'll continue these lessons tomorrow."

"Thank you for believing in me, Priestess," Marcus said.

"Of course," she replied softly. "I know you're capable of wonderful things. You just have to learn how to harness what's already inside of you."

We left the demigod training room. Priestess Chloe went one way, while Kallie, Marcus and I went the other. Rishi followed along at Marcus' feet.

"What are you two up to the rest of the day?" Kallie asked. "My schedule is free."

"Mine, too," Marcus said. "There's an indie film premiering at the theater this afternoon I wanted to go to. Do you want to come, Kallie?"

"Absolutely," Kallie answered. For a girl who wanted nothing to do with Marcus a few months ago, she seemed eager to spend time with him now. I wondered just how much of their connection had been a magical bond, and how much of it had been because they naturally worked well together. I was really glad they could be friends now without feeling pressured to be more, because it seemed like they really did get each other.

"Sorry, but I can't come with," I told them. "I don't get much free time these days, and I've got to take what I can. I'm working on a special project for Ava."

"Oh... *that*," Marcus teased. "I saw that in your mind, too, but I didn't want to say anything."

"That's it, you're officially banned from my mind," I said. "I don't want you ruining the surprise."

"I won't!" Marcus made the sound of a zipper. "My lips are sealed."

"They better be," I warned.

"Would you relax? You're so serious lately," Kallie said, and she punched my shoulder. "Lighten up every now and then, would you?"

I scowled. There wasn't much of a chance to lighten up. Not when there was so much on the line.

Kallie and Marcus went off to the theater, while I headed toward the music room. It was one of my favorite places in the palace, with all kinds of instruments for the royal orchestra. It was often a bustling place, even when the orchestra wasn't in session, because the Elves were such musical people that they enjoyed going there to practice. As the prince, I had free rein of the instruments and got to play with whatever I wanted.

I turned a corner, and my heart leapt into my throat as I rammed into someone. I nearly fell over, but caught my balance at the last minute. It was a little weird— servants in the palace usually gave me a wide berth, as it was seen as incredibly offensive to touch one of the monarchy without specifically being asked. But this person probably hadn't seen me coming. An honest mistake.

"Easy there," I said. "I didn't mean to run into you."

"My prince!" a woman cried. I didn't recognize her voice, but it could've been any servant or guard. She hadn't stumbled like I had. "Thank the gods I found you. You must come quickly. She's hurt— your one true love is in pain!"

Alarm bells went off in my head, and I immediately started to panic. Something bad must've happened during mystic training. Why hadn't I been informed the second it happened?

I quickly tried to connect with Ava through our bond, but I brushed up against an impenetrable wall. That usually meant Ava was sleeping... or that she was seriously hurt, and unconscious.

I tried to do the same with Oberi and was met with no response. That immediately made me worried. I should've been able to contact at least one of them, and I couldn't reach out to either.

"Where is she?" I demanded.

"Follow me," the woman urged.

I ran to keep up with her, and we twisted through a maze of hallways. I assumed we were headed toward the temple, but it wasn't long before I lost my bearings.

I slowed and turned around, trying to use my magic to figure out where we were.

"Are we going the right way?" I asked the servant girl. "I don't know this part of the palace."

"This is the right way," she said. "It's just downstairs."

My Air magic sensed an empty column rising upward through the palace— an elevator shaft. I figured Ava must've taken the elevator, so I headed for that immediately.

The servant girl grabbed my arm, but I was freaking out too much to remind her that was against the rules. "It'll be faster if we take the stairs."

I didn't know this part of the palace, and all I wanted was to get to Ava quickly. I followed hastily beside her. Her stone-like grip on my arm didn't release as we hurried along, until we began to descend a twisted staircase. I was getting more anxious with every passing second, so I took the lead. The air grew colder around us the deeper into the basement we went. Heat radiated off torches burning on the wall, which I was sure provided the only light. I heard the servant girl behind me slip a torch off its sconce to carry, to help her see as we descended.

"This has to be the cellar, where the royal stores of wine are kept," I mused aloud.

I didn't know why Ava would be down here, but I guess it wasn't unlike her to go exploring, especially in cave-like places where she might find a hidden passageway. It was the anthropologist inside of her. I just hoped she wasn't seriously injured. Why hadn't she talked to me about this before she went wandering off?

She wouldn't. That didn't make any sense. She always came to me about everything before she went and did it. That was the agreement we'd made, and she'd never broken it. Was she led into some kind of trap, where she thought something was safe but was actually dangerous? I didn't think the Elves would put her at risk, but the mystics were desperate to contact the goddesses, so maybe something had gone wrong.

"Was this part of her mystic training? Is that why Ava came down here alone?" I demanded.

"Who's Ava?" the servant girl asked innocently.

I stopped dead on the stairs. "My wife. You said the princess was hurt."

"Oh, *her*," she sneered. The way she said it tickled a memory in the back of my mind, but I couldn't quite place it. "I said your one true love was hurt. I never said anything about Ava-Marie."

Something was very wrong here. My magic tingled through the stairwell, and for the first time, I actually paid attention to it. I hadn't been listening to my magic because I was so worried about Ava, but I finally recognized that the woman standing beside me wasn't an Elf. That's when I noticed the energy signature of the servant girl following me.

She was a vampire, and I wasn't entirely sure—

I didn't finish the thought before she shoved me *hard*, with enough force to send me plummeting. I went tumbling head over heels down the stairs. My head smashed against the wall, then again on the corner of a step.

I came rolling to a halt at the bottom of the stairs. My heart hammered, though I was no longer worried. I was *pissed*.

I groaned and struggled to get to my feet through the ache in the back of my head. I felt completely disoriented. I never managed to stand before I heard the vampire rush toward me.

"Your true love is right here!" she cried, before I felt the heat of the torch she carried coming straight for me.

The torch slammed hard into the back of my head with the force of the vampire's blow. I felt cinders burn into my scalp, and the world faded to nothing.

WHEN I CAME TO, I couldn't make sense of my surroundings.

The back of my head pulsed in pain, and my guts twisted with the weight of a heavy sickness. I was sitting upright on a hard surface, some sort of chair, but that was about all I could process.

I tried to move, only to meet restraint. Cold, hard objects wrapped around my wrists and ankles. My heart hammered as I tried to yank free of the shackles, but no matter how much I struggled, I couldn't break free. I tried to pull my magic to the surface, but found it only made the sickness in my gut tighten.

I realized in horror what was going on. These weren't just any old shackles — they were made of inferichite. Whoever had restrained me had been cautious, because these inferichite cuffs were large and heavy, and there were two per limb. These were nothing like the cuffs the Warden used on us in the Institute. Back then, the inferichite was just enough to keep my demigod powers at bay, but they still allowed me to cast elemental magic. These were more like the cuffs they fitted on us in Cellblock 9. There was so much inferichite that it made me sick to even try casting my Air.

I tried reaching out to Ava or Oberi through our bond, but the inferichite cuffs had shut that down.

I was completely alone.

I turned to my other senses. I could tell I was in a large space, because I could hear a fire crackling from a hearth at the other end of the room. The warmth of a smaller flame flickered a few inches in front of me, like I was surrounded by candles. Various scents surrounded me— all delicious and enticing. The savory smell of prime rib and the pleasant scent of risotto filled my nose. It was strange, because I'd think that if I were to be kidnapped, I'd be thrown in a musty, rotting dungeon. Wherever I was, it was a nice place.

And roses. There were so many damn rose petals around they almost overpowered the scent of the food. They were all over the floor under my shoes, and scattered all over my clothes. What the hell was going on?

I ran my fingers over the armrest of the chair I was shackled to, and I realized the material was smooth, but not cold enough to be stone. Intricate carvings ran up and down the wood.

I pushed a little harder past the inferichite, because I *had* to make better sense of my surroundings, and without my magic, it wasn't enough information.

I sensed the air swirling around the area, and I realized I was in a long room with a high ceiling. A table that must've been able to sit twelve people expanded out in front of me, and I sat at the head of it.

I had to be in some sort of fancy dining room. I sensed someone at the other end of the table, though they didn't breathe.

"Finally, you're awake," a woman purred. It had to be the vampire girl who'd lured me to the cellar. "We can finally eat!"

She sounded more happy than sinister, which was really fucking weird for a captor.

"Forgive me if I'm not hungry," I said through gritted teeth. There was very little that could keep me from scarfing down such delicious-smelling food, but this bitch had accomplished it. I was almost certain every dish at this table had to be poisoned.

She rose from her chair, and her heels clicked on the floor as she made her way over to me. "You're not even hungry for some chocolate cake, Charlie? I know how much you love it."

She ran her hand over my back, and it made my skin crawl. She held a plate under my nose, and the sweet smell of chocolate cake filled my nostrils.

"Tell me what's going on," I demanded. "Where's Ava?"

"Back at the palace, of course," she said.

"She isn't hurt then? You lied," I accused.

"Ava was merely taking a nap with that *dog* of yours," the woman sneered. "I don't know why you care so much about her when I'm around."

"Who are you?" I growled.

She set the plate in front of me and took the seat beside me. The hem of her silk dress brushed my ankle. She reached out to trace her finger along my arm. My insides curled, but I couldn't get away from her.

"Oh, Charlie." She let out an innocent giggle. "Haven't you figured it out by now? I left you so many clues."

I tilted my head, but I had no idea what she was talking about. "Clues?"

"Didn't you get my roses?" she asked. "I wanted you to know I was there in the palace."

I didn't know what she meant, until a memory of roses came back to me. "The morning after the engagement party," I realized. "*You're* the one who left those cut-up roses at my door."

So it wasn't some elaborate prank Alistair pulled off while he was drunk. Shit. We should've made sure.

"Of course it was me," she snickered. "Don't you recognize me?"

I tried to place her voice, but I couldn't make the connection. Then I thought of the way she sneered the word *her* when talking about my wife, and it clicked where I'd heard that tone before.

"You're the servant girl from our engagement party," I realized. She'd been trying to flirt with me that night when I approached the dessert table— and insulted my wife to do it. It'd made me uncomfortable then, and I was beyond uncomfortable now.

"Servant girl?!" she balked. "Charlie, how could you possibly reduce me to *that*? It's true I was at your party, but I was only there to keep an eye on you. I've been watching you for a very long time. You're a very hard man to get alone. The prince is always surrounded by guards, and I can see why, because you deserve to command an army. It's so *you*."

She gave another high-pitched giggle. "It's funny, referring to you as the prince now. I remember when you were just another hunk in fight club. I used to come to your fights at the Institute. I always bet on you, of course. I watched *every one*."

So she'd been an inmate. My mind raced with the possibilities of who this girl could be. She sounded like she was my age, but I couldn't think of anyone from the Institute who'd go through all this trouble to kidnap me, apart from the Warden's demigods. I could tell by her magic she wasn't one of them, and she didn't seem affected by inferichite, either.

Most of the inmates at the Institute had died, and if they hadn't, they'd joined The Mission. My friends and I were the only inmates I knew who'd made it to Ilamanthe. I knew even fewer vampires from the Institute— and most of them were enemies. The only vampire I could think of was Scarlet, and I'd spent enough time with her in the fight club's training area to know this girl wasn't her. The voice wasn't right.

She had to be from The Mission, because despite her friendly tone, she was certainly no friend of mine.

"I'm going to ask you one last time," I growled. "Who. Are. You?"

She giggled, like she thought of me as nothing less than amusing. "I suppose it has been a while, hasn't it? It's me, silly! Danielle!"

I felt the blood drain from my face, and as a vampire, I was certain she sensed it. Danielle had barely been on my radar my whole time at the Institute, but I remembered she was on the bus that brought us to the Institute the day we arrived. She was buddies with Naya, and though Danielle had mostly kept her distance, she'd always been a little *too* nice to me.

Ava had despised Danielle, and had insisted to me more than once that Danielle had a thing for me and I needed to take it seriously. I barely thought about it, because I didn't think a little crush was a big deal. After all, I'd never considered her a threat.

Apparently that had turned out to be a big mistake.

"Finally, we're alone, and we get to enjoy the proper date we always deserved over a candle-lit dinner," she continued.

"I'm not interested. I'm an engaged-married man, Danielle," I pointed out. I had a wedding coming up, but who knew if I was going to make it, now that I was in Crazy Town with a vampire who obviously had a sick obsession with me.

She cackled. "You're so funny, Charlie— always making jokes. You can't be engaged *and* married. Sit back and enjoy your meal. Isn't it lovely? The Warden procured it himself."

I figured a stupid crush should've died out by now, but Danielle seemed a little more than obsessed. She was delusional, really.

Unfortunately, I'd dealt with my fair share of crazy. If I wanted answers, I was going to have to play along. I forced my heart rate to slow.

"You don't say," I said smoothly. "That's very kind of him to... set up this date. We must be in his home, then?"

"One of them," Danielle confirmed. "A manor in Celestial City. He's not here, though."

Of course not. He'd sent Danielle to do his dirty work, though why he trusted her, I didn't know. There had to be more to this plan than it appeared.

"I suppose the Warden sent you after me because you could get into Ilamanthe undetected," I said.

"Yes. I'm a very valuable asset to The Mission," Danielle said proudly. It was like she was repeating what the Warden had told her.

Danielle wasn't a demigod like the others. She wouldn't trip my grandfather's wards like the Warden or Esther would. It was clear the Warden wanted to get me out clean, without inciting a supernatural fight.

It seemed Danielle had been biding her time, waiting to get me alone so she could knock me out and portal me to Celestial City. Danielle couldn't create a portal, but Esther sure as hell could. That had to be how we got here.

I wondered where Esther was now. Though I nearly vomited, I forced myself to push past the inferichite and expand my magic outward. My magic brushed up against demigod powers just outside the room— four of them, guarding the entrances. It was like they were waiting for something. If they came in here, they'd get sick from the inferichite, but they could've killed me while I'd been knocked out. I didn't get it.

I had to let my magic fall, because I couldn't hold it any longer without puking. That little bit of effort to resist the inferichite had drained me. I'd broken inferichite before using strong emotion, but these inferichite crystals were much bigger than the ones I'd previously shattered, and unless all four of my friends were here with me, I knew I didn't have a chance of destroying them.

So I needed to keep Danielle talking. At least long enough to buy my friends some time to find me. Ancestors, I hoped they knew I was missing by now, because I wasn't sure how long I could keep this ruse up... or what Danielle would make me do in the meantime.

"So what's going on here?" I asked. "The Warden obviously needs me alive; otherwise, I'd be dead by now. What am I, some sort of bait?"

"I'm not supposed to tell you that," Danielle said. "I'm just supposed to keep you occupied."

Ugh. Danielle wasn't going to crack unless I put in some effort. I had to act like I was interested in her. Otherwise, she wouldn't tell me shit, and if I was in this situation I might as well try to gather some intel.

Danielle was clearly in love with me. I had to use that to my advantage. I knew I could con anyone, but fuck, even considering this felt like cheating on Ava. That thought made me want to hurl more than the inferichite did, but Ava would want me to stay alive no matter what. I had to play Danielle's game if I wanted to get out of this.

"Come on... darling," I purred. I nearly choked on the words. "I'd like to get to know you better. We never got a chance back at the Institute to... talk. I want to know more about you."

"Very well." Danielle seemed to settle in, because her silverware clinked against her plate as she began eating. Vampires didn't *need* to eat, but they could if they wanted to, just to enjoy the taste.

She didn't seem to notice I was still shackled and couldn't lift a fork, but it was better that way. I'd rather die than eat anything the Warden had prepared. It was like she was pretending I was here of my own free will, rather than being dragged here and chained up.

"Perhaps you'd like to hear the story of how I was sentenced to the Institute. I never got to tell you," she offered. "I thought it was unfair, at first. After all, it's technically not *illegal* to take the man you love back to your house and tie him up. Couples do it all the time!"

Delusional didn't even begin to cover it. If Danielle thought kidnapping was anything like BDSM, she was sorely mistaken. At least I bothered to *ask* Ava first before I got the ropes out.

Danielle sighed. "He didn't understand. We were so in love. Drake and I were the perfect couple, he just didn't see it... didn't see me. He never said hello, and we didn't speak before the day I brought him home, but I saw the way he looked at me when no one else was around. He didn't realize the special connection we had, and I knew I had to make him see it. I kept him in my basement and figured I'd let him out once he understood what we meant to each other. But Drake turned on me. When he escaped, he reported me to the United Supernatural Union."

Danielle let out an obnoxious noise. "He was a dragon shifter, so *of course* the incident was treated like some crime against the fae. See what I mean by unfair?"

"Completely," I purred, though I absolutely didn't.

"I was angry at Drake for what he'd done. It wasn't right for him to dump me like that out of the blue," Danielle raged.

Her voice softened. "But then I saw *you*, and I realized it was fate that I was sent to the Institute! Drake meant nothing to me anymore, because the moment I met you, it was clear I was being led to my true mate the whole time."

I wasn't exactly following along, because vampires didn't have fated mates the way the fae did. This bitch was even crazier than I thought.

"Of course. I understand now. I *am* your true mate," I added, playing along. I didn't think I sounded convincing, but Danielle didn't seem to notice. "The Warden must've sensed it, too. That's why he sent you after me."

"I knew you'd understand!" Danielle cried happily. "He said if I help kill your friends, I can keep you!"

What a dumb bitch. She couldn't actually believe he'd keep his word.

"I knew from the day we met that it was destined to be between us," Danielle gushed. "You held the door open for me on our first day of class, remember?"

Yeah, that made her *so* special. I held the door open for everyone.

"One day, you brushed up against my hand in Commissary when you picked up a muffin," she continued. "I knew you felt it, too. I couldn't stand the thought of you not touching me. Then there were all those times I was behind you in the cafeteria line, and you left the last croissant for *me*!"

Damn, I didn't even know the Institute *had* croissants in the cafeteria. That would've been awesome.

"I saw you push Scarlet off of you that day in the cemetery, and I knew you must've been thinking about me," Danielle said. "It was clear all I had to do was get you alone, and we could finally be together. I tried for so long. Every day you walked to your factory shift, I was there walking behind you. I could never get close with your dog and *that bitch* around, but you're all mine now!"

Danielle rose from her chair and came to sit on my lap. I nearly vomited all over her right there, but I couldn't exactly shove her off. I still needed answers.

Danielle ran her fingers through my hair, and I noticed it was tangled in the back, matted with something that was probably blood. I winced, because the area was sensitive and still hurt. "I know you didn't really love Ava, because you broke up with her. Then you were forced to *marry her* to survive, and she ended up in that nasty wheelchair. It was obvious you only stayed with her because you felt bad and couldn't leave. But you don't have to feel obligated to *her* anymore. You're free!"

I wasn't sure how much longer I could keep it together. For her to suggest this was beyond disgusting. Danielle never let me get a word in, though.

"I'm more of a woman than she'll ever be! I know you can feel it, Charlie." Danielle shoved her boobs in my face— and they were so fucking huge I couldn't breathe. I tried to inhale, but the fabric of her dress nearly suffocated me.

"I got a boob job for you!" Danielle raved as she drew away. "I know how you like your women busty. I'm bigger than Ava now!"

Fuck, this was getting out of hand way too quickly. I should've listened to my wife. She said this bitch was obsessed with me, and I didn't believe her.

I had to get Danielle talking about the Warden again, or there was no point in playing along.

"Danielle—" I started, but she cut me off.

She grabbed my face with both hands, forcing my chin to tilt up toward her. "See me, Charlie! I *know* you can. I know you've seen me through all that haze, because I saw you looking at me all the time at the Institute. *Our love* cured your blindness, because I was the only one you *could* see. You were always looking at me. You don't have to fake it anymore."

For fuck's sake. I guarantee all those times she thought I was *looking at her*, my head was just pointed in one direction. She took it as a sign that she'd restored my eyesight.

"Danielle—" I tried again.

"I had a shrine of our love in my room at the Institute," she gushed. "I used my Commissary points to print out your mugshot. I saw you drop a candy wrapper, once, and I kept that, too."

She gave a light giggle. "I also had your midterm essay from Rehabilitation Skills. You did such a lovely job typing it up."

What the hell? So *that's* where that essay ended up. I'd fucking got an F for that essay because Professor Ziva didn't believe I'd turned it in, and I *knew* I had. She hadn't let me redo it, either. Danielle must've snatched it off the stack of essays before Professor Ziva had a chance to grade them.

"We're certainly devoted to one another," I cut in, before Danielle could say anything else. "That means we're on the same side. Perhaps you can tell me what I have to look forward to. I've been so eager to join The Mission, but... ah... *that girl* wouldn't let me."

Talking about Ava like that made me physically ill, but she had to play the bad guy if I was getting back to her.

"It's going to be grand!" she exclaimed. "The Warden figured if he stormed Ilamanthe with you demigods there, it would only end in destruction and casualties, and he doesn't want all those Elves to die. They're too useful to him. But he had the brilliant idea that if I took *you* and lured your friends out, he could kill them and take Ilamanthe no problem, imprisoning all the Elves."

I chuckled under my breath. "That's so like him— never taking on a fight he isn't certain he can win. He's very cautious."

My tone held amusement. Danielle clearly missed the insult that was there.

"Oh, yes," she agreed. "He's very methodical."

"And patient," I added. "What does he want to do with the Elves? Use their power? It's weird he doesn't just exterminate them all, like the fae tried to do during the last Great Supernatural War."

"I'm not sure..." Danielle mused. "Maybe he just likes them because they're beautiful. Like you."

Ick. Please shut up.

"Surely he's been working out a plan all this time," I insisted. "What has he been up to? Making more demigods?"

"He tried, for some time," she admitted. "But he's moved on from that. Too many people died because their bodies couldn't contain the power. Plus, he's got to take power from Esther and Mad Dog to do it, since they're natural-born demigods. They get sick for days after his experiments, so he put an end to them. He figured it's better to put his best fighters to work rather than try to make more demigods and fail every time. He doesn't want to keep giving up his power."

Of course. That's something he'd hoard for himself.

"How does he maintain loyalty?" I wondered. "I understand that Esther's on his side, because she's his niece, but what about Mad Dog, Naya, and Deuce? What has he offered them? Why don't they just kill him and take over?"

Danielle laughed so hard it shook my shackles. *"Kill him?* Charlie, no one can kill the Warden. Why do you think the dark gods are working for him? Even they can't destroy him."

My heart rate picked up, but I forced it to slow so Danielle didn't notice. Angels were immortal, but only in the sense that they didn't age once they reached adulthood. They could still be killed by a number of other means, and I was damn sure a god had the ability to kill any supernatural, demigod or not.

But the dark gods couldn't kill the Warden. That was absolutely terrifying. If they didn't have the power to get rid of him, who did?

"How can you be sure?" I asked.

"I saw it," she stated simply. "I witnessed the dark gods try to destroy him, but no matter what they did, he wouldn't go down. He didn't even get hurt."

Terror spread throughout my body and pinned me to the chair. I couldn't imagine the type of power it would take to protect himself like that. It had to be one hell of a spell… or maybe not a spell at all. Perhaps it was the Warden's special demigod power— like how I could make illusions into solid reality, or how Kallie could manipulate time.

Still, there had to be *some* way around this power, so we could kill him for good. Even the greatest supernaturals alive had weaknesses.

"Demigods aren't an easy bunch to kill," I pointed out. "How does he plan to do it?"

"Esther had a job before she came to the Institute," Danielle explained. "She used to kill angelic Deacons on the council for the Warden. She has experience killing angels. She can kill demigods, too."

I shuddered. If Danielle was right and she wasn't making up stories, there was literally no way to kill the Warden. It didn't matter what kind of power we were packing, because he was completely invulnerable to all attacks.

I didn't understand how we were going to win this war. The Warden had to die if things were going to come to an end. If we couldn't kill him, eventually he'd find a way to kill us.

If I wasn't dead already.

"Let's not waste our time talking about the Warden." Danielle ran a finger down my face, then across my neck. "Your blood smells so good. Everyone else's blood is like water. Yours is like the finest wine harvested from the best vines of Napa Valley. I want a taste."

"Danielle, don't—" I warned, but it was already too late.

Danielle tossed her hair to the side, draping it over my shoulder as she pressed her sharp fangs to my neck. Pain sliced through my skin, and I felt my blood leaking out of me as she fed. I let out a hiss, because it was incredibly painful. I struggled away from her, but there was nothing I could do as long as I was shackled to this chair.

Something brushed up against my bond just then. I couldn't *hear* Ava the way we usually communicated, but past the inferichite cuffs, I could tell that she was close.

And she was *fucking furious*.

Danielle pulled her mouth away from my neck, and I felt warm blood gush out from the incision wounds there. She rasped, "It tastes so good. I can't wait to feed on you all night."

I was already lightheaded from being fed on, and I felt my head lolling. But

I still managed to force out, "Thank you, Danielle. You've provided me with some very crucial insights. Unfortunately, I believe it's time for me to depart."

"What do you—?"

Danielle didn't get a chance to finish her sentence before a high-pitched cry pierced the air from outside the room. Something blasted through the wall, though it couldn't be very big. It was like a bullet had been shot. I heard a body hit the ground outside the door.

That's when the chaos erupted.

Screams filled the air, and I heard the clang of knives clicking together. Something heavy landed against the wall outside, shaking the whole room. Mad Dog's deep voice echoed throughout the manor as he yelled obscenities at his attackers. Naya shouted, and Deuce's cry cut off mid-yell as another blow shook the house.

"*Give me back my husband!*" Ava screeched.

Joy flooded through me at the sound of her voice. She'd found me!

"No!" Danielle screamed, leaping out of her chair. "No, she can't be here!"

She scrambled for something on the table, and I heard liquid sloshing in a glass. Before I knew what was happening, Danielle was behind me, yanking my head back by my hair.

"If I can't have you, no one can," she sneered.

Danielle shoved a glass between my lips and tipped it back. Wine filled my mouth. I refused to swallow. The wine gurgled out my mouth, spilling down my front as I choked on the liquid. She was going to drown me.

"Drink, goddamn it!" Danielle screamed. She tossed the wine glass aside, and it shattered against the wall. She grabbed the whole fucking bottle and shoved it so far down my throat I gagged. Wine slid down the back of my throat. My energy instantly drained, as if the wine itself was made of inferichite.

The door burst open, and Danielle cackled. "You're too late!"

"Get your hands off my man, you vile bitch!" Ava cried. Oberi's hooves smacked against the marble floor as she entered, and the Fire from her horn elevated the temperature in the room to an uncomfortable rate. I knew Oberi had carried Ava in here, and both of them were dead set on taking revenge.

My head lolled as I felt more blood trickle down my neck. It was obvious what Danielle had been doing in here, and it sent Ava into a mad rage.

Oberi let out a terrifying bray, and Fire shot out of her horn as she galloped forward. Danielle dodged out of the way, but that didn't stop Ava. I heard the blade of a knife slide across the table as Ava snatched it up, then Oberi went charging her way.

A harsh wind blew by as Ava launched herself off Oberi's back. Danielle grunted as Ava landed on top of her. The sickly sound of a knife tearing through flesh filled the room. Danielle screamed. She had super strength and speed, but Ava's assault had slowed her down.

Ava didn't stop. She screamed at the top of her lungs as she stabbed Danielle in the heart over and over again, until I was certain there was no heart left. Oberi commanded the flames from the hearth to spray onto Danielle's body, and the vampire ignited. Danielle wailed in suffering as the flames consumed her, but Ava remained on top and kept going, sinking the knife into the flesh long after Danielle's cries of pain ended.

I heard Kallie and Marcus rush in from the other end of the room. Kallie ripped Ava off of Danielle's charred corpse, snapping, "Ava, cut it out! She's dead already."

Ava didn't listen. She crawled back to Danielle's corpse and continued stabbing with a gurgle of insane laughter.

"Screw it. Charlie, we've got to work together," Kallie demanded. "We need to use simultension to overload the cuffs and break them."

"Okay," I choked out. I was still feeling queasy.

"Ready?" Marcus asked.

"Ready," I said. Kallie took one of my hands, while Marcus took the other. Our magic combined, funneling into the cuffs. My head spun, and my body swayed, but I didn't stop until I heard the crack of stone. The cuffs fell off my limbs and onto the floor, and I finally felt like I could breathe again.

Charlie! Oberi cried. *Ava's lost it!*

Oberi's hooves hit the ground, and she whinnied loudly, but Ava continued to sink her knife into Danielle's chest, even though she was long gone.

"Ava!" I jumped out of my chair and grabbed her wrist as she drew the blade back once more. "Ava, it's all right. I'm right here."

Her whole body trembled beneath my touch. The knife clattered out of her hand as she reached for me. "She hurt you, Charlie."

"It's over," I told her, getting to my knees beside her. "Danielle's gone."

"And we don't have much time!" Marcus added. "We've got to go, before the Warden shows up."

"Give us a fucking minute," Ava snapped. She wrapped her arms around my neck, and I squeezed her close to my chest. Her healing magic filled me up as we embraced, knitting together the wound on my neck.

Ava ran her fingers through my hair, catching in the tangle on the back. She gasped. "What did that bitch do— oh *no!* She ruined your *beautiful hair!*"

I reached back to feel, and I found a good chunk of my hair was missing, the ends all crusted and burnt. I had a bald spot the size of my palm, and some of the scalp had been singed. I winced as I pulled my hand away. "She knocked me out with a torch."

"You can worry about his hair later," Marcus demanded. "Right now, we need to get out of here."

"I'm not going anywhere until this is fixed! My poor baby, what did she do to you?" Ava cooed. She put her hand to the burn. I felt the injury heal, and my hair grow back to its usual length.

"There. That's better," Ava said proudly, stroking my head like I was her pet. "*Now* we can go."

"This place is warded down tight," Kallie pointed out. "We have to get out of the manor so we can portal out."

I hoisted Ava onto Oberi's back. She'd sliced open the saddle straps to launch herself at Danielle, so I used my illusion abilities to mend them before I refastened them around her legs. We hurried out of the room, into a large foyer.

The commotion from earlier had died down, but Mad Dog was still yelling obscenities. I heard the tearing of fabric, then Eddie's voice as he said, "Oh, put a sock in it!"

Mad Dog's insults turned to muffled screams as Eddie shoved something in his mouth.

"You won't get away with this!" Deuce sneered from somewhere on the floor.

Heavy footsteps approached, but my magic recognized them as friends. It was the twins Asa and Ares. Gavyn cleared his throat from nearby. The Elvish Associates had shown up and somehow kicked the demigods' asses, though I didn't know how they managed.

"What *happened* here?" I asked.

"The Elvish Associates have a few cameras scattered around the palace," Marcus said. "The picture isn't great due to all the magic, but once they realized you were missing, they pulled up the footage. They got Danielle on camera, and we recognized her."

"You bet your ass I recognized her," Ava seethed.

"Uh, yeah. Ava lost her fucking shit when she realized it was Danielle who took you," Marcus added.

"Told you she was nuts," Ava grumbled.

"Sorry, pidge," I said. Ava huffed.

"The Warden wouldn't take you to an imprisonment camp, as he wants to watch you personally," Asa added. "Abigail knows where the Warden keeps his prisoners, as she was once imprisoned here before, so we portaled here to get you out."

"Thanks for the rundown," I said flatly. "But I meant what happened *here*, to all these demigods."

"Oh, it's simple really," Eddie said. "While on the way to rescue you, I was overcome by a strong magic, an urge to protect, really, and it awakened my Elvish powers! By the goddesses, I'm a Grand Master! I can phase solid objects in and out of existence, almost like *reversing* illusions. I can phase through walls and the like as if they're nothing. I siphoned Deuce's super strength and punched him into the floor. It was quite thrilling, really— unlocked something deep inside of me. I phased the concrete foundation around him, and now, he's stuck. Just his head is poking out!"

Just as he said it, my foot landed on something soft, and Deuce let out a scream. I'd literally just stepped on his face.

And I did it again, too. And a third time just for laughs.

"Elyx is stationed outside the manor with a sniper rifle," Ava explained quickly. "He shot Esther in the wing to slow her down, then Asa and Ares snuck up behind Mad Dog to siphon his strength. They used knives to pin him to the wall. Gavyn took on Naya."

"I siphoned her wings and her super strength," Gavyn said. "I beat the crap out of her before locking her and Esther up in a safe down the hall, but it won't hold them for long."

"We need to kill them while we have the chance," I said.

Ava gave a hollow laugh. "Oh, believe me. I'm burning this place to the ground the second we're out of here."

"Come on. Max is waiting for us outside!" Gavyn called.

I didn't want to risk staying another second and facing the Warden. Because if what Danielle said was true about him, we weren't ready. Not even close.

But you know what? Deuce was stuck in the floor, and he wasn't going anywhere. He couldn't fight back, and I had a few minutes to take care of this fucker. I swore not long ago that the next time I encountered Deuce, he was going straight to hell. Deuce was as good as dead.

I took a step forward to do just that, but I found that the movement made my head spin. Suddenly, my body felt feverish when it hadn't been before. An intense wave of dizziness overcame me, and I was briefly aware that I'd staggered forward. Eddie caught me, holding me upright.

"Charlie?" Ava asked in worry. "Are you okay?"

I tried to say something, but instead, something caught in my throat. I heaved, and without me realizing what was going on, I was vomiting a thick substance that poured from my mouth and onto the floor.

"He's been poisoned! Hurry!" someone barked, but I couldn't be sure who it was. I'd lost all my bearings.

Several heavy hands landed on me, and they lifted to raise me onto Oberi's back, situating me in front of Ava. A horrible sickness swelled in my gut.

"Danielle made me drink the wine..." I slurred. I gagged again, and tasted copper.

An enraged cry tore from Ava's lungs. "These bitches are going to learn to never touch my man!"

Oberi took off running toward the doors, and our friends quickly followed. Fire crackled, and the waves of heat nearly seared my skin. Ava had lit the mansion aflame. The warmth quickly shifted to an icy chill as Ava blasted another spell at the walls, ordering her blue Fire to consume it all. The dying screams of the trapped demigods echoed through the air.

I received a brief moment of satisfaction before everything disappeared.

ava-marie

FOURTEEN

This couldn't be happening.

Oberi surged into a gallop, and we left the others behind us as we burst through the double doors of the Warden's shitty manor. This place was warded up the ass, so we had to get off the property in order to cast a portal and get out of here. I held on to Charlie, clutching him tightly so he didn't fall off. He lolled in my arms like a rag doll, spent of all energy, and my panic grew to an immeasurable rate as the flames raged around us. My fury at what Danielle had done to Charlie made the fire grow larger, consuming the mansion and turning every bit of it to smoldering cinders. I hoped Esther, Naya, Mad Dog, and Deuce had extremely painful deaths, because that's what they deserved for hurting my husband.

We passed the bodies of dead guards stationed around the manor. Oberi leapt over them like they were nothing, and she was right, because they *did* mean nothing if they had helped cause this. The Elvish Associates had taken them all out so we could get inside the mansion.

In the distance, dots had appeared in the sky above tall, golden skyscrapers. They were only growing closer. I saw wings, and even from here, I could make out the expression of my most hated enemy. The Warden and a whole angel army was on their way to capture us.

Go ahead and try. I had burned this mansion to ash without bothering to blink. I was more enraged than I ever had been before, and I knew if anyone got in my way now, I'd put them in the ground before I gave up a second more of Charlie's life.

Max was waiting for us once I was past the manor's open gate and on the empty streets of Celestial City. She gazed at the blood soaking Charlie's shirt and didn't ask any questions. She pulled a pocket mirror from her jacket and projected it forward. A portal bloomed ahead, and Oberi charged through it just as I heard the Warden give a cry of frustrated rage.

Oberi stepped out of a mirror that led to the palace hospital wing, followed by our friends. The portal snapped shut behind us, preventing anyone from following. Now that we were in a safe place, I put my hand to Charlie's heart so I could heal him.

My fingers glowed white as I surveyed his body. The light grew in intensity as I forced my powers through his systems. I hadn't noticed before when I had healed the vampire bite and regrown his hair, because the poison had been so small, but clearly it had grown. A sickening feeling overtook me as I found the poison sifting through his bloodstream. It was sticky as it clung to the inside of his throat, his stomach, his lungs, a vile substance that tasted disgusting and foul.

When I prodded further, my entire soul quivered as I recognized something familiar— the sting of inferichite.

"I can't heal this," I said in terror. "There's still poison in his blood. It won't clear."

"What do you mean?" Eddie asked, an edge of denial in his voice. "You can heal anything, princess."

"Whatever the poison is, it's made with inferichite. My healing abilities aren't driving it out," I raged. "All I can do is survey the effect it's having on him."

"Let's try to clear it together," Marcus suggested. "Fuse our demigod powers with your healing magic. The poison has to leave, then."

My heart started in hope, because that was the only thing that I figured would work. Marcus moved forward, along with Kallie. They reached up to put their hands on top of my own as I rested them against Charlie's torso. I could feel their abilities mending with mine as I used simultension to join our powers together, and drive the poison away.

I felt my windpipe closing off from air as I realized that wasn't working, either. The inferichite was stubborn. It had latched on to Charlie's demigod magic, and was using it to resist our own. The poison drained him whenever I tried to remove it, sucking energy from his organs and weakening him further than he already was. We couldn't destroy the inferichite in his system without killing him, but at the same time, we couldn't heal him at all if there was still inferichite in his body, either.

"Stop," I demanded, and my friends drew back. "His body can't handle it. If we keep going, it'll make everything shut down."

"But..." Marcus had gone paler than a ghost. "If we can't use simultension, then how are we gonna make him better?"

I didn't have an answer, and that made me nearly go insane.

Let's get him in a bed, Oberi offered. *Then we can evaluate further.*

She sounded very worried, which concerned me even more. If Oberi didn't understand what was going on or how to fix it, with all her experience and wisdom, then who would?

We hurried inside the hospital, where a variety of doctors and nurses walked around the wing's lobby. When they turned and saw Charlie, many of the Elves started screaming.

"What is wrong with the prince?!" a doctor demanded. Charlie threw up again, and more blood splattered out from his mouth and onto the floor.

I nearly passed out. That was a lot of blood to lose, and he didn't have much more left to give. Marcus pulled Charlie off of Oberi and laid him on the floor, turning him on his side so he didn't choke.

I didn't have to ask for a wheelchair, because Kallie had already brought one. She helped me off Oberi, and the second I was in my chair I was wheeling toward Charlie. I tried to heal him again, and again, but the inferichite pushed my magic back and refused to allow me to chase the poison out.

Two nurses wheeled out a gurney, but I screamed, "Leave him alone! No one can heal him like I can!"

I didn't trust doctors, not after my spinal injury. They'd fuck him up more than he already was.

Ava, we need help with this, Oberi demanded. *What we're doing isn't working!*

I knew we did, but it was equivalent to sawing my torso in half to allow anyone to touch Charlie when he was in this dire of a state.

Elves placed Charlie upon a gurney as he continued to gurgle up blood. He wasn't conscious, but his face was ashen, and his body wracked with tremors. The poison was getting worse by the moment.

"He's been poisoned. I need a private room. Someone fetch my brother and my mother immediately," I barked.

"I—" the doctor stuttered.

"I am the princess of Ilamanthe! You will do as I say!" I screeched.

Not a damn soul dared to ask me any more questions. They wheeled Charlie into a large room filled with surgical equipment, potion vials, herbs, and everything else we could use to treat this. Charlie was moved from the gurney to a bed, which could be prepped for surgical purposes if we needed it. A nurse drew his blood to test it.

"I need to know what properties are in that poison. I want a full report the minute you get the results back," I ordered.

"Yes, princess," a nurse replied, and she ran off to the lab with a tube of Charlie's blood.

The doctors and nurses rushed to get Charlie hooked up to an IV and a heart monitor. Doctors cut off his bloody clothes and threw them away, until he was covered only by a thin sheet. He shivered, and as I touched his skin again, my fingers grazed his ice-cold arm. He shook underneath my touch. Even though he was out of it, his body was still reacting to the effects of the poison.

Oberi changed into a phoenix. She flew to the bed, landing at Charlie's side. She fluttered her wings and skimmed her beak over Charlie's chest, using her healing magic to observe him.

My heart withered and turned cold in my chest as Oberi said, *I do not have the power to heal this. It is beyond my ability. Charlie's body cannot work against the inferichite, so any magic I may use to heal him is useless, because his system will not respond.*

"That's impossible! You brought me back from death!" I demanded. "You can cure this!"

I cannot do that again, Oberi argued. *What I did for you, I was only able to accomplish once, and was a different kind of magic. It was a gift given to me by the gods to save one of you if death came, and death has already happened. My healing magic is strong. But I cannot heal what I do not know, and this poison is strange to me. I have never met it, not in all my eons of existence. I have never encountered a poison that prevents me from healing the body, as this substance turns the system's own organs against the host, and fights us off besides. Anything we can do will be countered by the poison.*

"There must be something," I insisted.

I'll try to use my magic to stop the poison from working, in order to buy us time, Oberi stated. *If I resist against it, you can work on finding a cure.*

It wasn't enough. One of the nurses called out, "Edwyrd and Abigail will be posted at the door, should you need them."

"Fine." Where the fuck were Ez and Mama? They needed to be here!

A second after I thought that, they stormed in. They didn't ask questions, just went to Charlie's bedside immediately and hovered their hands over him. Their Anichi magic glowed as they surveyed the situation. Ez's gaze darted from Charlie's face to his abdomen, while Mama squeezed her eyes shut in concentration.

"I need help. I don't know what this poison is, or what the active ingredient may be, but it's got inferichite in it," I pleaded. "We can't force his body to get rid of the inferichite without killing him, but the poison is killing him, too. Even with all our power, everything we try just backfires."

Their hands stopped glowing as they drew back their healing magic. Ez sent Mama an anxious look, which she shared.

"*What?*" I asked.

"It's a combination poison," Ez said thickly. "It's got inferichite in it, which prevents *you* from helping, but I can sense it's been mixed with noxite, too, which means me and Mom can't do anything to get rid of it, either. No healer can."

The Warden had really thought this through. His soul belonged to me, the next time we dared to meet.

"What if we all try together?" I suggested. "I'll use simultension to fuse your magic with mine. I'm invulnerable to noxite, and inferichite doesn't affect you. Maybe if we work together, we can overpower it."

"It's worth a shot," Mama said, and the three of us grabbed hands. We made a circle with our conjoined grasps, our arms hovering over Charlie's form.

I *tried.* I wrapped my magic around my brother's power, and my mother's, with so much force it nearly yanked their abilities out of them. My mother was a powerful elemental, so I shouldn't have been able to do that so easily, but I found even her magic crumbled like melting snow the minute I demanded it show up to serve me. I pushed our magic into Charlie's veins and attempted to force the poison to leave, but despite my best efforts, it wouldn't budge.

Ez let out a rasping sound and dropped his hand from mine. He put a hand on the wall to steady himself, as if I'd gone too hard and too fast.

"It's not working," he said. "The inferichite is preventing you from getting rid of the noxite, so we can't get past it to heal him."

Mama went to check Charlie again. Her fingers roamed his chest, and her eyes darkened. "The poison is manifesting into a growth, like a cancer. There are tumors spreading all over his body, and they're getting bigger the longer we wait."

No. No, no, *no.* I wouldn't let this happen.

We kept trying, and an hour passed, but there was absolutely no effect. If anything, Charlie only seemed to get worse.

"The blood draw is in, princess," the nurse replied breathlessly as she hurried in.

"What did it say?" I asked. She gave me the paper without a word, and I read over the results quickly.

Inconclusive. Of course. Just like inferichite, the properties and chemical compounds inside the poison weren't anything recognizable on Earth. The

Warden had probably gotten all kinds of awful ingredients from his buddies in hell, then put it all together to make this terrible poison. And if the ingredients used in the poison didn't grow here, that meant we probably didn't have anything on this planet that could counteract them.

I threw the results on a nearby counter and demanded, "Get Marcus in here."

He must've been standing right outside the door, because he heard my voice and came in. "What do you need?"

"There's noxite in the poison as well. You're a Curse Breaker, so you can take it out," I said. "That way, Mom and Ez will be able to get past the inferichite, because I can't, and they can remove the poison."

Marcus leaned over Charlie. He grasped Charlie's arm and closed his eyes, trying to concentrate.

A few moments later, Marcus buckled to the floor. Ez rushed forward to hold him up, and I demanded, "Well?"

"I can't get rid of it, though I tried," Marcus insisted, rising back up again.

"You've drawn noxite out of people before!" I cried.

"Yes, but the inferichite is fortifying it, which means I can't do a damn thing unless we get rid of the inferichite *first*!" he yelled back.

I made an angry noise and pushed him away. "If you're not going to help, just go."

Marcus didn't argue, but he also didn't seem upset with me. He did as I asked, thank the ancestors, and gave me some space.

Charlie vomited up another spray of blood, which dribbled down his chest and constricted his airways, choking him. Blood got all over the white sheet, and on Oberi's feathers. She didn't react, merely let out a wary coo. A doctor moved in, checking the heart monitor.

His heart rate was faint.

"He needs a blood transfusion! He's already lost a quart or more!" I barked.

"We can't run the transfusion without first attempting dialysis," the doctor responded. "There's a chance the dialysis machine can clean his blood and get rid of the poison. If we give him new blood now, his body could become over-stressed with the introduction of the transfusion and the poison, and reject the donation, not to mention the new blood will become tainted with the poison once it's introduced."

"Well get it on, then!" I shouted. Why were we sitting around talking about it when we needed to take action? I placed my hands on Charlie's arm, and my Spirit magic observed how his body responded as the doctors did their best to start dialysis. Ez and Mama leaned against the wall, waiting for me if I needed them.

I didn't like how worried they looked.

The Elvish healers tried everything. They used every antidote they had on hand, from the *serpens spelunca* antivenom to all kinds of spells and potions. Other Anichi healers arrived to help, but like Ez and Mama, their magic was useless against the combination poison in Charlie's blood.

Not even dialysis was working. The machine filtered out the toxins in his blood, but the poison kept reproducing itself, so it did nothing to get rid of it.

Charlie was having trouble breathing. His rasping gasps for air made me feel like I was choking. They'd given him a medication that managed to stop the vomiting, at least, so he wouldn't drown in his own blood if we put him on a ventilator.

Do you want to leave the room? Oberi asked warily as they started prepping the breathing tube for insertion.

"Fuck no." I wasn't leaving him alone even if the world started ending. I held his hand and watched, refusing to shut my eyes or look away as they inserted the breathing tube and fitted a mask over his face, because I'd be damned before I allowed him to go through this alone. There was a lump in my throat that reminded me of how painful the bruise from my own breathing tube had been when I'd survived the Infernal Underground, but I pushed that memory aside, because it was useless to me now. No trauma, memory, or pain was worth anything if it didn't help me save Charlie now.

Once he was stabilized, the doctors switched to experimental antidotes that had never been tried before, and could be dangerous. It was a sign of how desperate they were.

It didn't help. Nothing did a damn thing to stop the poison from advancing. The Warden had created this new formula just for us, and there wasn't a cure for it. The doctors had given Charlie so many medications and treatments I was worried it was making him worse.

Surgery was discussed, but it was discarded as an option almost immediately. They couldn't perform surgery to remove the growths— in the time we'd been working, the poison had wrapped itself so tightly around his organs that if they tried to cut the tumors out, the surgeons would kill him in the process.

Oberi was doing her best, and my Spirit magic could tell that her abilities were slowing the growth of the tumors. But although she could slow the poison's hold, she couldn't prevent it completely. We'd have lost Charlie already if she wasn't doing her best to hold it off.

Charlie was clearly fading. His skin had turned ashen, and his lips had gone gray. His body sagged into the mattress with all the appearance of a corpse long since dead.

The doctors and nurses stood in a circle, unmoving. They weren't sure of what else to try. Mama held Ez, who was trying to wipe his face and not let me see.

I took a deep breath, held it, then exhaled.

"Leave me," I demanded coldly. "All of you. There's nothing more you can do."

Saying nothing, the crowd dispersed, leaving me alone with my Familiar and my husband. My shoulders shuddered as I barely contained my rage.

Useless. They were all useless. If Charlie was going to make it through this, it had to be up to me. Everybody else needed to leave me alone so I could figure out a solution.

I surveyed his condition again. My expression dropped the moment I laid my hand on his chest and used my Anichi magic to assess the situation. At this rate, Charlie would be dead within the hour. And there was jack shit I could do to prevent it.

But that was shitty thinking. I didn't give up, because I was stubborn, and Charlie was, too. We'd pull through this, like we always did. I just had to come up with a way—

The door banged open. My teeth gritted together as I heard Cameron's voice cry out, "Let me in!"

Cameron entered, and his approaching footsteps made it clear he wasn't going to take no for an answer unless I shoved it down his throat.

I wrenched my wheelchair so I could turn myself around. "Get out of here, Cameron. I don't want you here, and neither does Charlie."

Cameron's face turned red with rage, but his anger was pathetic compared to my own. I'd like to see him try to get his way.

"How *dare* you attempt to keep me from seeing him. I have the right to say goodbye to my son!" Cameron bellowed.

What a coward he was. Charlie wasn't gone yet, and I'd be cold in my own grave before I allowed him to slip away. Where was Cameron's spine? Charlie needed his dad to *fight* for him, like I was. He needed his dad to not give in.

It was clear the only person in this room who would go to war for the incredible man lying in this bed was me, and I couldn't be distracted by some simpering Elf who pretended to have some kind of claim on the son he'd created and forgotten.

"You want to show up and be a dad now when he's dying?" I spat. "He's needed you in the past few months, and where have you been? Partying and fucking off and doing ancestors know what else."

"You won't speak to me that way. I am his father!" Cameron demanded.

"You are nothing because I say you are! I am the Holy Mother to the Elves, the symbol and messenger of Idril and Carolyn on this earth, and you will not command me!" I bellowed. "You are not welcome here!"

"But—"

"LEAVE!"

Cameron might've had more authority than me as the Crown Prince, but he listened to my order all the same. He ducked out with his head bowed low, tail tucked between his legs.

I had no regrets about throwing him out. He was pitiful and would only get in my way.

Was that really necessary? Oberi asked dully. She'd been holding off the poison's growth for some time, and was getting tired.

"You tell me." I went to lay my hands on Charlie again, but they fell to the mattress as I heard more footsteps behind me, this time, lighter and slower.

My hands bunched in the sheets as I snapped, "I said no one can come in here."

"You have authority over all in Ilamanthe, child, save for me."

The gentle voice that met my ears gave me pause. I turned my chair again. Emperor Cassiel was standing in the doorway, not demanding I let him approach, but instead, asking to be invited in.

"Are you here to say goodbye, too?" I asked harshly. I wouldn't let anyone do that, because this wasn't the end. Not yet.

"Of course not. I know who you are, princess. You will not deny your beloved Charlie the comfort of having his grandfather at his side in this time of need."

My lip quivered. "You can come in."

Cassiel strode toward me with a gentleness I could never imitate. He took a chair beside me, near the head of Charlie's bed. "You have half the staff quivering in fear. You are as terrifying as a lioness, or perhaps, a wyvern defending her mate."

I had to be terrifying— be mean, be vicious and ruthless and all these terrible things. No one else would go to the lengths needed to save Charlie, and I had to protect him from whatever happened. He was vulnerable right now.

"It's my job to defend him when he can't defend himself," I said. "It's always been that way."

"Who are you protecting him from?" Cassiel asked quietly. "The Warden? The world? Himself?"

I didn't know. Because the worst had already happened, and I hadn't been able to protect Charlie from the people who'd already hurt him the most.

For the first time that day, I broke down into tears. Cassiel put his warm hand over mine in comfort.

"What am I going to do?" I wailed. "We've tried everything. It's hopeless!"

Oberi dropped her head and made a low note, but Cassiel didn't crumble. He looked... sad, and definitely worried, but he wasn't panicking.

"There were many Elves who said that about me, when I was bitten by a *serpens spelunca* many years ago," Cassiel said lowly. "And yet here I am decades later, because Aponi refused to give up when all others did."

I didn't say anything, because I was still crying.

Cassiel went on. "When I was bitten, there was no antidote or cure for such a venom. Everyone who had been bitten by a *serpens spelunca* died, and there were no exceptions. Healers and alchemists tried for many years to find a cure for the venom, and failed miserably. But my wife succeeded, and she created an antidote that saved me and thousands of others when it had never been done before. Do you know why?"

I shook my head, and Cassiel said, "It is because she believed she could. Everyone told my wife that it was hopeless, and that she couldn't cure me, but Aponi refused to give up. She worked on that potion tirelessly until she found something that worked. She saved my life, and that hope blossomed into love."

"Love isn't enough to save people. If it was, so many people I loved wouldn't have died," I wept.

"But like Aponi, you are not the kind to give up and let this poison take him," Cassiel pointed out. "My wife saved me from the venom. You can save Charlie, too. You are an extraordinary demigod, princess, the best of our people. I know you will rescue the prince from this fate."

Cassiel rose from his chair. "I will leave you be, so you can concentrate."

He left the room, and I was alone again. It strengthened me that Cassiel hadn't said his goodbyes. He truly believed in me and knew I could save Charlie. His presence had been comforting, and it'd cleared my mind enough so I could think.

Cassiel was right. I could do this. I just needed to pull myself together, so my Familiar and I could figure out a solution. Oberi wavered, close to falling off the bed.

"Oberi, stop," I said weakly. "If you keep trying to resist the poison, it'll kill you, too. Then I'll lose both of you."

I will not die permanently. I will simply become deceased, then regenerate a few minutes later, Oberi insisted, though she sounded exhausted.

"It still weakens you every time you die and come back. You need to save what's left of your strength. I may need your help yet."

Oberi pulled back her magic, and I felt the poison surge forward. It was advancing quicker than ever because Oberi wasn't holding it back, but I don't think it mattered. Charlie had already suffered too much damage to his organs, anyway. Even if I got the poison out of his blood, he'd still be in danger, because his entire system needed to be healed now for him to recover.

My fear turned to rage as I thought that none of this would've happened in the first place if Danielle hadn't gotten involved. I should've killed her before I left the Institute, but I'd waited too long to make her meet her end. If Charlie died, I'd find a way to portal to hell, locate Danielle, and kill her all over again. And I wouldn't stop. Somehow, I'd find a way to resurrect her again and again, and slaughter her in increasingly gruesome ways to make her pay, until her soul ceased to exist due to the suffering.

She'd still be getting off easy. Nothing could be as painful as me losing my husband. She had no idea the damage she'd just caused. An eternity of torture wouldn't be enough to satisfy my longing for revenge if she took him from me.

No. I wasn't allowing that to happen. Charlie belonged to me, and nobody, not Danielle, the Warden, or the gods themselves would steal his life. Whatever fate had planned, *I* was the one who got to decide if he lived or died.

And he would live, if I commanded it. He wouldn't leave me here.

"You don't get to die unless I tell you that you can," I whispered to him. "So hold on, and keep fighting this. I'm going to figure this out."

Charlie let out a wheezing breath, like he'd heard me. I steeled my nerves. Right now, Charlie wasn't my husband, or the love of my life. He was my patient, and my patient was going to expire unless I put my mind to work and outwitted the Warden yet again.

And speaking of the Warden...

The Beast appeared in a corner of the room, skulking around the area and seeming arrogant as all hell. My lip lifted into a snarl when I saw him, but I wasn't the only one who saw him this time. Oberi was a part of me, and although my bipolar didn't affect her, she could recognize what I saw. She didn't react, but allowed me to process as I needed to.

The Beast's face curled into a sick smile. "Looks like I've finally found something that works. After Cellblock 9, I didn't know what it was going to take. The four of you are particularly difficult to exterminate, but I've gained the upper hand."

"Fuck you. I'm smarter than you, you smug bastard. I'm better than you, I'm stronger than you, and you've never beaten me yet," I sneered. "You're not going to win this time, either."

The Beast raised an eyebrow. "That may be true, but you have more to lose than ever before. I suggest you get moving. There isn't much time left."

The Beast gave a cruel laugh as he disappeared once again, and Oberi tilted her head. *I didn't know you were having visions of the Warden.*

"My psychosis finds weird ways to fuck with me, Oberi. It doesn't help us now."

She let the matter drop, and I went back to figuring out what to do. Since I'd tried everything but praying, it might as well be a last resort.

Goddesses, I pleaded, reaching out to Idril and Carolyn. *I am your Holy Mother, an Elvish mystic of your temple. Help me save your son, and rescue the prince from certain death.*

I didn't get any sort of response, energetic or otherwise, because I don't think they heard me. I wasn't sure they could help even if they tried.

Coyote Spirit and Whale Spirit were most likely too far off, in the middle of fighting a battle with the dark gods. I didn't think they'd show up, either. Coyote had a hard time crossing the boundary from the spiritual realm to Earth the last time we'd spoken, and at the time, his power had been limited in helping me more than giving advice.

Even so, I tried anyway. I prayed to them, and prayed and prayed, and got no answer.

After moments of sitting in silence, I dug in my pocket. I withdrew my mother's compass, which I carried with me always. It was one of the very few things I still had from the Institute.

I lifted the compass to my mouth, to whisper into it. "Lindsey and Miranda, are you there? I know you can't cross the divide, but I need assistance. My husband's been poisoned, and we aren't sure how to heal him. Nothing's working. Send us your aid, if you're able to do what you can from the Ancestral Lands."

I clutched the compass in my hands, and watched as the arrow wildly spun out of control, pointing me toward nothing. I wasn't sure what I was waiting for — an audible response, a message, something. But what happened next was certainly something I did not expect.

Two spirits began to rise from the compass. They appeared at first to be a glittering mist, rising from the compass' face and hovering around the room. Then, they began to materialize.

The shape of a dire wolf, nearly the size of a wolven, took form in the room. It had massive muscular shoulders and a proud stance. Riding on the wolf's back was a tiny, furry creature that looked to be a cross between a sugar glider and a bush baby. The creature had big ears, two curled horns on top of its head, and big blue eyes— a kurble. As their spirits became solid, the wolf's coat became black, and the kurble's pure white.

The kurble chittered. He let out a trill as he waved his bushy tail.

I smiled, and extended my hand to the creature. "I know you."

The kurble jumped off the wolf's back, soaring through the air to land on my hand. He scurried up my arm, then raced across the bed and sat on Charlie's stomach. He sat up on his haunches, rubbing his tiny paws over his nose and furry ears.

I can hear them both speak, so I will translate, Oberi noted. *They are spiritual guardians that protect your family from the Ancestral Lands. Lindsey and Miranda sent them. The wolf is here to guard the room against any dark spirits that may interfere. The little one, to help you heal.*

"How did they cross the broken boundary?" I asked. The wolf began stalking near the door, raising his lip in a low growl, while the kurble let out an indigent squeak.

Your mother has a special attachment to that compass, and your family's guides can come through it. These creatures have a connection still remaining on this Earth that other ancestors do not, allowing them to cross the boundary. The little one is very powerful, and the wolf has strength of his own, but they cannot stay for long. We must hurry, Oberi insisted.

"What must I do?" I asked the kurble. Oberi waited to hear what he had to say. The kurble gave a chitter, and whatever he'd said had even surprised Oberi, because she nearly toppled over in astonishment.

"What? What did he say?" I demanded.

Oberi peered at the kurble out of one eye, as if she wasn't sure she was hearing things correctly, before she said, *The poison is a substance they know well, one that grows in the Eternal Torment. It latches onto the host, creating tumors that feed off life energy until the host dies a painful death. In order to heal Charlie, you will need to destroy the poison and the organs that it is attached to at the same time, then* regrow *new organs in their place. I will keep him alive while you are doing this, so the organs have time to generate.*

I thought about the practicality of this. Demigods could make something out of nothing. We could create our own energy, and I had the specialty of healing, so why couldn't I make Charlie new organs, too? It was part of my demigod magic, so in theory, I had the capability.

It was similar to Charlie's illusion magic. He didn't just make illusions, he made them into real physical objects. He'd regrown Sprigs when he was just a dying plant, and gave him sentience. I couldn't make a body out of nothing, but I could regrow what was already in front of him. I needed to remake him, craft his organs so they were brand-new.

Still... I didn't know of anyone, demigod or otherwise, who had done this before. Not in history, or even myth.

"How do I do it?" If we fucked this up, Charlie was definitely not coming out of this.

You have already done it, Oberi marveled, with a shocked look at the kurble.

Once before, when your father was in the hospital. You replaced his lungs. This is not a tool you can use on just anyone. This is magic that you may only perform on someone you deeply love.

Memories of my father suffering from pneumonia flooded into my mind. I was still in high school, and hadn't even gotten my magic yet as far as I knew, but I remembered how I'd laid my hands on his chest the night before he was supposed to die, and the bright light that I'd seen just before passing out.

No wonder my father hadn't had any breathing issues since.

Tears threatened to spill as I realized the blue eyes I'd seen that night in the hospital had been this little creature's. He'd come to help me heal my father then, as he had arrived tonight to help me heal my husband.

"We need to recraft everything," I insisted. "It's the only way to help him."

We can do it. The guardian can help us, and we can pull from Charlie's abilities as a demigod to give us fuel. The small one will help you get past the inferichite, because as an ancestor, he has the ability to push it aside so you can do your work, Oberi stated, looking to the kurble for confirmation. The little creature nodded sharply. *You must clean out everything— all the medicine, potions, and antidotes. Everything must go, and the failing organs must be destroyed with the tumors, so his body can be remade anew. Nothing can be left behind.*

"Will this kill us?" I questioned. When I had healed Ez from sepsis, it had taken all my strength, and this was way worse.

You are much stronger now than you were before. Your will is more powerful than this poison, and it will not take our lives, but we must act now, Oberi insisted. *His heart is failing.*

The heart monitor was barely showing a pulse. It wouldn't be five minutes before Charlie would be gone.

"Okay. Let's do this," I said firmly. I sprawled my hand over Charlie's torso. Oberi laid her beak on my knuckles, and the kurble pressed his tiny paw into the back of my hand. I didn't think I'd be able to feel him, since he was a spirit. Yet I felt his soft paw caress my skin as a light began to shine throughout the room that was brighter than any I'd ever seen before.

I started with Charlie's heart first, because might as well. I sought the poison that was taking his heart over and was unable to move the tumor wrapped around it, even with everyone's help. So, I commanded the organ to die. I felt Charlie's heart wither and blacken, disintegrating into nothing at my command as the tumor died.

When the heart faded away, so did the poison, because it had nothing left to hold on to. The inferichite wasn't able to cling to anything, and therefore, lost its power.

The sound of the heart monitor going flatline absolutely rattled me, but I felt Oberi's magic pulsing, and I knew she was using her power to keep Charlie's blood pumping. I ignored the noise of the machine and focused my attention instead on making a new heart.

I was skilled in healing, but I didn't understand most systems, or how the body worked. I didn't know the various chambers or vessels I needed to create in order to fix him.

No matter, though. When I told his body to form a new heart, it *did*. A new organ magically formulated there, replacing the one that I'd destroyed. Charlie's body knew what it needed, and knew what to do, forming a new heart at my command. When I pulled back my healing magic, I found with relief that the new heart began beating on its own, without my assistance.

When I was certain that his heart was better than new, I moved on to the blood and replaced that, too, giving him an entirely new life force that was fresh and clean of the toxin. Without the poison in his blood, it couldn't spread to more parts of his body, which was a benefit. All we had to do now was clear out what was already there.

I moved on to Charlie's lungs next. The ventilator breathed for him as I disintegrated his old lungs, growing new ones. His lungs materialized almost immediately, and I knew it was because I had experience replacing this particular organ from healing my father. Once that was done, I fixed his stomach and intestines, which were hoarding a massive sticky glob of poison. It took time to clear out, and sweat began to bead across my forehead as I replaced his entire digestive system, starting from scratch.

I heard the wolf give a snarl from the other side of the room. Out of the corner of my eye, I watched as the wolf jumped in mid-air, snarling and snapping his jaws as he tossed an invisible foe into the wall. A piece of stone broke off the wall, though I wasn't sure what hit it. It looked like the wolf was battling some dark force I couldn't see.

Dark spirits have arrived to stop you, sent by the Warden. They don't want Charlie to heal, Oberi rasped. *The wolf is fighting them off.*

Didn't care. That wasn't my job. The wolf continued to growl, and he threw the invisible force into the door as I moved on to healing the rest of Charlie's organs. Medical supplies were knocked aside, and a cart was tipped over as the wolf fought off the evil entities.

The wolf chased the dark spirits into the hallway. Marcus will deal with it, Oberi stated, though her voice was strained. *We're almost done, Ava.*

Thank the ancestors, because I couldn't keep this up. His liver was the only organ left to be healed— I'd replaced all the others. It was going to be the most difficult, because the liver was what filtered all the body's toxins, and most of the poison had ended up there due to his poor liver trying to metabolize the poison and failing. I felt my magic wavering, on the edge of failure, but I yanked on Charlie's demigod magic to support me. His power came surging through the minute I asked, and I used that energy to give me strength as I faded the infected liver into nothing, and forged a new one in its place.

I searched his body avidly for more poison, and didn't find any. The kurble chittered happily, and Oberi said, *It is done. The poison is completely gone.*

I sagged in my chair, on the edge of delirium. I'd regrown what had been damaged. But would it be enough?

I began sobbing as I watched color return to Charlie's complexion. I reached out to touch his skin and found that it was once again vibrant and warm. "He's going to be okay!"

Yes, he is, Oberi said wearily. *We have cheated death once again.*

I bawled into my hands. The little kurble scurried up my shoulder and sat there to give me a kiss on the cheek. The wolf approached from the side, giving a satisfied growl.

They must return to the Ancestral Lands now, Oberi noted. *But they will be around, even if you cannot see them.*

The kurble gave another trill, and the wolf grumbled lowly. Their spirits faded from my eyesight, though I sensed their presence lingering throughout the room.

Oberi hopped off the bed and changed into a husky, *I will find assistance. He is healed, but he will need rest... as will we.*

I couldn't move. I was too busy weeping in relief.

EVERYONE HAD RUSHED in the moment Oberi had retrieved them. There were questions from a lot of people on how I'd done it, and I gave the most basic of explanations, because I was honestly too overwhelmed to go over everything.

I told my parents about the spirits that had arrived to help me. Needless to say, both of them were completely floored by the arrival of our family's guardians, and shaken up. They took a private room in the hospital to console each other, grieve, and rejoice as I returned to Charlie's side.

The doctors had taken the breathing tube out and unhooked him from all the monitors, as it was clear he didn't need them. He still hadn't woken up, but I wasn't surprised. He'd been through a lot and needed time to recover.

I refused to let anyone help me. The doctors wanted to monitor me and check me over for any damage that may have been caused by the extent of my magic, but I wouldn't let them. They could worry about me once Charlie woke up and we knew he was all right. I wasn't leaving his bedside until his eyes opened, that was for sure.

"*Please* leave me alone," I snapped, pushing Ez's hands away. He was trying to check if I was good, which was unnecessary, because I was certain I was fine.

"Ancestors, Ava, you're impossible!" Ez snapped.

"Would you stop acting crazy and let people help?" Kallie demanded. She'd been arguing with me to let the doctors do an evaluation for fifteen minutes, and was getting more pissed by the second. "There's no reason to act ridiculous now. Charlie's fine."

"We *think* he's fine. We don't know for sure if my spell had any side effects," I worried.

Kallie rubbed her face. "If you don't get looked at, Charlie's gonna be pissed when he wakes up. He hates it when you don't take care of yourself."

"Fine by me." I wasn't the patient here.

Marcus stormed in. He carried a vial in his hands, which he shoved into my lap. "Ava, *drink this.*"

His tone was so aggressive that he was the only person I didn't argue with. I looked at the contents through the glass vial and figured it was a simple healing potion. I uncorked the bottle and drank. I found it tasted like grapefruit juice.

When the potion's effects kicked in, I instantly felt pain ebb away that I didn't know was there. I'd been so hyped up I didn't realize I was experiencing any flare-up symptoms, in my spine or my body. *Now* I noticed, and they were aggressive. My muscles ached as if I'd moved the universe itself to fix Charlie. Guess I kind of had.

"Thanks," I said, handing the empty bottle back to Marcus.

"I brewed it myself. I figured you would need it," he said. "You don't have to worry about it counteracting any of your medications. Everything I put in there is safe."

"Well, I really appreciate..."

I staggered in my chair, because all of a sudden, I started getting very sleepy. I registered that the potion had left a faint aftertaste, one of a sleeping herb I recognized.

Marcus smirked. "I might've slipped in a sedative. Nighty night."

"You little bitch," I grumbled. That's all I got out before I slumped in my chair and went to sleep.

I must've been sleeping for a few hours, because when I woke up, the morning sun was beaming through the windows. I'd been moved to a separate room in the hospital and given my own bed.

Marcus was sitting at the edge of my bed with a wry smile. "Rise and shine."

I scowled as I roused. "That was a dirty trick."

"We had to put you down and give you a time out. You were out of control, even after you fixed him," Marcus said. "Ez checked you while you were sleeping, and he said everything's all good. We had to make sure. Sorry, not sorry."

"How's Charlie?" I asked. I was concerned the organs I gave him might suddenly fail, or some other catastrophe would happen.

"He's up and talking. He's already been looked at, and he's in perfectly good health," Marcus informed me. "We told him what happened. You can see him soon, but first..."

Marcus' gaze shot across the room, and I lifted my head to see he wasn't the only one here. His parents were in the room as well, looking rather worried.

I gave Marcus an inquisitive look. "What's going on?"

He wrung his hands. "We know what you're going to try to do, Ava, and we all agree it isn't worth the risk. I've asked my parents here to help talk you out of it."

"And what exactly do you think I'm going to do, Marcus?" I demanded.

He drew a deep breath. "You replaced Charlie's organs. Now that you know what you can do, we're afraid you're going to try using this power to replace the nerves in your spine."

I might as well get on with replacing my heart, too, because it nearly stopped beating at the suggestion. I'd been so worried about Charlie, the thought of replacing my own spine hadn't crossed my mind.

But now that Marcus mentioned it, it wasn't such a bad idea. The angel surgeons had fucked up my spine during surgery, all while my healing magic was trying to repair the damage, and everything had healed wrong. Now I'd utilized power that went far beyond any average healer. Why couldn't I use it to replace the feeling that I'd lost? I certainly had a better chance of going up against the Warden if I was agile on my feet.

Marcus knew that, too, so why was he acting so apprehensive?

I looked at Nadine and Lucas. "Forgive me, but why are *you* here? If I have a chance to repair my spine, shouldn't I do it?"

"That's what we want to speak with you about," Nadine said gently, taking a step closer to my bed. "Marcus told us that healing magic has failed to repair your injury thus far because supernatural forces were involved. As we understand it, your own healing magic set the injury, and therefore, no magic has been able to undo the damage your demigod power already caused."

"We've never seen healing magic like what I performed on Charlie before, though," I said. "My power is stronger now, so I should be able to overpower whatever spell I used to set the injury in the first place. I could make a full recovery and walk again! Isn't this great?"

I turned to Marcus, but he had a solemn look on his face. My voice turned cold. "You're acting like this is a death sentence rather than a beacon of hope."

"It's not going to work," Marcus stated firmly, like he was certain of the fact. "I don't want to shatter your hopes, Ava, but I also know it's dangerous to even attempt such a spell. My parents can explain better than I can."

Lucas cleared his throat. "When Marcus was very young, our enemies used his own power against him. Enemies of ours used Marcus' magic to cast a curse, which prevented us from telling him about his demigod abilities, until he learned of them himself."

"Marcus has told us about this curse before," I said. "What does it have to do with me?"

"We tried many things to break this curse," Nadine admitted. "We even tried to use Marcus' own powers to break it, the same way our enemies used his powers against him. But nothing worked. We were able to determine that once a demigod uses their magic on *themselves*, even their own power cannot reverse the spell— whether the demigod intended to cast the spell or not."

"Please, Ava," Marcus begged. "We're only trying to help. What you did to help Charlie was incredible, but if you try to reverse what your demigod magic already did to you, you only risk doing more damage. When a demigod casts a spell like this on themselves, that spell will always remain permanent."

I got that he was worried, but wasn't he taking this a bit too far? Marcus was a warlock, and I was an Elementai. We didn't know if my powers would have the same effect as his. He was too scared to brave the risks, but wasn't it at least worth a try, considering the potential reward? If I could regrow all of Charlie's internal organs— nerves, blood vessels, and all— then I didn't see why I couldn't fix a few nerves in my spine.

My lips set into a thin line. Marcus and his family had my best interests at heart, but they didn't know the lengths I'd go through to test my limits.

"Thank you for your concern," I said evenly. "You have nothing to worry about."

Marcus breathed a sigh of relief. "I'm so relieved to hear that, Ava. I knew you would listen."

Eh, only sort of. I'd learned from Kallie how to twist my words, and I wasn't exactly *lying* to him.

Nadine looked a little shocked, like she expected me to push back. The woman didn't even know me, but I sensed she had a bit of fire in her back in her day— probably still did. She relaxed a moment later, though.

Lucas gave a kind nod. "Then we'll leave you to rest. Thank you for your time, princess."

"I'll be right back in," Marcus assured me. He led his parents out into the hall, and his muffled voice came through the door as he thanked them for coming to speak to me.

Nadine and Lucas' warning shook me a bit, but not enough to rule out the option completely. I didn't get what the big deal was. The least I could do was *try*. I was alone, and no one was here to stop me. I might as well see if gaining back my ability to walk was even a possibility.

I placed my hand on my stomach, right above the area where my spine was damaged. With my healing magic, I could feel the foreign rods in my spine, and sense the bundle of nerves that had been completely damaged. All I had to do was disintegrate them, then regrow them.

I decided to test it only on one nerve, in case Lucas and Nadine's warning held any real merit. Better to be safe than sorry.

My healing magic curled around a singular nerve, and I felt my power burn it away. I thought it would be ungodly painful, because I was literally destroying a nerve, but I didn't feel a thing at all.

Of course not, because there was nothing left *to* feel. That was almost more terrifying than the pain.

I concentrated on replacing the nerve, like I had with Charlie's organs. My hand glowed a bright white, until my power seemed to smash up against a brick wall I couldn't penetrate. I tried again and again to replace the nerve, to regrow it, but nothing worked.

I started to panic. Nadine and Lucas had been right. I couldn't counteract the botched spell that had healed my spine in all the wrong places.

Please, don't let there be any more damage, I prayed.

I pinched my upper thighs— *hard*. There was still a dull sensation there, like always, but it seemed weaker than ever before.

Marcus was right about the risk. I had done some serious damage that was now irreversible.

I had the thought that I could destroy the rest of my nerves that weren't firing right, to alleviate some pain, but that would also impair any and all sensation I had left in my legs, and I already had so little left. If I kept going with this, I was really going to hurt myself.

I hated to admit it, but I was glad Nadine and Lucas came to warn me before I did anything stupid I couldn't undo. I wasn't trying this again— that was for certain. Otherwise, I'd lose the little feeling I had left.

I hated that tears rushed to my eyes and ran down my cheeks at the realization that there was no way out of this. I'd accepted that I wasn't going to walk again a long time ago, but I couldn't help there being a small prayer of hope tucked away inside of me that one day, something would be able to fix me, or I'd be able to fix myself. That prayer dried up and withered away as I realized the truth.

I was never going to get better. This was permanent. I could perform miracles to heal other people, but I couldn't heal myself. I could replace Charlie's organs, but I couldn't replace what my own magic had set in stone without me being aware of it.

I was such a powerful demigod. But my demigod magic couldn't do the *one thing* I was most desperate for it to do, and that wounded me incredibly. I was helpful to others, but useless to myself. All these magical spells, potions, and medications I'd tried to fix my spine were nothing but disappointments. They were all the same, leading to identical undeniable outcomes.

I wiped my tears away and struggled to take in a few shaking breaths. You never stopped grieving when you were disabled, for the life you could've had, the life you desperately desired to live but would never receive. I'd given myself hope there would be a chance I could go back to the girl I had been, but I'd learned already that girl was dead and gone. I needed to accept myself now for who I *was*, not the person I wished I could be. I had to love my body the way it'd turned out to be, not hate it for not being the body I wished for.

I was worthy even though I was in a wheelchair, and stronger than anyone else in this palace. It was okay the spell hadn't worked. I accepted my body for what it was. I'd done my best, given it a good try, and that was all I could expect from myself. Though this treatment hadn't worked, and so many others hadn't either, I knew it would be okay.

I was still me. That was all that mattered. Charlie and my friends loved me no matter what, and I loved me, too. I didn't need to make myself into something different to earn that love. I could still be sick and receive it generously.

Even so... there would always be a piece of me that wanted things to change. But that piece of me didn't have to believe I was worth any less because of it. And it wouldn't, because that wasn't the truth. I was valuable just as I was. I had to acknowledge that.

A few minutes later, I'd pulled myself together and Marcus returned to the room. "Ready to see Charlie?"

"Finally." I wasn't waiting a second longer. Marcus helped me from the bed back into my chair. I found that I was too tired to roll my wheels, or even use the button on my chair that would move me forward, so Marcus pushed me.

Okay, so they were right to knock me out, because casting the spell on Charlie had affected me more than I thought. While we were in the hallway,

Oberi came flying in from a separate ward. The phoenix landed on my chair, a bright sparkle in her eye.

"You look much better," I said, and she reached out to preen my hair.

Marcus gave me some healing treats. I am in tip-top shape thanks to his astounding Alchemy magic, she replied. *I hope you had a nice nap.*

"Splendid."

Marcus wheeled me into Charlie's room. Happiness spread across my form as I saw he was sitting up in bed, appearing perfectly well. Emperor Cassiel was there. He gave me a kind smile, as if to say he knew I could do it.

Charlie felt my presence and immediately reached out for me. "Pidge."

I took his hand as Marcus moved me to his bedside. "Oh, Charlie." If he could call me by my favorite name, all was right again in the world.

"You regrew my organs." His thumb moved over the back of my hand, and I didn't bother to resist a delightful shudder.

"I do what I want."

"Still... that's incredible magic. I'd say it's hard for me to believe that you pulled it off, but nothing's off-limits to you. Thank you so much for saving me."

"I'd never let anything happen to you," I promised. "Whatever happens, you'll always be safe if I'm there."

Kallie walked in, eating a bag of cookies. "Hey," she said. "Have a nice sleep?"

"You butthead! You let Marcus spike my drink with a sleeping tonic! I know you were in on it," I snapped.

"From what I hear, he had to, because you were being purposefully difficult," Charlie said firmly. "I'd ask what you were thinking, but you obviously weren't. Pulling off big magic like that then not letting the doctors make sure you're healthy is beyond not okay. You're in big trouble."

I huffed out a breath. "We can talk about that later. What the hell did Danielle *do* to you? When we burst in, it looked like you were having some kind of fancy dinner to satisfy her disgusting fantasies."

My blood nearly boiled out of my veins at the memory of her curled up on his lap. That was *my place*, and she'd taken *my man*.

"I kept her talking," Charlie said. "And if I'm being honest, what she told me isn't good."

"What'd she say?" Kallie asked, already appearing on edge.

Charlie seemed very frightened, which always scared me. Not much terrified my husband, so if he was concerned, we all should be. "Danielle told me the Warden doesn't want to attack Ilamanthe yet. It's like he's biding his time, because he needs the Elves for some kind of purpose. The more Elves that die in battle, the less he has to use for whatever awful idea he's got planned. He doesn't want to exterminate them; he wants to imprison them. It's why he hasn't attacked the city yet. That, and it sounded like he's threatened by us demigods. That's why he had to lure us away from the city, onto his own turf."

"If that's true, this goes beyond the war," I said. "It's not about winning and defeating the other supernatural nations. It's about taking control of the Elvish race and using their magic. For what, we don't know. We need to figure out what the Warden needs the Elves for, because whatever he's planning, it gives him even more power than he already has."

"He could capture the Elves easily if he makes more demigods and creates an army for himself," Marcus said in terror.

"He can't," Charlie said. "Danielle told me that he's tried, and they die every time, plus he gives away some of his power on each attempt. The demigods he has are the ones he's got."

"Well, that's good, because we killed them," Kallie said, crossing her arms. "But it's definitely concerning that we don't have an idea of what he wants to do with the Elves, and he needs us out of the way to do it."

Cassiel appeared contemplative as he took in all this information, leaning closer to listen.

"That's not the worst thing," Charlie warned. "Danielle said the Warden *can't die.*"

Marcus gave a *psh.* "He's an angel, of course he can't die."

"It's more than that. Danielle said she watched the Warden fight the dark gods. They were trying to kill him and take over, but they couldn't, because no matter what they threw at him, he survived it all. Apparently, his magic was so strong he put them in their place, and they had to listen. He was able to defeat and control multiple gods without a scratch on him," Charlie said.

I scoffed. "She was obviously lying. That, or she was so stupid that she believed whatever came out of the Warden's mouth."

"It makes sense, though," Charlie argued. "Nothing we've seen other people do has come close to even hurting the Warden, let alone killing him, and the dark gods wouldn't be working for him unless he has an edge over them. Otherwise, they would've killed him and taken The Mission for themselves by now."

"This is a problem, because if the dark gods can't kill him, we don't stand a chance, either," Kallie insisted.

"But how did he get so much power?" Marcus wondered. "I've never heard of any supernatural who literally can't die and are invulnerable to all attacks. Angels, Elves and vampires are immortal, but they can still be killed. It doesn't even sound like the Warden can be wounded without recovering."

"Maybe he's like Oberi," I speculated. "Even if you get him down, he'll just regenerate, and come back to life."

"Great," Kallie grumbled. "Like we didn't have enough problems on our hands. Now the Warden is basically a god himself."

"Exactly," Charlie growled. "If we want to kill the Warden, we need to learn how to kill a god... and I don't even know if that's possible."

Nobody in the room said anything, because it might not be. I didn't know of any stories or legends which told of a god dying, in any supernatural religion.

But I hadn't heard any legends about a supernatural regrowing organs, either, and I'd done just that for Charlie. I knew, deep in my gut, that I'd kill the Warden one day. I was certain I would. Impossible things were possible for me. I just had to learn how.

"Is Ilamanthe safe now that the Warden knows our location?" Marcus asked. "I can't imagine what's so important that he's holding off going after our city."

"I think that's the point," Charlie said. "He's trying to capture all these other cities first, and we're the final boss. Ilamanthe is still protected by demigods, but I'm certain he's already working out another way to draw us out so he can take the city for his own. It sure doesn't help that we're losing soldiers to The Mission, as that weakens our defenses by the day. Soon the Warden will be done with whatever he's doing with the Elves, or get impatient, and come for us here. We should be very, very afraid."

Cassiel finally spoke. "If he wants a fight, then we'll give him something to fight. Our wards are strong; I'd like to see him try getting through them."

Cassiel started for the door, but Charlie asked, "What's your plan?"

"I'm going to fortify our wards right away, as well as order a city shutdown," Cassiel stated. "No residents will be allowed in or out of Ilamanthe. Only your team and our military will be permitted the use of portals."

Cassiel left the room to get to work.

"The Emperor will keep the city safe," I said, and I squeezed Charlie's hand. "Let's focus on getting the rest of the Divinity Keys. Then, once the Elven Gate is open and the Elves are safe in the Blessed Haven, we can deal with the Warden once and for all."

OVERDOING it put me back a couple of days. I had to stay in bed for most of the week to recover, because I was too tired to get out of it. My spine felt like it was on fire for days, and it'd been hell dealing with the agony. No medicine or healing magic had worked to make it go away. I'd had to let it pass on its own.

I got in trouble with Charlie for not letting the doctors help me. I wasn't allowed to practice any magic for the rest of the week. He didn't even let me attend demigod training, which I thought was really unfair. He'd commanded me to stay in the Jacuzzi tub all afternoon and eat chocolate-covered strawberries instead.

I mean, not a bad trade-off, but still. I wanted to *help*. I'd upset my dom, but if my actions had put us any closer to saving the world, I'd have to suck it up and take the luxurious punishment.

Charlie didn't go to demigod training, either. He was still recovering and spent most of his time in our suite resting.

My bachelorette party was on Saturday, but I was concerned about leaving Charlie alone in the suite... even though he was never really alone, because there were guards and servants stationed everywhere.

Of course, I'd thought that before, and Danielle had sunk her claws into him.

"I don't want to go. What if you need me?" I protested. I was doing my hair in the vanity mirror, because even if I wasn't going outside the palace, I still wanted to have big fluffy curls.

"Eddie is right outside to grab me whatever I ask for, and if I need you, someone will come get you right away," Charlie promised. "This is your bachelorette party. You shouldn't miss it. You need a chance to have fun."

Kallie had been planning this party for weeks, and I guess it would bum her out if I had to cancel. "Okay, fine. I'll try to relax."

I tied a big white bow into my hair, and Charlie said, "Have a great time, pidge."

"I will. Be back in the morning."

Kallie and the girls were planning on keeping me all night. I could only imagine what those sluts had planned. I smoothed down my slim white dress before Oberi escorted me out the door in her unicorn form.

Women cheered when I entered the Ladies' Court. The entire area had been decorated in black and pink— our wedding colors. Balloons and banners were hung over the area, and near the pool was a table that was laid out with fruit parfait cups, a chocolate charcuterie board, and a champagne bar.

"Congratulations, bitch. You're getting married again!" Kallie slipped a sash around my shoulders that read *The Bride* and fashioned a mini-veil into my curls underneath the bow.

Opal, Abigail, and Ivy were here, along with a variety of Elvish girls I'd met. Everyone was here to celebrate my wedding, and I couldn't be more honored that all my friends had come by to support me.

We started the party by having a tea party and playing party games. We played a fun truth-or-dare game that was bachelorette party themed, where everyone had to draw a card. The prompts were hilarious. Ivy had to give Kallie a piggyback ride while making donkey sounds, Abigail and Opal had to swap bras, and Oberi had to do a belly-dance— which looked completely silly in her unicorn form. She shook her big butt more than anything, and she knocked a poor Elf girl over. My card said I had to get into an embarrassing position and take a group photo. By the time we'd worked our way through all the cards, my stomach hurt because I was laughing so much.

After the game, we got massages and spent some time relaxing in the hot tub and sipping on our drink concoctions. I'd mixed raspberries into my lemonade and felt really refreshed. I watched Oberi swim around the pool in her narwhal form while I sank further into the water. Charlie was right. I needed this.

"Isn't this so wonderful?" Abigail asked, toasting her glass to the party. "Your wedding is going to be a celebration fit for a fairytale."

"It feels magical and all, but I don't know if I can believe it's a fairytale quite yet." I was a princess, but I was also a mob wife, after all.

"You should!" Opal burst. "You guys are everywhere! I can't turn the TV on without seeing a story about the proposal!"

All the Elvish tabloids had front-page articles about our upcoming wedding. Pictures of Charlie and me were on every page. I knew Cassiel must've put them up to it.

The fanfare was nice and all. It was crazy, seeing how obsessed people were with us. The Elves actually acted like they knew us personally. I'd been in the spotlight as a daughter of a chieftain, but I'd never had this much attention.

"Ilamanthe is so different from Malovia," Kallie said. "In my country, the monarchy looks the wrong way and the fae press rips them to shreds. The Elves don't think their monarchy can do any wrong."

"It's a difference in culture," I responded. It was in fae nature to criticize and complain constantly; they had high standards that no one on this earth could attain, but they still expected perfection even when it was impossible to achieve. Elvish society was run more like a mob, where any disapproval of the monarchy was dealt with swiftly, either through condemnation of society or... literally.

When we got out of the hot tub, girls started handing me gifts. I unwrapped a rainbow popsicle dick, designer makeup, a silk robe with slippers that I could use to get ready on my big day, and a bridal emergency kit, with all the little things I could need at the last minute before I walked down the aisle.

"This is great, you guys. You really know how to make a girl feel special," I swooned, surrounded by wrapping paper.

"Hold on. We've saved the best for last," Kallie teased, turning a corner.

I was curious. What could it be? But then my jaw dropped open, and my breath was stolen from my lungs as Kallie came out from behind the corner, bouncing in on a big, blow-up, six-foot tall penis.

"Meet Perky Peter," Kallie said proudly, and she stood the blow-up in front of me. "He's *very* happy to see you."

Tears came to my eyes and almost spilled over as I gazed at the magnificent monument to masculinity standing before me. By the ancestors. It was so *beautiful.* I'd never received such an outstanding gift.

"I love it!" I wrapped my arms around the blow-up and squeezed it as hard as I could, smushing my face into it.

"Geez, don't pop it," Kallie grumbled. "It took me thirty minutes to blow it up with air."

"It ain't the longest your mouth's been on one, cupcake," Ivy quipped, and Opal spat out her drink.

"Did you think about what you're going to get the prince for a wedding present?" Abigail asked, nibbling on a piece of chocolate. She handed one to me, and I took it, chewing on the caramel.

"I'm not sure. I know he's got something big planned for me," I mused.

"Is it in his pants?" Ivy asked. Opal giggled as she cleaned up the mess she spat out with a napkin.

"Most brides do boudoir photos, but... oh." Abigail's face fell, like she hadn't realized what she'd said until she'd already spoken it out loud.

"I know," I said regretfully. "It'd be nice to dress up in lingerie and take sexy pictures for him, but he can't see them. So that idea's a bust."

"Maybe you can in your own way," Kallie offered. "His hearing still works, after all."

Inspiration hit me like a flooding wave, and a satisfied smile spread over my face. I clinked my glass together with hers. "Kallie, you are a genius."

The girls took turns hopping around the edge of the pool on Perky Peter. Ivy bounced a little *too* eagerly and went floundering into the pool. I laughed so hard it was difficult to breathe.

As the afternoon grew long, the door to the Ladies' Court opened, and in walked my Grandmother Eleanor. Grandmother saw me clutching Perky Peter proudly as I wheeled around the snack table and gave a long, drawn-out sigh. "Ava, my dear, it's time to move the party on to other events. I expected you fifteen minutes ago. You need to pick out your wedding dress. The wedding is two weeks away."

"But I can't find anything I like," I whined.

Not for lack of trying— the Elves had brought me dozens of wedding dresses to try on since I'd gotten engaged, and I didn't like all of them. They were all extravagant, gorgeous, beautiful... but they weren't *me*. I knew my friends were tired of watching me try stuff on and wanted me to pick something already, but they didn't understand. This was my wedding, and I wanted my dress to tell the world who I was, not only as a person, but as the future Empress of Ilamanthe. My dress would be the topic of conversation throughout the empire for years to come, so it had to be just right.

"I think I may have a solution," Grandmother offered. "Though it's only an option. I won't be upset if you say no."

I was intrigued. "Where is it?"

"In my sewing room. We can go there now, if you wish."

"Okay!" I balanced Perky Peter on my lap and attempted to wheel forward clumsily. It tottered off and bounced on the ground.

Grandmother rolled her eyes. "I am *not* allowing you to accompany me to my room while you are in possession of that obscene object."

"Come on! Everyone should see how grand he is!" I objected.

She narrowed her eyes. "Leave it, Ava."

I grumbled, but propped Perky Peter against a wall and promised him I'd be back later. My friends followed me to my grandmother's suite, which was a few halls down from the Ladies' Court. When we stepped inside her quarters, my grandfather was at the kitchen table, hunched over a group of artifacts. He waved, and I suppressed a giggle. It was a missed opportunity my grandfather hadn't seen me carry in a six-foot blow-up dick. He probably would've fallen on the floor.

"Here it is," Grandmother said as we entered her sewing room, and she turned on the lights. "What do you think?"

I was in complete awe. On a dress form in the middle of the room was the most spectacular ball gown. It was ballerina pink, sleeveless with a sweetheart neckline, a tulle corset with silk ties, and layers upon layers of a full, poofy skirt. Rhinestones, pearls and silver gems decorated the front of the dress, making the entire gown shimmer.

It was stunning on the dress form. I couldn't imagine how it would look on *me*.

"I was making it as a graduation present. It's one of the few things we took from Kinpago before we left," Grandmother said. "But perhaps it's meant for your wedding instead."

"It's pink!" Kallie exclaimed.

"It's *perfect!*" I gushed. I wheeled myself toward the dress and caressed my hands over the poofy skirt. "Oh, thank you, Grandmother. I couldn't have imagined a more stunning gown."

"It's certainly fit for a princess," Abigail agreed.

"Do you think the Elves will care about the color?" Ivy worried. "It's far from traditional."

Kallie scoffed. "Ava could wear a paper bag to her wedding and the Elves would worship her for reinventing style. She can do no wrong by them."

"Definitely," I agreed. "White's not my color, anyway."

"Yeah, we all know you ain't no virgin," Ivy teased.

I circled the dress, looking it over. I put a hand to my chin. "Well, the dress is *almost* perfect."

"What does it need?" Grandmother asked, already grabbing a notepad and pencil.

"Well... I've been reading about tactile wedding dresses," I confessed. "They're gowns for brides who are marrying blind spouses. These dresses usually have more textures to them than regular wedding dresses."

It was one of the reasons I'd been having such a hard time finding a dress. I wanted something Charlie could see in his own way, not something everyone else would love. He was my groom. I wanted to look pretty *for him* more than anyone else.

"We'll add a skirt with a raised texture pattern, a few embroidered flowers, and more beading on the bodice, and alter it so it fits your chair properly," Grandmother suggested. "If we get your mother's help, and ask the Elvish seamstresses to step in, this dress can be altered and ready by your wedding day. We'll have your first fitting tomorrow."

"Thank you so much, Grandmother." I reached out to hug her. "I can't believe you made this just for me."

"Of course, my dear," Grandmother said, stroking my hair. "Anything for your special day. Ancestors know I won't allow my granddaughter to get married in anything but the best."

I spent the rest of the night goofing off with my friends in the Ladies' Court. We didn't go to bed until almost two in the morning. We all crashed in one of the attached suites, which had a ton of beds in it. I fell asleep holding the blow-up dick, because I loved it that much.

I woke up a couple of hours later, when everything was still dark. I hadn't meant to, but my earlier idea had gotten me so excited I guess it was hard for me to stay asleep.

The other girls were still out of it. I smiled. Time to put my plan into motion.

I got into my chair, then silently rolled out of the room and down the hallway to an isolated bedroom in the Ladies' Court where nobody was around. I shut the door, locked it, and pulled myself onto the bed.

One of my bridesmaids had given me a vibrator as a gag gift, but the joke was on them, because I was going to use it. I turned it on, grabbed my phone, pressed *record,* and slipped the vibrator under my panties. I made sure to put my phone by my mouth and be as loud as I dared.

When I was done, I saved the recording to a file, attached it to a text message, then sent it to Charlie.

I could barely contain my excitement. When Charlie woke up, he was going to get a big surprise.

THE MOMENT I woke up the next morning, I felt Charlie prodding at my mind.

Come see me when you're ready.

He was my dom and I always obeyed him, but he gave me permission to come when I was *ready,* so I wasn't going to show up until I knew he couldn't take it anymore. I smiled and giddily buried my face in the pillows.

I wasn't going to go running his way, that was for sure. I could edge him, too. I took my time enjoying a late brunch with my friends, gossip over lattes and a bit of shopping in town before I finally moseyed my way back to our bedroom by one o'clock. Oberi remained at the Ladies' Court to sunbathe, promising me she'd be back later.

I'd barely rolled in our bedroom door before Charlie grabbed me. He lifted me into his arms, spinning me around the room before he growled, "I leave you alone for one night and you send me a recording of you getting yourself off?"

"Uh-huh." I looped my arms around his neck and asked, "What are *you* going to do about it?"

His tone darkened as he said, "You're supposed to come when I call."

"You didn't give me a specific time, so how was I supposed to know? I came *eventually.*"

"And you're gonna come again." He carried me through the mirror that led to the Sanctuary, and when I saw what waited inside, it gave me a thrill.

In an open area by the bed there was a sling hanging from the ceiling, suspended on several anchors. It had a spinning swing seat, as well as adjustable straps that had fabric cuffs for the legs and ankles.

A sex swing. *Now* we were talking.

He spent all that time this morning that I'd used to make him wait setting up the room. I could only imagine what he had planned on doing to me.

He threw me on the bed, then went tearing off my clothes without any further conversation. My breath raced as he slipped me into a lace lingerie set. It left absolutely nothing to the imagination— the bra was a strappy underbust band, with tiny triangles that barely covered my nipples, and the panties were sheer, a double-strapped waistband with a thong-cut back. I might as well not be wearing anything at all, and that was just fine by me.

He was more unrestrained than he usually was, tossing me around as he dressed me like his personal doll, and I was enjoying it. There was no time to be gentle or romantic, because all either of us wanted right now was to be rough.

Once I was dressed, Charlie put me down in the swing, then immediately went to fasten the cuffs. He velcroed two cuffs around my ankles before reaching out for a nearby rope and tying my wrists together. Once they were bound, he fastened them into a larger singular cuff and pulled tight.

"You need to slow down. You're still recovering." I didn't want him to push it and end up overexerting himself.

"I'm well enough to do this, trust me. That little recording of yours made sure of that," he said roughly. "Lean back."

He didn't give me a choice, because he pushed my shoulders backward. The swing adjusted, and I felt completely weightless as I laid backward, the seat and the cuffs supporting my weight as I was suspended from the ceiling.

Charlie got down on his knees and immediately planted his face between my legs. My eyes rolled back in my head as I felt his tongue on my core, and I gasped in extreme pleasure. His tongue on my apex instantly made me breathless, and wanting more.

As the feelings within me welled, Charlie suddenly stopped. He got up, going to the dresser I wasn't allowed to touch. I nearly whined, but he grabbed a vibrator that was a similar shape and size as he was. He inserted the toy as he continued to massage my clit with his tongue, and ancestors, I couldn't understand why it felt so damn good right now. I don't think it ever had before, and we'd had some pretty incredible nights.

"You act like you don't turn me on and drive me crazy," Charlie said as he tasted me. "Why are you such a bad girl?"

I couldn't respond. I was already too far into delirium. I found myself crying out with small whimpers, and Charlie breathed, "Make those sounds, pidge. Just like you did last night."

My head lolled, and my breasts heaved as I gasped for air. He kept edging me, getting me to the brink just before I was about to come, then he backed off — again and again.

"Let me come," I pleaded. This wasn't fair.

"You didn't come when I called, so now you get to see how you make me feel."

I might've felt regret for being such a brat, if this wasn't so blissful. I was almost crying by the time he backed off again— tears leaked out of my eyes.

"Are you going to behave next time? Or are you going to pull another stunt like that?" Charlie asked roughly.

"I won't. I promise," I begged. "Let me come, please."

"As you wish." Charlie tossed the toy aside, got to his feet, and unfastened his pants. He pulled on the straps and the swing adjusted, so that my legs were at a ninety-degree angle toward the ceiling, my back tilted toward the floor. My head hung completely upside down, my hair trailing against the tile.

I'd told Charlie before I wanted him to fuck me while I was hanging from the ceiling, upside down. Looks like he'd put his mind to it and figured out how. Good boy.

Charlie placed my legs against his torso, so my ankles were laying on his shoulders, then shoved his dick into me. I let out a moan, and he began railing me like never before. The springs that the swing was suspended on added for extra bounce, and gave even more power to his thrusts. I felt like I was flying as he slammed into me, and I closed my eyes to experience the sublime release. I was tied up and bound to this swing, but had never been more untethered. This swing was amazing. It made me feel free. We had complete freedom of movement with it, and with the cuffs holding up my legs, I had more support than I typically did. His cock went deep, and I felt myself begin to convulse. The sight of him fucking me, with my legs splayed across the front of his suit, and that dark look in his eyes... I lost it. My eyes closed as my body hit its peak, and waves of pleasure broke out all across my form, so powerful I felt myself reeling.

When I came, Charlie chuckled lowly under his breath and uttered, "Good girl."

With a strength that required everything in me, I managed to open my eyes. I let out a few loud moans, and my head turned to the side.

The Beast. He was standing in a darkened corner of the Sanctuary, watching what we were doing. Ugh, what was *he* doing here? This place was for me and Charlie only. It was off-limits.

The Beast appeared completely disturbed. His lip curled as he observed us with a look of complete revulsion.

I couldn't help it; I let out a deranged laugh, locking eyes with him as my gaze told him silently that I didn't give a shit about him, and for all his efforts to stop me, I was completely unaffected by his pathetic attempts to destroy my life. It was hilarious to me that the Warden could do nothing to me here, and arousing that I was able to do whatever the fuck I wanted, when I wanted, and he wasn't able to stop me.

"What's so funny, my good little bad girl?" Charlie asked, and he fucked me harder.

The Beast faded from my sight, and I managed to strain out, "I just love how you make me feel."

Charlie's controlled breaths turned into ragged pants. "Good, because I can't hold back any—"

Charlie didn't have the ability to finish the sentence, because he came. He gasped and held on to me tightly, and I came again, mixing our two climaxes into one powerful harmony. His feelings ricocheted through our bond, and I rode them with delight as he came down from his rapture.

Charlie staggered away, then put a hand on the wall to steady himself. I noticed through our bond his consciousness flicker for a moment, and I became concerned.

"Please sit down," I pleaded. That had been a lot of activity, for him still recovering.

He stumbled to the bed and sat to take a few deep breaths. "It was your fault for getting me so worked up."

"I'm sorry, baby," I crooned, but I really wasn't. Not after all that.

"It's okay. I forgive you," he said with a sly smile.

I was still hanging upside down, and by now, I could feel the blood draining to my head. "Um... can you get me down?"

"Sure." Charlie slowly got up and refastened his pants. He released the cuffs binding my limbs and picked me up out of the swing. He carried me through the mirror and out of the Sanctuary, then set me on our bed.

"Can I leave my wrists tied in the rope?" I begged.

"For a little bit," he said. "I want you in that lingerie a while longer."

He laid beside me as the Mediterranean breeze blew through the open balcony, filling our bedroom with warmth. His fingers skimmed over my skin absentmindedly as we talked, which we liked to do after we played. We could converse for hours, talking about anything and everything. If we didn't have any responsibilities, we could lay here all day.

Charlie moved closer to me, then winced as his ribs laid on a hard object stuck in the covers. "Ouch."

He shifted on the bed and dug under the covers. He pulled out a notebook with a thick spine, and said, "A book? Why is this here?"

"Oops. I was writing in that yesterday," I apologized. "I must've left it in the bed. Sorry."

"What's this?" he teased, flipping the pages. "A diary of our adventures? Should I call a servant to read it out loud?"

"Don't." I laughed. "It's not for anyone's eyes but us."

"Oh?" he asked curiously.

"It's a notebook, containing three lists," I said. "One list is for all the places I want us to travel to, once the war is over. Another list is for all the places I want us to have sex— all the positions, and all the different toys I want to try. That list is pretty long."

"You'll have to read it to me sometime," Charlie said, sounding amused. "I have my own ideas I'd like to add."

"I'm sure. We'll be working our way through it for the rest of our lives." It sounded so delicious. I couldn't wait.

"What's the third list?" Charlie asked curiously.

I frowned. "The last list doesn't even have a full page."

"What's on it?"

Might as well be honest. "It's a list of people I want to kill."

Charlie didn't even flinch— or react at all— like my answer was something as benign as a list of clothes I wanted to buy, and not a murder sheet. "Who's on the list?"

I blinked as I mused on the names. "Before we killed them, it was Mad Dog. Naya. Deuce. Esther."

"And at the top?"

My voice was cold as I said, "The Warden."

Charlie was far from surprised. "You want to kill him more than the rest of us."

"Absolutely." My teeth gritted as I thought about how much I hated him. "I dream about it all the time— how amazing it would be to finally kill him. When you're making love to me, I laugh, because even though it's wonderful, *nothing* on this earth would make me feel as good as you do, other than taking the Warden's life. Murdering him would be ecstasy. I've got a few pages with ideas, theories on how we could take him out, ways we could put him in the ground."

I sighed. "I don't think any of them would work, especially now that we know he's invulnerable to almost anything, but I'll come up with how to kill him someday. And it's fun, because even though it's not realistic, picturing fantasies of how I can make him suffer gives me satisfaction. It delights me."

"It's one thing to keep it in your head, but why put it on paper?" Charlie asked.

"I have this kill list because I want to end people who hurt us, before they hurt anyone else. And I need to remind myself that even though we live in paradise here, I can't forget that I need to make certain people pay."

"The Warden's horrible, but it's not your responsibility to get rid of him, pidge. At least, not your responsibility alone. We can do it together."

I said nothing. Charlie asked, "Is that all who's on the kill list?"

I paused. "There's a name on the list you might not like."

"Who?"

"Your dad. Cameron Wahkin."

Charlie's brow furrowed. "Why is my dad on the list? I don't forgive him for what happened, but killing him is a little extreme."

I turned on my back, sighed and looked up at the ceiling. "He acts like you should forget about your childhood. Even if leaving you behind was out of his hands, it's okay for you to be upset that it happened. I don't like that he believes you can just move on and forgive him. Especially when he doesn't want to put any work in to fix it."

"You can't kill my dad, pidge."

"I wasn't going to. I wouldn't hurt you like that," I said softly. "But he makes me feel that way, so he's on the list."

I scoffed. "He might be the only person who makes it off of it."

Charlie lifted me into a sitting position on his lap. "Whatever is going on with you, I'm here for you. You're never going to suffer through it alone."

"I know." I put my forehead to his and happily breathed him in. "No matter what I'm going through, I'll always have you."

I was vaguely aware of a soft knock, and a small voice that asked, "Princess?"

The door creaked open. I heard a soft, strangled gasp. I looked up and saw that Abigail's face had gone pale as her eyes locked on the ropes around my wrists. She gave a terrified glance to Charlie, spun her wheelchair around, then hurried out of there.

Ooh. I'd forgotten Abigail was coming by today to escort me to my bridal fitting. She'd come in at a pretty bad time.

"What was that?" Charlie asked as he heard the door sharply shut.

"Abigail saw us with the ropes," I said as I held my wrists out for him to untie.

"Do we care?" Charlie asked, and he loosened the ropes before he pulled them off, setting them aside. "She's your lady, and loyal to you. She's not going to spread it around."

"Yeah, but that's not really the point," I said. "You should give me a moment with her."

"As you wish." Charlie nipped at my ear. "Can't say I won't listen to that recording again though, and be back for more later."

I giggled, and he helped me change into proper clothes before placing me in my chair and leaving our quarters. He had something to do for the wedding, but he wouldn't tell me what. I was already bubbling with anticipation at what the surprise might be.

I rolled myself into the living area of our suite and noticed that Abigail was already there, looking meekly at the floor.

"Could you have someone get us some tea and snacks?" I asked. "We need to talk."

Abigail didn't hesitate. She ducked out to speak with another servant, before venturing back in. I was already waiting at a small round table for her. I didn't say a word as an Elvish maiden brought us chai tea and a plate of decorated spiced cinnamon cookies, leaving the room with a bow. Abigail poured me a cup of tea, though she didn't make one for herself.

I ate a cookie before I said, "We should talk about what you saw."

"I am your lady, and I serve the crown," Abigail said in a flat voice, glancing at my wrists where the ties had been. "It is not my place to question anything the prince does, and I understand my position. I should've waited for you to call me in before entering, and I didn't, as I forgot my place. Forgive me. You have no need to explain anything."

"I'm not obligated to explain. But I want to." I put the cookie down. "You're worried he's hurting me. As you said, you are my lady, and you've sworn to care for me. So I want to show you that I'm not being hurt."

Abigail visibly swallowed. "Permission to speak freely, princess?"

"Of course."

"You may *believe* that he's not hurting you, but I don't see how such a thing can *ever* be good, especially not for a woman," Abigail insisted. "This... bondage is dangerous. It's... it's not a real relationship! He's using you in a sick way!"

She nearly burst while saying the words, and I reached out to take her hand. "It is, and it's safe. He's not using me. This is something we both enjoy."

"Has *he* convinced you of that? I bet this was his idea," Abigail spat.

"This is something we've done for a while, and everything's consensual," I insisted. "It seems terrible because you don't understand. I want to know what you've assumed, so I can answer your questions."

Abigail looked increasingly worried. "My princess, there are rumors about the palace. Not about you and the prince, but about... *others* who participate in such activities."

Where was this going? "Rumors about who?"

Abigail drew her hand away from me and began twisting a napkin in her grasp. "Well... Prince Cameron is an upstanding gentleman, and as far as I've heard, would never consider anything so heinous."

She dropped her voice and leaned forward. "As for the Emperor... there are whispers of what he and the former queen used to do in their bedchamber alone... and what is said truly shocks me."

Okay, so Cassiel and his wife had been into some kinky shit. I could see where Charlie had gotten it from. Cassiel seemed like the type of person who could go to some really dark places if he wanted to. He was noble and gentle on the outside, but I bet he'd done a bunch of twisted things to remain on the throne. If he was anything like Charlie— and I knew the two of them were a lot alike— there was a monster inside of him he didn't let out unless he had to. But when the monster unleashed, he enjoyed every minute of it.

If possible, Abigail's voice became even lower. "In fact, there are even those that say she died *because* of it."

"People make up silly rumors about BDSM all the time, because they don't understand it," I told her. "I'm certain that's not true."

But yet... holy shit. What if it *was?* So what's why Cassiel's wife had died before her time. He'd fucked her to death.

What a way to go. I could only be so lucky.

"You think this was Emperor Cassiel's idea, and he told Charlie to do this?" I did my best not to laugh.

"Yes, but you're insinuating that's not the case," Abigail stated.

"It's not. Some people can take this lifestyle too far, and it can get abusive. But for other people, it can actually be a safe choice. It's all about how well the couple communicates."

"How? Explain it to me." Abigail's eyes flashed. "As far as I'm concerned, all this is about is a woman being subservient to a man."

"This lifestyle isn't dependent on gender roles. A man can be submissive to a woman, in this kind of situation, and couples with queer identities can participate, too. If you'll have an open mind, I can tell you more."

Abigail held a breath, then let it out. "Very well. I'll listen to whatever my princess has to say, because I want to understand the situation, and be sure you're safe."

I leaned back in my chair. "Charlie and I are full-time dominant and submissive. We know our roles, and we live them out at all times, including outside the bedroom. If I listen to what he tells me, then he rewards me."

"But is this something you need to do?" Abigail asked.

"For my mental health, yes. But also, no. I can be *Charlie's* sub, but I could never be anyone else's. I love this life and the dynamic we have, but he's my one and only, and I could never be intimate with another person like this, because even though it's a lot of fun, it requires me to be excessively vulnerable. And he's the only man I could ever be that open with."

"And how does he... dominate you in a respectful way?" she questioned.

"We've created our relationship to be respectful by default, because we both have our needs, and if we don't get what we need from this, it doesn't work," I said. "He needs me to trust him. He needs me to know that he's going to respect my boundaries, and take care of me after he pushes my limits. This kind of situation doesn't work if he doesn't love me and I don't love him. What we have is a power exchange, where I'm giving him something valuable, and he's giving that back to me. I know some people are into this kind of lifestyle for just the dynamic, but that's not us. I'm his equal, but I'm also his submissive. And he never pushes me to do anything I don't want to do. I have full control."

Abigail seemed to muse on this. "How does this lifestyle work, in a practical sense outside of the bedroom?"

"I have rules I have to follow," I explained. "Charlie set them for me, but we discussed them beforehand, and I agreed to all of them before we actually put the rules into practice."

"Rules?" Abigail seemed slightly repulsed. "What kind?"

"Well, for example, some of the rules are very straightforward. I have to take a nap after lunch every day, so I don't get too tired. My nails always have to be done— because I like doing them, and because Charlie appreciates it when they're nice. I have a set bedtime, and a time to wake up. I have to eat three meals a day, and when we're being intimate, I do my best to do as I'm told. He'll give me commands to follow, then reward me with pleasure when I listen."

"Does he tie you up every time?" Abigail questioned.

"No. We don't always get kinky. Sometimes we just have normal sex. And sometimes the rules change due to circumstance. For example, I wasn't feeling well over the past week, so I had to rest more. One of my rules is I have to make Charlie's coffee for him in the morning, because even though the servants can, I *like* doing that for him, because I consider it *my* thing. But because I was sick, he told me I had to stay in bed while he made his own coffee, and that made me very grumpy."

I gave a shrug. "A lot of our rules fly under the radar. In public, people wouldn't think I'm being submissive. They'd just think I was doing something nice for my spouse, or taking care of myself. Charlie has a *lot of rules* for that. He wants to help me improve in life and meet my own goals, as well as keep me relaxed. So the rules he sets center around that. The whole point of having rules is for me to *enjoy* having to follow them, so I can get pleasure out of pleasing him, and he can focus on making me happy."

"What if you break a rule?" Abigail wondered. "What happens?"

"I would say the punishment suits what rule I broke. For example, if I skipped my nap that day, I would have to take an extra long one the day after, to make up for it."

"He doesn't hit you, does he?" Abigail asked softly.

I felt absolutely repulsed by the thought. "No. Charlie won't physically hit me in any way. Plus, spankings don't work on me, because I see them as a reward instead of a punishment. They turn me on, and that's the opposite of being disciplined. A lot of the traditional punishments don't have any effect. For example, putting me in time out would just make me think something exciting is coming later. And that's another reward. He's got to get creative to want to deter me from misbehaving. Also, he never withholds attention or sex from me. That's abusive, and I'm the kind of person who needs sexual contact to stabilize my moods and keep me grounded."

"I know it's not my place to ask, but what about in the bedroom?" she whispered. "I know some couples like striking each other with…"

She shuddered, and whispered lowly, "*Paddles.*"

Angelic purity culture had really done a number on this poor girl. I wanted to help her, because even though it wasn't my obligation to teach her about safe, kinky sex, I didn't think anyone else would. Ivy had been a big help to me when I'd started exploring, so now, I wanted to pass on that knowledge.

"We haven't used crops or whips yet, but I'm into the idea. Charlie's hesitant, because he doesn't enjoy striking me, not even in a sexy way. But I get a vote, and I'm sure with enough convincing I can push him to try it." I raised a coy eyebrow. "He might be the head of our family, but I'm the neck that turns his head, so to say. And I know my opinion has a powerful influence."

"So who's really in charge, him or you?"

"Him. He's the boss, always. But he always takes my thoughts and feelings into account, so in the end, I typically get what I want, anyway." I sighed. "And sometimes I don't make the best choices, so it's easier on me for him to make those decisions for me. Especially when my bipolar is out of control, because when my mind is all over the place, it's hard to keep centered. He *becomes* my center."

"So are they rules, or more like guidelines?" Abigail asked.

"If he gives a command, I'm obligated to follow it," I said. "For example, the other night, I *really* didn't want to do any stretching exercises for my physical therapy. But Charlie said I had to, and I'm submissive to him, so I did as he asked. But I felt better afterward, because I hadn't realized my muscles were really sore, and I needed to stretch them in order to get the muscles to release. Charlie did, because even without our bond, he can sense micro changes in my behavior that I don't necessarily notice. Then he can direct me toward what I need. I'm not the best at taking care of myself, so I need the extra guidance and help."

"This sounds like you have to do all the work and he gets off with no responsibility," Abigail grumbled.

"Oh no, he has rules, too," I explained. "One of his rules is he can't come home to me later than seven o'clock, because the time from dinner until we go to bed he's promised exclusively to me, and that's my time to have him to myself. Unless it's a Thursday, of course, or a Sunday."

"What happens *then*?" She sounded terrified.

"Thursday evenings are friend days. He'll go out with Marcus or Chancey, and I'll see Opal or Kallie, or go see my family. On Sundays we have alone time by ourselves, so we can recharge for the week. But honestly, we don't use a lot of that alone time on Sundays, because we like spending the free time we have together."

I took a sip of tea and continued. "He also has to be open and honest with me at all times. He's not allowed to conceal things from me. He has to be patient, and not let his emotions overtake him when I'm not doing as I'm told— because sometimes, I don't. I try to obey his orders as much as I can, but I'm a brat, and I like being one, and he likes my bratty behavior. I know when to push his buttons and when to behave. Sometimes I'll mess up just because I want his attention, and he knows that. So there's a balancing act we both ascribe to. But if we really don't like a rule, or it's not working for us, we can agree to throw it out. It's a constant work in progress. I like my role because I get pampered a lot. Charlie spoils me, and I show him I appreciate that by being submissive to him. It works for both of us."

"But do you *belong* to him?" Abigail insisted. "In a way that's possessive, and not loving?"

"I don't love the idea of ownership, but he owns my body, and I own his, so to say. I'm not his property, but his treasure. He knows that he belongs to me, and he's dedicated to my needs, wants, and desires in all areas of life. And he knows that I adore him, and will do what he asks because I do. We're both committed to improving ourselves, because you can't maintain this kind of lifestyle without growing together. It takes work, like all marriages do."

Abigail nodded. "I see. Although I don't quite understand, I think I can acknowledge this isn't hurting you. And if this is what you truly want, and your choice, I have no business getting in the way of that."

"We're really in a good place," I said dreamily. "This setup works well for us, because we know what to expect out of each other and ourselves."

"I'm glad," Abigail responded. "All I wish is for my princess to be happy."

I finished my tea and said, "I don't mean to intrude, but you've never been with anyone, have you, Abigail?"

"No," Abigail said sadly. "I prefer the female variety, myself, but I've never even been on a date. Or been kissed."

"It'll happen at the right time," I promised. "And when it does, all that waiting will have been worth it."

"I hope so," Abigail said sadly. "It was really hard, being a lesbian in angelic culture. I had to hide all the time, and pretend to be someone I'm not. I've suppressed so much of myself that it's difficult for me to even admit that I like girls in private, because it still seems wrong. It goes against what the Almighty One says, and that feels like a sin."

"It's never a sin to be who you are," I told her. "What Charlie and I have isn't so different than the relationship between you and me."

"How so?" Abigail asked curiously.

"You are my lady-in-waiting, and you serve me. You listen to my commands, and follow my orders. I have authority over you, but that doesn't mean I get to treat you however I want," I said. "You and I have to trust each other, like Charlie and I do."

"Okay. I think I get it now." Abigail nodded. "You're serving Charlie, but he's also serving you. And trust grows as the connection deepens."

"Exactly. You shouldn't be afraid to be who you are, Abigail, at least not in Ilamanthe. People are accepting here."

"It's just..." She took a deep sigh. "Whenever I find myself having feelings for another woman, I just see my father's face, and those feelings instantly feel filthy. He would be sickened by me if he knew who I truly was. He doesn't want to have someone like me for a child."

"What your dad wants isn't important, because this is your life, and you deserve love," I insisted. "To trust that Charlie will take care of me, I have to trust myself. And you need to trust that your heart is leading you in the right direction."

Abigail straightened her shoulders, as if the weight of the world had been lifted off her. "Thank you, princess. You are very wise."

"I've just been through a lot of stuff," I explained. "Wisdom comes with the territory."

"Indeed." Abigail turned her chair. "We need to get to your dress fitting. Your grandmother is probably very cross that we're late again."

Cross wasn't the word for it. I was fully expecting to get yelled at the minute I arrived. Being a princess meant nothing when your grandmother thought she ruled over all.

I could sense Oberi was waiting for me at the dress fitting, and getting a little impatient. She wanted to see me in my dress and gush over how pretty it looked. We left Charlie's quarters and ventured into the hall, on our way to my grandmother's suite. My guard, Eldin, followed behind.

I went to say something more to Abigail, but stopped when a figure crossed our path and stood in our way. I gasped in a mixture of shock and relief when I recognized who it was.

It was Professor *Hemlock*. Her clothes were tattered and dirty, and her face was covered with dozens of bruises and cuts. Her hair hung mangled and ratted around her thin jaw, and her skin gave off a gaunt, sickly appearance.

She was *alive*. I couldn't believe it! She must've escaped the Warden!

"Professor!" I was so happy to see her. I wheeled forward to give her a hug. "You're okay!"

Hemlock didn't respond to my gesture of affection. Instead, she reached into her robes and pulled out a thin, bloody dagger, her mouth sinking into a snarl.

I halted my chair, and my insides flipped inside my abdomen. "Professor?"

"You must die!" Hemlock screeched, charging toward me. Abigail screamed. I found myself frozen, unable to comprehend that my favorite teacher was actually *attacking me.*

"Princess!" Eldin cried, charging forward to save me. She drew her sword, and I shut my eyes tight as Hemlock raised her dagger high, aiming to bring the blade down upon my throat.

charlie

FIFTEEN

Ava-Marie had left me feeling delirious. It was torture waiting for her to arrive back in our room after the voice message I woke up to. I craved her all day, but truth be told, the wanting made her taste even sweeter. I allowed her to act like a brat sometimes because honestly, there were parts I liked about it, too.

I'd been dying to get her into the Sanctuary for a week, ever since she healed me from the poison, but neither of us had felt well enough to play until now. Hell, I'd gone so hard I nearly passed out myself. I'd wanted to show her just how much I appreciated everything she'd done for me— when she tracked me down at the manor in Celestial City, then brought me back from certain death. The thought of Danielle still churned my guts, and I wanted Ava to know there would never be anyone else in this world for me but *her*. Then she sent me that voice recording, and fuck... did it make my head spin. I'd certainly showed her my appreciation.

It was Sunday, so I was free to roam the palace as I pleased. There were no training sessions with my grandfather or meetings I had to be at today, and I'd given Eddie the day off so he could spend time with Alistair. When I wasn't with Ava, there was only one place I wanted to be.

I entered the music room, which was completely deserted on a Sunday afternoon. It was one of the grandest rooms in all the palace, with a high ceiling that each note resonated off of perfectly. Eddie had said the tall, arched windows were adorned with red drapes, and an ornate chandelier hung from the ceiling. A mahogany grand piano sat in the center, surrounded by other instruments and upholstered chairs. It was quiet here, a place all my own. That was perfect, because I liked having this time to myself. I didn't want people knowing what I was up to, or it might get back to Ava.

I took a seat at the grand piano and ran my fingers over several keys, enjoying the beautiful resonance the strings gave off. This instrument was nothing like what I'd played before. I'd learned to play on a second-hand piano that hadn't been tuned in years and had two broken keys in the upper register. Then there was the organ back at the Institute, and I was certain some of the pipes had been cracked or dented, because it just couldn't sing the way this grand piano could. Every note vibrated at the proper frequency, resounding in perfect harmony within the other notes in each chord.

I pressed the keys, and it was a bittersweet sound. It reminded me of the piano at the Institute that the guards had smashed. Back then, I wasn't sure I'd ever get a chance to play again. But here I was, in a palace all my own, with access to all the musical instruments I could ever desire.

I warmed up by playing a few chord progressions and parts of various songs I'd memorized over the years, then started playing the song I wrote for Ava. *Pigeon's Croon*, I called it. It was a slow, soft melody in a major key, with a progression of high notes that mimicked the race of my heart whenever Ava was around. I'd crafted the tune with care, knowing there were no words that could communicate the way I felt about her... but maybe this music could. It was a soft lullaby, mixed with the incredible high of the passion and desire we shared.

Most people wouldn't think of us as a lullaby kind of people. To the rest of the world we were angry, reactive, and harsh. But when I was with Ava, I felt calm, safe and loved, and that's exactly what this song portrayed. She hadn't heard it yet, because I was saving it for her wedding present. She was going to be so surprised.

The longer I played, the more I got lost in the music. When I was playing piano, it was like the music could carry me away to a different world. I hummed the tune lowly under my breath while my fingers moved over the keys. I pounded the notes harder as the music crescendoed, growing to its peak.

I fumbled on a few keys. Fuck, I thought I had it that time.

I practiced the melody slower, making sure I had it down, then started a few measures before the crescendo and built it up again—

Hands wrapped tightly around my throat from behind, bringing the music to an abrupt halt. The piano keys clashed as I was yanked to the side. I was caught completely off guard as the assailant wrenched me off the piano bench and threw me to the ground. My head smashed against the floor, leaving me momentarily disoriented. My attacker jumped on top of me and curled his hands around my throat. I tried to suck a breath, but the air wouldn't come. He was strong, I'd give him that.

Who the fuck did this guy think he was, attacking the prince in his own palace? I was getting pretty sick and tired of this shit.

I quickly reached out with my magic to assess who it was. If it was another one of the Warden's vampire cronies, I'd make sure the execution was a grand celebration. I'd laugh all the way to the pyre, then set the damn thing aflame myself.

Except... it wasn't a vampire. Several types of magic hit me all at once, and I couldn't make sense of it. I didn't know *what* this guy was.

I blasted him back with my Air magic, and he went flying across the room. Music stands crashed to the ground, and chairs squeaked.

I got to my feet and stalked toward the intruder. "The Warden really thinks he can send in anyone to get the job done?" I growled. "It's going to take a lot more than that to kill me."

I grabbed him, and my hands met armor, similar to what the guards all around the palace wore. I yanked the man upward. He had already recovered, though, and was obviously well trained. He kicked off the ground and did a flip, until his legs were curled around my neck. He twisted his weight, dragging the both of us to the floor. I searched for super strength to siphon it from him, but it wasn't there. That ruled out shifters, vampires, and merfolk. He definitely wasn't an Elementai.

I landed a blow to the side of his head, but he only squeezed harder. I gathered all my strength and spun my body, forcing him into another cluster of chairs. We engaged in a scuffle on the ground, and I finally broke free of his hold. I smashed a fist into his face, and he let out a pained groan.

I searched his magic again, looking for something that I could use. I noticed something that didn't seem quite right. It was reminiscent of Kallie's magic, but deep at this man's core, I could tell he wasn't fae. There was some sort of illusion on him— an enchantment he couldn't get away from.

I tangled my magic in his and siphoned it for my own. The fae magic was easy to manipulate because it was a lot like my Elf magic, only stronger. The illusion was more concrete than an Elf's, but I'd been growing my powers, and it was easy to break.

As the illusion fell away, the origin of his magic became clear. He was an Astromancer.

What the hell was an Astromancer doing in the palace? They didn't like to get involved in wars between the supernatural communities, and I certainly didn't expect one of them to be working with the Warden.

But what did I know? The only Astromancer I'd ever met had been my counselor back at the Institute, and he wasn't here now—

"Don't try to stop me, Charlie," the assailant growled. "You won't get away from the Warden this time. We'll kill you and your wife if it's the last thing we do!"

My blood turned to ice. There were very few people I recognized just by the sound of their voice, but I knew the cadence of his speech far too well. I'd sat through endless weeks of therapy sessions with him.

I didn't get it. He was a Demigod Guardian... he wouldn't hurt me. There was no way.

But here Professor Takahashi was in the flesh, threatening to end my life. Takahashi had been missing, along with Hemlock, since we left the Institute. I didn't understand how he got here, or where he'd been all this time.

"What's going on?" I demanded.

Takahashi didn't bother offering an answer. He threw himself at me, but this time, I was prepared. I spun out of the way, then used a quick maneuver I'd learned in fight club to pin his arm behind his back. I heard the tear of tendons and the snap of the joint popping out of the socket. Takahashi let out a pained cry. He went fucking crazy, screaming curses and gnashing his teeth at me like he was a wild dog. I couldn't imagine what possessed him to do such a thing. He was always such a kind-hearted man.

Looked like his kindness had run out. I figured he must've been bewitched. I tried to break whatever hold the spell he was under had on him, but I couldn't do it, which shocked me. With my Elf magic, I should've been able to break anything.

Guess I was going to have to do this the old-fashioned way.

I grabbed Takahashi by the back of the head and slammed his temple downward onto the hard back of the nearest chair. I heard the crunch of bone as his nose connected with it, then the splatter of blood as it sprayed every-where. His body went limp, and he slumped to the ground.

The heavy footsteps of guards flooded into the room. They'd obviously heard the commotion, and they quickly grabbed Takahashi and dragged him away from me.

"What are your orders, sire?" one of them asked.

"Prop him up on the chair," I spat. "We need to interrogate him. This was no ordinary attack."

As the guards hoisted him into a chair, I quickly dug in my pocket and grabbed my phone, then spoke a quick command. "Call Max."

Max picked up on the first ring. I didn't give her a chance to speak before I was already barking into the phone. "Get everyone you can to the music room now. We have shit to discuss."

"We're on our way, your highness," Max said, before hanging up.

Oberi, get here fast! I snapped through the bond.

I'm a little busy, Oberi insisted before slamming our bond shut. I didn't know what she was being snippy about, but I didn't have time to convince her to give up whatever she was doing.

I stepped forward to check Takahashi's pulse and found it still beating. I'd hit him with a hard blow, but only enough to knock him out. I quickly conjured handcuffs with my illusion magic and slapped them over his wrists.

A barrage of footsteps pounded into the room. Marcus let out a gasp. "Dear Goddess, what the hell is going on *now?*"

"What happened here?" Max demanded.

Several others were with them— four Elves and a vampire. The vampire's magic rolled off him in waves, an energy signature I'd become used to during our demigod training sessions.

I really wished Danny wouldn't have come. I didn't have the time or energy for his shit.

"Isn't it obvious?" Danny asked in that cocky tone he always used. "Charlie got his ass kicked by this old man."

I didn't know what gave him that impression, considering I wasn't the one tied up, until I touched my forehead and noticed I had a lump the size of a goose egg. I bet the bruise looked pretty damn nice, too.

Marcus pushed past Danny and hurried to kneel in front of Takahashi. "He's not an old man. He's our counselor, one of the Demigod Guardians. Charlie, he looks like he's been tortured."

I let out a gruff laugh, but it hurt to even talk. "Not exactly. He tried to kill me, and I fought back. He's stronger than he looks."

"I don't understand," Max said. "It goes against everything the Demigod Guardians stand for to hurt one of you. If he was any threat, he'd never make it past our borders. I don't know how he got in."

"There was some enchantment cast over him when he got here," I explained. "It was a fae illusion that must've concealed his features. I broke the spell that disguised him, but he's still bewitched. I can't seem to break whatever's got him brainwashed."

"He's wearing Elvish armor," Marcus noted. "Someone must've put an enchantment on him to make him look like a guard. That's how he slipped past security."

Danny paced around Takahashi's chair, boxing both Marcus and me in. He clicked his tongue. "Something else ain't right about this. The smell of his blood. It's..."

Danny paused to assess the blood splattered across the floor. He moved toward Takahashi, and I heard the old professor let out a groan.

"Ew!" Marcus cried. "You licked blood off his *face?*"

"I put it on my hand first," Danny said defensively. "How do you want me to figure out what's wrong with him?"

"This isn't time for a snack," I growled. Vampires were so gross.

"Relax," he said nonchalantly. "Fuck, I'm not *drinking* his blood. I'm searching for traces of magic, and I can tell it's vampiric. Your friend here is being compelled through blood magic. Strong stuff, that is. Judging by the power I'm feeling, he's being controlled by a demigod. That's why you couldn't break it."

"That's impossible," I stated. "The Warden gave up on creating more demigods, and the only one we knew who could do this kind of thing was Mad Dog. He perished in the fire at the Warden's manor in Celestial City."

"You sure about that?" Danny asked skeptically.

My stomach dropped. I *thought* I'd been sure, but now I was starting to question it.

Takahashi groaned. He was starting to wake.

"How do we break the spell?" I asked Danny.

Danny paced around to my other side— taking his sweet time answering the question, I might add. He clapped me on the shoulder. "Your guy Mad Dog might be a vampire demigod, but so am I. I've got you, boo."

"Don't ever call me that again," I warned, but Danny was already getting to work. I heard him kneel down next to Takahashi.

"What's he doing?" I whispered to Marcus.

"Danny's running his hands over Takahashi's arms. His eyes are glowing red— like, redder than usual," Marcus explained. "Strange red tendrils are filtering out of his body. Danny's dissolving them into the air."

Danny stood. "There. He should be back to normal."

Takahashi stirred.

"Did it work?" I demanded.

"Charlie?" Takahashi's tone was so weak. He sounded completely beaten down. "Where... where am I?"

He had no idea where he was. This was bad. "You're in the music room inside the palace in Ilamanthe," I told him gently. "You were compelled to come and kill me. Do you remember any of that?"

Takahashi gave a weak groan as he tried shifting in his seat. "I recall being captured at the Institute and held prisoner by The Mission. Professor Hemlock was with me. They... tortured us. For months on end."

A hollow pit opened in my stomach. Had I known what they'd endured, I'd have worked to get them out.

No, I *would* have got them out. I regretted not being there for them.

"We did our best to withstand the interrogation, and gave nothing of value to The Mission," Takahashi promised. "Everything the Demigod Guardians know, we kept safe."

"How did you get into Ilamanthe?" I asked. "My grandfather fortified the wards around the city days ago. You shouldn't have been able to get through."

"We've been here for a week posing as guards, so we must've slipped through before the wards were fortified," Takahashi said. "We were compelled to attack once we had ample opportunity, and today was our first chance. Believe me, Charlie, I didn't want to do this, but I could not fight the compulsion."

"Hemlock," Marcus said thoughtfully. "She must've been compelled to put the illusion on Takahashi. She's a powerful fae sorceress, and I wouldn't be surprised if her magic could make it past our wards undetected. That's how he got into the palace unnoticed."

I started barking orders. "I want the Elvish Associates to alert all guards. Get Ava somewhere safe, and find Hemlock. Danny, go with them. If Hemlock's being compelled, they'll need you to break the spell. Max, call the infirmary and tell them to bring a gurney. Takahashi needs medical attention."

"We're on it, your highness," Max obeyed.

The others filtered out of the room, while Marcus and I turned back to Takahashi.

"I'm sorry for what The Mission put you through, Professor," I said softly. "But we need to know more. Did you overhear anything while you were being held captive?"

"I know very little, I'm afraid." Takahashi swallowed audibly. "Professor Hemlock and I were both in a poor state when they came to compel us. Though I overheard the Warden speaking. There was a fire on one of his properties, and the demigods he controls were inside. They got hurt, but the Warden arrived in time to order his soldiers to pull them from the flames. Mad Dog, Deuce, and Naya all bore scars from the fire, but Esther was able to heal herself, and got out unharmed."

Fucking hell. Esther and the others were still out there. What was it going to take to kill these people?

"The Warden said he'd tried to kill you already, and since that hadn't worked, he would send me and Hemlock to perform the assassination," Takahashi continued weakly. "He thought since you trusted us, you'd let your guard down, and we'd get the job done. He ordered Mad Dog to compel us and send us in. The Warden's plan was to have us infiltrate the palace quietly, but Mad Dog had other plans. His magic was impatient."

I scoffed. "Mad Dog fucked that one up. He clearly doesn't know how to use trust against us, and he botched his spell."

"Yeah," Marcus agreed. "I bet he's never trusted anyone in his life. Doesn't know trust from his asshole. All he knows is violence."

I sighed. "Well, this time, violence didn't work."

"He's certainly being punished by the Warden now," Takahashi rasped. "Gods have mercy on him."

Hell. I couldn't imagine what kind of torture they'd put our teachers through to have Takahashi feel sorry for Mad Dog. He was a gentle guy, anyhow, but to show forgiveness to an enemy after what he'd been through meant the Warden was probably submitting Mad Dog to horrible pain right now.

I put a hand on his shoulder. "You're safe with us now, Professor. Let's get you all healed up."

A team of medical staff arrived then, and I undid Takahashi's handcuffs and helped him onto the gurney. Marcus and I followed the medics to the hospital wing.

On the way there, I overheard Takahashi literally *weeping* in what seemed like relief. Shit. I felt terrible for him. It was awful, listening to a poor old man cry.

"Takahashi looks *bad*, dude," Marcus murmured. "He's basically skin and bones. There's nothing left to him. What The Mission did to him was really fucked up."

"Did you read him?" I asked.

Marcus shuddered. "Yeah. I touched him when I helped lift him onto the gurney. He and Hemlock were held in an underground room for months, far below ground. There were no windows, or any light. No sun or stars. Everything was reinforced with noxite. They had no magic, and food was withheld for weeks. The Warden came down frequently to watch them be interrogated. They used everything— magic, torture devices. Blood was just... all over the place."

Marcus sounded sick as he added, "When he got angry they didn't comply, he gave them to his guards to torment."

A disgusting sickness welled inside my gut and paralyzed all my senses. The Warden had done the same to me in Cellblock 9; once he'd drained my power, he'd handed me off to his vampire guards to have fun with. They'd blood let me with every instrument they could get their hands on.

I hadn't even endured that for very long, and I couldn't think about it without wanting to scream. I'd blocked out that small part of my life since it'd happened, because I didn't think my sanity could take it if I faced what happened down in Cellblock 9 again.

Hemlock and Takahashi had gone through the same... *for months.*

"It won't go unpunished," I promised. "We're going to make The Mission suffer."

I felt Ava brushing up against our bond before we arrived at the hospital, and I realized I hadn't been paying attention to my bond since Oberi cut me off. We hurried through the doors to the medical wing, and I could hear Ava and Kallie speaking to one another nearby. The staff wheeled Takahashi away, while Marcus and I rushed over to the girls.

"Hemlock and Takahashi are in the palace," I blurted, before anyone else could get a word in.

We're well aware, Oberi replied, ruffling her feathers from the back of Ava's chair. *Didn't I tell you we were busy?*

Fucking hell. Hemlock had gotten to Ava first, and I'd been too preoccupied to notice. That scared me, because even though our bond was strong, things still went unnoticed even in the most trying of times.

I ran my hands over Ava's arms, searching for signs of injury, but I found none. "Are you safe?"

"Rattled, but I'm fine," she admitted. "Can't say the same for Hemlock."

"What happened to you?" I asked desperately. I hated that I hadn't been there for her.

"Hemlock was waiting for me in the halls. She sprung out at us, but Eldin stopped her, and held her off," Ava explained.

"It wasn't her," I insisted. "She and Takahashi were both compelled— by Mad Dog, no less."

"We figured that," Kallie said. "It was too good to be true that we got rid of those fuckheads forever."

"By the time Oberi pinned her, Danny showed up. He lifted the compulsion on her. She's recovering," Ava explained.

Kallie huffed. "Regardless, they're here now, and that's good news. If anything, the Warden did us a favor by sending them here. Now they're back with us, and safe, but the Warden's infiltrated the palace twice now. Who's to say he won't try—"

"He won't get to you again," a booming voice came from behind us.

It was obvious who he was, because the atmosphere changed when he entered the hospital wing. Voices turned to whispers, and people scurried out of his way. The Emperor commanded respect so casually that I didn't even think he noticed. It was completely natural to him.

Ancestors, I wanted to be just like him one day.

My grandfather must've just received the news of the intruders, and he did *not* sound happy. "This is the second time Doctor Taurus' assassins have infiltrated the palace, and I daresay I don't trust my own security force. We diverted military forces from the palace to fight The Mission, and that was nearly a fatal mistake. I'm increasing our security force— again. No one will get in and out of the palace without me knowing about it. Our empire could have lost you both today, and it'd have devastated all of Ilamanthe."

"Believe me, *seanari*, it'll take a lot more than a compulsion spell to kill us," I told him.

"I don't care what Doctor Taurus tries next. He *won't* hurt either one of you," Cassiel insisted. "Neither one of you are free to roam the palace on your own. Your guards will follow you wherever you go. I don't care if they have to watch you piss; you will remain in their line of sight at all times. Do you understand?"

I wanted to protest, because it sounded a lot like being locked up all over again. I didn't make my guards follow me everywhere, and I gave Eddie days off, like today, because I enjoyed my freedom.

But I understood why my grandfather insisted we take these precautions. At first, I thought he was being overly cautious with his security detail following him everywhere. Now it made sense. I didn't like it, but it was a whole lot better than ending up dead— which had nearly happened twice in less than a few weeks now.

"I understand," I told him.

I don't like taking orders from your grandfather, even if he is the Emperor, Ava said through the bond. *We're in charge here, too.*

He's just trying to keep us safe, I replied. *If you don't want to take orders from him, take them from me. You've got a curfew now and rules to follow, pidge. If you choose to act like a brat, I will punish you accordingly, and believe me, it won't be the fun kind.*

I could feel Ava wavering, because she liked being a brat and having her way, but knew as well as I did how crucial this had become. *Fine. I'll behave,* she agreed.

I turned back to my grandfather. "When can we see Takahashi and Hemlock?"

"They're with the healers now," he said. "You'll be able to see them once they're stable."

We sat in the waiting room for over an hour, until a nurse came out to tell us Hemlock was awake. We decided Ava and I would go visit Hemlock first. Kallie and Marcus could visit Takahashi, because we didn't want to crowd either of them.

I wheeled Ava into the room. Oberi flew off the back of the chair and landed on the bed beside Hemlock. I could feel her working her healing magic through the bond.

The healers did well, Oberi noted. *She's doing much better now.*

"Ava, Charlie," Hemlock said, sounding relieved. "It's so good to see you."

The way her voice sounded shocked me. Hemlock was such a strong person — so strict, no nonsense. She was a fae in every sense of the word, because she was tough and endured no matter what came her way.

But now... she didn't sound that way anymore. She seemed fragile and weak. Her typically strong tone was so subdued.

I had the thought that even though Hemlock and Takahashi were here with us now, the Warden might've taken them from us anyway. They weren't the same people anymore as a result of his torture, and I hated him for it.

Ava kept on the facade of everything being normal even though it wasn't— because I couldn't, and she knew it. "It's good to see you, too, Professor." Ava wheeled herself forward and planted herself at Hemlock's bedside. "We had no idea where you'd gone all these months. We've been so worried."

Hemlock gave a gasping cough. "It doesn't matter what I've been through or where I've been. The important thing is that you're safe, which is what Hiroto and I did our best to maintain."

Ava and I shared unease across our bond. "You didn't have to do that. You could've given in and saved yourself."

Hemlock let out a harsh laugh. "There are far less important reasons for me to resist Doctor Taurus, the littlest of them being that I despise him. It was nothing to endure what he put us through in order to protect you all."

"What did they do to you?" Ava whispered, and I heard her voice quiver. Like Takahashi, Hemlock must've looked terrible. I was happy not to see it; I wanted to pretend like they were as they always had been, not tormented by the worst of the world.

"Nothing I didn't survive," Hemlock replied, and she didn't elaborate. I understood why— she didn't want to burden us with what she'd been through, though I knew most of it from what Marcus had told me, and she didn't want to relive it by recounting it now.

Hemlock shifted on the bed. "But you... Ava. A princess, and the Holy Mother to Elvish kind. I couldn't be more proud. I heard you two are getting married again."

"We are," Ava gushed. "I absolutely can't wait. We need you to be there—no, we *need* you to officiate the ceremony. You married us the first time, you should marry us again."

"I love that idea, but we need an Elvish mystic to marry us, pidge," I reminded her. My grandfather had made that part *very clear* during our wedding planning that we had to get married in the temple.

"So? We'll make Hemlock a mystic, then," Ava demanded. "She's been studying the Elves for decades. She knows more about their religion, culture and lifestyle than anyone. She should be accepted by the Elves as one of their own and installed as a religious figure at the temple— that is, as long as she's open to it."

Hemlock gave a light laugh that seemed very pained. "A dream of mine, once considered foolish and out of reach. But an Elvish mystic... I never thought I'd get the chance. If it's possible, I absolutely will take the rites and join their ranks as a mystic."

"I'll talk to the temple," Ava said in excitement. "I'm sure they'll induct you as a mystic as soon as possible, if only to please me."

"It would be a great honor to be a part of the Elvish temple," Hemlock said. She gave a tired sigh. "I will be happy to marry you once again. Hopefully I will be strong enough to perform the ceremony."

"You will be," Ava promised. "I'll come in and heal you myself every day. We'll even put the wedding off, if we have to."

My grandfather was *not* going to be okay with that idea, but Hemlock wheezed again and said, "There will be no need. I will be strong enough to wed you when it is time. Go, now. I need rest, and neither of you should be worrying over a silly old woman like me."

"We *will* worry over you. Very much, every day until you're well again," Ava insisted.

"Then I'm sure I'll be well again very quickly, if only so you can be at peace," Hemlock said.

We had to leave, because Hemlock sounded too tired to talk anymore. We left the room. We barely had time to close the door behind us before we ran right into Eddie.

"I'm *so* very sorry, my prince," Eddie apologized profusely. "I heard what happened. I should've been there to protect you."

"I ordered you not to be, Eddie. It wasn't your fault," I stated.

Eddie gave a nervous laugh. "Well, I suppose you did. I am just glad that I am not being replaced, like the others on the palace's security council."

"Replaced? Like, fired?" Ava questioned.

"Oh no, princess," Eddie said, sounding very serious. "The Head of Security, General Ibrahim, as well as his second, Colonel Amilda, were both executed immediately after it was discovered the prince was attacked yet again within palace walls."

"What?" Ava screeched. "They're *dead?*"

"You must understand," Eddie replied, sounding confused. "They had their second chance after Danielle infiltrated, and they blew it. The Emperor was not going to allow them to fail a third time and put the prince at risk yet again. They were happy to kneel before the executioner, to atone for their humiliation at failing the royal family. Death was the only way to repay the crime they had committed, and they were glad to pay the price."

Eddie's voice fell in shame. "The Emperor knows you favor me, and that we are close. It is the only reason my head is currently still on my shoulders. Otherwise, he would've found Charlie a new guard."

"But that's absolutely ridiculous!" Ava yelled.

"Ava, quiet down," I ordered. We didn't need anyone overhearing us.

I have to agree, Oberi spoke up. *That does seem barbaric.*

"Your safety is paramount here within the palace," Eddie stated. "This time, not only Charlie was attacked, but *you* were also in danger. The Emperor nearly lost his mind when he was told the princess was nearly stabbed within his walls. It is a mistake that must be accounted for."

Eddie's tone grew cheery once again. "But regardless, we must press onward! I will not leave your side for anything, my prince! Not ever again!"

I nearly let out a groan. There went any private time I had to breathe without Eddie being there to ask if I needed him to do it for me.

We returned to our quarters. Eddie reassured us that we'd have privacy within our room, but anywhere else we went in the palace, we'd be thoroughly watched.

"Eddie's brainwashed," Ava hissed under her breath the minute we were away from him. "Can you imagine! Cassiel orders these people to die, and they just... do?"

"Look at the family we're in, pidge. This is how things run around here, how they've been run for thousands of years," I insisted.

"Charlie, it's fucked up your grandpa killed those guards," Ava said fiercely. "They might've made a mistake, but it didn't warrant them dying, let alone being *happy* about walking themselves to the execution block!"

"Maybe those guards didn't deserve death, but they definitely fucked up by letting Danielle into the palace, along with Takahashi and Hemlock," I pointed out. "Something could've happened to you— something *did* happen to me, and the only reason I'm still here to talk about it is because you're exceptional at pulling miracles out of your ass. I wouldn't be here if I didn't have you, and we're important to the Elvish people. We can't die; otherwise, the Warden wins. One mistake could cost us this whole war. If he has to send a message to prevent one of us from literally dying, then so be it."

Ava paused, thinking this over. "I still don't think it was right."

"You don't have to. When I'm Emperor, you can help me call the shots, but it's my grandfather's palace now. That means we have to play by his rules—which I'm more than willing to do, if it's going to keep you safe."

She huffed. "I just don't want to be locked in a cage."

"That'll never happen," I promised, and I leaned down to give her a kiss. "I'll make sure of it."

⛓

A WEEK PASSED since Takahashi and Hemlock arrived in Ilamanthe, and they were doing much better now, though I couldn't say they were back to normal. They never would be. *Normal* was a long-lost concept now. The Mission had put them through heinous torture, and it wasn't the kind of thing they'd ever forget.

But Hemlock and Takahashi were strong. If anything, their experience had only made them more resolute. They were going to take down the Warden with us, and failure wasn't an option. The minute they were released from the hospital, they were already back to work with the Demigod Guardians, meeting frequently with Professors Amber and Wykoff, and helping the Elvish Associates fortify the city.

I was pissed about what happened and angry that the Warden had ever gotten his hands on my teachers. I needed to hit something, and my friends knew me well enough to know it, even though I hadn't admitted it out loud.

Marcus had planned a bachelor party at a boxing club in the city, but since the palace was on high alert and security followed me everywhere, he decided to bring the boxing club to me. They'd transformed one of the state rooms into a temporary boxing arena, complete with a professional boxing ring and a set of bleachers for the others to watch when they weren't in the ring. Alistair had set up a whole bar with a keg, and Eddie had ordered a bunch of junk food from the royal kitchens. We drank and laughed and beat the shit out of each other.

Alistair finally went into the ring like he'd wanted to all these years, and he had Marcus on the ground with his arm twisted behind his back in under a minute. Rishi yowled, and Pig tackled him, until the cats were engaged in a match of their own. Rishi won, so Marcus and Alistair agreed they were even.

Eddie was hesitant to fight, because it wasn't in him to hurt someone unless it was to protect me, but I convinced him it was good for practice. He was pretty bent out of shape that he hadn't been there with me when Takahashi attacked, and he was looking to make it up to me. Once he got in the ring with Ezekiel, Eddie was laughing maniacally. Eddie was a natural, and poor Ez was pretty beat up by the end of it.

Chancey and I went at it for what felt like hours. We'd always wanted to get in the ring and see who was better, but the last time we did it, Captain wanted us to fight to the death. This time, we got to go at it properly— no cheating, no using magic, and no kill shots.

It was fantastic. I'd had the time of my life whacking him around, and he felt the same.

Chancey ended up tapping out, and we both stumbled to the edge of the ring with massive black eyes and a couple of missing teeth. Nothing the healers couldn't fix up. I didn't think the royal cleaners would be pleased about all the blood sprayed across the tile, but it was whatever. I had the best time with my buddies that day, and I felt a hell of a lot better about all the shit that had happened recently.

The wedding was quickly approaching, and Ava had requested a meeting with her mother before we got too distracted with last-minute wedding preparations. We didn't like being apart from each other if we didn't have to, so I tagged along. Eddie accompanied us, along with Ava's guard Eldin.

Liam seemed surprised when we showed up at their quarters. "Peanut! What are you doing here?"

"We came to talk to Mama. Is she around?" Ava asked as I pushed her inside. Oberi ruffled her feathers from the back of Ava's chair.

Sophia came out of the bathroom, and a small creature *meeped* from her arms. It shook its fur and sprayed water all over me.

"I just got done giving Buttercup a bath," Sophia said. "You must be here about your pictures. I've picked out a few highlights, but I'm not done going through them all."

Yesterday, Ava and I had spent most of the day in the gardens with her mother, taking engagement photos. Ava *loved* photoshoots, and I'd do anything to make her happy. The whole thing had taken hours, and Ava had at least six outfit changes.

"Come on, I'll show you." Sophia set Buttercup down, and the kurble immediately jumped down and raced to another room with aggravated chitters. Ava's mom led us to the bedroom, where her laptop was set up on a desk. I heard her let out a gasp as she said, "Oh, no! I didn't realize I'd left a cup of coffee—"

Her words cut off, and I heard her move something aside as she hissed, "Ugh, Jonah!"

What happened? I asked Ava through our bond.

It looks like a coffee cup spilled all over her open laptop, but it's just a piece of plastic shaped and dyed to look like a coffee spill, and a styrofoam cup, Ava replied humorously. *My uncle must've snuck in here and planted it as a joke. He and my mom have had a prank war going on for over twenty years.*

"I'm going to get him back good next time," Sophia grumbled. She started clicking keys on the laptop.

"He clearly hasn't forgiven you for putting shaving cream inside his pillow," Ava said with a laugh.

"Laptops are off limits, he knows that. Rules of the game. I'm going to have to elevate my next prank," Sophia replied, sounding devious.

Ava laughed, and I smiled. I thought it was cute that Sophia and Jonah were still goofing around decades after they'd left college. I wanted my friends and me to stay that close, no matter how old we got.

There's almost nothing in their bedroom, Ava noted. *They weren't given much time to evacuate Kinpago. Only their most treasured items from the house are here.*

That's not fair, I replied telepathically. *I'm sure there's a lot of history they miss.*

I felt Ava's curiosity pique as she explained to me, *There's a framed abstract painting above their bed. It's multi-colored, with a variety of splotches and splatters of color all across the canvas. There's no rhyme or reason to it.*

I wondered what it could be. An abstract painting seemed to be a weird thing to save from their old home while fleeing for their lives.

"Hey, what's that?" Ava asked her mother.

Sophia paused. "Oh, that? Don't mind it. It's just a painting your father and I made... uh, *together,* to replace one we'd lost during the Hawkei Civil War."

I'm guessing they didn't use paint brushes, Oberi joked.

I wasn't going to go there, because I wasn't interested in knowing how Ava's parents got it on. Like, good for them; I hoped Ava and I were still banging hardcore after twenty years of marriage. But it's not like I wanted to picture my in-laws like that.

"Oh, I love it!" Ava squealed as Sophia clicked a button on her computer. "Charlie, in this one you're sitting on the edge of the fountain with me on your lap, dipping me into a kiss."

I smiled at the memory. I didn't really care for the photos themselves, but our time together in the gardens— hugging her close and goofing around— had been really fun.

"Oh my ancestors! *This* one is it!" Ava was so excited that she yanked on my sleeve. "It's the one where Oberi's in unicorn form, and we're both on her back. I'm sitting backwards on Oberi facing you, and I'm holding your face in my hands. Our foreheads are touching, and it's *sooo* cute. My pink silk dress is flowing in the wind. I want this framed in our quarters!"

I placed a hand on her back. "Anything you want, pidge."

Sophia clicked through a few more photos, and Ava raved about them all, but nothing could compare to the photo of us on Oberi's back. She talked about it all throughout the session.

"That's all I've gotten through so far," Sophia said. "I'll show you more later."

"I want a whole book of them!" Ava requested brightly.

"I'm sure we can get one printed," Sophia offered.

"Thank you so much, Mama. I really appreciate it, but we didn't come for the photos," Ava admitted.

Sophia sounded confused. "What can I help with?"

"I've been thinking a lot about what happened with Charlie in the hospital," Ava said. "I can't let Charlie— or anyone else— get into a situation like that again where he was poisoned and I couldn't help. I need to be able to heal people whenever I have to. My Anichi powers still aren't everything they could be. You're the most advanced Spirit caster I know, so I need you to teach me what to do."

I hated that this was weighing on her, because it wasn't her fault that she'd struggled to heal me. It was the fucking Warden's. He'd done everything he could to circumvent her powers, and she still saved my life. That alone showed how incredible she was.

Ava wasn't as helpless as she thought she was. I suspected she knew that and that's why she brought me along. She needed me to be a part of this lesson so that when she doubted herself, I could remind her how strong she was.

Sophia stood. "Of course I'll help, honey. Let's go outside. The terrace is lovely."

We stepped through a sliding glass door attached to the kitchen. My Air magic swirled around the area, and I could feel that we'd stepped onto a terrace that was large and square. It was large enough to house a dragon. As members of the royal family, her parents were given a large suite at the top of one of the tallest towers. We walked along a brick path, and a small fountain trickled at the center of the terrace. I inhaled the sweet scent of potted flowers, and I felt the sway of small palm trees.

Eddie and Eldin remained several paces behind us. They didn't want to crowd us, but they wanted to be close so they could react quickly to any threats. Oberi landed on top of a palm tree to watch over us. Sophia led us to a small table surrounded by chairs, and I took a seat.

"I want to know everything an Anichi like me can do," Ava said.

"You're most familiar with healing magic, but our capabilities go beyond healing," Sophia explained. "Anichi means *spirit*, so we have the ability to manipulate spirit energy. Spirit is an energy that is all around us— within our bodies, inside the Earth, and even in light particles. Everything has a spirit, and we as Anichi can harness that power. We can use it to heal, as well as influence light."

"How do you use that practically in times of war?" I wondered. Ava had heard a lot of this from her mother before, but I didn't know a lot about Anichi magic, and I wanted to know more.

"Anichi can emit light from their hands to guide a dark path ahead, and they can bend light waves around themselves to turn themselves invisible," Sophia said.

My eyebrows shot up. "Invisibility? That's incredible."

"It's a complicated technique only the most advanced Anichi can do," Sophia replied. "It requires a deep desire to disappear to master."

Ava snorted. "That's the exact opposite of me. I want everyone to notice me when I enter the room. What can I say? I was born to be a royal."

"I still think you could do it, with practice," Sophia said. "You may find it useful one day."

"I want to try," Ava requested. "If I'm invisible, the Warden won't know I'm coming."

"Okay. Let's give it a shot," Sophia replied. "Picture wrapping light around your body, forming the molecules to your form—"

"Hey, I think I've got it!" Ava cried.

I obviously couldn't notice a difference, but Oberi said, *Ava's completely disappeared. I can't see her anymore, and I can't see her chair, either. She wrapped her Spirit magic around herself and is completely unable to be seen by the naked eye.*

Sophia sounded concerned. "Ava... that's incredible. It took me some time to learn invisibility magic properly."

"Well, I just accomplished it in seconds," Ava said proudly. I heard a *whooshing* noise beside me as she reappeared. "What else can I do?"

"You can use shields," Sophia listed off. "That's one of an Anichi's most important abilities."

"I've done that," Ava said. "I used a shield in the forest when the other demigods came for us, before Eddie portaled us to Ilamanthe. Now that I know how to do it, it's pretty easy, because I just want to protect my friends."

"You must realize that Anichi magic has duality, just like any magic,"

Sophia explained. "We can use it to protect and heal, but we can also use it to destroy and kill."

I felt a thrill go through Ava at the idea. She'd use any tools at her disposal to take down the Warden, and so would I. I couldn't be sure if Sophia noticed Ava's reaction, but she must've, because she was quick to add a warning.

"You must be certain with your intent before you cast a spell," Sophia pressed. "What we're able to do is not something to take lightly. People *will* die, and that's a decision we can never take back."

I didn't think Sophia *regretted* what she'd done during the Hawkei Civil War, but there was definitely a darkness to her warning that said she wasn't proud. She'd done what she had to in order to save her people, but she hadn't won the Hawkei Civil War unscathed. It'd left deep scars I wasn't sure I could comprehend.

"You can trust me, Mama. I know where to put my energy," Ava told her mother.

She was careful with her words, but I felt the meaning crystal clear. She'd already weighed who would die by her hand. She just had to decide the best way to take them out.

"Very well," Sophia said. "While your light can guide your way, it can also be used to blind your enemies. Your shields can be used to protect, but it can also crush those who get in your way. You can project a shield around them and squeeze, until their bones crush. Your healing magic can save your people on the battlefield, but you can also reverse it, to suck the life force from enemy forces. You can also concentrate your Spirit energy into orbs, to use as weapons."

"Great!" Ava said chipperly. "Let's try it."

Sophia drew a deep breath, as if demonstrating for Ava. "Spirit is a calm energy, and it takes careful discernment to feel into it and access—"

"Well, would you look at that?" Ava interrupted. Her Spirit magic flowed through the bond, and warmth blossomed across my skin, but I didn't know what she'd done.

Would you stop shining that in my direction? Oberi snapped. *You'll end up with* two *blind companions, and you'll have to be the eyes for all three of us.*

"You're emitting light?" I wondered.

"Yeah," Ava said proudly. "I can make my hands glow bright— like, *really bright*. If it were nighttime, I bet I could light up the whole palace like it was daytime. I can keep going."

"Not if you want the rest of us to keep our vision by the end of it," Sophia insisted.

The warmth on my skin disappeared as Ava pulled her magic back.

"Are you sure Spirit is calm energy?" Ava asked skeptically. "Because I'm pure chaos, and that was easy. Give me a harder one."

"All right. Let's see what you can *do* with a shield, besides just conjuring it," Sophia said. "Project the shield outside of yourself, around that rose bush. Then slowly compress your shield until it crushes the bush."

Ava had already gotten to work. The sound of snapping twigs filled the courtyard. At the same time, my lungs became heavy, like something was squeezing them.

Then I realized it was my Earth magic responding to her attack. I could *feel* the rose bush being squashed. The smell of roses filled my nose, but it wasn't a pleasant floral scent. It was the smell of death as the petals were pulverized to nothing.

I held my breath, each passing moment more agonizing than the last. The bush continued to snap and groan as Ava reduced it to shreds. I winced, and I wasn't sure how much more I could handle. My magic *ached*, and all I wanted was to bring the rose bush back to life, but I didn't want to stop her, either. Ava had to master this. It could be a way to beat the Warden.

Finally, Ava let up, and I sucked in a deep breath of relief. A breeze swept through the courtyard, sending a whirlwind of dust particles over my arm. Ava had squeezed so hard that the rose bush was nothing more than a pile of dust now.

"Sorry, Charlie," Ava said sadly. She could obviously sense my unease.

I sat up straighter. "We have to do what needs to be done to grow your powers."

"I don't need much practice," Ava admitted. "That was easy. Let's try reversing life force energy. That seems more complicated."

"This technique requires accessing your healing magic," Sophia told her. "Notice how your healing magic comes from a place of love and care. It can also be the opposite— you can pull from hate and destruction. To do this, you must reverse your healing magic, and draw the life force out of a living being."

"How's she going to practice that?" I asked. "She can't try on just anyone. She'll kill them."

"Wait here." Sophia got up from the table, then came back a few minutes later. She laid something on the table in front of us. I heard labored panting and realized it was some kind of animal.

"This rabbit is a Familiar that was bonded to an Elementai who died months ago," Sophia explained.

"I thought Elementai and Familiars couldn't live without each other, so if you killed one, you killed both," I said.

"That's true, but if the Elementai and Familiar are older, or if the bond between them was strained, the dying process for the remaining partner can sometimes take weeks after the first one is gone," Sophia said. "The Anichi healers and I have tried everything we can to help this Familiar's soul pass on, but he seems stuck here. This is an opportunity to teach you how to use your powers, Ava. Help this poor creature die so he can rejoin his Elementai, even in the inbetween place."

The rabbit panted harder. Clearly, this Familiar was in pain, and helping him to live on wouldn't do any good. The merciful thing would be to end his life, even if he couldn't get into the Ancestral Lands right now.

"I'll try. What do I need to do?" Ava asked, and she shifted to hover her hand over the animal.

"Instead of asking your Spirit magic to heal the animal, do the opposite," Sophia instructed. "Have your powers indicate to the body that it needs to start shutting down."

Ava cast the spell, and I could feel tingles of her power spreading out throughout the space, even though I was sitting right next to her. The rabbit gave a shriek and shuddered, twitching on the table.

"It's working, but he's fighting me," Ava said. "What do I do?"

"Sometimes, death is frightening," Sophia said. "Let your magic tell his soul that there's nothing to worry about, and he can go on to a safe place while continuing to draw his remaining energy out."

Ava did so. The rabbit gave a last breath, and the noise fell silent.

After a few moments, Ava said, "It worked. His heart stopped. I felt the moment he rejoined his Elementai. They're together now, even if they can't get into the Ancestral Lands."

"Very good, Ava," Sophia stated. "Now you understand that healing magic isn't just restoring. It is also taking."

Fabric rustled as she wrapped the rabbit's body in a blanket and took him into the house. "I will bury him beside his Elementai after our lesson. It's only right that they be reunited. No Elementai should be separated from their Familiar for long."

There was an ache in her voice I couldn't place and didn't understand. Ava turned to Sophia. "Mama, if I can do all this so easily, maybe there's more I can do— like how I healed Charlie in the hospital."

"What were you thinking?" Sophia asked curiously.

"Can you go get Daddy?" Ava asked.

Sophia hesitated. "Ava, I know you don't want to see your father suffer, but this won't be the same. We've had the best Anichi healers working with him for decades—"

"No, you haven't," Ava insisted. "I'm the best Anichi healer there is, and you didn't have *me*. Can't I at least talk to him about it and see what he thinks?"

Sophia sighed and stood from her chair. "You can talk to him, but ultimately, this decision is up to him."

Sophia left to go get Liam.

I turned to Ava. "You think you can heal your dad's illness the same way you healed me from the poison?"

"Why not?" Ava asked. "I regrew whole *organs*. Why can't I regrow my father's body?"

"Because his illness affects every organ and body system all at once," I said. "When you regrew my body, it was similar to transplanting one organ at a time. Your dad's condition would require you to destroy him altogether, and if you did that, there'd be nothing left to regrow."

"We don't know that," Ava argued. "At least let me talk to him."

"Even if you could heal him, you need to be prepared if he says no," I pressed.

"I know you wouldn't want to be cured of your blindness, but this is different," Ava insisted.

"Is it?" I shook my head. "I've lived most of my life as a blind person. I've learned how to navigate the world in my own way. If you were to regrow my eyes and give me my sight back, I wouldn't know what to do with it. I'd be too overstimulated, and I'd have to completely change the way I interact with life and learn a whole new way of being. My disability has never been the problem — the problem is the way people treat me. But here in Ilamanthe, where everything is accessible to people like us, I don't feel like my disability is a hindrance, because I'm given the tools I need to thrive. I like the way I experience the world, and I wouldn't want to have it any other way. I'm not saying all disabled people would feel the same, because we all experience life differently, but that's how it is for me. Maybe your dad likes the way he is, and doesn't want to change."

"I'm not sure I could regrow your eyes, even if I wanted to," Ava admitted. "You lost your sight due to a spell the gods created. I'm powerful, but I'm not more powerful than a god."

"Promise me you won't try," I pressed. "I gave up my sight to save your life, and if we were to reverse that, we could reverse the spell, and you might not survive that."

Ava scoffed, and I could tell she was rolling her eyes. "Fine. If you don't want me to try, then I won't."

I smiled. "That's my good girl."

Sophia and Liam returned to the terrace, and they both took a seat at the table.

"All right," Liam grumbled. "Let's move it along."

"Are you sure you want to go through with this?" I asked cautiously.

Liam grunted. "My illness has been a pain in the ass since I was diagnosed. I don't really expect to be cured, but I guess I'll just have to live with the inconveniences of not feeling like shit everyday if this actually works. What a tragedy."

Ava's voice brightened. "Mama explained to you what I want to do?"

"You want to try and cure my illness, but it's not going to work, so we might as well get it over with," Liam said. "Let's give it a shot, so I can get back to what I was doing."

"Daddy, you're such a pessimist," Ava grumbled.

"Whoa, back up," I balked. "I don't think you clearly understand what Ava's suggesting. She wants to destroy your organs and regrow them, like she did to me in the hospital, in order to cure your condition. You guys can't seriously think this would work? She'd have to completely regrow your immune system, and that's not something even the best healers in the world can do. Even if it *could* work in theory, Ava could kill you in the process. This isn't worth risking."

"Eh, if I die, I'm ready to go," he replied.

"Liam," Sophia growled, and he gave a skeptical snort.

Liam seemed anything but bothered. I couldn't believe him. Did anything shake this guy?

"Death isn't something you want right now," I warned. "In case you forgot, nobody's making it to the Ancestral Lands these days."

"I've lived through everything that's tried to kill me over the years, Ava included. She's not gonna hurt me now, believe me," Liam grumped.

"I'm not going to kill you," Ava insisted. "Just let me try."

Ava was stubborn, so Liam begrudgingly held his arm out for her to take. The warmth of her healing magic radiated through the area once again, though Liam didn't respond.

"Do you feel any better?" Ava asked hopefully.

"Just as spectacular as always, which means no," Liam replied.

"I need to try harder! Ugh!" Ava made noises of frustration as she worked her healing magic, which clearly wasn't doing anything.

After a few minutes passed, Sophia drew her hands away. "You're exerting yourself for nothing, sweetheart. Your father's illness hasn't changed."

"Gee, what a shock," Liam huffed. "I really appreciate that you tried, peanut, but I'm used to it. Really, it doesn't bother me that much anymore."

"I don't get it!" Ava said angrily. "How can I do so much, but I can't cure *this*? I was able to heal Ez from sepsis, I could regrow your guys' organs..."

"Disabilities and chronic conditions are a little different," Sophia stated. "Many supernaturals think they're a result of life contracts we made before we were born, and your magic can't override that, not unless that person wishes to change the contract they already made. You always need a person's consent to heal them before you do so; otherwise, the magic doesn't work. Spirit magic will fail to heal a person who's lost the will to live, and I'm assuming it doesn't work to heal conditions that supernaturals have chosen to undergo in order to learn life lessons to carry into the spiritual realm after death."

"But why would Daddy choose to be sick? That's so offensive to say," Ava argued.

"Because I like to live life on extra-hard mode to impress everyone else," Liam said.

"Daddy, this isn't the time for jokes," Ava grumbled.

Liam gave a huff. "It's not really a joke."

"Disabilities don't have to always be hard. Sometimes, they're just different," I pointed out to Ava. "Remember what I talked about when we discussed my blindness? If everyone in this world was the same, it'd be void of variety and life. Some people want to be healed, and some don't, and that's just fine. You know as well as I do that people don't have to be able-bodied to be whole. That's just the expectation society puts on us."

"Yes. And Anichi magic knows that." Ava sighed. "We've found the one thing I can't do, which kinda sucks."

"You can do everything else, so don't be disappointed," Liam said. "It's probably good you have some limits."

I got the hidden message there. If Ava had no limits at all, that wasn't a good thing, because she barely controlled herself as it was, and that was with me guiding her most of the time. If she was limitless, there was no telling what she'd try.

"I have a theory, but no one's ever done it before," Sophia said. "But you aren't like other Anichi. I want to see if it works for you."

"Ooh. What is it?" Ava gushed.

"Traditionally, the Elementai draw their magic from their Familiars, but talented Elementai like your father and I are able to draw magic from other sources. We call it intrafusion," Sophia said. "We can draw power from magical creatures that share our element, or from other elemental sources. In my case, I'm able to draw Fire magic from the sun, and your father can draw Water energy from the moon. Nivita and Yapluma should be able to draw power from the earth and the atmosphere, as those powerful forces correlate with their elements."

"What about Spirit?" Ava asked. "Would I have to pull from people's souls?"

"No," Sophia answered. "As you know, within our culture, we believe that everything has a spirit, even the rocks, the rivers, and the mountains. There is a spirit within the planet itself. It's the planet's life essence, which gives plants and animals the power to grow and thrive here. It's different from Charlie's Earth magic, where his power is tied to dirt, rocks and plants. There is a spirit within the planet itself, as the planet is a living being with her own soul. I believe that if you are strong enough, you can tap into the soul of the Earth and use her power, the way your father and I use other planetary bodies to influence our magic."

"That sounds incredible!" Ava cried. "I want to try it right now!"

"I thought so." Sophia laughed. "But to do so, we'll have to relocate to the gardens."

"Let's do it, then," Ava proclaimed. "There's no time to lose!"

Around a half hour later we gathered around Ava in the palace gardens, waiting to see what would happen. Ava sat on the ground as Sophia instructed her to do, her palm spread over the earth. Oberi perched in a nearby tree to observe.

"See if you can feel the Earth's spirit," Sophia gently prodded. "It should be like feeling any other soul, in any other kind of entity. View our planet as a person, and deep within, there will be a guiding light—"

Ava abruptly screamed, cutting her mother off. "I think I feel it!"

We held our breath in hesitation, and Ava started gushing. "Oh. She's *beautiful*. The Earth has a wonderful, divine feminine spirit. We're kind of alike in that way. She's nurturing and kind, and she reacts by instinct. She wants to feel joy and share that with others. She's extroverted and open, but vulnerable, too. She loves to just *be*, rather than *do*. She's creative and gentle and sensitive, but there's a side of her too that's emotional. Her tears fill our rivers, and her volcanic eruptions and earthquakes demand our attention. She doesn't want to be alone— she wants to co-create with us and collaborate."

Spirit magic swelled through the bond. I could feel Ava drawing the magic from the Earth, pulling it into herself.

"The Earth is connected to everyone and everything," Ava said quickly. "Her spirit is tied to the spirit of the ocean, and the soul of the mountains. Every rock, animal and plant resonates and responds to her energy. She's so powerful. Her soul seems to go on forever."

The ground shook a little, and I held my breath. Whatever was going on, this was powerful magic.

"Slow down, Ava," her mother pressed. "You don't want to overwhelm yourself."

Ava blew a breath. "I'm barely getting started."

She continued to pull magic from the Earth, and it seemed to surround us with warmth at all angles. It wasn't hot like her Fire, but more like a comforting blanket.

But even blankets could strangle you. I felt a shift the more Ava worked. Nutrients in the soil converted into Spirit energy at her command. The plants around us began to wilt, and the grass started to die. A bird squawked in a tree above us before falling from its branch and making a *splatting* noise on the brick path as it died. I felt the trees bend as they started to wither, and a few boulders in the rock garden split in two.

"What's she doing?" Liam panicked. "She shouldn't be able to draw this much power."

"I'm not sure," Sophia wavered. "Ava, hold off."

Ava kept pulling. Oberi leapt from her perch and began making circles overhead, flapping her wings frantically and screeching loudly. *Ava, you're drawing too much!*

She didn't hear our Familiar. Ava continued to draw from the Earth's soul, a sort of madness permeating our bond as she siphoned the spirit of the Earth's energy. Thunder began to crack overhead, and the area developed a coldness I couldn't shake as an incoming storm started to grow.

She was scaring the shit out of me. This had to end, before there were permanent consequences.

"Ava, *stop!*" I shouted.

Ava followed my command immediately. The magic subsided, and the warmth returned as the storm dissipated. Everything went back to normal, but the plants and animals she killed remained motionless, and the rocks lay shattered only a few feet away.

"I'm sorry. I— I didn't mean to," Ava stammered. "I didn't realize how much I was taking. It felt so easy."

"You're more powerful than I anticipated, which makes me think this isn't an Anichi power," Sophia mused. "I believe this is a demigod power connected to your abilities— something that only *you* can do."

"I don't understand," Ava said. "If you and Daddy can draw from the sun and the moon, why can't *all* Anichi do this?"

"They should be able to, but not to this extent," Sophia said. "Other Anichi can pull from Earth's spirit for energy, but it seems you have no limit. If that's the case... you could manipulate the Earth's soul beyond what any supernatural could ever dream of before."

"You could use the Earth's energy to heal *itself*," Liam said in wonder.

"What does that mean?" Ava asked. "This spirit energy is everywhere, so if what you're saying is true, I could use it to heal the entire planet— not just rocks and trees, but the souls of people at large, the collective energy of the universe... everything we are."

"It appears so," Sophia said.

"If I can do that, then I can heal the Warden's heart. I can heal the bastard, so he stops being a giant dickhead and starts striving for peace! Nobody else needs to die!" Ava insisted. "We could bring an end to this war! I need to at least *try*."

Ava didn't wait for permission. The magic around us grew in intensity again.

Nerves shuddered through my body, because I didn't think she understood just how powerful she was. It was dangerous to pursue a theory like this without properly testing it first. She could end up destroying everything, like she had my organs— only there wouldn't be anything left to put together again.

I felt myself pull back, resisting her magic. "Ava, you need to stop before someone gets hurt. We don't know what kind of consequences this could have."

"Either I heal the Warden, or he destroys us all," Ava insisted. "This *has* to work."

"Ava, don't—" Liam cried, but he didn't get the words out before a massive blast of energy blew us back. It was like a slap in the face, and knocked me off my feet. Liam and Sophia fell down too, and I struggled to get back up as the pulsing waves subsided.

I felt Ava's entire body slump as she said in defeat, "I can't get to him. It's like he's blocking me off."

"Because healing magic needs *consent*, Ava, like we talked about earlier," Sophia said sternly. "You can't heal the heart of everyone on this planet, especially not people who don't *want* to be healed."

I scoffed, because she was absolutely right. The Warden had no desire to stop killing people and become a good person. He didn't want to be healed. He was perfectly fine having a dark heart, going around committing evil deeds for as long as he could. Even if Ava could fix him, he wouldn't want her to.

"Let's try on a smaller scale," Liam suggested. "Try healing the plants you nearly killed."

"All right," Ava agreed. "At least it's something."

Ava tried again. Wilted plants sprang upright again, swaying in the breeze like she'd never stolen their power in the first place, and the bent trees righted themselves.

I felt her healing magic brush up against me, but a part of me was scared how easily she'd done all that. Ava didn't have Earth magic. She shouldn't be able to revive the plants— yet she'd tapped into their spirits and done something I'd never witnessed before. It wasn't just scary. It was unnatural beyond belief, and I was momentarily stunned at just how powerful my wife was.

I resisted her magic, and that proved to be a dark mistake. My skin began to sag on my cheeks. My limbs became heavy, and my joints ached.

Sophia gasped and rushed to me. "Charlie, what's happening?!"

The more I resisted Ava's magic, the more it felt like years were being shaved off my life. That only made me more terrified, and I pulled away more. I tried to tell Ava to stop, but I couldn't find the words.

Eddie rushed forward. "Princess! As the Guard to the Emperor's Heir, I demand you stop at once. You're hurting him!"

Ava shifted, and she gasped when she saw what she was doing to me. She pulled back instantly, and I sagged raggedly against the ground. The pain ebbed out of my joints, and my skin smoothed back into place. My whole body shook.

Ava's voice wavered. "I don't understand. I didn't draw enough magic to hurt anyone that time. That shouldn't have happened."

"I resisted you," I admitted, still trying to catch my breath. "It's not going to work— this healing thing. Like your mom said, you need consent. You could've kept going and destroyed me, but if you're going to heal, you need everyone on board. It's like you said; the spirit of the Earth wants to work in collaboration."

"But why do I need consent to heal, but not *take*?" she questioned. "That doesn't seem right. I don't need consent to pull from the Earth's soul and take her energy, but I need it to actually do any good."

"The Earth's soul is connected to everyone, including you," Sophia said. "You aren't just pulling from the Earth's spirit, you *are* the Earth, and so are all of us. You don't need consent to draw from yourself."

"But if everyone just got on board, and let me help them, we could stop all the bad stuff in the world!" Ava protested.

"That's not how it works, peanut," Liam said. "You need to work together with people, not force them to make the right choices."

"I understand that," Ava insisted, but I wasn't sure she did. Ava would continue to push the limits, and I feared what would happen if she went too far. She could kill herself if this spell got out of control.

"Perhaps that's enough practice for today," Sophia said hastily. "We should let Ava rest. She cast a lot of magic this afternoon."

"You've learned a lot in one session, peanut," Liam added. "You don't want to overextend yourself."

We all left the gardens. Sophia and Liam went on ahead, while Eddie and Eldin hung back a bit. I pushed Ava's chair forward, and Oberi landed on the back of it.

Ava huffed. "I don't know why we need to stop. I'm not tired at all. My parents don't think I can *handle* it."

I'm certain they're just trying to keep you safe, Oberi said. *They don't understand how powerful you really are. Magic like that would've killed both of them, and they're talented supernaturals.*

"We need to be careful," I added. "This kind of magic isn't something you can just play with."

"I know that," Ava snapped.

"No, Ava, I don't think you do," I pressed. I stopped her chair and rounded to the front of it to kneel beside her. I needed her to *really* listen to what I had to say, because she'd scared me today. "This power might feel like nothing to you because you can handle it, but it's important to recognize your own strength. This is an incredible ability you have, and you can't let it get out of control. You keep saying you understand, but you don't know how far you could take this. None of us do. We have to be careful, so you don't exceed your limits."

Ava rested her hand on mine. "I know you're scared, Charlie, but I'm not. I have this gift for a reason, and I will *always* use it to help people. If I'm meant to heal the Earth, then that's what I'm going to do. When the time is right and I'm strong enough to pull this spell off, I'm *going* to cast it, and heal everyone at once. We all have the option to choose bad decisions, but I'm not going to do that. I'll use this ability for good, and only good. I promise."

Ava was firm in her conviction, which told me she believed every word she said. She was certain she was going to use this power to help the world.

Though what I feared most was this ability getting out of hand, because if Ava lost control of this magic, she could destroy it. This kind of power had personal consequences for everybody.

So I had to do my best to keep her magic reigned in. At any cost.

ava-marie

SIXTEEN

When my eyes opened on October eleventh, one thing crossed my mind.

Holy shit. I'm getting married today.

I was already married, but... I was having an actual *wedding*. Not something I'd chosen at the last minute, not a choice to save Charlie's life, but a real commitment. One that I was going to make in front of the whole world.

The thought made a pit of anxiety grow and tighten within my stomach, and I didn't know why. I took a deep breath to try and settle it, but it didn't go away. Oberi stirred on the bed, shifting into a phoenix as she looked at me curiously.

The bedroom door *banged* open, and Kallie cheered, "Wake up, bitch! It's time to get married!"

Opal and Ivy came romping in, cheering behind her. I rubbed my eyes and sat up. I'd spent the night in a bedroom inside the Ladies' Court. I'd been out like a light, but now that I was awake, I immediately felt strange. I tried to place the feeling, but found that I couldn't give it any words. My failure to understand what I was going through only made my worry grow.

"You okay?" Opal asked, and she paused to take in my expression. "You look pale."

I swallowed a lump in my throat. "I just need some makeup. Let's go."

I got into the robe that I'd received at my bachelorette party, and my friends and I traveled to the palace temple together. Oberi flew overhead, cooing a wedding song. Before I could start getting ready I had to partake in rituals, both Elvish and Hawkei, to prepare me as a bride. These rituals would take place in the temple pool, in a room off of the main sanctuary and removed from the main chapel.

Charlie's half of our bond was quiet. We'd promised each other we wouldn't communicate at all until the ceremony started, but damn if it wasn't hard to reach out to him right now. It was weird for my head not to be filled with his thoughts. It felt strangely quiet.

When I got to the magic pool within the temple, my mother, Grandmother Eleanor, and the Great Mystic were standing beside its waters. Kallie, Ivy, Opal and Abigail were nearby. Everyone wore huge smiles, though I found I had to force mine.

What was wrong with me?

"Isn't this wonderful?" Mama gushed, like she'd been dreaming about this day since I'd been born. "You're finally getting married."

"Indeed. I never thought I'd live to see the day," a soft, warm voice said as quiet footsteps approached from behind me.

My heart lifted, for I knew that voice. Grandma Haloke had arrived, looking exactly as I remembered. Her long hair hung over her shoulder in a braid, and she still carried herself proudly, wearing Grandpa Liwanu's shawl around her shoulders.

"Grandma," I said, and I reached out to embrace her. "I'm so happy you came." I hadn't seen her in such a long time. I knew she'd come to Ilamanthe recently, but I hadn't been able to visit her.

This was the first time she'd seen me in a wheelchair. I worried she'd get upset, or look bothered, but she treated me the same as ever. I was grateful she didn't bring it up— I didn't want to relive what had happened, especially on a day like today.

"I wouldn't miss this wedding even if the ancestors forbade me to come," Grandma Haloke replied. "Eleanor and I made you a very special present."

"Yes," Grandmother Eleanor said with a twinkle in her eye. "You'll see it during the ceremony."

"I can't peek now?" I complained.

"It would ruin the surprise," Grandma Haloke said, appearing quite mischievous. People said I looked like her when I was concocting up a villainous plan, and I certainly could see it. She got the same smirk I did when she was plotting something. Though she was a Water elemental, I was sure some of the fire inside of me had come from her. She'd raised dragons for a living, after all.

Beside Grandma Haloke was her daughter. Jackie was my dad's sister, and technically my aunt. But she was only a year or so older than me, and we'd grown up together. She was more like my cousin than anything else. I knew her as Jackson growing up, but seeing her now, I knew she was always meant to be Jackie. Her hair was long, past her hips now, and she had the most elaborate cheekbones that I would *die* to have. She was even taller and thinner than I remembered. A model if there ever was one.

"Prison life did wonders for you. You look great," Jackie teased. "Maybe I should do a few years behind bars and work on my complexion."

Prison was no place for a girl like Jackie. I'd seen how the inmates had treated Ivy, and my friend was tough. My cousin didn't need to experience anything like that. Jackie deserved to be loved and accepted everywhere she went.

"Please," I said flatly. "Nothing could make you more beautiful than you already are. You've always been prettier than me."

"Nonsense. *All* of my children and grandchildren are beautiful," Grandma Haloke scolded.

"Well..." Grandmother Eleanor said, fluffing her hair. "You *are* beautiful, Haloke, there is no doubt about that, but I do believe that Ava-Marie takes after her mother. Sophia is quite gorgeous."

That was a round-about way of Grandmother Eleanor congratulating herself on passing down good genes, but nobody called it out— save for Mama, who dared to roll her eyes.

"Should we get started?" the Great Mystic asked, and the ceremony commenced. I wheeled myself to the very edge of the pool and looked down, taking in my reflection in the water.

Ancestors. I hoped no one else could see how scared I looked. My eyes seemed terrified.

"This is a great day for our people," the Great Mystic said, gesturing to the pool. "You will finally be joined with the prince in the way of our goddesses. Let us prepare you for the ceremony."

I gave no response, because once the ceremony began, I didn't feel like I could talk— my voice felt strangled in my throat. I simply slipped my robe off my shoulders and handed it to Ivy.

Underneath the robe, I wore a short Elvish slip in silver that was stitched with intricate designs of Elvish love knots. It was styled after the gown Caralyn donned before the night of her wedding to the goddess Idril, and was something every Elvish bride wore for her pre-wedding ritual. My friends placed me into the water, and the silver slip became soaked as I submerged myself into the pool.

"The night Idril fell in love with Caralyn, she came upon her bathing in a pool," the Great Mystic began. "From now until the time you are wed, these rituals will be a symbol for the love story Idril and Caralyn experienced, until they joined as one."

"This ritual also prepares your soul and body for the joining with the Great Spirit," Mama reminded me. "Today, you become a bride not just for Charlie, but for Him."

I took a deep breath. There was so much symbolism and sacredness in these ceremonies. They meant a lot to everyone, not just me. I wanted to prepare myself for this wedding the right way, so I could be sure I didn't let the gods down. This ceremony wasn't just about me and Charlie. It was about the Elvish people, and the Hawkei, and was a beacon of hope for everyone who lived in Ilamanthe.

As I sat in the water, the Great Mystic poured a vial of liquid gold into it, making the water shimmer. "The union between the Elvish goddesses is the joining of the masculine energy, and the feminine energy. Idril is a goddess, but this gold symbolizes her masculine power, the heat of the sun. Idril is a deity of war, strength, protection, and courage. She leads Caralyn and guides her to become all she can be."

The Great Mystic picked up another vial, one of liquid silver, and poured it into the other side of the pool, until the gold and silver were mixing together and swirling within the water. "In response, this silver, reflecting the glow of the moon, represents Caralyn's feminine magic," the Great Mystic said. "Caralyn gives Idril a safe, empathetic space where her spouse may rest and heal. She provides compassion, nurturing, creativity and love. When these two sides intertwine, they create a divine marriage. Like Idril and Caralyn, you and the prince must combine the masculine and the feminine into a singular being, one soul that can see the world through different perspectives, within one heart."

I understood. In Hawkei lore, the Sun was always chasing the Moon, as he was in love with her, but she was forever out of his reach. To be with her, the Sun had created gods and goddesses out of himself, and the Moon had responded in kind, so aspects of their souls could be reunited throughout the universe. I knew this wedding was a reenactment of that feminine and masculine energy today.

"Love has the power to induce great and wondrous change," the Great Mystic continued. "Idril's deep love for Caralyn changed her from a human to an Elven goddess, so they could live together in eternity. Charlie's love for you has transformed you into an Elf, and we have accepted you as one of our people. Allow his love to change you into a better person, as your love will change him."

I nodded, and the liquid metals glistened across my skin. Charlie had changed me— for the better, and for the worse. I was a different person than I had been before I met him; hell, even before I *married* him. I knew as time passed our relationship would continue to change and morph me, because I'd never stay the same person. I wouldn't be able to. I'd always have to keep growing, learning and shifting, and he'd do the same for me.

My mother, Jackie, and both of my grandmothers entered the water. This was the Hawkei part of the ceremony, and therefore, only Hawkei women participated. Each of them wore simple white dresses, and they surrounded me in a circle. I used my Toaqua magic to float my body upward, and laid back upon the surface as Grandma Haloke began to sprinkle oils of lavender and white sage upon my wet hair. She worked her fingers into my locks, washing the tendrils.

"All gods and goddesses are born from the Great Spirit," Grandma Haloke began. "This ancient Hawkei ceremony prepares you as a bride by washing your hair, the most sacred part of your spirit, cleansing your soul and providing blessings by the women of the tribe. Ava-Marie, I call upon Whale Spirit to bless you with courage. May she enable you to be brave— not only as a princess — but as a wife. Marriage requires courage, and facing your fears even as you want to run from them. I pray that you will be brave enough to battle whatever comes, and hold your ground as you fight by your husband's side."

"I'll be brave," I promised. This world could do its best to take Charlie from me, and I'd never let them do it. I'd fight until the very end for him, and even long after.

She moved aside. Jackie took her place, massaging the oils into my hair. "Ava-Marie, I call upon Eagle Spirit to provide you with virtue. Sometimes in relationships, temptation comes to play dirty. It makes you desire to hurt the one you love, if only because they've hurt you first. But forgiveness will bridge a way to healing, and being virtuous will help you to remember that despite pain, love endures... if you're willing to give it a second chance."

The lump in my throat got even bigger, and I wasn't able to respond. I knew marriage sometimes required you to forgive, even when forgiveness could be the most painful thing in the world to grant. But Charlie was worth it, and if I forgave him for whatever mistakes came down the line, he'd forgive me, too. We'd work together to create a better future for the both of us, not just ourselves. I would be tempted to strike out at Charlie if he hurt me, and he'd feel the same. But even if we slipped up, we'd find our way back to each other eventually, because we always did. Nothing we could do to each other would ever make us depart from this marriage. No matter what, we'd forgive each other, and move forward.

No one noticed me choke up, and Grandmother Eleanor came to wash my hair beside Jackie.

"I call upon Coyote Spirit to help you be clever," she began. "In marriage, you must not only pick your battles, but be smart enough to outwit whatever may come to challenge your love. Cleverness will enable you to make the best choices for your family. It will help you gain good standing in your community, destroy your enemies, and will keep your husband on the right path."

"Mother," Mama hissed under her breath, and I giggled. Everyone knew that Grandmother Eleanor had no problem keeping my grandfather in line.

"Charlie will be an Emperor, and you are his bride. It will be up to you to steer his decisions, which will ultimately affect thousands of lives," Grandmother Eleanor said, ignoring what my mother had whispered. "Cleverness will help you decide what outcome will be the best one. Not just for others, but for you. Be cunning. It may be what saves your marriage one day, when calamity comes to call and strength is not enough."

"I'll be cunning, Grandmother," I told her. "You know I always have been, and will continue to be."

As she moved back, my mother came close. She began washing my hair lovingly, and it reminded me of how she used to braid my hair when I was a little girl. Her soft, gentle motions made tears come to my eyes with the memory of how life used to be. That was all gone now. I wasn't a child anymore, and nothing could ever bring those times back. But though I was grown, I couldn't be more grateful, because my mother was by my side.

"Ava-Marie, you came from my womb. I birthed you into this world, and now, I place you into the arms of another," Mama said. "I call upon Phoenix Spirit, the goddess of Anichi, to bless you with the gift of renewal and reincarnation. Throughout your marriage, you will find that you and your husband will be born anew. There will come a time when he will no longer be the man you married, nor you the woman he wed. But no matter what circumstances you find yourself in, love can always start again. Rebirth is essential to a marriage, because both of you will reincarnate into new forms again and again, especially in times of pain and loss. Rise from the ashes, and each time you do, rise closer together."

I let out a sob, and tears trickled out of my eyes and into the water. I'd managed to hold it together this long, but I couldn't manage when my mother spoke. The tears demanded to come, because she was right. Charlie and I had changed so many times over the past two years, and though those transformations had been painful, they'd brought us closer together. I knew I wouldn't be the same woman fifty, twenty, or even five years from now, and Charlie wouldn't be the same man. But that wouldn't matter, because I'd continue to fall in love with him all over again, and he'd fall in love with me, too, no matter who or what I became. With this wedding, we were promising to grow together, and that's exactly what we would do.

When my mother was done washing my hair, she and the other women left the pool. I floated back upward into a sitting position, and my friends approached, kneeling at the pool's edge. Kallie, Ivy, Opal and Abigail sat in a circle around me, each of them holding a flower in their hands as they began the Elvish part of the ceremony.

"Before her wedding, Caralyn's friends came to sprinkle her with flower petals, and create magic that would strengthen her bond with Idril," Kallie began. She cast white rose petals into the water. "The fae goddess of time blesses you, Ava. My mother Neva looks upon this day favorably, and gives you the gift of long days. May you and Charlie grow old together, and as the years pass, may you never separate. The most valuable lesson I've learned as a woman is that the bonds we make aren't so easily broken. In the fae tradition, you are becoming a woman today, so let your bond with Charlie last no matter what time may bring."

I'd never felt more appreciated, or loved, than when Kallie laid the blessing upon me. My soul felt like it was buzzing, nearly ready to lift out of my body and float upon the air. Our eyes connected, and in that moment, Kallie and I shared something special— something I knew that even Charlie and I couldn't mimic, a connection that was just as deep and profound as any soul bond. She was my best friend, and I knew I could count on her to support my marriage and advocate for Charlie and me. Even if hard times came, Kallie would be there to help us stay strong, and tell me not to give up on him. Marriage wasn't just about the blending of two people, but the unity of one community. We loved each other, but Charlie and I couldn't do this alone. We needed support to stay married and be happy, and Kallie was offering that help to us if and when we required it. I'd never had a more faithful, more loving friend, and I adored the ancestors for sending her to me.

Opal approached, dropping hibiscus leaves into the water. "Within the gods of merfolk lore, there is Mytera, the goddess of motherhood. Ava, like me, you are a mother. You may not have a child as I do, but you care for and love everyone you meet, regardless of who they are or what they've done. You take care of your friends, and look out for them as a mother would. Because you are a mother to all, Mytera will watch over you and any children that you have, whether they are born from your body or simply from your heart. As you watch over others, Charlie will watch over you, protecting you with his body and providing whatever you may need or ask for. As you've decided and desired, he is your head of household, and I ask Mytera to give you the guidance you need to follow his leadership with faith, trust, and love. He will be your safe place, and it is you who will make his house a home."

I gave her an anxious smile, because all this talk of motherhood was a little nerve-wracking, even if she didn't mean it like that. But Opal was right. I *was* a mother, because despite not having any children, I cared for my friends like they were my own. I had to look out for everyone and make sure they were okay, putting others before myself no matter what. That was just the kind of person I was. I wanted to make sure everyone I loved was happy and safe, even if it cost me something. That kind of sacrifice could be draining sometimes, because I often forgot about myself in the end. But I didn't have to do it alone, because Charlie would be there to give me whatever I was lacking. I looked out for everyone else, but he looked out for me. He'd helped me handle my bipolar, tended to me after my spinal injury, and watched out for me every day, even when I was sick of managing myself. He took care of me gently, and always would until the moment I died. I knew that without a doubt. My heart swelled as I thought of how much my dom loved me, and I wanted to please him by following his lead until the end of my days.

Ivy stood at the edge of the pool, clutching the flower petals in their hand tightly. It almost looked like they were considering something deep— a decision was being weighed in their mind, one to speak up or back down.

Then Ivy tossed the petals in and said, "Look, the vampires only have one god, and we don't really follow him. Uraeus ain't really a god of weddings, more of a god of destruction, but you know what? Who needs him."

Ivy straightened their shoulders. "Precious, *my* blessing is better than any gift any god could give you. I'm right here, right in front of your eyes, and I ain't going anywhere. I'll be here to protect you, and protect your marriage for as long as you wanna be with him. I bless you with passion and desire. I pray that you will follow your heart and honor the longings of your body, that you will follow your darkest impulses and most secret inclinations, no matter how wicked they might be. These flower petals I dropped in? They're cardinal flowers, and they're rumored to bring love to the lives of elderly ladies. Cause I hope that even when you're ninety, you and Charlie are still having the same crazy, kinky and devoted sex you're enjoying now. I love you, precious. Don't forget that, because I'm always gonna be here, no matter who stays or who goes."

"Thank you, Ivy," I whispered. I felt reassured by their promise, because I knew I could always count on them. When I had been at the lowest point of my life, Ivy had been there. I wouldn't be getting married today without Ivy's support. They were the reason Charlie and I had made it this far, and the reason my husband and I were getting along so well. Without Ivy's guidance and love, my marriage wouldn't have made it. I wouldn't be with the man I loved if Ivy hadn't been there to bestow their wisdom and give me their shoulder to grieve on when my world was falling apart. They taught me how to love myself first, and for that, I was eternally grateful.

I heard the rushing beat of wings, and Oberi landed beside the pool. She dipped her beak into the water. The effect made ripples as she said, *I provide you with the blessings and the protection of the mutabeecha. The companions of the Great Spirit, beings who exist outside the boundaries of time and space, are here with you now. May they surround you, and may the sanctity of their connection keep you and Charlie intertwined, as my existence, and heart, binds you together as one.*

Several people gasped, and my eyes widened as the water around me began to *glow*. A white sheen spread throughout the room, the light reflecting off the ceiling and bouncing off the stained glass. I lifted my hand and saw that my body was glowing, too, a dazzling halo erupting off my golden skin.

When Oberi withdrew her beak, the glow subsided. She blinked at me with her pretty black eyes. *I will do my best to love you and keep the two of you safe. As a Familiar, my duty is to enable the two of you to have a relationship that is strong, intimate, and kind. It is all I can do, and all that I desire from my life.*

I started crying again— because, you know, how *was* I supposed to keep it together when my Familiar performed beautiful magic like that? Even if the entire world fell apart, and Charlie and I didn't know how to start again, or had forgotten how to love, Oberi would always be there to bring us back together. She bound us as one, and the connection between the three of us was powerful and deep. Nothing would separate us, now and forevermore.

The Great Mystic spread primrose flowers over my body, which fell upon my wet hair. "With the completion of this ceremony, I complete the rite that transforms our bride into Caralyn, so she may wait for our prince, her Idril. Arise from this pool, and become the goddess."

My friends lifted me out of the water, and I dried off using my Toaqua magic. As they placed me back into my chair, I felt renewed and invigorated— like I was a different woman than I'd been before going into the water with all the blessings my friends and family had bestowed upon me.

Even so, the disquiet burning in my chest remained with me. Oberi cocked her head, like she felt it and didn't understand.

"Now that the rites are over, we must hurry, princess," the Great Mystic said. "There is much to do before the ceremony."

"Yay! Now for the fun part," Opal gushed.

When we got to the bridal suite where I was supposed to get ready, we found a whole waffle bar with mimosas ready for us. I was almost too nervous to eat, but I managed to have a small breakfast before the stylists got started on my hair. They fashioned it so it was falling free down my back in big, beautiful curls. It took over an hour to do my makeup, because I was very specific on having glittering silver eyeshadow, winged eyeliner, and a nude mauve lip gloss, with a dusting of glitter over my cheekbones. I did *not* lay on a spa table for three hours last week getting lash extensions for them to go to waste, after all. My choice of manicure for the wedding was an almond-shaped nail with sparkling diamond tips and a thin, gold French edge. When in Ilamanthe, be extravagant.

Around two o'clock, Elrye strode in. She was the official planner for the royal wedding, and appeared horrified that I was still in my robe. "The wedding is soon to start, and the princess is not in her dress! What is the bride *doing?*" she yelped.

"*Helping everyone else!*" several people cried out at once.

It was true. After getting my hair and makeup, I'd fashioned Ivy's hair, put on Opal's makeup, and was currently zipping Kallie into her dress.

I froze as Elrye scowled, crossing her arms. "Princess, this is *your wedding*, not everyone else's. May I remind you that *you* come first?"

"Sorry!" I turned my chair around and hurried away. I couldn't help it if I wanted my friends to look pretty, too. As I headed to change, my bridesmaids were running around the room, chatting loudly, eating snacks and hurrying to yank on their dresses. All of my bridesmaids were wearing long black gowns, the bodice embroidered with pink flowers— everyone, save for Kallie. As my maid of honor, she wore a special off-the-shoulder black dress with see-through, long lace sleeves and a skirt that draped behind her when she walked. Each of my bridesmaids wore floral crowns of twisted branches, decorated with dark green leaves and small pink and white flowers.

My mother and I went behind a large curtain in the bridal suite, to conceal the dress until the big reveal to my friends once it was on. The Elves had a special wheelchair made for my wedding day— it was painted white, and adjustable, with removable handles and armrests. The back of the chair was folded down, and the seat attached on top of it, so the skirt of the ballgown could fall over the sides and the wheels. When I sat on the chair, it didn't appear that I was in a wheelchair at all, merely sitting down. I couldn't really move around when the chair was like this— only stay in one place. It would be like this during the ceremony, then for the reception, the chair would be adjusted again with all the parts reattached so I could move around.

I bounced my hands up and down on the fluffy skirt, examining the layers of tulle. I was in my perfect pink dress. No turning back now.

I couldn't really wear heels anymore, because they put my legs in an awkward position in my chair, and put more pressure on my hips than I would've liked. My feet had also developed a more pronounced arch since I'd been paralyzed, so it was a pain in the ass to find heels that fit, anyhow. Instead, I wore dusty pink pointed flats with rhinestone embellishments and big bows on the heels.

Finally, my mother placed a dazzling veil into my hair, at the back of my head. The edge of the veil was bordered with diamonds, embroidered apple blossom petals spreading throughout the piece. It was long, cathedral length. I was counting on my bridesmaids to make sure it didn't get tangled up in my wheels at any time during the ceremony.

"You're dazzling, Ava," Mama said softly as she took me in, brushing my curls back as tears welled in her eyes. "The perfect look for a bride."

I swallowed thickly. "Is it normal for me to be this... nervous?"

"I suppose it depends," Mama mused. "Do you know what you're nervous about?"

"Not really," I confessed. "I know I want to do this, and I want to be married to Charlie. I want the big wedding, and I want to celebrate our love."

"But?" Mama asked softly.

"But..." I sighed. "I'm so afraid. I *know* this is the right choice, but it's like my ego is telling me not to take the chance... because if I'm in love, there's a risk I could get hurt."

I could articulate some of my feelings now, because I'd been thinking about them all morning. Charlie had hurt me once before. What if he did so again? I didn't think that would happen, but I was also afraid of proclaiming my love to him in front of the world, then running the risk of being told I was wrong. My intuition told me he was the only man I would ever love, but what if my intuition sent me astray?

"Don't let your anxiety talk you out of taking a wonderful leap of faith," Mama said, and she kissed my cheek. "Sometimes, it's the most terrifying thing in the world, to follow our hearts and do what we know we've been fated to do. Do you believe you and Charlie are destined to be together?"

I nodded. "Absolutely. There's no doubt."

"Then love him no matter what comes," Mama encouraged, squeezing my shoulders. "A long time ago, your grandmother told me the more I opened up to your father, the more he would open up to me. It'll be the same for you and Charlie. If you open up to him, and give him your heart freely, you can trust that he'll keep it safe. Keeping your heart closed and trying to protect yourself isn't going to prevent you from experiencing pain, my daughter. In fact, it's more painful to *be* alone. Closing him off will hurt him just as much as it'll hurt you. Even if someone you love does something to shatter your heart, what matters is if he'll be there to pick up all the pieces, and mend them together again. I know Charlie is that person for you. All you have to do is believe it for yourself, and trust that if pain comes, it'll pass to transform into happiness again."

I nodded. "I understand. You're so wise, Mama."

"Wisdom gained from being married to your father all these years," she quipped. She grabbed the curtain and said, "Now, are you ready?"

I nodded. When the curtain was pulled back, my bridesmaids immediately started crying.

"Oh, precious, you look so lovely!" Ivy wept, and they dotted at their eyes with a handkerchief before giving me a hug. Other girls swarmed around me, weeping and saying how spectacular I looked.

I knew I'd never appeared so divine. My gown made me feel powerful, strong, and beautiful. Even though my emotions were fighting me, I warred back, because I refused to allow my anxiety and fear to ruin this incredible day.

The time for the ceremony was getting closer. As the bridesmaids rushed to grab their bouquets, Kallie took my hands and squeezed them. "Ava, that dress describes every part of who you are. You've definitely found your place in the world since becoming a princess."

"I hope so." I gave a troubled sigh. "I just hope I don't mess this up."

Kallie's eyebrows knitted together in concern. "Are you getting cold feet?"

"No," I said, but it felt like a lie. "I mean, I don't know. Something feels *off*."

I nearly tangled a hand in my hair, until I remembered that we'd *just* gotten it perfect, so I forced my hand to remain in my lap.

"Everyone out! Give the princess some time to relax before we begin!" Elrye cried. "The ceremony will commence in a half-hour. Places, everyone!"

My bridesmaids rushed out of the suite. Kallie stayed behind and squeezed my hands again. "Whatever happens, today, tomorrow, or in the future, you're going to be okay. Any decision you make, right or wrong, is going to lead you to be the woman you're going to become. Charlie loves you more than life itself, and I know you feel the same way about him. There's nothing to worry about, not when you two have been through hell and back and come back stronger every time. If there's anything you two have taught me, it's that love always wins."

I felt the tension in my gut lessen significantly. "You're right, Kallie. Thank you for being here."

"You're welcome." Kallie's face became troubled as she added, "Even though I feel like I'm taking Monica's place, in a spot that was meant for her. I'm sorry she's not with you today, because she should be."

"You're not replacing anyone. You're uplifting and supporting me," I said firmly. "I know Monica is here in spirit, but she can't be here for me today like you can, not in the same way. And I miss her today... more than I've ever missed her in my entire life."

My voice cracked, because it was true. I knew part of the reason I felt so awful is because it was unfair Monica wasn't here today. I'd had to rush into the bathroom after my hair was styled to break down and cry, because I missed her so much. It was *so fucking wrong* she wasn't here, because I wanted her at my side more than anything on my wedding day. I wanted to watch her expression as I showed her my dress, see her tears as I came down the aisle, reach out to touch her as I adjusted her bridesmaid crown. I was mad at the ancestors, the gods, and the universe for stealing her away, because she should be here.

She wasn't. Yet Kallie was. I found tears welling up in my eyes as I added, "But I know that she sent you to me, and I couldn't ask for a better friend in the entire world. I loved Monica so much... but I'm starting to realize that I love you even more. I couldn't marry Charlie without you, and wouldn't want to. Charlie's my twin flame, but you're my soulmate. I couldn't think of anyone better to stand in her place."

Tears beaded the corners of her eyes. "Oh, Ava." Kallie hugged me, and I embraced her back. "If I could pick anyone in the world to have by my side for the rest of my life, it would be you."

"Always." Even if, ancestors forbid, something happened to Charlie and the whole world withered away, I had a chance to get by, so long as Kallie was there to hold my hand.

I held Kallie close, until she drew away and said, "I have to meet up with Marcus. Cross your fingers that the best man didn't lose the rings."

"Unlikely." I laughed. Kallie placed a loving kiss on the top of my head before she wandered out.

Oberi was the only one still in the room with me, resting on a perch near a wardrobe. Oberi hadn't said much all day, merely observed the routine of the bridal suite with interest. She hadn't even eaten, which was so unlike her.

Oberi, help me, I thought. *I don't know what to do.*

She ruffled her feathers. *Love persists in spite of conflict.*

What does that mean?

It is possible to contradict yourself, Oberi pointed out. *You can feel multiple things at once, things that are true, and untrue. What you want and what you fear are at odds, and you need to choose a side on what to believe in.*

But I don't know *what's true. The feelings are too complicated,* I thought in frustration. *I don't want to feel like this on my wedding day.*

What does your intuition say?

I tried to swallow the massive lump in my throat again, and failed. *I don't know. Everything seems so loud. I can't distinguish between what's my anxiety, or what's intuition, and trying to decide what to listen to is only making my fear worse.*

Your intuition will never lie to you, Ava. Intuition is quiet, and can be ignored if you so choose. Most likely, your intuition will only say something once, and you know it like a truth in your heart. Anxiety cannot be ignored. It keeps worrying endlessly on a wheel until you are forced to pay attention to it. When your intuition tells you something, even if it is upsetting news, you won't feel pain, but rather, will be at peace. And peace is not the feeling anxiety provides.

Well, I definitely don't feel peaceful now. I wish Charlie were here. What do you think he'd say?

Oberi preened her feathers. *Why don't you ask him yourself?*

He'd opened the door so quietly I hadn't even heard him come in. I felt the color drain from my cheeks as I saw Charlie standing six feet away from me.

Ancestors, he looked so handsome. His tailored suit, dress shirt and tie were all a shade of deep black, his hair slicked back. It reminded me of how he'd looked the night of the Villain's Ball, and the memory nearly swept me away.

He was so... perfect.

But I wasn't supposed to be looking at him, not for another half hour.

"Charlie, what are you doing here?!" I hissed. I couldn't believe he'd snuck into the bridal suite.

He didn't budge an inch. "I knew you needed me, so I came."

"You're not supposed to see me before the wedding!" I said in despair.

Charlie smirked. "Well, I can't really *see* you."

"That's not the point," I grumbled. Now we were going to get bad luck for speaking before the ceremony. My nerves were right, and this wedding *was* cursed.

"I felt you freaking out all day. I tried not to engage, but it became impossible," Charlie said. "Something's on your mind. Let's talk this out."

I let out a great huff. "I *guess* we can talk. But don't touch my dress yet. It was supposed to be a surprise."

"What's this about?" Charlie took a seat across from me— close enough he could reach out and take my hand, but not get anywhere near my dress, thank you very much.

"I'm just... scared," I confessed.

"Scared of what?" Charlie pressed. "Is this too big of an event? I knew I should've told my grandpa to tone it down—"

"It's not that," I began. How did I get my meaning across without breaking his heart?

I didn't have to, because Charlie knew me so well that he guessed. "You're worried this is the wrong decision."

"Yes? No?" I wondered. "I don't know. It doesn't make sense to me."

I didn't understand why I felt so anxious. It wasn't like I didn't *want* to do this. I loved Charlie. I'd live for him— I'd *died* for him. Having this wedding should've been easy. For fuck's sake, we'd been legally married for a year already, and it had been wonderful. I didn't get why I was so scared to do this, scared to participate in a religious ceremony that, really, didn't change anything about the structure of our relationship.

But there was a terrible fear in the back of my mind that though this was a happy day, full of joy and love, it could eventually turn into something that I would regret.

Charlie moved closer to me. I did my best to scoot the edge of my dress away. "Pidge, if you don't want to do this, we can call everything off right now."

"No!" I insisted. "I want this... more than anything in the entire world. You're my husband. You're everything I could ever want."

"Then why are you so scared?"

"Because I'm afraid of what's coming," I said. "We don't know what's out there waiting for us. Marriage is supposed to be forever. What if something happens to tear us apart?"

"Then we'll fix it," Charlie replied simply.

"I'm not afraid of getting married. I'm afraid of losing you," I said, and my throat choked up. "We got married at the Institute, but that was a legal ceremony, not a religious one. What we're about to do is a vow to the ancestors and the goddesses. It secures our bond even more, so if we lose each other, it's going to be that much more devastating. I'm terrified to declare my love for you, because someone could come along and take you from me because of it."

"No one would ever do that, pidge," Charlie promised. "There isn't a god, demon, or man that could ever take me away from you."

"But what if something happens that we can't fix?"

"I don't think it's a *what if*, but when," Charlie said calmly. "People aren't perfect. We make mistakes— you and I make a lot of them. But we always come back from it, no matter who or what comes to challenge us. I'm not afraid of anything except facing this world without you."

My throat tightened at the confession, and I nearly started crying again, because that was exactly how I felt. "I'm not either. We can get through anything, as long as we're together. I want this wedding— I want *you*. I know I do."

"Then I'll be waiting for you at the end of the aisle." Charlie gave my hand one last squeeze before he stepped away. I counted his steps as he wandered out, already wanting to be at his side again. Oberi gave a soft coo as he left, but said nothing more.

I knew what I felt for Charlie couldn't be wrong if I desired him this badly. He left me alone in the room, and I turned so I was facing a floor-to-ceiling golden mirror mounted on the wall.

I observed myself and had the thought I'd never looked so pretty. I stared into my eyes, realizing this was one of the greatest moments of my life, a chapter that would mark where the rest of my existence would go. After waiting for all these years, I was actually a *bride*. It was insane to me. I had pictured this day in my mind for so long, and now, it was actually coming true. This felt like a dream I could wake up from any second.

As I took in my reflection, I realized I'd been letting my anxiety run the show, worrying myself with constant variables and *what ifs*. The story I was telling myself was overshadowing my love for Charlie, and I wouldn't let that happen anymore.

Intuition is quiet. Oberi's words came back to me, and I closed my eyes so I could just... feel.

There, underneath the worry and the fear of unexpected pain, was certainty. As I listened to my intuition, I felt an immensely deep sense of peace, and a complete knowing that this was the right choice. No matter how nervous I felt, or how many second thoughts I had, my intuition told me that this was what was always meant to be, and my fears were merely that... thoughts that couldn't harm me, unless I let them. My mother was right. Trying to protect myself from pain would only make the pain worse, and though I knew that pain would come, I was certain there'd be much more happiness to experience than there ever would be sadness.

No fear of the future, or of what may happen, would separate Charlie and me. Whatever happened, we'd figure it out, and we'd do it *together*. Even if one day something awful came to pass and I regretted the choice I made, this marriage still wouldn't be a mistake. We belonged to each other. I knew that in the deepest core of my soul. My gut wasn't telling me that this was wrong— it was telling me that this was *right*.

Now all I had to do was follow my intuition, and take a leap of faith.

I took a few, calming breaths, collected my thoughts, and straightened my shoulders. I was ready.

A few moments later, Hemlock wandered in. She was carrying a book from the temple, an old tome that had been passed down through the centuries to marry royals within the Elvish temple. She was wearing the silver robes of a mystic and appeared brilliant. The bruises on her face had healed, so she resembled the professor I once knew...

Almost.

As she stood before me, Hemlock took a breath. "Oh, my dear. You are the grandest princess I ever did see on her wedding day."

"Thanks." I gave a soft smile. "All ready to go?"

"I came by to check on you before we begin," Hemlock said. "Is there anything you need?"

"No." I shook my head. "Just ready to get this show on the road."

"Indeed." Hemlock took me in again, then unexpectedly began to weep. It was sudden and heartbreaking to hear, although the tears barely lasted a moment or two.

"Professor, is there something wrong?" I asked in alarm. I knew people cried at weddings, but this seemed... different.

"Don't worry about me, girl," Hemlock said quickly, wiping at her eyes. "Nothing but silly tears from an old woman. I won't bother you like this on your wedding day."

"It's not," I demanded. "What's wrong? I need to know you're okay."

Hemlock gave a quiet sniff. "It is merely... I wish my child had survived, so I could've seen her as a bride."

A piece of my heart broke off. "Your child?"

"Over twenty years ago, I lost my daughter. She was around your age when she died. She was a student at Arcanea University, where I taught alchemy and enchanting," Hemlock replied.

I felt that busted piece of my heart dissolve into dust at her pain. "What happened?"

"She became involved with the wrong people, unfortunately," Hemlock said sadly. "My mate was an Unseelie fae, and he was killed for the fae's hatred against all dark magic. Callista never got over her father's death. She sought revenge against those that had killed him, and wanted to bring equality to Malovia for all fae. But she tried to change the country through violence, and eventually, it cost Callista her life."

"That's truly awful. I'm so sorry for your loss," I said. Hemlock had lost her mate, and her daughter. I couldn't imagine how alone she felt.

"Callista wasn't a bad girl. Merely someone who desperately wanted to stop others from suffering. She thought the only way to change the world was by using force and pain," Hemlock stated heavily. "I tried to help her heal, but my actions weren't enough to stop her from meeting a horrible fate. After Callista's death, I realized that I had failed her."

"You could never fail her. You did all you could to help her get back on the right path," I insisted.

"But it wasn't enough," Hemlock replied. "I swore to myself if there *was* a child out there that I could save, a girl who had found herself on the wrong side of things but was looking for a way to make them right again, I'd be there for her. I would set her straight, and help her find her way in life before it was too late. I couldn't save Callista, but I could save someone else. That's why I came to the Darke Institute to teach. I wanted to help girls like Callista... help someone like you. You remind me a lot of her. I confess, Ava, when I think about my daughter, I see *you*."

A deep affection spread like warmth throughout my body, because I didn't know Hemlock felt that way about me. I realized we were close, but didn't know exactly what I meant to her until now.

"I know I can't replace what you lost," I said. "But I hope that reigning in my wild and crazy ways has given you a bit of comfort. You're the kind of teacher that *should* be instructing at a reform school. You actually care where kids end up. And you care about me— you cared even when I didn't care about myself, and it might've saved my life. So thank you for looking out for me and being there. Because even though I couldn't have my mother at the Institute, I knew that I always had you there."

Her face crumpled, and she raised her arms. Hemlock wasn't able to reply in words; all she could do was stoop down and give me a hug. I hugged her back, because I cared about her just as much as she cared about me.

"I'm so happy to be marrying you and Charlie all over again. You two always look like you're so in love," Hemlock said, wiping a tear away from her eye. "It's an honor to do this for you."

"I wouldn't want anyone else," I reassured her. "Thank you. For marrying me and Charlie, for watching out for me, protecting me... everything."

Hemlock cupped her hand to my cheek and whispered, "My dear, there is nothing you need to thank me for. Truly, I do not want you to feel regret for what I experienced at The Mission's hands. I was more than happy to do it, all for you."

Hemlock left then, because I don't think either of us could talk further without both of us breaking down. By this time, the ceremony was about to start. Oberi jumped off her perch and changed into a unicorn. As she did so, my father opened the massive double doors and stepped in.

Daddy's eyes widened, then immediately watered as he took me in. He spread his arms wide as he said, "Oh, baby. You look every part a princess."

"Thanks, Daddy." I embraced him, squeezing his broad shoulders tightly. "Tell me the truth. Do you *really* accept Charlie? Are you okay with me marrying him?"

"Of course I am, peanut," Daddy hushed. "I know there's no better man in the world for you than him. You love him, and he loves you. That's the only thing that matters."

"Will you be here for me, no matter what happens?" I asked. "Charlie and I can't do this alone. We need our families, and we need support."

"Every step of the way."

A rush of tears trailed down Daddy's cheeks. "I never thought I'd make it to this day. I thought... you know. But the ancestors answered my prayers."

I understood. He thought his disease would take him from me before he got to see me become a bride. But fate had smiled upon us and been kind. I thanked her for it, because I didn't think I could get married without my father by my side. I reached out to wipe his tears away, but as I did so, my magic froze the tears into ice.

I paused to observe them as the tears floated off of Daddy's face, hovering in the air in front of us. As I watched, I saw the ice crystallize, gleaming under the light. They'd solidified and turned solid— like diamonds.

The tears floated in the air at first, before they twirled downward and landed upon my skin. Threads of ice materialized between them and joined the tears together, forming a dazzling silver necklace. I touched the shimmering necklace and found that it was just as solid as something forged from metal and gems. This piece would be permanent— a creation of my demigod magic. I couldn't create illusions, but the power of my demigod abilities had forged my Spirit and Toaqua magic together to make something out of deep love.

Daddy's shock was clear on his face. "Your magic has no limits, does it?"

"I guess not." I touched the necklace with awe. "I didn't know I could do that. Now I'll get to wear your love whenever I need you there."

"It's a gift you'll have forever, even when I'm gone." Daddy's voice choked up, though he forced his way past the tears. "There's nothing you're incapable of, peanut. And I couldn't be any prouder than to call you my daughter."

Daddy stood and squeezed my hand. "Come on, peanut. Let's get you married."

Oberi walked to us. Daddy lifted me out of my chair and onto her back, so I was sitting side-saddle. He fitted a diamond bridle onto Oberi's face, then grabbed one of the reins to lead her out the double doors and to the hallway that connected to the temple. A servant came to take the bridal wheelchair to the altar, where it would be waiting for me.

By this point, the ceremony had started. All of the bridesmaids and groomsmen had walked down the aisle in pairs, except for Marcus and Kallie. I heard *Ave Maria* playing from the temple's interior behind the doors, and felt my stomach dip yet again— but this time, it was in excitement. I honestly couldn't wait to get out there.

Kallie draped my veil so it was hanging over Oberi's rump and trailing onto the floor, then placed a light purple bouquet into my hands. It was made of cascading clematis flowers, cut and arranged from the gardens that morning. Clematis flowers symbolized love that was unchanged throughout the passing of eternity, and I thought that was a wonderful flower for Charlie and me.

Plus, the lilac color went well with my pink dress.

Marcus' mouth was open as he took me in with a gaze of awe. "You look incredible."

"I sure hope so. This took all morning," I replied, smoothing down my dress and hoping everything stayed in place.

Marcus hooked his arm with Kallie's and brought her to his side so they could walk together. Neither one of them seemed weirded out by the close proximity. In fact, both of them gravitated closer. In their free hand, Kallie and Marcus were carrying framed photographs. Kallie had a picture of Monica— Marcus, of Marty.

It was a special thing Charlie and I had requested. We couldn't have Monica and Marty here with us today, but Kallie and Marcus had become what we'd needed in the darkest time of our lives. It was an honor for them to stand with us today.

Kallie and Marcus stepped through the double doors. My father, Oberi and I remained out of sight, so we wouldn't ruin the big reveal.

Eventually, we heard the song end, and a new one began— a piano ballad that Charlie and I had composed at the Institute together over a year ago. That was my cue.

"It's time," Daddy said. "Are you ready, Ava?"

I took a deep breath, gathered myself, and nodded. By participating in this ceremony, I was fulfilling my soul path and everything that had been planned for me. I felt certain of that. Now all that was left to do was become joined with my destiny.

I felt my breath sweep away as Oberi carried me into the temple's hall. My father walked at the unicorn's side, holding my hand as we journeyed down the aisle.

The temple was more elaborate than I'd ever seen it be. Burning white candles hovered in the air above the congregation, and the smell of incense, lavender, cinnamon, and sage levitated throughout the room. Pendant amaranth flowers in a dark pink color hung from the temple ceiling in the thousands.

Amaranth. The flower of love that endures despite great difficulty.

The temple was absolutely packed. There wasn't a seat left in the house. People gasped, and a few Elvish women wailed as they took in the sight of my dress. My eyes scanned the room quickly, my breath still caught in my throat. I saw so many faces I knew in a flash, smiling at me like I was the grandest thing in the world. All of my family members clustered together in the pews, looking thrilled.

I realized that time was passing too quickly, because we were already halfway down the aisle and I hadn't had any time to take it all in. Oberi noticed my thoughts and slowed her steps, so I could rejoice in the moment. I glanced toward the front of the room and nearly laughed as I saw our bridesmaids and groomsmen all lined up. Marcus, Ez, Chancey and Alistair were standing up front as groomsmen, Eddie was off to the side, serving as Charlie's guard. I tried to take in and memorize each of their expressions, but it was hard, because my heart was beating so fast and time was moving so quickly.

At the altar, a trellis had been set up. That trellis had been lined with greenery, white asphodel flowers scattered throughout the eucalyptus leaves.

Asphodel. The flower of love that survives even death.

The Emperor had been very adamant about every flower that we used in our wedding, insisting each bloom had to represent something important for our relationship. I'd figured we'd chosen well. The colors were no mistake, either— pink for romantic, youthful love, and black for the steadfastness and seriousness of the commitment we were making. Charlie and I were very certain of the choice we were making, and we wanted everyone to know that we considered it to be forever.

My eyes found my love. He was waiting at the altar for me, his hands clasped with a huge smile on his face. Time had moved so quickly just seconds before, but it suddenly stopped completely. The entire crowd fell away, until I was certain all that existed was just me and him. Nobody else mattered in this world but us, and he was the only person that was alive to me. My soul honed in on him, and I forgot that this wedding was happening at all, because the only center my universe needed was him.

The biggest grin that I'd ever seen him have spread across Charlie's face, and I saw two tears slip out of his eyes. He wiped his eyes quickly, the smile seemingly permanent on his face as Oberi finally stopped at the altar.

Daddy reached up to take me down from her back, and as he carried me, I whispered in his ear, "I love you, Daddy."

Another tear dropped down my father's face, and he set me into the bridal wheelchair. Kallie, Ivy, Abigail and Opal immediately went to adjusting my dress and veil around the chair, and when they were done, Kallie took my bouquet.

I figured Charlie was going to stand, but the groomsmen passed a silver chair down the line. Charlie set it across from me, sitting down so he was at my level, indicating the two of us were equals.

My eyes immediately welled with tears. I didn't know he was going to do that.

Charlie reached out to take my hands. Once he did, I immediately relaxed. I found that I could finally breathe.

There was nothing else to worry about. The waiting was over, and we were here, joined in this temple together. Now would be the best part.

My gaze traveled down to our entwined hands, settling on the date inscribed across our left ring fingers in black ink. *October 11*, the tattoos read. The font matched the names that were permanently inked across our wrists... his name on mine, my name on his. We'd had Marcus tattoo the date on our fingers back at the Institute after our first wedding. Now here we were exactly one year later, declaring our love in front of all our friends and family who didn't get to be there the first time. Like the tattoos, our love was permanent, and would be a mark on the world that would never fade.

The music concluded, and Hemlock began the ceremony. "Hail the goddesses Idril and Caralyn, and hail the prince and princess, who are to be wedded upon this day."

"*Long may they reign,*" the crowd responded in unison, before the temple went silent.

Hemlock spoke loudly as she stated, "In Elvish tradition, Elven couples are required to undergo a handfasting, and live together for one year before they are officially wed. Today marks the one-year anniversary of the prince and princess' legal wedding. Therefore, I pronounce that they are ready to be joined together in the eyes of the goddesses. We will commence with the rites that will make them as one. We will begin by casting a circle spell, enshrining the couple with our protection."

Four mystics stepped forward, each carrying musical instruments like flutes and drums. They began to circle, moving in a ring around us as they played. Elves valued music above all other art forms, and they used it in most of their ceremonies to perform ancient magic.

Hemlock rang a bell. "I summon the goddesses. Speak now, and let their energy cleanse your space."

One of the mystics circling us beat a small drum, and Charlie said, "I speak to the east, for you are my first dawn, my new beginning."

My heart skipped, and the next mystic rang a wind chime. We'd gone over all of this in rehearsal last night, but I was still worried I'd forget something. There were so many Elvish religious rites to learn, and I'd far from mastered them all.

But the words came naturally to me as I said, "I speak to the west, for you are my last twilight, my final ending."

A mystic played a light tune on her flute. Charlie said, "I speak to the north, for you are my everlasting winter, my place of home."

The last mystic shook a tambourine, and I added, "I speak to the south, for you are my eternal summer, my passion burning."

When the circle was complete, the mystics drew away, and Hemlock said, "The protective circle has been cast. For those that came before, and those who are yet to be, for all the spirits that walk this realm, and all that roam in the Blessed Haven, for all who have come to bear witness today; receive this union, and give it all your blessings. You two who have come to be joined, all life is an endless circle. You will journey together through this life and under the stars until you come to live amongst them with your ancestors in a land forevermore. Your family, your friends, and your people will provide a strong foundation for your marriage. Will you lean on them, and take sacredly the vows you are about to speak?"

"We will be faithful in our love, and our will to remain as one," Charlie and I recited in unison. He squeezed my hands, and a flood of warm emotion rushed through my torso. Even now, it was so hard to believe we were doing this. I was shaking.

"Times of abundance will come, as well as times of trouble," Hemlock said. "Charles, do you vow to take Ava-Marie as your wife, to celebrate with her your victories and carry her sorrows, to share your wealth and come together in poverty, comforting her in illness and rejoicing in health, believing in faith and braving through doubt? Do you vow to be honest and always offer your forgiveness, knowing you cannot wound her part of your soul without harming your own as well, enduring by her side, forsaking all others, for now and forever, until this life shall end and you join together in another?"

"I do," Charlie said sincerely. His voice nearly trembled as he said the words, and I felt a great wave of love wash over me like the ocean at sunset.

"And Ava-Marie," Hemlock began. My spirit flipped inside my chest. "Do you accept Charles to be the husband of your heart, to celebrate with him your victories and carry his sorrows, to share your wealth and come together in poverty, comforting him in illness and rejoicing in health, believing in faith and braving through doubt? Do you vow to be honest and always offer your forgiveness, knowing you cannot wound his part of your soul without harming your own as well, enduring by his side, forsaking all others, for now and forever, until this life shall end and you join together in another?"

"I do," I whispered. Another tear slipped out of Charlie's eyes, and I saw his lip quiver.

Hemlock's voice went a little dry as she said, "Do you, Ava-Marie, vow to submit to your husband, to give to him your obedience and heart, following his headship and commands, remaining devoted in all things?"

"I will," I replied.

"And Charles, do you vow to protect, defend, and lead your wife, becoming her sanctuary, building a home to keep her safe, laying your life down for hers in every circumstance, swearing to never abandon her side?" Hemlock asked. She nearly rolled her eyes, but resisted, ancestors bless her.

"I will," Charlie promised.

We'd added this part in, at the disapproval of Hemlock and despite the scowling of the mystics. This was our damn wedding, after all. We'd followed all the traditions, but this was one small addition to our vows that we'd written ourselves and wanted to keep, so the temple was going to have to learn to live with it. Nobody else had to understand what it meant, but we did, and it was special to us.

"We shall now commence with the making of the bridal spell," Hemlock said. A mystic brought a small pillar before her, topped with a silver bowl. The mystic combined dried rose buds, cinnamon, rosemary, and raspberry leaves, crushing them together and mixing as one.

"These herbs provide romance, abundance, protection, and fertility for your marriage," Hemlock said. "Grown from the earth, they contain the deep magic that will bind this marriage in sanctity."

She spooned the dried mixture into two small pouches, tying the ends and handing them to us. "Keep them in your pockets— Charles' on the left, and Ava-Marie's on the right. After the wedding day is done, tuck them someplace safe, and treasure them until the end of your days, until the satchels are buried with you when you are returned to the ground."

Both Charlie and I slipped the satchels into our respective pockets— which my dress had, by the way. They only made it cooler. The satchel felt heavy in my pocket, weighed with both hope and responsibility.

"We will now exchange the rings," Hemlock stated. She looked at Marcus, who hurried her way. He tripped before he got there and nearly dropped them. I gasped, but he caught them at the last second as a blush spread across his face.

Hemlock shook her head. Marcus gave my ring to Charlie, and his ring to me, before dipping out of there as quickly as he could. Charlie took my hand in his softly, and I noticed his grip was a little unsteady.

"I give you this ring as a reminder of my everlasting commitment to you," Charlie said, and he placed the ring gently onto my hand with trembling fingers. "Our love has no beginning and no end. I choose you as my love, the lost piece of my soul, to live as one everlasting."

I slipped Charlie's ring on, absent of nearly all thought except how perfect this moment was. "I give you this ring as a reminder of my everlasting commitment to you. Our love has no beginning and no end. I choose you as my love, the lost piece of my soul, to live as one everlasting."

Hemlock smiled as I finished the promise, and my brother came up from the back of the groomsmen line. Ezekiel was carrying an old vase, painted with Hawkei designs that had two spouts. The vase had been used at my parents' wedding, and was one of the few things they'd saved from Kinpago.

"The bride and groom are not only Elves, but also Hawkei," Hemlock said to the congregation. "Therefore, some Hawkei traditions have been incorporated into this ceremony, to honor the ancestors and the heritage of these two individuals. In Hawkei tradition, the bride and groom drink tea from a vase with two spouts, symbolizing the separate lives of the bride and groom, uniting into one. In Elvish, the bride and groom drink sweetened wine from one goblet. This tradition from both sides will be united, as the couple will now take a shared drink of Elvish wine from a traditional Hawkei wedding vase."

Charlie took the vase from Hemlock as she said, "Drink carefully, my dear."

He tipped it back, and I took a sip. The wine was delicious— I wanted more the moment I tasted it. It was symbolic of my desire for Charlie, and how I'd never be able to quench my thirst for him no matter how much time passed. Charlie drank from the vase, then handed it back to Ez after we'd polished off every drop.

Ez was near weeping, and his lip trembled as he whispered, "Love you, big sis."

I smiled fondly at him, and he took the vase away as Hemlock raised her hands. "Ava-Marie's grandmothers have come together to make a wedding quilt for the couple," she said. "The quilt shares the couple's wedding colors and features the intricate design of infinity knots. In Elvish culture, these knots symbolize an everlasting loop, a reminder that we are connected to nature and each other in an eternal cycle that will always bring us back to each other. This quilt will be placed on the shoulders of the couple and wrapped around them, to signify they are creating a new home, making a new family, and are forever bound together."

Grandmother Eleanor and Grandma Haloke came up from the pews. Suspended between them was a gorgeous, hand-stitched quilt featuring a variety of intricate Elvish knots. This was the surprise my grandma had hinted at. The designs seemed never-ending and flowed into each other, until I couldn't tell where the design began or ended.

Just like Charlie and me.

As the blanket was draped around our shoulders, Oberi changed from a unicorn into a phoenix, flying over to suspend herself on the quilt between us. She gave a loving coo as she nestled her beak in my hair.

My grandmothers stepped aside. After the quilt was wrapped tightly around us, Hemlock said, "The ceremony is complete, and you are now married. I now pronounce you prince and princess, husband and wife. Prince Charles, you may seal your love for your bride with a kiss."

Charlie didn't waste a second. He kissed me, and ancestors if it didn't bring me back to one year ago, when we'd kissed for the first time as husband and wife in the Institute's chapel. We might as well have traveled back in time, because his kiss roused something deep in me... something we'd done over and over for thousands of years and couldn't wait to do all over again in our next lifetime. This time around, things had been better than I could've ever dreamed. Oberi let out a little song as she perched on the blanket between us.

Flower petals began falling, but I wouldn't have noticed if I didn't sense their weight in my hair, or hear the crowd celebrating our love with exhilarated applause. I felt myself getting swept away by Charlie's kiss, once again breathless, flying and falling all at once.

Charlie was mine, and I was his. I couldn't imagine a better way to start off our forever.

And this forever would never be stolen from me. I'd kill anyone who tried to take it away. There was no more him, or me, just *us*— a soul united in love, and *nothing*, not the gods or The Mission or the Warden himself, would ever tear us apart.

Our love would always win. So let the world do its best to destroy us. Even if there was no tomorrow, I wasn't afraid of what was coming next, because if I had Charlie there'd always be something left to fight for. I'd always remember us just like this, young and ready to take on whatever the future had in store.

Charlie was my one and only. I'd never love again after him, never love anyone else— he was the only man I wanted, needed, or desired, for now until my soul ceased to exist.

I'd be his wife for all infinity, until the last days of existence came. And even then, there'd always be a whisper in the universe of what we were and how much we'd meant to each other. Our love was something that had sparked at the beginning of eternity, I was sure of it.

Eternity, I was sure, would never be enough. But it was a pretty damn good place to start.

Ava and I had been married for a year already, but this ceremony was different. Back then, we'd been forced into a marriage, but here we were a year later, choosing each other all over again and declaring our love in front of our entire kingdom.

When my grandfather first suggested it, I figured the ceremony would more or less act like vow renewals, but it was *so* much more than that. I felt like I was marrying Ava for the first time. Nothing was rushed this time around, and I could actually *sit* with the excitement all morning. My face hurt from all the smiling.

I couldn't wait to be in the same room with her, so I went to visit her before the ceremony. I felt her anxiety, so I needed to be there to support her. I knew she wouldn't leave me at the altar, but I couldn't say I wasn't relieved as hell when I heard Oberi's hooves walking through the temple. I'd told Ava I'd be waiting for her at the end of the aisle, and by the Great Spirit, I held my promise. I could never express the joy I felt when she chose to join me.

When we spoke our vows, I felt them deep in my soul, like a contract we'd made long ago was finally being sealed. I didn't think I could love Ava-Marie more than I already did, but by all the gods in the Blessed Haven, I loved her more than ever now. I was certain that neither of us would exit this temple the same.

Thunderous applause drowned out the sound of celebratory flutes. My lips were still on Ava's, and I never wanted the kiss to end. I kissed her again— over and over again, as if no amount of kisses would be enough to show her just how much I loved her.

Save it for the honeymoon, lovebirds, Oberi teased. *It's time to go.*

I scooped Ava into my arms and carried her down the aisle. I left her chair behind, knowing someone else would grab it for her later. She draped her arms around my neck and squeezed me tightly, like she never wanted to let me go. Gleeful laughter escaped her chest as she waved to the guests as we passed. I practically danced down the aisle, and I felt like I was floating on air... maybe I *was.* I couldn't be sure, because all my attention was stolen by the woman in my arms.

"This way," my grandfather said. I hadn't even realized he'd followed us.

He wasn't the only one. Other guests flooded out of the temple doors, cheering for our union. I felt someone remove the quilt from our shoulders, taking it to our room for safekeeping.

"It is tradition to present the royal couple to the city following their marriage," my grandfather explained. "Your guests will remain here at the castle, enjoying a cocktail hour until you return. Enjoy the parade, for you two have earned it."

Cassiel guided us into an open-top carriage, and Oberi fluttered down onto the seat beside us. I set Ava onto the velvet bench. Her dress was so big it covered my legs.

The carriage driver snapped the reins. The sound of hooves hit the cobblestone as we were guided toward the palace gates. The gates creaked open. It was quiet for only a moment before I heard a roaring ovation erupt from outside the castle. Ilamanthe residents had gathered along the streets to witness our parade, and they cried out in celebration when they saw us coming.

It's the prince and princess!

We love you, Charlie!

Ava-Marie is the most beautiful bride!

"Charlie, I feel like a real princess!" Ava raved.

I squeezed her hand. "That's because you *are,* pidge. You better start believing it."

Ava let go of my hand to wave to the crowd, and I did the same. Flower petals rained down on us in all directions. Above us, I heard the sound of large wings flapping, and for a brief moment, the warmth of the sun left my skin.

Ava gasped. "Charlie, there's an air force above us made of all types of magical creatures— dragons, alicorns, phoenixes, you name it. They're all wearing the Elven Union's military crest. There goes Julian with them! Other military officers are stationed along the parade route, and they're saluting as we pass."

I beamed. My grandfather really knew how to put on a spectacle. I'd be lying if I said I didn't enjoy it just a *little* bit.

"This is one big parade," Ava commented. "There are musicians and acrobats ahead of our carriage, along with floats that are decorated with all kinds of flowers picked from the royal gardens. The residents are throwing flower petals from the rooftops. There are so many that it looks like rain. The whole city is celebrating our wedding."

I heard a beautiful song being sung ahead of us in Elvish. "Where's the singing coming from?"

"There are performers riding the floats, wearing gorgeous outfits. They're singing wedding songs to accompany the music," Ava explained. "Your grandfather really went all out."

I'd say. We passed by the barracks, and the cry of a general giving orders rang out over the sound of the parade.

"It's the Elvish army, dressed in uniform. There are hundreds of soldiers here in formation," Ava replied. "They're raising their swords in unison to give us a royal salute."

I waved at them, and a rustling noise sounded as all the soldiers bowed in unison. As we left the barracks, a cannon was set off behind us, and the people cheered louder.

"Prince, princess, show us a kiss!" an Elf cried from the sidelines. Had to be a reporter. Dozens of other voices begged alongside him.

Might as well give the people what they want, Oberi suggested, and she nudged me with her beak.

I grinned and grabbed the back of Ava's neck to bring her in. We kissed, and the click of cameras went off in the background as I gave the papers something to feature on the front page tomorrow.

"A taste of what's coming tonight?" Ava teased.

"My hands are going to be all over you," I whispered, and she let out a giggle.

We turned down another side street, and Ava unexpectedly grabbed my arm. Oberi beat her wings. *There's a little girl standing off to the side, holding out a flower for you to take.*

"Stop the carriage!" Ava called out. The carriage was brought to a halt, and seemingly the whole parade.

I wasn't sure what she was doing, until I felt her gesture to someone beside the carriage. Another person entered. The carriage didn't shift, so the person who entered couldn't have weighed much. It was probably the little girl.

"For you, princess," she said, and the petals brushed my hand as she held it out. She could barely talk. I didn't think she was more than three years old.

Ava took the flower and laid it on her skirt. "Thank you so much. What a lovely gift."

"Your crown is so pretty," the little girl said, sounding awed. "I wish *I* could be a princess."

"Well, why not?" Ava reached up to take the tiara off, then set it on top of the little girl's head. All around us, the Elves gasped in disbelief that Ava would give such a priceless gift.

It's so big it's almost falling off and into her eyes, Oberi said with a laugh.

She'll grow into it, Ava replied. I wondered if she was talking more about herself and not the child.

"Wow!" the little girl said. "It's so sparkly!"

"Keep it. As a gift from your princess," Ava said sincerely.

The little girl squealed in joy. "Thank you, princess!"

She darted off the carriage, and the people around us cheered even louder. The noise around us swelled to resemble a sports game and not a parade as the carriage moved forward.

"That was very thoughtful," I commented.

"I've got a dozen tiaras at home, and I don't need it. I've still got my wedding veil in," Ava replied. "She should get to feel like a princess for a day."

Ava was so good at being a princess. Much better than I was at being a prince. She made me look good next to her. Ava was such a star, and it was all I could do to bathe in her light.

Plus, the press had clearly eaten that up. The cameras had been going a mile a minute when Ava had put that tiara on the little girl's head. My grandfather was going to be pleased at all the positive reception.

"They really love us, don't they?" Ava asked quietly as the Elves continued to scream, cheer, and cry at our appearance.

"Yeah, they do," I said. "This is a special day for them as well."

Ava's voice dropped as she added, "I just hope I can be the princess they deserve."

"You are, and you will be." I squeezed her hand for reassurance. No matter what we would face in our upcoming rule, she'd always be the perfect royal. I was the one who needed to measure up.

The parade must've lasted for at least an hour. It seemed that we'd covered every street in the city. I didn't think there was a single resident who hadn't witnessed us pass by. We were covered in flower petals, and the music was still going on.

Fireworks exploded in the sky as we returned inside the palace gates, and the city continued to be vibrant and loud. My grandfather said that today had been declared a city-wide holiday. The Elves would be partying throughout the night until dawn to celebrate the wedding, all across Ilamanthe.

The carriage stopped in front of the palace doors, where Eddie was already waiting for us. "Your highnesses," he said with a bow. "The Grand March will begin as soon as you are ready. I have the princesses' chair here."

I scooped Ava into my arms, then helped her down from the carriage and into her bridal chair. She was very particular about the way her dress hung, and Eddie was more than happy to get on his hands and knees to straighten it out. Oberi changed into a husky and followed behind us.

Eddie led us inside and down several hallways. We stopped beside a closed doorway, though I could hear chatter coming from the other side. "Wait here. I will let them know you've arrived, and you will be announced before you come in."

Eddie walked off, leaving us alone. It occurred to me this might be the last time Ava and I would get a spare moment to ourselves during the reception.

"I got you something, pidge," I said as I reached into my suit jacket.

"A present? Charlie, you didn't have to do that!" Ava's voice raised a few pitches.

"I didn't *have* to, but I *wanted* to." I pulled out a small velvet box and opened it. Inside sat a pure gold necklace in the shape of tiny handcuffs.

Ava drew a sharp breath. "Oh, Charlie! I love it!"

I don't think those are going to fit her, Oberi cracked.

"Shut up," Ava playfully jabbed back. "I want to wear it!"

I took the necklace out of the box. "I wanted to get you something that would always remind you of our wedding day. I wasn't sure if handcuffs were fitting, but they felt right for *us*. I couldn't get the gold right with my illusion magic, so I had the royal jeweler custom make it."

Ava took off the necklace she was wearing and gave it to Oberi to keep safe. I secured the clasp of the handcuff necklace around her neck.

"It's perfect. I'm never taking it off!" Ava raved. She wrapped her arms around my middle. "Thank you, Charlie."

"You're welcome, pidge." Now she would always know she was mine. I never wanted anything else.

Eddie's footsteps approached. "Your highnesses, it is time."

Double doors opened in front of us, and trumpets blared. Eddie cried, "Presenting His Royal Highness Prince Charles Majestica, Grand Duke of Ilamanthe, and his bride, Her Royal Highness Princess Ava-Marie Wahkin, Grand Duchess of Ilamanthe."

We entered an expansive room with a tall ceiling and polished floors. Our guests applauded, and chairs squeaked as people stood to give us a standing ovation.

The ballroom is gorgeous! Ava gushed telepathically. *All the doors are trimmed in silver, and a glittering chandelier is hanging above us burning black candles. Diamond streamers are hanging from the ceiling. The lights are dimmed to give a dark ambience. Our guests are seated at tables around the perimeter of the room, and a string quartet is set up in the corner. The curtains and table-cloths are in black, and there are massive bouquets of pink flowers for the center-pieces. A multi-tiered wedding cake in black with pink roses is in the corner. It's a perfect wedding for a pair of villains.*

Ava didn't have to describe the room to me for me to know how wonderful it was. I could *feel* the joy in the air as our guests welcomed us with a booming fanfare. It was hard to believe they were here for *us*, celebrating our union. The first time we got married back at the Institute, our union was treated as a nuisance. Here, our love was celebrated. I couldn't imagine a better way to show Ava just how much I loved her than to declare it in front of all our family and friends— hell, our entire nation.

We were guided to the front of the room, where our wedding party was already seated at a head table. We passed by a table where our parents sat, and my father stood to shake my hand.

"Congratulations to you both," Cameron said. "I'm very happy for you."

He was being really nice, and I didn't know how to respond to that. It was easier when we were yelling at each other.

"Thanks," I told him. I didn't know what else to say.

Cameron sniffled, and I thought for a second he was crying about my wedding. To hide his emotions, he quickly added, "Wish I'd have gotten a wedding as lovely as this. Your mother and I had to get married in secret, so we never got the big celebration."

There it was. Of fucking *course* he had to make this about himself. My father was *jealous*, and he had to make sure I knew it. I wasn't going to let him ruin this special day, though.

"Didn't you and Drea have a royal wedding?" I asked, trying to keep the harshness out of my tone.

"Yes, but it wasn't the same," Cameron admitted. He wasn't going to drop it.

"Yeah, well, I wouldn't have all this if it wasn't for my *seanari*," I said. I left it at that, then turned away and led Ava up to the head table.

"What a prick," she mumbled under his breath. "So he didn't have the wedding he wanted. Doesn't mean he has to ruin it for us. He could suck it up for a night."

I pushed her chair in at the table. "Don't worry, love. This is *our* special day, and nothing he can say will ruin it."

I took a seat next to Ava, and Oberi hopped onto a chair beside me that was reserved especially for him. He sniffed the air, then licked his lips loudly. He was practically panting. *I smell meat!*

Servants came around with our first course, which was a Greek salad made with fresh tomatoes and bell peppers tossed with delicious feta cheese. Ava ate all of her salad, which was a good sign. She was feeling well today. I was worried she'd have a flare-up on this most important of days, but we'd gotten lucky, because she was thankfully at her best.

Oberi turned up his nose. In his words; *salad is what real food eats.*

As the servants came around with platters of food for our main course, my stomach rumbled at the delicious smell of lamb and roasted veggies. The perfect blend of basil and garlic burst across my taste buds when I took a bite. I tried to slow down and savor every bite, but it was difficult when it was so damn good.

Ava gave a slight sigh and whispered under her breath, "I wish I had gotten my way on this one."

"It's my grandfather's favorite. We had to compromise on something," I offered.

"I don't mind eating meat, but I'm not a fan of consuming innocent little babies. It feels like we're offering up a sacrificial lamb," Ava argued. "The Warden would probably love this meal."

"Then it's the only thing he and I will ever agree on," I said, and I greedily took a second helping, because I couldn't get enough. This was great.

"You can have it, but I'm not eating it. There's plenty of other food here, like these delicious rolls," Ava said happily.

Oberi scarfed down his lamb chops and barked at a server to bring him more. They came back with a plate piled so high I could feel the heat coming off it. I had no doubt Oberi would eat each and every item on his plate.

"Oberi, mind your manners, please," Ava said as she gently sliced her vegetables. "This is a *royal occasion.*"

As the royal pup, I can do whatever I want, Oberi stated proudly. *I request that the kitchen save all the leftovers and deliver them to my room promptly when the party ends.*

I sighed heavily. "Whatever you say, *royal pup.*"

Ava snickered.

Someone clinked their glass, and the chatter in the room died down. Liam cleared his throat, then stood. "I'd like to thank you all for being here today to celebrate my daughter's marriage. I cannot thank Emperor Cassiel enough for his hospitality, and for hosting such a wonderful celebration."

Liam paused to contemplate. "I love my little girl. I think that's clear to everyone who's ever seen me with her. I've adored Ava from the moment I found out my wife and I were going to have a girl over twenty years ago. She's the best of my life, and the light of my world. Years ago, she gave me a reason to keep fighting when I didn't think there was anything left to fight for. I swore the day she was born there'd never be anyone for her, because no one would love her as much as I did. I didn't ever want to give her away, because she was just too precious, and too special. But then I met Charlie, and I realized how wrong I was."

I was shocked. I didn't think Liam would say anything about me in his speech, and if he did, I didn't think it would be anything good. But Liam went on. "Charlie, you're a good person. I've seen you be a good husband, even when Ava's pushing your buttons. At first, I didn't think the two of you fit together, but after seeing how you interact together, I know now that there were never two people that were better meant for each other. You take care of her in a way that I never could, and you understand her better than anyone else in this world. Our family is more than happy to welcome you as our son."

Despite trying to hold my emotions back, I found myself choking up. It was really nice that Liam supported me and accepted me for who I was. Ava put a hand on my arm, sounding teary-eyed herself.

"My wife and I are here to support you both, and we will until we join the ancestors, and even beyond," Liam stated. "You two have been married for a year now, so you already know how it is. Marriage isn't simply a piece of paper, or a legal arrangement. It's a commitment to be the best you can be for one person for the rest of your lifetime. It changes the fundamental makeup of who you are, for better or worse. Marriage is easy, it's hard, and everything in between. If I can leave you both with one piece of advice, it is this; The world will never stop throwing things at you, and things will always change, but what's important is that your love remains consistent and something you both can count on. As long as you have each other, you can face anything together. To Ava and Charlie."

"*To Ava and Charlie,*" the crowd toasted. They didn't address us by our official titles, which was nice, because it meant we were surrounded by friends. These people knew us on a personal level, and it was everything I'd dreamed of to have them here today.

My father stood next. "That was a lovely speech, Liam. I suppose now it's my turn."

"Aw, fuck," I mumbled under my breath. *Here we go.* I reached for Ava's hand under the table and squeezed it. She held onto me tightly. I'd told her Cameron couldn't ruin our wedding, but I had a feeling he was about to prove me wrong.

"What can I say?" Cameron started.

Nothing. Sit back down, Ava cracked telepathically.

That made me smile, and I squeezed her hand even tighter.

"Charlie, ever since you were a little boy, I knew you were destined for great things," Cameron said. "I remember the day you were born. You were so small when I held you."

You deserve a Father-of-the-Year Award for that, considering it was the only time you were there for him, Ava growled.

I chuckled under my breath. *He's certainly trying to win himself some points with our guests,* I joked back through our bond. *They can all see right through him, and I bet he knows it.*

Cameron cleared his throat, then slurred, "Just a tiny little baby. You were walking by the time you were six months old."

By the ancestors, Charlie's a miracle baby! Ava exclaimed telepathically.

I cracked a smile at that one, and I had to hold back a laugh. *It certainly has nothing to do with my father's shit memory.*

Cameron let out a snicker. "You were such a fussy baby. You'd drive me nuts with your crying, day in and day out, but I let your mother handle all that."

Is he drunk? I asked Ava. I hadn't noticed before when we were talking to him, but now, it was unmistakable.

He looks fucking plastered, Ava complained. *I bet he was like that at the ceremony, too.*

Eh, Elvish tradition? I bet it won't even take an hour before he's stumbling back to his quarters, Oberi cut in.

We're taking bets now? Ava teased. *I'll give him at least an hour and a half. He'll have twelve glasses of wine in him by then. I think he's already on glass number three.*

Ah, so that explains the speech, I quipped. *I never thought he'd actually get up and say something.*

Oh, he's saying something, all right, Oberi said.

"It's not easy being a parent, you know," Cameron rambled on. "You need to be strong, make hard decisions, and there are a lot of sacrifices."

What was he talking about? My dad had been around when I was a toddler, but I was barely three years old when I'd been taken away from him, and we'd hardly talked since I got to Ilamanthe.

"Kids don't like to listen," Cameron complained. "You give them the world, and they throw it back in your face. They do what they want and don't like to obey. As a father, there were dreams I had to give up and money I had to waste, because I had a child and he was supposed to come first."

The reception hall was stunned into silence. Embarrassment began to creep across my skin, and I felt my cheeks redden. Ancestors, this was *mortify-*

ing. I couldn't believe my father was humiliating me like this, in front of all our guests.

I'm going to kill him, Ava thought, and her Fire began to smolder between our interlocked fingers.

Just let him finish. My grandfather said that murder wasn't exactly *unusual* at an Elvish wedding, at least not historically. According to him, it was only fifty or so years ago that an Elvish wedding was considered boring if at least one body wasn't getting dragged out of the reception hall at the end of the night. But I really didn't want my beautiful bride getting blood on her dress. She liked it too much.

"I was still the best dad that I could be," Cameron slurred. "Despite the circumstances. Charlie and I had to spend a few years apart—"

A few years? I thought angrily. *More like my entire life!*

"—And he went through some hard times. Most of you have heard that he grew up on the streets, doing unmentionable things in order to survive," Cameron ranted. "And I feel bad that I couldn't be there for him as a father should, even though I did my absolute best to. Sometimes, life happens."

He was talking about the absolute worst time of my life when this was supposed to be the happiest day of my existence. It made me feel like absolute shit.

"Should we get up and stop this?" I heard Chancey murmur to the other groomsmen a few seats down from me. They mumbled back, not sure what to do.

"The lesson here is to never forget about family," Cameron ranted. "And son, I know you're a prince now, but don't let the riches and fame go to your head. It can be really hard, having all this money and being a part of the royal family. But there are benefits to being a Majestica. Your wedding guests here will certainly be giving you some elaborate gifts, but don't forget the presents will be going into the royal treasury, where *all* of us can share it."

So much for not letting the riches go to your head. Jewels always ended up in the royal treasury, so they'd be shared amongst the family, which really meant he'd benefit from our wedding gifts anyway. As if the royal family didn't already have enough. He was making this all about him when this was supposed to be mine and Ava's day. What's more, he was trying to profit off our guests. What the hell was he thinking? This was insane.

I honestly couldn't believe Cameron. My grandfather's lessons had changed my life, and I knew my dad had gone through the same teachings. Did Cassiel's words not have any effect on him at all? He wanted the benefits of being Emperor, but not any of the responsibility.

I guess that was a theme of his, because he wanted to have the title of being my father and brag to people about having a son, but he didn't want to actually do any of the work. My father and I were complete opposites, because I would go to any lengths to make sure my people thrived, and I would give up anything if I had a child of my own. Cameron wasn't willing to sacrifice a bit of comfort to be a ruler or a parent, and I realized he didn't deserve to be either.

Cameron chuckled. "Remember, Charlie. Your duties as a royal aren't as important as your family. Your mother isn't here today, and I'm sure, like all of us, that you regret that she isn't. Because you can't get time with your loved ones back once they're gone."

It really hurt when he brought up my mom, more than anything else he'd said. I wished he'd stop. It wasn't like it was her choice not to come to this wedding. She was dead... because she'd died for me. My dad had made sure to remind me of that on my wedding day.

I gripped Ava's hand so tightly I was sure I was restricting circulation, but she didn't let go. Unexpectedly, I felt another hand slip into mine. Marcus held tight to show his support.

I grasped his fingers back and didn't pull away. I was a pretty masculine guy, but all that bravado was walking out the door right now, and I needed him to help me at the moment. I was grateful as hell for him, because besides the comfort, his hand in mine prevented me from getting up from his chair and socking my old man, which I *very much* wanted to do. I'd rather get in the boxing ring with six vampires, because that couldn't be more painful than this speech.

Cameron's voice got high-pitched. Man, he really was wasted. "His best friend, Martin, he seems like a nice guy. And that Katrina girl he hangs around with is really swell. And my daughter-in-law, Ava... well, I'm proud of her, too. I've heard she has a beautiful voice, and she plays piano in every one of her videos. She's written three whole songs!"

Ava had certainly written more than three songs. She had whole albums she'd finished before she'd even left high school. We'd written dozens of songs together at the Institute alone, and I was the one who always played the piano, not her.

My dad didn't know us at all, and this was the proof.

A chair scraped backward, and I just *knew* my grandfather was interrupting. He had to be embarrassed, too. I was surprised he'd let it go on for as long as he did.

"That's enough, my son. I believe our other guests would like to speak," Cassiel said gracefully, smoothly saving the situation.

Cameron hiccupped. "Oh. Okay. I'll wrap it up. I guess what I'm trying to say is, I'm proud of the man you've become, Charlie. Cheers to the happy couple."

"*Cheers*," the guests echoed, though their response sounded really awkward. Cameron had none of the qualities my grandfather had as a leader, and damn, it showed now.

Cameron sat back down, and I could finally breathe. I wasn't sure I believed him when he said he was proud of me, or if that's just what he was *supposed* to say, but I'd take it, so long as that awful speech was finally fucking over.

Marcus hurried to move things along. "I guess that means it's our turn."

Kallie stood and clinked her glass, getting people's attention. "For those of you who don't know me, I am Princess *Kalina* Nowak of Malovia, and I'm the maid-of-honor."

"Yeah— and I'm the best man. My name's Marcus, not Martin," Marcus said.

Ava and I were already laughing. We couldn't hold it in, not after that ridiculous speech from my dad. It sounded like the two of them had rehearsed this already.

Marcus continued for Kallie. "Of course, it would be traditional for the two of us to give a big speech, but Ava and Charlie are anything *but* traditional."

"Just look at their wedding— they did the whole thing backwards," Kallie cracked. "You're supposed to hold the ceremony *before* you get married."

"I couldn't wait!" Ava joked. The crowd laughed along with us.

"And so, in true Ava and Charlie fashion, Kalina and I have decided to go untraditional and put on a play, rather than a speech," Marcus announced. "We present to you the *true* story of Ava-Marie and Charlie's marriage."

He clapped his hands loudly. "Places, everyone!"

All along the head table, chairs squeaked as our friends stood to make their way to the center of the ballroom. Even Oberi hopped down and followed behind the rest of the wedding party. Ava and I were both stunned into silence, because we didn't know they were planning this. I couldn't imagine what they had in store.

"Oh, ancestors," Ava whispered. "They have *costumes*."

"Costumes?" I asked.

"Kallie's in a leather jacket, and Marcus put on a wig," Ava groaned.

I was intrigued. This was going to be interesting, at the very least.

"Our story begins on a warm summer day in a distant land known as Kinpago," Alistair narrated dramatically. "The sweet maiden Ava was taking a stroll through the streets of her home when she unexpectedly ran into the tall, dark and handsome Charlie."

"Who are you calling a sweet maiden?" Ava called out, and the crowd laughed hysterically.

Two pairs of footsteps came from either side of the ballroom before crossing paths.

"Ooph!" Marcus said dramatically as he bumped into Kallie, giving a girlish croon.

"Watch it, sweetheart," Kallie grunted in a masculine voice. She'd made me sound like a fucking caveman. I wasn't *that* broody. "What do you think you're doing in a rough part of town like this?"

"Oh, just fucking off, as usual!" Marcus chirped, and the audience laughed. Ancestors, his female voice was *horrible*. It was obnoxious and totally overdone. I grinned at how good he was at it.

"I didn't mean to bump into you— except, I totally did, because I use my bad boy persona to act tough when I don't have to," Kallie grumbled. "What's your name?"

Marcus giggled like a little schoolgirl. "My name's Pigeon! I'm called that because my brain is the size of one, at least when it comes to men!"

Ava let out a spewing laugh, slamming her hand against the table. I was glad she was having fun.

"Pigeon? I'm going to call you pidge," Kallie replied. "That's a nice name for a pretty girl."

"Am I a pretty girl?" Marcus squeaked, and the crowd roared.

"The prettiest I've ever seen. I'm Charlie. Now do what I tell you to and run along. This part is important, because you're going to be doing a lot of that in the future."

"Okay!" Marcus peeped, then he sighed dramatically as he flounced away. "Oh, my. That man was *so* gorgeous. He's like a world tour... for my vagina!"

Ava bust a gut laughing, then quickly added under her breath, "I told Kallie that in *confidence!*"

I smirked. "You really thought that about me?"

"Yes, but it's missing context, all right?" Ava said. "And you can't tell me I was wrong."

I beamed. "You certainly weren't."

The play continued. I sat back, wondering what these two would come up with next.

Marcus let out a dainty croon. "Mm... I can't find my wallet. Perhaps I dropped it on the beach. I'll go look!"

Marcus began skipping across the ballroom. He gasped, stumbling backward as he oversold his surprise. "What is that? Oh, it's my Familiar! I've finally bonded. Her name is Oberi."

Oberi shifted into a Fire unicorn and trotted up next to Marcus.

"You stay away from my Familiar!" Kallie shouted, coming on scene. I swore, she made me sound more stupid with every word she uttered.

"No one asked your opinion," Marcus shot back. "Go away, you big, strong man you."

"Now, now, children." Ezekiel entered, using a gruff tone I could only assume was an impression of his Grandpa Elliot. His voice sounded muffled—like he was wearing a fake beard. "Let's not get too carried away. You have both bonded to the same creature, and you have no choice but to work together. Ava, show Charlie around school and don't get into any trouble. Don't even *think* about stealing a boat and running off together."

"Hey, my grandfather had a great idea!" Marcus said once Ezekiel exited the stage. "Perhaps we should steal a boat and run off together! It's not like anything could go wrong!"

"That's a grand plan!" Kallie raved.

"That isn't how it happened," I grumbled to Ava, while she snickered.

Our friends started clapping and stomping their feet, mimicking the sound of a storm.

"Oh, *no!*" Marcus cried dramatically. "These waters are too rough. Good golly gee, I think I broke a nail!"

"I'll show you rough," Kallie rumbled, and I snorted.

"How dare you! I would never sleep with a brute like you— except, I totally would!" Marcus screeched.

"*Lower your sails and turn back to shore!*" Chancey called out. It sounded like he was speaking through a megaphone.

"Oh no!" Marcus gave a high-pitched yelp. "It's the police! Quick, Charlie. Sail faster!"

"You're under arrest," Ivy practically sang in a smooth voice that made this sound more like a porno than anything. I was *certain* it was intentional. Metal clinked together, and I realized they'd brought real fucking handcuffs as props.

Yep— a real porno for sure. This certainly wasn't appropriate for a royal affair, but then again the Majestica family weren't your typical royals, either. I could hear my grandfather chuckling from the nearest table.

"You can't arrest me!" Marcus panted, and now *he* sounded like the one who was in a porno. "I'm the daughter of a chief!"

"Sure you are, and I'm an Emperor's grandson," Kallie said sarcastically. This got a big laugh from the audience.

The scene quickly shifted, and all our friends rushed to center stage.

"Order!" Ivy called seductively. "Order in the court!"

Great, now they were a horny judge, too.

"Your honor, my client is innocent," Opal insisted, playing her part well. "Ava-Marie was never on that boat."

"Charlie's the criminal!" Marcus whined, stomping his foot. "You'll never believe what he did. Your honor, he stole. My. Wallet!"

Ava leaned over to me and whispered, "Well, they got one thing right."

"Well, we can't separate you two, and also, we like the sexual tension, so you are both hereby sentenced to the Darke Institute for Supernatural Offenders," Ivy announced, banging a gavel.

"Anywhere but there!" Marcus feigned dramatically. "I'm too hot for prison!"

Our friends dragged him off, while Kallie took centerstage. "Perhaps this pidge is not as bad as she seems. I feel terribly sorry for her. If only I could understand my feelings, then I could articulate what I feel about her. Sadly, my emotional intelligence is equal to that of a kumquat, so I'll just ignore what my heart is telling me and misinterpret it as anger. Me punch things, me feel better."

I sputtered. Okay, I'd been a *little* oblivious, but that was pushing the envelope a bit, right?

"I hate him, Oberi," Marcus whined from his side of the stage. Oberi stomped her foot and gave a loud neigh. "It's Charlie's fault we're in this prison. He's complete trash."

Kallie whipped off her leather jacket and spun it around over her head, then tossed it across the room. It smacked me across the face, and I laughed hysterically.

"Who wants to go for a swim?" Kallie cried. "Look at me, all hot and shirtless! My swim trunks don't fit, so that just means you can *almost* see my junk past my happy trail, and I'm too inconsiderate to pull them up!"

"Those *abs*!" Marcus raved to Oberi. "If Charlie's trash, consider me a raccoon, because I love garbage!"

The crowd completely lost it at that. Ava and I laughed so hard that we were leaning against each other. This was fucking hilarious. They were playing their parts so well.

"Fast forward a few years, and our two star crossed lovers were in a tight predicament," Alistair narrated. "As the story goes, anyone with Elvish blood at the Institute was taken away, to where, no one knew, by the Warden himself."

"*Boo!*" The crowd jeered, and I smirked. Boo indeed.

"The Warden discovered that Charlie had Elvish blood, and there was only one way to save him— through an arranged marriage, conceived by the princess herself!" Alistair announced.

"Charlie, we need to get married so the Warden can't kidnap you, and that's the *only reason*," Marcus peeped. "It's not like I secretly love you or anything."

"Yeah, I understand. You want to save me, not be with me. At least, that's what I think, because like I said, feelings are hard for me to read. Or have," Kallie grunted.

Ava socked me in the arm, and I cringed. That hadn't been one of my finest moments.

"So marry me!" Marcus cried. "There's an officiant in the chapel right now. We can get married, and I can pretend that I'm not totally head over heels for you, even though it's obvious to everyone else!"

"Cool, I guess. I must stay completely rigid, so you can't understand what's going on with me and we can fight about it later, like we always do," Kallie stated.

"It's so true!" Ava yelped. It sounded like she was crying laughing.

Eddie stood in as Professor Hemlock. "Do you—?"

"*Yes!*" Kallie and Marcus both said in unison.

"Then I declare you man and wife," Eddie said. "You may now kiss the bride."

The crowd erupted into cheers, and Ava and I clapped loudly. "Aw, Marcus dipped Kallie down into a stage kiss. How cute!" Ava exclaimed.

"Yeah, a *stage kiss*," I said sarcastically. I knew what he was trying to pull. *Just friends* my ass.

"There you have it!" Alistair announced. "The true story of the prince and princess's marriage. Though another year of hardship would pass, it was on their wedding day a year later when they found their true happily ever after."

Marcus took center stage again, and this time, his voice had turned serious. "Ava, Charlie, we cannot thank you enough for the joy your love has brought into our lives. You guys created a safe place at the Institute for each of us to make friends and find our forever family. Your love is bigger than just the two of you, because it's influenced us all. It is because of you that all of us are here today."

"Thank you for all the laughs, all the memories, and most importantly, our friendship," Kallie added. "Congratulations to the not-so-newlyweds."

The room burst into applause again. I found my throat tightening up, because after the comedy show they'd just put on, I hadn't expected them to get so serious. I raised my glass and took a sip of wine, trying to hide my response.

Our friends returned to the head table, and Oberi came over to nudge her nose against my cheek. *Your turn, Charlie!*

"What are you talking about?" Ava asked. "It's Charlie's wedding. He doesn't need to give a speech."

"It isn't a speech," I told her gently. "I have something else planned."

I got out of my chair as the servants rolled a grand piano to the center of the ballroom. The room quieted as I sat; everyone was curious what I was going to do.

I softly played a high C note three times, before launching into a C major arpeggio and then adding more complicated melodies in the lower register. It was soft at first, growing in intensity as I played the keys faster. The acoustics in the ballroom were beyond comparison, and my music twinkled like stars against the high ceiling. As I got into the song, I leaned forward, and my face hit a microphone I hadn't realized had been set up there.

I got an idea. I didn't even think about it. I just started singing, improvising the lyrics to my melody as I went. I never thought about adding words to this song— lyrics were Ava's thing, and the piano was mine. But when I was there, lost in the moment, the words just spilled out of me. It was like they existed all along inside of me, and I didn't know they needed to come out until now.

You were a light among the dark
When I didn't even know that night had fallen
A beacon to my broken heart
Somehow I heard you calling

When the day broke
You were the sunrise
The cosmos rearranged
The morn' you called my name

Call it fate; call it destiny
Say the ancestors led you to me
All I know is this is meant to be
Even gods can't take you from me

I clung to the pigeon's croon
And somehow made my way to you
We've been set free; now we can fly
This world is ours 'til the day we die

We can tear it down or rise above
Because there's nothing stronger than our love

The melody faded as the song came to an end. I knew it was custom to repeat a chorus, but somehow, the song felt perfect just like that. I leaned back on the bench as the final chord reverberated through the ballroom. I could feel Ava's emotions pouring into me through the bond. She was crying; I already knew it.

Charlie, that was beautiful, Ava told me telepathically.

It's how I feel, pidge, I replied.

Only a moment later did I remember we weren't alone. I'd been so lost in the music— so lost in *her.* The crowd went wild with applause.

I stood from the piano, and the servants quickly came to wheel it away. I never once took my focus off of Ava-Marie. I approached the head table, but instead of going to sit down, I took her hand. I gestured to the string quartet, and they began playing a slow song for our first dance.

"Hold on," Ava said. "I've got to unlock my chair's wheels."

I shook my head. "You don't need your chair, pidge."

I scooped her up in my arms, and she gave a little yelp. I carried her onto the dance floor, then gently placed her feet on mine. I held her around the waist to keep her upright. My heart filled with joy as I began to sway her back and forth.

Tears leaked from Ava's eyes and landed on my suit coat. Her voice cracked as she said, "Charlie, we're dancing."

"Of course, pidge," I whispered. "It's our first dance."

"I didn't think I would get one." She sniffled, then squeezed me tighter and buried her face in my chest. "Thank you for this, and for the song, too. It was lovely."

"Anything for you, my love."

I truly meant it. Whatever she wanted, she could have. Everything I did, I did for her.

Ava leaned in closer and whispered, "I got you something too, but it's for later."

My dick hardened, because I could only imagine what she had in store. I was thankful at that moment for her huge dress, because it hid my hard-on when all eyes were on us.

I barely registered the guests, though. I was so mesmerized by my wife as I spun her around the dance floor. Holding Ava close like this on our wedding night was something I could only ever dream of, but here it was, really happening.

My fingers trailed over her dress. There were so many bumps and ridges from rhinestones and sparkles that it was a lot to take in, and there were raised dots on the skirt. It was like Ava had chosen the beads just for me, so I could experience the beauty of her wedding dress like all our guests— then I realized that she *had*. She wanted me to see this dress just like everyone else could. I was so touched.

"Remember our first dance at our *last* wedding?" I asked.

"That silly reception at the Devil's Playground." She laughed lightly. "Our friends made us."

"I was so worried at the time. I thought you hated me," I confessed.

"I wanted to dance with you. But I was too scared."

"There was never anything to be afraid of, pidge. We belong together."

I took in every sensation of her body against mine, and the beat of her heart against my chest. I was so overcome with joy and love, and I never wanted this night to end.

The song eventually concluded, and our guests applauded. All of our friends swarmed onto the dance floor, surrounding us at all angles.

"We're so happy for you guys!" Kallie squealed as she threw her arms around the two of us.

"This wedding is even better than your first," Marcus cut in, squeezing us tight from our other side. "You should do this every year."

I laughed. "If I could, I'd marry Ava every day for the rest of my life."

"And beyond," Ava added.

I beamed. "Every day for the rest of forever, because that's how long we're going to be together."

"Forever," Ava mused in my arms. "I can certainly live with that."

Marcus sniffled. "All of us, together forever. It's so beautiful!"

I sighed heavily, but really, I was masking my feelings as I choked up. "I suppose you guys aren't going anywhere, huh?"

"Come in here, all of you!" Ava cried.

A different slow song began to play as all of our friends gathered around, wrapping us in a group hug. Nobody moved to end it, either. We began swaying back and forth. The group dance felt slow and intimate. Kallie and Marcus pressed in around us, while Ivy hummed to the beat. Alistair and Eddie rocked side by side, while Ez and Opal leaned on each other.

Chancey was bawling— I knew, because it was right in my ear.

You know what? My dad had screwed up his speech earlier, but *this* was my family. I'd die for any one of these guys. We'd been through some mad shit and slayed some wicked foes, and we were still fucking here, and we were still friends. All of us were together, and that's how it always should be. I never wanted that to change.

I had to fight every day to prove that I was worthy growing up, and sometimes it felt like I was still fighting the entire world, all the time. I never thought I'd be good enough, but my friends insisted that wasn't true. I needed these people to remind me who I was every single day. I was more than just the ups and the downs; I belonged to them. When I was at my weakest, they promised I was strong, and they held me up when I just went numb to it all. The person I was lived inside of them. I couldn't fail, not when I had these guys to back me up.

My friends believed in me when I didn't believe in myself. And I believed them, too, when they said they loved me. That was the biggest miracle I'd ever experienced.

The song ended, and the group slowly broke apart. I was really grateful to have that moment with my friends. Whatever happened, even if things didn't stay the way they were now, it was a memory I'd always cherish.

Okay, enough with the sappy stuff. Now it's time for some real *music,* Oberi demanded.

"Woohoo!" Kallie yelled. "Let's party!"

Oberi stomped her hooves at the DJ, and fast-paced music began to boom over speakers set around the ballroom. Our friends let us go to begin spinning or twerking across the dance floor. Eddie brought Ava's chair, and I helped her into it. She kept on dancing the whole time, shimmying her boobs against me and grabbing my ass as I shook it in her direction.

"All right, *now* it's a party!" a grating voice called from beside us. A vampire who reeked of alcohol and blood stumbled against me. He must've had several bottles of wine by now, because it took a lot to make a vampire drunk.

I groaned. "Go away, Danny. You weren't invited."

"I crashed!" he stated proudly, before rubbing his ass against me to the music. I shoved him *hard*. He stumbled, but didn't fall over.

"Actually, *I* invited him," Ava said.

"And I'm having a great time!" Danny cheered. He threw his hands upward, and a splash of wine landed on my pant leg.

"Danny, you're drunk," I complained.

"Shh..." Danny hissed, coming in close to me. "Don't tell anyone, because it's a secret... but getting drunk is what you *do* at weddings."

"Get drunk somewhere else." I put my hand on his face and pushed him away.

Danny laughed. "Lighten up. It's supposed to be the happiest day of your life!"

Danny stumbled off to another part of the dance floor.

"Oh, be nice to him," Ava scolded playfully. "He's just here to party."

"Well, he can party somewhere else," I said, before taking her hands in mine and spinning her around.

Danny completely fell from my mind as we continued dancing to upbeat songs. This was supposed to be a royal affair, but neither Ava nor I held back. We groped each other and shook our asses, spinning all over the dance floor like we owned it— and we fucking *did*. This palace, this nation, this *world*... it was ours for the taking. Now that we were officially joined in marriage under the gods and the ancestors, it felt as if we could do anything and not one fucker alive was going to stop us.

The song changed to a slow song, and Ava gave a heavy sigh. "Whew! I need a drink."

"I'll get it, love," I offered.

I went over to the drink table, and Ava followed. I was filling a glass of punch when the hairs on the back of my neck stood. I didn't understand why, until I heard the voice of Ava's aunt behind me.

"Ava. Charlie," Maddie said.

I turned to her, though my tone was stilted. "Maddie. I trust you're having a good time."

"It's been a great wedding," she said. "I'm very happy for both of you. Happiness like this is something we must never take for granted."

Aw, fuck. I just *knew* she was going to come in here with her *end of the world* bullshit. This wasn't the time or the place for her to issue some warning about our prophecy.

I kept my cool while I handed Ava her glass. Before my wife could say anything, I extended my hand in Maddie's direction. "Would you like to dance?"

Maddie hesitated a moment, then said, "Yes. Thank you."

"Have fun!" Ava called. She thought the gesture was innocent, but really, I was trying to get her aunt away from her, so she didn't ruin Ava's special night.

I guided Maddie onto the dance floor, and we began to spin in slow circles. Nearby, Marcus and Kallie's soft voices drifted over the ballroom. They'd been hanging on each other all night and hadn't been apart all evening. I thought something like this would trigger them, but they were laughing, and seemed perfectly fine.

I'd broken their bond. But to be honest, I wasn't sure if things were completely over between them yet. They still acted like there was something there, especially at this wedding. The two of them were behaving like a couple, dancing together and whispering softly, though they'd both promised me they were just friends.

I supposed we'd see.

"Congratulations on your wedding, Charlie," Maddie said.

"You didn't come here to congratulate me," I said coldly. "You came to give me another warning."

"I could try, but it wouldn't do any good, would it?" Maddie replied in an equally cool manner. "You've made your choice already, and there's nothing I can do to stop it."

"No," I told her as we stiffly swayed. "I decide the fate of my prophecy, so it's already done. I don't care if the evidence proves otherwise. Ava and I have already won. We *will* defeat the Warden."

"I cannot change your mind, but I will leave you with this," Maddie said. "Don't lie to yourself, Charlie. If that is the way you truly feel, then so be it. But don't let your confidence overshadow what you know to be true. Eventually, the truths you are hiding from yourself will come to light. You can't run from that."

I tilted my head. "Why would I run from something I'm not afraid of?"

"Because you *should* be afraid of it, Charlie," Maddie responded hollowly. "We all should."

I was grateful that the song ended then. An upbeat melody came on, and Kallie rushed to my side in an instant.

"Charlie, come *dance* with me," Kallie begged, dragging me away. "Marcus is being a limp dick and went to get cake."

I didn't afford Maddie so much as a goodbye. I think she got the message.

I spun Kallie around, and she laughed gleefully. "You and Marcus seem to be having a good time," I called over the music.

She leaned in and said, "We're having the *best* time."

Unexpectedly, she reached out to give me a hug. "Thank you *so much* for breaking our bond. Marcus and I have never been better. We're such good friends now that there's no romantic pressure hanging over our heads. We can actually have deep conversations without fighting."

"I'm glad to hear that," I told her, though I wasn't sure I was completely buying it.

"I didn't think our friendship would survive after the bond broke, but we actually get along now," she confessed. "You cleared the air so we could start from scratch. It really did set us free."

"I'm happy for you guys," I said honestly. "I just want what's best for you two."

Ava joined us again, and Kallie dropped it. We danced with our friends for hours, and time seemed to fly by. In the distance, we heard a clock tower strike midnight, and still, we continued spinning across the dance floor and laughing until we couldn't breathe. Several guests came by to greet and congratulate us, saying goodbye before they retreated to their quarters, but most stayed to drink, dance, and celebrate.

It must've been past two in the morning when Alistair snatched the microphone from the DJ booth. "As the night wears down, we have a special grand finale performance for the bride and groom. Folks, put your hands together for Ivy and Jonah!"

Ava squealed. "Oh my ancestors! This is going to be *epic!*"

Eddie rushed to my side with a chair and forced me into it. Ava and I sat in the center of the dance floor while a pumping bass shook the entire ballroom. An explosion sounded, and streamers and confetti rained down on my head. An old Lady Gaga song burst through the speakers, and Ivy's beautiful singing voice filled the room. The crowd cheered, though Ava's voice was the loudest.

Ivy's heels clicked against the marble floor as they strutted forward. They stopped directly in front of us, then tickled me under the chin with a feather boa. Ivy circled us, and Ava whistled loudly.

"That dress is sexy as *fuck*, Ivy!" she cheered.

Ivy didn't miss a beat. They spun around, then sat right on my lap and twerked their ass. Strands from their long hair got stuck in my mouth. I threw my head back in laughter. Ivy was only on me for a second before they threw their leg over Ava's chair and gave her a lap dance. Ava whooped and hollered.

The beat dropped for the chorus, and Ava's Uncle Jonah came on stage, his voice blaring through the speakers. Ivy and Jonah coordinated perfectly, with Ivy singing a matching harmony. They began to dance in a choreographed motion, and though I couldn't keep track of the movements, Ava did her best to describe it to me.

My uncle went all out! she raved. *He's wearing a sexy red sequin dress and the biggest blonde wig I've ever seen!*

At the second verse, Ava squealed so loud it could be heard over the music. "Ahhhhhh! There are *stripper poles* coming down from the ceiling!"

Ivy and Jonah spun around the poles, whipping their hair so hard I could feel the air coming off it with my magic. Smoke machines hissed, and I coughed as the smoke filled the dance floor.

I'm getting in there, Oberi insisted. She didn't care if she was invited or not; she strutted up between them, her hooves smacking the floor to the beat of the song. She spun in circles so fast that she got dizzy. She was forced to shift into a husky, or she was going to fall on someone and break their legs. Oberi stumbled to the side, his head landing in my lap. I shoved him off of me, and he went strutting around the dance floor again.

By the end of the song, fireworks were going off around the room, and embers rained down upon us. Ivy grabbed my hand and dragged me out of my chair, and Jonah pushed Ava forward. We spun and danced around, while our guests stormed the dance floor with us.

We were surrounded from all angles. Another song thumped a deep base, and suddenly, people were pushing and shoving each other. I heard the sound of punches and kicks connect, and panic swept through me.

"Ava!" I cried out. I was too far away from her, and I didn't know where she'd gone. Then I heard her laughter, and I knew she was safe.

I'm okay, she told me through the bond. *Jonah got me out of the way. I'm with Kallie getting drinks. Go have fun!*

A heavy hand landed on my shoulder, and my grandpa's gruff voice came from behind me. "There's nothing to worry about, my boy! A brawl at the end of the evening is an Elvish wedding tradition. Didn't you know?"

A fist came out of nowhere and smacked me in the face. I didn't know where it'd come from, though it wasn't my grandfather's. Pain shot through my nose, and blood trickled down my face. I tasted copper. Chancey's maniacal laughter faded as he raced away from me before I could get him back.

A huge grin spread across my face. It was like the Villain's Ball all over again, and I *lived* for the high of a fight.

"I fucking love the Elves!" I cheered.

I shoved my grandfather, and he hit me back. It wasn't enough to hurt—more like I was roughhousing with the father I had never had. I laughed gleefully as he got me in a headlock. I punched him in the stomach and ducked out of his arms. I dodged away from him and could still hear his laughter far off.

Oberi scurried up to me and bit my pants. He tugged, though not enough to rip fabric. He was being playful. I tried to kick him off, and he snapped his jaws at me. His sharp canines dug into my leg. Thankfully, he didn't draw blood, but it still hurt.

"Ow, Oberi!" I protested. "That's a bit harsh, don't you think?"

So siphon some of my strength, Elf boy, he teased. *Show me what you've got!*

I wrestled him to the ground and curled my arms around his neck. He spun in circles, dragging me along the floor, but I didn't budge.

Fine, I yield! he insisted.

I hopped off his back. As soon as my feet were back on solid ground, someone shoved me again. It had to be a vampire, judging by how strong they were. I tried to siphon his strength, but I noticed his magic was just as strong as I was. Fucking Danny.

I shoved him, and we ended up in a bloody brawl on the floor, both of us laughing the whole time. It felt really good to finally punch this guy in the face. I'd been waiting far too long for it. He landed a few good punches himself, and I could feel a bruise forming above my eye. He was one of the few guys who could actually give me a run for my money.

Danny slipped away, and I ended up smacking a few strangers before getting into it with Ez for a bit. I went easy on him, though, even though he was crushing the life out of me. I couldn't tell the difference between his grapples and bear hugs.

I stumbled off the dance floor laughing more than I think I ever had in my life, blood dripping from my face and all over my suit. My stomach was starting to hurt, and I couldn't stop smiling. Someone caught me and helped me stand up.

He dusted off my suit coat, and I realized it was my grandfather. "You seem to be enjoying yourself."

"Very much!" I cried. "This is the best night *ever*. Thank you so much for doing all this."

"It was my pleasure," he said. "This is everything I wanted to give you, and everything you deserve. I hope the night has been wonderful, despite your father's words at dinner."

My smile started to fall. "It didn't ruin anything, promise."

"I want to apologize. He doesn't mean to hurt you, but he's never been good with words."

"I understand," I stated. "I don't need him, because I have you."

My grandfather paused, like he didn't expect me to say that, before he cleared his throat. "Before you go, I would like to leave you with one last gift. Would you like to see your bride?"

My heart stalled. I hadn't even thought to ask him before, and now, I wanted nothing more. "Yes," I said eagerly.

Cassiel took my hand, and images began to flit across my vision. I saw the whole day play out from his point of view as memories of the ceremony and reception filled my head.

I witnessed Ava being carried down the aisle by Oberi, wearing her wedding gown and appearing more dazzling than a goddess. Her beautiful brown eyes were sparkling with light as her black hair cascaded down her back, her incredible lips lifted in a soft smile.

I couldn't imagine anything more beautiful than she was. In the heavens or here on Earth, it didn't exist.

His memories changed, and he showed me Ava's face as she listened to my song. Tears welled in her eyes, and she looked at me like there was no one else in the world for her. I witnessed myself holding Ava on the dance floor, her feet propped against mine as I spun her in circles. My face was buried in her hair, and my eyes were closed as I took her in. She rested her head on my chest, happiness beaming from every part of her.

I began to cry when my grandfather showed me those images. I'd seen Ava only once before when I'd brought her back from the Ancestral Lands, and that had merely been her spirit. Now I got to see her in the flesh, as she was day to day. I couldn't describe how much it meant to me to have a picture of her in my mind, forever, a piece of her I could hold on to and never let go. It was obvious Ava and I belonged together, because there was nothing more incredible than having her by my side.

"Thank you," I told him when the visions ended. "I didn't think I could love her any more than I already do, but I just keep falling in love with her over and over again."

"And you will for the rest of your life," he promised me. "Even when life changes, your love for Ava never will."

"I'm not ready for things to change," I admitted. "I love it here in Ilamanthe."

"Life never stays the same, but that doesn't mean you can't be happy in every stage of it," Cassiel said. "After all, you must start making heirs soon, and that is a beautiful stage of life to be in!"

I laughed. "Yeah. I'm really going to enjoy the *making* part."

"Well, you best get on it, son!" he joked. "It *is* your wedding night."

I'd certainly been looking forward to *that* part of the night for a while. Kind of weird for my grandpa to suggest it, though.

I found Ava near the head table, eating a slice of cake with Kallie. Oberi was beside her in unicorn form. The girls were snickering under their breath.

"Enjoy the *rest of your night*," Kallie said with a giggle, before I heard her grab Marcus and scamper off.

"Ancestors, is that all anyone can think of around here— consummating our marriage?" I joked.

"It's all *I'm* thinking of," Ava teased. "I've been thinking about it all day, really."

I leaned down to whisper in her ear. "I suppose we should do something about that."

Ava shivered, and fuck, I was hard already. "Take me back to our quarters," she whispered. "*Now.*"

"Gladly." I scooped her up in my arms and placed her on Oberi's back, then climbed on behind her. I held her to me, so she could keep her balance as we walked forward.

Our guests cheered as Ava waved them goodbye. Oberi trotted out of the ballroom. She took us down long hallways and wide corridors until we were far away from the reception.

"I saw you talking to your grandfather," Ava remarked. "What did he say?"

I chuckled. "He wants us to start *making heirs*."

"Oh, yes, we should get on that right away," Ava teased sarcastically.

I paused for a beat. "I know you're only joking, but what do we *really* think about it? I never thought I'd be a dad, because I didn't think I could provide for a kid, but I always *wanted* to be a parent. Now we *can* give our kids the best life here in the city. But I wouldn't want to have a child unless it's what you really want."

Ava seemed to ponder my question for a long time. "I'm not sure. Before, I was absolutely against having kids. But that was because I thought I'd be a bad mom."

"You'd never be a bad mom, Ava," I whispered. I couldn't imagine why she'd think so. She was such a good person.

"I don't know. I think I could imagine having kids, yet I'm still on the fence. I'm open to it, at least. But I'm not bringing a child into this world as long as the Warden is still alive. He's dying by my hand before I *ever* let him touch one of our babies. If we ever get around to making heirs, it won't be until this war is over."

"I agree. We can talk about kids again when we're ready, and when he's gone for good."

This world was too dangerous to bring a kid into while the Warden was still living. It would just be Ava and me, for now, and I was more than happy with that.

The temperature dropped as Oberi cut through an open courtyard. A large fountain trickled ahead of us.

Oberi blew a breath, like she was displeased. *Don't I get a say? My Familiar instincts are telling me it is time for you to have a baby, and the time to make it is right now!*

"We would, but there isn't enough room up here," I cracked.

Oberi skidded to a halt beside the fountain, clearly offended. *I am not your sex toy! If you want to make a baby, you can do it right here.*

Then she *bucked us off.* Ava and I screamed as we went flying into the fountain, and water surrounded us from all angles. I inhaled a bit of water and gasped as my head resurfaced. Ava shook water out of her hair. We'd landed on our asses in the pool, and the water was up to our chests. The fountain had a tiered structure in the middle that poured water down on all sides like a waterfall, but the base of the fountain was so large that the droplets from the center never touched us.

"Real mature, Oberi," Ava said. "You're lucky water isn't going to ruin this dress."

Oberi ignored her and began trotting away. *I'll cast a protection spell around the area so you two can be alone. Charlie, don't come out until you've put a baby in her!*

I laughed as Oberi's hoofsteps completely faded. In fact, I didn't hear her at all, as if the spell she cast blocked out all noise outside this courtyard. We were certainly alone.

"Oberi's not offended," I said. "She just wants us to get on making babies *right now.*"

Ava snickered as she wrapped her arms around my neck. She commanded the water to float her legs over top of me, until she was straddling me. Her dress billowed around us. "You're still on birth control, so it won't work anyway... but we might as well try, right? It'll be fun."

Her lips pressed against mine, and passion swelled between us. A primal wanting came over me, and my head spun as I dragged her even closer to me. The water was a bit chilly, but it barely registered as my cock became rock hard for her.

"I literally can't wait to get you back to the room," I gasped between kisses. "I'm going to do you right here."

Ava gave a gleeful snicker. "We've never done it in a fountain before."

I smirked. "Sit back and relax, my love. There's a first time for everything."

Ava gasped as I kissed the sensitive area below her jaw. Slowly, I guided her onto her back, and she used her powers to keep herself afloat. I trailed kisses up and down her chest, until my fingers found the buttons of her dress. I slowly undid the dress as she let out little moans with each kiss. The dress loosened, and the fabric tickled my skin as Ava's water magic carried it away. She wore lace lingerie underneath, and my fingers trailed over it, taking in every detail. There was ribbing along the bodice, along with smooth ribbons outlining her breasts. I shuddered as my fingers grazed over her nipples.

I trailed my hand downward, and I gasped when I found how thin the fabric was between her legs. I pushed the lace aside, and Ava moaned as I slid two fingers deep inside of her. I just about lost it right then and there. My lips met hers, and I placed my other hand against the back of her neck to pull her close. Her tongue rolled over my mouth as she clutched to my suit coat in desperate wanting.

Fuck this suitcoat. It was wet and heavy, and it was in the freaking way.

I shrugged the coat off, and Ava began to undo the buttons on my shirt. As we deepened our kisses, the water within the fountain began to swirl around us. Ava's magic swept by to remove my clothes, and soon, I was on my knees stark naked in the fountain. Ava's bare skin rubbed against mine as I drew her close.

The water lifted us upward until Ava was able to lay on her back, completely supported by her magic. I floated on top of her, then thrust my hips once until I was buried deep inside her. Ava let out a cry of pleasure as I filled her up completely. We moved slowly, drawing out the sensations as I moved in and out of her.

Ava moaned as I increased my speed, the water rocking her up and down. I didn't think she realized what she was doing when the water began to swirl around the fountain. We floated in circles like we were drifting down a river.

Ava seemed to be supporting her weight just fine with her magic, so I began roaming my hands over her body. I cupped her breasts, and she arched her back for me. Slowly, I pushed the fabric of her lingerie aside, and I squeezed her nipples between my fingers. She gasped.

"More," she begged.

My heart hammered as I wrapped an arm around her waist and pulled her closer. I sucked her nipple into my mouth as I thrust upward.

"Fuck," she breathed.

The water between us changed. Tiny water currents swirled around my cock, and it felt *really* fucking good. Certainly reminded me of some of our toys back in the Sanctuary. That's when I realized Ava was doing it on purpose. She was using the water currents as a vibrator.

She obviously really liked it, because the rest of the fountain responded to her magic. Waves began to swell and fall to the rhythm of our passion. Shapes formed in the water around us, and when I ran my hands over them, I found that she'd made a herd of tiny unicorns that galloped across the surface of the water. They almost felt solid, until I pushed too hard and my fingers went straight through them. Around us, water crystallized momentarily, before the warmth of Ava's Fire magic melted them. There was a beautiful ebb and flow to her magic, and I was eager to see what her magic might do when her passion reached its peak.

I couldn't hold back any longer. I bit down on her nipple while I grabbed her ass and thrust deep inside of her. Ava let out a cry that would've echoed through the halls of the palace if Oberi hadn't cast the protection spell. I pulled out of her, then buried myself deep inside her again. She cried out even louder this time.

I silenced her with a passionate kiss. Ava tugged on my hair as desire surged through our bond. Her magic faltered for a beat, and our heads dipped under water. I didn't care, though, because my wife had already taken my breath away. She kissed me under water over and over again, and her magic swirled around my cock. I braced my feet against the bottom of the pool to thrust into her even harder.

Ava could hold her breath longer than I could, because she was Toaqua. She wrapped her arms tightly around me and commanded the water to flip us over. My head broke the surface. I inhaled a deep breath, before dipping my head back underwater to kiss her again. We spun several more times, until she was on top. She took a breath, then joined me under the water again.

We did this over and over, twirling within the water until we broke the surface together, panting. I guided her to the middle of the fountain, where the center tiers rained water down in a circle. Ava giggled as the water trickled over our heads, until we were beneath the waterfall completely. A stone bowl-like structure stood above our heads, and the waterfall concealed us in our own little world.

I pinned Ava against the smooth stone structure that rose at the center of the pool. I kissed her again as I increased my speed. I thrust upward once, then twice, and that's when I lost it. My mind went completely blank as I spiraled into an incredible orgasm. I moaned loudly, the sound echoing off the stone above us.

Ava gasped as I filled her up. She clung to me tightly, and the water she'd been commanding vibrated hard against her clit. She drew a deep breath as she reached her peak. The high of my orgasm continued as she contracted around me and waves of pleasure swept through the bond. Water swirled around us faster, turning the fountain into a tumultuous sea. Our passion seemed to tangle together until it felt as if we weren't in the pool anymore, but somewhere else entirely where only our souls could reach. For a brief moment, I felt as if Ava and I were one.

We were both panting as we came down from the high. The water calmed. I held her tight in my arms and pressed my nose into her hair.

"Pidge, that was fucking great," I whispered.

"Yeah," she sighed. "I'm not sure you put a baby in me, though. We should probably try again."

I chuckled happily. "I could go forever if you asked."

"So keep going," she begged breathlessly.

And we did. We must've been rolling around in that fountain for hours. I lost all sense of time, because all I could make sense of was Ava's body against mine. We only stopped when Ava became too tired to keep going. It was probably a good thing, because if we hadn't, I would've been more than happy to drown in there.

I carried her out of the water and set her on a bench nearby. She sagged onto it with a blissful sigh. I felt around in the pool until I felt the fabric of our clothes.

"I can dry those off, but good luck getting me back into that dress," Ava said.

I draped her dress against the side of the fountain. Honestly, I couldn't make much sense of the layers of clothing I'd been wearing earlier.

"I'll leave our clothes here for a servant to bring back to our room," I offered. "In the meantime, we can't roam around the palace naked."

"Why not? I don't mind who sees," Ava said coyly.

"Well, I do. You're all mine, and no one else's. I'm not sharing one bit of you."

I waved my hand, and magic settled over both of us until my illusion magic had created beautiful silk pajamas for us both. Mine was a shirt and pants— practically a suit— and Ava's was a short nightgown.

The fabric rustled as Ava ran her fingers over it. "This is perfect."

I scooped her up in my arms, and she leaned her head against my shoulder as I carried her out of the courtyard. Oberi's protection spell fell the moment we left. We weren't far from our quarters, so I only had to turn down one hall before I was carrying Ava into our suite. I got a thrill when we walked through the door, because I realized I was carrying her over the threshold, as wedding tradition dictated.

I set her on the bed in our room, then pulled the blanket over her. I slid into bed beside her and snuggled close.

"Do you want your present now?" Ava whispered.

I tilted my head. "I thought what happened in the fountain *was* my present."

She snickered. "That was a given. I have something else for you."

I sat up straighter. "Oh?"

Ava leaned over the nightstand, then clicked the remote. The TV on the other side of the room turned on, and Ava pressed a few more buttons before I heard the sound of Ezekiel's voice coming through the speakers.

"*Shh...*" he hissed. "*It's starting.*"

I furrowed my brow. "Um... recordings of your brother don't exactly turn me on. What is this?"

"Keep watching," Ava said playfully.

Hemlock's voice came then. "*Dearly beloved. We are gathered here today to join Charlie Wahkin and Ava-Marie Mitoh in holy matrimony. Have the two of you prepared your vows?*"

"*Oh, um...*" I heard my own voice say.

"*We have vows,*" Ava said over the TV.

Tears beaded in my eyes. "It's our wedding video," I whispered. "From our first wedding at the Institute. Ez was recording the whole time?"

"Yes. He saved it before he escaped the prison," Ava said. "Today's ceremony was a celebration of our love, but whatever your grandpa says, we've already been married for a year. This was the *true* start of our relationship. Before we were married, we were messing around, but we weren't dating for most of it. Even when we were, we didn't have a lot of time to be boyfriend and girlfriend. Everything about us being together has been about our marriage. No one else is going to understand this video but us, so I kept it for just me and you, because this is where we started."

On the video, Ava was already halfway through her vows. "*I promise you from now on, you will never be alone. And so, I vow to follow you on all future adventures, because being with my worst enemy is the greatest adventure of all.*"

Tears streamed from my cheeks as I listened to my vows from a year ago. So much had changed since then. "*Ava-Marie, I vow to serve you as your bonded partner from now until the day we die, no matter how long that might be.*"

I pulled Ava tightly to my chest and kissed the top of her head. "I love where we started, but I love us even more now. That guy in the video was wrong, though. I don't vow to love you until the day we die, because I vow to love you longer. My love for you will never end, pidge. *Never.*"

Ava melted into me. "Mine either, Charlie. A year ago was the beginning of our love, but today... today was the beginning of forever."

ava-marie

EIGHTEEN

"What are you doing, Ava?"

Marcus' voice echoed across the gardens. It was starting to get a little chilly— autumn had finally arrived in Ilamanthe with the end of October, and the leaves were starting to turn. I sat underneath an olive tree, contemplating to myself quietly while Eldin stood guard.

My wedding had been wonderful, and Charlie and I felt like we were so in love. The day had been completely magical, and held so many memories I would cherish forever. It was good to get back to normal life, though, and we'd happily settled into a routine of being husband and wife once more. It was everything I ever wanted... even if I had to admit to myself that as perfect as things were in Ilamanthe, they weren't perfect everywhere. I knew that intimately. We had our happy ending here, but until things were happy all around the world, I couldn't rest. Not while the Warden was still out there.

"Just... feeling the energy of the Earth," I said as Marcus took a seat on a stone bench beside me. "With fall here, it's like I can feel everything dying."

"I figured only a Nivita would be able to sense that kind of change in the earth," Marcus said.

"Earth with a capital E— the energy of the planet, not just the rocks and trees. It's different now," I noted. "Now that I know what I can do, everything feels like it's... changed."

"You're talking about your demigod power?" Marcus asked.

"Yeah." I wasn't the type of muse on things, but my newfound abilities had me perplexed. "We know I can take magic from the Earth's spirit, but I've been looking inside of her lately, and it's like there isn't much to give. She felt so powerful when I first connected with her during my training with my mother, but I've reconnected since, and it's like she's... sick."

"That's not good." Marcus frowned. "Do you think you might be able to fix it?"

"I actually wanted to talk to you about it," I started. "This isn't just the changing of the seasons. I feel like Earth's energy is being drained. It's pulling on my demigod magic— something from the spiritual realm. You have Death magic. Can you feel it, too?"

"I can try to tap in." Marcus shrugged. "It will work best with simultension — your Spirit magic with my Death magic."

He reached out for me, and I placed my hands in his. Marcus closed his eyes and drew a deep breath. My Spirit magic tingled up and down my form, and I could feel it tangling with the dark energy Marcus gave off. Together, we reached deep into the Earth. A pit seemed to form in my stomach the deeper we dug. I shifted in my chair, because the feeling made me very uncomfortable. I wanted to pull away, but Marcus' hold on me tightened. He squeezed his eyes shut tighter, twisting his head to the side. He felt it, too.

"You're right," Marcus noted as he pulled back. "Ava, I think the spiritual realm is pulling energy from Earth. They're connected. With the gods fighting, and the Blessed Haven ripping apart, the spiritual realm is taking power from the earthly plane to stay alive."

"No wonder the Earth feels weak." I shuddered. "But Earth only has so much to give, and the spiritual realm needs to keep taking in order to remain active, since it's not able to sustain itself anymore. Supernaturals are constantly pulling magic from the spiritual realm in order to cast, so all that magic has to come from somewhere. If the Blessed Haven isn't providing it, Earth has to make up the difference. But what happens when the planet doesn't have anything left to give?"

Marcus swallowed. "I think that if that *does* happen, Earth wouldn't be the only thing that would be destroyed. The spiritual realm would be ruined, too."

"It would be a dire situation if such a thing were to happen," a deep voice said. I turned to see Emperor Cassiel standing a short distance away. He must've overheard us.

"Your majesty," Marcus blurted, and he fumbled to his feet to give a clumsy bow. I dipped my head as the Emperor joined us and took a seat on the stone bench.

"I hope you don't mind my intrusion, but this seems like a grave matter," Cassiel began. "I believe Mister Taylor is right when he says that if the Blessed Haven keeps taking energy from Earth, both planes of reality will eventually collapse."

"That truly means the end of everything," I said ominously. "No Earth, no spiritual realm... all the souls, in both planes, would be destroyed with the collapse. There'd be no life or afterlife. Everything that has been or ever was would cease to exist in one moment."

"Everything we *know*," Cassiel said. "Remember, energy cannot be created nor destroyed, save by gods or demigods, and neither demigods nor deities themselves would have control over the situation. All of that energy would have to go somewhere. Perhaps into the creation of a new world, one that may be better than this one."

The suggestion felt heartless, as if it was worth sacrificing all the innocent lives on Earth for something better.

"I don't want there to be a new world; I *want* to save the one we have," I growled.

"As we all do," Cassiel replied. "Ava, since this power to influence the Earth's spirit lies with you, I can do my best to advise, so we can avoid this situation altogether."

"You're a powerful Elf, but I don't know if we can find a solution to this," I said heavily. "The only way to stabilize things is to get the Blessed Haven up and running again, and it's breaking apart because the gods are fighting. The only way to prevent this is to stop the Warden, find the Divinity Keys, and open the Elven Gate as Charlie's prophecy foretells."

"Or surrender," Cassiel said simply.

Marcus gaped, and I instantly recoiled. "How can you say that?" I demanded. I didn't care that I was speaking harshly to an Emperor. *No one* should suggest we give in to the Warden. "Even if we were to give up, the Warden would rule everything, on Earth and in the Blessed Haven!"

"Yes. And we Elves would be exterminated, along with anyone else who disagreed with the Warden's rule, and all the love and light would eventually go out of the world, to be replaced by pain and suffering," Cassiel said gently. "But wouldn't it be a better alternative than all of nature and time being consumed by the breaking of the Blessed Haven entirely, and all souls being destroyed? There are more important things in the universe than us— things that have existed for time immemorial, that will continue to exist long after supernatural kind is gone. Isn't it worth our sacrifice to preserve that?"

"That's no world I want to live in," I spat. "No afterlife, either. It might as well all be gone if it's run by a dictator like the Warden."

"That's a very heavy choice to make," Cassiel stated. "You are a princess, Ava. These are very difficult choices that affect everyone. No matter what choices you make as ruler, someone will always have to pay the price. Sometimes we have to consider the greater good."

I despised that way of thinking. *The greater good.* It was a pathetic way to think and talk. I didn't believe we had to make sacrifices to get to where we wanted to go.

We just needed to deal with the Warden the hard way, and be done with it.

I huffed. "Well, it doesn't *matter*, because I'm not going to let that happen. The Blessed Haven isn't going to collapse, and the Earth isn't going to be destroyed. I'll give up everything I have to make sure that never comes to pass."

"I know you speak the truth, Ava. You will do what you must to protect all of us. I've been certain of it from the moment I met you," Cassiel praised. "This is a frightening situation, but if we band as one, we'll pull through it. You and your friends will bring an end to this war, so long as you stick together."

"Doesn't the Warden understand what he's doing?" Marcus asked. "He has to know that by convincing the dark gods to fight our deities, the Blessed Haven could break, and destroy everything else along with it."

"I believe if we've figured it out, he must know as well, but Doctor Taurus is a man who will take calculated risks to get what he desires," Cassiel said.

Of course. Because it was his way or the highway. The Warden didn't mind making a gamble on all of time, space and eternity if there was a chance he could be at the head of it, calling all the shots and making all the rules.

Screw him. Nobody decided what was going to happen to our world but *me*, because I would always make the right choice. We were saving it from the Warden, and kicking his ass on his way out.

"I don't care what the Warden has planned, because it's not coming true." I sat up higher. "Charlie and I are going to end him, then once we do, we're going to rid this world of suffering. Since we're demigods, we'll be strong enough to put an ending to misery and pain. Once the Warden is out of the way, it'll be easy."

"You can't avoid suffering, my child. No matter how much you try to," Cassiel said kindly. "The world is always innately suffering, and there is no way for anyone to stop it."

"That can't be true." I felt my fingers ache as my hands clenched. "*I* can be powerful enough to change it. If I'm a demigod, and I can't use my magic to end *all* suffering, then why should I even bother having my abilities? Why does it matter that I can perform incredible feats of magic if I can't use it to make the world a better place *everywhere*? I'm strong enough to stop anything."

"Not even a god is powerful enough to end suffering. If they were, don't you think they would've done so? Don't you think your ancestors would've interceded on your behalf if they had that ability?" Cassiel questioned.

"They can influence things," I argued. "We've seen it before."

"Yes, but even the influence of a deity is limited," Cassiel pointed out. "Not even a god has infinite power, enough to override free will."

I raised my chin. "Well, it doesn't matter if all the other gods and demigods were unable to do anything to prevent suffering, because none of them are *me*. I'll be the first one."

"Ava, my dear, you cannot survive without taking life from something else." Cassiel laid his hand gently on mine. "Even if you refuse to eat meat, you must still take the life of a plant to consume it. Otherwise, you will starve. Creatures must die to fertilize the ground so nature can continue to grow. The designer labels you love so much— how can you absolutely prove they weren't produced through unethical means? We could go on and on. There is a purpose to suffering, for if there wasn't, it wouldn't exist."

I felt my hand grow cold under his. "There is no purpose in suffering. Perhaps death, but not pain."

"Why not?" Cassiel asked softly. "Does it bother you to consider that could be a possibility, for suffering to have meaning? Do you have to believe that purpose has to be *good*?"

I shifted in my chair again. Marcus wasn't saying much, that was for sure. He was staring at me, expecting me to have some stereotypical answer.

But I wasn't giving him one. I thought differently from most people, and that was part of my identity. I wouldn't cave on this because other people figured the problem was too hard to solve. Not when there were solutions right in front of us, solutions society refused to integrate.

"We can make a completely equal, ethical society," I argued. "Look at Ilamanthe. I have no trouble getting around in my wheelchair here, and neither does Charlie, even though he's blind. We've fought society so long for accommodations that should be standard, but they're considered radical in the rest of the world. That's only a small taste of how perfect things are here. If the Elves can do it, so can everyone else. The world doesn't have to be the way that it is."

"Perhaps." Cassiel shrugged. "But much of that requires societal change to get there. The Elves have always had an accommodating culture, so it wasn't much of an effort or a debate to install these practices. In other cultures, you'd have a much tougher time. Decades, or even centuries, could pass without people ever changing their minds."

I let out a dark laugh. "I'd figure out a way."

"Why do you think you're responsible for the world?" Cassiel questioned. "Why is it on your shoulders to stop the suffering of everyone in it? You are only one woman."

"Because I'm *better* than everyone else," I demanded. "I'm stronger, braver, more powerful. I'm willing to put more on the line and make choices others won't. Other people don't have the capability to change the world, but *I do*. You must understand. You're an Emperor! You have enough power and soldiers at your command to make a true difference."

Cassiel tilted his head. "Do you think I'm a bad person?"

I was shocked he'd ask. "Of course not," I insisted. "You're good."

"But I've tortured and killed people," Cassiel stated.

"That was to save the Elves."

"Does that make it right because I had a good *reason*?"

I couldn't reply. It was hard to imagine Cassiel, soft and gentle as he was, being any sort of monster.

Though I knew he was. He'd done things in the dark that I probably couldn't imagine. Things that I bet were far worse than what Charlie and I had ever committed.

"We've built a paradise in Ilamanthe, yes," Cassiel added. "But don't think it didn't come at a cost. Some people had to suffer in order for us to get here. As much as you'd like to change the world, it won't happen without someone getting hurt."

I flattened my lips. "I'm sorry, Emperor, but I don't believe you." I stood firm in my belief, because no way was I bending on this one. "We can make a just world for everyone without having to make any sacrifices. Everyone can come with us, and everyone can benefit. We just have to find a way."

Cassiel smiled. "Never change, my child. You are exactly what this world needs, even if you fail."

"I don't lose," I told him with a smirk. "You'll see."

Cassiel laughed. "I never had to wonder why Charlie is so devoted to you. Even I, set in my ways as I am, feel inspired to call up a banner and join you."

"He's been different since he's been in Ilamanthe," I said. "You've changed him in such a wonderful way. Charlie hasn't said so, but I know he really loves you."

Cassiel's eyes glimmered. "I hold deep affection for him as well. Although I would never say this to Cameron, my son and I never quite got along, even as he was growing up. He never wanted to take the job seriously. But in his stead, Charlie is everything I hoped for in a future Emperor. We are very much alike. I see myself as a young man in him. Just as I see so much of my wife in you."

Cassiel raised my hand and kissed the back of it before he stood. "I am afraid I must be elsewhere, my dear. There are generals I must speak to about our next attack against The Mission. If you need me at any time, merely call, and I will come to you at once. You are the hope for Ilamanthe's future, now."

Cassiel's elegant robe skimmed the grass as he left, and I let out a tired sigh before glancing at Marcus.

"I've got to go to the temple for mystic training, and I don't think I can get there on my own," I said wearily. "Push me?"

Marcus nodded. "Sure."

I felt myself falling asleep in my chair as we left the gardens. The wedding had been great, but it had worn me out for days afterward. I still wasn't fully recovered, but I couldn't keep pushing off my mystic duties. I needed to go to the temple and try to contact the Elvish goddesses yet again... not that they'd managed to answer so far.

"You didn't say much back there," I grumbled as Marcus and I made our way back into the palace. "You could've helped me out a little."

"I didn't know what *to* say," Marcus stated. "I'm not sure what to believe, really."

"You can't be buying what Cassiel said," I argued. "Suffering is a *choice*, one people choose to inflict on each other. Society just has to choose to stop hurting itself. Don't you believe that?"

Marcus seemed thoughtful. "I don't know, Ava. Kallie committed her entire life to stopping suffering in Malovia, and she nearly drowned in it. That was just one country. She would've lost her mind if she hadn't been sent to the Institute while trying to take down all the bad in her nation. How do you think you can stop all the terrible things from happening all over the *world*? It just isn't realistic. You'll go crazy before you manage it."

"I don't care," I said stubbornly. "The rest of you just haven't figured it out yet. I'm smart enough to find a way."

The Great Mystic appeared impatient when I showed up at the temple doors, which was saying something for a five-hundred-year-old Elf.

"Princess, you were supposed to show up an hour ago," the Great Mystic scolded.

Marcus hastily dipped out, not wanting to be yelled at himself.

"I'm sorry, Valindra. I was speaking with the Emperor," I told her.

Not a lie, but that wasn't my reason for showing up late. I'd been struggling with a bad flare up all morning and didn't want to let anyone at the temple know. I had zero energy, and a lot of body aches. If they saw I was in pain, they'd insist I needed to rest, but we didn't have time for that. Now that I knew what I did about the Blessed Haven, we needed to beat the Warden *now*, and there wasn't any time for me to take a day off.

The Great Mystic's eyes softened. "Oh, the Emperor. Of course. Any conference you have with him is more important than what we're doing here, most certainly."

I used what bit of strength I could to push myself toward the front of the temple, smiling as I observed the sunlight coming through the windows. This temple held such fond memories for me now. Whenever I entered it, I was reminded of how beautiful our wedding was. It nearly swept me away into dreamland whenever I roamed its halls.

"Princess, please," the Great Mystic said, and it snapped me out of any daydreams about my wedding day. "We simply must get started."

I hid my shaking hands in my skirt. "Very well. Let's begin."

The mystics prepared me for the ritual to speak to the goddesses by bathing me in the blessed pool and dressing me in a golden gown, painting shining symbols onto my skin as they always did. The ceremony for contacting the Elvish goddesses was similar to my induction as the Holy Mother, without all the fanfare, and was the same every time. I did this every week, only once, as it took too much energy to be performed more often. The rest of my mystic training was centered around learning about the goddesses, and all the various rituals and spells the Elves used to connect with them.

I felt bad for the mystics, going through all this work just for me to never get any answers. My visions remained unclear each time I went through the ceremony. I was wondering if I couldn't hear the goddesses, or if the goddesses couldn't hear me.

The mystics laid me upon the stone altar, and I closed my eyes. As the Great Mystic began her chant, I found myself falling into a trance, although it was different this time... it felt similar to the way I'd fallen into the first vision when I'd become the Holy Mother. During my other attempts to speak with the goddesses, I'd remained conscious, although I'd gotten fragments of images.

Now, I was fading. The goddesses were finally sending me a message! I eagerly dove into the darkness, awaiting what the Elvish goddesses had for me...

I SAW WAR, and a sky that was on fire. Thousands perished under the weight of incredible magic that was impossible to stop. Armies marched across the land, cutting down anyone in their path. Leaders bowed, and kings surrendered. Nothing was able to stop the conquering of nations and lands on the planet Earth underneath the rule of one who wanted to control it all.

I watched, one by one, as the Elvish race died out, a line of people toppling over into graves until there were none left standing. Plants withered and died, and chasms blazing with the fires of hell opened in the ground. Screams of torture echoed across barren landscapes. Among the bodies strewn across battlefields, supernaturals of all races were locked in chains. The prisoners were all carted away to become slaves.

A palace flashed in my mind, one I knew well. It looked unlike anything I remembered. All the shine from the golden trim around the doorways had weathered, and the water in the fountains had been replaced by thick red algae. Twisted vines grew up the side of the palace walls, and weeds invaded the stone walkways. Several towers had been toppled over, the remnants of stone still lying in forgotten heaps. The towers were nothing more than graveyards now. Overhead, dark storm clouds swirled, and all that could be heard was the howl of the wind.

A middle-aged woman lay on the stone path underneath the castle, her black hair covering her face. A dark pool of blood spanned around her head, and hundreds of feet above her, there was an open window. People rushed about, screaming that she had thrown herself from the tower's edge.

The vision changed again. I saw an old man sitting upon a throne, a lopsided crown atop his gray head. His hair was long and scraggly, marred across his face, and his tangled beard lay over his tattered clothes. His sunken eyes appeared dead as two prisoners were dragged into the throne room and placed before him. He stared out the window and waved his hand without a second thought. The prisoners dropped dead in an instant. They didn't even get the chance to scream before their bodies were reduced to ash.

Everyone in the throne room bowed to the king— everyone feared him. The man on the throne appeared to have no remorse for anything that was going on around him, merely stared coldly ahead, as if all of this meant nothing to him. The pained roar of a dragon-like creature echoed in the distance, proclaiming his grief for all to hear.

In the distance, I heard the voices of two women— their words were indistinguishable, but they called out to me, their Holy Mother, as I found myself sinking back into the dark...

My eyes shot open, and I took a deep gasp as if I'd broken the surface of the ocean, writhing on the altar as I emerged from the trance.

Charlie stood above me. I didn't expect him to be here, but he was, hovering at my side and appearing grave. Oberi was tucked into his left arm, and she looked weary. The phoenix stirred with a withered chirp, as if she'd just awoken from some terrible nightmare. The other mystics gathered around the altar in a circle, hands over their mouths and clutching their necks.

Valindra had wrapped her cloak around her shoulders, though she still appeared cold. She shivered as I looked at her.

"The whole temple became dark when you fell into the vision, princess," the Great Mystic informed me. "Thunder rolled and shook the whole palace. It was certainly an omen from the goddesses."

The sun was beaming through the windows now, so the event must've passed quickly. Charlie helped me sit up. My head was still foggy and filled with memories of what I'd seen.

"Why are you here?" I mumbled, grabbing Charlie's arm to steady myself.

"Oberi fainted in mid-air during my meeting. I picked her up and came running to you," Charlie said. "You must've seen something important."

"I did," I replied. "Carolyn and Idril heard me this time; I'm sure of it. They sent me a message at the end of the vision, though their voices were muffled and I couldn't understand what they were saying. I think they're trying to get through to me from the Blessed Haven, but they just can't."

"What'd you see?" Charlie asked, kneeling beside the altar.

I explained to him, and the other mystics, the contents of my vision. The longer my words went on, the more terrified the mystics became— a few of them broke down in tears.

"It wasn't a very long trance, but a clear one," I finished. "I think the goddesses are trying to warn us of what's to come if we don't stop this."

"Can you interpret this vision for us, princess?" the Great Mystic questioned.

I hesitated. "I'm not a *naderei*, so it's difficult for me to know what the goddesses wanted me to see for certain."

Then I swallowed thickly. "But I think I can understand what that vision meant. It was a potential future, one the goddesses want us to avoid."

What do you believe you saw? Oberi asked. Charlie placed her on the altar, and she struggled to stand as she peered at me.

"In my vision, I saw the Warden's armies marching across the land. He killed everyone who opposed him and took over the entire Earth," I began. "No one was able to stand up to him, and anyone who tried was immediately killed. Millions of people must've perished, and I don't think any Elves survived. Under the Warden's rule, the Earth began to die. The entire planet looked barren."

I held back a shudder. If the Earth was still around, at least the Blessed Haven had endured in this future... but it was a future that wasn't worth living through.

"What about the old man on the throne?" Charlie asked, appearing scared himself.

"It was the Warden, I know it. I don't know how far in the future this was, but it could've been a thousand years or more. The Warden had aged, and the war appeared to take a great toll on him. He looked so old that I barely recognized him, but I *know* it was him," I stated. "His eyes were sunken, like they are now, and he seemed completely heartless. He succeeded and got everything he wanted, but it still wasn't enough to satisfy him. He will always be cruel, no matter what he achieves, and nothing he does will bring him the utopia he desires."

The temple was silent, save for the weeping of the other mystics, but we couldn't sit around and be fearful now. Not when the goddesses had given us a warning we needed to act on.

"My vision is *going* to happen if The Mission wins," I said firmly. "What's coming is worse than what we imagined. We have to make sure that future doesn't come to pass, at any cost."

But who was the woman who fell from the tower? Oberi asked, nudging me. *What does that mean?*

I had to force myself to choke out the words. "I think... I think the woman who jumped from the tower was *me*."

Charlie went pale. He grasped me firmly, stuttering, "Where was I? I wouldn't have let you—"

"I didn't see you in the vision, which means the Warden must've killed you and our friends. I know none of you would let me remain captured unless you guys couldn't do anything about it." I was nearly crying now; imagining all of this, considering losing Charlie and all my friends, almost caused me to break down. "He eliminated you and the other demigods, then took me and Oberi prisoner after the war was over. *That's* why I heard a creature roar in pain. It was Oberi. The Warden conquered Ilamanthe, then captured the palace for himself. He took me as his personal pet and kept me in a tower, but it came to the point where I couldn't stand it any longer, so I fell to my death to escape him."

I felt sick inside. Becoming the Warden's favorite toy... it was a potential future that *could* befall me. Otherwise, the goddesses wouldn't have warned me about it. It made me want to end my life now, just to avoid the possibility of that ever occurring.

"I would never let that happen to you," Charlie growled fiercely.

"It's going to, if we don't prevent this from happening," I insisted. "I won't be the Warden's prisoner. I know killing myself is something I would do to get away from him."

"So we must make certain the Warden never conquers Ilamanthe," the Great Mystic stated, with renewed vigor. "The life of our princess, and of our people, is at stake."

"Why would the goddesses send you this specific message? We've all known what's been at stake since the start of this war," Charlie said.

"Maybe we weren't taking it seriously enough," I mumbled. "We knew that the Warden wanted to conquer the entire world, but knowing that and seeing it firsthand are two completely different things."

I leaned against his chest and wasn't able to suppress a soft moan of pain this time. My back felt like it was on fire, right above the vertebra where I lost all feeling.

"My prince, I implore you, the princess needs rest," the Great Mystic said.

"I'm taking her back to our room immediately," Charlie replied as he helped me into my chair, though he more or less carried me into it. "I don't want anyone disturbing us for the rest of the day, understood?"

"Yes, my prince." The mystics bowed out of the way, and Charlie hurried to push me back to his quarters. Oberi was too worn to fly, so she rested on my lap. Eldin had been standing guard by the temple doors, and she followed close behind us as we left.

On the way back, Danny called across the hall, "Hey, you two! Wait up, it's important!"

I could practically feel Charlie grinding his teeth as he replied, "Not today, Danny."

Danny used super speed to run from one side of the hall to the other to catch up with us. "We got a lead on that list of vamps you pulled from the strip club. They're congregating in New York, and we've finally got a chance to find out what they know about the vampire key's location. We need to put together a team now, because we've got a good shot at intercepting this information."

Charlie stopped pushing my chair. At the mention of a new lead on the vampire key, I felt myself sag in both relief and exhaustion.

I went to say something, but Charlie shook his head and said, "No. It'll have to wait."

"*Wait?*" Danny asked blankly. "We've been waiting around for weeks on a new lead, and *now* you wanna sit around? Not a smart move, pal."

"Ava doesn't need this—" Charlie started, before I put a soft hand on his.

"Charlie, no. We need to handle this," I insisted.

"You've been through a lot. You need a break," he demanded.

"In a minute. Let's take care of this first," I begged.

Charlie appeared thoroughly depressed, but I said through our bond, *You're not making me do this. We don't have a choice right now.*

Charlie's shoulders slumped. "Fine, hurry up. You guys better have something good."

"Oh, believe me," Danny started. "It's more than good. It's closer than we've ever gotten."

My body screamed in protest. All I wanted to do was go back to my room and go to bed, yet I couldn't, because we had a job to do. I remembered the sunken eyes of the old man on the throne and recoiled. I told myself if I didn't want to become the Warden's prisoner, I needed to keep going so I could avoid that fate.

I was so tired. Not just today— tired of doing this, tired of living this way. I wasn't sure if this war would ever be over, but I supposed it only would be when I decided to stop trying. That would never happen, so we had to carry on.

When we got to the training arena, Eddie, Marcus, and Kallie were waiting for us, along with Ivy and Chancey. Danny leaned against a wall. I rolled to the center of the room, where a large whiteboard had been rolled out. On the whiteboard were the faces of all the head mobsters in Salvatore Bianchi's mob that knew something about the vampire key, and all the knowledge we'd acquired about them since.

"Prince, princess, glad to see you here. The Elvish Associates have found a valuable piece of intel," Eddie began.

"What is it?" Charlie asked.

"We've discovered a rare chance to learn more about the vampire key, one we're not going to get again," Eddie started. "Usually, Salvatore sends his top underbosses all around the world to do his dirty work on separate jobs. Next week, he's concentrating all of them in New York, inside a hotel he owns."

"All of them?" I raised my eyebrow. "That seems risky. If someone blows the place up, all his cronies are dead. Why would he take such a risk?"

"It is our belief this is something of a yearly summit for the vampire mob," Eddie said. "Salvatore calls all his top people in, and they have meetings about the expansion of the mob's projects and endeavors around the supernatural community. All of the men who know something about the vampire key are going to be there."

Kallie laughed. "What do you know? Even the mob has work conventions."

"This is our chance, then," Charlie muttered. "We can't risk tracking these people down one by one and interrogating them. Once we try, Salvatore will find out, and he'll bring all his mobsters back into the safety of his base. We have to get everything we can from these people all at once, at the same time."

"That sounds impossible. How are we supposed to manage that?" Danny asked.

"We'll have to don disguises and infiltrate the meeting," Eddie announced. "Marcus has a powerful potion to disguise our team that he made with his uncle, which worked well for us in Vegas. It will withstand any magical wards or alarms."

"I doubt it's enough," Danny said skeptically. "Salvatore's got top security in these places, and even with our people, I don't think we're going to be able to get inside."

Kallie crossed her arms in front of the whiteboard. "Well, we have to. We know that each of these mobsters has a piece of information related to the vampire key, and to put the puzzle together, we need to get that info from each of them. They're not going to tell us, which means we need to be able to read their minds. Marcus can do it. He's been training for this very moment."

Ivy stepped forward. "Mind reading can work, but Danny's right. We can *maybe* get one or two people past my father, but Marcus is going to need more back-up than that. If we're all in disguises, my father will know something's up. We can't fool him. I have a better idea. My father wants to get his hands on me, and he wants the rest of you in his grasp. So we should give him what he's asking for."

"I'm not following," I said. This already sounded like a risk.

"This convention is happening, and my father will have all his cronies in one place. We can't pass up this opportunity," Ivy insisted. "I'm going to reach out to my father and tell him I want back in the mob."

"Ivy, no," I demanded. "Don't sell yourself like this for us."

"Listen for a sec," Ivy persisted. "I'll convince my dad that we need him. I'll stroke his ego and tell him exactly what he wants to hear, that the Warden's too strong and we can't take him on by ourselves. I'll pose an alliance between the Bianchi gang and the Majestica family against The Mission. Joining the Elvish crime family and the vampiric mob together into a union is going to be an offer my dad won't be able to refuse. Everyone knows that this war is going to be determined by demigods. If it wasn't, the Warden wouldn't be busting his ass to try and capture you. If Salvatore wants to win, he needs to get his hands on some of his own, and you guys are the only candidates still alive that haven't joined The Mission."

"Is Salvatore going to buy that you're handing us over to him?" Charlie asked skeptically. "He's going to suspect it's a trap."

"It doesn't matter if he does," Ivy replied. "My dad is going to be cautious, but by the time he figures out we've fooled him, we'll be out of there. I'll tell him we want in, and to sweeten the deal, we'll put on a circus."

"Like, an act, or an actual circus?" Marcus questioned. "I don't see how this is going to help us."

"A real one," Ivy said. "We'll offer to show off your demigod powers in a grand show, for all his vampires to see. My dad is interested in seeing what you guys can do. Plus, being immortal gets boring, and the vampires who've lived for centuries are always looking for a way to shake things up. A supernatural circus is something different and interesting. It'll be a big draw. Even if they suspect something, one night of amusement to them is worth the risk. And these guys are cocky. They're not going to think they'll be attacked at a circus, and if they do, they'll be certain they can handle it."

"So we put on a circus. Then what?" Charlie asked.

"We use Marcus to get the information we need," Ivy said, smacking their hand into their fist. "While we're putting on a distraction, Marcus can use teleinsight to read the minds of the mobsters who have information on the vampire key, and piece the puzzle together."

"Is Marcus skilled enough to pull that off?" Chancey asked. "He just started learning teleinsight."

"I've been practicing with it every day, and I've gotten stronger. It's no easy task, but I think I can read the minds of these mobsters without much of an issue," Marcus replied. "We just need to get them in the same room, and I'll be able to do it. I *know* I can."

I looked Ivy's way. "What do you think, Ivy? Will this really work?"

"I'm certain. My dad will buy whatever I say, because if anyone hates the Warden more than us, it's my father," Ivy insisted. "My dad knows the Warden is gonna come sniffing around Chicago eventually, and if he's got the rest of the supernatural world in his pocket, it ain't gonna take much for the mob to fall under the Warden's influence. The vampiric government has already sided with the Warden, so my father knows his days are numbered. If he wants the mob to survive, he needs more firepower. That's where demigods are useful to him."

"But Salvatore Bianchi isn't going to welcome you back into the mob with open arms," Charlie protested. "He'll assume this is a trick."

"Let him," Ivy said, shrugging. "I know my dad. It'll be interesting to him, to play a game of power. He wants to know if I'm a better mobster than he is, if I can outthink him— I *know* that eats away at him. Plus, he wants his chance to either eliminate or join the Majestica family. The only way he can destroy the Elvish mob as his rival is to team up with them or eliminate the Elvish heir. I'm practically handing Charlie to him on a silver platter if we do this, and despite any hesitations, he'll see that as too good an opportunity to pass up. He'll be suspecting his gangsters to be ambushed at the circus, but when that doesn't happen, he'll spend all his time wondering what we're playing at."

"And when none of his mobsters get hurt, he'll be convinced your offer is genuine," I said. "They won't even know Marcus read their minds. When it seems clear to Salvatore that Ivy actually *wants* to be welcomed back into the mob, we have another in."

"So it's simple. We go in, put on a big distraction, and while the circus is going on I'll read the minds of Salvatore's gangsters to find out what they know," Marcus stated. "Nobody gets hurt, Salvatore doesn't find out anything, and the job stays clean."

"The job never stays clean with us," I mumbled.

"We'll go ahead with this plan. We need a few days to map out the details, and Ava needs to rest before we go," Charlie insisted, gesturing to me.

"That'll give us enough time to publicize the event and lure these mobsters in," Marcus said.

"I need time to reach out to dear old dad," Ivy said scathingly. "He'll be suspicious, for sure, but I also know he'll be frothing at the mouth to get his hands on the rest of you and one-up the Warden. Trust me. He won't be able to resist."

Marcus nodded. "Everyone needs to get ready. We've always said our lives have been a circus— well, now it's time to become one."

A WEEK LATER, we stood outside a massive circus tent at midnight, waiting to execute our plan.

The circus was set up on a hotel property that Salvatore owned in New York City, in a massive tent that could fit over a thousand people. We were getting ready in a smaller, secondary tent that was set up next to the big top. Marcus, Kallie, and Alistair were already waiting to begin their performances, while Danny, Chancey and Ivy were finishing getting ready with us. At any minute, the show would start.

The packed crowd actively chatted inside the tent— true to Ivy's word, every vampiric mobster had shown up to see what the circus was all about. Now we just had to hope our plan worked.

"You guys owe me big time for putting me in the same room with Salvatore Bianchi," Danny grumbled as he slipped on a sparkling red shirt. "He's been looking for my ass for ages, and now I'm wrapped up in a pretty bow on his doorstep."

"He's not getting his hands on any of us," Charlie promised. "The Elvish Associates are waiting on my say so to get us out."

Charlie and I were part of the acrobatic act, so we wore matching costumes — me, a glittering silver leotard, and him, a set of black pants and a white button-up. I finished off my makeup in front of a fun mirror in the setup tent. The mirror appeared as natural as any prop in the circus, but really, it was our way out. Once the circus was over with, we'd use the fun mirror to escape back to Ilamanthe before Salvatore tried to catch us, which he most certainly would do.

Ivy was decked out in the best costume I'd ever seen them wear. They wore a black corset with gold fringe, and black panties with fishnet tights. The red jacket they donned had pointed coattails, long sleeves, buttons with gold chains, and was absolutely covered in rhinestones. Their outfit was complimented by thigh-high black heels and a glimmering top hat.

The entire ensemble was absolutely marvelous. They were playing the part of the ringleader, and they suited the part perfectly. Red lipstick and false eyelashes brought the look altogether.

"A little daring with your dad around, don't you think?" I commented. "I thought we were trying to convince him you wanted back into the mob."

"I need to come as I am. He's not gonna believe me if I show up looking like a man," Ivy replied. "We got in a big argument when he came to visit me at the Institute. He told me he didn't buy the act and knew that I was dressing like a male just to please him. Said I'd always be a dirty little queer."

My fists tightened in rage. "I hate him."

"Well, I *am* a dirty little queer," Ivy said with a wink. "And since my dad knows it, might as well go all-out. He'll hide his disgust until he thinks he's got the rest of you in the bag."

"You look adorable, dollface," Chancey said, and he gave Ivy a kiss. "Save that outfit for later."

I really hoped Ivy wasn't pushing their luck. We were dealing with the second most-dangerous man in the world, right after the Warden. If this went wrong in any way, we'd be risking our lives.

We put in earpieces so we could communicate throughout the show if need be. Ivy peeked out of the set-up tent once before they said, "Everyone is in place. Come on. Show's about to start."

We entered the big top through a slit in the back and took our positions around the arena, waiting for our turn to perform. I had brought a spare wheelchair to the circus, as I didn't want to risk losing my main one if we had to get the fuck out of here in a hurry.

I left the spare wheelchair to the side as Charlie hovered me upward, to the top of the tent. I sat on a platform and looked down at the crowd from above. This was where I would host my act, but it also served as a good look-out spot. I'd be watching the mobsters, as well as Salvatore, to make sure they didn't try to pull a fast one during the performance.

Salvatore was sitting in a fancy booth at the top of the tent, looking like he'd rather be anywhere else. Good. He was here, at least, which meant he wasn't out plotting our demise somewhere else. We could keep an eye on him.

The palace orchestra had sent some of its members along to provide music and aid the suspense. Haunting, creepy carnival music played the interim as a singular spotlight shone in the middle of the arena. Ivy stood on a red-and-gold striped pedestal, lifting a golden cane aloft as the spotlight beamed upon them.

"Welcome, welcome, debauchees and degenerates, freaks and fiends, to the greatest supernatural show on Earth!" Ivy announced.

Applause filled the arena, and Ivy gave a dramatic twirl on the pedestal. "Prepare to be amazed and have your mind twisted as our performers dazzle and delight unlike anything in this world! For our first act, we invite you on a trip across the sea. A wild beast, captured from the mysterious forests of Malovia, only to be calmed underneath the hand of our brave and mighty monster tamer! Behold as Marcus the Magnificent compels this deranged wolf to perform tricks for your amusement— that is, if the creature doesn't cause him to meet his end!"

Marcus was the one doing all the work, so he had to go first, so it wouldn't appear unusual when he was still lurking around the area. He stepped into the arena, wearing a red vest and black pants. In his hand he carried a rolled-up whip. Hoops and platforms were set up in a circle around him.

Danny and Chancey pushed a cage on wheels into the arena. Kallie was locked inside in her wolf form. We'd messed up her fur and put foam around her mouth for show. She banged herself against the bars of the cage, snarling in rage. The crowd looked on in interest.

"Observe how Marcus the Magnificent tames the wolf with nothing more than a whip and his words—" Ivy said, but the sentence was cut off as Kallie broke open the door of the cage and burst free. She charged toward the crowd and grabbed a vampire in her jaws, shaking him roughly. The vampire screamed, and several onlookers shouted, reaching for their pistols. Marcus approached, cracking the whip. Kallie dropped the vampire and backed off, bowing her head. The vampire that had gotten bitten yelped and scrambled away.

"Stay back, everyone!" Ivy proclaimed. "The wolf is vicious. More than one onlooker has lost an arm to this maddened animal!"

Marcus cracked the whip again. Kallie charged at him, but Marcus put out a hand. Kallie acted as if she'd been blasted backward. She rolled on the ground, howling in mock-pain, and the crowd gasped.

"Now that Marcus has the animal under his spell, watch as he guides it to perform tricks!" Ivy cried. Marcus cracked the whip, and Kallie sat back onto her haunches, rising up to paw at the air. He circled around her, crying out orders, and Kallie did a pirouette before she climbed onto a nearby platform and poised to jump. As Marcus wiggled the whip, Kallie began leaping through the hoops. The crowd applauded in surprise.

I focused my attention on the hoops, and they burst into flames. Astonished cries came from the audience. Kallie pretended to balk at the fire, but Marcus shouted and cracked the whip, and she jumped through all the flaming hoops with ease. When she landed again, Marcus pulled himself onto Kallie's back, and she began running around the arena in a dead sprint. The vampires began chatting amongst themselves in amazement as Marcus hung on to Kallie's fur, flattening himself to her body as they jumped through hoop after hoop. One of the flames from the hoop caught his pant leg, but I quickly put it out before it could spread further.

"Observe as he rides the monster through the flames with no saddle, no bridle, merely his will!" Ivy called. "This is a creature completely under his control!"

I could almost feel Kallie rolling her eyes from here. Kallie came to a stop in the middle of the arena, rearing onto her hind legs and giving a vicious snarl. When she came down onto four legs, Marcus slid off her back and did a spectacular tumble, rising back to his feet to give a bow.

Show off.

The vampires loved it. They cheered in excitement as Marcus guided Kallie back into her cage with the whip. Once Kallie was locked away, Danny and Chancey came forward again to wheel her out of the big top. Marcus took another bow to amp up the crowd, and the applause grew louder. He headed toward a ladder at the edge of the arena and began climbing it upward.

"Marcus the Magnificent will now complete his act by walking the tightrope, finishing his performance by diving twenty feet into a pool!" Ivy gushed.

Below me, a pool magically appeared in the middle of the arena, and the crowd *ooed* with wonder. Marcus stumbled on his way up the ladder and had to fumble to grab onto the bars. The crowd laughed, thinking it was part of the act, but Marcus had actually almost fallen on his way up.

I didn't know *why* we'd picked Marcus to do the tightrope, because he was clumsy as they come, but he promised he could do it. Here's hoping he didn't splatter himself all over the arena floor.

Marcus took a deep breath to steady himself as he stood on the platform before the tightrope. Then he took a step— one that was too forceful. He staggered onto the tightrope, and the crowd held its breath as he struggled to maintain his balance. He floundered his arms like a chicken as he took a couple of staggering steps forward, and the tightrope bowed under his weight.

He was holding himself up by his telepathy magic, clearly. He couldn't walk a straight line most days down a ten-foot-wide hall. Marcus wobbled down the tightrope like a baby learning how to walk, until he got to the middle. The band beat the drums rapidly, and Marcus drew out the moment by putting his arms over his head before he swung downward off the tightrope.

He was *supposed* to roll into a tuck like an Olympic diver, but Marcus didn't really do much but flounder through the air on the way down. He used telepathy magic to break his fall, though not so much that it was noticeable. Marcus splashed into the pool, and the audience cried out.

He didn't surface right away. The crowd waited on bated breath as Marcus remained at the bottom of the pool, holding his breath for as long as he could.

"It appears that Marcus' act has gone terribly wrong, folks," Ivy said in a somber tone. "A tragic end indeed for this warlock of immense talent—"

Marcus burst out of the pool, throwing his arms up and sucking in a breath. A couple of vampires in the stands leapt to their feet, and others cried out in amazement. Marcus couldn't swim, so I had to use my Toaqua powers to float him to the side. Marcus pulled himself out of the pool, and it vanished as Ivy lifted his arm and said, "Marcus the Magnificent, everyone!"

The crowd continued to applaud. Now that Marcus' act was done, he slipped to the side and donned a red robe that was hanging on a hook. The pocket of the robe contained his wand. He busied himself by pretending to set up the next performances, moving the hoops to the side and getting the plat-forms out of the way.

But I wasn't fooled. I saw the concentration on his face as he worked his mind reading magic. His eyes darted here and there as he scanned the minds of the underbosses sitting in the box beside the arena, and every now and then, his hand dove in the robe's pocket so he could use the wand. By the looks on the mobsters' faces, they didn't suspect or notice a thing. They had no idea Marcus was rattling around inside their heads. We needed things to stay that way.

Ivy was the best showperson on this planet, and they managed to keep the crowd's attention on them and off of Marcus as they proclaimed, "Our next act features a damsel whose power rivals her beauty. Kalina the Incredible will inspire you with her feats of magic, as she is the greatest illusionist ever to be born!"

Kallie looked nothing like the rabid wolf she'd been moments before as she strode into the arena, wearing a shimmering purple leotard and a sparkling cape. She cast a spell, and wisps of purple magic burst from her fingers as three elephants appeared inside the arena. They appeared as real and solid as flesh-and-blood elephants would be. Several vampires within the stands appeared shocked. Kallie made the illusion elephants dance, hold each other's tails, and sit on platforms. She then climbed onto the back of one of the elephants and did tricks herself. She performed a handstand and a backflip on the back of the elephant as it wiggled its trunk to give the audience a wave.

"Bringing these mysterious creatures to our circus isn't the only thing Kalina can do," Ivy stated. "Observe as she transports all of us to the plains of Africa itself!"

The big top changed, and the crowd let out noises of terror as the scene shifted. Daylight, hot and sweltering, encompassed the area. Long yellow grass bloomed everywhere, and mountains could be seen in the distance. Gazelles and zebras ran by, while a cheetah chased after them. Hyenas and baboons cackle before a loud roar silenced it all. A male lion stalked around the elephants, growling and baring his fangs. If I didn't know any better I'd swear we were right in the middle of the Serengeti.

Kallie was so damn good. Most faeries would've killed themselves trying to make more than a few people see such an intricate illusion, and she was able to cast the spell on hundreds of people at a time without breaking a sweat.

The vampires were actually terrified. The big, bad mobsters whimpered and held each other, unsure of what was going on. When they realized that the sunlight didn't burn their skin, and that the animals weren't real, they got excited. They started pointing out the different animals and whispering to each other, clapping when the lion roared or the elephants started trumpeting.

Salvatore Bianchi looked hideously greedy as he stared at Kallie below. I'd been watching him this whole time, and he'd appeared bored during Marcus' act, but he was definitely excited when Kallie showed off what she could do. He knew that kind of illusion power could be useful to him.

He'd never touch Kallie. Not so long as I was breathing.

Kallie made the illusion fade so we were back under the big top again, then slid off the elephant's back. All of her elephants turned into purple sparks that dazzled upward, and she gave a performative curtsy. The applause for her act was even louder than Marcus' dive.

"And now, the Amazing Alistair will perform one of his incredible card tricks!" Ivy announced, and Kallie ran out of the arena.

Alistair stepped into the ring and began shuffling cards. "Pick a card, any card! You, sir. How about you? Take a card, and I will guess what it is with my *amazing* mind-reading abilities!"

"BOO!" the crowd yelled, giving him a collective thumbs-down. Clearly, this wasn't impressive enough for them.

"Who are you booing at?" Alistair demanded, whirling on one of the nearest vampires. "You want a show, I'll give you a show!"

Alistair tossed his deck of cards aside, and they rained down around him. He lifted his hands, and two vampires stood to face each other. He'd gotten into their heads and was puppeteering them around, like he had when he killed Professor Mazur. The vampires both threw a punch, and they socked each other in the nose at the same time. A thunderous *boom* sounded through the tent as their marble-like skin connected.

The other vampires roared in laughter. He was getting a rise out of the crowd, that was for certain.

"IS MY ACT BORING NOW?!" Alistair raged.

Ivy quickly rushed in front of him, before he could get us into any real trouble. "And that's it for the Amazing Alistair!"

Alistair grumbled and stomped out of the ring. "Boring, my ass. I'll show you *boring*." His puppeteering magic fell flat, and the vampires who'd punched each other sat back down, holding their noses. Danny and Chancey hurried to set up the next act.

Ivy's gave a flourish of their hand. "Now, undoubtedly, the best part of any circus— or the worst, depending on who you're talking to— the motherfucking clowns!"

The spotlight centered on Oberi as he entered the big top in his husky form. I couldn't resist giving a wide smile and a little squeal. Oberi looked so lovable. We'd fitted a red nose onto him and painted his face to look like a clown. He had a big polka-dot bow attached to his collar and a multi-colored skirt. I seriously couldn't handle the cuteness.

Oberi pushed a baby carriage into the center of the arena, and Rishi popped his head out. Rishi wore a jester's hat with jingly bells and a ruffled collar with pom-poms attached. I honestly couldn't tell who was more endearing.

The crowd *awed* at how cute they were. Well, what do you know. Even vampiric mobsters had a soft spot for adorable animals.

Even so, I saw Ivy shiver. They'd made it very fucking clear before we started planning this circus that they *hated* clowns. We'd insisted no circus was complete without them, and Ivy had compromised by putting the animal companions in clown costumes, but they'd certainly complained about it all the way.

"Watch, laugh, and applaud as our... *ugh*... clowns perform ploys for your amusement," Ivy grumbled.

The band switched up the music to a comedic tune. Rishi hopped onto Oberi's back and rode him like a horse as Oberi raced up and down a seesaw and through a tunnel. Oberi climbed into a tiny toddler bike, his front legs hanging off the handlebars, and pedaled with his back paws while Rishi stood on his head and meowed. The crowd laughed along, enjoying the games. When he got to the other side of the arena, Oberi got off the bike and jumped on a trampoline. Rishi followed him, giving yowls as the husky bounced him high into the air.

This is quite fun. I enjoy the circus life, Oberi said as he catapulted Rishi across the arena. Rishi landed on a separate trampoline and started bouncing back and forth between the two.

Maybe when the war's done, we'll take the act on the road, Charlie replied sarcastically on the ground.

Oh, wouldn't that be a delight! Oberi said, thinking he was serious. He and Rishi balanced on balls and rolled them carefully to a high platform in the middle of the arena. Rishi climbed up the ladder that was on the platform, then jumped through a hoop Oberi held at the bottom.

As Oberi and Rishi kept the crowd busy, I surveyed the audience. The underbosses, along with the rest of the mobsters, still seemed fully enthralled in the circus. I noticed Salvatore had ducked out for a moment— concerning— but he came back to his seat and watched Rishi perform his tricks with a raised lip of disgust. Guess he wasn't a fan of clowns, either. Below, Marcus moved different platforms and stands for Oberi and Rishi to use, but his brow was furrowed in concentration.

"Marcus, how's it going?" I whispered into my earpiece.

"*I've scanned about half of them,*" he hushed back. "*I've got some of what we need, but you need to buy me more time.*"

The circus still had a few more acts. I hoped Marcus could finish up before then.

Oberi and Rishi finished off their act elaborately. Rishi scaled across the tightrope upside down, clinging to it and scampering across before dropping and allowing Oberi to catch him. Oberi jumped up, and Rishi landed perfectly on his back. Oberi's tail wagged a mile a minute as he and Rishi took their bows.

You're up, pidge, Charlie said.

Salvatore was starting to look impatient, and we couldn't have that. I needed to make sure his eyes were on me. Otherwise, there was a possibility he'd figure out what Marcus was doing, and I wasn't going to let that happen.

"I now ask that the audience direct their attention to the ceiling of the big top, where our next act will take place," Ivy proclaimed. "Become enthralled by the fiery blaze of our next act, and observe the power of the Diamond Empress."

The warmth of the spotlight was on me, and it reflected off my dazzling outfit, making the entire area around me sparkle. I lifted my hands, and two fireballs ignited in both of them. The platform I was sitting on caught ablaze, burning brightly as the flames licked my form. The swing began to move back and forth at Charlie's Air magic, swinging like a trapeze as I manipulated the flames around me. His powers secured me in my seat, so I kept my balance and didn't fall.

"See how the fire touches her body, but she doesn't burn!" Ivy exclaimed. "Observe as she manipulates the flames to her will!"

I pushed the fireballs together to create a stream of flame. They forged into one, and I manipulated the fire to morph into a unicorn, which galloped above the crowd, before shifting the flames into a dragon. The fiery dragon beat his wings, and embers trailed down from above as the vampires looked upward nervously. They didn't like fire, as it was one of the things they were vulnerable to. It was important for them to know they couldn't fuck with me.

I left the Fire dragon to fly around the room on its own as I took two batons at my sides, lighting them aflame. I swirled them around in complicated movements, tossing them into the air and catching them as they were still burning. It was a simple baton sequence I'd learned in cheerleading, but it was impressive, because the flames licked all along my arms and hair as I tossed the batons, leaving my body unharmed.

I took one of the flaming batons and inserted the end of it inside my mouth. The flames burned across my lips, and I blew out a breath. A plume of flame erupted from my mouth, one that was large and aimed toward the audience. The flames ended before they touched anyone, but still, the vampires could feel their heat, and they were astonished.

As the crowd was still gaping in amazement, I shifted the Fire in the room to change colors. The red dragon became blue, and sapphire flames burned around me as I showed off my specialty to the crowd.

"The Diamond Empress is the only caster in the world who is able to create blue Fire— a cool substance, one that is created of both Fire and Water, an energy that even the most powerful creatures are vulnerable to, in this world and the next! Nothing can survive its touch!" Ivy said.

I could feel Salvatore's covetous eyes roam the edges of my blue Fire. He definitely wanted magic that could kill anything he desired, and my blue Fire was it.

"To aid her in her performance, the Diamond Empress will be accompanied by her husband, who is none other than the Elven Prince," Ivy shouted.

Even so, I could tell their tone was nervous— if any part of the circus could go wrong, it was this one, because Charlie's appearance could set everyone here off.

I extinguished my flames, and the fiery dragon turned into nothing more than smoke. Whispers of shock traveled all around as Charlie walked into the arena below me. None of the mobsters could believe that the Majestica heir was right here, in a literal den of vipers. A few of the underbosses looked up, waiting for Salvatore to give them an order, but Salvatore shook his head. The show would go on.

"The Elven Prince and the Diamond Empress will now perform acrobatic tricks from above," Ivy added, and my trapeze slowed to a stop. "Now, let me be clear. The Elven Prince is completely blind; he has no sight, no ability to see where his partner may be. They must be in perfect tandem for this not to become a tragedy."

An aerial silk, created out of an illusion by Kallie, suddenly appeared at my side. It was hooked to the top of the tent's infrastructure and would hold our weight. Charlie flew up to hover beside me. He wrapped the silk around his arm and torso, then reached out the other to grab me around the waist. Charlie held me close to him, and I felt our rapid heartbeats beat together as one. Charlie used his Air magic to swing us around the arena in a circle, twirling our bodies as the silk twisted with the gusts of wind. The crowd sighed in awe as the two of us spun in the air, flying over the arena in beautiful patterns formed by Charlie's magic.

We scared the crowd when Charlie pretended to drop me. There were a few screams, but Charlie caught my wrist at the last second, and I used momentum to swing back upward. His magic pushed me around until I was back against his chest again, in the place where I belonged. He was holding me, and we were flying, and everything seemed so beautiful. I clung to Charlie and looked up at his gorgeous face as our bodies wound around each other and our breathing synchronized.

"I love you," I said, and I kissed him. He kissed me back, and we soared together with our mouths forged. It was so romantic I could die right then.

"The epitome of true love," Ivy drawled dryly, in a way that was meant to say; *Ava, that wasn't part of the act.*

I didn't want it to end, but we had to stop flying sometime. The aerial silk lost the momentum it had and slowed down. Charlie deposited me back onto the trapeze that was still hanging in the middle of the arena, then hovered himself back to the earth.

Ivy raised their arms as they cried, "Now, for the most dramatic part of the act! A trust fall, from the height of the big top! The Diamond Empress will count on her husband to catch her as she falls. If he misses, it will be her doom!"

"How will he catch her if he can't see?" A vampire cried from the audience — he actually sounded worried. I suppose these vamps weren't all heartless.

"The connection between the Diamond Empress and the Elven Prince is very strong," Ivy swore. "But its strength will be tested today."

This was much taller than where Marcus had jumped from, but I trusted

Charlie with my life. I let myself fall backward, and I spread my arms out wide as I plummeted downward. Cries rose from the audience as I fell, and my hair whipped across my face.

Then I felt Charlie's Air magic buffet me as I neared the ground, lessening the impact as I fell into his arms. Charlie cradled me against his chest, and the crowd went wild.

"A perfect landing!" Ivy cried. "Please give a round of applause for the Diamond Empress and her Elven Prince!"

Charlie didn't bother to stick around as the crowd cheered, but immediately went to carry me out of the arena.

"You all right, pidge?" Charlie asked.

"Never better," I said, and I kissed him again. He nuzzled against me. I wished we could go home right now to get some private time in the Sanctuary. I felt desperate for his attention, and Charlie knew it, too.

"Soon," he promised as my thoughts passed him by. When we were outside the big top, he set me onto Oberi's back. She'd changed into a unicorn at this point and was waiting for the next phase of the plan.

The crowd sounded like it was complaining through the next act. Oberi maneuvered me closer to the tent, and I poked my head in through a flap to see what was going on.

Chancey was up, and it didn't look like the vampires were impressed by his strongman demonstration. He was lifting a car with one hand, but the crowd was booing and throwing disposable cups of blood at him. One splattered onto his shirt, and Chancey let out a string of curse words.

"He ain't even a demigod!" a vampire complained. "Why are we watching this?"

"That's nothing. I can do that!" another mobster called out.

"Oh, yeah?" Chancey lost his temper and threw the car. I cringed as the vehicle flew into the audience and hit a couple of vampires. The car hurriedly vanished— Kallie was hiding on the other side of the arena behind a platform, and she had conjured the illusion for Chancey to use.

None of the vampires had been hurt by the flying car, though a group of them looked pissed. They clambered to their feet, fists bunched and fangs clenched.

Ivy scrambled to save the situation. "Our strongman can take on multiple opponents at once! Who in the crowd would like to test their skills against him in a boxing match?"

All the vampires that had been hit by the car immediately charged at Chancey, their arms outstretched. These mobsters definitely wanted to give him a piece of their mind, if not outright kill him.

"You wanna fight me? Bring it on!" Chancey yelled. He grabbed the first vampire that had climbed into the area by the shirt and started laying him out. Three more vampires jumped into the arena, but Chancey's fists went flying, and the mobsters went down.

Angels were just as strong as vampires, and Chancey's punches were nothing to scoff at. He'd practically been raised in fight club at the prison, and this was a call back to those days. Chancey laughed as he beat the crap out of whatever vampires that came near. A few mobsters got hits on him, but for Chancey, this is what he did for fun, so despite the black eyes and bruises he got in return he always came out on top. By the end, a bunch of mobsters lay in a heap on the big top's floor, and Chancey raised his fists in victory.

Now the vampires were happy. They were cheering at the violence, arms raised and calling for more blood.

One of the vampires Chancey had beaten was still conscious. He staggered to his feet and pulled a switchblade from his pocket, advancing on Chancey. Ivy gave a gasp into the microphone— they weren't sure whether to play along or to step in to save Chancey.

A blur of color passed by, and the vampire holding the knife fell on his ass as he was knocked sideways. Danny was the next act, and he stepped in, racing by with super-speed as he snatched the knife out of the mobster's hand. He threw the knife at a nearby target, and it embedded in the middle. The vampires, who had the attention span of a gnat, immediately swiveled their heads to watch Danny pull knives from a holster around his chest, tossing them at targets that dropped from the ceiling and rotated on a circular platform. Every time he threw a blade, it hit the bullseye.

Danny had told us he could do an act with throwing knives, but I was amazed at how skilled he really was. I wasn't sure where he'd learned to throw them, but he was truly a master.

While Danny was tossing knives, I searched the room for Marcus. He was leaning on a pole, appearing dazed with his mouth hanging open. I could tell he was tired. Utilizing this spell on a big group of people was wearing him out.

"Marcus, you need to look busy," I hissed into the earpiece. He jolted back to life and pretended to fiddle with some ropes hanging near the underboss box.

"*Marcus, are you good?*" Kallie asked, her voice coming through the earpiece. She was still hiding behind a platform, but she looked very concerned as she stared at Marcus from the other side of the arena.

"*I just need to read one more guy,*" Marcus replied wearily. "*I've almost—*"

The circus fell to silence as Salvatore Bianchi rose to his feet. Every vampire in the hall quivered, and Salvatore cleared his throat to say, "As entertaining as this has all been, I'm afraid the circus must now come to a close."

"What?!" Ivy snarled, looking up at their father. Their grip tightened on the golden cane as they spat, "We had a deal!"

"Deals can be modified, and though it's been amusing, I tire of watching you and your circus freaks," Salvatore said coldly. "You were always an embarrassment to me, even as a child, and the performance stops here. All of you—take the demigods into custody. And kill my son while you're at it."

"Aw, come on," Danny complained. "I didn't even get to finish my act and get fired through the cannon!"

This wasn't good. We were counting on Salvatore letting the circus finish before he made a move to capture us. We definitely hadn't expected him to try to kill *Ivy*. Guess Salvatore wasn't as concerned about the future of the mob as he was making sure Ivy didn't continue to humiliate him. Rat bastard.

Vampires started firing their pistols. Oberi galloped to the center of the ring where Ivy was, and I immediately threw up a shield. Charlie, Kallie, Alistair, Marcus, and Chancey rushed to my side and took cover behind it. Bullets, noxite darts and otherwise, bounced off the surface of the shield and deflected, taking down the same vampires that had fired them.

The Elvish Associates had been hiding in places all around the circus, inside of boxes and props just in case something like this went wrong, and now that their prince was in danger they immediately took action. I saw Gavyn explode through a box and go flying through the crowd as he cut heads from torsos, which went rolling along the ground. Max and Eddie siphoned vampiric magic from the mobsters, which enabled them to move with super speed and rip vampires apart with incredible strength. Asa and Ares were in the stands, shooting vampires with rifles that left holes the size of my fists in the chests of our enemies. Wooden stakes whizzed from a high platform, where Elyx had been stationed with a modified crossbow. The stakes struck vampires straight in the heart, killing them instantly. The Elvish orchestra went from musicians to killers in an instant as they pulled hidden weapons from their instruments and started dropping bodies.

The Associates weren't the only allies here. The Emperor had ordered other guards to come with us as well, and soon, the entire circus was a mess of Elves and vampires going for blood.

Salvatore Bianchi wasn't an idiot. Vampires were falling quickly, and he knew it would be impossible to stop all the Elves here to get to us. He cast a despising sneer at Ivy before turning away, taking his head vamps with him and leaving the rest of his mobsters as target practice for the Associates.

Asa and Ares were heading our way. I opened up a spot in the shield for them to slip through, and their grips tightened on their rifles as they approached.

"We need to go, sire," Ares said to Charlie. "Salvatore has fled for now, but if we stay in the area he'll send more of his men in, and we'll soon be outnumbered."

"I'm not done yet," Marcus said in a panic. "There's one guy I wasn't able to read!"

"Who is it?" Charlie asked.

"Purple shirt, scar over his left cheek," Marcus said, pointing.

"Then he's coming with us," Charlie said roughly. "Asa, Ares, go get him."

The two Elves took off, and I had to open up the shield again to let them through. One of the flying bullets snuck through the opening and hit me in the arm as it flew by. Blood went everywhere, and I cried out in pain. My shield fell completely and I gasped, putting a hand to my arm.

"AVA!" Oberi screamed, sounding deranged.

"Pidge, stay with me!" Charlie gasped in alarm.

"I'm fine," I breathed, using my magic to heal the wound. The bullet popped out as I knit the muscle back together. I tried to put up the shield again, but it was too late— we were already exposed.

"Everyone get down!" Ivy cried, and my friends flattened themselves to the floor as more bullets flew over their heads. Marcus tried to put up a shield, but he was too weak, and it faltered. Alistair was too busy killing vampires by puppeteering them around to help his friends, so we were left unshielded. He forced one vampire to lash out with his fangs, slicing another's head clean off his shoulders. He was laughing the whole time, not caring if we were exposed, only that he got his revenge on the mobsters for mocking him.

Kallie put up a shield, but it didn't expand fast enough in time to cover me. Vampires came storming toward us. As I reeled on Oberi's back, she let out a cry of rage. I felt her shift, fur becoming scales as my Familiar grew to an immense size.

Oberi was changing into a wyvern, and he was too big to fit inside the circus tent. He spread his wings wide, and the entire big top came crashing down on top of us. Fabric covered me, and I couldn't see where we were going or where my friends were.

"Pidge!" I heard Charlie cry, but his voice was muffled and sounded far away. Where was he?

Though we couldn't see, the mobsters couldn't, either. The sounds of fabric ripping and tearing could be heard all around as vampires attempted to claw their way out of the circus tent.

Oberi was a rampaging animal. All I could do was hold on as he stormed around, smashing vampires under his feet and ripping them to pieces with his teeth. He'd gotten tangled up in the circus tent when it came down, and attempting to break free was making him more infuriated.

"Oberi, change back!" I ordered, but he wasn't listening. All he wanted to do was protect me, and seeing me be shot had brought back memories of the Infernal Underground. He'd taken the bullet for us when Jaymin had shot him, and seeing me get hurt like that drove him insane.

Unexpectedly, a burst of Air lifted the big top off of us, sending it spiraling into the sky. Another stream of Air yanked me off of Oberi's back, and I didn't have any chance to hang on. I was pulled downward by a powerful gust of wind, and I slammed against Charlie's body as he caught me. Once I was in his arms, the large tent collapsed back onto the ground again, covering the vampires and Oberi's back half.

"It's time to go. Everyone else is already out," Charlie said. "The Elven guards are holding off the vampires so we can leave." He proceeded toward the fun mirror inside the set-up tent, which was still standing.

"Oberi, let's go!" Charlie called out.

Oberi laughed as he watched three vampires die under the searing pain of his venom. Then he turned and changed into a husky, racing after us. I held on tight, and Charlie carried me through the mirror and back home.

The portal took us straight to the throne room, where the rest of our friends were waiting. Marcus leaned against a wall, looking sick, while Alistair played with his deck of cards wearing a smug grin.

Danny, for once in his life, didn't appear cocky, but rather relieved. "Thank fuck," he said quietly to himself. "Don't know how many times I'm gonna get away from that guy by the skin of my ass."

Chancey had his arm slung around Ivy's shoulders, who appeared quite sour.

"Screw my old man," Ivy grumbled. "He's always gotta take the piss out of everything, don't he?"

Kallie had already fetched my chair, and Charlie put me down in it as my chest tightened in anxiety.

"Oberi—" I breathed, and I patted his head. "I'm so glad you're safe."

Savage beasts, he grumbled. *Tore them right to bits, yes I did.*

"Oh, Oberi," I said, and I threw my arms around his neck to hug him. "You bad doggy!"

"Oberi, why didn't you listen to Ava?" Charlie scolded. "You could've gotten hurt."

They harmed what was mine, and so, were not permitted to survive, Oberi stated bluntly, before he licked my cheek.

"You went off the rails," Charlie accused. "You need to follow orders, and do as you're told! What if we were *both* in trouble, and you weren't paying attention? What if you had to pick between Ava and me, because there wasn't a chance we'd both make it out? We'd *all* be dead if you ignored her like you did back there!"

Oberi appeared horrified at the thought of having to pick one over the other. *Do not say such things. How could I ever choose? I love you both equally. Such a thing would be impossible.*

"The good news is, the operation went well," Eddie said cheerfully, before Charlie could start ranting again. "The prince and princess are safe, which is our top priority."

"What about the other Elves?" I asked, worried. We'd left many of the guards behind in order to get here.

"They all have their own pocket mirrors and are capable of escaping on their own," Eddie assured me. "If not, trust me when I say that they are happy to lay down their lives for the monarchy, princess. The vampire key is more important than any of us."

I didn't want anyone else dying for us, but Charlie seemed unbothered by Eddie's words as he asked, "Is the mobster here? The guy we need."

"We got him, sire," I heard Asa say as he came through the mirror. "He didn't get away."

Asa and Ares had entered. They were dragging a vampire with them, who'd been forced to kneel. He wore noxite cuffs and appeared ruthless.

Charlie strode in front of the mobster. "You know something about the vampire key. A piece of information Salvatore Bianchi entrusted only to you. Tell us what it is."

"Or what?" The mobster laughed, then spat on the floor at Charlie's shoes. "I've dealt with tougher bastards than you, kid. You ain't getting jack outta me."

Charlie grabbed one of the daggers holstered to Asa's belt and stabbed it into the vampire's side, between his ribs. The vampire cried out in pain, and our friends around the room froze. Nobody had been expecting that. Not even I was ready for it, because it'd happened so fast. At the action, Chancey and Danny shared a wary glance.

"There's more to come if you don't talk," Charlie promised.

"Fuck... you," the vampire seethed, speaking through the pain.

Charlie stopped trying to reason with him, and instead demanded, "Marcus, do you think you can cast the spell again and read this guy's mind?"

Marcus looked even worse than he did when I'd gotten here. He was bent over his knees and breathing heavily. Kallie rubbed his back. She shook her head at me, which I took to mean he wasn't doing well.

"I... can try," Marcus said. "But if I'm being honest, I'm running out of juice. I don't know if I can perform the spell again without passing out."

"Fine. There are other ways to get it out of him," Charlie said.

I was momentarily stunned, wondering if he was suggesting what I think he was, until Ares said, "We're the specialists in this area, sire. You don't need to participate in this. We promise we'll get what you need out of him."

"I have to oversee this," Charlie insisted. "Marcus, I need you with me. Just in case you can get into his head."

Marcus nodded. Asa and Ares began dragging the mobster out of the throne room... probably to some undisclosed torture area somewhere in the palace... and Charlie followed, Marcus in his wake. I went to trail behind, wanting to see how this would go down.

"Go back to our room, pidge," Charlie told me. "You don't need to be a part of it."

By his tone, that was definitely an order and not a request. I hesitated, then told myself he was right. This wasn't the job of a princess, but a prince's work. I knew my role and what it entailed, and this wasn't it.

Everyone else kind of... dispersed. We all went our separate ways without speaking, though Kallie sent me a glance that held all kinds of questions. Were we really going to let the boys do this?

Guess so. I gave a shrug in response. It's what Emperor Cassiel would do, I was sure, and if Charlie was truly to follow in his footsteps, he had to get his hands dirty like a Majestica man. I couldn't say I liked it, but I knew it was what had to be done.

Cassiel's words from days ago came back to me. He believed someone always had to suffer for the greater good, and it pained me to admit that someone *would* suffer for us to get to the vampire key. What bothered me more is that I was going to let it happen.

This mobster was one of the bad guys, though. He was going to get what was coming to him. It didn't matter if he was the one suffering, because he was an awful person, so his suffering wasn't one I cared about.

Kallie did what she was good at. She disassociated from the situation, and let it go. Oberi followed me out, dutifully shadowing my every move. He was acting as my bodyguard at the moment and didn't want me to be farther than a stone's throw away.

I tried to keep my mind off of what I knew had to be happening. I had dinner in the dining hall, then had the servants help me take a bath in the spa area of the Ladies' Court before heading back to my room. My mind kept wandering back to the mobster, but I was pretty cold about it. I didn't have any feelings or regrets about what I knew Charlie had to be doing right now. He'd shut his part of our bond off from Oberi and me so we didn't experience any of it.

It was almost... easy. Too easy. I wondered what kind of people we'd become, and how far we'd fallen, to be okay with torturing people, and found that I didn't care.

That was the scariest part.

When I was almost to Charlie's quarters, I heard a concerned voice ask, "Ava? Can we talk to you?"

Chancey was leaning against a wall, along with Danny. Both of them had clearly been waiting for me to show.

"What about?" I asked, feeling a little cornered.

"Let's go somewhere private," Danny offered, and he led us to a parlor room that was wholly abandoned. He checked all the closets and locked the doors before he turned to me with a rough gaze.

"Look, you and Oberi gotta listen," Chancey started. "There's something wrong with Charlie."

My heartbeat immediately quickened in fear, and Oberi stirred beside me. She changed into a phoenix, leaping onto my chair. "Wrong? Is he sick, or—"

"Let me clarify," Danny began. "My magic tells me there's something wrong with Charlie's *desires*, and if he doesn't change his way of thinking, it's gonna fuck us all over."

My mood immediately soured, and Oberi cocked her head. *This* was what they had dragged me aside for? They were wasting my time. They didn't have the right to question my husband. Nobody did, and the fact that they were pissed me off. I hadn't missed the glance the two of them shared when Charlie stabbed that vampire.

"Is this about him torturing that guy? Because we need intel," I argued.

"No. It's worse," Danny said.

I turned to leave for the door, but Chancey blocked my path. "You need to hear him out." He jerked his head toward Danny.

Suppressing my irritation, I faced the vampire again and crossed my arms.

"Spit it out," I demanded. "What do your demigod powers have to say?"

Danny fiddled with his hair, appearing extremely nervous. "I don't talk about what my powers can do with just anyone. I usually keep it to myself. But it's gotten to the point where I can't ignore it anymore. I *had* to tell somebody, and Chancey seemed like the first person who'd be willing to listen. I just hope I can convince you, too."

"You're not doing a very good job of it," I sneered.

"Then let me be clear," Danny said harshly. "When Charlie got here, my powers told me his only desire was to keep you and his friends safe. But those desires have changed over the past few months. They've gotten more reckless, dangerous. He's thinking about something. I can *tell* he's plotting something he ain't telling the rest of us, not even you."

"You really think my husband would keep secrets from me? You really think he *can*? We share a bond!" I burst. How *dare* they suggest Charlie was lying to me. It was unthinkable!

"There are ways to get around a bond. You know how easy it is to shut Charlie out if you don't want him to know what you're thinking, but what you try to hide is petty shit to spare his feelings," Danny demanded. "Whatever Charlie's keeping from you is way bigger. And I *know* he is— his desires plainly tell me he's keeping secrets."

"Okay, big shot, so what's he hiding?" I sneered. "Since you *know his desires* and all."

"That's the thing. I can't tell," Danny said in frustration. "It's something *big*, something that involves all of us. I don't think he's worked out the details yet, because it seems like the desire is confused. I don't even know if he's conscious of it yet. But it's there, underneath the surface. I was hoping you'd have some idea of what it could be."

"He hasn't mentioned anything to me." This was a pointless conversation. I nearly turned away again, but Oberi beat her wings, telling me to stay.

"According to you, he tells you everything, right?" Danny snapped.

I bit my lip. "Of course he does. If Charlie had something in mind, he'd share it with me."

"That's not what my powers tell me, and demigod magic doesn't lie," Danny argued. "He hasn't decided what he's going to do, and we don't have much time to convince him to take a different path. If we even *can* at this point."

"What do you want me to do about it?" I asked coldly.

"You've gotta talk to him, Ava. Out of all of us, you've got the best chance of making him crack. He needs to tell us what he's considering," Danny insisted. "Then, once we know, we can talk him out of it, whatever it is. Or help him to achieve it, if it's a good plan after all. Dark desires don't mean devious intentions, and if it's something cruel against the Warden, it could be good for us. I just don't like that he's keeping it from the group."

"You ever think you could have it wrong, and your magic could be lying to you?" I asked Danny, glaring him down.

Danny nodded. "Sure. I've been wrong before. But I got a gut feeling about this one."

I rolled my eyes and looked toward the angel in the room. "I'd expect this from Danny, but not you, Chancey. I thought you were Charlie's friend, but you're throwing accusations around without any proof."

"Look, I've always respected Charlie," Chancey said, spreading his arms wide. "But I've never been *afraid* of him. I am now. You wanna tell me why that is?"

I steeled myself. "I *won't* be afraid of Charlie, no matter what you two think he's capable of."

"You need to be, because we all should," Danny hissed.

"Lemme tell you something," Chancey started. "Cassiel isn't a bad guy. But he's got a bad job, and nobody stays the head of the Elvish crime family for as long as he has without making some questionable decisions. Now he's teaching Charlie how to do the same thing."

"Yeah, and Charlie's just doing his job. I'm sorry if you couldn't handle being in his position, but he's doing exactly what he needs to. We need a villain if we're going to beat the Warden," I demanded.

"You aren't listening. He ain't the same, Ava. There's a part of Charlie that ain't Charlie no more. Just the guy who was trapped in Cellblock 9," Chancey said grimly. "I know you destroyed the Institute and all it was, but that piece of him is always gonna be stuck down there. Cellblock 9 for him is what the Infernal Underground was for you. You can't look me in the eye and tell me that I'm wrong."

Rage quivered inside of me, threatening to burst out and light the room around me ablaze. I went down into the Infernal Underground and didn't come back out. I refused to even *consider* the same thing had happened with Charlie when it came to Cellblock 9.

I shook out my hair, to try and appear that I was keeping my cool. "I don't know what you guys are talking about. He's doing better than ever since we got to Ilamanthe!"

Oberi cooed in agreement, and I knew I was right. She wouldn't agree with me if I was in denial.

"Would the Charlie that lived at the Institute be happy to torture someone to get information out of him?" Chancey questioned. "We both know the answer to that."

"Those prison kids wouldn't have survived out here," I spat. "We're alive today because we're willing to do things we weren't before. If some lowlife gangster has to endure a little pain for us to get our hands on the vampire key, I'm not going to lose any sleep over it, and neither is my husband."

Chancey shook his head. "I'm telling you, something's not right with him. What they did to him down in Cellblock 9 screwed his wiring up. He ain't the same person."

"I understand your concern, but there's nothing to worry about," I said shortly. "I'm his wife. I have it under control, and if he does end up slipping, I'll be there to shut it down."

"You can't keep him on a leash," Danny warned. "One day you're gonna find he's broken the chain, then he'll be there to bite your hand."

I scoffed. "Charlie? You've got to be kidding me. He'd never hurt me."

Danny turned his back on me. "You don't see what we see because you don't *want* to see it. But you will. Just make sure you're at a distance when he goes off, so you don't get hurt."

I was done with this conversation. I unlocked the doors and wheeled myself out of the room. Danny and Chancey, the bastards they were, hushed into a low conversation.

"Told you she wouldn't listen," Chancey grumbled, and the door swung shut behind me.

I was aggravated, but maybe Danny had a point and it was worth looking into. "What do you think about this, Oberi?" I asked. "Do you think they're right?"

Oberi bristled her feathers and responded, *I think they're wrong, in a way. Charlie has always acted like Charlie. This is just a new side of him we haven't seen before, a piece that he hides, and now it's being coaxed out. He could be concealing something for all we know, but maybe it's not for sinister reasons. He probably doesn't want any of us, especially you, getting hurt, and if the plan he's concocting is dangerous it'd make sense to keep us out of it.*

"If that's the case, we need to talk to him about it before it gets worse."

I didn't want to completely invalidate their concerns. I was annoyed they were taking it this far, but I might as well look into it.

I got ready for bed once I returned to the room. I didn't expect Charlie to be back so soon, but he came in only an hour after I got there.

"Hey," I said as Charlie sat on the other side of the bed. Oberi, who was laying as a husky across my legs, lifted his gaze. "Back so soon?"

There was blood on Charlie's button-up that wasn't his. It should've bothered me, but you know what? It didn't. He took it off and tossed it in the hamper.

"He didn't make it," Charlie said roughly. "We didn't get what we needed out of him before he corked off."

I didn't like Charlie's tone. Terror tightened in my throat, but I told myself to settle. "Did we get enough information from the other mobsters to know where the key is?"

"Let's hope so. Marcus is piecing together what he found out."

I nodded, then dared to ask, "How'd you kill him?"

Charlie was emotionless as he responded, "You don't need to know, pidge."

My insides flipped nervously. "Was that the right move? Salvatore will go looking for him, and we'll need to hide the body."

"It was what we had to do. Asa and Ares have it handled."

I trusted the Elvish Associates to do their job. After all, this is what they'd been trained to do, and what the Elves had done for thousands of years. Torture and disposal of enemies was in the job description.

I wish I could say the thought was hard for me to stomach, but it wasn't. It was just what had to be done.

"Do you think we have enough clues?" I worried.

"I hope so. We'll talk about it in the morning, pigeon. It's been a long day."

"Okay." I paused, and Oberi perked up his ears as I asked, "Charlie? Are you... keeping something from me?"

"Huh? What would make you ask that, pidge?" He moved closer to me.

I immediately felt bad for asking. I knew he would never keep secrets from me, and as his sub, it wasn't really my place to question him. But I had to make sure, just in case.

"If there's something you're not telling me, I don't want you to be afraid. I can help. You don't have to protect me," I started. "If there's anything that I don't know, you can tell me now."

"Of course there isn't," Charlie insisted gently. "You know everything about me."

Do I?

I grasped his fingers and interwove them between mine. "I'm just worried about you. If there's something on your mind, I want to help."

Charlie lifted a dazzling smile that made me turn to water. "Don't worry, pidge. I'm better than ever." He gave me a kiss on the cheek. "I swear on us, there's nothing to be concerned about. It's always gonna be you and me, till the end. I'd never do anything to hurt you. Remember that I promised to take care of you? Everything's fine."

I knew through our bond what he said was genuine. He wasn't lying; I could tell that much.

"Okay." I kissed him back. "Goodnight, Charlie."

"Goodnight, pidge."

I cuddled into his arms and checked in with Oberi. Her thoughts were passive, telling me she was certain Charlie was being honest, and that she didn't think there was anything to worry about.

As my husband held me tight, I figured the guys were being paranoid. Danny was misreading Charlie's desires, whatever they were. Even if something bad *did* happen, and Charlie made a mistake, it didn't matter, because I could save him.

Even if he did the worst, and became bad... he'd change for me.

Charlie wasn't the person he'd been when we were at the Institute, but that was for the best. Maybe a piece of what Danny said *was* true, and Charlie was becoming darker, turning into a villain that was worse than the rest of us.

I wouldn't blame my husband if he was turning into a monster. If we were going to beat the Warden, he had to become one.

Otherwise, we weren't going to win. And if we lost, I would belong to the Warden... forever.

Charlie wouldn't let that happen to me. So let him be evil. He could burn this whole world down to the ground, and so long as I went with him, I'd be happy with that.

I would let the entire universe fall before I became a trapped bird in a cage. As long as I didn't end up in that tower from my vision, I was more than content to let the worst happen.

charlie

NINETEEN

The mobster hadn't caved. I was less than pleased about that, but I couldn't lie and say I wasn't satisfied by the ending he received. Sliced his head clean off his shoulders myself. He wanted to keep his lips locked? Well, he'd never open them again, that was for sure.

Didn't matter. Marcus had gathered enough information from the other mobsters.

Ivy knew more about the vampires than any of us, and they provided additional insight that I was certain would get us to the vampire key. I'd lain awake all night coming up with ideas, and I'd formed a solid plan by the next morning.

I met my grandfather for breakfast to discuss my plan. The last thing I wanted was a repeat of the bank in Paris, so I needed his consultation on this.

"I know you don't want me getting my hands dirty," I stated when I finished explaining my plan. "But if we're going to pull this off, I need to do it my way. I need to be there."

"I agree. This couldn't be a better plan if I came up with it myself," Cassiel said.

I nearly reeled back in shock. I expected my grandfather to tell me that it was too risky, and to let him take the reins on this one, but he didn't. My plan didn't involve him or any of our parents, and after the way they'd reacted when we'd committed the bank robbery, I'd have expected him to put up a bigger fight.

"You really think I can pull this off?" I asked.

He placed a hand on my shoulder. "I believe in you, Charlie. You weren't ready for this when you went to Paris, but you've progressed in our training

553

sessions since then. The fact that you came to me for my opinion beforehand shows that you're ready. I want you to pull off this job, and you have the perfect team to do it. Show me what you've learned from everything I've taught you."

"I will," I promised. "I'm going to get the vampire key. You won't be disappointed."

I meant it with every fiber of my being. We'd lost the vampire key in Paris, and I wasn't going to let that happen again. I would become everything my grandfather wanted me to be.

My friends and I gathered around the conference table in the Elvish Associates' meeting room later that day. I stood at the head of the table, facing the others. Ava sat by my side, and Oberi dutifully stood in husky form beside her. Marcus, Kallie, Chancey, and Ivy were there, along with Eddie and the Elvish Associates.

"Everyone's here," I said. "Let's begin."

"What about Alistair and Danny?" Marcus asked.

"They're sitting this one out," I replied.

Truth was, Alistair was a loose cannon who'd go off script at any chance he got, and we needed everything to go according to plan. Danny couldn't be trusted, either. He was shit at following directions, and he'd run off to do his own thing like he did when we time traveled. I wasn't going to bother telling either of them what we were up to.

"Here's what we learned from the circus," I started. "Marcus discovered that the vampire key is located inside The Devil's City."

"I don't know what that means, though," Marcus mused. "We're headed to Vegas again?"

"That's *Sin City*, dummy," Kallie said.

"According to Ivy, The Devil's City is the name for a casino in Chicago," I explained. "It's the worst kind of place— a hub for vampires and considered exclusively supernatural territory. The building towers over sixty stories high in downtown Chicago and acts as its own independent city, filled with bars, restaurants, shops, gambling dens, spas— you name it. The vampires don't leave, because they don't have to. It's ripe with illegal activity, like drug trafficking and worse. It comes as no surprise that the vampires are holding the key there, because The Devil's City is owned by Salvatore Bianchi."

Marcus tapped his fingers against the table. "Hold on... Ivy, didn't you grow up in Chicago?"

Ivy cleared their throat. "I was born in Hawaii and lived with my mother and her merfolk pod for a while, until I left to live with my dad in Chicago. More specifically, I lived in The Devil's City— spent my whole teen years there. I named The Devil's Playground after it, actually, because that was all I ever knew. The Devil's City was like my own personal playground. I never thought my father would keep the vampire key so close to himself, in such an obvious spot where so many people could stumble upon it. I thought for certain he'd hide it away in some remote location. My father continues to find ways to surprise me."

"This is a good thing, because it means Ivy has intel we wouldn't be able to obtain otherwise," I said. "I've asked Ivy to put together everything they can remember about The Devil's City."

Ivy stood, and pages rustled as they spread large sheets of paper over the table. "I know this place like the back of my hand— every nook and cranny, every ventilation shaft. It's all in my head."

"This is a big place, but luckily, Marcus was able to obtain additional information about the key's location," I continued. "One of Salvatore's men from the circus revealed that the key is located on the second from the top level, which puts it just below Salvatore's office."

"There's only one room it could be in on that level," Ivy said, stabbing their finger to one of the pages. "It's in this room *here*. It's always heavily guarded by security, and it's got a pin pad on the door."

"That room is our target," I said. "We already have the code to the pin pad, as revealed by another one of Salvatore's men. Another vampire's thoughts indicated that the key is kept inside a home safe with a dial lock. This is going to be easier to crack than the vault at the bank, because it uses a simpler locking mechanism."

"So we get to the safe, then what?" Ava asked. "You crush the metal door open with your Earth magic?"

"It isn't enough to rely on my Earth magic, because Salvatore wouldn't hide this key in any average safe," I said. "Salvatore knows demigods want the key, and he'll have thought ahead— either with a fail-safe like the bank, or even with inferichite if he's managed to get his hands on it. We don't know what safeguards he might have in place, so our best option is inputting the combination, so we don't trigger any magical alarm systems."

"Do we know the combination?" Kallie asked.

Marcus cleared his throat nervously. "Unfortunately, the vamp we captured last night had that information and he... uh... didn't crack."

I heard it in Marcus' tone. He thought I'd gone too far.

I did what I had to do. That fucker was never going to talk.

"We'll have to move forward without that information," I said coldly. "You can crack the safe, can't you, Kallie?"

"Yes," she stated confidently. "If it's a combination lock, I can break it."

"The last bit of information we obtained from Salvatore's vamps was the security measures in place around the target room," I continued. "There are two guards stationed in front of the room at all times, as well as one guard at the corner of each hall. This level is crawling with security, but I'm confident we can make it past them— or if we have to, take them out."

"How do we do that without getting caught?" Ava asked.

"Everyone will have their respective jobs to help us get in and out of The Devil's City clean," I began. "Our best time to strike will be two days from now."

"Why so soon?" Marcus asked.

"Because that's when my father is hosting his annual gala, the Blood Moon Ball," Ivy explained. "It's a big party he holds every year in the ballroom on the top floor of The Devil's City. Vampires never sleep, so the party goes on from one night and into the next. It gives him and his business partners a chance to mingle and make deals."

"He just had his annual convention in New York, and now he's throwing a ball?" Kallie asked.

"He's a very busy man. Or, to put it bluntly, he throws a lot of fucking parties to keep his morons entertained so they don't get into trouble," Ivy replied. "Most of the vampires bring... *extra guests*. Guests who never leave. My father pays a price for them, so all guests need to be properly vetted. Security is going to be diverted toward the gala."

Ava gave a shudder beside me, and she spoke in a disgusted tone. "You're talking about blood slaves. It's a gala to get valuable people into the building and trade them amongst top mobsters."

"Yes," Ivy said regrettably. "I know what you're thinking, Ava, and it's not going to happen. We can't break these people out. We can slip out with the vampire key while my father is distracted with the gala, but we're never going to get those blood slaves past him."

"If we get the vampire key and win this war, we can free those blood slaves when the time comes," I added. "It's imperative that the key is our one and only focus, because we can't afford any distractions. We need the vampire key so we can open the Elven Gate and save the afterlife, or no amount of rescuing people will bring them salvation."

"All right," Ava agreed, though I could tell she didn't like it. "We go in for the key and the key alone."

"We can't cross paths with my father," Ivy added. "That's a hard, fast rule we all need to play by. If he gets you in his sights, he will *not* hesitate to kill you by any means necessary. You already got past him once, and Salvatore Bianchi *never* lets anyone escape. The fact that you did once is already a miracle, and you can bet your pretty little asses you won't get away a second time. He'll either take you into custody to do with you as he pleases, or he'll kill you on the spot."

"Which is why we won't be crossing his path," I continued. "We'll be accessing the building from the bottom up, to avoid the gala."

"How exactly do we do that?" Kallie asked. "We can't just walk through the front doors. Surely they have alarm systems that will detect us immediately, even if we use illusions to disguise ourselves."

I smirked. "We don't have to go through the front doors, because we have our own way in. Listen carefully, because everything must go according to plan."

The room went silent as everyone leaned in to listen.

"Our home base will be at the Scarlet Grand Hotel eight blocks from The Devil's City," I explained. "The hotel is owned by an Elvish-vampire hybrid who is a rival of Salvatore Bianchi's. He's worked with the Majestica family before, and he's an ally of ours that Max is already in touch with. The hotel is heavily warded, so we'll be protected from being tracked by Salvatore's people. We'll set up at the penthouse suite, which has a clear view of The Devil's City's tower. Asa and Aries will be on the ground, going undercover as security officers who will hack into The Devil's City security feed and sending that information back to Max and Gavyn at the Scarlet Grand. The Elvish Associates will cover our tracks on the cameras, as well as use them to help us navigate the tower. We'll all have earpieces to stay in contact. Elyx will be stationed on the hotel roof. He'll be standing by to take out any potential threats on the target floor via sniper rifle."

"I should stay with the Elvish Associates at the Scarlet Grand," Ava offered. "We need a back-up plan in case communication goes down. I'll be able to telepathically communicate with Charlie. Plus, I'm clever, and I can piece stuff together quickly without getting distracted. I'll be able to watch the cameras and know what you need to do if something goes wrong. You need someone who can make hard decisions on the fly, and I'll be able to do that."

I nodded firmly. "I was thinking the exact same thing, pidge. As for the rest of you, you'll be on my team, infiltrating The Devil's City. I expect this to be a clean job, but I'm also planning ahead for any and all potential mishaps. Which means Oberi will be coming with me in case anyone needs to be healed. Let's hope we don't need her."

Ooh, yay! Oberi exclaimed. *I was hoping to be in on the action.*

I began pacing around the room. "We will strike during the daytime, beginning at ten in the morning. Vampires have a hard time moving around in daylight, and it will be difficult for them to follow us outside if we run into any snags. By then, the Blood Moon Ball will have been going on for several hours, and security will have lowered their guard. The gala will continue throughout the day and into the night, so we'll have time to pull this off while Salvatore is distracted. We can't portal into the building, because we've never been there before, so our portals won't be precise enough. We could end up anywhere in the casino, and we can't take such a risk, though we can portal out once the mission is complete."

I'd circled the whole table and stopped at my spot in the front of the room again. "Ivy's our guide to get us inside and to the right place. We'll start at the storm sewers. The same network that runs beneath the Scarlet Grand also runs under The Devil's City. There isn't direct access to The Devil's City through these tunnels, but all we need is to get under the building, and I can use my Earth powers to dig our way upward. Since we won't be entering the building through any known access points, it shouldn't trip the wards or alarms. For added security, Marcus will brew a potion that will ward us from tipping off the vampires. I'll dig a tunnel up through the boiler room in the basement, which Ivy has outlined in their blueprints. From there, we'll access the service elevator shaft and climb our way to the target floor. That way, we'll avoid all cameras and security."

"What about once we reach the target floor?" Kallie wondered. "That place is going to be crawling with security."

"That's Marcus' and Eddie's job," I said. "They'll be several steps ahead of us, acting as spies so we can circumvent any obstacles in our path. Marcus can use his Seer powers to read minds and detect if anyone is coming our way, as well as break any wards we might encounter. We have to be careful, though, because that will raise alarms, and we want to do this without alerting anyone. Eddie can phase people through walls, like he did in Celestial City, as well as get us out of danger quickly if something goes wrong. Rishi will be on site with Marcus, as an extra pair of eyes and ears. Once we get to the target floor, we'll have to move quickly, because we want to get in and out without raising any alarms. That's where you come in, Kallie."

I drew a breath, because this is where we *needed* the plan to work to stay undetected. Otherwise, it was going to turn into a bloodbath. "Once we're out of the elevator shaft, Kallie will need to stop time for as long as she can, so we can get to the target room and break in before Salvatore's people can come after us. If we *do* run into any vampires, Chancey will be along as our muscle, holding off any guards so Kallie and I can keep moving. Once Kallie and I reach the target room, we'll take out the final security guards and input the door code we retrieved from Salvatore's men. Kallie will crack the safe, and I'll have a mirror along so I can portal us all out."

"You really think we can pull this off without Salvatore knowing we're there?" Marcus asked.

"Yes, but we'll have to work quickly," I said. "Once we arrive in Chicago, we risk Salvatore finding out, even if we're warded from tracking. He has eyes and ears everywhere. We can't lose this key again, so we have to get to the key before Salvatore is alerted of a threat."

"We can give ourselves twenty-four hours," Ivy added. "That's it. Otherwise, we risk the key being moved again."

"Who's to say the key hasn't already been moved?" Kallie asked. "We already had a run-in with your father once."

"It's dangerous for my father to move the key unless he knows it's safe to do so, or unless he detects an immediate threat," Ivy replied. "He wouldn't trust anyone else to move it but himself, and once he does, he has to set up a whole nother system to keep it safe again, and dismantle the one he's already got set up. There are multiple people after the key, including the Warden. It's safer in The Devil's City than it is anywhere else, even if he suspects someone's coming for it, because as long as it's there, he can defend it."

"What if something goes wrong?" Marcus questioned. "Someone could get hurt."

"That's why we've got multiple people on each job," I said. "If something happens to you, for example, Eddie can clear a path for us. Last time, things didn't work out because we didn't account for potential hiccups. We need to expect that *anything* can happen, and be able to pivot in any situation. During the bank robbery, Kallie couldn't portal us out, so I'll have a pocket mirror so we've got two portal makers. If Kallie can't stop time, Chancey's along to buy us time to fight our way out. If we run into wards, you can break them, and if you can't, I can siphon the magic and break them anyway. Let's hope that doesn't happen, because an Elf breaking a ward is going to be worse than a witch, and it'll draw a lot of attention. But it's something we need to consider if things go sideways. Furthermore, if something happens to Ivy and they can't guide us, Ava will be back at the Scarlet Grand monitoring the cameras and telling us where to go."

I crossed my arms. "But this only works if everyone follows orders, no questions asked. With Ava watching the cameras, she's going to see things we won't, and we won't have time to hesitate. We need to trust each other on this."

"We trust you wholeheartedly, your highness," Eddie said.

"Charlie may be a prince here at the palace, but in Chicago, he's our boss," Ava added. "Everyone here needs to listen to him without hesitation."

I smiled. I liked the sound of that.

"You've got it, *boss*," Kallie said.

I clapped my hands. "All right, team. We've all got our jobs. Let's put our final preparations in order and get some rest. We move tomorrow night."

People started to get up and leave the room. "I'm going to stay with Max for a bit," Ava told me. "I want to learn about her tech before I use it. I'll meet you back in the suite."

I took her hand in mine and brought it to my lips to kiss it. "Make sure someone escorts you back."

"I will," she promised.

As we were leaving the room, Marcus approached me. He fidgeted with his hands so much that it was audible. He kept his voice low so the others wouldn't hear. "Charlie... can we talk?"

His tone sounded serious, and I didn't think it had anything to do with the vampire key.

"Yeah, sure," I told him, keeping my voice steady. "Let's find somewhere private."

I took Marcus aside. Oberi and Rishi followed us down the hall, until we found a secluded alcove nearby. Eddie remained close, though he stood guard and gave us space. "What's up?"

Marcus scuffed his foot on the ground. "The thing is... I don't know if I'm ready for this job. I thought I was, but I'm worried I might do something stupid that could screw up the whole operation."

"Like what?" I questioned. He needed to get to the point.

Marcus drew a deep breath. "I need to be honest with you. I was really uncomfortable watching you torture that guy. I know I shouldn't be, because of what we're up against, but I can't lie to myself. Even though you were the one torturing him, I was still watching, which meant I was participating. I don't know if I can stomach that again. I need to figure out what I'm willing to do to win. I need to know where my line is, because I didn't the other day."

"Marcus, we need you to pull off this heist," I started.

"I know, and I want to be a part of it," Marcus insisted. "But I need to figure out what I'm willing to do, and what I'm not, because I don't want to be put in a position where I'm going to freeze and screw all this up. I could potentially be in a situation where I need to kill someone, and I can't hesitate to pull the trigger. I'm not asking you to take me off the job, Charlie. I'm asking you to help me figure out where I *belong* on the job, and I can't do that without knowing how far I'll go."

Marcus' voice started to waver. "I realized some really important stuff in the last couple of months, and there are some big decisions I have to make. I need to do this *before* The Devil's City, because you need me at the top of my game. I can't be thinking about this stuff when we're doing this heist, because I don't want this to get in the way and make a mistake. You guys have been telling me to get my shit together for years, and I need to do it now."

"How can I help?" I asked. I *wanted* to help him, but I didn't understand why he was coming to *me* about this and not speaking to someone like Ava. She'd be able to work with him through this emotional stuff better than I could.

"I just need to talk it through, I think," Marcus admitted. "And you have experience with this kind of thing. I don't blame you for what you did to the vampire; I know we have to do whatever it takes, but I think you know how far you're willing to go. I don't. I'm just wondering... how did you know what you're willing to do? At what point did you figure out where you draw the line?"

If I was being honest with myself, I didn't think I'd *found* my line. I was almost certain I'd do *anything* to take down the Warden. There weren't any boundaries for me.

I didn't think I could tell Marcus that, though. He was looking up to me now, asking for my advice like a big brother. Maybe I didn't know *my* line, but perhaps I could help him find his. We needed to figure out how far he could go if we wanted to obtain the vampire key, because one single moment of hesitation meant the difference between pulling off this heist and being eaten alive by vampires.

Marcus helped me find myself in the Institute's chapel when I underwent my spiritual awakening. I could still hear the melody of his harp playing in my mind. It was time I returned the favor. I didn't know any spiritual ceremonies that would help him, but if we were going to do this, we needed to dig deep into his psyche.

There was really only one way to do that with Marcus, and *talking it out* wasn't going to do the trick. Perhaps that's why he'd come to me and not Ava. I had an idea, and I prayed to the Great Spirit it worked.

"This is going to take a while," I warned Marcus. "We shouldn't talk about this in the middle of the palace halls. Go back to your quarters and change into something casual. I'll meet you at the main doors in fifteen minutes."

"All right," Marcus said, without bothering to ask what I had in mind. He scampered off, and Rishi followed.

Eddie approached me. "Is there anything I can do to be of service, your highness?"

"Actually, there is, Eddie," I told him. "I'm going to need a few things."

I rattled off a list of items I needed. Eddie didn't want to leave my side, because he insisted on *guarding* me, but I told him that Marcus and I needed to do this alone.

Fifteen minutes later, I had changed into a black t-shirt and slacks, standing in front of the palace doors. Oberi was in her unicorn form and hooked up to a carriage, while Eddie had quickly retrieved the supplies I'd asked for and stored them in a trunk behind the seat. The chill of night crept over my skin, and the city was quiet.

Marcus met me there, and Rishi immediately jumped into the seat behind Oberi. "Where are we going?" he asked.

"You'll see," I replied, clapping him on the back.

Marcus and I climbed into the carriage, and Oberi took off out of the palace gates.

"You want to know what your limits are, Marcus?" I asked as we wove through the streets of Ilamanthe. "Then you need to get in touch with your dark side. You need to *test* those limits. You can sit around all day dreaming up imaginary scenarios and what you might do in those situations. The reality is you don't know what you'll actually do until the decision is right in front of you. Are you going to fight back? Are you going to run? You only get a split-second to decide."

"Can't I prepare myself?" he asked.

"Absolutely, and that's what we're going to do," I told him. "But we're going to start with something simple, and we're going to see what your bad side has to say about it. From there, we can decide what limits to test next."

I hoped he made a decision tonight, though, because we really didn't have time to be fucking around. He needed to figure this out now, before we left for Chicago.

Marcus hesitated. "I don't know if I have a bad side like you do, Charlie. I'm a good person who's done bad things, but those were mistakes. What if I want to be good?"

"What if it's good to be bad?" I asked him. "When I was torturing that guy, I wasn't thinking about how bad I was for hurting him. I was thinking about the good that could come from it. If we don't get answers, the Blessed Haven is fucked. Isn't it worth hurting one guy to save the world? I don't buy into the bullshit that the world is black and white. What if you didn't have to worry about whether you were good or bad, only had to exist just as you are?"

"And what is that, exactly?" he wondered. "What am I?"

I tilted my head. "Well, you're an artist, aren't you, Marcus?"

The air shifted around us, and I could sense tall buildings rising on either side of us as we entered a narrow alleyway. Oberi nickered and came to a halt. I hopped over the side of the carriage and opened the trunk, displaying over a dozen cans of spray paint.

"You... want me to paint?" Marcus questioned.

I grabbed a can of spray paint and shook it. "Hell yeah. You want to see what your bad side looks like? Why don't we do something bad in this abandoned alleyway?"

Marcus chuckled lightly as he hopped down from the carriage. "Painting isn't *bad*. I'm not hurting anyone."

I cocked an eyebrow. "Isn't vandalism illegal?"

"Um... I guess?" he replied. "I suppose someone owns this building and wouldn't appreciate me destroying their property."

"Destruction? But I thought it was art," I said with a smirk. I popped the top of my spray can. The canister hissed as I sprayed an X over the wall.

This looks like fun! Oberi exclaimed. He shifted into a husky and slipped out of his reins. He and Rishi approached the wet paint I'd just sprayed onto the wall. Their paws made a squishing sound as they pressed them into the wet paint, then started placing paw prints all over the wall.

"I think I get what you're saying," Marcus mused. "It's bad to vandalize, but it's good to make art. So the good thing cancels out the bad."

"Uh, no... not exactly. More like... being bad doesn't have to be a *bad* thing. Maybe it's okay to be bad."

Marcus absorbed this for a moment. "Do you really think I can get to a place where torturing someone feels like a good thing?"

I shrugged. "You tell me. You've got limits that clearly I don't have. At what point do you start to feel *bad*?"

I sprayed another X on the wall, but Marcus didn't answer. "Come on," I encouraged. "Paint something. You've done this a million times."

"Yeah, on Institute walls and shit," he said. "The Institute deserved it."

"Bullshit. You told me your rap sheet. You have a bunch of misdemeanor charges from tagging buildings in Octavia Falls before you got to prison."

"Yeah, but I did that to people who were assholes," he protested. "We don't know who owns this building, and I could really hurt their feelings."

The building was owned by the royal family, but I didn't tell him that. Marcus needed to get in touch with his inner villain to see how far he'd go. It was simple and harmless, but if he couldn't spray paint a fucking building like he had a million times before, he'd never make it through the first stage of the heist.

"Who's to judge who deserves what?" I asked. "Maybe it doesn't matter what people deserve, and morality is merely a tool for control. People can call us bad, and so what if we are?"

I pressed the spray can into his hand. "Following the rules has never worked for you, Marcus. If you want to feel good, you need to do something bad. There are no consequences for people like us, because this world is ours for the taking. You get to decide just how bad you want to be. No one else gets to tell you what to do. It's time to stop thinking about everyone else and what they think of you. What about Marcus' feelings? What does *Marcus* want?"

"I want... I want to paint a mural." He shook his spray can. "I want to release my demons. It's like they're caged inside of me, and I need to set them free. The only way I know how to do that is through painting."

"Do it," I told him. "What are those demons saying, Marcus? Let them run wild."

Marcus began spraying the wall, and he didn't stop, either. "They're saying; *You're bad, Marcus, but you aren't bad enough. You don't have what it takes to be on this team. You're going to fuck up, and everyone's going to blame you.* It's black, and it's dark, but it's other colors, too. Where's the blue?"

Marcus turned from the wall to rifle through the trunk. Spray cans clattered onto the pavement as he tossed colors he didn't like aside. He found what he was looking for and began spraying again. I leaned against the opposite building, listening to the hiss of the paint as he moved across the wall.

Marcus started rambling, as if I wasn't here at all. "My depression is a navy blue, almost gray. It's like the color of the clouds as a storm begins rolling in. It's a gloomy day when all the colors turn hazy and you can't see the sun, so you don't even know what time of day it is. I need some highlights."

Marcus grabbed another can and began adding detail to his painting.

Oberi stepped back, coming to my side. *He's barely started, and it's already beautiful. He's painting storm clouds, and they look so realistic.*

"My trauma... ooh, that's red." He popped off the cap of another can. "It's like lava, bubbling up inside of you, searing you to the bone. Sometimes you can push it down, but it creeps up on you, and sometimes it explodes!"

Marcus let out a maniacal laugh.

He's painting a hellscape, Oberi told me. *There's a volcano beneath the clouds, with rivers of lava streaming through cracks of black stone.*

"Then there's the rage," Marcus continued. His voice had taken on a crazed tone. "Fuck, I already used red— no, rage is more than that. It's like an explosion. It's yellow and orange and blue, colors of fire and flame... exploding dynamite. No, lightning!"

Marcus sprayed three quick streams of paint to create a lightning bolt. "Then there's the BPD, and that's... that's *all* the colors. It's everything combined into one. All my emotions brewing together, until I can't make sense of them and can't separate them, either."

I stood back curiously as Marcus put his borderline personality diagnosis onto the wall. I didn't know how his BPD would show up in his art. Marcus must've spent fifteen minutes on this part of the painting, before he stood back to admire his work.

"It's a monster..." he said breathlessly, like he'd only just realized what he'd done. "I know you can't see it, Charlie, but he's taller than I am— eight feet, at least. He's big and heavy, with a fat belly like a troll. He's made of all different colors. I can't even tell what color he is, because he's got splotches of every shade imaginable on him. He's only got one eye, like a cyclops. I don't know why I drew him that way. Maybe because with BPD, I can get so single minded. Once I put my sights on how I feel, it's hard to convince myself of anything else. It doesn't matter if it's true or not. All I know is the stories I believe about myself. He's got long claws and sharp teeth, like he's going to sink his fangs into me and never let go. He's not going to eat me, because that would be too merciful. He just lets me dangle out of his mouth and watch me bleed. Ooh, he likes the taste of my blood. He wants me to scream and suffer. But I'm not going to let him do that. He's a demon on my past, and he can fucking stay there."

Marcus gasped. *"That's* what they are! I've been fighting demons and monsters, not storms and volcanic eruptions. I need to start over."

Rishi gave a cry, and Marcus took a few steps back.

"You're right, Rishi," he said. "I can't calm a storm or force the lava back into the earth. I can't fight nature. But I can fight these fucking demons. I can *kill* them. I can leave them behind and keep on trudging up this mountain so I can transcend these clouds. These motherfuckers think this storm is bad? They haven't seen the kind of storm I can create!"

A hint of a smile touched my lips, because I felt like we were really getting somewhere. I didn't want to distract Marcus, though, so I didn't say anything.

Paint cans clattered across the pavement as Marcus kicked a few aside to get the ones he wanted. He shook the paint can in his hand. "All right, depression. You aren't these clouds; you're a demon. Let's see what you look like."

Marcus kept on painting, personifying his demons into real-life paintings. Hours must've passed as Marcus worked, muttering under his breath every now and then. I remained patient, letting Marcus depict what he wanted. Oberi described the paintings to me as they were created, giving them life.

Marcus painted his depression as a gray fog monster, with empty black eye sockets and a dark pit at the center that could suck him in. "Depression fucking sucks, man," Marcus ranted as he painted. "Some days, you're just in this haze, void of color and all hope. And then sometimes, you fall into this deep, black pit it feels like you'll never crawl out of. It's funny how the brain is wired to survive, but when things get really bad, the only solution your brain can come up with is to end it all. How's that possible? How can something that does everything to keep us alive be driven to such a dark solution? Only demons can do that. This demon sucks hours from your life, drains your will and your hope, and slowly crushes you. You don't really want to die, but you can't see another way out. You either lay in bed all day, waiting for the monster to claim you, or you power through the pain. Well, I'm going to choose a different path. I'm going to slay that fucking monster."

He kept on working, painting his trauma next. "People say trauma makes you stronger, but it doesn't. It breaks you, hurts you, makes you sensitive and vulnerable. You back off from everything and everyone, because you're so afraid to feel that way again. You don't know who to trust, because now you know that the people you love can hurt you... or you can hurt them. Trauma makes it difficult to concentrate or make a simple fucking decision. It gives you PTSD and nightmares. Trauma doesn't just happen in the moment, but it latches on and sticks with you, until it literally alters who you are."

Marcus shouted toward the sky. "Well, guess what? You can let me fucking go, because I won't let you latch on to me any longer!"

He's painted his trauma as a lamprey-like creature, Oberi told me. *It's a giant red eel with circles of razor-sharp teeth. It's creeping along the blackened rock with the other monsters, as if searching for something to devour.*

"Rage?" Marcus continued. "Well, she's a strong monster. She's got muscles bigger than my head, and fangs as big as Rishi. If she gets me in her hands, she could crush me."

It was interesting to me that Marcus identified his rage as a woman, but I didn't know why.

"Rage lashes out," Marcus continued. "She doesn't give a fuck who or what she destroys. She only knows that things aren't right, and somehow, she needs to put it back together again. She cares *too* fucking much."

Rage is bipedal, Oberi described. *She's got huge hands, bulging muscles, and teeth like a lion's. She doesn't have eyes, though.*

"She can't see where she's going," Marcus said. "She just reacts. She just *destroys.* I'm not going to let her keep destroying my life."

He picked up another can of spray paint. "Self-doubt is a tiny little monster, but he's fiercer than all the rest. He's a little gremlin, skittering between the others so that you don't even notice him until he's right on top of you. He makes you question your worth and convinces you to back down, even when you want to put up a fight. He can force you to retreat before the fight has even begun. And if you find yourself in the middle of the battle before he can convince you otherwise, boy, does this little guy make you feel like the smallest living thing on the battlefield. He can suck your soul dry, until you've lost everything... even the people you love. When he's got a hold of you, there isn't anything you wouldn't give up, because you don't believe you deserve it anyway. This little guy can go fuck himself, because I deserve the world!"

His self-doubt is only a foot high, with a naked round little body, small eyes, and spindly arms and legs, Oberi told me. *It's the tiniest little thing.*

Marcus stood back to view his painting. The moments ticked by, and I waited for him to say more, but he didn't. He just kept on tapping his foot.

"It isn't done," he mumbled after a long silence. "Something's missing."

I stepped forward. "The way you described it, these monsters are marching toward a destination, aren't they? They've got their claws out and their fangs bared like they're ready to battle. What are they fighting, Marcus?"

Rishi meowed loudly.

Marcus drew a sharp breath. "The mural is missing *me*. All this time, I've been fighting against these monsters, which means the painting is missing the warrior. I've got it, Charlie!"

He clapped me on the shoulder, and wet paint soaked into my shirt. I didn't even care. I smiled proudly as Marcus rushed to gather more paint cans that he'd sprawled across the alleyway.

"I used to be afraid of all these monsters," Marcus started as his paint can hissed. "But I don't have to be afraid anymore. I said trauma doesn't make you stronger, but that doesn't mean I'm not stronger than I was before. The trauma didn't make me strong, but you know what did? Perseverance. Healing. Hope. I'm not there yet, but I'm sure as hell farther along than I was before."

Marcus ran out of paint in one can and quickly tossed it aside to grab another. "I'm not afraid, because I know that if these demons haven't consumed me by now, they never will. I've had the tools all along to fight them; I just didn't realize that's what I was doing. No, no, no... fighting isn't the answer. That's what I've been doing all this time, and it's only worn me down. Maybe I don't have to fight them anymore. Instead, I have to become their master. They can't rule me anymore, because *I* rule them. I know how to direct my rage. I'm never going to get rid of her, but you know what? She's strong because she cares, and that is *not* a weakness. She's like a mother defending her children, and I can do the same. Instead of turning that rage inward or toward those I love, I can direct it toward the Warden to *save* the people I love."

I realized then why he'd personified his rage as a woman. He saw the side of rage that was caring, kind, and nurturing— that even in the midst of battle, one could fight from a place of love.

Marcus' footsteps disappeared, and the sound of his spray can came from high above my head. I realized he'd levitated himself off the ground to reach a higher portion of the mural. "My depression is a gift because it shows that I care, and I feel more deeply than others. Most people in this world don't give a damn. With my BPD, I struggle with relationships because I care so damn much, and I want to be perfect for everyone. My self-doubt shows me where I can focus my energy to heal myself. It shows me the parts of me that need more love. I have so much love to give, and I'm finally ready to give it back to myself. My mental health isn't a burden, but a tool, and I'm going to use it to make my life better and not worse."

Oberi wagged his tail and began panting. *Charlie, I see what he's painting now! It's all coming together. He's painting a cat that looks like Rishi. It's over twelve-feet tall! The cat is facing the oncoming monsters with its claws braced in the dirt. It's baring its teeth, like it's holding off the monsters.*

Something powerful seemed to surge through the alleyway. I didn't think it was magic, but I swore I could *feel* Marcus' emotions coming through the painting just by hearing Oberi describe it. It was powerful art; that was for certain.

I realized that Marcus hadn't just created a painting— he'd made Spirit Art. Ava told me some time ago that if a supernatural put enough of themselves into a creation they made, they sealed a fragment of their soul into the project that would remain attached to the piece forever.

I knew what Marcus had made now was a piece of Spirit Art, because the energy of his soul radiated powerfully off the painting he was creating. He was so immersed he didn't even realize a part of his soul was being sealed into the design. He hadn't tried to make Spirit Art, but it was something that happened naturally, because he put so much heart into this project.

"I've painted a cat," Marcus told me. "He's not fighting off the monsters, because he doesn't have to. He's standing guard, holding them off so they can't hurt me anymore. This cat is you, Charlie. He's all the good things I've had at my side all along— your friendship, my parents, Ava and Kallie and everyone who's been here all this time. He's my hope, and he's my dreams for the future. He's all the good things that fought the demons away."

Marcus' feet landed on the ground, and his spray can clinkered to the pavement. "I... I didn't realize..."

Marcus sank to his knees as sobs broke from his chest. I knelt beside him and placed a hand on his shoulder.

"Marcus," I said softly. "You never had to fight this battle alone."

He wiped the tears from his eyes. "You guys have told me that before, but I didn't believe it until now. I thought my demons controlled me, but the real fight was between me and the cat. I wasn't letting him defend me."

Marcus grabbed my shirt and sobbed into it. His tears dripped onto my chest. "It's time to set him free, Charlie! I don't have to fight off the bad to unleash the good. I can find the good *in* the bad, and use it to my advantage."

I clapped his back. "Yes, Marcus. That's exactly it!"

His shoulders shook as sobs racked his body. "Finally! Finally, I can be free."

Rishi meowed loudly, as if in warning. I wasn't sure what he was trying to communicate, until Marcus' sobs came to a sudden halt. He slumped into my arms, and I realized he was passing out. I caught him before he could fall completely to the pavement and hit his head. His body jerked several times, like he was in the midst of a terrible nightmare. Marcus had fainted, and it hadn't come with any warning.

I didn't realize what was happening until the alleyway completely disappeared around me. An image invaded my senses.

I SAW A DARK, desolate landscape all around us, with rivers of lava cutting through the blackened stone. The sky above us was black, without a single star in sight. It seemed like we had entered Marcus' painting, though I didn't know how that was possible. I noticed the edges of my vision were hazy, like the images my grandfather projected into my mind when he was replaying a memory.

I realized Marcus was having a vision, and I'd just been sucked into it.

I looked around for Marcus, but I didn't see him anywhere. He must've been close by, though, because his magic provided me with a frame of reference for the images I witnessed— filling in any gaps in my understanding of the shapes and colors that overwhelmed my senses. It was like I was viewing the vision from afar, as if I'd left my body and was hovering above the scene.

I peered down onto the dark landscape. Nothing but black rock stretched as far as the eye could see. Glowing rivers of lava flowed out of active volcanoes, and smoke billowed upward. Screams echoed in the distance, and the roar of monsters filled the air. It looked like a hellscape out of a horror story.

A shadowy figure took shape behind the steam of active geysers. It appeared as a man, walking upright on two legs, but he was larger than any man I'd encountered before. He must've stood at least eight feet tall, with broad shoulders and bulging muscles. As he came closer, I saw that he wasn't a man at all, but some sort of demon. He had the head of a ram, with thick curved horns growing out of the top of his head. His body was covered in fur, and he had long, sharp claws.

I wasn't afraid of him, though. Unlike the monsters in Marcus' painting, he didn't have fangs or a thirst for blood in his features. Instead, he had a curious look in his dark eyes.

In the distance, a woman's voice called out. "Please! Help me!"

"No one has called upon me in centuries," the demon uttered to himself. "I have been forgotten."

It didn't seem forgotten by everyone, because the woman cried again, "Lord demon, come to me!"

A portal bloomed in front of the demon, shimmering around the edges with powerful magic. He stepped through the portal, and I was transported through the vision with him.

The demon stood in a dense forest, and the moonlight shone overhead. Several paces away a woman knelt in the dirt, her quiet sobs piercing through the night. She had brown hair and pale skin, and wore a long, simple dress. Through the trees, I could make out a large stone manor. Something told me this vision had taken place many centuries ago, sometime in the late Middle Ages.

"You are a powerful sorceress to have summoned me," the demon said in a deep voice.

"Please," the woman begged in a shaky tone, keeping her head down. She spoke in an accent that I thought sounded Malovian. "I have prayed to my gods for many moons, and none have answered my prayers. I only seek your help, and I will give up anything in return— including my soul, if that is what you wish."

The demon took a step toward her, and she shuddered. "What help do you seek?" he asked.

"I wish to be free of my master," she said, though she wouldn't lift her gaze to look at the demon. "He is very cruel to me."

She reached a shaky hand to her shoulder and drew back her sleeve, to show the demon bloody slashes across her back. They had clearly been inflicted by a whip, and several were raw with infection.

"I do my best to please him, but if I make a mistake, my master locks me in the cellar for days to starve," she said. "I see the whip almost every day. I cry out in pain each time he lays me down to share his bed. Today, I spilled a pail of water while doing my chores, and I was punished severely."

The woman began to sob, and her tears landed in the dirt below her. She curled her knees to her chest, then showed the demon her feet. The bottoms were an angry red and oozing with blisters. It looked like her master had forced her to stand upon hot coals until there was no skin left on the soles of her feet. I didn't know how she'd managed to walk out here into the forest.

Then I noticed the dirt all over her hands and knees, and I realized she hadn't walked out here at all. She'd crawled out here to beg for mercy from a demon, because selling her soul to a creature of the Eternal Torment was a better alternative than serving her master.

My heart broke into a thousand pieces for her. I couldn't imagine treating any woman like this. She deserved to be protected, and instead, she was beaten and abused. The man who possessed her deserved a fate worse than death.

The demon curled his hands into fists, and his tone became enraged. "Where is this master?!"

Her voice shook, and she peered over her shoulder. "He is sleeping in the house. Please, take me away. I do not wish to go back there."

The demon wore a look of sympathy as he knelt by her side, though even on his knees, he towered over her. He reached out a hand and gently placed a finger beneath her chin. The woman shied away, until he guided her face toward his. For the first time, she looked at him. Tears streamed down her cheeks as she gazed upon his face. She appeared to see him in a way no other had before.

"After tonight, you will never have to return here," he promised. "I am a demonic god, and I will do everything in my power to grant you your wish. Now show me where to find him."

The woman couldn't walk, so the demon lifted her into his arms. She wrapped her arms around his neck, and he carried her like she was as light as a piece of paper. The demon stomped through the forest, his angry footsteps shaking the ground. He grunted and moaned in rage as he burst through the front door of the manor. The door blasted clear off its hinges and splintered into a hundred pieces in the middle of the foyer. The demon let out a terrifying roar that made the walls shake.

The house broke out into a ruckus as people woke to the sound of the intrusion. An older man in a nightcap skidded to a halt at the top of the stairs. "What is the meaning of this?" he demanded.

The man's eyes went wide when he saw the demon, and he clutched at his heart.

The woman clung tight to the demon's neck as he cradled her in a single arm. "That's him," she whimpered.

The demon gently set the woman on a chair near the door before turning his maddened gaze on her master. He stomped up the stairs, the wood cracking beneath his weight. "You are a wretched beast, and have issued your final punishment."

The master of the home scampered backward, tripping over his own two feet. "P-please, what is it you want? Jewels? Riches? T-take whatever you want."

"You have taken this woman's life, and that is of more value than anything you can possibly offer me," the demon sneered. "And so, I'll take your soul, in exchange for the one you damaged."

The demon swiped his long, sharp claws, and the master's pleading cries instantly died. In three quick swipes of his claws— one right after the other— the master's body had been completely dismembered. Blood spurted across the walls, and limbs fell to the floor in a heap. His torso, now in two pieces, landed on the lower level of the house, and the master's head rolled across the hardwood. Servants who had come to investigate the commotion screamed and quickly fled.

The demon stared down at the master's body, which was oozing a puddle of blood across the floor. The demon shook in rage.

"Even a demon would not be so heartless," he stated coldly. He turned from the master's body and slowly descended the stairs, reaching a gentle hand out to the woman.

She turned her gaze up to him, but she was no longer shaking in fear. Instead, she stared up at the demon with admiration in her eyes. Then, she bowed her head to him. "Thank you. In exchange for fulfilling my wish, I pledge that you are my lord. I will give my soul to you now, and you may do with it what you will."

"No," the demon stated, though his voice changed. His body shrank several inches, and the horns and claws disappeared as he took on the image of a man. He was tall in his human form, at least six feet, with a muscular build and dark hair. He wore a long black cloak and knelt at the woman's side again. "I will not take your soul, for you have already given enough to your master. You do not deserve an eternity in an endless abyss."

"Neither do you," she whispered. "What you did was merciful. You deserve a place among the gods."

"The gods do not want me," the demon replied. "I am not desired there."

"Then stay with me," the woman pleaded. "Be my lord here in this realm, and don't return to your hellish underworld."

He hesitated, like he never thought there was another option for him. "I will stay here on Earth for a while... to protect you. We will go far away, and you will never have to return to this place."

"How far?" she asked.

"As far as you wish."

"Take me out of this country," she begged. "My own people sold me to this man and claimed I deserved it, because I was born a dark magic user. My gods did not answer my prayers. I do not belong here."

"Then we will start a new life somewhere else."

He went to pick her up again, but she quickly said, "I think I can carry myself now."

To my surprise, black wings appeared out of her back. They were shaped like butterfly wings, with pointed edges, but they were sheer rather than velvety. In the light, the black wings shimmered purple and blue. She fluttered her wings, and they carried her several inches off the ground.

"Though my wings and my fae magic will always be a part of me, I do not wish to be Arcanean any longer," she told him. "My own people cast me out, and Malovia has become a foreign land to me. They have made it clear that as an Unseelie fae, I am not welcome there. I am no longer a fae sorceress, but something other."

"You will become something new," the demon promised. "I am called Santos."

"It is nice to meet you, Santos, my lord above lords," she replied. "I am Miriam."

She took the demon's hand, and together, they left the manor.

THE IMAGES WASHED AWAY, and I gasped as I was yanked from the vision. I felt the hard ground beneath my knees once again. Oberi nudged his wet nose into my arm, and Rishi meowed while he pawed at us. I was still holding Marcus, and he was growing heavy in my arms.

"Holy shit! Marcus!" I shook him.

He groaned as he came to. "Dear Goddess. I just had the most intense vision."

"I know!" I cried. "Somehow, you sucked me into it. I saw everything. How did you *do* that? When you sucked me into your visions before, I didn't see images."

Marcus sat up. "I guess my powers are getting stronger. I never felt so *present*. It was so clear, like I was there myself."

"Same," I remarked. "That was your god and goddess, wasn't it? The demon fell in love with her, and they gave birth to the first witches. Miriam and Santos are the mother and father of all Miriamic people."

"Yeah, but it can't be real. Mother Miriam was a witch; she got her powers from Santos. She wasn't an Arcanean fae sorceress— *oh, shit!*"

Marcus smacked the palm of his hand to his head. "How could I have never seen this before? Of *course!* It makes perfect sense."

He grabbed me by the shoulders and shook me. "Don't you see? It all adds up. In the vision, Miriam says she was born a dark magic user. She was Unseelie fae! Santos was a demonic god. Witches always knew we had demon blood running through our veins, but that's not all we are. We were always half Unseelie fae, half demon. *That's* why our magic is so similar to the Arcanea. Our Mentalists can do telekinesis like the fae's wolven faction. Our Seers feel emotions like the griffins. Our Mortana are warriors like the dragons, and our

Alchemists brew potions like the fae. Our Curse Breakers can even break fae magic, because it's so similar to our own!"

He got to his feet and started pacing. "It's all coming together. The fae and the witches lived in Europe at the same time, before the witches came to America to escape the witch trials. Witches use wands and crystals, just like the Unseelie fae! A tattooed mark appears on a fae sorceress when she's ready to bond, the same way a tattoo appears on a witch when their powers awaken."

Marcus paused for a beat as he realized something. "Even some of our last names are the same. My dad told me about a reaper he encountered when he was my age— Edgar Nowak was his name. That's Kallie's last name, too. I didn't think much of it, but now it's obvious that much of the witches' and the fae's lineage can be traced back to the same families. Santos and Miriam's kids had children of their own. I bet some of them married other Unseelie fae who were being persecuted at that time."

Marcus blew a breath of disbelief. "We have all these stories of Mother Miriam trying to hide her magic from the fae. She even wrote her grimoires in Latin, so the fae couldn't read them. It's because she was Unseelie, and if they discovered she was using dark magic— hell, used it to summon a *demon* and then mate with him— she'd be put to death!"

He stopped pacing. "Somewhere along the way, the coven lost this knowledge. Then again, knowledge wasn't the only thing we lost. If this is true, and my people are half fae, half demon, then our magic changed through the generations. Women lost their wings, and the men lost their ability to shift into magical creatures. We lost our fated mate bond. But we gained other powers through our demon ancestry, like the power of necromancy. Mother Miriam must've hidden this information to protect us, because the fae persecuted witches and put them on trial. She said she didn't want to be an Arcanea anymore... so she became a witch."

I stood up. "What does all this mean? You must've had this vision for a reason."

"It must be a lesson about what it means to be good and bad," Marcus said thoughtfully. "Miriam's people claimed she was bad, because she wielded dark magic. And Santos was labeled a demon because he was outcast by the other gods. They're telling me that just because people *think* you're bad doesn't mean that you are. They loved each other and created a whole new supernatural race out of their love. Santos made Mother Miriam into a goddess because he loved her that much. He killed Miriam's master, but that didn't make him a bad guy. He was *protecting* her."

Marcus thought about it for a moment. "But there's got to be more to it than that. I mean, holy shit, my goddess was an Unseelie fae! Mother Miriam must be trying to tell me something about me and Kallie, right? I mean, I'm trying to bring my demons to light, and my relationship with her is the one piece I still have yet to resolve. It's like Mother Miriam and Santos want me to know the witches and the fae need to be united, because they're really one people. Kallie was supposed to bond to an Arcanean fae, and I guess in a way, she kind of did, because that's what my distant ancestors are. Our relationship didn't make any sense before, and maybe that's why it was so intense. But now I understand. We aren't some fluke or freaks of nature. This was always meant to be. Kallie and I... we were meant to bring the fae and the witches *together*, and unite them into one people, because that's what we are. Our kinds have been at war for centuries, but they don't have to be anymore. The witches and the fae aren't two separate nations, but one."

"Does that mean you want her back?" I asked.

Marcus hesitated. "If she wanted me back, I would get together with her in a heartbeat... but I don't think that's what this vision meant. It's not about what I need to do in the future, but about coming to terms with the past. It's showing me that we weren't wrong to bond, and it wasn't a *bad* thing. Even if I can never have Kallie back in that way, I can learn from it. I know now that I might not have all the answers, and that doesn't make something wrong. I just need to trust the process and put my faith in my deities. I don't have to be in control of everything all the time, because there are forces at play working *for* me that I'm not even aware of."

"That's a beautiful message," I said. "And really powerful."

Marcus sniffled. "I think I get it now, Charlie. I don't have to be good, because that's not who I am. It just isn't in my blood. I'm bad, and that's okay. Thank you for everything, Charlie. You have no idea how helpful this was. I'm ready to take what I know now and put it to use. You don't have to worry that I'll hesitate in The Devil's City, because I'll pull the trigger if I have to."

I clapped Marcus on the back. To say I was proud of him was an understatement. "It's good to have you on board."

"I'll say," Marcus said breathlessly. "I need to tell Kallie all about this right away!"

I laughed, and we headed toward the carriage. "Let's get back to the palace. I have final preparations to make with the Elvish Associates, and we need rest before we leave tomorrow."

I thought about the vision on the way back. What Marcus had just discovered about Mother Miriam and Santos was powerful knowledge. It could bring the fae and the witches together— two sides that had been at war for centuries could be joined into a single nation.

Though that union would have to wait. To bring them together, we would first have to defeat the Warden.

Which meant stealing the vampire key right from Salvatore Bianchi's hands, no matter what it took.

ava-marie

TWENTY

Our plan was in place. Now we just had to pull it off.

We were leaving for Chicago tonight and staying at the hotel until morning, when we'd begin our heist. Vampires couldn't move in daylight without magical tools or potions to protect them, so hosting our heist during the day when they'd have the sun as an obstacle was part of our strategy.

At midnight, I drove my car through a massive mirror set up in the royal garage in order to portal to Chicago. Charlie and Oberi sat in the passenger's seat, while Marcus, Rishi, and Kallie were in the back. Kallie had left Alette behind in her room, as we figured it'd be safer for the faekin. Chancey, Ivy, and the Elvish Associates followed in a white van behind us, ready to make their move.

When we came out the other side of the portal, I looked from left to right. We'd emerged into a massive garage underneath the hotel, which had been cleared out for our vehicles, save for a few high-profile cars stored in the corner. We parked the cars, then took a set of elevators up to the main floor.

The lobby of the hotel was splendid. Candelabras stood next to black pillars, which drew your eye to the cathedral-like ceiling. Lovely frescoes depicted classical paintings of angels, demons, and vampires, portrayed by an accomplished artist. Marcus seemed very impressed by the paintings, unable to keep his eyes off the ceiling. The rest of the room was cast in dark tones, Persian rugs splayed across the hardwood floor while art deco furniture was placed carefully around the room. Whoever decorated this hotel had been very particular, and clearly took pride in making it appear stunning.

A beautiful man wearing a pressed suit was there to greet us. He had gorgeous, flowing hair, and he moved with the most refined grace.

"Welcome to the Scarlet Grand Hotel," he purred, shaking our hands. "My name is Dorian Abbot. I am the hotelier of this historical enterprise and wish to welcome you. I am honored that the prince and princess themselves have chosen to grace our doors."

He was a vampire, for sure, but also very Elvish. A regular supernatural couldn't tell, but I'd spent enough time in Ilamanthe to pick out Elven features, and Dorian had slightly pointed ears and high cheekbones that were signature Elvish traits.

"Thank you for having us," Charlie said as he shook Dorian's hand. "My grandfather sends his appreciation."

"There is no need for your gratitude. I am here to serve the Emperor and his kin, as I have done all my life," Dorian said, giving a slight bow to Charlie. "My full hotel has been reserved only for you, to conceal any rumors of your arrival from Salvatore Bianchi, and my staff is here to serve you. I would also like to add that anything I can do to be a thorn in the side of Salvatore Bianchi is a personal treat. He and I have had many quarrels over the years."

Gee, someone else who hated Ivy's dad. What a shock. Guy should be dead by now, with all the people who despised him.

Dorian turned Ivy's way and nodded politely to them. "Welcome, Ivy. It is good to see you again."

"Hey, Dorian," Ivy said hoarsely, and they averted their eyes. Chancey went to grab their hand.

"You'll want to stay aware when you enter The Devil's City tomorrow," Dorian noted. "This is the most popular time of year for visitors to the casino, and it will be infested with shady characters from all the magical races, not just Salvatore's men."

"I thought it was only for vampires," Marcus said.

"The Devil's City is a supernatural casino, and magical folks of all kinds can come in and out. Vampires aren't the only magical beings who come to visit its temptations," Dorian informed us. "It is one place of refuge during the war where all magical beings, regardless of race, may interact."

Yeah, sure. Salvatore was definitely racist, but he certainly had the belief that everyone's money spent the same, especially on cheap slots that probably never paid out.

"Isn't it risky for Salvatore to put a casino right in the middle of downtown Chicago, where even the humans can see him?" I asked. "It's not exactly hidden."

"The doors of The Devil's City are open to everyone, even humans," Dorian said.

"They let humans inside?" Marcus questioned, shocked. "What about magical secrecy?"

"You don't understand, my boy. They let humans *in*, but they do not let them out," Dorian replied.

Ugh. I got it. Any humans who chanced going into The Devil's City immediately became food or were sold as blood slaves. No need to keep magic a secret when you killed or enslaved everyone who walked in.

"Why hasn't the United Supernatural Union gotten involved?" Kallie questioned. "That seems like a big violation of international magical law, to let humans into a place for supes, then to sell off said humans to be fed on."

"The Union tends to look the other way when it comes to Salvatore Bianchi and his dealings," Dorian said dryly. "Unfortunately, he has a lot of power here, and any attempts the Union has made to arrest him have only led to their own officers being killed. In awful ways, I may add."

At least we didn't have to worry about Union reps crawling around Chicago looking to bring us in, but that wasn't necessarily a good thing. If even the Union was scared of Salvatore, we needed to be more careful than we already were.

"I will not take more of your time," Dorian said kindly, and he handed Eddie a set of key cards. "The Elvish Associates have been given their own rooms. The prince and his court will stay in the penthouse suite, which is our grandest chamber. I hope you will be comfortable staying with us, and if you need anything, merely ask, and I will run to your aid."

"We appreciate it," Charlie said, and he turned back toward the elevators. "Come on, guys. We need to get to bed."

We took the elevator up. The Associates ducked out on the second to the topmost floor, while we went all the way to the top.

"You know Dorian?" I whispered to Ivy as we headed up.

Ivy dropped their gaze, looking a little ashamed. "He helped Danny and me out when we were down on our luck. I used to bring clients here every now and then when I could manage it, because it was the only place I felt safe doing my job. Dorian didn't approve, but he gave me a room for free to do my business, and he backed me up when my dad tossed me out of the mob. He kicked me out when he learned I was using in one of the rooms, though. I haven't been back since."

"Maybe you can patch things up with him," I offered.

Ivy shrugged. "Maybe."

The penthouse really was grand. The suite was massive, with a kitchen and dining room suited for twelve, a widescreen TV placed in front of a large sectional sofa, a balcony that overlooked the city, and a dozen rooms. We had the top floor all to ourselves.

I rolled onto the penthouse's balcony and looked out. The Devil's City was only eight blocks away from the Scarlet Grand Hotel. The Scarlet Grand was taller than the buildings surrounding it, so I had a clear view of The Devil's City. It was a massive, mostly windowless tower, with only a line of windows streaking the outer corners. The building sparkled with colorful spotlights which lured gamblers into the casino. I knew that place was crawling with vampires, strippers and all kinds of illegal activity. It rose into the sky, several stories higher than the Scarlet Grand, and looked absolutely intimidating.

Not to mention phallic. I swear, Salvatore was compensating for something.

Charlie went to take a shower, which left me an opening to speak to Marcus in private. I had to talk to him before we went through with the plan. I quietly approached Marcus, who was rummaging for snacks in the stocked kitchen.

"Did you do what I asked?" I said quietly. Guilt sank like a rock into my stomach, but even so, I *had* to double check.

After the circus, I'd discussed what Danny and Chancey had brought up to me with Marcus, and asked him to use teleinsight to get into Charlie's head and see if he was keeping any secrets. I really didn't want to, but Oberi had encouraged me to ask, because she'd thought it was a good idea to have certainty. I despised the thought of rooting around in Charlie's head without his permission, because he'd made a promise long ago that he'd never do that to me. But Danny's words kept eating away at my conscience, and I needed to be sure.

Marcus nodded as he took a bag of cookies down from the cabinet. "Yeah. Sorry, Ava, but I didn't find anything. Everything in his head is stuff we've already discussed. As far as I can tell, Charlie isn't hiding secrets from us. The fact that I could get into his head at all is proof of that, because I shouldn't be able to access a demigod's mind without consent, and Charlie's not blocking me."

"I thought so." I dropped my gaze, ashamed that I'd mistrusted my husband.

Now I was sure Charlie wasn't planning anything devious. And I was angry at Danny for swaying me toward disbelieving Charlie's promises. "Thanks, Marcus. Ancestors, I feel awful. What kind of a wife am I, to do something like this to him?"

"Hey, don't feel bad. I'm his best friend, and I said yes," he said, giving a remorseful frown. "I wouldn't have agreed if I didn't wonder that something was up."

"Did you really think there was?"

He shrugged. "He has been acting kind of... *different* lately, and that's why I agreed to do it. But maybe that's just the mob boss coming out in him. Cassiel's been pushing him to be all he can be. I don't blame him for starting to crack under the pressure."

That had to be it. If Charlie was stressed out that his grandpa had such high expectations of him, I needed to be here to support him, not judging his every move. I promised myself that I'd trust Charlie fully from now on, no questions asked.

The heist was going to begin at ten, which meant we had to get up early. It was already one o'clock in the morning, so everyone went off to bed without much more than a goodnight. Kallie and Marcus lingered on the living room couch while Charlie and I went off to our bedroom, which obviously was the biggest.

The four-poster bed was almost as soft as the one back in our quarters in Ilamanthe. I sank into it, feeling absolutely luxurious. Oberi was already snoring at my feet. As Charlie waved his hand, the candles in the room that were burning went out, leaving us in darkness.

"You could pour some of that wax on me if you like," I teased as he slid in next to me. This was all so sexy, pulling off a heist, and now Charlie was all shirtless and delicious beside me. We were in a new place, and it was fun to think of having sex in a fancy hotel.

Charlie kissed me with a smile and whispered, "Later, when we get back home. Then I can fuck you as much as I want."

Oh, he was teasing me, drawing out the suspense. I was a little disappointed, but not much, because my eyes were already drooping shut. I wasn't sure how much energy I had for sexy times, anyway. I was out like a light in a matter of moments.

Loud noises from the room next to us woke me up a while later. I rolled over— Charlie was still fast asleep next to me. I checked the clock and saw that it was three in the morning.

I wearily wiped my hair away from my eyes and listened closer. What was going *on*? It sounded like someone was pounding the headboard against the wall as hard as they could.

My suspicions were confirmed when a few moans, one feminine and the other masculine, drifted through the wall next to mine. I scowled and put a pillow over my head, but it still didn't block it out.

Geez, Chancey and Ivy are really going at it, I thought irritably. *Can't they quiet down? It'd be nice to get some sleep around here.*

You and Charlie aren't the only ones who copulate from sunrise to sunset, Oberi grumbled back. Apparently, the noise had woken him up, too. *How do you think I feel?*

I didn't respond, because I didn't feel like it. The noises were still going. For fuck's sake, did nobody around here know how to have ninja sex? There were other people in the penthouse, too.

The moans only got louder, but I grunted, ignored them and went back to sleep.

After getting dressed the following morning, I went to the hotel's lobby to get coffee from the barista downstairs. In less than an hour, the heist would begin and we'd take the key from Salvatore. I couldn't wait to get on with it and be done. One step closer to fulfilling our destiny, we just had to kick in the balls of a vampiric mob boss. Easy enough.

When I arrived downstairs, I saw Kallie sitting at a table in the hotel's café. The hotel was all but deserted except for the staff, since Dorian had reserved the whole place for us. Kallie was dressed in her black heist suit, but was slumped over the table, looking at a cup of coffee that had certainly gone cold. Both hands were in her hair, and her eyes were bloodshot and haggard. She wore a strained, disturbed expression I'd never seen on her before.

"Hey," I said, and I rolled up to the other side of the table. "Are you all right?"

Her lip trembled. "Marcus and I had sex last night."

I didn't know whether to be shocked or elated, but either way, a huge grin spread across my face. I realized that I hadn't overheard Chancey and Ivy last night— it'd been *Kallie and Marcus.*

"Oh my ancestors, for real?! How? What happened?" I asked. "You need to give me details! Girl, I'm so happy for..."

My joy faded, and my words fell away as Kallie began *sobbing.* She folded her arms on the table and her head fell into them as tears cascaded from her eyes. "I don't know what happened! Everything's just..."

She couldn't finish, and started crying harder. My heart fell to pieces, and I hurried to roll around the table to give her a hug. "Oh, Kallie! Did something go wrong? Did he hurt you?"

I couldn't imagine Marcus ever doing something like that, but Kallie was clearly upset for a reason.

"No," she wept. "It was everything I hoped it would be, but now it's all awful—"

"Start from the beginning," I encouraged, and I reached out to take her hand. "Tell me everything."

Kallie sniffed, and her tears slowed. "Okay. So last night, after we arrived at the hotel, neither of us could sleep. We were both really excited about the heist, and just kept talking about it. Everyone else went to bed, so Marcus suggested we go to his room to keep talking, so we didn't wake anyone up."

I could see where this was going. "You didn't want to leave."

"No. And he didn't want me to leave, either." She wiped her eyes. "We were up talking for hours, and I got really tired. He said if I wanted to crash in his room, I could, so we both laid down."

"More went on than just that," I stated doubtfully.

"Yeah. It was like, two in the morning when we finally stopped talking. I figured we were going to sleep. Then Marcus just said my name, and... kissed me."

Oof. "You guys didn't have a conversation or anything?"

"There wasn't any time! I just wanted him to kiss me *so badly*. He hasn't in months, Ava. I wanted him to touch me again, and I think he wanted the same thing. Next thing I know, clothes are coming off, he's got me flipped over... and we did it."

She looked down at the table. "I don't regret it. At least, I didn't when I was in the moment. Now, I'm not so sure."

Well, from what I'd overheard, it didn't sound like anyone was having a bad time. Quite the opposite, in fact. I shrugged. "Okay, how was it?"

Kallie's eyes got misty again. "It was wonderful. It was everything I ever wanted, and everything he would never give me. It was just perfect, for both of us."

"If it was perfect you wouldn't be crying like this, Kallie."

"I'm crying because of what happened *this morning*," Kallie said. "After we had sex, we went to bed, and it was still great, because he held me in his arms all night. This morning he got up before me, and when I woke up, I heard him taking a shower. So... I got up and joined him."

"And you did it again," I guessed. They'd certainly had a wild time.

"Yeah!" Kallie threw up her free hand. "And *that* was awesome, too!"

"Did either of you guys try to *talk* about this?" I asked. I tried to keep the judgment out of my voice, but hell, I was frustrated with both of them at this point.

"That's where it all went wrong. After we'd gotten done fucking in the shower, I held him and asked him what all this meant."

Kallie's expression completely crumbled. She burst into tears again, and her voice raised a pitch as she cried, "His face just... got all red, and he just looked absolutely mortified. Like he was *embarrassed* or something about being with me. He just... got out of the shower and left. Before he walked out, he said; *Sorry, this isn't right.* I know what that means. He's running away again... running away from us."

Kallie's tears increased in intensity until she was crying harder than I'd ever seen her before. I squeezed her hand, not sure of what to do or how I could help, because nothing I could do would fix her broken heart.

"This must've meant something to him. It was his first time," I encouraged. "He's never done it with anyone else, but he wanted *you*, Kallie. If he didn't, he would've held back. It's so obvious."

"If it meant something, he'd tell me, but he didn't," she replied hopelessly. "I might be the only person he's ever slept with, but so what? Maybe he was just tired of being a virgin and knew I'd put out."

"You *know* that's not true," I said. "Sweetie, Marcus loves you, even if he can't say it."

"I can't do this again. I can't," Kallie said, her tone tighter than before. "I can't keep crawling into bed with someone who won't make me his, begging for scraps of love that he won't give me. I thought we were doing so well lately. We were getting along great, being such good friends... I really *did* figure it was over between us. In reality, I was just falling for him harder than I had before, and I kept denying to myself that's what it was."

"Kallie." I rubbed her back, knowing there wasn't much I could say.

"It doesn't matter that Charlie broke our bond. It doesn't matter that he's no longer my mate and that we don't share a magical connection anymore. I *still love him.*" Her entire body shuddered, grieving the loss of someone she deeply desired and couldn't have. "I don't know what it's going to take to make these feelings go away, because they never will! I'm always going to want him, and he's never going to choose me. He'll just use me and cast me aside, so he doesn't have to commit. I'm at the end of my rope, Ava. I don't know how I'm going to survive if he keeps doing this to me... and I keep letting him. I don't want to live like this anymore. Not if it hurts this bad."

Fuck. Marcus. Overwhelming anger welled in my chest and crashed over me, nearly making my body ache. As much as I cared about Marcus, I hated him for doing this to Kallie. I'd be happy to burn him alive right now.

"Is there anything I can do?" I asked softly, though my real thoughts were, *Don't worry, girl, I'll find a big enough hole to put him in.*

"I just need to be alone, and try to process this," she choked out. "Thanks for listening, but what you and I do isn't going to make a difference, because he's never going to change."

She stared at her coffee again, and I took it at a clear sign that she was done talking. I left the café, to give her some space. She was absolutely devastated by Marcus' latest rejection.

Which I was going to make him deeply regret. Right the fuck now.

I forgot about the coffee and started searching the hotel's main floor, looking for Marcus. The Scarlet Grand was a massive hotel, so I had a lot of ground to cover. Charlie was making his way toward me. He appeared to be a criminal mastermind, dressed in all black with his magical pistol holstered to his side. I went rolling by him at a higher speed than usual, which caught his attention. Oberi was on his shoulder as a phoenix, and she peeped as I sped by.

"Pidge, I've been looking for you. Where are you going?" he asked warily.

"I'm off to kill Marcus," I said simply. "You can join if you want."

"What'd he do this time?" Charlie groaned, following me.

"Marcus and Kallie slept together."

Oberi squawked in alarm, beating her wings. Charlie sucked in a breath, held it, then let it out in a long sigh. "Great."

"Yeah, twice. And he ran off this morning after it happened a second time without giving her any explanation. She's completely devastated."

"That's uncalled for." Charlie scowled. "We need to do something about this. It's gone on for far too long."

"I'll say. And if it has to be permanent, so be it," I said casually.

Are you sure you two should get involved? Oberi asked, but neither of us answered.

We finally found Marcus in the shopping area of the Scarlet Grand. The hotel had its own boutique stores, and he came out of one carrying a small square bag.

Oh, he went fucking *shopping*, taking a page out of my own handbook. *When things get hard, just blow some fucking cash, it'll make you feel better!* I really wanted to deck him.

"Hey guys," he said. "You ready to—"

"Screw you, Marcus!" I spat. "I'm not tall enough anymore to punch you in the face, so the dick will have to do!"

I pulled back my fist to do just that, and Marcus floundered away, but Charlie snagged my arm before I could swing. Oberi hung onto his shoulder for dear life. "Pidge, hold on a minute."

"This asshole hurt my best friend!" I shouted. "Nobody bangs my girl then takes off the next day without paying for it!"

Marcus' face fell. "You guys know about that?"

"Yeah, we know," Charlie said harshly. "Marcus, what were you thinking?"

"I wasn't, not really," he admitted. "I don't think either of us were."

"You should've used at least one cell in that pea-brain of yours to think before you left her in the shower all alone!" I shouted. "I found her in the café *crying* because of you!"

Marcus appeared crushed. "I didn't mean anything by all that. I wasn't trying to hurt her feelings."

"Well, you did," I said. "And now you've ditched her, *again*. Can't you get your shit together?"

"I didn't ditch her," Marcus insisted. "I just needed a minute to catch my bearings, all right?"

"Because you were going to come up with another excuse as to why you can't date?" I accused.

"Because I was *terrified*," Marcus said, and he truly sounded it. "I was going to *propose*."

My jaw dropped. "What... really?"

"Yes! Don't look so shocked," Marcus said sourly. "I wanted to ask, truly, but I felt like I was going to pass out, to be honest. Then she asked me what we were, and I realized I was totally unprepared."

His response floored me. Before he'd left the shower, Marcus had said; *Sorry, this isn't right.* Kallie had taken it as him turning her down, but now I realized Marcus had just chosen a really stupid way of telling her he wanted to do this *properly.*

"I didn't have a ring to give her, and I can't ask her without that, so I rushed down here to get one," Marcus explained. "I know it's last minute, but I can't go any longer without asking her. It's driving me crazy we're not engaged. We should be. I should've asked her to marry me a long time ago."

"Why this sudden change of heart?" Charlie asked. "You've never been ready to take this step before."

"Because ever since I did my ceremony and faced my demons in that alleyway, I've realized what I want out of life, and what I want is her," Marcus said firmly. "I don't care what's standing in our way or what we've been through, because that doesn't matter. Kallie and I should be together, and I'm done getting in our way."

"Well, hallelujah to you for finally seeing the light," I said grumpily. "Think she might want to know all of that?"

"Look, I planned to tell her everything last night," Marcus started. "I invited her back to my room so we could talk, but not about the heist. I wanted to spill everything to her, and lay it all on the table. I was going to tell her I love her, that I don't care that the bond is broken and that I want us to be together."

"So why didn't you?" Charlie demanded.

"I couldn't get the words out," Marcus confessed. "I tried, I really did, but I just felt scared, so my hands started doing the talking for me."

"Yes, because sharing a bed isn't going to lead to disaster." I waved my hands around. "Oh no, I've fallen, and my dick *just happened* to slip in!"

"It wasn't like that," Marcus shot at me. "We were just kissing at first, but then we kept going. I went to tell her to stop so we could talk about this, but what came out of my mouth next wasn't exactly words, and by that point neither of us wanted to quit."

I could only imagine. *Kallie hold on*, probably turned into a couple of moans, loud gasps and *Fuck, baby, right there.* I swear, I wanted to murder these two. This was a constant problem with them. If they'd just communicate every once in a while instead of denying their feelings then jumping into bed when they couldn't take it anymore, their relationship wouldn't be so messy.

"Marcus, you guys needed to talk about this *before* being intimate," Charlie growled. "You should've established the relationship and what you both wanted before going that far."

"I know that, but neither one of us controlled ourselves, or went to stop. We just lost it." Marcus pinched the bridge of his nose. "I think we wanted to be together so badly nothing else mattered in the moment."

"Sex isn't a mistake." Charlie crossed his arms. "It's not something you just fall into."

"No, but it's damn hard to resist when you've been denying each other forever and you just can't anymore," Marcus shot back at him.

"She doesn't get it," I said. "She thinks you guys messed around, and now you're going to leave like you always do."

"What? How could she think that?" Marcus gasped. "I didn't leave her. I just came to get *this*, so I could do this the right way!"

Marcus dug in the bag and showed me a small black ring box. He really was serious about this.

"She doesn't know that, Marcus. She just thinks you're abandoning her again," I pointed out.

"I don't want her to think that. I *never* want her to feel abandoned like that ever again," Marcus stated. "I was a jerk back then, but what we shared last night was real. I want her to know that, and I want more of that for us. I don't ever want to let her go."

"So this is just a huge misunderstanding!" I said in relief. "You can talk to Kallie, apologize, explain what you really meant and ask her to marry you! It'll all work out!"

"Definitely." Marcus straightened with a resilient nod. "I messed up, but I can fix this. I want Kallie to be my wife, and I want to be with her. It's not enough to be dating, not after everything we've gone through. We should be married, like you guys are. If she rejects me, fine, but I won't be a coward anymore. At least she'll know how I truly feel about her."

"She's not going to reject you, man," Charlie assured him. "But the longer you drag this out, the more she's in pain, and we have to leave soon. You need to set this straight so both of your minds can be on the mission."

"Exactly." Marcus subconjured the bag and hurried forward. "I need to find her, so I can tell her right away."

Charlie, Marcus and I headed back to the café. I hoped I'd get to witness it all, and see Marcus ask her. That would be amazing.

This is good, this is very good, Oberi muttered. *Perhaps now, all this drama is behind us.*

I sure hoped so. I really wanted Marcus and Kallie together, so I could fangirl over them like a proper best friend should, and this miscommunication stuff was getting really old. This was their chance to finally be a couple! I was so excited.

Except now, I was starting to get worried. We'd come back to the café, and she wasn't here, but her coffee was, sitting half-drank on the table.

Where was she? We were supposed to start the heist in fifteen minutes.

"This isn't right. I left her right here," I said in concern.

"Is she back at the penthouse?" Marcus asked.

Charlie was already making a phone call. He shook his head as he hung up on Eddie. "She's not up there. Nobody saw her come back from the café."

"Saw *who* come back from the café?" a familiar voice asked.

Ivy and Chancey walked in. Chancey was looking impatient. "Are we ever gonna start this thing? Time to hit the road. I ain't got no patience for bullshit today."

"Yeah. Neither of us got any sleep, what with Charlie and Ava keeping us up all night," Ivy grumbled grouchily.

"That wasn't us," I said, with a pointed look at Marcus. He blushed a deep red. Ivy seemed positively delighted.

"Oh, so it was *you*," Ivy said deliciously. "Finally grew a pair of balls and showed your lady what's up, huh?"

"Yeah, but I fucked up the talking part," Marcus said lamely. "We did it, but I was too chicken to tell her how I feel about her first."

Ivy sighed and put their face in their hand. "Marcus, I'm gonna kill you."

"Wait until we find Kallie." Marcus seemed really nervous. "Guys, have you seen her?"

"We haven't seen her all morning," Chancey said, suddenly appearing alert.

The color blanched from Marcus' face. He sprang into action, running toward the counter where the barista was stacking cups.

"Excuse me, did a woman with blonde hair come in here?" he asked loudly, getting her attention.

"Yeah. She left ten minutes ago with some guy," the barista replied.

Some... guy? This didn't make any sense.

"He left this note before they went out," the barista said, clutching a piece of paper. She extended it out to me. I took it. I unfolded the paper, reading letters crudely cut out of a magazine and patchworked together.

She belongs to me.

I recognized the signature trait, because he'd left similar notes behind on occasions when he'd slaughtered girls he considered prizes. I'd seen it in the crime photos Charlie researched for his Advanced Criminal Justice project. My hands began to shake, and the paper quivered in my hands.

The Dollmaker.

The minute I thought it, shared horror passed between Charlie and me. He grabbed onto a nearby chair to steady himself, and Oberi crooned lowly.

"Ancestors," I whispered, and nearly gagged. "He's got her."

"Who's got her?" Chancey asked frantically.

"The Dollmaker. Valen Christoffer," I whispered, and a horrified tear slipped down my cheek. "Kallie's ex."

"The psychopath who *murdered* all those girls in Malovia?!" Ivy screeched. "It just can't be!"

"This is one of his signatures. I *know* it is. I've seen it before when Charlie did his criminal profile," I said miserably, raising the note in the air. "Somehow, Valen found out we were in Chicago, and he waited until she was vulnerable enough to take her."

Charlie's features had gone pale. "This can't be right. The Dollmaker always strikes at night. If he really took Kallie now, it goes against his M.O."

"Kallie's the girl he's fixated on this whole time," I pointed out. "He's not going to stick to his M.O. if he saw his chance to take her. Those other girls were a fantasy of his, but Kallie's always been his ultimate target."

"No," Marcus whimpered, and he backed away. "No, he can't... this isn't... *fuck!*"

Marcus lost his shit. He punched a nearby picture, and the glass broke. Shards cut into his hand, and he started bleeding everywhere, but Marcus didn't feel it. He picked up a nearby side table and broke it across his knee, sending the legs scattering. I jumped in my seat. Chancey ran forward to restrain him, and held him in place. Marcus fought back, but he couldn't match the strength of an angel. The barista freaked out, giving a scream and running out of the café.

"Take it easy, pal," Chancey said. "You gotta keep a clear head."

"Are you fucking *kidding me?*" Marcus screamed. "The person I love is in the hands of a serial killer, and you're telling me to *keep calm?!*"

"She left ten minutes ago, which means we might be able to get to her before he does anything," I said in a rush.

"Chancey, start looking around the hotel for Valen. We don't know how far he's taken her," Charlie said, immediately giving orders. "Try to stay out of sight."

"I will," Chancey said, already heading toward the door.

"She wouldn't leave with him willingly," Marcus raged. "She'd put up a fight. How did he just walk out with her?"

"Check her drink. It's still here," I said quickly.

Marcus snatched the only coffee sitting out and held it in his hands. The coffee glowed a bright purple at his alchemy magic, and he stated, "It's been tampered with. Some kind of heavy magical sedative."

"He must've gotten into the hotel and slipped the drugs into her coffee without the barista seeing," Charlie growled. "We don't know how long he's been here."

"Give that to me," Ivy ordered, and Marcus handed them the coffee. Ivy sniffed it again, and their lip curled. "This isn't just a sedative. It's a compulsion charm, a powerful one made by a strong-ass vampire. If she drank this, she'd be forced to do whatever he said until it wore off."

"That's probably what he used on her before, when he compelled her to kill her brother," I said in horror. "Kallie and I talked about this. She suspected Valen was working with vampires, using compulsion items on his victims that vampires gave him, and this is proof. He's in Chicago for a reason— no wonder the Union hasn't been able to track him down, if he's got vamp friends around here who are willing to hide him."

"Ivy, you need to stay here in case she comes back, or in case Valen returns," Charlie said.

"I'm on it," Ivy said dangerously. "If this fucker comes crawling around, I'll rip his throat out."

Marcus stared down into the cup, and his features darkened. "My Aunt Talia gets visions of the past through touch. Perhaps I can, too. I should be able to follow his path and see where he took her."

Marcus closed his eyes, and his head twitched to the side, like he'd just witnessed something very troubling. His lips curled back into an angry sneer. "I see the fucker in the café. Kallie's eyes are completely glossed over, and he's ordering her to follow him. She's going along with it. She's trying to resist the compulsion, but the sedative makes it hard for her to disobey, so she can't fight back. I see them leaving... come on. They went this way."

Marcus sprinted out of the café and took the front door out of the hotel. We quickly followed. The November air was chilly, and the sky was completely overcast.

Marcus tried touching things to get a vision, but he must've not found anything useful. He raced down the street and began grabbing random people. He shook them to read their minds, trying to see where Valen had taken Kallie.

"Did you see him? Did you see where he took her?!" he yelled in a crazed manner.

He didn't find anything and angrily shoved people to the ground, screaming his desperation and acting insane. People scrambled to get away from him, glancing over their shoulder as they ran away. Rishi yowled as he did so, giving hisses of rage.

Marcus doubled over to catch his breath; he was practically hyperventilating. He steadied himself on a nearby lamp post, and almost immediately, his form went rigid. "Hold on. I'm getting something. I see them on the sidewalk... Valen's ordering Kallie to cast an illusion around them to conceal themselves, so nobody can see them leave. He says once the spell is cast, she's to get on his back—"

Marcus gasped. "Valen's going to shift into a wolven and fly Kallie out of here. But her concealment charm is strong... I can't break through it!"

Marcus started to panic, and now he *was* hyperventilating. "I've lost them. I don't know where they've gone. If he shifted to fly Kallie out of here, he could be miles away by now!"

Charlie grabbed Marcus by the shoulders. "Marcus, we need you to focus. Is there anything else?"

Marcus closed his eyes again and gave a shudder. "I see Kallie following Valen outside. She's walking forward. That's it."

"What else?" Charlie pressed.

The crease between Marcus' brow deepened. "Before Kallie cast the concealment charm, Valen brushed up against the side of the building, against some plaque. It was accidental, but he might've left some sort of energy imprinted on the object. Maybe I can get something from it."

I quickly surveyed the area and saw the plaque Marcus was talking about. I rolled over to it and began reading. *Chicago Landmark*, it read, before listing off all kinds of historical details about the Scarlet Grand Hotel.

Marcus put his hand on the plaque, and concentrated. His Seer powers worked quickly, and Marcus' eyes shot open as he said, "I couldn't see where he was going to take her, but I caught an impression of a name... Rupert Berenwald. It's got to mean something. Thoughts and intention are energy, but they're difficult to imprint on objects. The fact that I'm able to pick up on this at all means this information is really important."

Charlie yanked his phone out of his pocket and stabbed the screen. He began barking into it. "Max, Kallie's missing, but we might have a lead. Look up everything you can about Rupert Berenwald."

I could hear Max's voice through the phone. "I'm on it."

A keyboard clicked in the background, and I held my breath. Max better find something right fucking now, because I was ready to burn down this city for my best friend.

"Rupert Berenwald was an architect; a vampire, actually. He designed the Scarlet Grand," Max said.

"Did he design any other buildings in Chicago?" Charlie demanded.

Max clicked the keyboard again. "Yes... there was an entire neighborhood that he constructed decades ago, but that area looks completely deserted now. The groundwater in that area became polluted from a local factory nearby and forced everyone to leave. The city's left it abandoned."

"That must be where he took her!" I cried.

"Let's go," Charlie said. We dipped back inside the hotel, and Charlie used his pocket mirror to make a portal. We went through, and came out on the other side in a dilapidated residential area that didn't look like it'd been inhabited for twenty years or more.

Since the area was deserted, Oberi changed into a unicorn, and I got on her back. Marcus subconjured my wheelchair. Charlie and Marcus immediately dispersed in different directions to look for her.

I took off on Oberi, galloping through the abandoned streets. We rounded corners and went down crooked alleyways, but found nothing. Just graffiti, trash, and broken items that had been discarded long ago.

I met up with Marcus and Charlie a short time later. They'd been running around like I was, and clearly hadn't seen a thing. Rishi gave a mournful yowl.

"We've covered this whole block, and there's nothing here," Marcus moaned.

Charlie shook his head. "I don't think Valen's here. I'm scanning the area with my Elf magic, and I don't feel any magical traces."

"What do you *mean*?" Marcus asked. "According to my vision, this is where he ended up!"

"But it wasn't his final stop," Charlie stated. "If it was, we'd have found him."

"Then where the fuck is he?!" I yelled, feeling hopeless.

Charlie didn't answer. He was out of ideas, and so was I.

"Fuck this," Marcus snarled. He conjured items from his stash, and they sprang into his hands. One was a white rose, the other, an alchemy knife.

"Marcus, what are you doing?" I asked, already feeling scared.

"A powerful fae locator spell, from Kallie's grimoire," Marcus stated. "It'll show us the way he went."

"But you're not a fae! You're a witch, so the spell won't work!" I argued.

"According to my vision of Miriam and Santos, we know that witches are descended from Unseelie fae. Faerie magic is in my blood, no matter how far back it is, so I'm going to harness it to pull off this spell," Marcus rasped. "It's time to prove my theory that witches and fae are blood related, and this is the best time to try."

"And if the spell backfires, what happens?" I asked.

His face was grim as he stated, "If I fuck it up, it could kill me. And since I'm a witch using fae magic, it probably will."

"*Marcus!*" I yelled.

"I don't care!" he screamed. "I'll do *anything* to get her back! If I'm dead, you guys find her, okay? It doesn't matter what it takes!"

We couldn't lose both him and Kallie in one day, but Marcus was determined to go through with it even if it killed him. He used the alchemy knife to slice into his hand, then pressed his blood into the petals as he screamed, "*Fae ancestors of the briar, lead me to my heart's desire!*"

Kallie had used this spell before. I hadn't been there to see it, but according to Charlie, when she had tried to use the spell to find the merfolk key, it had sent her into a vision that had nearly taken her life.

I was terrified the same thing would happen to Marcus, and Kallie wasn't here to pull him out of it like he did her. But that didn't happen. The spell *worked.* I watched as a magical thread formed in the air, one that connected to Marcus' chest and formed a glowing line that hovered before us, leading us to Kallie.

"Let's go," Marcus said viciously, starting forward. We followed the thread as it led out of the abandoned area and to a large body of water sitting beside a vacant warehouse that stretched on in both directions as far as the eye could see.

The Dollmaker had taken her across Lake Michigan. The thread hovered over the water. In the distance there was an island that looked like it was a hub for some sort of factory. The thread led there, waiting for us to follow.

"She's there," Marcus breathed. He looked at the island with longing, desperately wanting his love.

I immediately conjured a boat out of ice with my water magic, gesturing for the boys to get into it as Oberi and Rishi hopped inside. "Come on, let's go. If a human sees us, I don't fucking care."

The boys didn't care, either, because they jumped into the ice boat and held on. I propelled the ice vessel toward the island faster than any speedboat could go. Even if a human did see us, my water magic was blasting us across the lake so fast they'd consider it a trick of the light, and it was dark and gloomy out. Winter was setting in, and the entire area was cold. I didn't think anyone would see us through the fog. We made it to the island in less than a minute, and I slowed the boat down as we came to the shore.

The place smelled like sewage and molten metal. These factories had been abandoned, too, and were leaking chemicals into the soil. Once we got on land, Oberi helped me onto her back. We followed the magical thread past the rusting buildings, though we crossed droplets of crimson liquid on our way. We came upon signs of a struggle— metal barrels recently overturned, along with a rusting sign with fresh blood on it. Kallie had been fighting the compulsion spell and tried to get away here, but Valen had kept her in captivity.

Marcus ran, and we followed. We turned down twisted lanes and alleyways to follow the thread around buildings, until I started to get dizzy. Where was she?

"Here!" Marcus yelled. We turned down an alley between the factory buildings, and my being absolutely trembled as I saw there was a woman lying at the end of it.

We'd found her. She looked so cold and forlorn. Kallie was lying on her side, her cheek flattened against the pavement, one arm splayed out on the ground and the other hanging limply against her torso. Her face was swollen with bruises, and I could tell from here some of her limbs were broken.

He'd beaten the shit out of her. My breath caught as I saw that she laid in a pool of her own blood, scarlet red still dripping from the multiple slashes in her skin. Valen had stabbed her multiple times, then cut her body open for his own pleasure. Once he was satisfied, he'd left her here to bleed out, like all his other victims.

I would do my best to save Kallie. But whatever happened to her, Valen wouldn't live to see the sun set, and his death would be far from painless. I promised her that.

Marcus got to her first. He rushed to Kallie's side and fell to his knees, freely weeping as he hovered his hands over her broken body. "Kalina," he whimpered, and that sound carved a hole inside of me that cut so deep, the person I was bled out.

I skimmed the area but didn't see anyone else, not even a shadow. Valen had fled. He'd probably gotten done by the time we arrived and was long gone. This was how he always killed— he liked to blood let his victims, then come back later to admire his handiwork. The sick fuck couldn't even stick around to finish the job himself. The longer it took his victims to die, the more thrill he got out of it.

Fuck him. We'd take care of his ass later.

Oberi cantered toward where Kallie lay. Once she got to her, Oberi knelt to the ground. I immediately slid off of her back and to Kallie's side, trying to figure out where to start repairing the damage.

Ancestors, there was just so much. Her skin was so ashen. I'd never seen a person turn that shade of gray unless they were already dead. We might've arrived too late.

I dared to touch Kallie's shoulder, and gently brought her forward so I could check her back. I didn't realize I was crying, but I had to be, because tears fell from my face as I looked at the jagged gashes that were cut through her jacket, two of them side by side, from the top of her shoulder blade to the base of her spine. They were the worst cuts and bled the most, staining her clothes and her skin red. Rishi put a paw on Kallie's leg, mewling softly.

"Her wings are gone," I choked out. "Valen's got them."

Charlie's thoughts flitted across my mine, and mixed with the revulsion was wrath. The Dollmaker had taken her wings as a fucking *trophy*.

I turned Kallie onto her back, though it wounded me to lay her onto her severed wings. I checked her pulse, and my own stopped when I realized there wasn't a heartbeat. With a quick check of her lungs, I found those weren't expanding, either. "She's not breathing."

"Goddammit." Charlie summoned Air magic to inflate her lungs, but that didn't work. I stirred my Toaqua magic to make her blood flow, but nothing happened.

Her body was refusing magic. Both of us felt it, and we panicked.

Charlie began performing CPR. He started on chest compressions while I summoned my Spirit magic. My hands glowed white, lighting up the entire alley as I brought the power of my soul to life in order to save my best friend.

"Oberi, help me," I ordered, and she changed into a phoenix to lend her aid as I set my healing magic to work. Marcus paced above us, both hands in his hair as he hyperventilated and sobbed at the same time.

Ancestors, there was so much blood. She'd lost at least four pints. She couldn't lose any more, or she'd die, and she was still hemorrhaging from all the wounds on her body. Her organs were shutting down. Some of them, like her heart, had stopped already, and Charlie's compressions on her chest were the only thing keeping it beating. Once he got to thirty, he bent over to breathe life into her lungs, giving her two rescue breaths, desperately trying to buy me enough time to stabilize her.

I could force these cuts to heal and regenerate the blood in her body. That was the most important step to saving her life, and I'd fix the rest later. But there was a problem. Despite my magic pouring into her body— and it was— and my command for magic to knit the wounds back together, nothing happened. Her skin glowed with my power, but the wounds remained intact and continued to bleed.

"What's happening?" Marcus wailed. "Why isn't it working?"

I went deeper, ignoring her bodily injuries and focusing on finding her life energy. Ancestors, it was fading. Barely a flicker of a flame inside her chest, it dwindled like a dying candle. Her body was nothing more than a half-filled vessel, holding back the only part of her spirit that hadn't yet broken free. So much of it was gone now, more afterlife than earthly.

I latched on and tugged at Kallie's soul, telling her to keep fighting. I pleaded with her to hold on, because she knew I could heal her and get her help.

Kallie's spirit felt weak and frail. She was telling me she loved me, and she cared, but she couldn't do this anymore. She didn't want to live in a world where something like this was capable. Even if she had to go to the in-between place where her soul would be trapped, unable to venture into the afterlife, it was better than whatever this existence was. She wanted me to let her go.

I almost did, because it should've been her choice. But I wouldn't until I knew for sure this was truly the call she wanted to make, and she had unfinished business here.

She didn't want to talk to me. She needed Marcus. He had to be the one to convince her to walk away from death.

"Marcus, you need to talk to her. I can't heal her if she's lost the will to live," I said harshly.

"Talk—" he said weakly. Charlie continued performing CPR, ignoring us. "Why? Why isn't she fighting?"

"Because she doesn't want to. Healing magic is Spirit magic. My magic isn't working because her soul isn't responding. You need to convince her it's still worth it!"

"What am I going to say to make her want to keep going?" he gasped with sorrow, and Rishi wailed beside him. "I'm not the person to do this— I've tried to kill myself *twice!*"

"Marcus, if you don't convince her to stay, she's going to die!" I snapped. *"Bring her back."*

That seemed to snap him out of it, because he moved closer to Kallie. He reached out to grab her hand, which was stone-cold by now. "Hey pretty girl, I'm here," he told her. "I'm not going anywhere. I'm *right here.*"

Kallie's soul flickered, but only a little bit. I couldn't heal her, but I could at least stop the blood from flowing out. My magic held it in place, hoping Marcus would find the right words to say.

"I'm sorry for everything I put you through," he started, speaking through his tears. "I'm sorry this happened. I didn't leave you this morning. You're the love of my life, and I want us to be together. I want to experience everything with you. I love you *so* goddamn much, Kallie. You're my best friend, and you're the woman I want to marry. I truly fucking mean that, with all my heart. I don't want to be anywhere if you're not here with me, and there's nothing I wouldn't do to love you exactly like you deserve to be loved."

Her life force energy got a little stronger. I went to heal up the wounds, but her soul cringed away, telling me she wasn't ready yet.

"Hey, remember all the things we planned to do together during those long nights we spent in the Criminal Lair?" Marcus asked, cracking a weak smile. "We'd sneak out overnight, and talk about all the places we're going to visit. Well, we're still going to do all that stuff. You're going to show me the art museum in Malovia, and I'll show you a sunset in Octavia Falls. We'll build a castle of our own on an island in the middle of the ocean, and no one will be able to take it from us, because it'll be *ours.* Remember that painting you asked me to make? I finally finished it for you, and it's so fucking beautiful, just like you. I'm going to hang it up in the entrance hall in our castle, right when people walk in, so when everybody looks I'll point to it and say that she's my wife, because I want to show you off to the world."

Charlie went to continue compressions, but I held up an arm to hold him back. Kallie was letting me help now, though she was still wavering on the decision to stay or go. I began to stitch up wounds, and the cuts on her body healed as I brought forth my power. Oberi focused on regenerating her blood, and color slowly began to come back into Kallie's skin as the phoenix repaired what she could. Kallie's heart began to beat again, and air finally flowed into her lungs.

Marcus went to lightly stroke her hair. "You told me your favorite girl name is Lilith, remember that? I didn't say so, but I loved it. Lilith is the most badass name ever. It would be perfect for a little girl that would look just like you. But we'll never get to use it if you're gone, and we're not meant to be separated. Not like this, not ever. We go to the Blessed Haven, we go together, when we're older than dirt and we've seen all we wanted to see, and do all we wanted to do. But not now. Not like this. You and me have all these dreams, and we're going to do them together. We're going to conquer the world, pretty girl, I promise. But you've gotta stick around so we can see all these places, and do all these things. You wanted to be a queen to save people, but right now, you need to save yourself."

I moved on to her organs now. Valen had stabbed several of them and left puncture wounds that left her organs in shreds. Normally, these kinds of wounds would require surgery, and be beyond a normal healer's power to mend. But I was a demigod, and it wasn't anything I couldn't fix. I would move mountains and reset the Earth's place in the cosmos before I allowed Kallie to fade away like this. I healed holes in her stomach and intestines while Oberi fixed up her liver and kidneys, mending them so they were whole again. I didn't need to replace or regrow anything, so that was a good sign.

Marcus' voice sank even lower, into a strained and desperate whisper. "We never got to test the limits of my art and your illusions, and when we combine our magic, miracles happen. We have so much left to discover together. We're going to create so much for this world, and for ourselves, and there isn't anyone else I'd rather do it with. I knew you were the one for me the second you came into my life, and I'm not letting you go now. What we have, we've had forever, maybe in another life or a thousand lifetimes before, but I'm not giving up a single day with you.

You light up the entire fucking world for me, Kallie. This place is going to be a whole lot darker if you're not in it. I might be the Lord of Death, but you're my Mistress of Time. And death doesn't mean anything if time isn't here to send him her love, or hold his hand."

I let out a sigh of relief as I felt Kallie's soul flood back into her body, no point of it remaining on the edge of the afterlife. She'd decided to come back.

"It's working," I breathed. "Marcus, keep talking."

He leaned closer, whispering to Kallie things that I couldn't hear. I didn't need to listen. If they wanted to be in their own private universe, let them, because all I cared about was if it helped Kallie recover.

As I healed her, I came across a foreign substance in her system. It was the sedative Valen had given her. I dissolved the sedative immediately, and Kallie's body began writhing in pain.

Fuck. She was still out of it, but the sedative had been acting as an anesthetic. Now she could feel everything. I rushed to heal her further, but there was still so much work to do, and I couldn't do it in the middle of this shitty alleyway. It'd take too long, and we were exposed out here.

"She's stable, but it won't last if I don't continue my work," I said in a rush. "We need to get her back to the hotel."

"I'm getting help from the Associates." Charlie spoke madly into his phone before he shoved it back in his pocket. "Let's go."

Charlie took a pocket mirror out of his jacket and projected it outward, blooming a portal. The hotel was only a few miles away, and Kallie's body could withstand traveling that short of a distance... I hoped.

Charlie conjured a gurney with his illusion magic, and he hovered Kallie's body onto it. Oberi changed back into a unicorn, and I hefted myself onto her as Charlie pushed the gurney through the portal. Marcus was still by Kallie's side, refusing to let go of her hand.

When we got back to the hotel, Mom and Ezekiel were already waiting for us, along with a whole team of Elvish medics. The Associates had clearly worked fast to portal them here. My brother appeared horrified when he saw Kallie lying limply on the stretcher.

"Who did this?" he asked hoarsely.

"Doesn't matter. Help me," I demanded.

The medics had set up Kallie's bedroom in the penthouse as a makeshift emergency room, and they hurried to utilize the medical equipment they'd brought. We rushed to get there. Chancey and Ivy were standing in the living room, and their expressions were crestfallen when they saw her. Ivy started sobbing, and Chancey's expression became gravely wounded as he witnessed Kallie barely hanging on to life.

The medics gave Kallie an oxygen mask, and set her up with an IV and a heart monitor while Mom, Ez, Oberi and I continued to heal her. Charlie stood at the back of the room, and Marcus remained with Kallie, holding her hand as Rishi mewled at his feet.

I was glad for the support, because I was getting tired, and so was Oberi. Mending Kallie's organs and replacing her blood had worn me out and taken a lot of my strength. Thankfully, Mom was a strong healer and Ez's magic had been improving, so they were able to mend the rest of Kallie's injuries without much help from me.

Eventually, we cleared away the bruises from Kallie's pretty face and restored all of her broken bones. We cleaned the blood off of her and got her into a clean hospital gown.

Unfortunately, there were mental scars we couldn't heal, and I knew when Kallie woke up she'd have to deal with them. Who knew what Valen had put her through, besides the obvious injuries on her body. The mental torture, and the memory of what happened, was going to be far worse than the physical injuries we'd fixed.

We left Kallie to rest. She still hadn't woken up, and that was probably for the best. I looked at my Mom and said, "You guys need to get back to Ilamanthe. It's not safe for you here in Chicago."

"Kallie needs us. Until she's strong enough to go back through a portal across the ocean, we're staying," Mom said firmly.

I couldn't argue. I needed help here.

My brother wavered on his feet. He looked close to passing out. "Do you think she's going to be all right?"

"She will be," I said, and I reached out for his arm. My Spirit magic immediately set off alarms when I touched him, and I added, "Your blood sugar is low."

"I was studying all day, and in med class. I didn't get a chance to stop for dinner," Ez mumbled.

"Ez, you need to eat something," Mom said firmly. "That was a lot of work we just did, and you're sick, too."

"I guess so," Ez mumbled. "No use having two people laid out in a hospital bed. Can't take care of patients if I don't take care of myself."

"That's right." Mom looked at me. "Ava, do you mind if we take a break?"

"Go ahead," I stated. "There's not much more you can do right now."

Mom nodded, guiding Ez out of the room. "Be back soon."

When they had cleared out, I glanced at Marcus. "Get into the bed with her. She needs you to hold her. Touch will stabilize her heartbeat and help her oxygen levels recover."

Charlie had done the same with me after my spinal injury, and it had really helped. I remembered even now how much better I felt when he'd been lying beside me. Kallie needed that right now.

Marcus didn't ask questions. He clambered into bed beside Kallie, carefully maneuvering around the tubes for the IV and oxygen mask and cradling her against him.

A few minutes after Marcus had laid beside her, Kallie's eyes weakly fluttered open. She went to pull at the oxygen mask, but Marcus did it for her, taking it off and laying it beside her. I kept an eye on the oxygen monitor, but her levels were stable. She could go without it for a bit while we talked.

"Marcus?" Kallie seemed astounded that he was right next to her, faintly grasping him back. "What's... what's going on?"

"I love you, pretty girl," Marcus said, and he kissed her. "I'm sorry I ran off this morning. I was just nervous for what I was about to ask, but I'm not anymore. I want us to be together, all right? I want a relationship, the commitment, all of it. You're my girlfriend now, okay? I'm here for you forever, and I never want to let you go."

Kallie marveled. The look in her eyes was sparkling and full of light as she gazed at Marcus. The joy emanating from her was so powerful I could feel it from here. She truly felt like this was some kind of dream, or that she'd won the lottery. It was the sweetest thing to see in the world.

"Okay." She laid her head against his chest, and gave the slightest of smiles. "I love you too, Marcus. Let's be together."

They nestled their heads together, and I melted inside. Rishi jumped up on the bed and settled between them, purring so loudly it echoed around the room.

Oberi ruffled her feathers, and Kallie settled into the pillows to look at me. "You guys got to me not a second too late," she said quietly. "It was really bad this time."

This time?

"Do you want to talk about what happened?" I asked carefully. "You don't have to, if you don't want to."

"Might as well. You guys should know the details, and I don't want to go over it ever again, not after today."

Kallie leaned into Marcus, and he held her closer. Kallie's voice wavered as she said, "I remember taking another sip of my coffee, but not much after that. When I came to, I was in some sort of alleyway, and I felt sick. Valen knew he couldn't take me in a fair fight, so he drugged me. I could do magic, but the drugs made me so confused it was hard to cast a simple spell, and I knew I'd been compelled. He gave me just enough to keep me delirious, but not enough so I would pass out. He wanted me to remember everything."

This was all stuff we knew, and I was terrified to hear what came next. Kallie gave a shudder and went on. "He wanted to drag it out. He punched me, broke my bones. I tried to take swings at him, but the drugs made me so uncoordinated. I never got a hit in. Then... he started stabbing me. Just... cutting me open. I was bleeding everywhere. I knew I wasn't going to make it out."

"Did he..." I couldn't get the words out, but I'm sure she knew what I meant. Everyone did. Charlie stiffened across the room, and Marcus went pale.

Kallie stared at me. Then she did the most unexpected thing. She *laughed.* She let out a loud, startling cackle, one that turned into a series of coughs.

"Fuck... him," she choked out, still laughing. "Oh, Ava, he *tried*, but he couldn't get it up. His tiny little dick was all limp and pathetic. I laughed at him and spat in his fucking face."

Her smile died, to be replaced by a deathly countenance devoid of all hope. "That was a mistake, though, because after I did that, he took my wings. He sawed them off while I was still conscious, because he wanted to hear me scream. He didn't get what he wanted, though, because I passed out from the pain before he even got to the second wing. I didn't wake up again after that, until just now."

Marcus nestled his head into her hair, and Charlie said, "We're glad we found you, Kallie. We wouldn't be able to handle it if we lost you."

"You got to me this time," she whispered. "You missed your chance twice before."

Marcus went paler than before, and I hushed, "Kallie, tell us what happened."

"I went back. Three different times," she said, and she started to cry. "I used my time powers to try and change the situation, so the Dollmaker never hurt me, and I never got captured."

Her tears amplified into sobs. "But it didn't work. He got me, all three times, and no matter what I did, it didn't change the outcome. And every time I tried, his torture just got worse. I was able to put myself back in my healthy body, up until the point where I drank the coffee, but I couldn't go back farther than that because of the drugs. The first two times, I had enough strength left after he beat me to go back and try to reverse things. I waited for you guys to find me then, but you never showed. I knew if I waited any longer, I was going to die, so I had to use my remaining strength to go back in time. This last time, he took my wings, which he didn't do before, and I wasn't able to influence time after that. I passed out thinking this was the end, and you guys weren't going to get to me before I died."

"What changed this last time?" I asked.

"I left the coffee cup," Kallie explained. "The first time around, the drugs started to hit when I got up from the table to leave the café. I threw away the cup just before he got me. When I went back a second time, I already knew that he'd drugged me. I threw my half-drank cup away, thinking the less drugs in my system, the more I could fight him, but I couldn't go back far enough to reverse what I'd already drank. You guys didn't make it in time, so I went back one last time to leave my cup there, so you'd know something was wrong and look for me sooner. You arrived just in time."

Tears leaked out of Kallie's eyes as she closed them. "It's all running together. I can't remember exactly what he did to me *this* time, only the details of all three events. It won't stop."

My stomach churned in absolute terror. Kallie had relived this three times over. We hadn't saved her the first two occasions, and barely managed to save her this time.

We'd failed her.

"Let's go back and kill Valen before he ever takes you," Charlie suggested. "Kallie, I know we promised not to use time magic unless it's absolutely necessary, but *this* is necessary. Then you'll never lose your wings."

"I *can't*, Charlie," Kallie wept. "You don't understand. Now that the Doll-maker took my wings, my power... it's not as strong as it was. I can't shift anymore. I can't stop time. I've *tried*, and nothing happens. All I can do is basic fae magic. I'm *useless* to you guys now."

"You're not useless. You're everything," Marcus promised, brushing her hair back from her eyes.

"Who am I if I can't be a wolf?" Kallie asked, in deep pain. "I've been a shifter since I was sixteen. What good am I if I can't be who I truly am?"

"You're mine," Marcus said, and he kissed her again. "You don't need to be powerful to be the incredible woman you are. I know I have everything I need right here."

"I should've had Alette with me. Faekin protect their faeries." Kallie wheezed. "She would've warned me before he drugged me. It was foolish to leave her behind in Ilamanthe."

"Don't blame yourself," Marcus insisted. "It's not your fault that monster attacked."

Kallie's eyelids fluttered, and she sank against Marcus as if everything in her was spent and worn. "I'm really tired."

"Go back to sleep." Marcus kissed her head. "You need your rest. We'll be here for you when you wake up."

Kallie didn't say anything more, just let out a few sobs before she passed out.

The minute she was out of it, Marcus broke down. He covered his mouth to silence his weeping as tears free flowed down his face. His entire body was quivering so hard it made the bed shake.

"Marcus, go get some air," I said gently. It was okay for him to cry, and understandable, but if Kallie woke up again and saw him like this she'd get very upset, and we had to keep her relatively calm if she was going to recover.

He nodded and got off the bed, heading for the door. Rishi stayed behind, remaining on the bed at Kallie's side.

It was silent as the grave with just Charlie and me inside the recovery room, Kallie's chest rising and falling as she slept. I glanced at the clock. Valen might still be in the area. We were already late on starting the heist, but it would have to wait. Valen was out there. We couldn't start the heist if he was still prowling around, because he was still a threat. Oberi stood at the foot of Kallie's bed, her eyes black and hungry for vengeance.

I directed my eyes toward my husband. I yanked on my end of our bond, demanding his attention, and I got it. Charlie stood rigid, waiting for whatever I was about to say.

My tone was dark and full of feminine rage as I said, "You need to take care of this."

He got what I meant. Charlie gave a short nod, then left me to watch over Kallie while he went to handle the job he was born to do.

TWENTY-ONE

va had asked me to handle things. So I fucking would.

Marcus stood outside the door. He was still crying, but I heard him pause for a moment and take a ragged breath as I came out.

"We need to kill him." I didn't say anything else. I didn't need to. Marcus didn't reply, just stood there.... trying to handle it all.

He was falling apart right now, but he didn't have the luxury to. Not when this beast had hurt the woman that belonged to him.

When a few long moments had passed, I sneered, "Kallie vowed to kill the Dollmaker, and he nearly killed her. She can't do it, so we're going to do it for her. This bastard messed with the wrong family. No sick fuck does this to one of *our girls* and gets to walk away alive."

Marcus sniffed and cleared his throat. His voice grew closer as he wiped his face and said, "All right. Let's find this motherfucker and make him pay."

"I'm going with ya," Chancey mumbled. I hadn't realized he'd been there, but I didn't care if he was. He wanted to come along, fine by me. If there were three of us, it'd be a hell of a lot harder for Valen to slip away.

I didn't want Ava to see what we were going to do, because it wasn't going to be pretty. How I'd killed the vampire mobster I'd tortured to death was going to look like a pleasant death compared to what we were going to do to Valen once we found him.

"Where do you think he is?" Marcus asked. His voice was straight again, and I was glad to see he'd pulled himself together.

"I've studied this guy," I stated. "He'll return to the scene of the crime to get his fill. I'd bet anything he's still on that island, re-living what he did to Kallie over and over."

Marcus grabbed his pistol, and a *click* sounded as he released the safety. "He's going to wish he'd never been born," Marcus said darkly, and we headed out.

We portaled back to the island. I thought about what it'd felt like to give Kallie CPR. How easily her chest had caved in when I'd given compressions, absolutely no resistance, and how cold her lips were when I tried to breathe into her lungs.

I'd known she was dead the moment I touched her, or good as. I almost told Ava not to even try— that she was too far gone, and saving her was something that wasn't possible.

But Ava proved me wrong as always, and thank the ancestors she did, because we'd almost lost Kallie today. Observing Marcus as he completely disintegrated at the loss of his love was triggering beyond belief. It'd been like reliving the Infernal Underground all over again, except this time, it was Marcus pleading for Kallie to come back, instead of me reaching out for Ava beyond the grave.

The day the Underground had caved in on Ava was— and would always be — the worst day of my life. And I knew today would be the worst day of Marcus'.

But I could deal with my trauma later. I had to shut my emotions off in favor of winning at all costs. That's what my grandfather had taught me, and that's what I would do. We'd handle our business with this guy, dispose of him, then go after the key. It was as simple as that. Feelings would only get in the way right now. I was the leader, and I was the only one pushing this team forward. Get in, get out, get it done. That was all that mattered. If we let the Dollmaker go and allowed him to live, he'd come back. He'd find Kallie again, and make sure to finish her off next time.

No fucking chance. We were putting Valen in the ground— *today*.

Not to mention this asshole threw a wrench in my plans, and I couldn't let my grandfather down. We were eliminating this piece of garbage from the planet, then we were getting back to business and going after that key. We were already running way past our schedule, and the clock was ticking.

I wasn't a guy that lost. I won, every time, and this degenerate fuckhead had bested me once. I wouldn't let Valen live long enough to do so twice.

He'd know we were coming, but let him... this guy always wanted an audience for his work, and if he wanted to play games, I was willing to play. We'd show him he was nothing more than a pawn on a board full of powerful pieces, and it was checkmate, bitch.

We stepped out of the portal and headed to the place where we'd found Kallie first.

"Do you think he's around?" Marcus asked lowly.

"Oh, he's around," I replied. "In fact, I bet he's watching us right now."

"In that case, why not see if he'll bite?" Marcus seethed.

He took a deep breath beside me and began to yell. "Come on out, Valen! I know you can hear me! I only want to play... with your organs."

A hissing laughter echoed throughout the factory grounds, but I couldn't tell where it was coming from— the dickhead was using illusion magic to project his voice. *You'll never find me, warlock. I'll kill you one by one, then use your bodies as my toys. I need some new dolls.*

Metal clanged loudly as Valen used a pipe to bang on the walls. It was distracting, and there wasn't a clear source of where it could be coming from.

"He's in one of these alleys," I noted, just as we turned a corner.

The metallic scent of blood filled the air, and I knew it was the same alleyway we'd found Kallie in earlier. My foot caught a rock, and I stumbled to catch myself on the side of the building. Cool, sticky liquid coated my hands, and I could still feel the remnants of Kallie's magic flowing through it.

It was Kallie's blood, smeared all over the wall. He'd painted the area with it after we'd left.

"Guys," Chancey said in a hoarse tone.

A noise of rage erupted from Marcus' throat. He immediately spun around and went storming out of the alley, screaming, "VALEN! I'm coming for you!"

Valen's haunting laughter vibrated around the area once again.

"What did he do?" I asked Chancey.

"He took Kallie's blood and used it to draw on the walls of the alley," Chancey told me under his breath. "Her name, gruesome pictures of what I think is her face. This character's really messed up."

That was a light way of putting it. I turned to follow Marcus, trailing the noise his shoes made as they crunched broken glass and discarded trash underneath his feet.

"Come out, come out, wherever you are!" Marcus sang. His voice had developed an eerie quality to it— one I hadn't heard in months, not since we'd left the Institute. A shiver ran up my spine as Marcus' breaths became ragged and shuddering. He sounded like some sort of monster hunting for his prey.

I will never be found. The Arcanea Alliance failed to bring me in, and the woman who swore to kill me has fallen, Valen responded in a creeping resonance that made the windows on the buildings creak. *You cannot take me, little warlock.*

"It's too late for you to run away!" Marcus conjured a high-powered battle orb, and it went sizzling to my left. The entire building beside us caved in and crumpled once the orb hit it, and the smell of smoke rose into the air.

Playing hide and seek with a serial killer wasn't how I'd planned on utilizing my morning, and recess was over. Marcus conjured another orb and tossed it into a different factory structure. I listened to one of the smokestacks groan as it toppled over and crashed into the lake.

"I know you're scared!" Marcus screamed. "Why not come a little closer, so I can enjoy watching the sparkle leave your eyes as you *fucking die?!*"

I think the falling buildings must've scared Valen and made him realize who exactly he was dealing with, because he didn't respond. He was definitely fleeing, and we couldn't let him do that. I turned on the spot, trying to get some sense of where Valen was or where he might've crawled off to.

I scanned the area with my magic, but I couldn't read a signature. My senses were fucked up by Kallie's blood, because her magic was stronger than Valen's, and it was everywhere. It made Valen hard to track.

"I saw a shadow over there," Chancey said, grabbing my arm to lead me. We ran that way, but Marcus sprinted past us. We ended up in some sort of epicenter of the factory's hub— I could tell, because the air was expansive here, and the wind currents had more space to move.

A barrel toppled over behind me, ringing out as it hit the concrete. Footsteps slapped against the ground as the fucker took off running. I instantly went for my pistol and raised it to fire. I gave three shots, and Air magic blasted outward. Dust and rocks hit my face as my shots made holes in the side of a building, and some of the residue cut into my cheek and made me bleed. Valen didn't cry out, so I knew I didn't hit him.

Marcus fired off his own gun, but he swore, so his shots must've missed. Chancey darted forward, but he let out an *oof* and stumbled to the ground. Valen had socked him in the stomach and kept going.

This fucker was fast. We had to be quicker. Valen's footsteps became soft, and I figured they'd turned into paws. He thought he'd shift into a wolven and run out of here. Not fucking likely.

"I don't think so," Marcus said. "It's rude not to play with your friends."

A yelp that sounded like it came from a hurt dog cut through the air, and I heard Valen scrabble his claws against the pavement as Marcus' telekinesis magic yanked him backward and threw him into a set of wooden boxes. They smashed on impact, and Valen groaned as he changed back.

He scrambled to his feet to make a run for it in the other direction, but Chancey and I blocked his exit before he had a chance. I reached out to grab one arm as Valen attempted to run by, and Chancey caught the other. Together, we rammed our shoulders into Valen's body and used all our strength to toss him forward. He flew twenty feet and smashed against a wall, breaking chunks out of a wall he slammed into.

My Air magic rushed up around us, and I noticed we'd tossed Valen down a dead-end alley, the only exit being the outlet where the three of us stood.

"Nowhere to go now," Marcus uttered, letting out a demented laugh. He staggered toward Valen, and I heard him crack his knuckles.

Chancey went to move in, but I put a hand on his chest to hold him back. "He belongs to Marcus. We're just here to make sure he doesn't slither away."

"Fine by me," Chancey said darkly. "I'm gonna get a kick outta watching this."

"You're awful at hiding," Marcus seethed as he circled Valen. "I've already found you."

"And?" Valen scorned. "Why should I give a shit about you?"

"Let me introduce myself. I'm the nightmare that lives inside of you, and I am going to haunt your *fucking dreams*."

Marcus kicked Valen in the face as hard as he could. I heard a smacking sound as his shoe connected with Valen's nose and broke it. Valen gave a cry of pain, which was quickly followed by the sound of fists pummeling into flesh. Blood spurted from his nose so far that droplets hit my pant leg. Marcus must've been covered in it. It made my heartbeat race and got me pumped.

"Wow, I can see why Charlie likes this!" Marcus cried as he pummeled Valen in the face again and again. "I'm having a *great* time!"

Magic pulsed through the area, an energy signature I was used to. It was Marcus' Curse Breaker powers, and his magic surged the way it did when he broke wards. Only this time, he wasn't breaking any ward. He was stealing Valen's powers, much like an Elf would, though Marcus couldn't utilize fae magic himself. Still, witch magic was similar enough to Valen's that Marcus was able to manipulate it and force it to change course. He drained Valen of his power so he couldn't fight back, making the shifter pathetic and weak.

A battle orb sizzled in Marcus' palm, and Valen's scream echoed across the island as the battle magic seared his skin. The smell of burning flesh filled the air.

Marcus' crazed laughter was even louder than Valen's screams. The dark side of Marcus— the deranged villain living inside of him— had returned. It hadn't emerged since we'd escaped the Institute, and I'd once thought it'd been a one-off psychotic break. But Marcus was losing it, and this time, he was remembering every moment of his missing sanity.

I understood now that *this* was who Marcus really was deep down. There was a part of him that lay deeply submerged unless Kallie was threatened. Now that darkness had been awakened, and Valen was going to experience the full wrath of the demonic rage that was Marcus' fury.

"You wanna fight back?" Marcus asked patronizingly, and he let Valen's body fall to the ground. "You weak, disgusting, sorry excuse for a piece-of-shit thing. I suppose I *could* let you try and stop me."

Valen gave an enraged yell, until his cries of anger turned to pain. There was a sloppy, gory sound, and I realized it was Valen's eye. Marcus was using Mentalist magic to puppeteer him, forcing him to claw his own eyeball out.

"Ew," Chancey said, sounding grossed out but not disagreeing. "Put that thing back in. It's hanging on by a thread."

Valen wailed in unimaginable agony before Marcus dropped him back to the ground, and the shifter gave a shriek.

"Oh, that's right. You *can't* fight back, because I'd never let you," Marcus taunted. "I'm not even going to let you get a cheap shot in. You won't put a scratch on me, but I sure as hell am going to fuck you up."

"Go to hell," Valen seethed. "I'm not afraid of you."

"What are you talking about? *Everyone's* afraid of me, because eventually, I come for you all. Haven't you heard? *I'm* the Lord of Death!" Marcus cried, giving a mock bow. "And death's knocking on your fucking doorstep. DING DONG, I'M HERE!"

Marcus fired his pistol twice. His magical bullets hit and blew chunks out of Valen's legs that splattered against my jacket. Off with the kneecaps, I guess. Valen's cries of agony were so loud, I figured they were going to crack the windows.

"If you're going to shoot me, be done with it!" Valen raged. He slapped a hand to his face— probably the side that was holding his dangling eyeball in.

"You think I'm going to kill you off right now? Like *this*?" Marcus cackled. "No fucking way. You've got a long way to go, shithead."

Marcus kicked him again, this time, in the stomach. Valen coughed a few times, and it sounded thick, like he was hacking up globules of blood.

"This was a good place to be a bad boy," Marcus said. He knelt by Valen, who was pathetically trying to crawl forward. "But it's a good place for *me* to be a bad boy, too. No one's going to hear you scream out here."

"You're fighting on behalf of some wench who swore herself to me before she even met you," Valen hissed. "I was the one she pledged herself to at our Choosing before the King's Contest even began. She swore to Neva, the Phantom Doe of Shadow and the goddess of time, to be my mate forever, and she turned her back on that promise. Don't forget, she was *mine* first."

"That's where you're wrong," Marcus spat. "No one is going to love her like I do, no one is going to understand her like I do, no one is going to *fuck her* like I do. You are a pathetic shitstain on the underside of her shoe, and I'm having a blast removing it."

Valen's fingernails could be heard as he drew them across the concrete. Marcus dragged him by his feet several paces away from us, and the magic in the air increased as my Air magic felt Valen be lifted into the air by Marcus' telekinesis, hanging him upside down.

Metal scraped as Marcus lifted a discarded metal pipe off the ground. Valen began to whimper. He was breaking already? How disappointing. He acted like such a big badass while he was on the streets murdering young women, but he sure turned into an overgrown crybaby when it was time to pick on someone his own size. I was *loving* that Marcus was torturing this bastard. I wanted to experience it again and again.

"You know, I was never very good at baseball. I always missed when it was my turn at bat," Marcus said, and the pipe whooshed as he twirled it in circles beside him. "But I don't see how I *can't* hit a home run with a target this big."

Marcus slammed the pipe into Valen's arm, and I rejoiced as it broke on impact. Valen didn't even have time to cry out before Marcus broke the other one. Marcus swung the pipe as hard as he could, breaking bones Valen probably didn't even know he had, beating the absolute shit out of him.

I was merciless. This sicko had made so many poor girls feel exactly like this— terrified, helpless and in unimaginable pain— before he'd taken their lives and humiliated their remains after. I had no sympathy. In fact, this was the most fun I'd had in a long time.

Marcus had busted Valen's skull open by the time he tossed the pipe to the side. I'd heard his head crack on the last hit. Blood dripped onto the ground like rain, and Valen gave a groan of suffering, though he didn't perish.

Valen was like a cockroach— hard to kill. No wonder people like him never died and continued to roam the earth poisoning society with their shadow. At least we could have fun watching him suffer. It would've been boring and dull to give this fucker the easy way out, and he didn't deserve a single ounce of mercy.

"Daddy's thirsty for blood," Marcus sang. "You know, Kallie taught me a lot about swords, though I've never used one before. Luckily, I happen to carry her sword with me in case she ever needs it, and it's *her blade* that's going to sever you apart. Isn't that poetic justice?"

The ringing sound of metal echoed throughout the air like a holy call as Marcus summoned Kallie's sword from his stash. "Let's see what your heart looks like, because I don't think you have one."

Metal sank into flesh, and Valen let out another howl. Bones cracked again, and I realized Marcus was cutting Valen open from the back, down the length of his spine.

I was impressed. Something like this would've grossed Marcus out even yesterday, caused him to vomit or cringe away. What Valen had done to Kallie had changed him, and there was no turning back from the evil he'd become.

Marcus nearly sounded disappointed. "Huh, your heart's not black. Color me surprised."

Marcus' fingers cracked as he crushed his hand into a fist, and I heard Valen's ribs buckle. The Dollmaker could barely utter a moan at this point. If he didn't die soon, he would any minute now.

We didn't have to wait long. Valen gave a dying moan, but Marcus cast a spell so strong I felt his Death magic ripple through the alleyway. It was like Marcus had shoved Valen's spirit back into his body. Marcus wasn't giving this fucker the satisfaction of death just yet.

"You're not going anywhere unless I say you are," Marcus hissed. There was the uncork of a bottle— a potion that Marcus carried, most likely— and a sizzling sound as Marcus poured it all over Valen's wounds. Valen cried out this time, his yowls high-pitched and louder than they had ever been before as the acid ate away at the open flesh.

"Burn alive," Marcus hissed, and the potion vial smashed against the ground as Valen continued to cry.

"Please," Valen pleaded. "Please, kill me."

"Oh, you're gonna *beg*, like a little bitch?" Marcus asked in a phony tone of concern. "Let me ask you a question. How many of those girls begged for their lives before you killed them? Did you ever care? No? Guess I don't give a shit, either."

Marcus stuck Kallie's sword into Valen's side and yelled, "Where are her wings?!"

"In a place... you'll never find," Valen rasped.

"*Tell me!*" Marcus demanded.

Valen gave a withering gasp. "Go... to... hell."

"Oh, I *will*," Marcus replied, and he gave another twisted laugh. "In fact, I'm going to be quite comfortable there, but I will *never* let you roam its halls."

The roar of hatred that emitted from Marcus was so terrifying, it almost made *me* cower. A powerful dark magical resonance, one that made my Elf magic marvel at how immense it was, ricocheted through the alleyway like a bolt of lightning. It made the earth quake and I stumbled forward, unable to catch my balance as I fell to the ground.

As I fell, I passed through some sort of spirit energy. Something materialized before me. I observed the soul that I knew had to be Valen's, giving a tortured wail as Marcus' magic held him in place, preventing him from escaping to the afterlife.

Then, in one exceptional magical burst, Valen's soul burst into ash. It exploded into an array of dust, coating me in his soul's energy. I wiped it off quickly, feeling disgusted, as the rest of his ether dissolved into the air.

Just before he'd died, Marcus had ripped Valen's soul out of his body and destroyed it. Valen would never go to the afterlife now, to any heaven or hell that would have him. He'd never reincarnate, and all of his past lives were gone. Marcus had effectively erased him from existence, as if he'd never been here at all.

But he *had* been here, even though Marcus had completely obliterated him. What he'd done to Kallie would continue to affect her for years to come. But at least now Valen couldn't hurt anyone else... here, or in any other lives going forward.

Marcus was absolutely raging, taking long and heavy gasps. I got to my feet and reached out to touch him. His shoulder was shaking underneath my hand. The psychotic part of him was gone. It had died down after he'd finished Valen, but he was still fuming.

"I didn't want to kill him yet," he said through clenched teeth. "I lost my temper and took it too far. I wasn't finished."

"He's gone now," I said firmly, squeezing his shoulder. "We took care of him, like we said we would. Now it's time to get back."

"You aren't still thinking about pulling off the heist, not after all this happened," Marcus insisted.

"We have to, Marcus. We still have daylight, and this is our only window," I said evenly. "I'm glad you made him pay. But Kallie wouldn't want us to miss out on the vampire key because of this."

Marcus sighed. "Guess you're right. I can't let Kallie down."

"No, you can't. Let's get back," I said.

We left Valen's body like the garbage it was behind us and portaled back to the hotel. Once we got there, Marcus immediately rushed back into the room where they were treating Kallie, and I followed.

"Did you get it done?" Ava whispered as I came to her side.

I nodded once, and Ava said nothing more.

"Marcus," Kallie wheezed. It sounded like she was awake again. "Where did you go?"

"I got him, pretty girl." Marcus sounded so sweet and gentle now. It was the complete opposite of the crazed killer he'd been moments before. "Valen's gone. I killed him, and destroyed his soul. He's never going to hurt you or any other woman ever again."

"He was mine," Kallie protested weakly. "I was supposed to kill him."

"He was *ours*," Marcus insisted. I heard him conjure her blade again, and lie it on the bedside next to her. "His blood is on your sword. I made sure to cut him open with it. He deserved to die just like all his victims did."

Kallie sounded astonished. "Marcus... there's no bigger honor for a fae, for you to kill their enemy with their sword."

"Of course there isn't. I was happy to do it for you."

Both of them got quiet, and I supposed they were off in their own little world. Ava tugged on my sleeve, and we left the room with Oberi to give them some privacy.

When the door closed behind us, I asked, "Is Kallie getting better?"

"She is, but there's no fucking way she can come on the heist. Kallie's down for the count," Ava said. "She can perform illusion magic, but she can't shift or stop time. I've healed her the best I can, but she can't come with us anymore. Even if she had access to her time powers, I don't think she can mentally pull this off. Not after what happened."

I wasn't expecting her to be well, but fuck, this sent our entire plan up in flames. "So what do we do now?"

"Mom and Ez are going to stay here and keep healing her. Once she's strong enough to make it through a long-distance portal, which should be by tonight, they'll take her back to Ilamanthe."

"And who's going to take her place?" I demanded.

"Come with me."

Ava led the way to the penthouse's kitchen, and I trailed her, but it was in silence. I was fuming. We should've had the vampire key by now, and we were running out of time to get it. We had to strike before nightfall, or this whole thing was a bust. I'd tried to account for everything, but I never thought the fucking Dollmaker would show up. The psycho was taken care of now, though, which meant we had to keep moving forward with our plan.

Max and Gavyn were waiting for us, surrounded by all kinds of tech noises, and the door to the penthouse opened. Two other voices halted me in my tracks as they entered, because I hadn't expected them to be here. It was Danny and Alistair. I just knew this was bad news. We were hours behind schedule, and now we had to account for these loose cannons.

"What the fuck are *you* doing here?" I sneered at Danny.

"Ava let me know about Kallie, and I came as soon as I could," he replied.

"Well, go home," I ordered. "We don't need you here."

"We just might," Ava countered. "Charlie, can I talk to you privately?"

Ava rolled out of the room, and I reluctantly followed her into the master suite.

"Pidge, you can't be serious!" I fumed. "You invited Danny and Alistair!"

"They deserved to know what happened," she said. "They're our friends."

I scoffed. "Alistair, yes, but that's a stretch for Danny. Forget about what happened with the Dollmaker; the fact that they're here has already compromised the whole mission. We might as well let Salvatore move the vampire key and hunt for it later."

"We didn't come all this way just to give up," Ava snapped. "Cassiel would riot if he knew we turned back now."

Ouch. She knew exactly where to hit me. I promised my grandfather I wouldn't let him down, and I wasn't going to let anyone— not the Dollmaker, and certainly not Danny— force me to go back on my word.

I paced around the room and ran my fingers through my hair. "We're running out of time. Getting that key is vital to the fate of the fucking world. It's now or never."

"Then we have to adjust our plan," Ava suggested. She reached out for me, and I stopped pacing. "We can do this. We just have to be clever. Together, we can pull this off."

I sighed heavily. "What were you thinking?"

"Take me with you. Kallie can't come along to crack the safe, so you'll have to rely on me."

"Pidge, you can't break open that safe the way Kallie can," I argued.

"I *can*," she insisted. "I've done it before. Back home, I used my water powers to break the lock on the safe in my parents' bedroom."

"You couldn't break into the bank vault, though," I pointed out.

"This is a different type of safe. The bank vault was a door, and this is just a box. I can break this tumbler system with my Water magic, and force my way in."

"And if that triggers alarms?" I asked.

"It's a chance we have to take," Ava pressed. "You planned for backups every step of the way *except* for cracking the safe. Let me come with, and we can do this together. We need to get the vampire key today, no matter what it takes."

The last thing I wanted to do was put Ava in any danger, but I didn't doubt her, either. I trusted that she could pull this off.

"You're our leader, Charlie," she added. "It's ultimately up to you, but I know I can do this."

Ava was right. I *was* the leader on this, and I had to get comfortable making tough decisions quickly. It's what my grandfather would do.

"Okay, you're with me, but we need to hurry," I conceded. "The longer we wait, the closer we get to sunset, and the vampires will be more active then. We have to move faster than we originally planned."

"Then let's discuss the change of plans with the others," Ava said.

We returned to the main room, where Max was clicking away at her keyboard. "Asa and Aries are ahead of us," she said. "We're already tapped into The Devil's City security feed. We have full control over the security system, so we can cover your tracks from here. Security won't know where you're at."

"Good, because it's time to move," I replied.

At the sound of my voice the others gathered around, waiting on my orders. Marcus left Kallie's room, taking my side.

"I'm with you, Charlie," he said. "Kallie wants me to do this with you guys, and though I don't want to leave her at a time like this, Ez and Ava's mom will take care of her. Kallie made me *swear* I'd get the vampire key and bring it back to Ilamanthe. She doesn't want our time in Chicago to be for nothing."

I'd say. If we missed out on the vampire key, Kallie's torment at the hands of the Dollmaker would end up being an unneeded sacrifice. We couldn't let that happen.

"Change of plans," I announced. "We're sending Kallie back to the palace once she's stable and getting her out of harm's way. Ava will be taking Kallie's place and accompanying us into The Devil's City. Everything else is remaining as close to the original plan as possible."

"I'm coming with," Danny insisted. "You're going to need me out there."

Fucking hell.

"You can take Ava's place and stay here on comms," I told him, because that was the safest place to put him.

"Like hell," Danny shot back. "I'm in on the action. I'm pretty good at causing a distraction when you need one, and something tells me you're going to need it."

"What kind of distraction?" I challenged.

Danny let out a cocky laugh. "Just trust me."

My grandfather had taught me that no job was bound to go perfectly, and that when faced with a problem, the best thing to do was work with it, rather than try to solve it.

You don't have time to solve problems when the clock is ticking, he'd told me. *You can only pivot. Find ways to turn that problem into a solution.*

I wasn't going to argue with Danny, because I knew he'd only cause more problems if he was left to his own devices. At least if Danny was with us, I could keep a close eye on him.

"All right, Danny. You're with us," I agreed.

"I'll take over the comms," Alistair offered. He plopped down in front of the computer. Pig jumped up on the table, and the keyboard clicked as the cat walked over it.

Alistair wasn't going to return to Ilamanthe, even if I dragged him there myself. Leaving him here where Max and Gavyn could watch him was our best option.

"Fine," I said. "Let's get moving."

We quickly gathered the last of our things. Gavyn supplied us each with an earpiece, so that we could stay in touch with each other.

Marcus placed a potion vial in my hand. "Everyone take this. It's a warding potion I made myself. It will disguise our scent, voices, and appearances. It will make us virtually undetectable."

I downed the potion, and the others followed. I felt the magic tingling across my skin, and I knew it was working.

"Danny, you'll need a sun-safe potion to protect you from the sunlight if we need to make a quick exit outside," Marcus added. "You're lucky I've got one on me. It should last up to twelve hours."

"Cheers!" Danny said, before downing the potion. I almost hoped it didn't work, because it'd be funny if his vampiric ass fried.

Oberi shifted into a unicorn. Ava left her chair behind, and I hoisted her onto Oberi's back. Rishi followed at Marcus' feet, and Eddie remained close by my side, braced to defend me at any moment. Chancey cracked his knuckles, ready for a fight, and Ivy walked alongside him. Danny followed us, but he thankfully kept his mouth shut. I think he finally realized how serious the situation was and that he couldn't fuck around right now.

We took a private elevator down to the lowest level of the hotel, which was deserted. I used my magic to shift the concrete and dirt beneath us, creating a sloping passage, until I felt my magic give way to a large tunnel beneath us.

"Quickly," I ordered. Oberi hurried through the hole I'd made, and the others followed.

I went last. The storm sewers were similar to long, circular hallways. They were tall enough to stand in, and although there were puddles of water beneath us, Ava cleared them aside with her Toaqua magic.

"It's a mile to The Devil's City," Ivy told us. "Come on. I know where we need to go."

We walked at a brisk pace and turned a few corridors until Ivy stopped in the middle of the tunnel fifteen minutes later. I knew we must be beneath The Devil's City, because I could feel the magic buzzing around us. It wasn't as strong as the magic in Ilamanthe, or even back at the Institute, because vampire magic wasn't as intense as the resonance given off by other supernatural races. That's why the vampires could still rely heavily on tech like security cameras when they didn't work so well at the Institute, because their magic didn't interfere with human technology as much. Still, there were enough vampires in the vicinity that I could sense them, even from underground.

"This is it," Ivy announced. "We should be right beneath the boiler room."

Gavyn's voice came through the comms. *"We've got a visual on the boiler room. It's empty. You're clear to go."*

"Everyone stand back," I told them.

They scurried back a few paces, and I lifted my hands. The ground shook, and debris rained downward as I shifted dirt, rock, and concrete above us. I was careful to make sure the earth was stable before ushering the others through. We crawled out of the storm sewers and into a large room whirring with equipment.

Goosebumps tingled along my arms, and I quickly scanned the room with my magic. I could feel Air moving in and out of the machines, but I felt no magical signatures nearby. The room was empty as expected.

"The service elevators are this way." Ivy started forward, and we all followed.

Though we were alone, we crept quietly past large machines and long pipes. I remained on keen alert, and I didn't pick up on anything until—

"*Eek!*" Marcus let out a high-pitched squeal, and Rishi hissed. Danny grunted, like he'd been hit by a heavy force. My Air magic swirled around two swiftly-moving figures. The vampires were on us in a split second, before any of us knew it, and they'd grabbed Marcus and Danny.

Danny gave a primal growl, and Chancey moved forward to beat the vampires to a pulp. I threw my hand out in one direction to shove Ava and Oberi behind me with my Air magic. My other hand lifted toward the vampires to cast a spell, but before I could shoot it off, Marcus gasped in pain. I realized if I cast the spell, Marcus would be caught in the crosshairs and probably get hurt.

Danny threw a punch at one of the guys, but he didn't get away from the guy holding him before he paused.

"Brant? Krew?" Danny asked in a bright tone. "What the hell are the chances?"

"What the fuck?" I snarled at Danny. "You know these pricks?"

"We have a history," Danny admitted. "Not a great one, obviously."

Chancey hesitated, then backed down. Eddie took a stance beside me, awaiting my instruction.

"Well, well, well." One of the vampires laughed. "Never expected to see you again, *Daniel.*"

"I don't want to have to hit you again, Brant," Danny warned. "We're friends, remember? You don't want to make an enemy out of me."

"If you're friends, you can let them go," I said. I really didn't want to leave a string of bodies behind if we could help it. It'd tip off Salvatore just as quickly as these two fuckers running back to him. The best option was to use Danny's friendship to our advantage, so these vamps didn't go reporting back to the boss.

"Friends?" the other vampire scoffed— Krew, I guessed. "We'd sooner kill these two than let them go. Salvatore will be very *interested* in speaking with you, Danny. And look, they brought the boss's little whelp. This day keeps getting better and better. Daddy's been looking for you, Junior."

"Fuck you, Krew," Ivy spat. "I'm not my father's tool."

"But you always have been," Krew replied. "Come with us now, or your friends are dead. Don't even think of casting any spells in here. Any rogue magic could hit one of these machines. An explosion like that would take all of us with it."

He was right about that, and I didn't want to risk hitting Marcus, either. I had to make a split-second decision, and the best thing to do was siphon the vamps of their powers. But when I tried, I couldn't sense their magic.

"Why can't I feel you?" I demanded. "You don't have any magic."

Krew gave a mischievous laugh. "We have *good* warding potions that make us undetectable to everyone, including our own cameras."

So that's why I hadn't felt them in the room with us, and why they hadn't been spotted by the Associates on the security cameras. An oversight I wasn't making again.

Ivy stepped forward. "You don't *really* want to keep working for my dad, do you? Come on, Brant. You looked the other way countless times when I was getting into mischief right here in this building. I know you hate it here."

Brant hesitated, like he couldn't argue with that. "Turning you in would guarantee one hell of a promotion."

"*Or* you could come with me and be free of my father," Ivy offered. "I made it out of this place; so can you. You told me the last time we talked you were sick of working for him, so come work for me instead."

"He'd have my head," Brant insisted.

"Not if he can't find you," Ivy said. "My father thinks he can beat us, but we've already escaped him once. We'll escape him every time after. So tell me, Brant... do you want to be on the winning side, or the losing? Because if you stay with my father, one way or another, you *will* lose yourself."

Brant's voice was small as he said, "I already have, Junior. If you really mean it, then take me with you."

"Screw you! You can't mean that!" Krew shouted.

"I do!" Brant insisted. "Junior's right. Salvatore isn't what he used to be, and I ain't sticking around if I've got better options."

"Good choice, Brant," Ivy said approvingly. "What do you say, Krew? You going to join us, too?"

"Over my dead body," Krew sneered. "You're a fucking traitor, Brant!"

Krew let go of Marcus and leapt on Brant. Before Danny could get between them, I heard the snap of breaking bones, then the tearing of flesh as Krew yanked Brant's head off his shoulders. The vampire's body slumped to the ground.

So much for not leaving any dead bodies behind. We couldn't let Krew walk now, because he was sure to run off to Salvatore immediately.

I lunged forward and clamped my hands around Krew's head, then twisted. I didn't know where I'd found the strength, because I certainly hadn't siphoned it from Krew. But I'd pulled a supernatural power boost from somewhere. Krew's bones snapped, and his neck crackled like broken stone against my touch. He was gone in an instant.

Ivy stumbled to the side. "Whoa, Charlie. You've taken a hit on my strength."

I realized I'd siphoned the super strength from Ivy. I had to be careful, because they needed their powers for themselves.

"*Wow!*" Alistair's voice came over the comms. "*That was impressive, Charlie! You show 'em who's boss!*"

"Stay off the comms unless you have information for us, Alistair." I tossed Krew's head aside, heaving heavy breaths. I turned on the others. "That was too fucking close! We can't let something like this happen again, or we aren't walking out of here with that key. We've got two bodies now, and we just got in. These bodies are going to be discovered quicker than we want them to be, because they'll be expected to report back to the higher-ups, and people will know they're missing."

"We can at least get rid of the evidence to slow Salvatore's people down," Ava suggested. She aimed her Fire magic, and warmth filled the air as her flames ate away at the vampires' bodies until there was nothing left of them.

I whirled on Danny. "You care to explain what just happened? How do you know these people? Every detail you leave out puts us at risk."

"There's not much to tell," Danny insisted. "I lived in The Devil's City for a while after my parents kicked me out. Ivy and I spent some time together, and they took me on jobs to help out. I never officially joined the mob, but I met a few guys along the way. That's it."

"You better hope that's it," I sneered. "Because if your mobster friends catch us off guard like that again, it's over. I won't hesitate to kill them, even if you're caught in the line of fire."

"Believe me," Danny replied darkly. "I won't be."

"I don't understand," Chancey said. "We shouldn't have been caught after taking Marcus' warding potion. It must've not worked."

"But I brewed it perfectly!" Marcus insisted. "I don't know what could've gone wrong."

"The spy in the palace," Ava sneered. "Someone must've sabotaged your potion. Just one wrong ingredient could make it ineffective, even if the magical signature remained."

That fucking spy again. We needed to figure out who they were, because we would never make any progress if someone was always sabotaging our moves.

I shook my head. "Nothing we can do about it now."

"What if the spy told Salvatore about our plan? Charlie, we could be walking into a trap!" Marcus panicked.

I paused. He was right. But we were already in the building, and the key was a hundred stories up. We were so close. Could we really turn back now, even if there was a risk?

Keep going forward, my grandfather would say. So that's what I decided we'd do.

"We don't quit until we have that key. Marcus, keep a close lookout for any potential wards," I warned. "Let's keep moving."

We hurried across the boiler room, but we didn't run into any other vamps. At the service elevator, Marcus and Chancey pried the doors open. I felt a column of air rising upward all the way to the top of the tower. Somewhere in the middle I could sense two elevator cars, but there was enough space around them that we could maneuver past them. This was our best way to navigate the building undetected.

"Let's move quickly." I ushered the others inside.

Ivy and Danny grabbed the side of the elevator shaft and began climbing. Marcus used his telekinesis to fly himself, Rishi, and Eddie upward, while I cast my Air magic to levitate myself and Ava. Oberi shifted into a phoenix to fly on her own, and Chancey spread his angel wings to follow up the rear.

Danny and Ivy climbed as fast as the rest of us flew. We moved at a quick pace, and I figured it would only take us a couple of minutes to reach the top. Floors flew past us in seconds. Ten floors, then twenty...

I sensed a shift in my Air magic, as if someone had opened a doorway overhead.

"Intruders!" a deep voice yelled.

"Fuck, we have company!" Ava cried.

I could feel her shock through the bond, and it was easy to read her. Two vampires stood several floors above us, peering out into the open elevator shaft. I reacted quickly, sending a column of Air upward to knock them off their feet.

"We have to move faster!" I shouted.

No sooner had I shoved those vamps backward did I feel another doorway open overhead. The sinister laughter of a vampire echoed off the elevator shaft.

"You have nowhere to hide!" the vamp called down to us.

Then the most horrible sound filled my ears— the sound of snapping cables, and the groan of metal on metal. The Air around me seemed to shrink. An elevator car was coming down on top of us!

"Everyone to the walls!" Chancey screamed.

I thrust my arms outward, and my Air magic pinned my friends against the corners of the elevator shaft. I lifted my arms to slow the elevator down, but my Air magic fought against it, like the vampires were using powers of their own to make it fall.

"Charlie!" Chancey panicked. He flapped his wings and threw himself on top of me, to push me out of the way. I landed hard against the side of the elevator shaft, squished between the wall and Chancey's chest. His wings spread wide, flattening us both there.

The elevator car swept past us, at a speed that seemed inhumanly possible. Chancey screamed in my ear... and then he was gone. His weight on me vanished, and his pained cry echoed up the shaft as he was dragged downward by the elevator car.

"*Chance!*" Ivy screamed, their cry echoing off the walls.

I leapt off the side of the shaft, free falling headfirst behind him as I used my Air to control my descent. Ava fell alongside me, trusting me to catch her fall. The others followed. Chancey's scream seemed to go on forever, until the crash of the elevator car sounded against the bottom of the shaft. Metal clanged and groaned as the elevator car crunched like a soda can.

"*Ouch, that sounded like it hurt,*" Alistair said.

"Not helpful," I barked into the comms.

Ivy had gotten there before any of us, and their panicked cries could be heard all around the elevator shaft.

"Oh no, no, no," Ivy whimpered, and their pleas made my heartbeat race. What if the elevator car had crushed him?

I landed on my feet on top of the elevator car, which was nothing more than a heap of metal now. I heard Chancey gasp below me, somewhere off to the side. He was still alive.

The elevator shaft housed two elevators, and the vamps had only cut the cable to one of them. Chancey lay on the ground in the space between the elevators, groaning in agonizing pain. He had to be pinned under it!

"*My wing!*" Chancey cried out in agony, sounding in incredible pain.

I flew to the ground and guided my Air magic to lay Ava gently beside Chancey. Oberi landed in phoenix form beside him.

"I'm going to heal you," Ava told him, before I felt her healing magic surge through the bond.

"Better be quick about it," Danny warned. "We've got company."

Above us, the scurry of hands and feet sounded from all angles. There were hordes of vampires *crawling* down the elevator shaft to get to us. Rishi yowled loudly. Marcus and Eddie were already getting to work prying open the nearest door.

Ivy sounded completely broken. "His right wing is crushed," they whimpered.

I went to walk around him, and my shoes splashed in the puddles of blood that were seeping out from Chancey's injuries.

"Leave... me," Chancey rasped. He sounded on the edge of consciousness, like he was fighting to hold on just to convince us to leave him there.

"I need to help you," Ava demanded.

"You can't... heal this," Chancey moaned. "Healing magic won't fix a broken angel wing. My wing stays like this, I'm gonna die... and I know there's no fixing it now. Just... leave me here. I'll be okay. I'm ready to go."

"We've got to get the car off of him!" I demanded.

"There's no time!" Ava cried. The crawling of the vampires grew closer, and I knew it would only be a matter of time before they were upon us.

We had less than a few minutes before the vampires got to us. If they reached us, they'd drag us off to Salvatore, and this would be all over. We didn't have time to contemplate a decision. Even if we managed to get Chancey free, I knew his wing was too mangled to function properly ever again, and as an angel, he couldn't live without them.

As the leader of this operation, I was prepared to make tough calls. I'd hoped it wouldn't come to this, but I knew I had to make one of the hardest decisions of my life. I didn't want to leave Chancey behind, but we had to. There was nothing more important than getting that key, and as much as I hated to say it, that included Chancey's life.

The thought flickered through my head in an instant. I tried not to feel anything at all, because I had to keep pushing the team forward. We just had to pivot when we met snags in the plan, as my grandfather taught me.

Oberi knew it, too. She shifted back into a Fire unicorn and stomped her hoof. I grabbed Ava around the waist and hoisted her onto Oberi's back. "We have to go!"

Ava pushed against me. "Charlie, we can't!"

"You... have... to," Chancey begged. His life was fading. He wasn't going to make it, and I couldn't waste time trying to save him when everything was on the line.

The vamps were closing in on us— and fast. I could hear their deranged laughs as they approached, scuttling down the walls like spiders closing in on their prey.

"We ain't leaving him," Ivy demanded. They shoved past me so hard I flew off my feet and landed against the side of the shaft with a heavy *oof*. "Chance, baby, I'm sorry. But I'm not letting you die on me."

"Ivy, *don't!*" Ava cried, but it was too late.

I heard the unsheathing of a blade, then the tearing of flesh. Chancey's agonized screams grew louder than ever. My stomach churned as I realized Ivy was slicing off Chancey's wing in order to save his life.

"Don't... Leave me... Kill me!" Chancey yelled, before his wails became even louder as Ivy sawed through the bone.

"I will never let you go," Ivy wept, though they continued slicing through the sinew on Chancey's wing. "Even if I have to hurt you to make you stay."

To lose one of your wings was one of the worst things to happen to an angel. To lose them both was a death sentence. Chancey would live if he kept one wing, but he'd forever be broken because of it. Half an angel, never able to fly again.

I didn't think Chancey would want that— in fact, I was certain he would rather be eaten alive by vampires.

Ivy, though, wasn't willing to allow him to die. Ivy kept going, using their blade to saw through Chancey's wing bone and feathers in order to cut him loose. Chancey's screams grew louder as he begged and pleaded with Ivy to stop, but it didn't do any good, because Ivy kept going. More warm blood trickled out along the floor, soaking my shoes.

There was a creaking noise above, and I realized with horror that the vampires had cut the cables of the second elevator car, which was now free-falling in mid-air. We had thirty seconds or less before it landed on us and crushed us all.

"Keep going, Ivy!" Ava yelled. "I'll take care of these vamps."

Intense magic laced in rage swept through the bond as Ava aimed her hands upward. An icy chill crept over my skin before being met with a blazing inferno as her blue Fire magic swept past me. Vampires screamed in pain as her flames licked up the sides of the elevator shaft. There were very few things that could slow a vampire down, but Ava's Fire was one of them. Her blue Fire was the most powerful of all.

The vampires turned to ash, the remnants of their bodies raining down on us. Marcus and Eddie yanked the elevator door open the same time Ivy hauled Chancey upward. We hurried out the moment the second elevator car crashed to the floor. It smashed against the spot where Chancey had been laying only a moment ago.

"Good thinking, Ava!" Alistair praised through the comms. *"Just like barbeque."*

I ignored him. "We've got to keep moving. Ava slowed the vamps down, but more will be coming. We can't keep going this way, because they could come from any floor before we make it to the top. We'll have to go another way."

And we had to move fast, because now we had even more dead vampires that would tip Salvatore off on our location.

We were back in the boiler room, the machines whirring from all angles. Ivy dragged Chancey forward and gently set him on the ground. Chancey didn't make a sound; he'd passed out cold. Blood dripped from his back as a result of his severed wing.

"Heal him, Ava!" Ivy yelled. "Bring his wing back!"

"I...can't," she insisted weakly.

"You replaced your father's lungs!" Ivy screamed, like she was being unreasonable.

"This isn't like that," Ava said. "I can heal Chancey's *wound*, but I can't regrow magical appendages, and angel wings are the hardest thing to fix!"

"It's no use, Ives," Danny said. "Once an angel loses their wings, that's it. They're done for."

"No!" Ivy raged. "He's still got one left. I'm not giving up on him."

"You have to, for the sake of the key," Danny argued. "He knew what he was risking when he signed up for this. We all did."

Ivy shot to their feet and began pacing back and forth. "This is my father's fault. I'm going to kill him; I *swear* it!"

I grabbed Ivy by the shoulders. They shook beneath my touch. "Ivy, you can't, not now. You'll get your revenge on your father, but we need to get that key first."

"Then I'll burn this place to the ground the second we get it!" Ivy shouted.

"No," I stated firmly. "If that's the way you feel, then you're off the job. I'm sorry, Ivy, but you can't come along if you're set on revenge. You're going to get someone hurt."

"Fuck you, Charlie. You wanna play boss, but this job is already fucked all to hell. Screw the plan— I ain't taking your orders no more. I *want* to see him get hurt!" Ivy raged. "I want to hurt my father. I want to *watch him suffer.*"

"Charlie's right," Marcus said. "You're bound to fuck up because you're so pissed."

"Believe me, if I get my father in my sights, I won't miss," Ivy insisted.

Ivy wasn't going to listen to me right now, and I couldn't have someone like that on my team. "I'm sorry, Ivy. This is going to hurt."

Before Ivy could react, I siphoned their vampire strength and punched them across the side of the face as hard as I could. Ivy went down, and they didn't get up.

"*That sounded like a nice swing!*" Alistair praised. Ancestors, he acted like he was listening to a wrestling match.

"Sire, you've knocked him out!" Eddie gasped.

"Ivy will be fine," I said. "Danny, drag Chancey back into the tunnel."

I spoke into my earpiece. "Max, can you send help to the storm sewers? Ivy and Chancey both need medical attention."

"*Asa and Aries are on their way,*" she replied.

I leaned down to pick Ivy up, then hoisted them over my shoulder. I hurried back over to the tunnel I'd created to get us in here, and I tossed Ivy inside.

Danny set Chancey down in the tunnel. Chancey made a ragged noise as he slowly came to.

He coughed a few times and rasped, "Thanks... for not leaving me behind... boss." His head slumped to the side again as he faded out.

That comment should've fucked me up. But to be honest, I didn't feel much of anything.

I used my magic to cover the hole so that Ivy couldn't use it to reenter The Devil's City, then I turned to the others. "New plan. Salvatore's men are going to be looking for us through maintenance access points, so our best chance is to take the route they'd least expect. Pidge, can you use your Spirit magic to turn us invisible?"

"If everyone stays close, I should be able to hold the spell," she said.

"What's our route?" Marcus asked.

Ivy must've gone through the building layout with me a hundred times before we portaled to Chicago. The staircase down to the boiler room didn't connect with the stairwell to the other parts of the hotel. To get to the staircase leading us upstairs, we had to ascend a level and cross the casino floor. It sucked that we'd lost our guide, but we didn't have a lot of options right now.

"We're going through the casino," I replied. "I hope you all like card games and slot machines, because we're about to gamble for that key."

Danny laughed. "The house ain't winning today. That's something I'll bet on."

We were all betting our lives on it. Ava hadn't turned this many people invisible all at once, and her magic could falter at any time, but it was a risk we had to take.

"Are you sure about this, Charlie?" Marcus asked. "Vamps have other senses. We could still be detected. They'll smell us before they see us."

"We're out of time, and it's a crowded place," I replied. "Our best option is to blend in with the crowd and move with them to get to the other side of the casino. If Salvatore already knows we're here, he's going to find us, which means we don't have time to debate on what to do. We just need to do it and get to the key."

Nobody else questioned me. Warmth surrounded me as Ava's invisibility magic enveloped us all.

"*Looking good on our end,*" Gavyn said through the comms. "*We can't see you on the cameras.*"

"Everyone be quiet and stay close," I warned. "If you wander too far outside Ava's magical range, you're on your own."

Marcus and Eddie took the lead, and we moved as a unit up the stairs. We came out in a deserted hallway, which I could only assume was filled with all kinds of maintenance rooms for employees only.

"We're approaching a door," Marcus whispered under his breath, for my sake as well as for the comms team back at the Scarlet Grand.

I heard a door creak open, and then came voices behind it. We entered a large foyer that must've been the entrance to the building. There were a few people crossing through, and several others behind a registration desk.

"*Still looking good,*" Gavyn said. "*Make your move... now.*"

We hurried across the foyer, until the sound of voices grew even louder, along with the pings of slot machines. The air seemed to close in around us as we neared the casino entrance. The casino was crowded, and there were at least a few hundred people inside, but there was no other way to get to the stairwell we needed; the guest stairs didn't go all the way to the top of the tower.

"Approaching the casino now," Marcus whispered. "Hang on... I sense some sort of ward here."

Marcus paused, and I could feel magic swirling around him. A slight buzzing sound whirred in my ears, until Marcus breathed a sigh of relief and it disappeared completely.

"That was it?" I asked. "You broke the ward?"

Before, Marcus had to transform spells in order to break them, but now, he just dissolved the ward without any effort.

"That was it," Marcus said proudly. "Easy as could be."

"*There's a group entering the casino now,*" Gavyn told us. "*The doors are narrow, so Ava's going to have to concentrate to move you each through single file. There's a group coming up behind this one. You'll have a ten-second window. And... move.*"

We moved quickly at Gavyn's instruction and slipped past the security guards and onto the casino floor.

"Something doesn't smell right," one of the security guards told the other. He sniffed the air, and I knew he was preparing to strike.

"*Fuck, they've caught you. Run!*" Alistair screamed over the comms.

"Stay calm," I started to hiss, but it was already too late. Rishi panicked and leapt from Marcus' arms, tearing across the casino.

"Rishi, no!" Marcus yelled.

"There!" the guard screamed. We'd certainly been caught now.

"Go!" I shoved at the others. The security guards raced after us, but since they couldn't see us due to Ava's invisibility magic, they had difficulty pursuing us at super-human speed. One of them rushed by so fast that Air billowed around us, but he was past us in a split-second. The other jumped toward us, but he landed flat on the ground.

Eddie yelped as he ran into someone, and I realized it was one of the employees at a blackjack table. Cards went flying into the air, raining down all around us. The warmth of Ava's magic disappeared around me, and I knew I had to be visible.

"There he is!" a guard yelled.

Ava's invisibility magic enveloped me again, and I took off running. I must've appeared to the guards for only a split-second, and they were already in pursuit. By now, there had to be at least five security guards tailing us.

We ran as fast as we could. Danny bumped into a poker table, and chips went flying across the floor. Oberi must've slipped on the chips, because she fell to the ground with a heavy crash. Ava gasped and tried to catch herself on the lever of a slot machine. An award-winning chime went off, along with the simulated sound of coins clanging together.

"Oh, hey!" Ava said brightly. "I won a jackpot!"

"No time." I shoved Oberi upright, and Ava clung to her mane. Rishi yowled as he rejoined us.

"*There's a restaurant along the outer wall, straight ahead of you,*" Gavyn informed us through the comms. "*Inside, there's a hall through the kitchens leading to the stairwell.*"

We raced through the restaurant and into the kitchens, pots and pans clanging as we passed through. In here, it smelled of copper, and I realized it was a blood bar. Two cooks stood in the kitchens, and they fled in fear when we entered. Someone else came through the back, and I sensed strong magic rolling off him. It had to be one of the security guards.

Marcus didn't even hesitate. The crackle of a high-powered battle orb came, then the vampire was blasted into the wall so hard that it crumbled around him. Before the vamp could get up, I heard metal slide across the countertop. Marcus grabbed a large knife— a cleaver, I guessed. He swung it at the vampire, and the bones in his neck snapped. The vamp was done for. Marcus really wasn't kidding when he said he'd been ready to do whatever it took to get the key.

"*All right. Go Marcus!*" Alistair cheered through my earpiece.

"Someone get Alistair off the comms!" I snapped.

"*Aw, but I'm having so much fun—*" he started to protest. I heard a brief scuffle, like Max had yanked the equipment away from Alistair.

"Marcus, you good?" I asked. I worried how he'd take killing someone, after everything we'd talked about.

Except Marcus didn't seem bothered at all. "Never been better, boss. Let's get this done."

Shouts came from outside the kitchen in the restaurant. Other vampires were coming.

"*You've got four more goons coming your way,*" Gavyn said.

I quickly barked orders. "Eddie, Danny, and Marcus, go ahead and clear a path upstairs. Ava and I will take care of these assholes."

The others went on ahead, while Ava and I faced the opposite doorway. The vampires burst through the door so fast it blasted off its hinges. I thrust my Air magic upward, sweeping all four of them into a fast current that halted their super-speed in its tracks. Ava blasted her Fire at them, and their screams instantly died as they perished in the flames.

"*Marcus and Eddie have cleared the stairwell,*" Gavyn said through my earpiece. "*Ava, Charlie, move now.*"

Oberi and I took off running, and we entered a tall, narrow stairwell that was only ever used in emergencies. I could feel a column of air swirling upward, and I knew there was enough space between the stairs that we could fly straight up. Marcus, Eddie, and Danny were already long gone, so I could only assume Marcus used his telekinesis to hover everyone else to the top.

I cradled Ava in my arms. Oberi shifted into a phoenix and took off flying above us. My Air magic swirled beneath my feet, and we began to ascend.

We were almost to the top when a massive explosion rocked the building.

Drywall cracked overhead and hit our heads. Ava and I were nearly knocked out of the air, but I caught us with my magic before we could go spiraling downward. An alarm blared, and Ava clutched me tighter.

"Looks like Danny really knows how to make a distraction," Ava said.

"What the *fuck* was that?" I barked into the earpiece.

"I'm getting the vamps away from the target," Danny replied. *"Took twelve of them out at once. You're welcome, by the way. I'm headed to Salvatore's gala right now. Gonna work some of my manipulation magic on those fuckers."*

He was going to make them fight each other. Now that the alarms were blaring, we needed the extra distraction.

"Whatever keeps them out of our hair," I replied.

Ava and I reached the target level, and Oberi shifted back into a Fire unicorn as we came out into the main hallway. I placed Ava on Oberi's back again, and spun around, trying to get my bearings.

Gavyn's voice came through my earpiece. *"We've got a visual on you, Charlie. Marcus and Eddie are two halls ahead, and a path has already been cleared."*

I guided Ava and Oberi into the hall. In the distance, magic exploded off the walls, and I could hear Eddie and Marcus screaming in rage as they fought off the vampires. The alarm overhead continued to blare.

We were out of time. We'd definitely been discovered, and if we didn't get to that key *now*, Salvatore would beat us to it.

By the time we reached the hall where I heard the fighting, Eddie and Marcus had already gone on ahead. The bodies of decapitated security guards lay sprawled out before us. I pressed a hand to the wall to climb over one of them, and my fingers met the hard chest of a vampire. He was stuck in the wall — like Eddie had used his powers to phase him there and trap him, before siphoning his strength to rip his head off.

"We just took out the last of them," Eddie said through the comms. *"Your path is clear, Charlie."*

"Eddie and I will stay on this level to take out anyone else who dares come close to the target," Marcus added.

"Marcus, you've got six vamps headed your way," Gavyn warned.

"On it," Marcus confirmed.

Ava and I reached the target room, and I felt around for the keypad. I entered the code we'd gotten from one of the men at the circus, and the keypad made an angry sound.

Either Salvatore had changed the code since we picked up the intel, or the alarm had put the area on lockdown. Didn't matter. We were getting through that room one way or another, and we weren't fucking around trying to get this keypad to work.

I placed my hands flat to the door, and magic surged all the way up my arms. I could feel a ward protecting the room. If I siphoned the magic, I was sure I could—

Magic exploded from my palms before I could finish the thought. The magic I'd siphoned had backfired, and the ward blasted a hole straight through the door. The floor shook, and dust hovered in the air.

"We've lost your feed!" Gavyn barked. *"The blast blew out the nearest security cameras."*

"It's okay," Ava replied through the comms. "The safe is just ahead. I can see it."

"Eddie, on your left!" Marcus shouted down the hall. More yells and sounds of attack came over the sound of the alarm, but Ava and I ignored them as we entered the room.

The moment we stepped through the crater I'd blasted in the wall, something changed. A *clang* came from overhead, and I stopped in my tracks as I felt all my energy whoosh out of me, completely draining my magic. There was only one thing that could make me feel that way.

Inferichite.

Oberi whinnied and stumbled back a few steps, but she crashed into something. I couldn't make sense of what was going on, because without my magic, I'd completely lost my bearings. I reached outward to feel my surroundings, and my hands clamped around cold bars.

Nausea slammed into my gut, and it became abundantly clear that a cage had fallen from the ceiling to trap us inside an inferichite cage. I could even feel the crystal sucking my power from beneath my feet.

"I've lost sight of Salvatore," Danny barked through the comms. *"Hurry up, because he'll be on you any minute now."*

Elyx's voice came through my earpiece. *"I've got my sights on his men. I can slow them down."*

I heard the click of a trigger through the comm as Elyx shot off his first bullet. People spread throughout the casino wailed in terror as the sound of shattering windows rang out over the building.

We were down to the last minute, and no amount of magic was going to get us out of this cage. We had to think fast.

"What are we going to do, Charlie?" Ava panicked. "The only way we've broken through inferichite before is with Marcus and Kallie's help."

"We can't use our magic," I said. "The only way out of here is through brute force. These bars are thin and brittle. The cage isn't made very well. There's *got* to be a way through."

Allow me, Oberi offered. She gave a high-pitched whinny and reared up on her hind legs. Ava clung to her back to hold on. I ducked out of the way as her front hooves came down on the bars so hard that the crystal shattered. In her unicorn form, Oberi weighed a thousand pounds or more, and the bars couldn't support her weight. Shards blasted everywhere, and several inferichite fragments hit me in the leg, cutting deep into the skin. I gasped in pain, reaching out to feel the blood that was seeping through my pants.

I couldn't stop now. I had to keep moving, no matter if I was hurt or not.

"Good work, Oberi," I said as I quickly slipped through the bars. Immediately, my Air magic swirled around the area, though I wasn't nearly as strong with inferichite in the room.

Oberi squeezed through the hole in the bars she'd made, and we rushed across the room to the safe. A chill spread over my skin as Ava summoned Water from the air. She filled the locking mechanism with water, then froze it, until we heard a *crack*. The door creaked open, and Ava gasped in delight.

"It's here!" she cried.

A loud whine erupted across the room, reverberating off the walls. It was louder than the alarm blaring overhead, and I was forced to cover my ears with my hands as the noise raked like nails on a chalkboard across my hearing.

A dark, chilling energy rose from the safe. It was some sort of curse, or perhaps a demon; it had to be. Before I could make sense of it, the energy swept past me— straight toward Ava.

"Charlie—!" she started, but her words choked off the same time I felt her energy change, and she was knocked off of Oberi's back. The link between our bond seemed to slam shut in an instant.

Oberi whinnied loudly. *A dark cloud rose out of the safe and went into her! She's been possessed!*

Rage filled my entire body. *Not on my watch.*

I reached for Ava where she sat on the ground, because whatever that dark energy was, I was going to siphon it out with my Elf powers. The moment I touched her, an ice-cold chill followed immediately by a blazing heat seared my fingers.

I jumped back. Ava had burned me with her blue Fire!

A deep, ethereal laugh bubbled up from Ava's throat. In a voice that wasn't her own, Ava said, "*You think you can steal from me?*"

Charlie, you have to get that demon out of her now! Oberi snapped.

"I'm on it!" I ducked to avoid a fireball the demon threw at me. It smashed into the wall behind me, and the room ignited into flames. The fire grew intense, licking up the walls and consuming the carpet.

I reached out with my Elf powers, but the demon resisted. I couldn't get a firm hold on him with my magic. I'd never tried using my powers on a being like him before, and it wasn't the same as manipulating a living person. There was something there I couldn't quite reach, like he existed on an entirely different plane than I did. His dark energy was complicated, and hard to manipulate.

I thought quickly, recalling all I could about demon possession. During our training for the Darke Games, Ava had frozen an allure demon out of Marcus. Maybe I could try that.

I immediately siphoned Ava's Water power and forced her body temperature to drop. I couldn't go too far, or I'd hurt Ava, but I had to push her limits to freeze this demon out.

Nothing happened. The demon only started *laughing*. It was a strange, terrifying laugh that overlaid a demonic voice over top of Ava's.

Obviously, this idea was a bust. Ava had told me most of her powers hadn't worked on the lichen during the Darke Games, either. I tried to create the blue Fire that was Ava's signature, but I couldn't pull it off. Even if I could borrow some of her magic for my own, I couldn't combine two separate elements like she could.

Whatever we were dealing with was a powerful demon. The more time we spent in this room, the more the inferichite drained my powers. We had to outsmart this bastard; otherwise, we weren't getting the key and we were probably going to die.

"Your punishment for theft will be death," the demon warned, before raising another fireball.

I dodged out of the way again, rolling across the ground. "Simultension, Oberi!" I barked. "My energy manipulation with your Spirit powers. Go!"

Oberi knew what I was thinking immediately. Our powers combined, creating a massive spell that latched on to the demon inside of Ava. With Oberi's Spirit magic, I could finally access the same plane the demon operated on. I grabbed a hold of him and yanked his spirit forward, using my Elf magic to manipulate his power.

The demon tore out of Ava's skin, and its smoky, ethereal form swept by me. As it touched me, I saw it for what it was— a dark cloud of black magic, with razors for teeth and claws that were a foot in length. He had no real form here, and he wasn't solid.

"Charlie, we have to banish him," Ava gasped, still sounding out of it. Demon possession was no easy thing to handle, and the demon's temporary hold on Ava had momentarily stunned her, making her unable to fight back.

We weren't witches. We had no spells that could banish a demon to hell the way Marcus could. And I wasn't sure it'd work anyway, not with the way things were going in the afterlife right now. If spirits couldn't make it to the

Blessed Haven, then I didn't think they could make the journey to the Eternal Torment, either.

But there *was* one place outside our realm I could send him.

I grabbed the pocket mirror from my jacket and shoved my arm straight into the middle of the demon's form. A portal opened within the mirror, and a terrifying screech filled the air as the demon was sucked inside, transported straight to the Mirror Realm.

I gasped a breath of relief as I felt the demon's dark magic leave the room. The second he was gone, I threw the mirror to the ground and smashed it with my foot. Glass crunched beneath my shoe, trapping the entity. That fucker was stuck in the Mirror Realm now, and there was no getting out.

Except now I'd just eliminated our way out, too.

"It's like Salvatore to put a curse on the safe," Ava spat. "He didn't trust his men enough to keep the key safe, so he trapped a demon inside to guard it. Asshole."

"Forget about it." Flames licked up the wall, and I coughed as the smoke filled the room. I was getting sicker with each passing second we remained near the inferichite.

"Grab the key, and let's go!" I barked.

Ava was close to the safe, and I heard the clink of metal as she grabbed the vampire key. "Take it," she said, shoving the key into my hand.

I clutched the key tightly. We finally had the vampire key in our grasp—literally. We weren't letting it go for anything.

"Pidge... any mirrored surfaces around?" I asked between coughs.

"None."

We needed to find another way out, because mirrors were the one illusion I always failed to create. I couldn't portal us out on my own.

I pressed my finger to my earpiece. "Mirror portal is a no-go. We need extraction *now*!"

No response came, and I realized our magic must've blasted out the comms. Ava and I were going to have to find another way.

Shouts came from down the hall. Salvatore was coming. We didn't have time to think about it.

"We're taking the windows," I decided. I pulled Ava upward and cradled her in my arms. I took off running out of the room, smoke from Ava's Fire billowing behind us.

"Straight ahead, at the end of the hall," Ava instructed.

Footsteps sounded behind us as Salvatore's men pursued us. Oberi galloped ahead, while I focused all my energy on creating an illusion. A harness wrapped around my legs, becoming solid in response to my thoughts. Another harness securely attached Ava to my front, so that he was straddling me.

Ready? Oberi warned. *One... two... three!*

The sound of shattering glass filled the hall as Oberi smashed through the window. Immediately, her shifting magic swelled through the bond, and she became a phoenix.

"Now!" Ava shouted. She turned her head into my shoulder, squeezing me tightly.

I jumped through the window, and for a moment, we were free-falling, nearly toppling in slow motion through the sky. I turned in mid-air, and a grappling hook appeared from my illusion, shooting upward until it snagged on the top of the building. A long rope connected us to the side of The Devil's City, and we went swinging back in the direction of the building like a pendulum. I braced my feet against the side of the building and kicked off again. We repelled downward at a rapid pace, leaving the vampires behind us.

Ava drew away from my chest and turned her gaze upward. "I don't get it. Salvatore's men aren't following us. Where'd they go—?"

Ava barely got the question out before a massive explosion detonated overhead. The blast rocked the whole building, and shattered glass fell to the city streets. A scream echoed through the air, coming closer, until it was gone a second later, the sound fading below us. Someone had *thrown a vampire out of the building*.

I dared to smirk in satisfaction. "Well, that answers your question. I guess Danny isn't so bad after all."

Ava's arms wrapped tighter around my neck, and she let out a ragged breath as we continued repelling off the side of the building. "It's hot, isn't it? Escaping with you— the key in our hands."

"Hot as fuck," I growled.

Then, Ava and I were kissing. It wasn't just *kissing*. It was a full-on, hot make-out session on the side of a skyscraper. Her tongue rolled over mine, and her hands moved downward to cup my ass. My stomach tingled in my abdomen as the thrill of the free-fall ignited a more intense desire for her. We'd fucking did it, and there was nothing more of a turn-on than pulling off a heist and getting away with my pidge in my arms.

I was born for it.

The ground came near, and Ava and I were forced to draw away from each other to catch our breath. I slowed our descent, and I landed softly on the sidewalk. Oberi landed beside us and shifted back into a unicorn. The street was deserted, because everyone had fled when the explosions started going off.

I undid the harness and placed Ava on Oberi's back. The key was still clutched tightly in my hand. "All we have to do is get to your car."

It should be this way. Come on, Oberi said.

She turned and started galloping down the street. I took off running after her.

I only took a few steps before something heavy came down on me. All my energy siphoned out of me in an instant, and I sagged under its weight. I swiped my elbows out to shove the thing off me, but it moved with me, like some sort of heavy-weight net. The nausea that hit me told me it contained inferichite, like tiny crystals had been embedded up and down the fabric. I tried to run, but I tripped over the net and crashed hard into the pavement. The inferichite touched my skin, siphoning all the strength I had left.

Footsteps sounded behind me— dozens, by the sound of it. Oberi was already several paces ahead, and I knew if she came back for me, she'd be caught.

We were already spent from the inferichite we'd faced earlier. If Salvatore didn't have another net for Oberi and Ava, the vamps would still take them out.

I said I wasn't letting this key go for anything, but I guess I was wrong. I knew at that moment that I'd sacrifice this key for Ava.

"Run!" I screamed.

"I'm not leaving you!" Ava shouted back.

"You have to, pidge!" I yelled. Then I turned my thoughts inward, and I spoke directly to Oberi. *You get her out of here, no matter what. I don't care what these keys mean to the rest of humanity or the afterlife. Nothing is worth giving up my pidge. Keep her safe, Oberi.*

I will, Oberi promised. I could feel the sinking in her gut through our bond. The last thing she wanted to do was leave me behind, but Ava's safety was a priority above all else— for both of us.

Her response didn't surprise me in the slightest. Turns out Oberi was a villain as much as the rest of us. She fled, leaving me behind.

"No!" Ava wailed. Her fists pounded against Oberi's side, begging her to fight the vampires to save my life.

It was already too late. The vampires caught up to me, and Oberi had disappeared around the side of the building. Ava's protests echoed down the street, but nothing she said could make Oberi turn back.

Vampires surrounded me at all angles. One of them pressed a heavy foot to my back so that I couldn't stand. I lay sprawled on the sidewalk face-down, the inferichite net over top of me.

Then came the slow, confident footsteps of a man who thought he knew it all, and the brush of silk fabric from his tailored suit. I already knew who it had to be— Salvatore Bianchi.

Salvatore gave a cold laugh. "I thought you might try to steal from me, *Prince Charles*. I didn't think you'd get all the way to my safe, though. I thought for sure that the inferichite cage would trap you for good, *if* you managed to make it that far."

"You were expecting us this whole time," I rasped beneath the heavy boot of one of Salvatore's vamps.

He gave a chilling laugh. "Of course. Who do you think hired the Dollmaker to capture you? A foolish mistake on my part, unfortunately, as he went rogue and targeted only *one* of you. But perhaps it all worked for the best in the end."

I gritted my teeth. This bastard had been responsible for Kallie getting hurt. He'd been working with Valen, probably for years, giving him compulsion tools to use on women in exchange for the Dollmaker doing his dirty work. He was a merciless fucker. "Why try to catch me? Why not just kill me, and eliminate the threat?"

"And let all your power go to waste?" he scoffed.

Salvatore squatted down to my level, like he and I were old friends having a chat. His skin didn't sizzle in the sun, so he must've had some power to protect himself from it.

"Ophio Taurus used you and your friends to make himself all-powerful," Salvatore said. "If I'm to go up against him properly, I need power like his. I've already been obtaining my own inferichite for a while now, biding my time until I could use it against a demigod... or *two*."

He laughed greedily as he turned to his men. "Go after the girl. Don't let her get away."

Most of the vampires left, racing around the side of the building at superhuman speed. Only two remained, along with Salvatore. I prayed to all the ancestors and the gods that Ava was already gone.

"You leave her alone!" I screamed. I struggled against the vampire holding me down, but the inferichite prevented me from siphoning his strength.

Salvatore chuckled, like he found this amusing. "You aren't calling the shots anymore, Charles— or Charlie, is it? From now on, you work for me. I believe this is *mine*."

He leaned down and snatched the vampire key straight from my hand. I tried to clutch on tight to it, but with his vampire strength, it was like nothing more than stealing candy from a baby.

Salvatore had caught me. My grandfather said I had to use each problem to my advantage, to think fast on my feet, because according to him there was *always* a way out. It didn't look like I had one here.

"Take him away," Salvatore said, nearly sounding bored as he got to his feet.

The squeal of tires came as a large van pulled up beside the curb. Two security guards grabbed me by the arms and hoisted me upward. I tried to fight them off, but my strength was completely gone. Doors opened, and I was thrown into the back of the van tangled within the inferichite net.

Salvatore walked away, and the van doors slammed, shutting me in. The van lurched forward, and my heart raced as I was driven away from The Devil's City and deeper into the city.

Leaving Charlie in Salvatore's clutches made me sick to my stomach. Worse, actually. I wanted to turn back and slaughter that vampire where he stood. It would only take a single fireball to end his life.

But Oberi wouldn't put me in danger for Charlie's sacrifice. She galloped forward until the sound of tires squealing up ahead met my ears. My car swerved around other vehicles, coming to an abrupt halt in front of me.

Marcus sat in the driver's seat, and Danny and Eddie rode in the back. Marcus flung open the passenger side door, and Oberi charged forward. My hands met the top of the car the same time Oberi shifted into a phoenix beneath me. I used momentum to hoist myself into the passenger seat, and Oberi flew inside to land on my lap. I slammed the door shut.

I glanced back in the direction we came to see a blur of vampires racing toward us. "Drive!"

Marcus stepped on the gas so hard that Rishi was thrown into the back seat. The streets of Chicago were crowded with vehicles, but Marcus swerved into oncoming traffic and dodged around the cars to get away as fast as possible. Tires squealed as he turned sharp corners. He drove up on the sidewalk and honked at pedestrians, who scattered out of the way— anything to get away from Salvatore's men.

Marcus was practically hyperventilating. "Fuck, we saw everything! He got *Charlie*! We've failed. They're going to kill him. We have to go back for him!"

I shot another glance in the rearview mirror. The vampires were gaining on us. "We can't go back for him if we're dead!"

I grabbed the wheel and yanked it to the side before Marcus could smash straight into an oncoming delivery truck.

"We have to go back to Ilamanthe," Danny argued. "We don't know where Salvatore's taking Charlie, and if we want to face him properly, we'll need an army of Elves to do it. I say we go back, get as many guards as we can, and rain terror upon Salvatore Bianchi."

"Marcus, take a right up here!" Eddie barked. "The only way back to Ilamanthe is through the Scarlet Grand. We're almost there!"

Marcus' hands shook on the steering wheel. I shot another glance behind us, and panic sent my heart hammering. We still hadn't lost Salvatore's vampires, and they'd catch up to us if we kept dicking around.

Marcus' features went paper white. He floored the pedal just as one of the vamps reached us. A *thud* sounded overhead as the vampire jumped on top of the car. We went tearing around another street corner, and the vampire flew off the vehicle and went rolling into the road. Marcus raced into the parking garage beneath the Scarlet Grand.

Along the outer edge of the parking garage were reflective surfaces. Eddie shoved himself over the middle console, holding a hand straight outward. "Faster!" he yelled.

The wall in front of us shimmered, and Marcus drove us straight into it. For a moment, I witnessed the darkness of the Mirror Realm around us as Eddie used his magic to portal us across dimensions. Then the palace gardens appeared, and we emerged on the other side.

Marcus slammed on the breaks. He yanked the car to the side, spinning it around until the back end smashed into a nearby fountain. We came to an abrupt halt.

Oberi shook her feathers from my lap. *That was a bit of a rough landing.*

Eddie gasped a breath. "We lost them!"

"Thank fuck," Danny grumbled.

Marcus whirled on me. "How could you, Ava? Charlie would never leave you. *Never!* Now Salvatore has Charlie *and* the vampire key. We accomplished *nothing!*"

"You know what Emperor Cassiel says," I told him bluntly. "Turn a problem into a solution. Mama, Ez, and Kallie should be back already. Get me my chair. We need to see the Emperor."

Marcus kicked open his door, and he came back several moments later with my wheelchair. Eldin, my guard, was with him. She'd already been outside the gardens waiting for us. Marcus crossed his arms and glowered at me as I situated myself in my chair. Oberi perched herself on the armrest.

"*I* won't be the one breaking the news," Marcus grumbled as he, Eddie, and

Danny followed behind me. "The Emperor is going to be furious with us for losing his grandson."

"Leave the explanations to me," I said firmly.

We reached the throne room, and two guards standing at the doors opened them. Emperor Cassiel lounged on his throne with a broad smile on his face.

And beside him sat Charlie, who was beaming from ear to ear. My heart lifted at the sight of my husband. Everything went just as we'd planned.

Charlie and Cassiel were surrounded by the Elvish Associates, who were laughing cheerfully. Alistair held a heavy net and tossed it over Pig, who batted at the ropes playfully. Ivy and Chancey were noticeably missing. I was certain both of them had to be in the hospital.

Marcus' jaw dropped when he saw Charlie there. He rubbed his eyes, like he thought he might be seeing an illusion. "What's going on? Charlie was caught. How is he *here*?"

Emperor Cassiel stood from his throne and reached his arms out wide. "Finally, you've all returned safely. It's wonderful to see you. I trust that you have it, princess?"

I smiled widely. "Charlie promised he wouldn't let you down, and he didn't."

I reached into my pocket and pulled out the vampire key— the *real* one.

Marcus gasped. His gaze darted from the key in my hand to Charlie, then back again. He turned toward the inferichite net Alistair was playing with. "I don't get it. Ava had the vampire key all along? How did Charlie escape?"

Charlie stood, smirking proudly. "Simple. Salvatore never captured me in the first place. The vamps who threw me in the back of the van weren't vampires at all. They were the Elvish Associates in disguise. They used the potion you made with your Uncle Grant to avoid triggering any magical alarms, along with the potion you used in Paris to take on the bank employee's identity. It was a perfect combination. Asa and Aries didn't infiltrate The Devil's City this morning *just* to hack into the security cameras. They were also taking down members of Salvatore's security team, so they could don their identities. Salvatore never knew the men guarding him were really working for *us*, and he believed the inferichite net to be one of his security team's latest toys."

"But what about the key Salvatore took?" Marcus demanded. "We were just down the street when it happened. We *saw* Salvatore take the vampire key from you."

"You saw him take *a* key," I said. "When we got to the vault, I pocketed the real vampire key. I gave Charlie a fake key he'd made with his illusion magic before we ever entered The Devil's City. Once we got outside the building, Asa and Ares threw the net on Charlie, and I pretended to protest as Oberi carried me away, to put on a good show for Salvatore."

"You did a wonderful job. Even I believed it," Charlie said smugly.

"Charlie was only a distraction for Salvatore, so that *you* could get away with the real key," Marcus realized. "Capturing Charlie in the inferichite net was your plan all along! That's so clever."

Danny crossed his arms. "You guys should've told us about this. It isn't okay that you kept this whole other plan from us."

"You didn't need to know everything," Charlie stated. "I did what had to be done. It was what my grandfather would do, and we pulled it off— quite spectacularly, I might add."

Cassiel clapped Charlie on the back proudly. "You got the vampire key, and that's what matters. Now, you have six of the seven Divinity Keys, and all that's left is the Astromancer key. You have all worked very hard, and now it's time to celebrate."

"Time to *part-ay!*" Alistair exclaimed.

I smiled, because after everything we'd been through today, I was relieved that all my friends had made it out alive. I thought a party would really help take the edge off for all of us. We hadn't celebrated a win like this in a long time, and I wanted to let loose at the idea of foiling Salvatore Bianchi's plans. "A party sounds great."

"Go put the key in the royal vault with the others, and enjoy the rest of your night," Cassiel said. "Take the day off tomorrow, too. You've earned it."

Cassiel left the throne room, and the Elvish Associates followed him. Charlie leaned down to pull the inferichite net off Pig's head, then began folding it up.

Danny scowled. "Charlie. Where did you get an inferichite net?"

"I had the Elvish Associates return to Darke Island to dig up what was left of the inferichite buried beneath the Institute's fence," Charlie stated. "The place has been completely abandoned, and the crystals were ours for the taking. I had it made in case we needed to use it against the Warden's demigods. Esther, Deuce, Naya, and Mad Dog won't be able to do anything if they're trapped in this."

Danny huffed. "Whatever. Don't even *think* of getting that thing near me."

"As long as you don't fuck up, you have nothing to worry about." Charlie gave a wry smile.

I pushed my chair between them. "Now, boys. Play nice."

Charlie finished folding the inferichite net and handed it off to Eddie, who left the room to store it elsewhere. "There's no problem here. Danny and I are *just fine.*"

Just fine, my ass. But Danny *did* help us get out of The Devil's City, and for that, I'd be forever grateful.

My friends and I left the throne room, and my guard Eldin followed us to the royal vault. We left the vampire key with the others, and then sealed the vault with iron-clad wards that even the other demigods couldn't break through. We knew the keys would be safe there, for as long as they remained.

We returned to our quarters, where we found the rest of our friends. Kallie sat on the couch wrapped in a blanket, sipping tea Abigail had brewed. Kallie looked much better than she had hours ago. She was talking with Ez and Opal, who were cuddled on a chair beside her. She still seemed pale, but Ez and Mama had healed the rest of her injuries.

I wanted to check in on her. "Hey," I greeted, and I came up beside her. "How are you?"

Kallie forced a smile. "I'm... I'm here."

That wasn't the best answer, but it also wasn't the worst. "I didn't think they'd let you out of the hospital yet."

"They didn't want to," Kallie said. "My mom and dad were there. They stayed at my side every second. I insisted I was fine, but they didn't want to let me out of their sight. I snuck out when I had the chance and came here. I don't want anyone fretting over me."

"I wouldn't, either." I reached out my hand and laid it on Kallie's. I was pretending to give a friendly gesture, but really, my Spirit abilities were reading her body. Everything was back to normal, like she'd never been hurt at all, and she could walk again, even though she was still tired. Mama had made sure to patch her up as good as new. Now the mental healing began.

"I really am fine, Ava," Kallie said. "Honest."

She wouldn't be swearing to me she was okay if she really *was*, which meant she was struggling with all this. But she'd come to me if she needed me, so I backed off. We didn't need to talk about the Dollmaker and make her relive everything that had happened.

I went to the other side of the party. Tahoma lay beside the couch, watching Sprigs climb a plant in the corner. Alette fluttered around Sprigs and tried to get him to play.

Ez got up from his spot on the couch and walked over to me. "We took care of Kallie," he promised. "She went through a tough thing, but she'll pull through it."

"Her mind's all fucked up," I whispered. I couldn't imagine the mental anguish Kallie was going through, even in a safe place surrounded by all her friends. After John had attacked me, it'd been all I was able to think about for months afterward. I was sure she couldn't get the Dollmaker out of her head.

"I know. It's gonna be like that for a while," Ez said. "But there's nothing our magic can do about that, and she was literally just attacked by a serial killer this morning. She's barely had any time to process. She needs this party, to get her mind off things and make her feel normal."

I hoped so. I really wanted this party to help. It was the reason we were doing this.

Kallie wasn't the only one acting off. Chancey sat in a chair near the window, staring out over the city. I think he'd just left the hospital wing. I noticed bandages poking out from the collar of his t-shirt. I think his chest and back were all wrapped up from where Ivy had cut off his wing. His tea was still steaming in his hand, and it didn't look like he'd taken a sip. Ivy leaned against Chancey and traced lines over his arm, though neither of them said anything. I thought Ivy was trying to cheer Chancey up, but Chancey appeared distant... or not even there at all.

"Did you do it?" Opal asked as she came up to me. "Did you pull it off?"

"We did," I said weakly. "Cassiel says we should celebrate."

Alistair approached the coffee table and touched the hot tea pot. "We can't celebrate with *tea*. Where's the booze?"

"I'll have the servants bring something," Abigail offered.

About a half an hour later, Eldin stood guard at the door while servants brought in pizzas with all kinds of topping combinations. They wheeled in a cart full of liquor, and Alistair began smelling the bottles, pouring shots when he found what he liked. Danny turned on music that shook the room, then grabbed one of Oberi's favorite tennis balls and threw it. She hopped off my chair and shifted into a husky, chasing after it.

Marcus caught the ball after a few bounces, then held it out of Oberi's reach while he jumped for it. "What is it, Oberi?" Marcus teased. "Oh, you want this? You're such a good boy."

Who are you calling a good boy? Oberi grumbled. *Give me the ball, you fool!*

Marcus obviously hadn't heard the insult. "Fetch!"

Marcus threw the ball, and Oberi tore across the room after it. I laughed as they played together.

Oberi caught the ball in his mouth. You're *the good boy,* he said, wagging his tail.

"Marcus, come over here," Kallie ordered. "I want to hear all about the mission."

Marcus obeyed her like a puppy dog and plopped onto the couch beside her. He draped an arm over the back of the couch casually and began to fill her in on all the details.

"I don't know, Oberi," I joked as he dropped the ball in my lap. I stroked the top of his head. "You and Marcus might have more in common than you think."

Oberi growled at me. *I take offense. Now throw the ball, please.*

"Oh, you said please?" I laughed. "Who's a good boy now?"

I threw the ball, and Oberi chased after it. He must've been upset that I called him a good boy, because he brought the ball back to Charlie instead. Charlie tossed the ball around and played with Oberi while I went to grab a slice of pizza.

Marcus and Kallie chatted from the couch. "Yeah, it was pretty intense," Marcus bragged. "I must've taken out at least a dozen vampires by myself. Chopped one's head off with a cleaver."

For once, Marcus wasn't exaggerating. Kallie's eyes sparkled as she stared up at him. Her eyes locked on him like he was the grandest thing she'd ever seen, looking at him in a way no one else had before.

Alistair passed drinks around, and the party got louder as everyone started to loosen up. I noticed Charlie had a drink in his hand. I was curious about that because we'd agreed we wouldn't drink anymore. But he was laughing as he played fetch with Oberi. It was nice to see the two of them having a good time, so I just let it go.

Alistair downed shots like they were candy, and it didn't take long before the alcohol hit him. He climbed up on the table and began shaking his ass, while Pig and Rishi danced around him. He placed his cane upright in front of himself, squatting down like he was straddling a stripper pole. He stumbled to the side and almost knocked over the teapot.

"Be careful, sir," Abigail scolded. She quickly grabbed the tray of tea from the table and wheeled across the room to get it away from Alistair.

"Take it off!" I called with a laugh.

"You like that?" Alistair wiggled his eyebrows. "I've got more where that came from."

Alistair ripped his shirt off and spun it around his head. I snickered and rolled my eyes.

Danny cupped his hands over his mouth and yelled, "Save it for the bedroom!"

"I would, but I don't see my man anywhere," Alistair grumbled. "Where's Eddie?"

Come to think of it, I hadn't seen Eddie since Charlie sent him out of the throne room with the inferichite net. He'd left shortly after Cassiel, so I could only assume the Emperor had given him another errand.

"Who needs Eddie?" Ivy piped up. "I'll dance with you!"

Ivy hopped up on the table to show Alistair some moves. Danny drank vodka straight from the bottle and twirled around the two of them. He must've been halfway through the bottle already and was stumbling a bit. I knew it took a lot to get a vampire drunk, but damn... he was going to wake up with one hell of a headache in the morning.

I was starting to get a little concerned about Danny's drinking habits. He was drunk whenever he got a spare moment, and never failed to reach for a bottle, even on days when there wasn't a celebration going on. I felt like he was hiding something. I wanted to talk to him about it, but I wasn't that close to him, at least not yet, so I decided not to bring it up.

Ivy made their way over to Chancey, circling their hips in his lap. Chancey glanced at Ivy, but his eyes were empty. He looked back out the window, appearing haunted. Ivy was trying to cheer him up, but it certainly wasn't working. Chancey just needed some time.

"Chance, you good?" Ivy whispered, looking concerned.

Chancey's reply was deadened as he said hoarsely, "Yeah, Ives. I'm... I'm good."

Ivy frowned, and tears formed in their eyes at Chancey's response. "Okay. I'll... I'll give you some space."

Ivy got off Chancey's lap and headed to a corner of the room. They stood there clasping one arm, looking at the floor and biting their lip.

I couldn't let Ivy feel this way. What had happened to Chancey was horrible, but it wasn't their fault. They'd done what they had to do to save Chancey's life. Chancey's wing was gone, but at least he was still here with us. If I couldn't help my angel friend, I at least needed to reach out to Ivy, and try to help them feel better.

"Over here, Ivy!" I called, trying to get their attention. "I need a celebratory lap dance."

Ivy looked up. "Gladly, sweet thing." Ivy headed my way, then twirled around and shimmied on my lap. Ivy's smile slightly lifted as I shook my boobs against their shoulder, and we laughed together.

This felt like fun. It was just a simple college party, something we all needed after the stress of the heist.

Ivy shot a glance over their shoulder. When they caught sight of Charlie, they glowered. They seemed to be expecting a fight.

I realized Ivy was waiting to get into it with Charlie, so they could chew him out about what happened in The Devil's City. Ivy was certainly pissed off that Charlie had sent him off the mission and back to Ilamanthe. It had taken away Ivy's chance to get back at Salvatore, and that was something Ivy couldn't forgive. Charlie plopped into an empty chair and devoured a slice of pizza, completely ignoring Ivy altogether.

Ugh. I could cut the tension in here with a knife. This was supposed to be *fun*. I was worried about my friends, and concerned this party wasn't giving them what they needed. Maybe this party was a mistake. Half the participants didn't seem like they wanted to be here. We were trying so hard to be happy, but maybe what we'd gone through to get the vampire key wasn't worth it. I didn't want any of my friends to suffer because of Charlie's destiny to unite the keys, and they were suffering now. We'd claimed the vampire key, but we'd had to sacrifice a lot to get it. If this party wasn't at least serving as a good distraction from all the bullshit we had to go through today, it might as well not be happening.

"Charlie, come on, get up and dance," I begged, and Ivy got off my lap. "We're supposed to be having a good time!"

Charlie licked the grease off his fingers. He wore a devilish look as he said, "You want a *real* party? Because this shit is boring. Let me spice it up."

Charlie spread his arms outward, and his Air magic pushed all the furniture to the walls. Alistair stumbled and nearly fell off the coffee table, but he caught himself. Kallie clung to the couch, looking annoyed.

Charlie lifted his hands, and an illusion formed in the middle of the room. A stage with a stripper pole in the center appeared, and a multi-colored disco ball emerged from the ceiling. Confetti rained down on us. I reached up to pull a piece of shimmering gold confetti from my hair. Charlie's illusion magic was getting *very* good. Whatever he desired, it became real.

Charlie smirked as he stepped onto the platform. He threw his jacket aside, along with the shirt underneath. A black tie appeared around his neck from his illusion magic. Fuck, I was getting all hot and bothered already. Those abs were to die for, and that tie was killing me. He danced so arrogantly, and it turned me the fuck on.

My husband knew exactly what I wanted, and he was so thrilled with the work we'd done that he was willing to give it *all* to me. That's what I loved about Charlie. He knew me so well.

"Now *this* is a party!" I cheered. "Give it all to me, baby!"

"Where are the dollar bills?" Ez cracked.

Along the edge of the stage, stacks of cash appeared. Ez and Opal each grabbed a stack and started tossing the bills at Charlie, laughing it up. Tahoma hooked an antler under a stack of cash, then tossed it in the air. Abigail blushed and averted her eyes.

Ez cupped his hands around his mouth. "Make it rain!"

My husband spun around the pole, then thrust his hips forward. Ah, fuck. I thought I might come right here. It did *not* seem appropriate for the others to be watching, but I couldn't say I wasn't getting a thrill over him being an exhibitionist.

Ivy noticed I was drooling over Charlie and shot a disgusted look at the stage. Look, if Ivy didn't find my man sexy, then that was on them. I'd been waiting for the day I got Charlie on a pole without complaining, and I wasn't going to let anyone ruin it. I laughed as I watched Charlie clap his hands, yank at his tie, and swagger across the stage, snapping his fingers to the music. He gave a slide and then a turn, pointing his fingers to the crowd.

Danny came up beside me and crossed his arms. "Charlie's going through great lengths to prove he runs this party, huh?"

Giggles bubbled past my lips as I watched Charlie shake it. He was being so silly. I'd never seen my husband act like such a spectacle. Usually he clung to the wall and tried to stay out of sight, and now, he was trying to be the center of attention. I found it adorable he was finally coming out of his shell. "It's harmless. He's just having fun!"

Danny shrugged. "Guess I never thought Charlie was the type to make an ass out of himself."

"Oh, screw you," I snapped. "We're here to have a good time. If you aren't, go get wasted somewhere else."

"*Psh.* Cool." Danny walked away, and I scowled. We were here to celebrate getting the vampire key. This wasn't some dick-measuring contest between Danny and Charlie.

And if it was, I was going to get some dick myself.

"I want a lap dance!" I called over the pumping base.

Charlie jumped down from the stage, then leaned over me as he whispered in my ear. "You looking for a private room, lady?"

My voice came out breathlessly. "Right here's just fine."

Charlie sat in my lap and moved his hips over me. I whimpered involuntarily. Fuck, I wanted him so badly right now. I didn't care *why* he thought he needed to give the room a strip tease. If he wanted to show everyone who was boss, fine. We could take this to the bedroom, and he could take charge there. I would love every moment of it. He was the king of this castle, and I was his bitch.

"You're certainly taking control," I whispered, and I bit his ear.

"Well, this is *my* party. I own this city," Charlie growled. "I just want to make sure everyone here knows it."

Alistair and Oberi hopped up on the platform and danced to the music. Pig and Rishi circled the stage, batting the cash off the edge. Tahoma went over to the floor-to-ceiling mirror on the wall and started dancing in front of it while making funny faces at his reflection.

I heard a slurping noise and looked over to see Kallie and Marcus were all over each other. They seemed to forget anyone else was in the room as their tongues slid inside each other's mouths. Kallie grabbed Marcus' curls and yanked on them. He moaned, then dragged Kallie onto his lap.

I was glad they were having fun, but jeez, guys, points for enthusiasm.

"Get a room!" Danny joked.

"If you need some condoms, I have some extra in my stash," Alistair teased.

Kallie pulled her mouth away from Marcus' and turned up her nose. "We don't *use* condoms."

"You guys aren't using protection?" I asked, floundering in my chair.

Marcus shrugged. "We didn't this morning, or last night. Pull-out's good enough for us."

Charlie frowned, and he got off my lap to tower over them. "That's not very effective. You guys can't be getting pregnant right now. There's a lot at stake. You should take the birth control I take, Marcus. It's one dose every three months. It's worked just fine for me and Ava."

"Sure, okay. I'll look into it tomorrow," Marcus said nonchalantly, like he wasn't taking him seriously.

Alistair tossed Marcus a condom, and it whacked him in the face. "Then you're going to need these tonight!"

Our friends roared in laughter.

All this talk of sex was making me hot and bothered. Charlie turned around so I could run my hands over his abs. A thrill traveled through my abdomen as my gaze lingered on his belt buckle. Gods damn, if we didn't get alone soon, I was going to end up blowing him in front of everybody, and I wouldn't care who watched, either.

"Charlie, I'm tired," I said quickly.

He leaned down, so he could hear me over the music. "What was that, pidge?"

I grabbed the tie around his neck. "I said, *If you don't take me back to our room right now, tie me up, and fuck me like there's no tomorrow, I'm going to scream until the guards come running.*"

Charlie smirked. "Oh, you'll be screaming, all right."

He scooped me up in his arms, and I giggled happily. I waved to the others. "Welp, it's been a long day. We're going to sleep!"

Alistair threw his head back in laughter. "Yeah. *Sleep.* You two just committed a crime, so we all know what *that* means."

Ivy rolled their eyes and said nastily, "For sure. Every time you guys do something bad, you two jump right into bed."

I beamed. "I can't help it if it turns me on to be bad. Kink shaming is for losers who aren't getting any, so enjoy *your* night, Ivy."

Ivy's mouth dropped open in shock. Okay, maybe that comment was kind of mean. After all, Ivy certainly wasn't getting laid tonight after what had happened with Chancey, but they weren't the only one who had a smart mouth. If Ivy wanted to be mean, I could play, too.

I smiled as I stared up at Charlie. He carried me to our bedroom and used his Air magic to wheel my chair in behind us. He locked the door, and music boomed loudly through the walls.

Charlie set me on the bed and unzipped my jacket. My nipples hardened at his touch. He tossed that aside and pulled my cami over my shirt, exposing my breasts. He began kissing down my neck, until his lips met my nipple and he pulled it into his mouth. He was rough, biting down just a little, and I loved every fucking second of it.

"More," I rasped, but Charlie drew away, teasing me.

My breaths grew shallow as I watched him undo the tie around his neck. I held out my wrists, wanting nothing more than to become a slave to him. We never got a chance to finish what we started when we were repelling down the side of that skyscraper, and I couldn't think of anything hotter than fucking my partner in crime after pulling off the greatest heist of the century.

"Fuck me, Charlie," I begged.

He smiled as he wrapped the tie around my wrists and secured it tightly. "You've been a bad girl today. You need to be punished, but *I* get to decide when that happens."

Charlie guided my arms above my head, and like a good girl, I kept them there. Charlie drew my pants down my legs, then slipped two fingers inside of me while he kissed my stomach. Hot damn, his lips on my belly were intoxicating. I wanted him to kiss me like this forever.

I watched in delight as he lowered his zipper and freed his cock. He was already hard and ready for me. He didn't bother taking his pants all the way off, because he was in such a hurry to take me. Charlie circled my clit with his thumb a few more times, until he was satisfied with my wetness. Desire flashed in his features as he positioned himself above me.

Then he filled me up, and oh, my fucking ancestors. My eyes rolled back, and I gasped as he moved over me. Charlie's lips locked on mine, and we started making out until sweat was dripping down our bodies. I placed my tied wrists around his neck, dragging him closer. Heat rose to my skin, but I felt some of that heat subside as Charlie siphoned my magic so he could tolerate my Fire. He moaned and squeezed his eyes tightly shut. Passion swelled through the bond.

"Charlie, come on me," I begged.

Charlie gasped at the suggestion, like there was nothing more he wanted to do. He pulled out of me and began pumping his cock. I watched him, feeling like there was no better sight in the world.

"Fuck, pidge," Charlie moaned, emptying himself all over my breasts.

I laughed deliriously as his essence spread over me, feeling high on life. "That was so fucking hot."

He smirked proudly. "Yeah? Well it's not over yet, my love."

Charlie ducked his head. He hooked my knees over his shoulders and began pleasuring me with his tongue. Air magic swirled around my nipples, gratifying me in a way that left me breathless as he kissed the deepest parts of me.

The high of Charlie's orgasm spilled into my own. I shoved my fingers into Charlie's hair and yanked hard on the strands as passion exploded through my body. Stars lit up behind my lids, and I screamed my delight over the sound of the music.

Charlie licked his lips. "How was that, pidge?"

I melted into the mattress. "You broke into my vault, and I liked what you took. Although, you left a lot of evidence behind, and that's going to get you in trouble. Maybe next time *I* can arrest *you*."

"I don't think so. You're never going to get cuffs on me. Let's get you cleaned up and into bed."

I scowled. "I don't want to," I said in a bratty way.

He cocked an eyebrow. "I wasn't asking. You need to get ready for bed. *Now*."

That turned me on even more. I liked it when he bossed me around like that.

I reached for his dick but he yanked the tie around my wrist, stopping me. "What did I say?"

I relaxed into the mattress. "Okay. You win."

Charlie undid the tie around my wrists, and he carried me to our private bathroom to help me clean up. By the time we cuddled beneath the sheets, we were so exhausted that we fell asleep immediately.

When I woke the next morning, I was snuggled in Charlie's arms. He'd had a few drinks last night and was completely out of it. He didn't even notice when I stirred, but simply groaned and rolled over. I, on the other hand, had slept *great*.

Emperor Cassiel had said we should take the day off, so I was going to spend it doing what I loved best— being pampered. I *really* needed to get my nails done, and I expected to spend the entire day at the spa.

I pulled myself out of bed and into my chair. I got dressed, then wheeled out into the main room. The stripper platform was still there from last night. Confetti and dollar bills littered the floor, along with empty liquor bottles. I wasn't sure what had happened after Charlie and I went back to our room, but it looked like things had gotten pretty wild. Pieces of a broken vase scattered the floor, and several pieces of pizza were stuck to the ceiling.

Ez and Opal were snuggled up on one of the couches, and Tahoma was passed out on the floor beside them. Alistair lay slumped over the armrest of one of the chairs, his mouth hanging open as he snored.

Danny was face-down on the ground, clutching an empty liquor bottle. Vampires didn't need to sleep, but it appeared Danny had enough liquor to knock him out cold.

Ivy and Chancey were tangled up on the other couch, Ivy curled in Chancey's arms. Oberi was in unicorn form sprawled across the stage, her collection of hats scattered around her.

Marcus and Kallie were notably missing. I was certain that meant they'd snuck off to one of their rooms to fuck before the party ended. Good for them, I guess.

Abigail was the only person who was awake. She carefully wheeled between people while she quietly placed trash into a garbage bag, trying not to wake them. In the corner, Sprigs' plant had been knocked over, and a mound of dirt had fallen out of the pot. Sprigs lay on Alette's back, and both of them were sleeping. Abigail wheeled to the corner and tried to lift the plant upright, but she struggled to bend far enough in her chair.

"You don't have to do that," I offered.

Abigail jumped in her chair and turned to me. "Your highness. I was hoping to have this cleaned up before you awoke."

I waved a hand nonchalantly. "I'm not worried about it. I have the day off, which means you should, too. I'm headed to the Ladies' Court to get my nails done. Would you like to join me?"

She gave another bow. "If your highness requests it, then it would be my pleasure."

"It would be nice to have some company," I said.

Abigail and I left the room. Eldin was still stationed at the door, and she followed at a close distance as we navigated the halls.

"So, things got pretty crazy last night?" I asked Abigail.

"I suppose so," she admitted with a giggle. "It was quite fun. I'm not usually invited to parties like that. It was my first."

"Really?" I asked. "Well, you're invited to *our* parties any time you want."

Around the corner, I heard a familiar voice. "Eddie, can I have a word?"

It was good to hear Eddie's name. We hadn't seen him since he left the throne room last night, and he'd never shown up for the party.

"Of course, my Emperor," Eddie replied. "What may I help you with?"

I paused. Both of them sounded pretty serious. They hadn't seen us, since we were still hidden behind the wall.

"It is regarding the intel we received last night," Cassiel stated. "Before you return to Charlie's quarters, I must make a request. You cannot tell the prince what we discuss."

I felt the blood drain from my face, and I instantly brought my wheels to a halt. Cassiel was hiding something from Charlie? That couldn't be right.

I signaled for Abigail and Eldin to stop. I slowly inched my chair forward until I could peer around the corner. Eddie seemed nervous as Cassiel gestured for him to come closer. He kept his voice low, but I was close enough to hear.

"I have thought long and hard about what we discovered last night, and I have concluded that it is best if Charlie doesn't know," Cassiel whispered. "He doesn't need to go to that awful place and experience what's happening."

"Forgive me, Emperor, but I do not understand," Eddie said. "Shouldn't the prince be made aware of this development? He should know what we found northwest of Flagstaff."

Cassiel dropped his head. "In time, he will know, once matters have settled. But for now, I wish to spare him and the others the turmoil. None of our people need to witness such suffering. We cannot send our soldiers there, as there's nothing that can be done. You know as well as I that these people cannot be saved. I give you this order as Emperor, Eddie. You must not tell Charlie that we found the Main Facility."

I nearly fell out of my chair. I couldn't have heard him right. My heart hammered as I listened closer.

"You will not speak of any of this to anyone," Cassiel ordered. "You will not mention the Main Facility at all or what has happened there. You won't tell Charlie or the others that the wards have fallen, nor will you discuss anything regarding the facility's location. Do you understand?"

"Yes, sire," Eddie said in a small voice. "I understand completely."

"Very good," Cassiel replied, holding his head high. "You may resume your duties."

Cassiel crossed his hands, then turned and walked off in the opposite direction. Eddie watched him go, but the moment he was out of sight, his shoulders sagged. He steadied himself against the wall for support.

I tore my gaze off him, though I swayed in my chair. I couldn't make sense of which way was up or down. The Warden's protective wards had fallen. The Emperor had found where the rest of the Elves were being held, yet he was just going to *leave* them there? He wasn't going to storm into the Main Facility and end the Elvish camps for good? I couldn't fathom the Emperor would be so heartless.

Our conversation from the gardens came back to me, and I recalled what he said about suffering. I believed Cassiel to be a good person, and I understood he had to make the toughest decisions as Emperor. Cassiel probably thought that sending his army to the Main Facility would cost us soldiers we couldn't spare, not when our armies were fighting The Mission on all fronts and barely surviving.

But if he thought he could just leave his people in the hands of the Warden to spare his own soldiers, then he was making the wrong call. I couldn't stand by and let this happen.

I whirled my chair around. "Come," I ordered Abigail and Eldin. "Eddie might not be able to tell the others about this, but we can."

We hurried back to the royal quarters as quickly as we could, and I stormed into the room. "Everybody up! We have matters to discuss."

Danny lifted his head and moaned. "Not with this headache, sweetheart."

"I couldn't give a shit about your hangover," I growled. "There are more pressing matters at hand."

Groans traveled around the room as everyone awoke. They must've noticed the urgency in my tone, because they all sat upright. Charlie heard the commotion and came rushing out of our bedroom, already fully clothed. Kallie and Marcus emerged from Kallie's room in bathrobes, squinting in the morning light.

"What's going on?" Charlie demanded.

"The Mission's wards have fallen. Your grandfather found the Main Facility," I blurted.

Charlie stumbled backward. We'd been waiting for this information for months, and I'd just dropped the news like a bomb. He steadied himself and straightened up. "We have to join the Emperor's Guard and go after the Warden."

"That's the thing," I urged. "Your grandfather isn't going to free the Elves in the camps."

Charlie froze. "What do you mean? We need to gather all our soldiers as soon as possible. If the wards have fallen, then we have an advantage. We need to liberate that camp before the wards are reinstated. What did my grandfather tell you?"

"He told me nothing," I stated bitterly. "In fact, he doesn't want us knowing at all. I overheard him ordering Eddie not to tell us. Eddie must've been with him all night, gathering this intel. That's why he never returned to our quarters. I don't think Cassiel has the soldiers to spare, because he's convinced he can't help the people imprisoned in the Main Facility. He believes they're a lost cause, but I won't settle for that. We have to at least *try* to free them, while we have the chance. Cassiel might not have the manpower, but we do. We're demigods, and we don't need an army to back us up. We can do this for him and free the people the Warden has locked up!"

"Your highness," Eldin protested. It was the first time she'd ever questioned me, as it wasn't within her rank to do so. "Forgive me, but you don't know what you may be walking into. If the Emperor doesn't want you to go, there's probably a good reason. I have to advise that you don't do this."

"You don't understand," I argued. "You don't know Cassiel the way that I do. The things he's said to me... I know the way he thinks. Cassiel has good intentions, but he doesn't want to help because he believes people will always suffer, and that sacrifices must be made for the greater good. He doesn't believe putting his resources into liberating the camp will be worth it, because it's a risk to do so. He'd rather keep his army stationed where they're at near Malovia, to keep The Mission at bay. He believes the victims at the Main Facility have to pay the price for the greater good, but if Ilamanthe is built off of letting these people suffer, then I don't want it. I want to live in a world where we help each other, and these people need us right now. Cassiel isn't even going to try. He's given up, but we won't."

"Then we're going," Charlie decided.

Alistair raised his fists. "Hell yeah. We'll fuck 'em up all right."

Chancey stood. "Ivy and I are in."

"Opal and me, too," Ez volunteered.

Wherever you need me, I will go, Oberi added.

"Princess, it sounded like the Emperor was only trying to protect you," Eldin noted. "Are you sure?"

"He doesn't need to protect us," Charlie insisted. "He thinks we can't handle this, but we proved yesterday that we can. We're better than this, and we're strong enough to take it, because these people need our help."

Marcus turned to Kallie and took her hands. "You don't have to come with. You're not strong enough, not after what happened yesterday. You need to stay here and rest."

Kallie shook her head. "I know you're worried about me, but I can't stay here if all of you are going. I *have* to help."

Marcus frowned, then nodded. "Then stay close to me, pretty girl. When do we leave?"

"Now," I said. "We need to get into the Main Facility before they reinforce the wards and we can't find it anymore. We don't have time to wait."

"How are we getting there?" Danny asked.

"I overheard that the Main Facility is located in Arizona, northwest of Flagstaff. There's nothing else in that part of the United States." I gestured to the large mirror on the wall beside me. "That information should get us close enough that Charlie can portal us from here and through any mirror on the facility's property. Arizona is several hours behind Ilamanthe, so it's still night over there. We can use the darkness to help conceal us."

Danny clapped his hands together. "Excellent, because I'm out of sun potion."

"Everyone get dressed," Charlie ordered. "We leave in two minutes."

Charlie wasn't fucking around. Everyone scrambled to get ready, and they were dressed quickly.

The door to our quarters opened. Eddie sauntered in with a dejected look on his face. He stopped in his tracks as all eyes turned to him.

"Looks like I missed a fun party." He forced a chuckle. He was trying to mask what had happened in the hall, but his tone came out completely flat.

"You don't have to pretend like everything's fine, Eddie," Charlie said, rather harshly. "We know my grandfather found the Main Facility."

Eddie's features paled. "I... I don't know what you're talking about."

Charlie gritted his teeth. "You can't lie to me, Eddie. You're my guard, and I order you to tell me the truth. You should've come to me the moment you found out."

Eddie chose his words carefully. "I don't understand how you learned of this."

"I overheard Cassiel speaking with you in the hall," I told him softly. "It's okay, Eddie. You can talk about it now. We already know."

Eddie took a step back. "I— I'm afraid I can't, princess."

Charlie's voice boomed across the room. "You can, and you *will*. Tell us everything you know, Eddie. That's an order!"

"Hey!" Alistair sneered. "You can't talk to my boyfriend like that."

Charlie gritted his teeth. "He's my guard, and I *own* him. I can talk to him whatever way I please."

The whole room had gone dead quiet as we all stared at Charlie. None of us had ever seen him treat Eddie this way before. Usually, I preferred when Charlie took charge, but this was on a whole different level I didn't like. Eddie was his guard, but he was his own person. He didn't belong to anyone, not even Charlie.

"I'm afraid you misunderstand, sire," Eddie said in a wavering tone. "There is very little I can say right now. What I *can* tell you is that as Emperor, your grandfather's orders supersede your own until *you* become Emperor."

"He's magically bound," I realized. "Charlie, you can't order him to do anything Cassiel doesn't want you to. Eddie's magically bound to you, but more than that, he's bound to the Majestica family, and there's a hierarchy even he has to follow. The magic prevents him from telling you anything Cassiel ordered him not to."

Eddie dropped his gaze. "Regardless of my orders, I do not regret keeping this from you. The Emperor doesn't want you to go, and believe me, you should not."

"Why not?" Charlie demanded.

Eddie twisted his hands together and opened his mouth several times, but he didn't answer.

"WHY NOT?!" Charlie raged, taking several steps forward.

I caught Charlie by the wrist. "Charlie, *stop*. He can't answer you, even if he wanted to. Emperor Cassiel ordered him not to speak of this. I think he's said all he possibly can."

Charlie got a disgusted look on his face. "If my grandfather has more authority over my guard than I do, how can I trust you, Eddie? What else has my grandfather told you to keep from me?"

"Nothing," Eddie insisted. "That I *can* tell you, Charlie. You must believe me. And you have to trust me when I say you don't want to go to the place you seek. You will only find—"

Eddie gagged, like he'd said too much and he was choking on his own tongue. Cassiel's orders prevented him from saying anything more.

"I guess we won't know until we go there," Charlie stated smugly. "Come on. We're leaving."

Charlie stepped up to the mirror on the wall, and the surface began to ripple as he created a portal. Oberi shifted into husky form and stood dutifully beside him, and Rishi followed. Everyone else gathered around the mirror.

Eddie hung back. "I do not wish to come, sire."

"Too bad," Charlie snapped. "You're coming. That's an order."

I turned to Abigail and Eldin. "You two stay behind. Buy us some time in case Cassiel comes looking for us. Don't tell him where we've gone."

I shot a glance at my brother's Familiar. The peryton was so big and an easy target. Ez wasn't going to stay behind even if I asked, but at least without Tahoma along, Ez wouldn't get hurt if his Familiar was targeted. Pig shrank back toward Tahoma.

"Pig and Tahoma will stay back, too," I said.

At that, I turned to the portal and followed Charlie through. The rest of my friends trailed behind.

Darkness enveloped me at all angles. All around me, my friends appeared to be floating in empty space. The light from endless mirrors flickered by us, and in the distance, a ghostly shriek echoed through the vast emptiness. We were inside the Mirror Realm, which I had become so accustomed to, but the sensation of passing through it usually only lasted a split-second.

Moments passed, and nothing changed.

Panic swelled inside of me. "Charlie!" I cried.

I had the horrifying thought that the Warden must be pushing against Charlie's magic, or that the Main Facility's wards had already been reinstated. We could become trapped here in the Mirror Realm, wasting away for eternity, unless Charlie found us a way out *now*.

All around me, my friends' terrified faces reflected off of spinning mirrors, until I couldn't make sense of what was solid and what was reflection. They started screaming in horror, their voices melting together into a sickening symphony.

"Hang on!" Charlie yelled. His voice seemed to echo distantly. "I'm finding a reflective surface to portal out of!"

One by one, my friends began to disappear. I couldn't make sense of where they'd gone.

Shit, shit, *shit*! We were going to be trapped in here!

"*Charlie!*" I screamed, crying out my last hope.

The shimmering ripple of a broken mirror with jagged edges appeared in front of me. Hands reached through the mirror and grabbed my arms and my chair. I screamed in terror as I was pulled through the portal.

Gravity shifted, and Charlie used his Air magic to steady me. My wheels landed on solid ground, though I was momentarily disoriented. I gasped for breath and looked around to see that all my friends had made it. I put a hand to my chest, trying to calm my raging heart.

As my balance returned, I found that we were in a small, empty bedroom. Thin curtains covered a miniscule window, and I could see that it was dark outside. We stood in a nice building that appeared newly built, and the temperature was comfortable. It didn't seem like the kind of place the Warden would hold prisoners. I assumed this was where the guards stayed... only, there was no one here.

A cot with no bedding stood in the corner, along with a vacant desk on the other side of the room. The only other item nearby was a large mirror that had been toppled over and broken. Beneath us lay shards of reflective glass; the largest piece we'd crawled out of lay in the center.

Marcus opened a drawer in the desk, but there was nothing inside. "This is weird. It's like nobody's been here."

Oberi went over to the cot and sniffed it. *This was someone's room, all right. I can smell the stench of angels in this place, though they left some time ago.*

The broken mirror indicated that someone had gone in a hurry, though otherwise there seemed to be no evidence that anyone had lived here at all. Everything had been completely cleared out.

"This is the guards' quarters," I said hollowly.

"They must've known it was only a matter of time before we showed up after their wards fell," Ez said thoughtfully. "The guards must've fled so they weren't discovered."

I listened closely for the sound of guards or the screams of prisoners, but I heard nothing at all.

That terrified me, and panic shook my frame. Something was *very* wrong.

I had the horrifying thought that Cassiel had waited too long. His words echoed in my mind. *In time, he will know, once matters have settled.*

Cassiel had been waiting for this.

I shuddered. "If everything's been neatly packed away, and the guards are gone, that means..."

Everyone else knew exactly what I was thinking, and I couldn't bear to finish the thought. My friends' faces fell, but I could see it in their eyes that they weren't ready to admit what we already knew.

We had to see it for ourselves.

Charlie walked toward the door. "Come on. Let's see if there are any survivors."

We left the bedroom and entered a long hall. We passed by other bedrooms, and each was as empty as the last.

Oberi kept his nose down, sniffing along the floor. He stopped at a closed door at the end of the hall. *There's something in here.*

My pulse quickened as Charlie opened the door. I didn't know what I expected to find— perhaps prisoners huddled in the corner, awaiting rescue.

Instead, we found a massive dark room lined with shelves so full, they were overflowing. The storage room had to be bigger than the rest of the guards' quarters combined. The room was full of random belongings, like glasses, jewelry, blankets, clothing, and children's toys. The piles of belongings stacked up to the ceiling and consumed the area. There was barely any room for my chair to get through. Cautiously, my friends and I entered the long room.

"What's all this?" Opal mused.

Alistair's cane hit a baseball, and it rolled across the hardwood floor. "Perhaps it's stuff the guards left behind?"

My stomach hollowed as I caught sight of a child's cup. I reached for it, and my heart ached as I pulled it down from the shelf. The cup had teeth marks from where the child chewed the spout.

I choked back a sob. "It's the *victims'* belongings," I rasped. "It's everything the guards confiscated from the people they brought here."

Eddie shuddered, and he shrank back toward the door.

Charlie ran his fingers over the items on one shelf— a framed photo of a witch family, a pair of worn moccasins, and a shell with the name of a merfolk pod carved on the outside. A traditional Elven wedding dress had been tossed haphazardly beside the other belongings, its beautiful train tailing to the floor. When Charlie touched the lace, he yanked his hand away, like he couldn't bear to take in any more.

"Let's keep moving," he ordered.

We left the room and turned down another hallway, until we came upon a door that led outside. I knew I wouldn't be able to navigate the camps in my chair, so Oberi shifted into unicorn form, and I hoisted myself onto her back. Marcus subconjured my wheelchair, then opened the door.

The night sky was dark, but floodlights lit the property. Outside, we had a full view of the camp, and my guts churned.

The first thing I noticed were the bodies strewn across the ground. Everywhere I looked, people lay face-down in the dirt. There were hundreds of them, if not thousands. The only sound that could be heard was the buzzing of insects feeding on the dead.

Worse than that was the smell. The stench of rotting corpses, mixed with sewage, hit me so hard I might've toppled over if I wasn't already sitting down. It was obvious these people hadn't been given proper sanitary facilities. It smelled so bad that my friends and I started gagging. Charlie waved his hands to try to control the smell in the air. His Air magic helped, but even he couldn't completely hold off the foul odors.

Kallie threw a hand over her mouth. Marcus wrapped an arm around her to pull her close, turning her into his chest so she didn't have to see it. Rishi sank closer to them. Chancey's features paled, and Ivy rubbed their eyes, like they couldn't believe what they were seeing. Alistair gripped tight to Eddie's hand. Ez and Opal both looked away.

I tore my gaze from the bloated corpses that were decomposing in the night to take in the rest of the camp. The property must've been dozens of acres wide. We were on one side of the camp near the edge, and I couldn't see the other side from here. A tall noxite fence with barbed wire at the top surrounded the property, and concrete guard towers were placed on each corner. Beyond the fence was nothing but barren desert as far as the eye could see.

Toward the far end of the camp was a collection of warehouses. A water tower that serviced the whole camp rose over a hundred feet high. I squinted across the landscape. The layout of the buildings seemed familiar, and I couldn't figure out why, until an image of the Institute flashed through my memory.

I clutched my stomach, because the realization was like a punch to the gut. "It's the Institute," I whispered. I pointed to a warehouse with a tower on top. "That looks like the cathedral, and that building over there has doors like the asylum. It's the same layout and everything, even though the buildings are smaller. The Warden *intentionally* built this place to look like the Darke Institute."

The Warden took pride in his prison— that much was obvious. This place was just an extension of what he'd built back on Darke Island... only much, *much* worse. There, he needed to keep up appearances for the United Supernatural Union. Here, there were no rules, and he'd taken every advantage of this lawless land for himself.

"We're too late," Ez breathed. "The Warden slaughtered all these people so they couldn't be liberated."

I shook my head. "I don't think so. These wards didn't fail by accident. The Warden *let* them fall, because he didn't need to hide this place anymore. There's no point now that there's no one left to hide. He... he wants to show off his work."

My friends remained silent, and I didn't blame them. There was so much to take in, and it was enough to make a person go mad. I felt what was left of my sanity disengage, crumble and be blown away as I observed the masses of bodies that were sprawled out all over the camps. They were nothing more than skeletons covered by skin. The Warden had starved them so badly before their demise, their empty eyes holding nothing but sorrow and pain.

These people had suffered miserably for months. All to serve the avarice of one cruel man.

I tried to cry, but couldn't. Tears wouldn't come, not even if I forced them to, because it seemed like a crime to cry over the fate of people who'd never had a chance, people who I hadn't been able to save. My sadness and grief meant nothing. Not when compared to what had been done to these poor people here.

Charlie started forward, Oberi at his side. We followed behind him like zombies, weaving between the dead bodies. I spotted witches lying beside dead cats. Elementai were sprawled next to small magical creatures like jackalopes and miniature dragons. I was certain the Warden had not permitted any larger, stronger Familiars to live once they arrived. Fae sorceresses lay face-down, their insect-like wings twisted angrily toward the sky. The pretty shimmer of a mermaid's blue hair was no longer visible beneath a layer of dirt.

There weren't very many angels, but the few I spotted barely had any feathers left on their wings. A vampire lay on his back, his eyes staring up lifelessly at the stars. His mouth hung open, fangs protruded as if in a permanent scream for help... a scream that didn't make a sound.

We passed by long tables lined with benches, like some sort of outdoor cafeteria. The tables were full of victims, and people lay slumped over bowls of unfinished soup. The sound of buzzing flies intensified as they swarmed the tables to feast on the rotting food.

It was like all these people had just... dropped dead in the middle of dinner.

Rishi jumped onto the table, eyeing each victim like he thought he might find a live one.

Danny furrowed his brow. "I don't get it. How'd all these people die?"

"Isn't it obvious?" Opal sniffled. She still couldn't look, and her face was curled into Ez's shoulder. "The guards lined them for a firing squad. That's how they do it at places like this."

Danny shook his head. "They aren't lined up, though. These bodies are everywhere. It's like they were all killed all at once. Nobody saw it coming."

"It must've been something like noxite gas, or a poison of some sort," Ez theorized.

Danny knelt beside a vampire to inspect the body. "That can't be it. A vampire would just hold his breath if attacked by gas. The only ways to kill a vampire are through decapitation, a stake to the heart, or fire, but there are no signs of injury. Normally people in places like this are treated so poorly they die of infection or malnutrition, but even if they were starved, there'd be signs of a struggle. Nobody ran or fought back. It's like they all dropped at once."

"Let's check the warehouses," Charlie suggested. "Perhaps we'll find more clues as to what happened here."

As we continued forward, it became apparent that this was more than poison. Pools of blood had dried to become nothing more than stains in the dirt. The further we ventured into the camp, the more apparent the injuries became. First came lacerations and minor wounds, until we came upon limbs completely missing from bodies. Holes had been blasted straight through people's chests.

Soon, the bodies became only parts. There was a foot here, a hand there, dismembered pieces amongst torn fabric that no longer resembled clothing. Then the dirt turned to a deep black.

We came upon a crater in the center of the camp, where dirt had been upheaved all around a circle at least twenty feet wide. The hole itself must've been ten feet deep in the middle. There were no bodies or remnants of *anything* within several yards of the crater.

"Whatever happened started here," Charlie said. "I can feel remnants of magic, but I can't identify it. I've never felt anything like it before."

"Something happened here, all right," Marcus said. "There's a huge crater in the earth, like a massive spell impacted the center of the camp. This is probably what killed everyone."

"What's all this black powder?" Ivy asked in a shaking tone.

Oberi sniffed the dirt, and Charlie knelt down to inspect the ground beside him. He rubbed the black powder between his fingers. "I can feel it's magical. It must be a residual of the spell."

I looked around, calculating. Something here didn't seem right. This camp was overcrowded with prisoners who hadn't had a chance to run from the attack. They hadn't even seen it coming. There were bodies all over the rest of the camp... except here.

It hit me like a cinder block to the chest. "It's the *people*," I realized. "Their bodies were reduced to nothing but ash. This spell disintegrated anyone who was standing too close."

Danny blew a breath. "One hell of a spell, I tell ya. These people were all ripped apart at once, dead as soon as the spell was cast. Someone literally walked in here and massacred these victims all at the same time."

"How's that possible?" Charlie wondered. "Even *we* couldn't kill this many people in a single blow."

"Why not?" Ez wondered. "You're demigods. You've got the power to kill them. Perhaps this is the doing of the other demigods."

I shook my head. "Not like this. There are too many different ways to kill supernatural beings, and they don't all die in the same way. Sure, I could kill five-hundred people at once by stopping their hearts, but they'd have warning once I began. They'd start running. But even if I did that, it wouldn't kill the angels and the vampires. We *could* kill this many people, but it'd be a bloodbath, and you'd see signs of a struggle. Not whatever this is. All these people died in seconds, and they didn't have time to run, or even see what was coming."

"So what kind of power can take out all supernatural races at once?" Alistair asked.

"I don't know," I replied hollowly. "Whatever weapon the Warden used goes beyond anything witnessed in this realm. It must've come from the gods themselves."

That was a terrifying thought, because it meant the Warden had access to power beyond anything we could imagine. Worse, he wouldn't hesitate to use it.

The Warden had deployed this weapon and then just *left*, without a single regard to the lives he took.

I was certain the Warden had *wanted* me to see this. He dropped his wards knowing I would come, and he left behind all the evidence as a display of his power. This was merely a message... a message for *me*.

He's coming for you Ava.

And he's leaving no survivors.

I shook my head as the voices invaded my mind. *No.* The Warden clearly had a powerful weapon, but that did *not* mean he'd won this. We had to keep going, because we *needed* to find survivors. There had to be a chance that we could still go up against him, despite what had happened here.

"Someone had to survive this," I said in a choked tone. "Let's keep going."

We continued past the crater, toward the warehouses that were built so much like the Darke Institute. I kept my gaze ahead, but Marcus continued to look around at all the dead bodies.

"It's strange, isn't it?" he remarked. "This place was built to hold the Elves, wasn't it? But I haven't seen a single Elf since we got here."

I swallowed the lump that rose in my throat. "Perhaps the Elves survived."

I dared to hope, because it would be the one advantage we had to stand up to the Warden's weapon... if there was anyone to stand up to him at all after this.

We entered the main warehouse, and despite the carnage we witnessed outside, I wasn't prepared for what we saw indoors. The warehouse was nothing more than a massive room with a tall ceiling and a dirt floor, metal walls surrounding us on all sides. Bunk beds were lined up in rows, and hundreds of bodies were crowded on the mattresses. There were multiple people on each bed, and they appeared to be sleeping, but the putrid smell of decaying bodies told us they were long gone. These people had literally been sleeping on top of one another and died immediately. No one had the chance to save them.

We kept on moving and made our way into the next warehouse. We all halted in the doorway, because after everything we'd seen, we didn't expect it to get any worse. But it was— so, *so* much worse.

Here, bodies that had long rotted were thrown into huge piles. Some of them were so far gone that they were mere skeletons now. The ones on top were fresher, but their skin was already sagging off their forms. These people had been dead for a while by the time the Warden's weapon killed all the other prisoners.

Nearby, one of the piles was made up entirely of hair and teeth. It was the only pile of human remains that wasn't rotting, as if the hair had been cut and teeth had been removed before the victims were murdered. Some of the hair was still in braids, though the base of the braids had been completely hacked to pieces.

I dared to guide Oberi closer to one of the mounds of bodies. I saw the pointed ears first, then witnessed holes straight through each of their chests.

"I guess the Elves didn't survive after all," Danny said in an empty tone.

I choked back tears. "Opal was right about the firing squad. That's what they did to these Elves. That's why there weren't any outside, because unlike the other prisoners, they'd already been slaughtered the moment they arrived. They piled them here to rot."

Charlie furrowed his brow. "This doesn't make sense. The Warden invaded Forevermore and imprisoned the Elves he captured because he *needed* them. He wanted their power. Why would he throw all this power away now? Unless..."

"He doesn't need them anymore," I finished hollowly. "Whatever he wanted from the Elves, he got."

"I bet you it's whatever weapon he used out there to kill all these people," Danny said.

A long silence stretched between us all, before Charlie turned and continued walking. We left the warehouse out the back.

In the distance was another building, smaller than the others. A fence blocked off that area of the camps, and tiny bodies littered the dirt behind the fence. I caught sight of blue fur, which I thought was a small Familiar at first, before a gust of wind swept past and it went tumbling across the ground. I realized it was made of cotton.

It was a teddy bear.

It hit me then that we hadn't seen a single child in all the rest of the camp. The Warden had separated children from their parents and locked them up behind that fence.

From a distance, I saw the bodies of toddlers and five-year-old children—tiny little ones who'd barely gotten a shot at life before the Warden had stolen it away.

The Warden was pure evil, and I had the sick urge to go see just how far he'd taken it. I *needed* to know. I started guiding Oberi forward.

"Please don't go, princess," Eddie whispered in a broken voice.

I paused and looked over my shoulder. "If the rest of you want to hang back, that's okay, but I need to see what the Warden has done."

Eddie kept his gaze down. "I'm not asking for myself, your highness. I'm telling you that you don't want to go over there. The injuries are great, and the lifeless stare of those children will haunt you forevermore. Trust me."

I saw something in Eddie's eye that I hadn't noticed before. It occurred to me that this must be harder on him than the rest of us, because he'd been held in a camp just like this for months before he escaped. It was torture like this that had lost him his eye.

But the longer I looked at him, the more I saw something else.

I narrowed my eyes. "How do you know what injuries they sustained?"

Eddie shook his head. "I cannot say, your highness."

That was all the confirmation I needed. Eddie knew, because he'd already seen them.

"You were here last night," I whispered. "Emperor Cassiel has already been here. You came with him. Cassiel ordered you not to tell Charlie, because he knew we'd want to come see the damage for ourselves. That's why he called this a lost cause... because he already knew all the victims were gone."

Charlie slowly turned toward his guard. "Is that true?"

Eddie kept his head down and didn't respond. It was his way of confirming the truth when he couldn't give a direct answer.

Charlie's hands curled into fists. "I don't care why my grandfather felt he had to keep this from me. He should've at least been *honest* about what happened here! We deserved to see this for ourselves."

Charlie whirled toward the children's area but Marcus cut in front of him, pressing a hand to his chest. "*No,*" Marcus insisted. "Fuck this. Eddie's right. We've seen enough. We don't need to see what happened to those kids, too. There's no reason to keep going."

"Fuck no, there isn't," Ivy snarled. "We shouldn't have come here at all. The Emperor kept this from us for a reason, and we still came here. I think we all know exactly why."

Ivy narrowed their gaze on me.

My voice shook. "What exactly are you saying?"

"You *really* want me to say it out loud?" Ivy spread their arms wide. "Fine. This was a stupid idea. We didn't need to see this shit and traumatize ourselves. Ava, the Emperor *knew* you would come no matter what he ordered you to do. That's why he wanted to keep this from you, but you just *have* to get your own way, don't you? You're so insistent on trying to save the world that it hurts people, and now, we hurt ourselves. You are *so* adamant about stopping suffering in this world, but you've made *us* suffer by bringing us here. You want to save people, but you never think about saving the people around you. You could've saved us from this, but you didn't. Now we gotta deal with it."

Chancey's voice got rough. "Don't go there, Ives. We didn't know. You'd think a whole lot differently if we'd gotten here in time to save these people.

Perhaps this could've been avoided if the Emperor would've been honest with us, instead of leaving us to come to our own conclusions."

"Yeah, blame Cassiel," Ivy scoffed. "I'm telling you he didn't want us coming here for a reason, and it's because he knows as well as the rest of us that Ava needs to save every person who's in trouble, even if they can't be saved."

"She's trying to do the right thing! You're being selfish!" Chancey demanded.

"If it's selfish of me to want to save the people I care about, then I guess I'm selfish," Ivy spat. "You want to know who I care about? Me. You. Us. Fuck the world right now. I've been miserable my whole goddamn life, and this shit ain't helping. All I got from coming here is just another fucked up memory that's going to haunt me for the rest of my cursed existence."

Ivy hugged themselves and turned away, trembling with each pleading, broken word. "We didn't get back at my father, and we sure as hell ain't getting back at the Warden now. I'm sick of adding people to my long list of revenge I gotta take. Hell, my list of people to take revenge on is so fucking long, I can't even remember who I need to get back at anymore. I just want to *rest*, and I can't do it, because Ava's over here thinking she can play the hero."

"Don't put this on Ava," Charlie growled. "I get it. You're looking for someone to blame, but this isn't her fault. You want to bitch and moan about how hard your life is? Look around at what happened to these people. At least you *have* a revenge list. These people will never get theirs. So are you going to lay down and take this, or are you going to help us end the Warden? Because that's where this shit has been leading all along."

Charlie began pacing, his words frantic now. "We needed to come here to see what we're up against. And we need to start putting a plan together *now*. We need to kill the Warden, and figure out how to stop him. If you don't want to be a part of it, then go back to the palace and enjoy your time off, because the rest of us have shit to do."

Charlie was starting to lose control. As much as he wanted to kill the Warden, I could see that, rationally, he was piecing together that it wasn't possible anymore. If the Warden could do something like this without consequences, that wasn't something we could stand up to. I could feel Charlie fighting himself through the bond, arguing with his logical mind that we could beat this.

It was terrifying to watch him actively lose it.

"You ain't thinking straight if you think we can take on this kind of power, because what happened here is nothing we have a chance against," Ivy sneered. "I know your grandpa told you to pivot with each problem, but this ain't one you can solve. I'm damn good at what I can do, but I know when I've been beaten. *We* don't have a chance of fixing this, so we need to figure out what the hell we can do to make it to the next day. If the Warden can do this to all these people, we're next."

"If he could do this to us, we'd be dead already," Charlie shot back. "We're stronger than him. We just need to figure out a way."

Ivy laughed in Charlie's face— literally. Ivy got so close to Charlie that their noses were less than an inch apart. Ivy's fangs protruded as they gave a mocking laugh.

It was completely insane, and I fell apart watching it. Ivy had been damaged from the moment I'd met them, but this... I'd had my hand in really wounding them this time.

Charlie didn't move. Just stood his ground without batting an eye.

"Ives, come on," Chancey sighed, grabbing Ivy's wrist. "Calm down."

"Calm *down*!" Ivy shouted, whirling on Chancey. Sobs broke from their chest, and tears began streaming down their face. "You don't understand what's going on here. I'm going to lose you. *We're* going to lose each other."

Chancey shook his head. "That ain't true."

"No, Chance. I'm not giving you up for a lost cause, because Charlie's leading us down one," Ivy snapped.

Chancey's shoulders fell. "Ives, please."

Ivy pointed a finger in Chancey's face. "Don't give me that shit. You're my *partner*. You're supposed to stand beside me, and if you can't do that, then fuck you."

Ivy stormed off, their vampire speed carrying them around the side of the building so fast I hadn't caught where they'd gone.

Chancey hesitated, then said, "They just need a minute, but Ivy's got a point. This was a dumb move. We shouldn't be here."

Charlie frowned, showing almost no emotion. "Look, if you guys can't handle what happened here, that's too bad. You need to see the reality of what the Warden can do, because sticking our heads in the sand and pretending like he's not hurting people is doing nothing for anyone."

"I'm with Ivy," Alistair piped up. "Eddie already went through this, and you made him relive it again. You shouldn't have made him come, Charlie."

Eddie didn't say anything, but my soul broke just looking at him. Tears streamed down his face, but he kept quiet so Charlie wouldn't notice. He never lifted his gaze from his feet.

"I'm sorry," Charlie said genuinely. "I shouldn't have brought you, Eddie. But everyone else needed to come."

Eddie's voice came out small. "I do as my master tells me. I must obey him no matter what it costs me."

His words sounded so shattered— like a piece of himself had already died in the service of his master. He'd given up so much to be Charlie's guard. I wondered how much more there was left inside of Eddie to give.

Ez stepped forward. "Look, we can't change what has already happened, or the choices we made that brought us here. We can only be here for each other now. We're all friends. This is a terrible thing, but we can't let this tear us apart."

"Ez is right," Opal agreed. "We're all in this together."

"That isn't fair, because some of us are handling this worse than others," Alistair argued. "Don't act like you know what Eddie's going through. Come on, Eddie. Let's go find Ivy."

Alistair grabbed Eddie's hand, and the two of them disappeared around the side of the building. Kallie stared after them. I witnessed contemplation in her eyes... like she thought about following them. She shrank close to Marcus, clutching him tightly, before turning her eyes back to the ground.

Kallie would never admit it, but I knew what it looked like for my best friend to be falling apart. She hadn't said a word since we'd gotten here, and though she'd insisted on coming, I felt bad for bringing her. I should've made her stay behind.

But I saw the look in her eyes. It was like she wanted to follow the others in order to get away from Charlie, because she couldn't stand to be near him right now, yet she literally couldn't move.

Marcus held Kallie tight. "Guys, none of us mean anything we're saying right now. We just need to leave."

Danny scoffed. "You just want to go home and forget about all of this, but we should stay here. The Warden might've killed all these people, but the guards at the camp helped him do it by imprisoning all these people here. We need to figure out exactly where these guards went, follow them, and kill them all. We can't let them get away with this."

Marcus narrowed his eyes at Danny, like he thought it was a stupid idea. "How are we supposed to find them? They left no clues behind."

Tears finally streaked my cheeks. Though I wasn't able to cry before, I couldn't hold myself back now, and my words fell like broken glass as water poured from my eyes. "I'm sorry, everyone. Ivy's right. I'm to blame. I'm the one who brought us here. I overheard Cassiel talking, and if I hadn't jumped to conclusions, we wouldn't be here."

"You did the right thing, Ava," Charlie insisted. "My grandfather should've told us. We did the best we could with the information we had."

I sniffled. "Oberi, What do you think?"

Oberi responded, though only Charlie and I could hear her internal thoughts. *You did your best, and you had good intentions, but sometimes, good intentions lead to horrible consequences. Unfortunately, this is something all of us had to go through. When terrible things happen, people need to come together as one, not fall away from one another. As much as you don't want to admit it, you all need each other right now.*

Opal wiped a tear from her eye. "What's Oberi saying, Ava?"

"He says Marcus is right," I translated. "There's nothing more to see here. We should head back to the palace."

Before Oberi could even turn, Ivy's voice rang across the camp. "Guys, come quick! We've got two live ones!"

My friends took off running, and I urged Oberi into a gallop. We followed Ivy to one of the guard towers. Next to the tower there was a hole in the fence just big enough for a small person to crawl through. It looked like it'd been mangled by the blast. The entrance to the tower was outside the fence, and Alistair knelt next to the open doorway.

"Come on," he encouraged. "It's safe."

Two trembling figures emerged from the guard tower. The first guy was scrawny and couldn't weigh more than a hundred pounds. I didn't think he could be more than fifteen years old, but he looked like a child with the way his tattered clothes hung off his starved form.

The other guy wasn't very big, but he wore a guard uniform. I instinctually drew back a fireball, but I paused when I witnessed a white tomcat with crooked whiskers emerge from the tower behind them.

"Ava? Charlie?" the guard said in disbelief. "It's so good to see you guys!"

I barely recognized him at first, because he was covered in dirt from head to toe. It was Ghost, a warlock student from back at the Institute. I recalled the guards trying to force him to sign up for The Mission, even though he didn't want to. Looks like in the end, he wasn't given a choice. Ghost had barely survived in fight club. I was surprised he'd outlasted the Warden's service this long.

"Ghost?" Marcus balked.

Before he could answer, the teenager's eyes lit up. "M... Marcus?!"

Recognition crossed Marcus' features, like the kid was so unrecognizable he hadn't noticed him at first. The kid scrambled through the broken fence and ran toward Marcus, practically body-slamming him in a hug. I'd never seen this kid before, and I didn't know how Marcus knew him.

Tears streamed down Marcus' cheeks. "Kellen? I thought I'd never see you again."

Holy fuck. It was Anya's younger brother— the kid Marcus left behind in Octavia Falls. Marcus had dated Anya before she died, and he'd gotten close with her little brother. He'd taken Kellen under his wing and started teaching him art, before Marcus was sent away to the Institute. He'd talked about Kellen multiple times, mostly to say how much he regretted never saying goodbye. Kellen had been like a little brother to him.

Kellen drew back. "You've put on some muscle."

Marcus squeezed his arms. "You don't know how happy I am to see you. There's so much I never got to tell you. I'm really, really sorry. None of this ever should've happened to you."

"You don't have to apologize. It's not your fault," Kellen promised. "I'm here because of *The Mission*."

He spat the words like they were poison.

Charlie turned to Ghost, who had crawled back inside the fence. "How did the two of you survive? The spell that took out the others should've killed you, too."

"After I was forced to join The Mission, they took me out of the Institute," Ghost explained. "The Warden made it sound like we were going to do good in the world, and I thought I could help. I learned pretty quickly that wasn't the case, but I did the best I could. I was stationed here as a guard. I tried to get people out, but never could, and almost got caught a few times. So I changed tactics and did what I could to keep people alive instead."

"He snuck us food," Kellen said. "He was the only guard that cared about us."

Ghost dropped his gaze. "I tried, but it wasn't enough."

"I was scared of all the other guards, but not Ghost," Kellen admitted. "We knew each other from back home. I was friends with his little sister— Mother Miriam rest her soul. She never made it out of Octavia Falls. Ghost used to drive me home from school, because I was just one block over from his house. He was my only friend here at the camps."

"Yesterday, the guards were told to pack up and leave," Ghost explained. "We weren't given a reason why, but I just knew something bad was about to happen. We only had minutes to evacuate. I was already on my way to sneak Kellen some food, and I knew I couldn't leave him behind. I snuck him out here to the guard tower so we could hide and wait for whatever was coming. Then... we heard the blast. There were no screams— just silence."

"Did you see what caused this?" Charlie asked.

"It was that creepy guy Ghost calls the Warden," Kellen spat.

"How was he able to do this, though?" Marcus asked. "This is beyond anything we've seen before. He must've gotten the power from somewhere."

"He's got demigod power, so he can create energy out of nothing," Danny offered.

"Demigods can create their own power, but there are limits even to what we can do," Charlie said. "We're still in mortal bodies, so we're still going to reach a point where we can't handle limitless energy. Eventually, we're going to get tired."

"He's got dark gods on his side that would give him the power and do the work for him," Danny pointed out. "He doesn't have to cast the magic himself."

Marcus' gaze shifted thoughtfully. "But what if he *did* do this by himself, without help? The Warden's demigod power is that he can't die, so he must be able to handle more magic than we can, because his body won't give out on him."

"He can still pass out, even if he can't die," Charlie stated. "He wouldn't be able to finish a spell like the one we saw."

Ghost shuddered. "I've had a theory for a while, and after what happened here yesterday, I'm certain I'm correct. It was my job to take the Elves to one of the warehouses, then pile up the bodies once the Warden was done with them. Once they went in, they never came out. He never said what he was doing with them in there, and guards were forbidden inside whenever he was here. But sometimes I was stationed at the doors, and I could hear the screams from inside. Every time the Warden walked out of that warehouse, it was like he was stronger than ever before. I can't explain it, because nothing about him changed outwardly. But there was this magical energy that rolled off him that was undeniable."

Ghost drew a shaky breath. "I think the Warden was using the Elves to gain power, like he did with kids back at the Institute."

"What does he need their power for?" Alistair asked. "He's already a demigod. You all saw it the night we escaped the Institute."

"Yeah, he's already a demigod, but like Charlie said, even demigods have limits, and their bodies will give out if they overexert themselves," Ghost said. "I think he was using the Elves' power to *increase* his limits. As a demigod, he can create power from nothing, but with the power of the Elves, that power can flow through him all at once. That's why he hasn't struck like this until now, because he's finally powerful enough to do anything he wants, and he's done using the Elves. He no longer needs to siphon their powers."

"Just because he was able to increase his limit doesn't give him ultimate power, though," Charlie insisted. It seemed he was grasping at straws. He didn't want to believe the Warden was as powerful as he was now.

If all of this was true, that meant the Warden had accomplished what he intended with the Elves. He didn't need them anymore. There was nothing holding him back from attacking Ilamanthe now. With power like this, he could take on all us demigods at once, and he would no longer care about the casualties. We were holding him off before, and that's why he had to lure us to his manor.

But none of that mattered now, and because the Elves were now useless to him, he was going to come for Ilamanthe the first chance he got. I had the horrible thought that he might already be on his way, and all of this was a ploy to lure us away from the city.

I furrowed my brow. It made sense, but something was missing. I knew there was. I just couldn't put my finger on it. "So the weapon he used here... you think it was *him*?"

"Well, yeah," Ghost said breathlessly. "He waltzed in here, and five minutes later everyone was dead."

"We saw him from the guard tower, lurking around all night," Kellen added. "We're pretty sure he knew we were here and left us alive to tell the tale. But we couldn't leave the tower as long as he was still sneaking around. Looks like we're safe now that you're here. You took care of him, didn't you?"

The blood in my veins turned to ice, and my throat became sandpaper. "Wait... you're saying he's still here?"

Ghost began to panic. "Well, he must be gone, or he would've attacked you by now, right? *Right?*"

Charlie's voice shook. "Or he was waiting for us to see what he'd done, like some sort of sick display—"

Charlie didn't finish speaking before an explosion rocked the entire camp. The ground shook violently, and the blow whipped us all backward. My friends screamed, and I was thrown from Oberi's back. I sailed through the sky and landed hard on my stomach in the dirt, the wind knocked out of me. It was like a massive bomb had gone off right beneath our feet, though I knew it'd been a powerful spell. Every inch of my body ached, and my ears rang.

A chilling laugh filled the air. It was the kind of laughter that made my heart stop beating. I dared to turn my gaze to the sky, and dread filled my core as my worst fear became true.

The Warden was here, and we were completely out in the open with nowhere to go. He was noticeably alone, as he was so powerful now that he didn't need his band of demigods to do his dirty work. He wanted to take me by himself.

The blast wasn't meant to kill us, only knock us down. Otherwise, how would I look into his sunken dark eyes when he finally destroyed my soul? We'd reached the final round of his game, and he wanted me to *know* he had won.

I realized he hadn't lured me out of Ilamanthe so that he could attack the city while I was preoccupied. He'd brought us here so he could kill my friends and take me prisoner. Only then would he conquer Ilamanthe, and wage war across Earth like I saw in my vision.

I *would not* let him take me. No matter what kind of power he had, I'd die before I became his prisoner a second time.

His white, feathery wings spread wide as he descended upon us, giving a broad and gloating smile. "I knew you wouldn't be able to resist my trap, Ava," the Warden taunted, his eyes fixed solely on me. "You're too soft of a person. You think you're such a villain, my dear, but no true villain has a good heart. Today, that kindness is going to be your reckoning."

TWENTY-THREE

The Warden was one sick fuck, watching us like a sadistic pig while we roamed the camp, waiting in the wings while we took in the devastation. He was showing off. He *wanted* us to experience everything he'd done and all he was capable of before he finished us off.

The spell had blasted us back fifty feet or more. I became disoriented as my head smashed against a large rock. I knew I had some sort of concussion, because it fucking hurt. Blood gushed from a wound on my head, and my pulse pounded in my ears.

The desert spun around me, and the Warden's words sounded like they were coming from under water. He'd appeared so quickly that none of us had a chance to react. I couldn't make much sense of anything, until I felt his magic swell once more. I knew he must be going in for the kill. If what Ghost said was true, then the Warden's power was unmatched, even for demigods like us. We were entirely defenseless.

Power that could rival a nuclear explosion burst toward us as the Warden cast his devastating spell— the same one he'd used to kill all the camp's victims at once. At the same time, my bond with Ava flared, and I felt all my magic drain out of me. Oberi gave a panicked cry, and I realized Ava was pulling from every resource she possibly could to cast her spell. Oberi and I both gave her our power, and Spirit magic exploded out of her. A Spirit shield stronger than any spell we'd cast before bloomed upward to encompass us all.

The Warden's power collided with Ava's shield, and the Spirit magic shattered. His magic blew through her shield and slammed into us, tossing us all back another twenty feet.

My breath left my chest, and pain radiated up and down my body as bruises formed all over. It felt like being pummeled by five dragon shifters all at once.

All around us, buildings screeched as they toppled over. The water tower crashed to the ground, making a huge sloshing noise as a wave spread across the camp. The Warden's blow had leveled the entire camp flat. Ava's shield was the only thing that had kept us from being torn to pieces.

Even now, she was the only one that had a chance of standing up to him.

Only a residual bit of magic remained within me, just enough to make out my surroundings. I didn't think I could cast another spell right now if I tried. Forget making illusions; even something as simple as creating a breeze or making a plant bloom would make me faint. Ava had needed every drop of our power to protect us from the Warden's blast, and now I had nothing left to give. The bond between Oberi and me seemed to flicker out of existence, though it didn't shatter. Oberi must've passed out.

Magic swelled one more time, and Ava gave a weak cry as she struggled to form another shield. It didn't come. Her first shield had taken everything we had, and it hadn't been enough. She was drained, exhausted, and unable to cast.

A different type of power bloomed in front of us, and I recognized it as portal magic. Loud shouts met my ears, along with the clang of armor. Battle magic sizzled through the air, and the Warden gave a primal scream that grew distant with each passing second. Someone had caught him by surprise and blasted him backward, but I couldn't make sense of who it was.

"You will not touch them!" a brave voice yelled. I realized it was my grandfather, arriving at the last second to rescue us.

"I will put you in the ground for hurting my daughter, you sick bastard!" Queen Emmaline's voice boomed over the area. She must've been the one to make the portal that brought backup here.

As I gathered my bearings, I was able to make more sense of my surroundings. I felt the powerful surge of Toaqua magic, as well as the chaotic buzz of a Death warlock's power. Kallie's mom wasn't the only one who'd come. Liam and Lucas were here, too.

"Your highness!" Eldin shouted. Her footsteps raced over to where I thought my wife had fallen, though I couldn't be sure. The desert continued to spin around me.

Someone grabbed my shoulder, dragging me to my feet. "Come on, Charlie!" Cameron's voice barked. "We have to go!"

I shoved at him weakly, but he held a firm grip. My limbs felt like they were made of sludge, and I could barely stand on my own two feet. The Warden's blast had taken a lot out of me, but I wasn't ready to give up. "We have to stay and fight!"

"Go, Charlie!" Cassiel barked from several feet away. "You never should've come here! You need to get out!"

Illusion magic filled the camp, and Emma gave a harrowing battle cry. The heavy sound of massive footsteps came, followed by the roar of a great beast. Emma had conjured an illusion monster that must've towered a hundred feet above us, and sent it charging at the Warden.

The Warden's maniacal laugh came in response. I heard the illusion monster groan in pain, then the ground shook as his magic took it down, shattering the queen's spell into a million pieces. Emma gave a cry of rage and sent illusion spells racing at the Warden, but he batted them all away, redirecting her own spells back at her. One of them hit her, and Emma gave a cry of pain as it forced her to the ground.

Our allies didn't miss a beat. Though Emma was down, droplets spread across the area as Liam drew water from the dirt where the water tower had fallen. His rage-filled scream filled the area as he sent a massive wave down upon the Warden with the intent to drown him.

The Warden merely flapped his wings and shot out of the water before blasting Liam backward. Liam grunted as the blast hit him, slamming into the earth.

Death magic permeated the camp, so strong the air began to develop a ghostly chill. Bones clicked against each other as Lucas' power surged out of him, turning his body into the skeleton of a reaper. I heard grunts of pain come from Lucas as he struggled to work his necromancy magic on the Warden.

"I'm trying to rip his soul out, but it's not working!" Lucas shouted, sounding frightened.

Shit. That wasn't good. Lucas was a master reaper, the highest caster of Death magic there was. If he couldn't rip the Warden's soul out, nobody was going to be able to.

The spell backfired, and Lucas went flying off his feet. He landed twenty yards from where he'd been standing, the sound of his clicking bones gone. He groaned as he stood upright.

It all happened within seconds, and it became abundantly clear that despite how powerful our allies were, they were no match for the Warden.

"It's not fucking working!" Emma cried. "He's impenetrable!"

"I'll deal with Doctor Taurus!" my grandfather shouted. "Get the children out of here!"

Another portal blossomed nearby at Emma's command. She started shoving people through, yelling at them to hurry into the portal and back to the city.

Fuck that. I wasn't going to leave my grandfather to deal with this alone. The small bits of power I had left surged through me, but I hadn't cast a spell before a hand that wasn't my father's landed on my shoulder, pushing me back.

I slumped to my knees, becoming weak as the rest of my power surged out of me and into another. Disbelief rattled my entire being. I refused to believe it, but when I tried to cast a spell and it wouldn't come, I had to face the truth.

Cassiel had siphoned the remainder of my magic for himself. He didn't want me to fight. He wanted me to flee, and be safe, while he took the blows *for me*. I sagged against the ground, and Cameron wrenched on my shirt to get me back upright.

My grandfather turned and sprinted toward the Warden, and I heard him draw his sword. Metal clanged, then came the sickening— or perhaps *satisfying* — squish of flesh and crunch of bone.

Something heavy flew through the air, smacking me in the stomach. Warm blood soaked into my shirt.

I realized that what hit me had been *the Warden's decapitated head*. My grandfather had just sliced his head from his shoulders!

Relief flowed through me so heavily I wanted to sob. Finally— after nightmarish years of fighting this horrible man, the Warden was fucking dead. My grandfather had killed him. This was all over.

Then... from below me came a horrifying sound. The Warden's *laughter*. I realized it was right below me, coming from the Warden's mouth, even though his head was no longer attached to his body.

Before I could fully process it, his laughter began to grow distant... like his head was rolling across the ground back toward his body, his hands commanding his disembodied skull to return to his headless body.

No. This couldn't be happening.

"This is impossible," Chancey gasped from a few paces away. "You decapitate an angel, and they die. *Every time*. I've never seen this happen before."

There was an awful, slick sound as muscle knitted back together and arteries mended themselves. The Warden cracked his neck as he placed his head back on his body, reattaching it like my grandfather had never cut it off at all.

"You are all fools," the Warden mocked. "I cannot die."

"Leave now, Charlie!" Cassiel ordered. "Don't come after me, no matter what!"

It absolutely petrified me that, for the first time in my life, I heard fear in his voice. My grandfather *never* got scared. He was always courageous, even when the situation was dire.

His tone told me that he knew we were going to lose, and that sacrifices had to be made for the greater good. Except this time... I was the greater good.

And he was the sacrifice.

Cameron yanked on my arm. My friends' voices disappeared as Emma, Liam and Lucas pulled them through the portal.

"We can't leave!" Ava yelled at Eldin, and I knew from the bottom of my heart she was trying to fight her guard off. "I order you to let me go!"

"I cannot," Eldin replied firmly. "Our orders from the Emperor are to get you out of here, and his commands are above yours."

"We have to help!" I shrieked. "Let me go!"

"You're not going anywhere," my father hissed, and he pulled me in the direction of the portal, despite me fighting him the whole way.

I would condemn myself to the worst pain the supernatural world knew before I allowed Cassiel to die here alone. I would *not* let him go down, and if he did, I would go down with him. I'd die with my grandfather, because that's what family did, and that's all I ever wanted. My father would not prevent me from perishing at my grandfather's side, because that's where I belonged. I drew my fist back and punched Cameron *hard* in the face. He reeled back at the blow, but his grip on me only tightened.

"We *have* to go!" Cameron screamed. He looped his arm around my neck to put me in a headlock. My concussion pounded with pain, disorientation growing stronger as I struggled to breathe.

"Where's your demigod army?" Cassiel taunted the Warden.

"Off following my orders in other parts of the world," the Warden replied coolly. "I don't need them to kill you all."

My father dragged me back while I struggled to free myself from his hold. The tingle of illusion magic filled the desert. My grandfather must've been using it to blind the Warden. It worked for a split second, giving my grandfather enough time to race forward. The Warden merely scoffed, and the illusion broke.

But Cassiel was already within arm's reach.

The Warden gave a gurgling sound as my grandfather grabbed him by the throat. The Warden's shoes made a scratching sound against the sand as Cassiel lifted him off the ground with one hand, strangling him.

I knew what his plan was. The Warden was too strong physically, but my grandfather knew exactly where to hit him. He was using his Elf power to turn the Warden's own memories against himself, pulling out the Warden's worst recollections and replaying them back to torture and weaken him. My grandfather wasn't usually powerful enough to read demigod memories, but when he siphoned my magic, it must've given him just enough of an edge against the Warden to do so.

"These memories... can't hurt me," the Warden rasped.

"Remember who you are," Cassiel urged. "Your father would be disappointed in you. You think you're so powerful, but you're merely a worthless, weak child who everyone thought would grow up to be nothing, and you're still nothing. Everyone picked on you and kicked you around, and instead of learning from your past, you just turned into the people you despised."

My grandfather's memory magic resonated throughout the camp in waves, so powerful that it hit me square in the chest. The desert seemed to close in on me, and my own screams faded until everything around me was happening in slow motion.

A heavy fist sank into my stomach, and images began to form inside my mind. I saw the remnants of the camp flying by me, until I was lying on my back in the middle of a crater formed by the impact of my body. I continued to scream, but my voice was far off in the distance. Without choosing to, I rose from the crater to my feet.

It was then that I realized what was happening. My grandfather's powers were so intense that he was projecting his memories of this moment outward, so that I could see what was happening in real time through his eyes. I didn't think he intended for it to happen. He was so focused on killing the Warden that his powers had flared beyond anything I'd seen him use before, and now, I was witnessing it all.

Cassiel stood to face the Warden. The Warden was at least fifty feet away, and he gave my grandfather a wry smile, like he merely found this amusing. In the blink of an eye, Cassiel shot a battle orb at the Warden that was crackling with power. It blasted straight through the Warden's chest, leaving a mangled hole where his heart should be. I saw organs, like his lungs, poking through the hole, as well as gnarled rib bones.

The Warden merely walked forward without missing a beat. His chest began to heal itself automatically, and the hole in his body that the battle orb had made became nothing more than a burn in the Warden's suit.

I felt my grandfather's panic like it was my own emotion. He took a step back, but the Warden had already spread his wings. He launched himself on Cassiel and grabbed him by the collar.

The Warden flew high into the sky, and the camp became smaller and smaller with each passing moment. Through my grandfather's eyes, I saw that our friends were already gone. Liam carried Oberi through the portal, until only Ava and I still remained.

The Warden must've flown my grandfather a mile up before spiraling downward, punching him through the sky. Cassiel spun through the air and landed on the ground so hard I heard the crunch of bones as the Warden's fists smashed him into the Earth.

Delirious pain surged through my grandfather's body, and he cried out in agony. Still, Cassiel didn't give up. He staggered to his feet, ignoring the pain of his broken leg and wiping the blood from his face as the Warden landed in front of him.

Cassiel lifted a hand, and tendrils of magic began to siphon out of the Warden. He staggered, forcing his crushed arm to remain outstretched as he struggled to take the Warden's abilities, giving moans of anguish as he did so.

The Warden merely smirked. "You cannot siphon my power, you filthy *Elf*. You will never be able to contain it, for I am more powerful than anyone in this universe has ever been."

Cassiel's body sagged, and he fell to his knees. The power he tried to siphon was already too much, and he couldn't take it. It was terrifying to watch. My grandpa was so powerful, and yet, the Warden acted like his power was *nothing*.

The Warden gave a smug grin as he stepped toward my grandfather. "I cannot thank you enough, Emperor Cassiel. You kept your people alive for all those years, so that one day, their power could become mine. My siege on Forevermore was merely the beginning. Now, I shall have the world."

Cassiel didn't have time to react. A bright light emanated from the Warden's palm and slammed into my grandfather's chest. His back arched, and his face turned toward the heavens. Complete anguish tore through me as my grandfather's cries echoed across the camp, and I screamed along with him.

My grandfather's pain permeated the memory, projecting outward so that I felt everything. The light magic felt like razor blades slicing through each nerve ending, separating muscle from bone and skin from flesh, scorching him into nothing more than fragments of skin and bone. The light magic tore away at Cassiel's body, consuming him as a covetous, unsatisfiable blaze.

The light grew in intensity, until it became blinding. An explosion sounded, and my grandfather's memory projection ended, until all images washed away from my mind.

Air swept by my feet, sending dust particles swirling around me. Embers fell upon my face from the sky and smeared across my clothes.

It... it was my grandfather.

The Warden had turned him completely to ash.

Ava's tormented cry died as Eldin dragged her through the portal. She had seen it all.

A chill spread across my skin as I felt the touch of a soul, and one last image washed through my mind. My grandfather's spirit ran through me on his way to the great beyond, and I witnessed his kind smile as he whispered, *"I love you, my grandson. I cherished the time we had together."*

Then... he was gone. It all happened so fast. I didn't even realize he was dead until his voice had faded from my mind forever.

Tears streamed down my face as despair consumed me, and I let out a cry of sorrow. I understood what grief was, because I'd experienced it so many times, but this was different. I'd lost the light that had guided me, and now, I was surrounded by darkness again. My grandfather had made me feel like I was a part of something, and now that he was gone, I might as well be out by myself on the streets all over again.

The palace, my title... it all meant jack shit, because it couldn't repair the damage my grandfather had left behind with his passing. It was an enormous loss, one that changed the fabric of who I was and molded me into someone different in a matter of moments without me realizing it.

I just wanted someone to *be there*, and not go away. Everyone I loved died, and if they didn't, they turned their back on me. I'd prayed my entire life to find a parent that gave a damn about me, and the second I got one, the universe ripped him away.

The Warden hadn't just killed my grandfather. He had trapped him in the in-between, never able to move on to the Blessed Haven. The Warden had imprisoned him, like he'd imprisoned me. Except this time, it was permanent, and my grandfather would have no escape.

Pure agony turned to unadulterated rage. Cameron yanked me toward the portal, but I gathered all my strength to pull away from him.

"I'm going to kill the Warden!" I screamed. I didn't care that I didn't have any magic at my disposal, that I was alone, that this was a useless attempt to stop a god. I'd murder that motherfucker with my bare hands for taking my grandfather away. I didn't need any demigod powers. I just needed my rage, and the Warden was going to feel every bit of my wrath before I took his worthless life. Every hurt and pain and bit of suffering that I'd ever been through, from the time I'd been born to now, surged out of me and begged to be summoned, so I could make someone else feel every awful thing that I'd ever felt in my meaningless existence.

I didn't care if I died anymore. I only cared if the Warden went down with me.

"He can't be beat," Cameron said, his voice choked with grief. "I'm sorry, Charlie."

A heavy blow hit me from behind, and that was it before the portal sucked us through and the camp disappeared completely. My mind went completely blank as I passed out.

My last thought was of my grandfather, and what he'd given up. He'd exchanged his life for mine, but it wasn't a gift that I wanted. He'd made the wrong choice. My enemies could take my life, because I didn't want it anymore. It wasn't worth living if I experienced these short moments of happiness and had them stolen away from me. I was tired of always ending up alone.

So I swore to myself that I wouldn't. Not ever again. No matter what I had to do, or what price I had to pay, I wouldn't allow anyone else I loved to be taken from me.

If I had to become a monster to do it, so be it. By the ancestors, I swore, I wasn't losing anyone else.

Even if I had to force them to stay.

TWENTY-FOUR

L ife didn't mean anything if it could turn out like this.

There was instant panic the moment we returned to Ilamanthe. We portaled back into the throne room where all my friends were recovering, sprawled out on the floor or hovering over their knees.

"Cassiel's dead," Ivy said weakly. "Fuck, fuck, *fuck*."

Eldin set me down. I managed to sit up from my place on the floor, and Oberi slowly came around beside me. I gritted my teeth in pain as I pulled myself onto her back. She got to her hooves as the throne room dissolved into a mess of screams and chaos. Servants and Elvish nobles had received word that Cassiel had perished, and now, the palace was crumbling from the inside.

Charlie was still unconscious from Cameron's blow. A group of servants carried him out, taking him to the infirmary.

I glared at Cameron with all the hatred I could muster. I knew he had to subdue Charlie to get him back to the city, but I wasn't going to forgive him for laying hands on my husband. When I had a spare moment, I'd make him pay, too.

But that would have to wait, because first of all, we had to make sure Cassiel's death wasn't in vain.

Cameron acted like he didn't notice my death stare and said aloud, "It's over! Doctor Taurus is too powerful! He'll be here any minute to storm Ilamanthe's gates! The city is going to fall!"

Cameron was so pathetic. Cassiel was dead and Ilamanthe was exposed, yet he was losing his head when it was imperative we took action.

"We need to fortify Cassiel's wards and boost it with a shield of our own," I insisted loudly, taking charge. Charlie was down and Cameron was useless. If there weren't any other competent royals around here to give orders, I sure the fuck would. The screams quieted down at my words, as I knew they would. I was the princess— these people needed me. The Elves in the throne room looked to me, waiting on my orders.

"Ava, you're still recovering. You don't have any magic right now," Daddy said, laying a gentle hand on my knee.

He was right. Shielding us from the Warden's blast had taken all my strength, but my rage was fueling my abilities. I could feel my magic beginning to spark, becoming stronger with each moment that passed.

"Just give me a little bit of time." My demigod powers would regenerate. We needed time to recover, but not much. "I need everyone who can make a shield at the outskirts of Ilamanthe, with me. It'll take everyone's power to do this."

"We'll come," Marcus said, holding Kallie against him.

"And me," Danny said. "We can use simultension to fuse my blood magic into the shield. Anyone who attempts to break the shield will have their magic siphoned, and the shield will continue to drain the Warden's magic the more he tries."

"That's good," I said. "We'll add layers onto the shield, so it'll have more defenses. He's got a lot of power— unlimited maybe— but it'll definitely slow him up. Even if it doesn't hold, it'll buy the citizens time to flee. We'll craft the shield so nobody can portal in or out of the city."

"I'll help too," Alistair volunteered, coming forward.

"The more casters we have to hold the shield up, the better," I confirmed.

I turned to Eldin. "I want my command broadcasted throughout the city. Every magic caster of every race is to come to the city's border and lend their aid. We're going to need everyone we can to make this shield as powerful as possible."

"Yes, princess," she said, bowing to me before running out of the throne room.

"What's the use?" Cameron wailed. "Nothing we can do will stop that man!"

I couldn't believe Cassiel, once the most powerful Elven Emperor on Earth, had raised this worthless excuse for a son. Cameron was no leader and couldn't even begin to fill a sliver of the void Cassiel had left. That meant I would have to.

"Shut *up*," I snapped, and Cameron blanched. "I'm sorry you lost your father, but Cassiel is gone, and we need to protect the city before the Warden destroys the rest of us. If Cassiel's wards fall, his death will have been for nothing. Go to the barracks and order the generals to start stationing soldiers around the perimeter. Hurry up!"

Completely cowed, Cameron obeyed. He hustled off, and the rest of us immediately left for the edge of the city. I hustled to take action, urging Oberi forward while my companions followed behind.

Supernaturals of all kinds were waiting for us when we arrived at the edge of Ilamanthe a short time later. Everyone was here; Kallie's parents, all of our aunts and uncles, the Demigod Guardians and all the Elvish nobles. Thousands had gathered to help me create the defensive barrier. Oberi carried me on her back as a unicorn as I approached the city's edge. The crowd followed me, waiting on my signal.

Though Cassiel was dead, I could still feel his wards holding across the city. He'd been powerful, so his magic had still held after his death.

"Peanut, be careful. You could hurt yourself," Daddy warned at my side, sounding worried. "No one has ever been able to fuse the power of so many different races into one spell before."

I narrowed my eyes. "Just fucking watch me."

I raised my voice, and Air elementals used my magic to project my commands to the crowd as I cried, "I need everyone to cast their magic at once! I'll do the rest!"

There was a resounding response from the crowd, then thousands of small shields began blooming all over the city, blossoming like white flowers as veins of magic grew across the sky. It was a spectacular sight, watching as the shields expanded against Cassiel's ward, but I didn't have time to observe it. My mother, Lucas, Nadine, Emma, Marcus, Kallie and Alistair were at the front near me, and their shields were the most powerful, growing to become miles wide.

I used simultension and began weaving all the shields into one, combining each shield into one massive barricade that fused with Cassiel's wards, preventing any kind of entry. I used intrafusion to combine other kinds of magic into the shield, melding the city's powers together into one. My magic sewed patches together into a protective blanket that covered Ilamanthe, so thick that the shield itself appeared to be a window several inches thick, expanding it across the city and over the beach a few miles off. When I'd fused everyone else's power, I called upon my own and funneled it into the shield, making it ten times stronger than it already was.

I wouldn't have been able to do this as a prisoner at the Institute, or perhaps even a few months ago. This kind of magic had never been attempted on such a mass scale, but I was *done* playing the Warden's games. He'd chosen the wrong bitch to fuck with, and I was going to show him how big of a mistake that was.

At the camps, I'd had to make the shield that protected us from the Warden's attack at the last second, and it'd caught me off guard, stunning me and leaving me weak. Now, I was fully aware of what I was doing, and I could craft this shield to stand up to any magical attack that came, even if that bastard showed up here right now.

When I was certain the shield was secure, I took Danny's demigod magic and channeled it into the shield, merging his blood magic with the protective power. Danny had a spectacular wealth of power at his disposal, almost as much as Charlie's, and I took every drop of it I could without harming him to make the shield stronger. The shield flashed a deep red for a moment before it returned to its usual translucence, indicating the blood magic had taken. Even if the Warden dropped a bomb on this place, the blood magic would suck him dry of power for at least a few moments afterward, I was sure of it.

When the shield was finally in place, I drew back my power. It shimmered above us, a round dome that sealed the city off from all invaders. I wished the Warden good luck with breaking through.

There wasn't so much of a whisper amongst all those people as the stunned expressions of Ilamanthe's citizens gazed upon me with reverence and awe. They seemed terrified of me.

Good. I was something to be terrified of.

Soldiers from the barracks could be heard marching out of the city, taking their places to stand watch at the city's edge. I turned Oberi, leaving the area without another word.

Nobody else would've been able to do that. Not a damn one of them. But *I* could. I was the strongest supernatural there ever was, and unlike the Warden, I was born that way. I didn't need to be a pathetic little welp and steal from others in order to gain strength, because I'd been created with it from the beginning of my existence. People bowed away from my presence, creating a path for me as Oberi carried me back to the palace, looking at me as if I had the power of a god.

Maybe I did. And that's why the Warden was still afraid of me.

Very soon, I was going to make his fear all too real.

SEVEN DAYS PASSED after Cassiel died in a monochrome, tasteless blur.

The entire city was in mourning. Ilamanthe had once been vibrant and full of life, but now the palace was quiet, and everyone dressed in black. People walked with their gazes toward the ground, heads bowed. There were so many whispers infecting the palace I often wondered if the voices were coming from around me, or were merely the ones echoing inside my head. Everyone in the city had loved Cassiel and adored him as a ruler. Now that he was gone, there was nothing left but grief.

And fear. People were so terrified. I could feel it every time they walked by. Just being in the presence of others caused my heartbeat to quicken in terror. I heard what people said. How were we going to defeat the Warden when Cassiel, the most powerful Emperor that had ever lived, had done everything he could to kill him and failed?

I didn't know. All I knew was that it was on *my* shoulders to take his life. If no one else had the ability to kill the Warden, I would. I just had to figure out how.

The shield remained untouched, and neither The Mission nor the Warden showed up to try and break it. It confirmed, for me, that my power was enough to hold the Warden off, at least for now. If he thought he could get past my defenses, he would've already tried. My shield would buy us some time to come up with a plan to put him in the ground for good.

The Beast appeared to me frequently now. He didn't say anything, just stood in the corner of the room and stared at me. I stared back, my thoughts lingering on the pointlessness of it all, wondering where any of this was going or why it mattered.

Cassiel's funeral would be in a few days, as Elvish tradition dictated that a mourning period of nine days had to be held before the ceremony took place on the tenth. After the funeral, Cameron would be crowned Emperor. Things would move on, but they'd never be right again.

Charlie stayed in his quarters and didn't come out. He refused the food the servants brought him and locked himself away in our bedroom for a week straight. I laid beside him at night, but that was the extent of our contact. He hadn't said a word to me since we'd come back from the camps. Just turned his back to me and pretended I wasn't there.

I knew he was grieving terribly. I couldn't imagine the deep, bottomless loss he felt. His grandfather, the only person who'd ever been a parent to him in the entire world, was gone. His grief devoured him, changing him into someone I couldn't recognize, nor reach.

I wondered if he blamed me. It'd been my idea to go to the camps, after all. I wanted to apologize and beg for his forgiveness, yet I was petrified at the thought of giving him more pain, so I said nothing.

Our friends weren't around. Like Charlie, everyone stayed in their rooms and kept to themselves, though the others had all coupled off. Chancey and Ivy, Ez and Opal, Eddie and Alistair... they leaned on each other. Since we'd been married, I didn't think Charlie and I had ever felt more apart.

Kallie and Marcus came by to talk here and there, but I told them Charlie wasn't ready and sent them off. Kallie didn't need to deal with this, not after what she'd been through with the Dollmaker, and Marcus needed to focus on taking care of her. I'd done enough damage trying to fix the unfixable. Repairing Charlie's broken spirit was my job, and no one else's.

Me? I was depressed as fuck, though I did my best to hide it from everyone, especially Charlie. Nobody else needed to be brought down due to how I felt... if we could sink any lower... but when I was alone, I completely crumbled into pieces.

Oberi was the only one who got me. He stayed by my side and wagged his tail, trying to cheer me up.

It's not your fault, dearest, Oberi insisted, laying his head on my lap as we hid in a parlor room that was far away from Charlie's quarters. It was late afternoon, and I'd come here to break down. I didn't want anyone to see or hear me doing it, so I'd taken off. This wasn't about me; I needed to be strong for everyone right now.

It is my fault. I stroked Oberi's ears as tears leaked down my cheeks. *If I had taken a second to think, Cassiel would still be alive.*

Charlie doesn't blame you in any way for his grandfather's passing. I can tell, Oberi promised. *Neither his thoughts nor his heart lay guilt upon you. You were trying to help people. The only one to despise for this atrocious act is the Warden.*

Even if Charlie didn't blame me, I wasn't sure if it mattered. Because I blamed myself.

After my tears slowed, I left the parlor room and took an elevator to the dungeons below the castle. The agony in my heart turned to rage when I saw Abigail in a cell against the far wall, exactly where I'd put her. She sat on the floor, looking sad and alone.

I hadn't seen her since we'd left for the camps, and you know what? I didn't want to.

If I wasn't going to blame myself for Cassiel's passing, then I blamed Abigail. Someone had told Cassiel that we'd gone to the camps, and I'd already confronted Eldin about it. She'd followed my orders and kept her mouth shut. Abigail was under no obligation to do the same, not the way Eddie had to follow Charlie's orders. Abigail had run off and told the Emperor we'd left the palace, and it was because of *her* that he'd followed us to the Main Facility.

The Warden had been right. Having a good heart had been my downfall, because I trusted others to think the same way I did. I believed Abigail to be good, despite her family ties to the Warden, but she'd sent Cassiel after us on purpose to get him killed. She was the spy in the palace. I'd been a fool to think it couldn't be her, because it was so fucking *obvious*. The only reason I hadn't sent her to the gallows yet was because I wanted to find out what else she knew about the Taurus family. I'd get answers out of her; it would only take some time.

Except my patience was starting to run out.

"Why are you here?" Abigail rasped. "You've thrown me down here without an answer, leaving me for days, and now you come to visit?"

"You deserve to be imprisoned for betraying my trust," I growled.

"Let me explain," Abigail offered weakly.

"I don't need your explanations. The Emperor is dead. You've done enough."

"I beg you to hear me," Abigail pleaded. "I never meant to cause harm, only to protect you, as is my purpose."

"Fuck you. You were supposed to be my lady, but you went against my orders. The second my back was turned, you went running to Cassiel to tell him what we were doing. You're the reason he ended up at those camps, and you're the reason he's dead now."

"I'm not bound to you like Eddie is to Charlie, princess. We do not share a bond, so I am not magically obliged to follow your orders. I have to do what's best for the good of my people," Abigail insisted.

"*The good of your people?* What don't you understand? Cassiel is *dead*," I spat. "You need to know your station. I'm the princess, and I make decisions for the people. That means you do as you're told."

"If I hadn't told the Emperor where you were going, my uncle would've found you all, and he would've slaughtered you in those camps. Cassiel bought you time to escape."

"Screw you. We could've fought the Warden. We could've *beat* him!"

"Forgive me, princess, but that is a foolish hope," Abigail snapped. For the first time, her voice rose in anger. "If Cassiel had not gone after you, my uncle would've killed all of you!"

My fingers dug into the armrests of my chair, turning my fingers white. "You don't know what I'm capable of when it comes to destroying that man."

And she didn't— I didn't even know, not until this point. If I had wanted to kill the Warden before, I desired to completely and utterly ruin his soul now. There would be nothing left of him once he met my wrath, and I assured myself it *was* coming. I was only furious Abigail had taken that chance from me, and that Cassiel had paid the price.

"Even after all this time, you do not understand," Abigail raged. "You are a powerful princess, and Charlie is your prince, but the Emperor is above both of you. Pardon me for speaking bluntly, but this is a mob. There is a chain of command to follow that you and the prince stubbornly insist on going against time and again, but one rule above all here is that you *do not* disobey the commands from those that are above you. Orders from Cassiel took priority over yours. The Emperor ruled that you and your friends were *not* to go into the camps. You did not follow his orders, so I had to step in."

"Enough! You don't get to speak to me like that!" I yelled. Oberi quivered at my voice, shrinking down, and my screams grew louder. "I thought you were a friend, but you know what? That was a stupid mistake on my part. I should've listened to my intuition and gotten rid of you from the start. But I didn't, and now I have to deal with having a traitor in my midst."

Abigail's expression remained passive. "I have no idea what you mean, princess. I can assure you, I am not involved in any plot against you or the prince."

I gave a cold laugh. "You're such a liar, Abigail. You offered to spy for me when we first met, but it's clear you want to play both sides. You're working for the Warden— it's obvious. He was there waiting for us at the camps. He knew we'd show up. You hurried to deliver him a message to let him know we were coming, then conveniently told Cassiel where we'd gone, so he'd show up to rescue us. We *know* there's a traitor in the palace, giving messages to the Warden. We have for months. I just didn't want to believe it was you."

"It's not me," Abigail insisted. "I've never betrayed you! I've only done as the monarchy demands!"

"Shut up, bitch. I gave you a chance, because I thought we were alike. I felt *sorry* for you because of what Esther did to you. I felt bad that she took all the feathers from your wings, and wanted to help you. I thought you could under-stand me because you're in a wheelchair, too, but now I see that was just a ploy to make me feel like I belonged here in the palace. I gave you the benefit of the doubt, and it was the worst mistake I've ever made. I'll never trust an outsider again."

Abigail said nothing, which was good, because if she spoke again I wasn't sure what I would do. "You're excused from my service," I spat. "I cast you aside as my lady. If I ever see you again, I'll *kill you*."

I left Abigail there and abandoned the dungeons behind me. If she was crying on my way out, I didn't acknowledge it. I didn't let my anger fade until she was gone from my sight, but even so, once I was alone again it only abated slightly. I was still so enraged... and I wasn't exactly sure at who. The Warden, Abigail, myself? All of them all at once.

That was pretty harsh, Oberi grumbled.

So what. She hurt my family. I won't let her do that again.

We don't have any proof that she's the traitor.

We don't have any proof she's not.

False accusations can be more misleading than not having any clue of the perpetrator at all. If she's not the traitor, and there's another mole in the palace ferrying information to the other side that we don't know about, we're in big trouble.

I'm not risking it. There's enough evidence here to prove she's up to something, which means she's too dangerous to let roam free.

This kind of thing is exceptionally dangerous to get wrong, Oberi warned.

I knew full well, but I didn't care right now. Whatever I had said to Abigail, I felt justified about it. It wouldn't bring Cassiel back, but at least it gave me some way to place blame that wasn't just on me.

It was around dinnertime by now, but I didn't feel like eating. I hadn't, not since I'd seen the emaciated bodies of the camp victims piled up in the warehouses, desperate for a scrap of something to sustain their lives.

But I would eat, because I needed to gain my strength— to fight. I had to get better, get healthier, become more powerful, because the next time I faced the Warden I swore to myself he wasn't getting out of it alive.

Yet on my way to dinner, I felt a sharp tug on my bond. I halted in place, shocked to feel it, because I hadn't in days.

Charlie's calling us, Oberi said, tilting his head. *Seems pretty urgent about it.*

I felt my heart lift in hope. Finally, he was letting us in. I turned the other way. "Let's go, Oberi. We need to be there for him."

Whatever Charlie wanted me for, I'd help. If he was ready to come out of his room and face the world again, I'd help him carry his grief. He was my husband, and everything we'd faced at the camps together had only made me care for him a hundred times more. I couldn't imagine losing him, couldn't imagine watching him suffer, and I wouldn't dare to let him slip away. I'd be there for him, and though I'd made a big mistake, I swore to myself I *would* make it right again. We'd go through this together.

Until... I arrived in Charlie's quarters. All of our friends were gathered in the living room, and everyone looked... anguished. It was a sorry sight, everyone dressed in black and in mourning. Ez's eyes were bloodshot, and Opal's cheeks were pale. Ivy huddled in the corner, their arms wrapped around their torso as they turned away from it all. Alistair slumped on the couch, seemingly defeated. Chancey appeared dumbstruck, like he didn't want to believe whatever had just been said.

Kallie leaned over her knees in the armchair, shaking with rage. Marcus had a hand on her shoulder to comfort her, but his expression seemed... dark.

Danny stuck his hands in his pockets and scowled at the floor, as if he'd seen this coming and had done everything he could to stop it, but it still happened anyway.

I knew we were all devastated by what had happened at the camps, but this was something different. The moment he saw me enter, Chancey sprinted toward me, reaching out his hands to plead.

"Ava, you gotta stop it," Chancey begged. "Eddie told us everything. The guy's lost his mind!"

"What?" I hardly got the word out before a group of people surrounded me. Everyone was talking all at once, and it was hard to understand.

"He's a complete nutso!" Ivy ranted. "I can get behind a lot of things, but this is totally fucked."

"I thought we were his *friends*," Kallie said bitterly. "He betrayed us."

"What's going on?" I asked, feeling overwhelmed. I shrank under the demands of them all, starting to drown. Apparently, Eddie had told them something about Charlie, but I wasn't sure what it was.

"He's not letting any of us in," Marcus said. "You need to talk to him."

My friends spoke over one another. The noise got louder and louder. I couldn't make out any words, just sounds, and they melded with the voices in my head until I wasn't sure who was saying what. I felt suffocated, until I threw my hands up and said, "All right! I'll talk to him."

Whatever this was about, I would get to the bottom of it. I wheeled myself forward, and my friends stepped aside.

Charlie had locked the door, but I knocked loudly and said, "Charlie? It's me."

The door unlocked. I held my breath as I went inside. Oberi shut the door behind us, closing me in.

Charlie stood in our room. His hands were clasped behind his back, like he was waiting for me. He moved forward to lock the door again, even though I hadn't asked him to.

I wasn't sure what this was about. But clearly this was going to be an important conversation.

Charlie beckoned me forward. "Come with me."

I wasn't going to be summoned like some kind of pet. Yet still, I followed, Oberi padding behind me with his hair standing on end.

My stomach knotted into pits of nausea. I was terrified of whatever impending bomb he was going to drop on me, because obviously it wasn't good.

Charlie went to the balcony, and I knew it wasn't an option not to follow. The November breeze blew my hair back as we stood on the balcony that overlooked the city. Charlie put his hands on the railing and asked, "Ava, what do you see down there?"

"I see what I always see," I responded. What was he trying to say?

"Potential," he responded. "Wasted potential, not harnessed by my father, not being used for anything except to lie in wait for the Warden to come here and ruin it all. It's potential that'll be ruined unless I harness it."

I was already expecting the worst. "And how do you intend to do that?"

He didn't answer right away. He bounced in place nervously, his jaw hardening before he rounded on me.

"I waited to tell you, because I couldn't stand the thought of you being disappointed in me," Charlie started. "But I've realized this is something that needs to be done."

"*What* needs to be done?" I demanded, grabbing his arm. "Charlie, tell me!"

"The Warden needs to be beaten. We've given him too much time to get stronger," Charlie stated. "The more time we give him, the more power he's going to amass, which means we can't give him any more. We need to do what we can to intercede him *now*, so I had to take drastic action."

"Drastic— we already have the power to beat the Warden! We're demigods!" I objected.

"Pidge, my grandfather cut his head off and it didn't *do* anything," Charlie said roughly. "We're way out of our league unless we start taking control."

"So we can't decapitate him, or blow a hole in him, or rip his magic out of him. We'll just have to get creative."

"Ava, you witnessed the kind of power he has. The only reason he hasn't come here already and destroyed the city is because he can't get past the shield you put up. That's our only hope right now, and it's not going to last. The Warden's got big guns, and he's going to use those big guns to break your shield eventually."

"Those *big guns* of his aren't enough to bring down our wards," I countered. "He's got a lot of magical power, but that doesn't mean he can get past me. I'm strong enough to hold him off."

"It doesn't *matter*. You're strong enough for now, but that won't last."

"The hell it won't," I snarled. "I don't care what the Warden does to make himself powerful— there will never come a day when he's more powerful than me. I'll be stronger than him *always*."

"Pidge, he has the power to destroy the entire city in one blast. He just has to know how to break your magic down, and mark my words, he's going to figure it out sooner or later. We can't keep hiding here and expecting that he'll never reach us, because it's not going to work."

"You're jumping to conclusions. If the Warden hasn't come for us by now, then we're strong enough to keep hiding. He has all this power and still isn't able to get past my defenses. If he could, he'd be here already," I pointed out.

"So what? He has control over Celestial City, Atlantis, Kinpago, Octavia Falls, and almost all of the vampire territories except Chicago, and Salvatore will be next on his list once he deals with us. Then he'll go on to bully the Astromancers into joining him, and they won't have a choice but to take his side. The only places we have left are Dolinska, *Hok'evale*, Edinmyre and Ilamanthe, and that's not enough to stand up against him. Not without a plan. He could destroy fae-owned territories or what's left of Elementai land within days. We need to stop him before that happens by fighting fire with fire, and throwing our army at his."

"This war is personal," I argued. "We need to target *him*, not all of his soldiers."

"You aren't listening," Charlie said. "There's only one way to beat the Warden, and I know how."

My heart grew heavy with terror. Sounds began swelling over the palace gardens— shouts, screams of horror, metal singing as weapons clashed. The sounds of the dying... something I never thought I'd hear in Ilamanthe... created a symphony of sorrow across the city streets as the music of battle began its plight.

"Charlie, what did you do?" I asked, my voice painted with horror.

"What I had to," he growled. "My father is a pathetic excuse for an Emperor. He can't lead us anywhere but into failure. If he rules Ilamanthe, we lose. My grandfather prepared me to take the Elvish throne, and I'm not waiting my turn in line. I'm overthrowing my father, *today*, and taking the city's army for myself."

I clutched at my throat. "You can't stage a coup against your father! Have you lost your mind?"

"Why not? I'm a demigod, so are you. We can do anything we want to," Charlie said forcefully.

I wildly grasped for excuses. "You're grieving. You're not thinking straight—"

"No, Ava. I've been considering this for a long time. I have to move forward, and fulfill the destiny my grandfather had in store for me."

"How are you even doing this? Who's fighting for you?" I demanded.

"The young guards of the city are loyal to me. They believe that I should become Emperor, and that Cameron needs to go. Max told me that a long time ago. It's only the old guard that's loyal to my father. I've already sent Eddie to deploy my orders. My Associates are leading the charge, and once my father is out of the way, we can do what needs to be done around here."

"And was Eddie happy to rally your soldiers against the rest of his family?" I asked sourly, knowing absolutely he wasn't.

"It doesn't matter what Eddie wants. He's sworn to me, so he'll do as I say."

"Why didn't you tell me about this?" I asked, and I moved closer. "You didn't go over this with me at all."

Charlie's answer, so cold, wasn't what I expected. "You didn't need to know."

My love for him turned spiteful. "So now you're keeping secrets in our marriage? That's not the Charlie I knew."

"That person doesn't exist anymore! I'm sorry if I'm not the man you wanted me to be, but I have to become something bigger now." He grabbed my hands. "But it doesn't have to mean anything for us. We love each other. So let's be together, and not let anything get in the way of that."

I searched his eyes and saw that this was the truth he believed. This was a worse reality than even my darkest nightmares could've conjured. No matter what I'd feared or imagined, it had never been this.

"You can still take it back," I begged. "Call off the guards, say you made a mistake. It doesn't have to be this way. The Elves shouldn't be fighting each other. We're killing our own soldiers! Your grandfather wouldn't want a civil war in Ilamanthe!"

"My grandfather would want me to do whatever it takes to win," he insisted, and he yanked his hands away.

"Charlie, don't you get it? This isn't a game! This is an insurrection!" I yelled. Behind me, Oberi let out a whine.

"Of course I understand," Charlie said, and he gave a twisted laugh. "Am I insane for enjoying the pain of my enemies? Am I mad for wanting to use the power I have to stop the Warden? If that's being crazy, then that's what you can call me. I personally don't care what labels people put on me. *Insane* is a term people give to the ones they're afraid of, and everyone needs to be afraid of me. It's the only way we'll survive."

"So you overthrow your dad, what next?" I asked harshly. "What's your grand scheme then?"

"We'll take the Elvish soldiers and go to our allies. I'll take command of *Hok'evale*, Dolinska, and any other magical city that's still out of the Warden's grasp. Then I'll unite the supernaturals we have together under the Elvish banner, into one army. Anyone who is able to fight, must. There can be no exceptions."

"You can't force people to fight for you," I said. Hot tears started burning at the corners of my eyes.

"I can and I will. Once we've got enough soldiers, we'll take everything we've got and face The Mission head-on. All our fighters, all our demigods. We'll corner the Warden and beat him back until we're able to put that bastard down. He can kill some of us; hell, he can even kill *most* of us, but he can't kill us all."

"You don't know that." I put a hand to my mouth to hold back the revulsion. "You're just sending people to slaughter, throwing whatever you can at the Warden because you're scared."

"If you aren't scared you aren't taking this seriously," Charlie hissed. "I've got to make hard choices, because I'm the only one who can."

"Okay, so let's pretend it all works out and the Warden's dead. You really think the supernatural community is going to forgive you once you've done this?" I snapped.

"You still aren't seeing the big picture. Ava, look at the opportunity we have!" Charlie said, spreading his arms out wide. "We're demigods, and we've been given this power for a divine purpose. The gods gave us our magic so we could set things right, and it would be wasteful not to use our abilities. Once we beat the Warden, the world is *ours*. We'll have such a powerful army that no one will be able to oppose us! We'll rule it *all*."

Tears began to fall from my eyes. This was everything I despised— everything I was against and didn't believe in. "Charlie, you're breaking my heart."

He wasn't listening. He was rambling on, ranting to himself in a frantic, deranged voice I'd never heard him use before. "There's only one way to stop war forever and make sure the world stays safe. I'm going to lead the Elves in a rebellion that's going to *crush* all the supernatural races, and bring them under our dominion. Then there will be no more fighting, and I'll have control over everything. Once we bring in the humans, we'll have world peace. Anyone who opposes us will immediately be put to death. The Elves are the original supernatural race and therefore are superior, so we *deserve* to rule over everything. It's the only thing that makes sense."

I was crying properly now. Charlie knew this went against my values. I put freedom and free will above all other morals, and he was trying to take that away from everyone, in the name of him becoming the ruler of it all. It was wrong beyond belief, and he knew I'd rather die than watch the world end up that way.

Yet... he had already considered my feelings on the subject, and he was choosing to go through with it anyway.

"How are you going to explain this to our friends? They'll hate you," I gasped through tears.

"So let them," Charlie stated. "They can either get behind me, or they can fall with the rest of them."

My already broken heart tore in two again. "Fall with the rest of them? You…"

I thought back to when we'd found Kallie in the alleyway, how I'd caught his fleeting thought that it was already too late to save her. "You were going to leave Kallie, weren't you?"

"I didn't *want* to," Charlie said, and he took a step closer. "But if it came down to her or the key—"

"No!" I pulled away. "I don't care if there were a million Divinity Keys in that safe! I would've picked Kallie *every time*."

"Then you don't understand what we need to do to win," Charlie replied. "For the greater good, we have to be willing to make some sacrifices."

Who the hell had I married? Who was this man standing in front of me whom I'd shared my deepest dreams, my life, my *body* with? I didn't recognize him in the slightest. In moments, the dearest person in my existence had become a stranger to me.

No, not a stranger. A monster.

"When did you come up with this?" I whispered. Danny's warning came back to me. I was horrified with the thought of how long Charlie had been plotting… weeks, months? And I'd known nothing.

My marriage was an illusion. It was created out of lies, and now, was being blown to pieces.

"I've been considering this for a long time. I didn't want to, at first, because it seemed so cruel, but now I know it's what has to be done," Charlie said.

He extended a hand to me. "Ava, be my Empress. Help me make this world ours, so it can be a better place for everyone. With me as the king of this planet, and you as my queen, we can end suffering forever. I know that's what you want more than anything. Once this is all over, no one else ever has to be in pain. We can bring justice, hope, accessibility and safety to the people of this world. We just have to get our hands a little dirty."

I didn't take his hand. I backed my chair away and stated, "The Warden wants to end suffering, too. And your plan sounds a hell of a lot like his."

"I think I'm finally starting to see his point," Charlie said through clenched teeth. "It's him, or us. All of this was going to happen either way. It simply comes down to who's stronger."

Oberi hadn't said anything this entire time, only listened to what Charlie had to say. But now he spoke up, coming forward with bared teeth. *Charlie, this is unacceptable. I can't let this happen.*

"You're just a Familiar!" Charlie screamed, and Oberi lunged away. "*I'm* your Elementai, and I say we do this!"

"I'm his Elementai, too!" I yelled, coming to Oberi's aid and planting myself in front of Charlie, to defend my beloved dog. "You're not the only one in control here!"

"Ava, the Elves need you. *I* need you," Charlie said firmly. "You can't turn your back on this. Do you want to become the Warden's prisoner, or do you want to rule with me? Because those are your options."

I never cowered away when I was backed into a corner, even by my own husband. My mind rushed to wickedly devise a plan. I had to do some damage control. I wasn't going to be able to talk him out of this, so I had to play the long game.

I could lie, and say I wanted to go along with his plan. Then I would manipulate him to change his mind about all of this. Over time, I could make him understand what he was doing was wrong, and he'd back off. We'd beat the Warden the *right way*, without using anyone, and we could still have our happy life at the end.

Charlie wasn't in his right mind. Once enough time passed, and he grieved his grandfather properly, I could set him back on a good path. He'd realize what he was doing was wrong, and then we'd put things back the way they should be. This wasn't really him— he was just hurting and lashing out. I was his wife. Nobody understood him like I did, and though I'd miscalculated, I could still rectify the situation. I'd promised Danny that I could control him, so I would. I could fix this.

I pulled myself together. "You're right. The last thing I want is to become a slave to the Warden, and if that happens, I won't be able to save anyone. At least if you and I are on top, we can do this our way. We don't have a choice if we want to keep people safe. I understand where you're coming from. We have to do this, to make the world a better place. So where are we going first?"

"You're not going anywhere," Charlie replied. "You're staying in the palace."

The world's axis shifted. I felt reality narrowing inward, enclosing me into a box that had little air to breathe as the earth tilted below me. "What?"

"You're too precious to lose," Charlie pleaded. He came before me on his knees, grasping my hands again, which were already turning cold. "You're not just valuable to me; you're priceless to the Elves as well. The Empress must always be kept safe."

He brushed back a lock of my hair and whispered, "Don't you realize how much I love you? That's why you have to stay here, where you're protected and won't get hurt. You've already died once. I can't bear to lose you again."

He'd turned into a raving lunatic. I guess we all had our breaking point. I should've seen this coming, but I'd willfully ignored it. Now I had to deal with the consequences.

"Do you really think this is the life I would've chosen for myself?" I asked, quivering with rage.

"Ava, I will give you whatever you wish," Charlie offered. "I'll make this life a paradise for you inside this tower, and you'll never have to ask for anything. You want it, it's yours."

"I'll have everything except my freedom," I spat.

"Because that's too much to ask for!" Charlie began pacing, walking the length of the balcony. "I know you want to travel, to explore and see the world, but that's not an option anymore. You're too much of a treasure, and we have too many enemies. You can still have a full life in Ilamanthe without leaving the palace. I'll make sure of it."

"That's not what I want!" I was bawling now. I wish I had some of that fiery courage I was known for, but I wasn't able to summon it against Charlie. At least, not at the moment, because I was dying inside. My entire spirit was decaying, and he could feel it, and he didn't care.

"I know what's best for you," Charlie said, dropping his voice to a gentle croon. "You promised me that I could make the decisions and you'd be okay with them. This is what I've decided."

"This is *nothing* like what we agreed to." I hated that he was using my choice to trust in him to lock me into a prison. I wiped more tears away with the heel of my hand. "The villain, keeping his trapped princess inside a tower. Might as well be a storybook."

"You're being dramatic," Charlie replied patronizingly. "You'll be living in luxury, and with our friends. I'll be here as often as I can. I adore you. I won't be apart from you for long."

You will not keep Ava in a cage, Oberi warned, and his hackles raised as he defiantly put himself between Charlie and me.

"I'll do whatever it takes to honor my marriage vows and keep her safe!" Charlie barked. "Why won't either of you accept that I'm trying to protect my wife?"

There was nothing left to say. I'd become empty. Charlie had hollowed me out and made me into a shell. He'd rather chain me up than lose me, and that was *nothing* resembling love.

I never wanted him to touch me again.

"I have important things to attend to. You're staying in our room until the rebellion is done." Charlie left the balcony and returned to the bedroom. I followed him, though I didn't know why. Maybe there was still a little protest in me, something that made me want to fight back.

"Charlie, don't go," I begged, as a last-ditch attempt to talk my way out of this. "Don't leave me here."

He went to the door, and as he opened it, I saw a full line of guards standing outside the room. I knew they were waiting for me.

"Charlie..." I whispered again. Another tear fell down my trembling face, and into my mouth. I tasted bitter salt.

He didn't even turn around to speak to me. "It'll be all right. Soon, you'll understand, and want things to be my way."

My tears slowed as I sneered, "Cassiel would've *never* done this to Aponi."

Charlie paused at the door. His response was heartless as he replied, "My grandfather didn't have someone like you."

Then he turned to the head guard. "Keep the princess inside. Don't let her out until I come to get her."

"Yes, your highness," the guard replied, giving a short bow.

Then he left me there. *He left me.* Charlie abandoned me in my new jail, closing the door and leaving our marriage in a complete state of destruction, so he could go on to do as he pleased and get what he wanted.

I ceased to feel as I realized this tower was just another prison I'd found myself locked in. The palace had become my new Institute, but it was far worse than anything Doctor Taurus had ever put me through, because this time, *Charlie* was my new Warden. My husband had become my captor, and everything I thought I knew about us, our love, and everything we shared exploded into dust. Memories shattered in my vision, days Charlie had spent by my side and nights I'd given up all of me to him.

I wasn't sure if it'd been real. I didn't know if it ever was. Whatever his motives, his reasons, doing this to me was unforgivable.

Oberi was in shock. He stood at my side, unable to function as he fought against the truth of what had just happened.

"I don't understand how we didn't catch this. We share a bond," I said brokenly. "We can hear his thoughts. Marcus looked inside his mind, and Danny felt his desires, but we still didn't see this coming."

He was lying to himself about what he truly wanted, Oberi said somberly. *It is the only way he could've misled us, and Danny and Marcus as well. To deceive us, he first had to deceive himself.*

At his words, I realized something crippling. I thought back to the vision the Elven goddesses had sent me not so long ago— the images that had flashed across my mind of the rampaging armies across the world, the old bearded king upon his throne, and the dead woman at the base of the tower.

The full truth of the visions hit me hard, and I clutched at my chest, feeling a sharp pain. The king I'd seen hadn't been the Warden, and the marching armies hadn't been The Mission. Those had been *Charlie's* soldiers, and the old king was Charlie himself. The goddesses had tried to give me a forewarning of what was coming. They had seen that Charlie would take the world over for himself, and that everything would suffer and die because of it due to famine and disease. The entire planet would turn to nothing but barren ash, all the realm's people at the mercy of a dictator-emperor.

The woman who'd thrown herself from the top of the tower was still me, but my end wasn't a result of being the Warden's prisoner. In my vision, I'd endured years of sadness watching Charlie rule over all, and my love for him eventually faded and turned to agonized hate. Charlie didn't let me wander free, nor did he permit me any sort of happiness within the palace except the kind he desired. One day, I wasn't able to take it anymore, and I jumped from the tower to end my life. The cry of the wyvern within my vision had been Oberi, grieving for me, as I abandoned Charlie to rule over his vast and empty kingdom alone.

This wasn't what could happen— I understood deeply that this was what *would* happen, if Charlie achieved his goal. He'd bring the entire world under his command and destroy it. I wouldn't be able to talk him out of it, no matter what I did, and any affection we had for each other would eventually wither away under the shadow of his greed.

I thought about the future, and what it held. I could tell Charlie of this new interpretation, but I already knew he wouldn't listen. The years would drag on by. I'd still be an Elvish mystic, but he wouldn't take my visions seriously if I foresaw something negative. He'd ignore my warnings and forge ahead anyway, like he was doing now. I'd become no more than a spiritual figurehead without any power, if I wasn't that already.

There were no options. Either the Warden was going to take over the world, or Charlie would, and both options would bring agony and anguish to anyone who managed to survive the all-encompassing war. Those who died in battle would be the lucky ones, for those who made it to whatever new world was built would live in misery until the day they died. Neither one of them would get to build the utopia they desired, for they would bring nothing but suffering.

Oberi observed every thought I had, trembling with each passing image as it flitted through my mind. *So the goddesses have spoken,* Oberi marveled. *If Charlie wins, this is what will be.*

"Yes. And we're powerless to stop it." I hung my head.

Oberi put a paw on my knee. *You are not powerless, for the prophecy is not yet done.*

He was correct. There was still one verse of my prophecy that hadn't been fulfilled.

A new world formed from gods of old,
One from ashes or one from light
The choice is hers alone

I still had a final, last option. One choice— a choice that I needed to make quickly.

The ending of my prophecy was never about us beating the Warden. It was always about me defeating *Charlie*. He had chosen to curse me to a cruel fate in order to turn the world to dust at his command. A fate worse than death was my destiny, and I knew that fate was one where I remained locked in a cage.

But I wouldn't be the only one. Charlie was going to lock us *all* in his prison, and we wouldn't be able to escape him on Earth or in the afterlife, because it was his destiny to open the Elven Gate. Once he did that, he would have control over the Blessed Haven. The Divinity Keys were going to give him that kind of power, and I'd put them right in his hands.

Yet I still had a chance to change this fate. I could save people by wiping the entire universe off the map, because being an eternal prisoner was worse than not existing at all.

I recalled the dying Earth from my vision the goddesses had sent me, and knew I couldn't allow that to happen. I needed to save this world from the person I loved, because the fate he would give it would be a more painful one than the ending I'd bestow.

My magic was strong, and you know what? I think this was where everything was leading to after all, right from the very beginning.

My mother had taught me that I could connect with the Earth's soul, and pull from it to strengthen my own magic. I'd tried to use that spell for good, and had desired to get stronger so that once I was powerful enough, I could use it to heal every soul and heart on the planet at once.

Now I accepted that spell would never work. There were too many bastards like the Warden roaming this realm, and they would never let me heal them, so that meant the world would always be this way unless I took a different path. Instead of using my connection to Earth's soul to heal the world...

I could reverse it, and change the universe forever.

I could feel the connection between the Earth and the spiritual realm, strained and fighting to survive. All I would have to do was tie my Spirit magic to that bond, and yank it tight. Once I did, both realms would collapse, and reality would cease to be. The Earth would be destroyed, along with all who lived on it, and the spiritual realm would die, taking all its souls and the gods within one energetic blast.

Everything in existence... would end.

I expected Oberi to freak out, but he didn't. He calmly resonated with my thoughts, taking the idea in.

"What's the point of living, Oberi?" I asked desperately. I wasn't sure if he could help me, but I needed some sort of excuse. Just one, to convince me to turn away from what I was considering.

I'm unsure, Oberi responded. *Perhaps before, I might've pretended to know the answers. But all my millennia of living cannot grasp, fathom, nor accept that Charlie has become this, or that his actions are going to ruin the lives of millions.*

"If this can happen to Charlie, and the world can make him into a monster like this, it can happen to anybody," I insisted. "He'll be worse than the Warden. He'll be more ruthless. I *know* he can be."

I took Oberi's furry face in my hands. "And then what'll I be? His pretty pigeon that he takes out of a gilded cage whenever he wants to play with me? He'll ruffle my feathers every now and then, but he'll *never* let me out long enough for me to spread my wings. Since the start, he's called me his little bird, and that's *exactly* what he's gonna make me into. I'm merely his pet, a sacrificial lamb he's willing to slaughter for his enjoyment. He's willing to bargain my freedom to get what he desires. Then what'll happen to you, huh?"

Oberi's big black eyes got sadder. *I will be his weapon, as he desires to use me as one. I am too powerful to be kept in a cage, and unlike you, I cannot die. Since he cannot lose me, I will become an asset, a tool of war against his enemies.*

"So you understand. This is the only way. It'll be beautiful. Glorious, even."

If he is capable of imprisoning you and taking away your freedom, as I did not think he would be, then he is capable of anything, Oberi said. *He is something we must protect the world from.*

"But can we protect it by ending it." It wasn't even a question, really. More of... asking permission.

There are far worse things than death, and this world has been left scarred by people like him. We cannot allow this to go on any longer, Oberi said firmly. *This cycle of suffering and purposeless pain needs to be drawn to a close. Whatever you decide, I will support you, and be behind you all the way.*

Clearly, he wasn't going to convince me otherwise, and I didn't want him to. "Do you really think this is the right decision?"

I cannot say, Oberi mused. *All I can say is that I love you, and trust you. If this is your choice as the prophecy says, then I am bound to your fate. May it be that something good comes out of this after all.*

"I think so. After all, energy can neither be created nor destroyed, save by demigods. If I destroy the Earth and the afterlife, all that energy has to go *some-*

where, so it'll recreate the universe and start everything over... give life a better chance. It'll be like the big bang, all over again from the beginning of creation, except *I'll* be the one creating the universe this time. If I sacrifice myself and everyone else, it could create a better world. An ideal world, one without all this hate."

It could, Oberi offered. *Or it could bring about a new universe full of calamity. Are you willing to risk that?*

I took a moment to really consider what I was contemplating. I thought about all the wars in the world, how they destroyed people's lives and ruined families. I thought about Kallie, what the Dollmaker had done to her, and all the girls in the future who would become victims to evil men. I thought about all those poor souls in the camps, and how cruelly they'd been treated before their miserable end. Nothing like that should ever be permissible, yet genocides similar to it had happened time and again throughout history, and they would continue to persist if something wasn't done.

Then I thought about all the vile, evil monsters who'd done all those awful things to innocents who didn't deserve it. Even if we killed the Warden, or convinced Charlie to stand down, another creature just as cruel as them would come in to take their place. And I figured if all those terrible things could happen in the world, it wasn't worth sparing anyway. I needed to protect others from enduring horrible things, even if protecting them meant ending their existence. I couldn't allow the afterlife to go on— the circle of reincarnation would just keep going, souls would find another plane of reality to return to, and the cycle would start up all over again.

No... if I was destroying everything, I was destroying it *all*.

No one would know if everything faded. They wouldn't have any comprehension of it, because they'd be gone. I would be, too. I could wipe out the entirety of suffering forever, for all of life in one single stroke. I had one thing the other demigods didn't. My demigod magic gave me a connection to the Earth, and I could break her spirit. Once that happened, nothing could stop this realm from breaking at the seams, sending a ripple of chaos through the other realms and destroying them all entirely.

It was all I ever desired, to stop the suffering of others forever, but I never thought it would end up like this.

But either way... if I did this, I'd finally get what I wanted.

Emperor Cassiel was right. Someone would always have to pay the price to end suffering. This time, it would be us all.

"I'll risk whatever it takes to make sure something like what happened in the camps never happens again," I promised Oberi. I landed on a decision.

There was still a small, bitter part of me that protested. A part that said this wasn't the only way and we'd find another solution, if I only gave it a chance.

I detested that Ava. She was weak— she still wanted to *play the hero*. She was desperate to save the world and all the people in it. She wanted to act like she was good inside, just misunderstood, when that really wasn't the case at all. She did everything she could to belong and gave away parts of who she was to try and fit the mold of the people around her, because achieving the status quo meant she'd finally be accepted for who she was. She was a girl that begged for scraps of love because she didn't feel like she deserved it, a girl who thought in black-and-white and only saw the world in one way. Right was right and wrong was wrong, to her. Things were simple and straightforward, and bad people deserved to be punished just as good people deserved to be rewarded.

That was a ridiculous concept. I wasn't a good person. I didn't know how long it was going to take for me to accept that. On top of it, I didn't want to be. Good people got used and mistreated. I was always going to be an outcast, and I was never going to be accepted for the person I was born to be. I was sick of carving parts out of my heart in order to fit into a role that wasn't mine. I knew the world wasn't black and white, and that everyone had good and evil inside of them. It only depended on what parts people chose to show. In this world we lived in now, *no one* was a hero. Punishments and rewards weren't given out depending on a person's actions, but by chance... and by people deciding what they deserved and taking it for themselves, despite any morals that might say otherwise.

I wasn't a hero. And I was tired of trying to play the part. There was a dagger inside of me that had been plunged into my back long ago by all the *good people* of the world, a dagger that cut deep and said that I'd never belong.

You know what? I loved that dagger. It made me who I was, and I was sick of trying to pull it out. If I didn't belong, I was more than happy with that. I'd bleed on all the fuckers who dared to get in my way. I didn't need anyone to love me but myself, and whatever decisions I made would be the right ones. There was no need to second guess myself anymore.

From deep inside myself, I summoned my Spirit magic. I put my hand on Oberi's chest, then lifted my fingers upward to project my soul out.

A piece of myself, a part of the spirit that I shared with Charlie, materialized out of Oberi's heart. She took form, hovering before me. She looked like me, had identical features and a cold smile, but she appeared younger.

And she stood, looming over me tall on two legs. This was the person I'd been before the Infernal Underground, and I'd still been holding on to her. I hadn't realized how tightly she'd been clinging to me. This was the person that had been formed from all my parents' stories, the hero that I'd dreamed someday I might be. If I was to do what needed to be done, she couldn't be a part of me anymore.

I couldn't show any mercy. I needed to kill her. She was hurting me and holding me back from everything I had the potential to become. I was burying her today, and turning her to ash.

The good girl I'd tried to be stared back with merciless eyes. "You can't kill me. You need me."

"I haven't needed you in years." My fingers glowed with blue Fire, and I raised my arm. "You aren't who I am."

"Wait—" she pleaded, but her words turned to screams as my blue Fire ignited her form. I wrapped tendrils of Spirit magic around her form so she couldn't move, binding her as the flames licked up her body. My flames consumed the part of my soul that still dared to hope I could be someone I wasn't, and she cried out in pain as her flesh singed away by the Fire. Smoke filtered from her body and through the open balcony, turning the sky black.

It should've hurt, but it didn't. I felt nothing but relief, and a sense of freedom that I was finally rid of her. Eventually, my blue flames burned only air, and I pulled back my power.

I had no regrets. That bitch had to die, because she wasn't strong enough to keep moving forward.

I felt lighter once she was gone, as if she had been holding me in shackles the same way the Warden and Charlie had. I would not become a prisoner to anyone— not even myself.

I sat taller in my chair as I turned toward the door, finally the woman I needed to be, finally ready to meet my destiny. They wanted a villain for their queen, and by the gods, I was going to give them one.

I was made for no man. I belong to myself.

I wrenched open the door, fully expecting that I'd have to take down a full battalion of guards on my way out. But I didn't have to— Kallie stood over them all with a bloody dagger in one hand, an illusion spell still burning in the other. Bodies of Elves were scattered all around the living area. I wasn't sure if they were dead or just knocked out, but I supposed it didn't matter either way— not with what I was about to do.

"Kallie," I breathed, and I rushed to her. She hugged me tightly, and I said, "I knew you'd never leave me."

Best friends before anyone else, that was what I truly believed.

"I wasn't going to leave you in there," she swore. "Never."

"Where's everyone else?" I asked.

"Watching the battle. The one he... started." Kallie couldn't bring herself to say Charlie's name. "I stayed behind, because I didn't trust him."

"He locked me up, Kallie." Tears beaded at my eyelids once again, but I wouldn't allow them to fall. Why bother to cry when my tears would soon cease to have meaning?

"I know. I was going to confront him, but I realized it would be a better idea to get you out." She sheathed her dagger. "What's the plan?"

I wasn't sure if she was going to understand. But Kallie knew me better than most people in this world, and we had a deeper connection in some ways than even Charlie and I did. There were things I could discuss with her that my husband just wouldn't get.

Clearly.

"He's not going to quit, Kallie. No matter what you guys do, he'll go forward with what he wants," I stated. "The only thing that's gonna stop him... is me."

"If you're going to fight him, I'll help," Kallie stated.

"No." I reached out to grasp her hands and squeezed them in mine. "I'm going to make sure he can't do this ever again. Or anyone else, for the rest of time."

Kallie blinked as she slowly caught my meaning. "You're going to do it? You're going to break the connection between the spirit realm and Earth, end the world?"

"The world, the afterlife, the universe... all of it."

Kallie nodded and squeezed my hands back. "Okay. I'm with you."

"Really?" I was shocked beyond belief. Didn't she want to give any kind of protest?

Kallie nodded again. "After going to the camps, I don't see the point in fighting anymore. All the bloodshed is just going to continue, even centuries after we're gone. Our descendants are going to forget about this war just so they can go fight in another."

Kallie's lips trembled as she struggled to hold the tears inside. "And I don't know if I'm strong enough to keep enduring flashbacks of what the Dollmaker did to me for the rest of my life. Or the fact that every day, there's another woman out there who's meeting the same fate, and I can do nothing about it. I love Marcus. But I don't want to keep living like this. I don't think it's fair for anyone else to, either. I just want it all to be over."

"It *will* be over, Kallie. We'll do it together, so not you or me or anybody else has to suffer anymore," I promised. "Best friends until the end."

"Always." Kallie shuddered. "You know Charlie is going to try and stop you."

I dropped her hands, and my mouth fell into a thin line as I steeled my tone. "I refuse to be afraid of my husband."

"Then let's go," Kallie said. "Where are you going to do it?"

"The beach, on the city limits," I told her. "It's going to be deserted. No one will be able to stop me out there."

"I'll find Charlie and the others. I'll distract them, to give you enough time to get the job done."

We hesitated, and it was for the same reason. I somehow managed to process that this was the last time I was going to see her... ever. There'd be no afterlife for us to reunite in.

It would be like that for everyone I loved. I would never see my parents again, my siblings, my friends...

I'd never see Monica again. I was willingly choosing not to. Ancestors, it nearly broke my will and made me turn back. Let Charlie and the Warden destroy it all, just so I could see her smile and say my name one last time.

Yet my cause was greater. I wished upon wish that maybe one day, the new stars that would be created from the fragments of our souls would come together, casting out stardust. Perhaps in another eternity, we'd be reunited again.

She embraced me again. "You've been the best friend I could've ever asked for, Ava. I wish things could've been different."

I hugged her back as tightly as I could, praying I could mold her into me so we didn't have to be separated. "It was the best, Kallie. You were one of the greatest joys of my life."

"And you mine." She lifted a watery smile as Oberi shifted into a unicorn beside me. Kallie helped me onto her back. I grasped Kallie's hand, locked onto her gaze, and held on for as long as I could before our fingers trailed apart as Oberi carried me away.

There were guards warring and killing each other in the halls, but Oberi swerved me around the various battles as we galloped through the palace. I glanced to my right as we passed the main hall and saw Cameron surrounded by his men, shouting orders as he battled Charlie's warriors off with magic and his sword.

All this death and unnecessary war, merely to decide who would rule over what. It was stupid. That cycle would end today.

Oberi burst into the gardens. Once she did, her body morphed and became larger, growing scales and wings. The wyvern lifted into the sky, taking flight and carrying me far away from the palace.

Oberi flew me toward the beach. As he did so, words that the Warden spoke to me years ago came back to haunt my thoughts, his voice creeping at the edges of my being.

One day, the four of you will have a disagreement, a difference of opinion that'll lead to division. Then it'll be as simple to pick you apart as it is to pick the wings off a fly.

Well, he was right. We were broken apart now. Charlie and me, our friends, all of us. But I wouldn't give the Warden enough time to divide our group in order to conquer them, because I was finishing them off myself. The best part about this was even though I was destroying the people I cared for, I was destroying the Warden, too, and he was going down with us.

As I flew over the city, I looked down. I observed Elves battling in the streets, fighting with each other and spilling blood as Charlie's side and Cameron's fought to take control.

Let them. It would all be over soon.

Then... my eyes locked upon a lone figure on the top of a nearby penthouse. I recognized her as I flew overhead. Our eyes connected, and her gaze... it looked so sad. But full of acceptance, like she'd been waiting for this day to come and no longer had to carry the burden of it upon her shoulders.

Aunt Maddie. She knew I was going to do this all along, because she'd foreseen it. She'd tried to warn me, but I hadn't listened. She could've killed me in my crib, stopped all this from happening, but she didn't. She'd left the choice up to me.

I was grateful for that. She'd done the job of a *naderei* and hadn't interfered, despite what she'd foreseen.

Oberi landed on the beach. I was still inside the shield, but it wasn't like that made a difference now. I held on to Oberi's head as he lifted me off his back, setting me in the sand. He shifted back into a husky as he stood beside me, waiting for me to take action.

The waves crashed onto the shore, my most beloved sound. As high tide met its peak, I gave a sad smile at the ocean I loved so much. The horizon line called to me as it always did, promising adventures I'd never have and incredible sights that I'd never see.

It was a shame we were losing all this beauty, the brilliance of the natural world and all its biodiversity. All because we couldn't get along.

An orange hue broke out over the sea, purple and pink colors racing throughout the sky. What a beautiful sunset. A perfect way to conclude our story.

Are you going to do it now? Oberi asked, and he tilted his head.

"Yes," I replied. It was the only way.

I put both hands on the ground, digging into the sand. I felt the Earth's energy deep within the ground, going down to the core of the planet. There was the bond that linked our realm to the spiritual one. The vibration of the Blessed Haven and all the afterlifes it contained sent an echoing call to Earth, and I felt that connection tremor as souls ferried back and forth along that tethered rope. Once I set off a chain reaction that couldn't be stopped, all of it would fall apart.

Harnessing all my power, I wrapped my Spirit magic around the rope and began to pull. Immediately, there was resistance, but I pushed harder. The bond began to crack under my pressure, and there was a great moan that spread throughout the land as the Earth started to protest.

I became enraged at this realm and outraged by her spirit. Back in the gardens with my parents, when I first felt Earth's spirit, I saw her beauty. She showed me her divine feminine energy, her desire to nurture and spread joy.

But she was in all of us— every human and supernatural on the planet— and while she could build mountains and create life, we were the part of her that would always be destructive. There was a dark side to her feminine beauty, and it was *us*. People would continue to sabotage each other— to starve, rape, murder, and abuse. This was never going to end, unless *I* put an end to it.

Images of war passed behind my lids. I recalled photographs and artist depictions of the Hawkei Civil War, along with stories my parents had shared with me. I thought of the wars all our parents had fought just to get us here; the Malovian Revolution that Kallie's parents won, along with the Miriamic Conflict that Marcus' parents fought so hard to resolve. It was all for nothing, because war had never really ended. The wounds caused by those wars only permeated through to the next generation, so that we would keep hurting each other over and over again.

I saw myself holding Monica's bleeding body in my arms, and I felt John force himself onto me. I heard the screams of Elves as they were slaughtered while trying to flee Forevermore. I could still smell the rotting corpses we'd found in the crypt beneath the Institute's graveyard. I felt the agonizing invasion of inferichite as Jaymin's spell invaded my magic in the Infernal Underground, and the crushing weight of death as my spirit was torn from my body that night. I still remembered the torturous screams of Cellblock 9 as the guards trapped us inside to torment us. Terror rocked my soul as I relived the night the Institute fell and the Warden summoned the dark gods. I recalled the devastation we'd witnessed at the Main Facility, and my heart shredded at the thought of all the lives lost there. I brought up images of the bloody battle back at the palace as my own people turned upon their brothers and sisters in arms.

I showed the Earth all of this, because if I was going to break her, I had to break her spirit— as she had done to mine.

The Earth's resistance was futile as I forced my magic to keep going, breaking the connection apart. This was going to take some time. A deep connection like this wasn't going to break unless I forced it to, and there was already so much strain upon it from the fight between the gods. Reality was bending. I only had to shape it to my will.

When I began breaking the connection, there was an immediate reaction. The firmament underneath me began vibrating, and cracks appeared in the ground over a mile long. Earthquakes rumbled throughout the area, and I watched as a skyscraper in the distance collapsed within Ilamanthe's borders, crumbling to nothing as an earthquake rattled it to the ground. The lovely sunset faded as the sky turned dark, and pitch-black storm clouds thundering with lightning raged overhead. A windstorm picked up, sweeping my hair around my face. I watched waterspouts form on the waves in the distance, waves that were quickly forming into a tsunami.

I was doing it. I was bringing a stop to it all.

I heard more screams resonate from the city and nearly held myself back. But I kept going, because I reminded myself these people deserved better, and so did I.

I wasn't doing this because I no longer loved Charlie. Not at all. I was destroying everything *because* I loved him. He was the fire within me, driving me onward, and he was the ocean inside my heart that gave me life. That fire would consume me and that ocean would drown me if I allowed it, so I was killing it, just like I'd killed my old life.

As I continued ripping apart the connection, figures materialized before me. The first was the image of a ghostly bear, so transparent I could hardly make him out in the quickening darkness. The bear transformed into a man, and my Grandpa Liwanu stood across from me, his eyes creasing in unhappiness.

"Ava, please. Think about what you're doing," he pleaded.

"No, Grandpa," I hushed. A tear slipped from my eye and into the sand. "This is what needs to be done."

The second figure was more solid. Coyote hunched down, dropping his head and approaching me with his tail between his legs. My spirit magic went so deep it touched the other realms, and they'd used it to cross the divide and come to me.

Ava, my love, I cherish you, Coyote begged. *This is not the way you were to go, not what your destiny foretold. Stop this, and come be with me.*

"I will not," I whispered. Forcibly, I sent them both away, and they faded as they returned to the other side.

I'd disappointed Coyote, all the gods, and everyone in the spiritual realm who'd given me a chance. They never should've let me come back to Earth and return to my life. I should've stayed in the Ancestral Lands. At least then, things would've been able to go on.

Or maybe I would've found a way to ruin it all, even in death. Who knew?

I heard a darling voice cry out, the wind calling my name as he approached from the east. What a precious thing, to hear my name fall from his tongue. Despite being furious with him, I wanted to see him... one last time.

Oberi lifted his lip, showing his fangs in a deep growl. I quickened my magic, urging it to go faster and get the job done, because I knew who was coming for me.

Charlie couldn't stop me. To save the world, or end it. I'd never thought I'd choose to end it. I'd always sworn I'd save the day, somehow.

But there was nothing left to be saved. We all knew that. Time to let it all go. As the prophet had foretold, this was my choice alone. And I wouldn't let Charlie take that choice away from me.

Not without a fight. And until my last breath, I was going to give him one.

charlie

TWENTY-FIVE

No one did great things without making tremendous sacrifices. I planned to be the greatest there ever was. That meant letting things go. I was willing to sacrifice my friendships, my reputation, and whatever good I still had left in me to become the ruler this world needed. It wasn't about making a choice anymore. The only question that remained was if I was strong enough to see my plans through. I swore I wouldn't break under the pressure, despite what it took to remain standing.

I had to lock Ava up. Not what I wanted, but what I needed. Ava didn't understand, but she would. With enough time, she'd accept that I couldn't lose her again and that the palace was the safest place for her. This was the right thing to do. She'd forgive me eventually.

I stood on a balcony off the throne room, listening to my soldiers demonstrate my power. The elder guard was experienced and wise, but the young guard outnumbered them at least two to one, and I knew there were some experienced soldiers who were wavering on supporting my father. My Associates had been ferrying me information for weeks, palace gossip that Cameron was a self-involved leader who cared more for parties than making decisions that would benefit his people. He wanted the luxuries of royal life, but not the responsibility of it, and the elder guard knew that. Soon, they'd buckle under the pressure and join me. Those that didn't, my soldiers would kill.

The revolution wouldn't take long. By sunset, my soldiers would claim Ilamanthe and they'd have my father in chains. I wasn't sure what I was going to do with him yet. It would be unwise to let him live, as he'd always pose a threat to my command, and I blamed him for pulling me away when there was still a chance I could've saved my grandfather's life. Cassiel was gone because of my father, and I wanted to punish Cameron for it.

He was still my father, though, and taking his life would be distasteful in the eyes of the public. I didn't *need* their trust, but this would be easier to do if I had it. I was already going to face some opposition from uprooting the line of succession. I could allow my father to live, keep him prisoner for a while until the city agreed that Cameron would've been a poor Emperor and nobody wanted him back on the throne. Then I'd let him go free, give him some meaningless position of ceremony within the palace to keep him busy and satisfy any whiners who still complained that I'd overthrown him.

The Elves valued power. This was a mob. I just had to prove I was more worthy than Cameron was, and they'd all fall in line.

I heard footsteps behind me. "I knew you were capable of some bad things. But I never thought you'd go this far."

Chancey's tone was full of accusation, but I wasn't going to let him goad me into an argument that would take my attention away from the mission.

"I'll do whatever I have to in order to make my grandfather proud," I responded. "Don't act like you thought I was some saint, because I never was."

"You need to call this off. People are dying, Charlie."

The screams of perishing soldiers rose up from the gardens, and I replied, "People die every day. Better they die for me than for someone else."

"Fuck you," Chancey spat. "When the hell did you turn so goddamn cold? I don't even know who you are anymore."

"Because you can't. Letting people get too close is a recipe for disaster." I kept my words even and plain. Fighting was a waste of energy right now.

"Your father—"

"*My father has no spine!*" I bellowed, rounding on him. "Do you think *he* has what it takes to defeat the Warden? Because we all know he's incapable of ruling a nation. I deserve to be Emperor. I'm stronger, smarter, younger and more willing to do what it takes. My father doesn't deserve to lick the bottom of my shoes."

"You could've told me about this," Chancey growled.

"What for? I didn't think I'd have to enact this plan for years, if ever. I was happy to let my grandfather keep the throne for as long as he lived, but I knew I would *never* allow my father to rule. Because my grandfather died so suddenly, I've had to set my plans into motion and take action quicker than I expected, so excuse me if this isn't going as smoothly as I hoped."

"You're a real piece of work, aren't ya, Charlie?" Chancey said in disgust. "Out of you two, I thought Ava was the crazy one, but you're proving to be nuttier than she ever had the capability of being. Say what you want about her being off her rocker, but she'd never pull something like this."

"Ava still wants to save the world. She doesn't realize we can't save the world unless we bring it under our control."

"*Your* control, you mean," Chancey flung out.

"Do you think any of this is easy?" I came closer to him, feeling my arms start to tremble. "I'm doing this to keep everyone alive and safe. We're lucky as all hell that my grandfather is the only one we've lost recently, and I'm going to make sure it stays that way. Nobody else has the balls to do what needs to be done around here. I'm *not* going to allow another one of the people I care about to die on my watch, not when I have the power to do something about it! So what if I'm willing to sacrifice a few soldiers and civilians— faceless, nameless people to me, people that I have no knowledge of? I don't care if they live or die! It's worth it to protect what means the most to me! I won't sacrifice that!"

"You already have! I could've *died* during that heist! I gave up one of my wings for you!" Chancey bellowed. "I'm never gonna fly again, and you know what? I thought it was a worthy sacrifice, because it was for *you*, Charlie."

I heard the tears in his voice, and I wished I could say it had an effect on me, but it didn't.

"And here you are, spitting in my face," he continued. "You were gonna leave me pinned under that elevator, and I even begged you to, because I believed if I died at least it'd be for something bigger than me."

Chancey gave a low, sickening laugh that was devoid of humor, only devastation. "I fell for that once before when I was a part of the Celestial Church, and I was stupid enough to fall for it again. We were brothers in the ring, and I thought we were brothers still, but you ain't nothing to me. You're just another psycho who has big guns, and by fuck you're gonna use 'em, aren't ya, Charlie?"

"You're damn right I am." I left Chancey behind me as I turned away, back to the balcony. "I'm sorry you gave up a wing for me, but now it's my turn to take flight. So watch me fly."

Chancey's voice was full of disbelief. "You really don't care at all, do you?"

"Whatever good was still left in me died with my grandfather. I'm glad it did. It was holding me back from everything I needed to become."

Chancey fell silent, giving up. I didn't care if his heart was broken. I'd have to do a lot more damage before this was all over. At least he was still breathing. I couldn't say the same for so many others that we'd lost along the way. He needed to be grateful for what I was giving him, and happy that he was still alive.

More footsteps entered— dozens of them. I was annoyed. Couldn't they leave me alone until this was over with? It really wouldn't take long.

I sensed that one of them was my guard. "Eddie, status report."

"Your plans are going well, your highness," Eddie rattled off in a disconnected, far-off tone. "Ilamanthe will be conquered before evening falls."

"Good. Stay close."

Cameron didn't have authority as Emperor until his coronation, so he couldn't order any of my soldiers to stand down magically. Even so, I didn't trust Eddie not to turn on me, so I made sure my orders were clear and he remained in a place where I could make sure he wouldn't go running off.

"Everyone's here," Eddie announced. "Kallie, Marcus, Ivy, Danny, Alistair, Ez, Opal... all your friends."

"Quite a liberal use of the word," Danny grumbled under his breath. "We've seen what you're trying to do, and this has gone too far. I *knew* you were up to something. I just couldn't put my finger on it. This plan has been brewing within you all along. You didn't even know what you were planning, yourself, but we should've stopped you long ago."

"You couldn't stop me, not even if you tried." I was tired of these insolent little games. Did he *really* think he could stand up to me?

"*That's* why you had the inferichite net made, wasn't it?" Danny asked, spite dripping from his words. "You didn't want to use it against the Warden's demigods. You kept it for *us*, just in case one of your friends got out of line and you had to get them under your control."

I shrugged. "I can trust my friends now, but that doesn't mean I can trust all of you forever. I needed a backup plan, if one of you decided to rise up against me."

Horrified gasps rose around me, but I didn't care. They weren't Elvish royals. They didn't understand that contingency plans had to be put in place.

I heard Kallie give a hateful huff. "Yeah. Some *friend* you are."

"Your perspective isn't important right now," I told her. "You tried to take your own crown and couldn't do it. I can't help it if you're jealous of me for succeeding where you failed."

Multiple people in the room emitted shocked exclamations, but I ignored them all. Kallie gave a comical laugh. "That crown wasn't worth it. And you're going to find out pretty fucking quick yours isn't, either."

"Where's Ava?" Marcus asked, and he didn't sound like he was fucking around. Whatever. He could be mad at me, too. I didn't care.

"Where she needs to be." They didn't need to be concerned about what I did with my wife. She wasn't theirs to keep.

"What the hell is that supposed to mean?" Ez shouted, storming my way. "Where did you put my sister?!"

"She's in my quarters, which is where she'll be confined until this is over with. Once I have control of the city, she can roam throughout the palace as she wishes, but she can't leave these walls. Not for the rest of her life," I stated bluntly.

I turned from them as I mumbled, "She's too valuable."

"You locked my sister in a fucking *tower*?" Ez screamed. "How fucking dare you. You know that's the biggest nightmare she could ever face. I should kill you where you stand."

"Stop trying to threaten me, Ez. It's embarrassingly pathetic," I told him, swatting his words off as if he was a fly buzzing in my ear. He might as well be.

"She's not yours to control!" Ez cried out.

"I care for her far more than any of you do. She's a danger to herself and others. This is the best option for her," I replied. "She's in that tower, and that's where she'll stay."

From behind me, I heard Kallie quietly whisper, "No, she's not."

I went still. I rigidly turned as I whispered, "What did you say?"

"I set her free." Kallie's words were triumphant, goading me. "She and Oberi are off to do what they promised they would."

I gave a scream of rage. I started toward Kallie, my arms outstretched, but Marcus planted himself in my way and shoved me backward.

"You hurt her, I will put you down, right here, right now." Marcus' voice was dark, daring me to take one step closer.

I was powerful, and I could take both of them down in an instant if they did anything to prevent my plans from falling into place. But I didn't want to hurt them. Not unless I had to.

"Kallie, why did you do that?" I asked desperately. "If Ava interferes, she'll stop this rebellion! All of this will have been for nothing!"

"She's not going to stop the rebellion. She's going to stop it *all*," Kallie stated bluntly.

Her words felt like dunking me in a sea of ice-cold water. A shiver ran down my spine and over my body, gluing me to the floor. I couldn't move, think, or feel. Since the rebellion had started, I'd been living in a dream, floating throughout space and unable to come down, but Kallie's words forcefully woke me up.

Hurriedly, I checked the connection between me and Ava. I found with terror that she'd shut me out. I tried to pry my way through, but her mind was a steel fortress, and she wasn't letting me in. Oberi wasn't responding, either, and his replies to my prodding questions were just as silent. I screamed through our bond for them to hear me, but neither of them listened. I couldn't even tell what Ava was thinking right now, let alone what she was doing or where she was.

Dear ancestors. Did that mean she'd already started?

"What... what does that mean, Kallie?" Opal questioned. She was asking the question aloud, but she didn't really need to, because I think we all knew.

"She's going to use her demigod powers to harness the Earth's soul, and break the connection between the spirit world and ours. When that happens, the entire universe will collapse, and everything will cease to exist. Our souls, our gods, our afterlife and nature itself will be destroyed, and there's not a damn thing Charlie will be able to do about it," Kallie said victoriously.

Several people in the room began to scream. Shouts of panic and despair went up all around, overpowering the sounds of battle outside.

"Why would Ava do that?" Ivy asked, sounding horrified.

"Ava's smart enough to know all of this is meaningless. Our pain is for nothing," Kallie insisted. "Why allow life to continue if it's just going to lead to agony?"

"Kallie, why would you support this? Why not stop her?" Marcus asked. He didn't sound judgmental, angry, or upset— merely shocked.

"Because the world is fucked up, Marcus. I love you so godsdamn much. More than anything in existence, that ever was or will be," Kallie pleaded. "But how can you ask me to keep living after what I've been through? How can you ask all the people of the world who've suffered so badly to keep suffering, when we can just end it all, and spare living beings the pain? Isn't this the more merciful way?"

"I know better than anyone what it's like to wish you could disappear," Marcus replied gently. "But this is an extreme answer to a problem that's been around for centuries, and it's not like we can take it back."

"This is the choice Ava's prophecy was talking about, and she's made it," Kallie said flatly. "None of us can do anything about it now."

"Fuck that. I ain't dying because Ava is going through some existential bullcrap," Ivy spat. "She don't get to make that choice for me. *I* get to put meaning on what I've been through, and decide if it's worth it or not. She wants to cry and carry on about the meaning of life, fine, but that's not my problem. Sorry she's having an inner crisis of faith, but I ain't going down for that. I'm not gonna let her take herself out, and the rest of us with her."

"Ives, that's not what this is about," Chancey argued.

"I don't give a shit. Me looking out for myself is what's kept me alive this far," Ivy shot back. "I adore Ava, but I won't take the fall for this one. I don't wanna live under a dictator on either side, but living is still living."

"No it's not," Chancey insisted. "I grew up in the Celestial Church, and I've seen what happens when only one guy has all the power. I don't want to live in a world like that, even if that guy *is* my best friend."

"You know what? I'm with Charlie. Why *not* use our powers to take over the world?" Alistair suggested.

"Alistair, how could you?" Eddie asked, sincerely sounding crushed. "Magic is to be used for good, not evil."

Alistair sneered, "Screw that. We'll all be in power if Charlie runs the world. I'm tired of getting kicked around all my life. It's time to rub everyone's face in the dirt like they did me. They showed me no mercy, so I won't give them any."

"You're delusional if you think Charlie's going to share anything," Kallie spat. "He wants it all for himself."

"That's not fair, Kallie." I couldn't believe she saw me in such a way. Even if I was on top, I couldn't do it all.

"Fuck you, Charlie. I know you," Kallie replied. "Any power you'd give up would be a farce, because you'd want your hands in everything."

"He can't run the entire world by himself, that's not possible. He'll have to delegate power, and it'll be to us," Alistair argued. "We could have all the power. If we control everything, we can get back at all those fuckheads who hurt us, every last one. In my opinion, it's a pretty damn good gig to be friends with the king of the world. Nobody would mess with us, and we'd get to make all the rules. You guys wanna pass that opportunity up, be my guest, but I'm not losing my shot at greatness."

"Your shot at power, you mean," Eddie replied. He sounded truly disappointed in his partner.

"Bullshit. This is the end of the line. It's Ava versus Charlie, and if you're not with us, you're against us. Who's side are you on?" Alistair demanded.

Ava versus Charlie. What kind of hellish world were we living in now?

"I'm not on Charlie's side. Far from it. But we can't let Ava do this, either. They're both in the wrong," Marcus stated.

"If you try to stop Ava then you *are* on his side, and you want him to take over," Kallie accused. "You can't have it both ways because only one person gets to win here."

"We can come up with another solution," Marcus demanded. "Everyone needs to take a breath so we can talk it out. Charlie needs to stop what he's doing, and so does Ava."

"Neither of them are going to," Kallie said. "So what's it going to be?"

"Marcus is right. We need to find Ava, then bring her back here so we can talk about this as a group," Danny argued.

"You aren't touching her. If we bring her back here, that monster will just lock her up again," Kallie raged. I *knew* she was pointing at me.

"I agree. Ava should be able to do whatever she decides," Opal said. "The prophecy says this is her choice to make, and we shouldn't interfere."

"Opal, you can't agree with this," Ez said, and the rest of them fell silent. Opal had a straight head on her shoulders and was more level-headed than the rest of us. She'd have a rational opinion, so everyone wanted to hear what she would say.

But it turned out her opinion was far from rational. Opal was quiet for a moment, before she said, "I don't know if I'll ever heal from what my father did to me. We all saw the terrible things that happened at the camps. Isn't it our duty to make sure something like that doesn't happen again?"

Ez stumbled back a few steps. "But what about Marina? Don't you want her to grow up, and live a full life?"

"I *am* thinking about my daughter, because I want her to stay innocent and safe," Opal replied. "This world isn't either of those things, and I can't always be around to protect her. It's not a question of if she'll get hurt, but *when*, and how badly. It's morbid, and sick, but what if this is the only way to protect my child?"

"You don't believe that, Opal," Ez swore. "You're sad and in pain, but I know you want Marina to live a long life. Taking that life away from her isn't solving anything. You're just becoming the person that's hurting her."

"Ez, I don't want her to go through anything like what I did," Opal whispered.

"I know your father hurt you, and there are pieces of you that are broken beyond repair because of it. But I'm glad that you're still here, and what we have together is worth fighting for," Ez promised.

More pleas and bargains went up around the room, from the various couples talking it out or arguing their own points. I drowned in them all, unable to take each voice in. Half of our friends were so emotionally bereft from what they'd seen in the camps, they didn't care if it all ended. The other half were so pissed off and full of rage they wanted to survive, so they could make the ones who did this pay.

Ava was right about one thing, at least. This world was a cycle of suffering. But did that really mean she had to end it?

"Enough," I said loudly, and the commotion ceased. "I don't care what the prophecy says, this is too big of a decision for one person to make on their own."

"But it's not, because some of us are agreeing with her." Eddie spoke up, and I was shocked that he had the courage to stand up to me. "This isn't just Ava's choice. Many of us throughout the world would take the same option, if the choice was in our hands."

"Eddie, you don't get a choice," I said forcefully. "You're my guard, so I order you to follow me. Now, go fetch the inferichite net. Then come with me, and help me search the city so we can bring Ava in."

Eddie hesitated. "You once told me I could disobey a command if I did not agree with it, and that itself was an order in which I'm inclined to obey. I do not agree with you or your plans, that you desire to usurp your father and take the world for yourself. Turning the world into a dictatorship is *not* what I spent my entire life training to do. No, sire. I will not follow you. My allegiance is to the princess, and if this is what she desires, then I will serve her only."

"I *order* you to follow me!" I raged. "I command you to bring the inferichite net to me, so we can use it on Ava and stop her from doing this!"

"I have hidden that sick object in a place where you will never find it, and even if you try, Ava will succeed before you are even close," Eddie spat. "I reject your command. I will not follow your orders. You will not touch our princess, and you will not stop her."

"I love you, Eddie, but you're a fool," Alistair said darkly. "You'll come to your senses once we put Ava down."

"If you desire to stop the princess, you'll have to get through me first," Eddie vowed. "I am no weak challenger to defeat."

Footsteps echoed throughout the room. People were taking sides within the throne room, preparing to battle.

If they wanted to fight, so be it. Let the strongest survive, because only those who were willing to fight for what *my* idea of the world should be deserved to be in it. My heartbeat stuttered and picked up the pace inside my chest as I realized couples were starting to face off.

Ivy gave a disgusted scoff. "This is dumb. I'm not here for the latest episode of *college kids have a mental breakdown, and it leads to the end of existence.* Sorry, but there's therapy for all that. You guys wanna let your trauma kill you, fine, but mine isn't gonna kill me, and I won't let Ava's trauma put me in the ground, neither. I ain't stupid enough for that."

"I don't wanna fight you, Ives," Chancey warned, and I heard the rustling of feathers that came from the one wing he still had.

"Then don't," Ivy replied coldly. "But if you get in my way, you're gonna have to."

"You guys are jumping to conclusions," Danny yelled. "Everyone needs to slow down and think!"

Danny was the only one who was keeping a cool head. But nobody was listening.

"Pretty girl, please. We just got together. We have our whole lives ahead of us," Marcus hushed. "Don't you want to experience more of that? We had so little time. You didn't come back to me in that alleyway just to give up now."

"The time we spent together mattered more than you know. But this is bigger than both of us. I have to believe that even if the universe is wiped out, we'll find our way back to each other somehow," Kallie promised.

"You can't beat me, Kallie." Marcus' tone was gentle and loving, pleading with her not to do this. I heard him summon a battle orb that he cautiously cradled in his hand. "Witch magic can overpower fae abilities."

"I don't have to beat you, Marcus." Kallie truly sounded defeated— a woman ready to take her last breath and be done with it. "I just have to buy Ava enough time."

Kallie struck before any more words could be spoken. She cast an illusion spell that went ricocheting by my head, and the entire room broke into chaos. Marcus tossed his battle orb and it exploded near the door, making smoke rise throughout the room. Eddie and Alistair called out gasps of pain as they hurt each other, but neither were backing down. A window broke nearby as Chancey tackled Ivy into a wall. Ivy hissed, and Chancey screamed as I smelled the unmistakable tang of blood spread throughout the room from their fangs.

"Opal, come on!" Ez yelled, and her body slammed into mine as Ez yanked her to the exit.

"Cut it out!" Danny cried over the noise. "This isn't helping anyone!"

I stood in the middle of it all, observing the destruction around me. Marcus, Ivy, and Alistair had chosen to fight for me, while Kallie, Chancey, and Eddie had taken Ava's side. Danny was trying to break it all up. Opal and Ez had decided to stay out of it and flee.

This was what villains did— we fought for power and betrayed the people we loved. This couldn't have ended up any other way.

That's when the entire castle quaked. A few stones slipped out of the walls and shattered on the floor. I failed to keep my balance and toppled over as the floor beneath me rocked, and the ground gave a shudder that was unmistakable. My Earth magic caught on to it right away.

It'd been an earthquake, a massive one, and it wasn't by chance. I knew Ava had started her spell to end all things. I scrambled to get to my feet and rushed to the balcony, tripping as the palace wavered again. My friends were so busy battling they didn't even notice that the earthquake had rocked the palace. They continued to toss spells at their lovers, and a couple of them grazed me, cutting open my clothes and causing blood to seep from small wounds.

I jumped off the balcony and used my Air magic to take to the sky. The area below me echoed with explosions— probably magic cast by my friends, who were running throughout the palace inevitably trying to kill their significant others. I flew overhead, using my Earth magic to sense where the epicenter of the earthquake was. I knew Ava would be there.

I sensed she was on the beach, along with Oberi. I flew in that direction, following our bond as it led me out of the city. Ava was at the same spot where my grandfather had shown me his memories of his wedding. I landed, and my feet hit soft sand. Ava's spell sent pulsing energetic waves outward, and I shuddered every time they hit my skin.

"Ava!" I cried, but she didn't respond. I hurried to approach her, but Oberi got in my way, giving a deep growl and stomping his paws in the sand.

"Oberi, move," I commanded. I went to step around him, but he snapped his jaws at me to stay back.

Stay out of this, Charlie. This is not your decision, Oberi warned.

I shouted over him, speaking directly to Ava. "Pidge, you need to stop! Let's talk about this!"

Ava didn't pull back her spell. Instead, the energetic waves became more intense, almost knocking me off my feet as she yelled, "You didn't want to talk earlier!"

"That was a mistake!"

"A mistake? Ha. It's a mistake *now*, because I'm not doing what I'm told, and because I'm a threat to you. That's the only reason you're out here."

One of the energetic pulses blew me backward, and I was knocked down. I struggled to get onto my feet as I said, "I acted irrationally. But we can still fix this."

"Hell yeah, you did. Oberi, take care of him."

Oberi's snarls got deeper. *Leave now, before I make you.*

"I'm not going anywhere," I growled, and I went to go around him. Oberi bit my hand, digging his teeth in and drawing blood.

I cried out in pain and punched him across the face to get him off. Oberi went sprawling backward, and his growls became deadlier as he morphed, our connection changing as his fur became scales and he shifted into his wyvern form.

Fine. Two could play that game. I yanked on our connection, and Oberi was unable to stop me as I siphoned power out of him in order to become a wyvern myself. I pulled at his magic, and my body shifted until I matched Oberi's strength and size, facing him as my tail twisted behind me. I lifted my leathery wings and roared, declaring a challenge.

Oberi, let me get to her. I don't want to hurt you. This was my last chance to convince him, but if I had to do this the hard way, so be it.

You already have, Charlie. It will be my last act of free will, to prevent you from coming near her ever again, Oberi seethed, letting out a monstrous roar to respond to my own.

He charged first. Oberi slammed into my front and tossed me backward. The tackle would've been enough to collapse a building, and it made my chest bruise. I opened my mouth and spat venom at him. Several streams of venom collided with his side, sizzling against his scales and making the air smell like burning flesh. Oberi snarled in pain, responding with venom of his own that I dodged.

I would've hesitated at Oberi's pain any other time, but now I was the one doing the damage. It was unfathomable, doing this to your own Familiar. I usually did everything I could to protect and care for him. I wanted to stop, even as I was hurting him, but I couldn't. There was too much at stake. Ava ignored us both, focusing her attention on the spell that was draining the world as we did our best to overpower one another.

Oberi rose on his hind legs to strike at me, and I copied him, swiping out with my talons. One of his wings smacked me on the side of the head, and I responded, using my wings like I did my fists to punch him in the sides. A spike on my wing caught his shoulder and tore as I was smacking him around, and more blood poured onto the beach.

Oberi screeched at the injury and swung at me with his tail. I ducked and smashed my shoulder into him, trying to knock him off his feet.

I wasn't fast enough, and the venomous pincher on his tail dug into my hip. I screeched as a sensation like fire rushed through my veins and made the entire area go numb. Oberi's venom temporarily paralyzed the limb, making it so I had to drag my right leg behind me in order to move.

Now that he'd slowed me up, Oberi took advantage. He stampeded forward, and my tail wasn't enough to stop his charge. He knocked my tail aside and reached out with his mouth, the acidic smell of his venom filling my nose.

Oberi bit down on my neck as hard as he could. His fangs sank in, scraping against bone. I let out an animalistic scream and clawed my talons at his legs to let me go, but he held on tight. Hot blood seeped from the wound and poured down my scales. I attempted to wiggle free, but he clambered on top of me and held me down with his weight.

Get off! I lifted my tail and stuck the barb into the side of his head. He groaned and let me go, backing off. He'd gotten away before I'd been able to deposit my venom, but the blow still hurt. My blood spilled against the sand from my torn neck, and Oberi hissed like an angry snake. We circled each other, both waiting for the other to resume the fight.

I can't believe you chose Ava over me! I roared in frustration. I couldn't help it; I nearly hated him right now.

You left me with no choice. You've become a mad prince, deranged with the idea of what could be, and I could not stand to let you harm her in such a way, Oberi replied— as if he didn't care about me. It truly sounded like he didn't.

That has nothing to do with it. You've always secretly favored Ava over me, I spat resentfully. *You love her more.*

Perhaps she is my favorite, Oberi— finally— admitted. *I cherish you, Charlie, I really do, but look around at our circumstances! You have forced me to choose, and if it comes down to protecting her or you, it will always be her. I apologize if that wounds you, but that is the way it has been and must be.*

You shouldn't be siding with her at all! Look what she's doing to the world! I declared.

Charlie, I tried to talk to you about this. When we left the naderei's *home months ago, I told you we needed to come up with a plan, just in case Ava got out of hand and we needed to subdue her. I begged you to see reason and play it safe, but you insisted that you had it handled and Ava would never consider doing such a thing. Yet here we are!* Oberi spread his wings wide, and the gust from them buffeted me back.

I never wanted things to end this way, I pleaded.

But they did. I am tired of you ignoring my warnings. I will not be your weapon, to be used to conquer the world as you please. I belong to Ava now, more so than I ever belonged to you. And it is she who will be this universe's judgment and reckoning.

Oberi attacked again, but I was waiting for him. As he attempted to strike, I dodged out of the way and latched my jaws on to one of his wings. I shredded it to bits with my teeth, breaking the bone. Oberi gave an immense cry of pain that broke my heart to hear, but I forced myself to keep going as I dug my claws into his back and tossed him into the ocean. He went sailing away at my strength, probably half a mile or more, before he crashed into the sea.

I couldn't hold on to my wyvern form, and I staggered back into my own body. Feeling was starting to come back into my leg now, and I could use it again. I limped forward, toward the sound of my wife's voice.

"Oberi, come to me," she ordered.

The waves rushed within the sea, and I knew Ava was using her Water abilities to bring Oberi back to shore. My bond flared as she healed him of the injuries I'd dealt, and I felt Oberi shift, her form becoming smaller as she changed into a unicorn.

I clapped my hand over my bleeding neck where Oberi had bitten me and stumbled toward my wife. Ava's spell temporarily paused, and the ground ceased to thunder as Ava pulled herself onto Oberi's back.

"Ava, why are you doing this?" I called as I approached. "You're taking things too far."

"I'm doing what was prophesied at the time of my birth," Ava proclaimed. "This is my destiny, and I have to follow it."

"Your *destiny*?" I demanded. "It's not your destiny to cast billions of souls to their doom!"

Ava emitted a disturbed laugh. "You don't get it. I want to end suffering *so badly* that I'm willing to end the universe and start everything over to do it, because no one should ever suffer while they exist on this planet."

"Life matters in spite of and *because* of suffering, pidge. It doesn't take away its meaning," I insisted.

"I don't believe that," Ava said through clenched teeth. "You and Cassiel might've shared that belief, but it's not one I follow. You want to become the one who causes all this pain. Don't you see how much suffering you will create, despite your good intentions to save the world? I've seen it, Charlie, and at the end of it all, you'll be the one to suffer the greatest. Let me save you from that. Let me save us all. I don't believe there's any meaning to suffering, so why not let me do as I will? The whole universal energy exchange system is messed up. We can't avoid suffering no matter what. For some to live, others have to die. It's a flawed system, one that I have to correct."

"That's not your responsibility. That's too much weight for anyone to have on their shoulders. We can't save everyone. All we can do is live as ethically as possible," I stated, trying to make her understand.

"You claim your way is ethical?! You think you're doing the right thing, but I've foreseen what you will become. You will kill and enslave all these people to try to force them into a better life, but you will never succeed, because I will stop you. I saw you in my vision as a mad king, and it's already starting. The old ruler I saw wasn't the Warden; it was *you*, Charlie. That is a future I will never allow to pass."

"You don't know that will happen. Your vision was merely a warning of the future, and we can choose to correct it, but we have to do it together!"

Ava chuckled. "So *now* you want us to have an equal relationship. Let me tell you something, it says a whole hell of a lot about our marriage when you think you can pull something like this and get away with it. I'm not yours to control."

"So you destroy it all?" I asked. "We can only do the best we can to prevent others from experiencing pain, but we can't change how the world works!"

"*That's not good enough*! I'm giving the universe a chance to start over, to recreate itself to be more fair, and develop a better system," Ava said wildly, clearly believing every word she told herself.

"You don't know if that's going to happen! You're taking a shot in the dark, and chances are you'll be sending everything into nothing more than oblivion!" I shouted.

She was talking nonsense— why didn't she see how psychotic all this was?

"I'm willing to take that shot in the dark," Ava replied. "As long as it gets me what I want. Why is oblivion so bad? No one is going to know they don't exist, so it's not going to hurt anyone."

"Yes it *is*. You're trying to protect people, but you attempting to heal this world is only making it worse. We still have a chance to make things better, but you have to work with me."

"Don't compare me to you," Ava said harshly. "I'm doing this for everyone else, unlike you, who is only doing it for himself."

"Pidge, don't punish the entire universe because I hurt you." If she needed me to get on my knees and beg, I'd do it. "Come with me to Ilamanthe. We can still rule together. Nothing is worth you doing this."

"Too late. I know you're capable of making this choice now, so there's no going back," Ava swore. "I never thought you were capable of locking me away, but you did. That proves to me that anyone can be corrupted by hatred and fear, no matter how good of intentions they have. And I'll damn this world to hell before I let you or the Warden take control of it."

"Please forgive me. We can come up with another way. We'll be great, you'll see. We just need to come up with a way where we both can win."

Ava shuddered as she said, "My prophecy says it's my choice alone to save the world or destroy it, and I've decided. So don't try to stop me, because I won't allow another man to make a choice that should've been mine. Not even if it's you."

Oberi gave a horse-like cry that sounded like a scream. She reared on her hind legs to throw sand in my face. She galloped in a circle around me, and I felt Ava's power growing, ready to use it against me.

Enemies to lovers back to enemies. Why did I think our tragic love story would turn out any different? I wasn't going to take her life, but if I had to hurt her in order to stop this, I would. I steadied myself, preparing to fight again.

The *whoosh* of roaring flames incinerated the area, though instead of being hot, it was cool. My Air magic noticed a swirling vortex coming straight toward me, one that extended toward the sky and met up with the clouds. Ava had created a tornado made of blue Fire and sent it spinning my way!

I immediately took to the skies to dodge it. I flew around the tornado, sweeping in a circle to avoid the cyclone's path. I struggled to resist it, forcing the wind currents to obey me as Ava's blue Fire reached out for my limbs. Her flames singed my clothes and made frostbite pop up along my skin, and I gasped in pain. The cyclone's power nearly ripped me into the sky, until I stopped running and turned to face it. I shot out a gust of Air that was so powerful it knocked the twister sideways, taking the energy out of it. The tornado disintegrated, though traces of Ava's blue Fire still burned in the air and all around me.

Ava was galloping below me on Oberi, but now that the cyclone was gone, she was temporarily exposed. I conjured illusion magic using my Elven abilities and followed my bond to take aim. Shackles sprung out of the sand and locked on to her wrists and ankles, yanking her off of Oberi and pinning her to the sand. I landed, holding the illusion spell in place so the shackles remained tight.

Oberi let out a screech, but Ava merely laughed. "Nice handcuffs, Charlie. Though they're not my favorite pair you've ever put on me. Too bad you'll never get to tie me up again, but you get credit for trying."

There was yet another combustion of flame, and my illusion magic began peeling away. I attempted to resist, forcing the shackles to hold, but my magic faded at Ava's touch. I realized she was using her blue Fire to melt the illusion shackles away, and they couldn't hold up to her vast power.

I took deep breaths, trying to recover my strength. She'd destroyed my illusion spell like it was *nothing*. A spell like that was powerful enough to hold a demigod, but Ava hadn't even flinched.

"My turn," Ava sang.

The beach was quiet, but only for a moment, for the sound of roaring water approached me from the right. My throat tightened, and fear overwhelmed my senses as I comprehended that there was a massive tidal wave rushing straight toward me, conjured from Ava's powers of the ocean.

I ran further up the beach, casting my hand behind me as I fell to the sand once again. I scrambled backwards to get away as I created a mountain out of the area around me. It took a tremendous amount of effort, but I forced my demigod abilities to rush to the surface to fight for me as I raised a wall of earth that was over a thousand feet tall.

It wasn't a second too late, because just as I'd stopped building the earth wall, the tsunami struck. The mountain of sand quivered and moaned, and sand went flying everywhere at the destructive power of the sea surge. The edges of the massive wave spilled over the top of the earth wall, but I'd managed to spare myself from the worst of the damage. My Earth magic cried out in pain as the cracks in the ground widened and grew larger from my creation of the mountain and the fall of Ava's tidal wave. We were completely ruining this beach.

"Are you ready to give up yet?" Ava asked. Oberi snorted, and her hoof stomped into the sand.

I clambered shakily onto my feet and rasped, "Not until you quit."

"Never."

She'd barely gotten the word out before she cast another spell. I reached out for her, but my hands were blocked by some sort of invisible force. Ava had cast a shield, one that circled around me and left no exit. I pushed against the glass-like dome, and as I did, it pushed *back*.

My knees began to bend, and I realized that the circular jail she'd put me in was getting smaller. If she kept this up, I was going to be crushed. I punched the walls of the shield, trying to get it to break, but it held up like bulletproof glass.

"Ava!" I cried, but she didn't respond. The walls of the shield only got narrower, closing me in.

This wasn't working. Ava was trying to kill me, but I was trying to apprehend her without seriously harming her. It made for a lopsided fight. I needed to do something drastic even if it caused her damage, because if I didn't, she was going to take my life.

I called on my Elf abilities again and focused them on Ava. I wasted no time siphoning her magic out of her before she could force the Spirit shield to crush me. It worked, and she lost control of the spell. When her shield broke, shards of it fragmented off, cutting my lip and eyebrow. My blood splattered everywhere.

I had some of Ava's Spirit magic now, though it wasn't enough to heal everything. I fixed up the worst of my injuries, including my bleeding neck, before I rose to face her again.

I hoped that would be the end of the fight, but it wasn't. Though I'd siphoned her power, Ava quickly regenerated, and through our bond I felt her magic instantly return to her.

I started to lose hope. I couldn't take her magic, not for any longer than a few seconds. I wasn't strong enough to stop her, only delay her abilities. Any power I stole, she'd take right back.

"You want to know something, Charlie?" Ava asked ruthlessly, while I was still spitting blood out of my mouth. "My gut told me you were going to do something like this. You were always headed toward villainy, always playing the bad guy with your guns and torture. It was like a game to you, because you wanted to make granddaddy proud and fit in with his mob, even though you didn't. You wanted to play the part, and you're still acting now. I hated those damn pistols. I'm so pissed that I let you pressure me into using guns. I think that's one thing I can't forgive myself for."

"What?" I asked viciously, wiping the stinging blood out of my eyes. "You said you were comfortable with it!"

"I wasn't," Ava spat. "I'd do anything that you asked me to, and you knew that."

My anger exploded. "I was asking you to tell me the truth, and you didn't. Don't put this on me! I trusted you to know where you were at."

"You shouldn't have done that, because I didn't even know! I've never been able to do that because of my bipolar. You've always been the one who makes sense of the world for me. You should've known better, and you ignored the signs in order to suit your own agenda!"

"I can't be your moral compass all the time, because there's things I don't know!" I raged. "I'm in your head *some* of the time, but it doesn't give me perfect insight on what's going on with you, so you need to communicate with me!"

"I can't communicate with you because you're a pathological *liar!*" Ava screamed at the top of her lungs.

Fury boiled inside me, giving strength back into my aching limbs. "Now you're just throwing insults at me because you don't know any other way to win."

"No, it's the truth! Too bad if it hurts! Charlie, you lie all the fucking time, without even realizing you're doing it! You lie to yourself, constantly, and delude yourself into telling your ego whatever story you want to hear, and *that's* why we're in this position now!"

I wasn't going to take this lying down. "You want to talk about me like *I'm* the bad guy? You're brutally honest. You wound people, because you don't know how to be tactful with the truth."

"Bullshit. You've never had an honest thought in your life. Yeah, I've been harsh with the truth, and I've lied a lot, too, but I never lied about how much I love you."

I gaped, hardly able to believe that messed up shit had come out of her mouth. "You doubt that I love you? Are you fucking *insane?*"

"Yeah, I am, and I'm fucking owning it. Because you chose to do this, I'm doubting everything you ever said to me, because I don't think someone could love me and want to keep me in a cage." Ava's voice cracked like thunder as she sobbed bitter tears of heartbreak, and out of all of this, it was the thing I regretted most of all. "Maybe you loved me, and maybe you didn't. Maybe I am the person you adored, or maybe I was just a convenient weapon for you to call upon whenever you needed me. It doesn't matter now. I'm ending it all."

"Ava, I'm *sorry* that I locked you away," I wept. "I never should've done that. It was wrong. I did it because I loved you so much, I wanted to keep you all to myself. I knew that went against everything you wanted, but I thought I was doing the right thing to keep you safe!"

"I get to decide what's right for my life! *Me!*" Ava screamed. "I gave you too much power, and I never should've let that happen. I purposefully looked the other way and lived in denial when I knew something was wrong. I loved you so much it blinded me to what I didn't wish to see. You're a monster, Charlie."

I gave an unstable snicker as I hissed, "You're a monster, too."

"Damn right I am. We're in agreement that we'll do whatever it takes to put each other down, so let's just kill each other and be done with it. At least we'll die together, because even now, I don't want to go down without you."

A crackle overhead made my Air magic tingle with electricity. Ava summoned lightning, and it was hot and out of control as it raced across the sky. Thunder rolled so loudly above it made my eardrums ache.

If I didn't get her under control, and soon, the universe was going to fall apart at any moment. She could sustain the spell to drain Earth's soul while she was fighting me, and I was running out of time.

I had to get twisted, and get into her head in order to slow her up. I brought my illusion magic rushing forth once again, and I caused it to conjure into something new. I pulled from our Familiar, taking the smallest piece of Oberi and fashioning it into an illusion, something living and breathing. I took from the part of Oberi that loved Ava more than she loved me, because it wasn't fair, and I had to make things even *somehow*. Oberi snorted in disbelief, and Ava showed the tiniest bit of weakness as she gave the smallest noise of torment.

My illusion magic created a duplicate version of Oberi, right down to the tail and horn. I created her so she was solid, living and breathing just like the real Oberi.

I think Ava was in disbelief, because she didn't do anything, not at first. The Oberi duplicate shot fireballs out of her horn at Ava. The real Oberi dodged, keeping Ava at a distance as the fake Oberi attacked.

If anything could hold her off, it was this. If Ava wanted to continue what she was doing, and get to me, she had to kill a piece of our Familiar. She didn't have the stomach to do it.

"You think an image of Oberi can stop me?" Ava hissed.

"It's not just an image. It's the real thing. This Oberi is just as real as the one you're riding on," I snapped. "It's a piece of her. A piece of us all. Oberi took your side, but there's still a part of her that's connected to me. If you kill her, you kill a piece of Oberi."

Ava gave a heartless scoff. "I've already killed a part of my spirit today. I can do it again."

Ava let out a high-pitched scream, and a firebomb erupted in the middle of the beach where the fake Oberi had been standing. Ava's wails echoed throughout the beach as the dying cries of the duplicate Oberi closed in around us. I felt the heat of the explosion coming the moment the firebomb went off, and I sheltered myself inside of an Earth shield that I enclosed around me as the flames rippled overhead.

When the detonation was over, I let my Earth shield drop and knelt to the ground with a shaking hand. My magic surveyed the scene. Ava had left a crater in the middle of the beach over twenty feet wide, and just as deep.

I was stunned. I couldn't believe she'd killed off a piece of our Familiar... a piece of our *joined soul*— without hesitating. She wouldn't have done that hours ago.

My fingers shook as I withdrew them from the sand. Ava truly was stronger than me. Any control or power she'd given to me in our relationship had certainly been a gift, and I'd squandered it. She was kicking my ass all over this beach without any problem. I couldn't even get a hit in on her, and here she was, making me her bitch without breaking a sweat. Only days ago she'd promised to get me in handcuffs, and she'd certainly kept true to that promise, because my hands might as well be tied behind my back while I was fighting her. I was nothing more than a doll getting tossed around at her whim, a toy to entertain her rage.

"You know, Charlie, you're *really* pissing me off today." I hadn't heard Ava use a tone full of hate toward me in such a long time, but loathing infected her voice now. "I think you like playing these twisted little games."

I whispered quietly to myself, "I think you like them too, Ava."

She'd heard me. Viciously, she responded, "Even if I did, it wouldn't matter much to you, because you'd still make me play them."

We'd done this for years, played mind games and gone back and forth, but Ava and I weren't playing the same game anymore. I didn't even think we were on the same chessboard.

I was stupid to think I could dominate her. I'd been so, so naive. Childish, cruel, heartless— there weren't enough words to describe how ignorant I'd been, any way to encompass the severity of the horrible mistake I'd made.

And that mistake was going to cost me more than anything I'd ever gambled on before.

I started gasping as something inside my chest contracted. Fragments of pain projected outward from the inside, and my being withered as an unknown force tore me apart, shredding my essence like bits of paper. This felt similar to when the Warden had sucked the life force out of me, but *worse*. I wasn't just dying. I was ceasing to exist.

I realized the awful truth, and felt that I might as well be perishing inside. Ava was using her Spirit magic to crush my soul. Whatever piece of me that was tied to Oberi was being torn apart, and it was all thanks to her.

"How does it feel, Charlie?" Ava asked. "How does it make you feel, knowing *this* is what you did to me?"

I'd never intended to make her feel this way, and if I had, I regretted any choice I had made that had led to it. Damn my plans, my kingdom, the world. I never wanted to do anything unless it was for her.

"Fine. If this is what you want, pidge, take me," I rasped. "Take my life."

The searing agony continued for a moment longer. Then Ava pulled her magic back, and I fell onto my side as I curled up in the fetal position, trembling as I did my best to breathe.

"I know I want to end the world," Ava said quietly. "But I don't know if I can end you."

I laid there on the ground and didn't blame her. I got it. She got it. She still loved me, and I still loved her. Didn't matter what we did to each other. We just couldn't escape it. We'd damn it all if it meant we could be together, but there was no coming back from this. There was no hope for our relationship now.

Not after what we had done.

Ava's spell continued to grow, wracking the ground with tremors and causing the sky to fracture above. A cry of defeat echoed from somewhere down shore, and it sounded like it'd come from Kallie. Her sobs were only twenty feet or so away, muffled as she cried into someone's front.

"It's all right, pretty girl. I've got you," Marcus said lovingly. I knew he had to be holding her.

Marcus had beaten her, but I didn't know if it meant anything. Not at this stage of the game. Farther away, Ivy said, "Stay down, Chance. I don't want to keep doing this."

Chancey moaned, but gave no other response. I recognized Alistair, heaving in pain. Eddie must've hurt him badly, though I couldn't tell what the injuries could be.

Our friends had followed us out here to the beach, fighting all the way. They'd finally caught up with us. They'd clearly planned to help either me or Ava, and now, they were going to jump in.

"Ava, we're here to stop you," Ivy screamed over the noise of the roaring tempest.

"You'll never stop me! No one can!" Ava cried.

Ice rushed past my face, and I realized Ava had cast another spell. There were shouts of pain, ones that melded into panic.

"I can't move!" Alistair shouted, and Ivy let out similar protests. She'd frozen Alistair and Ivy to the beach, and they couldn't do anything to get away.

I staggered to my feet, but my head swam. Marcus took action. He ran past me, nearly knocking me over on his way to get to Ava. His arm was drawn back, the Death spell in his hand grazing my face.

"You're giving me no choice!" Ava cried. There was the *whoosh* of a fireball and Marcus cried out, stumbling to the ground. I smelled burnt flesh, and Marcus wailed in pain as Ava's flames rushed up and down his torso. It quickly fizzled out into smoke, but Marcus still curled on the ground in pain.

"*No!*" Kallie screamed, falling to his side. He breathed heavily, trying to get up, but his injuries wouldn't let him.

This was my fault. I'd done this to my friends. I'd put them in this situation, and now, they were paying the price for it.

"Ava, draw back the spell!" I said again. I leaned into the wind, bracing myself against the roaring currents as I came closer.

"You're too late!" Ava shouted toward the skies. "Any moment now, all of this will be gone!"

"Ava, *please!*" Kallie pleaded, but the earth shook again, and didn't stop this time. The earthquake was so violent it rattled my bones, creating caverns in the ground. Skyscrapers within the city made creaking noises as the steel ruptured, falling into the pits and burning into the earth's core. Ava's maniacal laughter resonated over it all, the last sound the universe would ever hear.

"Charlie, *do something!*" Kallie shrieked. Now that she'd seen Marcus get hurt, she'd suddenly changed her mind, as she fully comprehended exactly what was happening. She now realized what was at stake and understood that she was willing to give up the world, but not give up Marcus. She wasn't just telling me to take action— she was giving me *permission* to hurt her best friend in the only way I had left, because there was no other alternative.

An idea rose to the surface. Something that had been on my mind since the start of this fight, It was magic that, until now, I'd been unwilling to try. There was *one* thing I could do to stop this. It was the only spell I hadn't tried, and it was now or never.

There was only one way an Elementai could lose access to their magic forever... if they lost their bond with their Familiar. And if I didn't take Ava's magic away, she'd destroy us all. There was no other choice.

A golden spiritual cord, gleaming like what I supposed was sunlight, hovered out of my chest and into the open air. It was two feet across and wound together with many strands, thousands of past lives woven into the threads. It was the strongest bond I'd ever come across. Probably the strongest bond there ever would be, in all of time.

The cord linked me to two beings, Oberi and Ava. Tears beaded at the corners of my eyes as I observed the spiritual strand tying us together. I needed to do this, but I didn't even know if I *could*.

But she was forcing my hand.

"Ava, don't make me do this," I warned. I took hold of the bond, praying with all my might she'd stop what she was doing, so I didn't have to go through with this.

Ava didn't listen, just continued what she was doing. I swore that I heard the very Earth itself begin to crack in half as her power accelerated, breaking apart the spirit of the world.

"You're not going to do anything." Her voice was certain, confident. "You'd never hurt me that way."

"Ava—" I begged one more time, but she didn't listen. Ava increased the intensity of her magic, and my friends screamed in terror as they cried out that the sky above had gone pitch black, plunging the entire planet into a world without light.

There were only seconds left before the universe disappeared forever. So, I did what I had to do.

A heart-wrenching *crack* rang over the ocean, and the physical effect was like having my body sawed in half, straight down the middle. It felt as if my flesh was being ripped from my bones by the jaws of a resentful beast that had crawled into my chest and started tearing outward. The worst pain imaginable permeated down to my bones. The feeling of ice covered my body as I felt the warmth of Ava's Fire leave me forever.

I couldn't sense where Ava had gone, and I started to panic. She ceased to exist entirely to me, as if she'd been stolen away from all realms. I reached out with my magic to find her, but my power found *nothing*.

A pit deeper than hell opened inside of me, leaving nothing but an empty void. My spirit fractured and bled out, spraying love and emotions everywhere and suffocating me with the need to breathe. I became nothing but a hollow shell, the wound of my soul covering me in loneliness.

I realized I'd never been truly alone before. Even before we met, Ava had always been there, her presence tangled intricately with mine. I felt her beautiful existence from the moment I could breathe, and now she was just... gone. There was a part of me that was missing, and I didn't understand how to fill the hole, because nothing and no one in this universe could mend a chasm this deep.

The moment I broke our bond, my purpose in this life and everything we dreamed of together faded. Ava toppled off of Oberi's back from the blow, crying out as she hit the sand. Oberi yelped as he was forced out of his unicorn form and into the body of a husky. Oberi barked loudly in protest. I could feel him attempting to shift into a unicorn or a phoenix, but both attempts failed.

The earthquake came to an abrupt halt, and peace returned to the beach.

The sun returned, for I could feel it shining on my face as the storm ebbed and the clouds parted.

I waited for something to happen, but magically, I didn't feel any different.

My soul, though? It was ripped to fucking shreds.

Then, I felt it. The intimate waver of a bond, still so recognizable to me.

Charlie, Oberi broke. *No.*

I could still hear him. Which meant...

Ava groaned. I felt tears slip from my eyes as she came to.

I checked again. Maybe I hadn't done anything irreversible. Maybe I'd just weakened it a bit.

What I wished for was whisked away by the wind as my spirit saw the golden cord once more, but this time, it was only connected to Oberi and me, leaving Ava out.

"What's going on?" Ava asked, clearly delirious. She was so used to our bond being there, she didn't recognize the obvious. She'd never needed to check before.

Nobody said anything. Everyone on the beach had witnessed what had happened, and like me, they were all in shock.

"Oberi," Ava whispered. "What happened, girl?"

Ava, darling, Oberi breathed, but I knew I was the only one who heard.

A few moments passed, until Ava stuttered, "I... I can't hear her. What's she saying? Why can't she talk to me?"

I opened my mouth to answer, but I wasn't able to respond. I was still a coward, because I couldn't admit to her that I'd been her undoing.

More long seconds dragged on. Ava's breathing quickened, and she began to panic as she cried, "Where's my magic? What did you *do* to me?"

"I... I took your magic away." I managed to speak this time, but my voice cracked. "I broke our bond."

Ava took in a shuddering breath of agony that pained me to hear, worse than anything else I'd gone through in my entire life. I'd been taking a risk when I broke it. Oberi had said when we'd discussed this before that if the bond broke, who he would remain tied to would be a fifty-fifty chance. I knew if I broke the bond, there was a shot that I'd lose my abilities and my connection to Oberi, and Ava would keep all her power.

That wasn't what happened. Oberi had remained bonded to me, and I kept my magic.

But I'd taken hers. Ava had lost her powers, her connection to her Familiar, and her bond to me, all in one stroke.

To stop her from doing the worst, I'd taken the source of her magic. I'd taken her soul. And I knew, without a doubt, it was the worst thing anyone had or could ever do to her.

A choice will be made by the twin of her soul, to save her and damn the realm, or curse her, and save us all. A fate worse than death is the chosen one's destiny.

Maddie's warning, and the final words of Ava's prophecy, came back to me in the most sickening way. This had been my choice, and this was Ava's fate.

"Bring it back, Charlie!" Ava demanded, and she began to weep. "Bring it *back!*"

My grandfather had made clear that once a bond was broken, it could never be repaired. What was separated was destined to remain apart.

I tried anyway. I attempted to reforge the connection between us, taking the golden cord that was hovering between Oberi and me and putting it back into her.

It wouldn't take. The cord sprang back, refusing to join with her again. It didn't even *recognize* her.

"I can't fix it once it's broken," I grieved. "It's... gone."

Ava wailed, and unimaginable pain ached throughout my core and spread over my spirit, turning it to stone. *This* was true suffering unlike any other. To be separated from the one you loved, and to lose the connection that brought you so close, was torture unlike any other. My bond with my wife was permanently severed. She had lost her Familiar, and lost her magic. We'd lost *each other.*

As Ava wept, I wasn't sure if any of this had been worth it. At our wedding dinner, she insisted we were taking the lives of blameless creatures for our own pleasure, and I'd done just that to her now. I'd taken away her innocent belief in our marriage and exchanged it for my own greed. I devoured her as my sacrificial lamb, and enjoyed every moment.

I regretted my decision to stop her, but it was too late now to go back and change it. I thought I had known suffering before— that living on the streets, growing up without a family, and losing the people I loved was the worst that could happen. But I was wrong. No suffering could compare to the feeling of losing oneself, because without Ava, I didn't understand who I was anymore.

She was right to try and end this— to end it all. But she couldn't anymore, because I had taken her magic with our bond, and I'd ruined her in the process. I wished we'd never met in the first place, because I never wanted this to happen to her.

Ava was always stronger than me, and that was clear now. Ava had tried to kill me, and she couldn't do it. She couldn't choose the world over me, but I chose the world over her, and it was a cruel thing to do. Ava loved me more than I loved her, because I had done this to her, and she would *never* do this to me. That's what made her stronger than I could ever be.

To save the world, I'd taken upon myself unimaginable suffering, and it just wasn't worth it in the end. I'd sacrificed myself, my love, and everything that meant something to us for the good of the world. That sacrifice ultimately meant nothing, because the world would continue to be a horrible place whether we gave ourselves up for it or not. The Warden would continue his rampage, evil people would continue to do terrible things, and there would be no heroes to survive to tell their tale... only villains who would always come out on top.

I tried to play the hero, because the hero always chose the world over the person he loved. I was wrong to do so, because the outcome I was promised turned out to be a lie. People said if you did the right thing and were a good person, that it would always turn out to be a happy ending.

It was a false and empty promise that I made the mistake of believing in. I'd swallowed the lie that doing the right thing was always the best way, and doing good was just. Now I realized doing good could be just as harmful as being evil, and we didn't get to decide the outcome. People who tried to make a difference were beat down by all the effort they put in to make the world a better place, only to find that nothing ever changed. It only got worse. Eventually, the world beat them down so much that the only remaining option was to give up.

I was no hero. Nobody was. I'd tried to make myself into something I wasn't, and that had demolished me completely— and I tore down everyone else in my path.

Ava was always destined to be the villain, and she'd stayed true to herself the entire time. She had chosen me constantly in every situation, but this time, I'd chosen others over her.

It didn't matter. Despite everything I'd done to protect people, our enemies were still out there, and they would rampage across the realms to continue this cycle of suffering that I could do nothing about. After this, we didn't have the heart to fight them anymore.

Now that we were apart, there was nothing left in it for me... for *us*.

Just silence.

END OF BOOK FIVE

Continue on to read a special excerpt from Book Six: *The Elven Gate.*

HIDDEN LEGENDS

Read more from the Hidden Legends universe! Each Hidden Legends series takes place within the same world, but in separate and unique societies. Every series stands on its own, and they can be read in any order.

ELEMENTALS, DRAGONS, & MORE

Academy of Magical Creatures by Megan Linski & Alicia Rades

SHIFTERS, FAE, & SORCERESSES

University of Sorcery by Megan Linski

WITCHES, DEMONS, & REAPERS

College of Witchcraft by Alicia Rades

Never miss a new release! Join our newsletter at hiddenlegendsbooks.com/fanclub/

THE ELVEN GATE
CHAPTER ONE

Charlie

Silence stretched for an eternity and back. The beach that quaked only moments ago became completely still, and I couldn't be sure of how long the stillness lasted. I felt completely detached from my body, as if I existed outside of all time and space entirely as I marched onward into Ilamanthe.

My powers noticed the magical signatures of soldiers surrounding me. I recognized them as the young guards who'd sworn to fight for me, though they'd turned against me now. Their hands gripped tight to my arms, and I couldn't find it in me to fight back. After what happened here, nothing mattered anymore.

An entire battalion of guards patrolled me through the city streets, escorting me to be judged by my father. My father didn't want to take any chances. I wasn't there to lead my soldiers in the rebellion, nor give orders on where to go and what to do, and so, the Elves fighting against my father's guard became disorganized. The soldiers had come for me because they didn't have a choice. When I was distracted, Cameron had clearly rushed to the temple and gotten the Great Mystic to coronate him quickly, so he could become Emperor and gain control of the palace's guard. Once he did that, he won automatically, because now the entire military was magically sworn to follow his orders without question.

My father had cheated to obtain the throne, because he couldn't beat me out of his own power or merit, though I hardly cared at this point. The crown, which I'd been so desperate to get my hands on earlier, seemed useless and trivial now.

More guards joined the battalion to give extra support as they marched me in the direction of Ilamanthe's palace. I could've taken them all out easily, but I just didn't care to. Why even bother? Everything that had ever mattered to me had been ripped out of my soul. Worse, I was the one to do it. Whatever punishment my father had waiting for me, it'd be child's play compared to the complete devastation that was losing my bond to Ava.

If he had any mercy at all, he'd take my life. Living this way just wasn't worth it.

Oberi caught my thoughts and gave a low whine at my side. He'd joined me once the guards had shown up to escort me off the beach, though I don't know why. He should've stayed with Ava... except, I realized that Oberi believed remaining at her side would only cause her more pain, in the aftermath of losing him and her magic all at once.

Ava... I'd left her there, broken on the sand and still screaming in pain. Our friends had rushed to comfort her, and that was the only consolation I had. At least she wouldn't have to be alone right now, and I was certain she wanted nothing to do with me at the moment... not after what I'd done.

Elves gathered on the streets gasped in disbelief as the guards took me in. Clearly, they were still in shock that the Elvish prince had attempted to overthrow his father. Whispers of shame and sadness were all around, coupled with the sounds of the dying. The city was still in turmoil, from the rebellion and from Ava's destruction, and the citizens were doing everything they could to heal the injured and pull survivors from the rubble.

Ava and I had really made a mess of things, except this time, the blowback from our argument had decimated an entire city. *Our* city. The Warden didn't even have to come here, because we'd already ruined it.

We were terrible people who destroyed everything we touched.

I was dragged to the throne room the minute we got to the palace. It was crowded, swarming with my father's Associates and council members.

The area instantly went quiet as I entered. I waited at the door for a moment, before a guard shoved me forward. I proceeded toward the throne at the end of the room with my head down. I could sense the weak magic of my father resonating off the raised dais. He sat on my grandfather's throne... which was now his.

As I walked, I heard the hushed voices of Elves all around me, whispering to each other.

"Deceiver," a councilwoman said.

"Such a disgrace," another added.

The degenerating slander continued all the way to the dais. I stopped when I got to the stone steps, and I waited. I bet Cameron thought I would kneel at the steps before him and plead for his forgiveness.

I wouldn't. Not even now. The only way I'd bow to this man is if he took my head and my body collapsed to the floor. As much as I hated the Warden, I'd rather prostrate at his feet than before the coward who was callous enough to call himself my father.

"Is it true?" Cameron demanded. "Did you sever the magic of our Holy Mother?"

I opened my mouth to speak, but no words came out. I hadn't been expecting him to talk to me about Ava first. The rebellion, my betrayal, all of those I could defend myself against.

I couldn't stand up for myself when it came down to hurting my wife. In that aspect, for wounding her beyond repair, I deserved every brutal pain that this world could give... and I was paying that price, even now, for merely existing without her was agony. Whatever Cameron could do to me would be nothing in comparison to the loss that was my love.

My lack of response told him all he needed to know.

"You insolent child," Cameron sneered. "Do you realize what you've *done?* If the princess has no magic, we are not only unable to contact our goddesses; we are also defenseless against Ophio Taurus! She was the most valuable weapon we had!"

"I didn't have any choice," I replied, nearly devoid of feeling, because it was just so hard *to* feel right now. "If I hadn't, she would've—"

"*Silence!*" Cameron shouted. He wasn't going to even let me explain. "Whatever the princess was in the process of, it was up to you to keep her in line, and you failed miserably. Worse than that, you attempted to take the crown from me, something that has never been done in the history of the Elvish monarchy."

"This boy is not one of us! He never has been!" an Associate cried, and other voices rose up to join his.

"He is an outsider who was never raised among us, and is not of our kind! Cassiel made a mistake taking him in. We should've left him on the streets, where he belongs!"

"This is an outrage! We were looking for trouble the moment we brought him into the city!"

"He is a greedy child, raised in hatred and spite by strangers we do not know, so he cannot understand our ways, no matter how hard Cassiel tried to instill our values in him. We cannot forgive this!"

"Enough!" Cameron bellowed, and the slurs halted as he spoke. "I am the Emperor, and I will decide his fate!"

"Sire, you know what must be done," a councilman encouraged. "This insurrection is unforgivable. We must take his life. Drea cannot become Empress, but she is still young by Elvish standards, and is able to bear children. You *must* produce another heir to rise after you, and wash this stain of your name."

I hoped to the gods they killed me, because I didn't want to live anymore. Ava, my friends, the world, they'd all be better off without me. I'd hurt all of them, and the death sentence would be more than a fair sentence for my crimes.

At least it'd be a mercy, because then I wouldn't feel like this.

But my hopes were dashed as Cameron replied, "I will not conceive another child. Not after this one has turned out to be such a colossal disappointment. I do not desire to be a father again, and I cannot take another chance that a second child would turn out to be even worse than he is. Charlie will still rise after me, and he will become Emperor after I am gone."

Outrage shook the walls of the throne room once again. "Your majesty, it cannot be so!" an Associate yelled. "We cannot expect this corrupt, depraved deviant to become Emperor after you step down! You cannot forgive your son for this!"

"We cannot blame him too harshly. After all, he was raised without a mother," Cameron argued. "Kelly wasn't there to guide him as she should've."

"Because Kelly gave her life for this spawn," another hissed. "An unworthy sacrifice."

He had no idea how much I wished that my mother had survived and I had died instead. If she didn't outright hate me from the afterlife, she had to be ashamed of me now. That was the only thing that held me back from wishing for death— the terror that somehow, I might encounter my mother on the other side, only for her to berate me and tell me how worthless I was, and that her gift of life to me had been for less than nothing. Because all of it was true... it had to be.

"Charlie will still rule, but it will be in time. He has much to learn before he does," Cameron stated.

My father came closer to me, walking down the steps until he was perched on the one above me, only a few feet away. Oberi pressed closer against my legs, his body tense in warning.

Cameron paused and whispered, "After all, your grandfather planted this idea in your head, didn't he?"

"*What?*" The word came out in a gasp. Was he really implying what I thought he was?

"Don't lie, Charlie. I know my father never wanted me to ascend to the title of Emperor. He made that very clear," Cameron sneered. "He put you up to all of this— betraying me, the rebellion, everything."

My grandfather would never do such a thing. Nobody disrespected my *seanari* like that.

"He *never* mentioned any of this to me, or conspired with me to plot the rebellion," I spat. "All of this was my plan, and mine alone!"

"Don't take me for a fool!" Cameron screamed, and spittle fell across my face. "You aren't clever enough, nor are you experienced enough, to have done this all on your own!"

I didn't even care that Cameron was calling me an idiot, only that he was slandering my grandfather's name. Blaming Cassiel for my actions was worse than cruel. Whatever Cameron said about grieving his father, he still was resentful toward Cassiel, even in death.

Even the Associates and the council members in the room seemed shocked. A few low tones of disbelief rang throughout, though nobody said anything to advocate for my grandfather's honor, the spineless weaklings they all were. They didn't believe the coup had been Cassiel's idea, but Cameron was Emperor now, and to go against him by speaking up on my grandfather's behalf meant death, or worse, so they kept their mouths shut.

"But it doesn't have to be this way," Cameron continued. "I can instruct you in the ways of our family, and correct what went wrong. Your grandfather taught you the wrong way, but I can fix what's been broken. I will mold you into a proper prince, one in my image, who will rule in the right way once you ascend to the throne."

"I'm not letting you teach me a goddamn thing," I raged. "You have nothing to offer me."

"I understand you're upset about the death of Cassiel, but he was my father. I knew him for far longer, and loved him more than you ever could," Cameron replied cruelly. "The loss of a grandparent cannot compare to the loss of a parent, and you are taking things too far, when you need to consider *my* feelings."

It was rare that I was ever left speechless, but somehow, Cameron had managed to stun me beyond belief. How dare he imply I wasn't allowed to grieve, that *his* pain was more important than my own.

"You didn't care about him like I did," I accused. "My grandfather never said it, but I knew he was ashamed of you as a son. He thought you were weak, and weren't fit to rule. I could hear it in his voice every time he spoke your name."

"Treason!" one of Cameron's Associates cried out, and the throne room broke into mad jeers.

I didn't give a damn, because there was nothing left between me and my father to save, so I might as well tell him how I felt. "I fucking hate you. You're no father of mine. I wish my grandfather was still here and *you* were the one who'd died! At least then I'd be rid of you, and he'd still be here—"

Cameron slapped me across the face. The blow was so hard it knocked me to the floor, and I fell roughly against my side.

Only a few hours ago, I would've hit back— punched him so hard he wouldn't be able to get back up again.

But I couldn't summon the heart to care. Let Cameron hit me. It wouldn't make any difference in how I felt. He could torture me, embrace me, do nothing at all, and all of them would come down to the same result.

I'd still be numb.

Oberi gave a snarl and charged toward my father. *Leave him alone!*

A yelp of pain reverberated off the walls, and Oberi fell to the ground beside me. I reached out to help him, but when I grabbed whatever had hurt him, I immediately recoiled as a sickness slammed into my gut. I recognized ropes, and realized with a sinking feeling that it was the inferichite net I'd had my Associates create for me. Eddie had given the inferichite net to my father, and hidden it from me. A short time ago, I would've considered him a traitor for it.

Now, I couldn't muster the strength to blame him. Not for anything.

Oberi yelped and writhed. A few guards pushed me aside as they came forward, and I heard something metal snap around Oberi's neck.

"As part of your punishment, your Familiar will be forced to wear an inferichite collar until further notice," Cameron said. "He will not be allowed to shift forms, or exhibit his magic, as you have proven to be a danger in our society. He will still be able to communicate with you, though the bounds of his powers are restricted beyond that. When you have learned to behave, the collar can come off. If you or your friends attempt to remove it, whosoever takes this collar off *will* be executed immediately. This is your one and only warning."

Oberi whimpered, and my hands trembled as they ran through his fur. The collar was thick and heavy. It made me sick to be near it, so I couldn't imagine how Oberi felt.

"How could you do this?" I asked, and tears stung at the corners of my eyes. "You have a Familiar. You know how unfair this is, and how much it hurts my creature."

"My Familiar would never conspire against the empire," Cameron stated coldly.

"Oberi had *nothing* to do with this!" I bellowed.

"When are you going to get it through your head that you have no control here?" Cameron picked me up by my shirt collar, then tossed me down again roughly. "The consequences of your actions affect more than just you, as your former Associates have become well aware."

Fear froze me in place. Were they already dead?

"Punish me, fine, but don't hurt my team," I begged. "They were following my orders."

"Asa, Ares, Gavyn, Max and Elyx will keep their lives, but they have been stripped of their duties and cast out of the monarchy's employment. They are no longer allowed on palace grounds, and must start over from nothing," Cameron replied. "Of course, no one will hire them nor take them in, due to the disgrace they've caused the family, but they will manage to survive."

"If they have any integrity at all they will take their own lives, to preserve what honor they have left," another councilman replied.

"What about Eddie?" I demanded.

"Edwyrd is bonded to you, and even I cannot break that bond that ties the two of you together," Cameron stated. "What you do with him is your business. He is the only remaining servant you will still have at your disposal, even if it displeases him to remain so."

The intent was clear; Eddie had asked Cameron if he could leave my service, and Cameron told him no. Remaining my guard was punishment enough for Eddie's crimes against the city.

"You will keep your title, as you need to in order to become Emperor after me, but you are stripped of all your privileges," Cameron continued. "You will not be given Associates, nor will you be allowed into the city. You will still be able to roam the palace as you wish, but you will be followed at all times by the guards, so they can keep an eye on you and report back to me your every movement."

"I'm not a child to be babysat." My words were cutting. Even now, though there was nothing left in me, I couldn't find it in me to not oppose my father. I'd given up my connection to Ava because of this, and I would be damned if that resulted in nothing, even if it only entailed gaining my father's spite.

"No. You are a grown man, one who must learn his place," Cameron snapped. "And you will learn the penalty for your disobedience."

He motioned to one of his guards. I wasn't aware of what was going on until it happened. A soldier grabbed my left hand, and I felt a dagger slicing through my left pinky. Blood spurted from the wound, and I screamed in indescribable agony as my finger was sliced off. Oberi whimpered as it fell to the floor, and I collapsed beside him, creating a puddle of blood on the marble beneath me.

I didn't even care about my finger, honestly. I was just screaming because it hurt, out of a physical reaction. I heard myself cry out, but barely registered the actual pain. It was nothing compared to the turmoil inside of me, *nothing* when placed beside the loss of a piece of me, which was Ava.

I was barely here anymore. Cameron could take my finger, my heart, whatever else he wanted. I needed nothing anymore, not unless I had my bond with Ava... and I didn't have that bond. I wouldn't ever again.

"Stop whining," Cameron scoffed at my cries. "It's the finger you use the least, for the gods' sake. I'm being nice. You hardly need it. Be glad I didn't take more, and that the monarchy still needs heirs; otherwise, your balls would be sitting in a box in my quarters."

Cassiel must've taken Cameron's balls after he got back from messing around with my mom, then, because it'd explain why he was so worthless now. I tried to say that, but I couldn't. I wasn't able to make any words with my mouth, because the pain was all-encompassing.

Ava was right to mistrust you, Oberi hissed at my father, his words biting. *And I will have my revenge on you, Cameron, son of Cassiel, if it is the final action I take before my breath leaves my body forever.*

I was the only one who'd heard it, but even so, a shudder ran up my spine.

Oberi couldn't heal my severed finger— he'd lost access to healing magic now that his phoenix form was gone, so I continued to bleed all over the room. Nobody went to help me, so I figured I'd probably bleed out.

That was fine. Let it happen.

"Cameron, stop this at once!" A female voice I didn't know echoed behind me, and footsteps rang across the throne room as someone ran to my side. She knelt beside me, grabbing my mutilated hand.

"Drea, he doesn't deserve any mercy," Cameron hissed.

It was my father's wife and guard, Drea. She came to my aid, even though I didn't deserve it. I felt soft cotton on my skin as she wrapped up my hand with a bandage before she stood to face her husband. "Whatever has transpired, he is still your son."

I'd judged Drea too harshly. She was a good person, someone who was able to prevent Cameron from doing the worst. The only thing she'd ever done wrong in her life was marry the pig that was my father. I felt sorry for her, being tied to a sinking ship like him.

Cameron relented. "Very well. Take him out of here. I do not wish to see him again until I decide to summon him."

I was dragged out by guards. I let them do it, because who fucking cared anyhow? My discarded finger was still lying on the floor, and I guessed that was where it was going to stay.

They threw me into my quarters. I stumbled into the living area of my tower, and Oberi yelped as another soldier tossed him in behind me. These Elves had once revered us, but now, they were treating us as the worst of the worst.

I supposed that was what we were.

As I careened forward, I fell into someone. That person grabbed me and held me upright. I immediately recognized Marcus was the one who'd caught me, and felt the magical signatures of several other people in the room, though I was so disoriented I couldn't make out who. People must've gathered here, waiting for me.

"Charlie…" Marcus uttered in horror. I could guess that he and all the others were staring at my bloody hand.

I didn't bring it up. Instead, I stood taller and choked out, "Who's… who's all here?"

"Me, Kallie, Ez, Opal, Alistair and Danny," Marcus replied, his voice even.

"Where's Ava?" I asked immediately. I wanted to— no, *needed* to— know where she was, because I couldn't sense her, and she was my beacon in this world. How was I going to navigate my life if she wasn't there to be my light?

"You don't need to know where she is right now," Kallie replied. "She needs some space."

That was understandable. I swallowed thickly. It wasn't lost on me that Ivy and Chancey hadn't turned up.

There was silence, until I heard Danny utter, "Dude, *fuck you*."

His voice quivered with rage. The next moment, he completely lost it. His fist connected with a stone pillar, and his hand went straight through it, sending bits of stone scattering to the floor.

"I can't fucking believe you," Danny growled, and he came closer to me. "You better feel *lucky* that your father only took a finger, because I want to rip your head off right now."

"You should," I said hoarsely. "Please."

Danny huffed. "No way. You don't get to take the easy way out. You're sticking around to clean up your shit."

He was so mad he couldn't keep talking, or he'd lose control. Danny stormed out of the room, and Alistair gave a hefty sigh.

"I can't believe we lost," he grumbled. "If you ever want to take over again, I'm right here by your side, buddy."

"Alistair, shut the fuck up," Kallie snapped. "This isn't about you right now."

Alistair sulked, and Ez exploded. He started toward me, shoving me backward. "How dare you, Charlie. I will *never* forgive you for this. You've broken my sister, when she already had so little that held her together. She doesn't have her magic now! She doesn't have her Familiar— *anything!* Do you think you had the right to do this to her?"

"No," I said hollowly. "Ava would've been better off if she'd never met me."

"You're damn right she would've," Ez snapped. "I should kill you where you stand."

"Ez, wait," Opal said kindly. She was holding him back, and I heard Ezekiel's gasping breaths as he struggled to obtain control of himself.

Then, his voice changed, from furious to despondent. Ez took a shattering breath and said, "Charlie... I hate you for taking Ava's magic away. I always will. But..."

His voice broke, and he started to cry. "I know how Ava gets when she's out of control. I know you had to stop her *somehow*. But did you really have to go that far?"

"She didn't give him much of a choice, Ez," Marcus mumbled.

Ez cried harder. "I get that. I... I've been there when Ava's on her warpath of destruction, and I know it's hard to stop. Charlie... I overheard you a few months ago, when you were talking to my dad on the terrace."

I froze. Ez was talking about the night I'd asked for Liam's blessing, before Ava and I had our royal wedding within Ilamanthe. I remembered the conversation well, and every word Liam said came rushing back to me now.

He'd warned me Ava would push me past my limits one day, and I hadn't believed him. I wished I'd heeded his warning.

Ez wiped his face and went on. "Dad asked if you had the capability to do what needed to be done to handle her. I know if it was my decision, I wouldn't have been able to do that to Ava. You had the strength to do what we wouldn't have been able to. My dad trusted you, and you made a promise. You fulfilled that promise, as awful as it is. I just wish it had never come to this."

Ez continued to sob, and I didn't say anything, just stood there. What *could* I say? Even if I apologized for ruining his sister's life, it wouldn't do any good. There wasn't any amount of forgiveness in the world that would compensate for what I'd just done.

"You guys act like this is all Charlie's fault," Alistair complained. "Ava's got some penance to make too, you know. If Charlie hadn't saved our asses, literally none of us would exist right now, so quit crying about what he did and go blame her."

"Alistair, *leave*," Kallie ordered. "Or I swear, you will *not* like where you end up once I'm done with you."

I expected Alistair to bite back a retort or make a threat, but he didn't. He left, muttering under his breath, though he made sure he spoke quietly enough that no one heard him.

"This isn't right," Opal said in frustration as she continued to comfort Ez. "Guys, we can't do this to each other ever again. You guys *fought your significant others.* Somebody could've gotten killed— somebody *did* get seriously hurt, and it was Ava."

"It's always Ava," Kallie said quietly. "She's always the one who has to bear the brunt of the sacrifice, to accommodate for everyone else's mistakes. She already lost the ability to walk before this, and now, she's lost the core of who she is. How much more are we going to take from her? How much more does Ava even have left to *give?*"

Her words were a gut punch straight to the core of me. Kallie spoke the truth. Ava was the one who'd lost the most out of all of us in this war, and always had been. What had happened on the beach was the worst blow of all.

I didn't want to keep hurting my wife like this. I didn't want to keep making the same mistakes.

Maybe I *was* bad for her. I'd tried to force things to be my way, and my wife had taken blows that were meant for me. I figured any consequences for my rebellion would fall back on me, but they hadn't. I'd lost my finger, the respect from my people, and any chance of having a relationship with my father, but Ava had lost so much more. I'd taken away her magic and Oberi, the foundation of who she was. My losses were pale and empty in comparison to hers.

"Opal's right. Today was fucked up," Marcus agreed. "We can fight the Warden, but we shouldn't be fighting each other."

"I know. This is the worst thing I've ever done, the worst thing that could've happened," I admitted, forcing out the words. "I am so, so sorry you guys."

"Sorry isn't going to cut it, Charlie," Ez said lonesomely. "Not after what you did."

A lump formed in my throat that was hard to speak past. "I know. Just... give me the chance to fix it."

There was a deep quiet, before Kallie said, "I don't know if it can be fixed this time."

"I at least need to be given the chance," I pleaded.

I literally felt the distaste rolling off the others when I made that statement, because I realized I was a hypocrite. I didn't want to give other people chances when I had decided to bring the world under my command, but now I was asking for one, even when I didn't deserve it.

Kallie's words wavered somewhere between bitterness and grief as she said, "I think it's horrible that you tried to take over Ilamanthe. But as much as I despise admitting it, you did the right thing breaking your bond. This was a last resort, and I *never* would've asked you to do this otherwise."

"Kallie—"

"No. Listen," she demanded. "I asked you to break your bond in order to save Marcus. That was the *only* reason, because I couldn't bear the thought of losing him. Don't make my sacrifice be in vain. Work this out with Ava, because if you've hurt her beyond repair, I will lose the last ounce of respect and love I have for you that I've still managed to cling to after the bullshit you just pulled. I've been through a lot with you, and that's the only reason I'm not walking away from you for good. You need to make this right. You need to heal what you broke. Prove to me that you still give a shit about Ava, and about all of us; otherwise, I'm done with you. That is, if I'm not already."

Kallie dipped out, and the others followed her, save for Marcus. Kallie's absence was tough to handle, because she wasn't the type to give second chances. She always laid down the law and told it how it was, and she made it clear that if I didn't mend things, I was worth nothing to her.

Marcus came closer to me, and as he did, I felt myself breaking down. It was easy to hold myself together in front of other people, but not Marcus. He'd seen me unravel before, so it wasn't so terrifying to fall apart in front of him again.

"It'll be okay," Marcus promised, coming closer. "We'll figure it out."

My shoulders shuddered, and I managed to ask, "How are your burns?"

Before Ava had lost her abilities, she'd burned Marcus to stop him from interfering with her plans to destroy the world. He'd been unable to move afterward, because the injuries had been so intense.

"They're healed. I found a healer to patch me up right away, but that's not important right now," Marcus insisted.

"Are you and Kallie going to be okay?" I asked. They'd just gotten together, and within a few days of their relationship being permanent, they'd participated in a full-on magical battle with each other— one where they didn't hold anything back.

"We're fine," Marcus insisted. "Kallie and I don't blame each other for anything that happened. We forgave each other instantly once it was all over. In fact, there was nothing to forgive."

"You guys got over it that fast?" I questioned.

"I can't blame Kallie for taking Ava's side, not after what happened with the Dollmaker," Marcus insisted. "I'd want everything to end, too, if I'd just survived a traumatic experience with a serial killer. And she gets why I had to take your side, because deep down, she didn't really want things to end, either.

She just wanted to stop herself and others from being in pain. A temporary lapse in judgment isn't enough to split us up."

"Even if it leads to something like this?" My tone was so... barren. My entire world had been turned upside down as a result of my own actions, and I still had my magic and Oberi. I couldn't imagine how Ava was feeling right now.

"You and Ava both made mistakes," Marcus said. "None of this is right, but we'll make it better."

Tears fell down my face as I grabbed at my hair and pulled. "I don't know how I'm going to repair this. Ava *has* to hate me."

"Hey, you guys will work it out," Marcus encouraged. "You broke my bond with Kallie, and that worked out. We're together now. You and Ava don't have a bond anymore, but you're still married. This is the toughest thing you'll ever have to go through, but breaking a bond doesn't mean destroying a relationship. You two can still pull out of this, and become stronger. Closer, even."

"You think so?" I asked.

Marcus was giving me back a little bit of hope, and I was terrified to believe in it. But I had to, because accepting the alternative was worse than pure hell. It was a sentence that tightened like a noose around my neck and removed all air, but wasn't enough to actually kill me, though I desperately wanted to suffocate, leaving me in a state of permanent suffering.

"Definitely," Marcus said. He put an arm around me and pulled me closer. "Bro, I love you. Your friends love you, even though everybody's pissed, and Ava still loves you... even if you've broken her heart."

"I broke more than her heart. I shattered her."

"She's got stuff to be accountable for, too," he encouraged. "Even if you started it, this isn't all on you. You guys love each other more than anybody I've ever seen. I know you can get through this."

I wiped my face. "Okay. I guess I'll wait for her to come back, and we can talk this out."

"That's the spirit." Marcus clapped me on the back. "You get ready to patch things up with Ava, and I'll go talk to Kallie. We can smooth all of this over."

Marcus' words were so level-headed that it gave me some courage. He was right. Marriage had good times and bad times, right? This was one of the bad— no, *absolutely atrocious*— times. I was certain there'd never be anything more terrible in our lives than what had happened today. Even if the Warden did his worst, it wouldn't be more than what Ava and I had already done to each other. If we were at rock bottom, the only way to go was up, right? It wasn't like things between us could get any *worse*.

I went into my bedroom. The moment I closed the door behind Oberi, he came toward me.

Charlie, does it hurt? Oberi asked softly, nudging my hurt hand. *What can I do?*

My infinite sadness instantly turned to rage. Even with the inferichite collar, I was angry at Oberi— and a part of me blamed him for what I'd done to Ava. He'd taken her side, instead of helping me to protect her by calming her down, and it had forced me to make a horrible decision. If I couldn't forgive myself, I didn't want to forgive him, either.

"Why are you trying to comfort me?" I seethed hatefully as I pushed him away. "Leave me!"

Because I still care! Oberi yelled. *Because I still love you, even though you are testing every ounce of patience that love has right now!*

"You didn't give a shit when you and Ava were kicking the crap out of me a few hours ago!"

Well things have certainly changed, as you now notice, because now we are all stuck here, Oberi snapped. *Ava's desire to end all things has now resulted in turmoil, no thanks to you.*

"I had to stop her somehow!"

Oh, yes, and we are all paying the price for it, Oberi growled.

"Quit blaming me! If you had taken *my* side, we would've been able to subdue Ava without me having to break our bond!"

I will never take your side, not after you planned to imprison Ava away.

"I made a mistake—"

A mistake! Oberi's guffaw was an absolute insult. You ruined us, Charlie! All of us! Ava certainly had her part to play in it, but it was you who started this whole mess, and I blame you alone for its consequences. None of this would've happened if you hadn't let the power go to your head. Ava chose to destroy the world, but you pushed her to do it. You know as well as I do that you are her anchor, and you steer her in the direction she goes, wherever that may be.

"How could I have predicted she'd go off the deep end?" I yelled back. "I knew she'd be upset about the restrictions I put upon her—"

Restrictions?! Charlie, you put her in a cage! If you cannot see the devastation such an action gave her, then you are even blinder than you appear.

"I cannot be responsible for everything that she decides to do," I spat back. "I can do my best to guide her, control her when she gets out of hand, but I can't take the blame when she decides to do something this radical!"

You fail to understand the kind of sway you have over her. These sick ideas that originate in her head don't just pop up without being coerced, and she wouldn't have done this if you hadn't forced her hand.

"Of course you're going to take Ava's side." I hugged my arms around myself and turned my back to him. "After all, she's your *favorite*, right?"

Oh, fuck you, Charlie. Oberi's livid voice rang out louder than I'd ever heard it before. *I think you fail to see the obvious, for I am certainly being punished for my heart going one way instead of another. Because for the love of the gods and all that is holy, when our bond was broken, I remained tied to you.*

Oberi gave a wail. *And now my Ava is gone. Taken away from me, never again to be reunited with my beloved. She cannot hear me, she cannot feel my presence. I have become nothing to her, and the part of her within our soul is lost. I cannot take any of Ava's soul forms— the unicorn, the phoenix, the narwhal, they are all gone to me now. I am bonded to you only, to the pieces of you that live inside of me, and the pieces of her are gone. Who am I now, except a being cleaved in two?*

"We could've prevented this," I argued. Goddammit, I was crying again. The tears just wouldn't stop.

We could've, but you did not desire to. You didn't take the prophecy seriously. None of us did. So now, we must deal with its outcome.

I didn't bother giving him a response. Either because I was weeping so hard or because I was just so upset with him, I couldn't tell.

Hours passed. I sat on my bed, and Oberi laid on the other side of the room ignoring me. We sat there in silence, ignoring each other's presence while we waited for Ava to return from wherever she was.

As the time passed, my mind wandered. Whatever my friends said about Ava taking responsibility, I still felt like this was all my fault. I'd driven Ava to want to end the world, and I was the one who'd broken our bond. I was a fool to think that I could end suffering, because now *I* was the one suffering, and worse yet, so was she... suffering beyond explanation.

I supposed I would just have to be the villain forever, because that's what I'd become. And if there wasn't any way to mend this, then I guessed I'd just die, because everything else felt just as pointless.

Even so, I kept telling myself that this situation wasn't hopeless. I knew I could get Ava back, and there were no limits on what I'd do to prove to her that I'd made a mistake and I needed to make it up to her. No matter what my grandfather had said, I'd find a way to restore our bond eventually, and repair our magical connection. Then, she'd forgive me, and we could move on. I *knew* we could work through this. Nothing had kept us apart before, so why would this?

I'd do anything to get her back. *Anything.*

The door to my room opened. I immediately stood, bracing myself. "Who's there?"

There was an infinite pause that dragged out the endlessness of time and space. Oberi held a breath, and I realized then who exactly had entered... my wife.

Something inside of me fractured and tore once again, cutting my heart to shreds. I'd never had to ask if Ava was *around* before. I felt her presence through the bond, and always knew where she was because of her connection to me. If she was far away, or close... I automatically knew. I didn't have to place her in my world like I did other people, because she always *was*.

Ava had become one of those outliers for me. A person in my world that I couldn't place.

A longing piece of me withered up and died inside. It was like losing myself all over again. I knew the bond was broken, and I felt the empty pit inside of me where that bond once connected us. But it was one thing to know it and another entirely to *experience* it like this. The emptiness was all-encompassing, to the point where I wasn't even sure Ava was here at all, and I'd only imagined she'd entered the room. She might as well be a figment of my imagination, because none of this felt real. How could Ava and I exist without one another? It seemed to defy all laws of nature.

Again, I was reminded that I was the one who did this to us.

I fell on my knees before her, crawling and begging. "Ava, *please*," I pleaded. "I'm so sorry. I never should've done this. If I could take it all back, I would. You were right. I never should've locked you up, never broken—"

I didn't get a chance to finish my sentence, because she whacked me *hard* in the chest with something that crumpled on impact and made a crinkling noise. I caught whatever she was holding, and found that it was a stack of papers.

"What... what's this?" I asked breathlessly, catching the papers and holding them in my hands.

Ava's response was distant. Her following words disintegrated everything that was still hanging on inside my chest, imploding any future we may still have.

"Divorce papers," she snarled. "Sign them."

Continue The Elven Gate to witness Ava-Marie and Charlie's love story come to a dramatic and stunning conclusion.

BONUS OFFERS

Find coloring pages, games, quizzes, and bonus content at hiddenlegendsbooks.com

Join *Orenda Academy: Hidden Legends Fan Group* on Facebook for all things Hidden Legends!

Check out the *Prison for Supernatural Offenders Official Playlist* on Spotify!

Never miss a new release! Join our newsletter at hiddenlegendsbooks.com/fanclub/

ABOUT THE AUTHORS

Megan Linski (left) and Alicia Rades (right) are best friends and the authors of the Hidden Legends universe. Both are USA Today bestselling authors of young adult and new adult fiction. Megan Linski is a coffee connoisseur who enjoys ice skating, horseback riding, and shopping. Her stories feature themes of community and friendship while advocating for the rights of the disabled. Alicia Rades is a mother who loves baking cookies, reading tarot, and binge-watching Netflix. She has a passion for personal development and strives to incorporate emotional-empowerment themes into her books. Both girls love nature, animals, sexy romances, and eating cheese.

www.ingramcontent.com/pod-product-compliance
Lightning Source LLC
Chambersburg PA
CBHW030324010826
48973CB00004B/852